THE YEAR'S BEST SCIENCE FICTION

TENTH ANNUAL COLLECTION

Gardner Dozois, Editor

ST. MARTIN'S PRESS   NEW YORK

For my Clarion West Classes,
the Class of 1988
and the Class of 1992.

Library of Congress Catalog Card Number: 85-645716
ISSN: 0743-1740

First Edition: June 1993

10 9 8 7 6 5 4 3 2 1

Paperback 0-312-09424-8
Hardcover 0-312-09423-X

CONTENTS

ACKNOWLEDGMENTS

The editor would like to thank the following people for their help and support: first and foremost, Susan Casper, for doing much of the thankless scut work involved in producing this anthology; Michael Swanwick, Janet Kagan, Ellen Datlow, Virginia Kidd, Sheila Williams, Ian Randal Strock, Scott L. Towner, Tina Lee, David Pringle, Kristine Kathryn Rusch, Dean Wesley Smith, Pat Cadigan, David S. Garnett, Charles C. Ryan, Chuq von Rospach, Susan Allison, Ginjer Buchanan, Lou Aronica, Betsy Mitchell, Beth Meacham, Claire Eddy, David G. Hartwell, Bob Walters, Tess Kissinger, Jim Frenkel, Greg Egan, Steve Pasechnick, Susan Ann Protter, Lawrence Person, Dwight Brown, Chris Reed, Dirk Strasser, Michael Sumbera, Glen Cox, Darrell Schweitzer, Don Keller, Robert Killheffer, Greg Cox, and special thanks to my own editor, Gordon Van Gelder.

Thanks are also due to Charles N. Brown, whose magazine *Locus* (Locus Publications, P.O. Box 13305, Oakland, CA 94661, $50.00 for a one-year subscription [twelve issues] via first class mail, $38.00 second class) was used as a reference source throughout the Summation, and to Andrew Porter, whose magazine *Science Fiction Chronicle* (Science Fiction Chronicle, P.O. Box 2730, Brooklyn, NY 11202-0056, $30.00 for a one-year subscription [twelve issues]; $36.00 first class) was also used as a reference source throughout.

SUMMATION:
1992

This was a low-key, low-energy year, for the most part, a recession year with a siege mentality firmly in place, gray, grim, unsmiling—and yet, it seems to me that many people were a little more gloomy and pessimistic than was actually justified by the year's *events*.

Yes, things of ill omen happened in 1992—there were major corporate shakeups and cutbacks at Bantam and at Pulphouse Publishing, for instance, with unadmitted buying slowdowns or freezes clearly in place at other publishing houses, and there may be worse to come. Some book editors were fired, or participated in the usual game of Editorial Musical Chairs, with former Roc editor John Silbersack moving to Warner, for instance, former Warner editor Brian Thomsen moving to TSR, former Bantam editor Amy Stout going to Roc, and former Ace editor Peter Heck going from Ace back to editing the Waldenbooks SF newsletter. For the first time in several years, the overall number of books in the related SF/fantasy/horror genres did not increase, and even began to creep back a little. Money was generally tight this year, and many mid-list writers were forced to take part-time or full-time jobs—if they could find them—in order to make ends meet. Fewer writers and editors went to conventions and professional gatherings, and when they did go, they were more likely to spend their time glumly sitting around discussing how depressing everything was.

And yet, certainly things could have been a lot *worse*. The American SF publishing industry has yet to be hit with the kind of really major and crippling collapse that afflicted British SF publishing in 1991 (although, of course, it could always be still to come), and even the British SF publishing industry is showing a few tentative signs of at least partial recovery. It certainly wouldn't be true to say that the SF publishing world in general had gone bust this year—the decline in the number of titles published overall is really quite minor so far, in the United States, at least, and although most of the major publishers *did* cut their lines back in 1992, many of the small-press publishers and smaller publishing houses were *expanding* at the same time, so that the overall decline in titles is almost negligible. Some genre books continued to sell quite well, and there were many genre titles on nationwide bestseller lists throughout 1992 (although, increasingly, many of these are TV/movie–related books, or gaming books, which is worrisome). The magazine market suffered (the imminent death and vanishing of the science fiction magazine was predicted again, as it has been predicted nearly every year since I first entered the SF world professionally, in the late sixties), the year's anthologies were rather weak, and overall it wasn't a terribly good year for short fiction in general (although so *many* stories now appear in the field annually, hundreds and hundreds of them, that even in a weak year there's still more than enough good stories among the chaff to fill a volume of this size easily), or for genre movies either (although it *was* a fairly strong year for novels).

Still, as someone who's been assembling Best of the Year anthologies, and Summations, since 1976, I can assure you that science fiction has seen a number of considerably *worse* years. Nevertheless, industry people did seem to be gloomier than usual this year, perhaps gloomier than they ought to have been realistically. Perhaps it was the fact that several of the most beloved figures in the field died this year, including Isaac Asimov and Fritz Leiber; perhaps it was the deepening of the nationwide recession generally, throughout 1992, or the Los Angeles riots, or the Presidential elections, about which many people were depressed right up until they heated up at last, almost to November. Whatever it was, several commentators were predicting the imminent death of the science fiction genre this year, in articles in semiprozines and fanzines, in letters and in postings on the electronic computer networks, and in private conversations. Even David G. Hartwell, usually a fairly optimistic sort, wrote a gloomy cautionary editorial for *The New York Review of Science Fiction*, warning that because of the increasing dilution of the form, "Science fiction could end this decade. Maybe it will. Maybe it (already) has." The coming death of science fiction was also predicted here and there by Charles Platt, Barry Malzberg, and others.

A bit of historical perspective may be in order here, since, as with so much else that happens in the SF publishing world, we have been through all this before.

By the beginning of the 1960s, for instance, after the furor and excitement of the *Galaxy*-era aesthetic revolution of the mid-1950s had begun to die away, after the inflationary postwar SF boom had gone bust and a recession had settled in over the SF publishing industry, wiping out dozens of SF magazines, many fans and professionals began to perceive the SF world of the late fifties as a dismal place, in Robert Silverberg's words, "a kind of fallen empire that had collapsed into eerie provincial decay." For the first time since the middle of the thirties (just prior to John W. Campbell's takeover of *Astounding*), it became possible to entertain seriously the thought that SF might have reached the end of its string and be on its way to extinction. Many critics and commentators were worried and increasingly glum over what they perceived as the sudden dearth of worthwhile SF, and the proliferation of "watered-down" nonkosher SF (including fantasy "masquerading" as SF), and it is probably significant that the winner of the fanzine Hugo for 1961 was a symposium with the title *Who Killed Science Fiction?*

Was science fiction dead, or dying?

With hindsight, it is easy to see that it was not. A great deal of good work, and even much evolutionarily significant work, was published throughout the early sixties, right through this supposedly dry and sterile period—the bulk of Cordwainer Smith's work, for instance, the best of Jack Vance's short work, incandescently strange work by Philip K. Dick and J.G. Ballard, as well as important work by Poul Anderson, Algis Budrys, Edgar Pangborn, Avram Davidson, Richard McKenna, Theodore Sturgeon, and dozens of others. Most of the new writers who would soon be the stars of the New Wave revolution—Samuel R. Delany, Roger Zelazny, Ursula K. Le Guin, Keith Roberts, Joanna Russ, Norman Spinrad, Kate Wilhelm, Thomas M. Disch, John Sladek, and many others—had *already* started their careers by the early sixties, and were busily toiling away in obscurity, attracting as yet little or no attention. And many older writers who were considered at the time to be "burnt out" can be seen in retrospect to have instead been within a few years of a revitalizing surge of new creative energy.

And yet, one of the most common *perceptions* of this period at the time was that SF was in decline, a long, slow dwindling-away into gray mediocrity, the ferocious fires of the early years of the fifties cooling into ash—and the evidence to the contrary seemed to register on few.

We went through this whole thing *again* some years later, in the middle and late seventies, in a low-energy recessionary period following the creative excitement of the New Wave revolution of the mid-sixties, when once again commentators were shaking their heads solemnly over the imminent demise of science fiction, scholarly articles were being written explaining why it was All Over, and some writers (among many others who were *also* plunged into gloom and despair in those days . . . for some very real reasons, it should be emphasized) were making a big public show of "getting out" of science fiction, renouncing a failing genre for greener and more lucrative pastures elsewhere. (Nearly all of them were working in the field again by the beginning of the new decade, if not before.) This was theoretically another dry and sterile period in SF—and yet, as David G. Hartwell notes in an article about the seventies in the December 1991 issue of *The New York Review of Science Fiction* (and as other commentators have pointed out), a tremendous amount of good work was produced during this "sterile" period, by writers as various as James Tiptree, Jr., Frederik Pohl, Michael Bishop, Ursula K. Le Guin, Gene Wolfe, John Varley, Joanna Russ, Robert Silverberg, Brian W. Aldiss, and dozens of others. As is usually the case in these episodes of postcoital *triste* that inevitably seem to follow periods of compacted "revolutionary" aesthetic furor, the evidence for SF's state of health would again be viewed with a very selective eye. As I pointed out at the time, in several of the "Best" anthologies from the late seventies, if you looked around carefully, you could see, even then, the seeds being planted that would soon bloom into a new period of energy and expansion and creative excitement.

And now, in the wake of the "Cyberpunk" revolution, and in a recessionary period following a boom, we're going through it all again. More or less.

No, history does not repeat itself in tidy one-to-one analogues; there are important differences between each of those historical situations, especially as far as the mechanics of the SF publishing world are concerned, differences that are too complicated to get into in detail in the space permitted here—and yet, I really feel that, in general, the pattern holds.

Of course, this can be dismissed as merely a *belief* on my part, something that

I take on faith alone—and yet, I can look around me, right here, right now, and clearly *see* the seeds being planted that are going to blossom in the years ahead. There are new writers out there right now who are going to be the Big Names of the nineties—hell, the Big Names of the first part of the 21st century, for that matter. Some of them may be in this book. Some of them have yet to be noticed. Some of them have probably not even made their first *sale* yet. But they're out there.

Right now, even as you read these words, there's some sixteen-year-old kid out there somewhere reading *something* that is blowing him or her away, sitting somewhere with a book or a story grasped tightly in sweaty fingers, eyes bulging out of his or her head, going "Wow! Wow! Oh boy oh boy oh boy oh boy!", and *that* kid, whoever he or she may be, is going to be the key figure, or one of them, in the next high-energy creative "revolution" to hit science fiction. What that revolution will consist of, I don't know, although I'd be willing to bet that Cyberpunk will be one of the elements that is swept into the meld, just as the New Wave was one of the elements that went into the meld for the creation of Cyberpunk. I may not like it, or even *recognize* it—few old fart editors maintain their receptivity or credibility through more than one such revolutionary up- heaval, and I've already been through at least two of them. But it's out there. And so is that kid in the grubby T-shirt, reading until the room grows too dark to see the page, because he or she can't bear to break away long enough to get up and turn on the light.

It was a gray and somewhat glum year in the magazine market, although there were some encouraging signs, and even a couple of potential success stories. Unlike 1991, it was a relatively quiet year—most of the major changes in the magazine market were already in place by the end of 1991 or the beginning of 1992, and what we've seen this year is the beginning of the working out of their *effects* . . . although, in some cases, the jury is still out on whether the overall effect of the changes is positive or negative, and we may have to wait until next year (or later) to know for sure.

Magazine sales were down almost across the board in all of the established magazines, including *Omni*, as the magazine field in general (not just SF/fantasy titles, or even fiction magazines) continued to struggle with the effects of the recession, which deepened throughout most of 1992. *Amazing* probably had the worst year, as its first full year as a large-sized slick-format monthly saw its circulation plummet disastrously, down 61.6 percent since last year, according to the newsmagazine *Locus*; this must particularly hurt *Amazing*, since a large- sized magazine is so much more costly to produce than a digest-sized magazine, so that expenses are probably *rising* as sales decline. Nevertheless, by the spring of 1993, parent company TSR was still committed to supporting them, according to editor Kim Mohan, who remains confident that sales will increase dramatically this year. *Amazing* is probably the best-*looking* SF magazine in the business, and you'd think that it would do well on the newsstands in its new format, but the problem may be that very few people *see* it there; its distribution is awful— it's almost impossible to find on newsstands in Philadelphia or New York, for instance; or at least I haven't been able to find it in those places, and I've been looking. It was recently announced that *Amazing* has signed on with a new national distributor, which will distribute the magazine starting with its April 1993 issue, and maybe that will help; let's keep our fingers crossed for them.

Aboriginal SF also continued to struggle throughout 1992, as did *Pulphouse: A Fiction Magazine. Aboriginal SF* skipped their Spring 1992 issue, and only published three issues this year, although they were large "double" issues—they are now scheduled to produce four quarterly "double" issues a year; financial considerations also forced them to drop the use of color for their interior illustrations, and their circulation continued to decline. As I reported last year, *Aboriginal SF* had laid off their paid staff (all work is now being done by volunteer labor) and applied to the IRS for nonprofit status in order to enable the magazine to continue to publish, but that status still has not yet been approved, and it may well be that the magazine's survival depends on what the IRS ultimately decides to do. Money problems also hit Pulphouse Publishing hard this year, causing the cancellation of many of their projects, and affecting *Pulphouse: A Fiction Magazine* as well. Last year, editor Dean Wesley Smith had been forced to give up on his ambitious but unrealistic original plan to publish *Pulphouse* as a *weekly* magazine, and had changed the publication schedule to a more feasible one of publication every four weeks, closer to the monthly schedule that is the industry standard—unfortunately, probably because of the upheavals at Pulphouse Publishing, *Pulphouse: A Fiction Magazine* was published extremely erratically this year, managing to produce only six of their scheduled thirteen issues, at irregular intervals; if they can't steady down to a reliable publication schedule this year, they may be in trouble, but the Pulphouse people are planning to devote more of their energies to the magazine now that many of their other projects are defunct or scaled down, so we'll see.

Money troubles also caused *Weird Tales* to publish only two issues this year, and to change format with the second issue to a full-size staplebound format from a somewhat smaller perfectbound format. This change may end up helping *Weird Tales* considerably, since issues in this format are much less expensive to produce (thereby increasing the magazine's profitability) and bookstore chains will carry it in its new size, where they would not carry it at its former size . . . which, of course, may help its chances of being displayed, and, therefore, of being bought. *Omni*, which went through a massive internal reorganization last year and moved its production facilities to North Carolina, also changed its format slightly, going from perfectbound to staplebound—the good news is that this makes the magazine considerably cheaper to produce (especially as its production has been consolidated with that of another general media magazine, *Compute*), which increases its profitability; the *bad* news is that much of the graphic style and flair that typified the old *Omni* has been lost in the process (the magazine now looks almost exactly like *Compute*, perhaps not surprisingly), and since much of the upscale appeal of *Omni* depended on the sophistication of its graphics and the slickness of its whole visual "look" (it was *the* chic thing to be seen reading on the Metroliner, in the old days), it remains to be seen what the overall effect of all this will be on sales. *Omni* also started a new original anthology series this year, which we discuss below in the original anthology section.

At the beginning of 1992, *Analog* and *Isaac Asimov's Science Fiction Magazine* (along with two mystery magazines, all formerly belonging to Davis Publications) were sold to Dell Magazines, part of the Bantam Doubleday Dell Publishing Group, which is a part of the international consortium Bertelsmann. In November, they were redesigned slightly and "relaunched" with new logos (which, for *IAsfm*, included a name change—or alteration, anyway—to *Asimov's Science Fiction*), and in early 1993 they changed editorial offices and editorial addresses, as Dell Magazines moved into a huge new office tower in Manhattan, along with Bantam, Dell, Doubleday, and all the other (formerly) far-flung pieces of the Bertelsmann American empire. The editorial staffs of both magazines remain intact, however, and so far other changes have been minor. Circulation was down somewhat for both *Analog* and *Asimov's Science Fiction* in 1992, but Dell Magazines is putting into action a massive push for new subscriptions and greatly increased newsstand display, and next year we'll begin to see what effect this has.

Circulation was also down slightly at *The Magazine of Fantasy & Science Fiction*, 18.6 percent, according to *Locus*, but not enough to offset completely last year's *gain* in circulation of 30.9 percent, leaving it still in better shape than it had been in 1990. The tragic death of Isaac Asimov in 1992 compelled some changes in columnists for *F&SF*, with Bruce Sterling and Gregory Benford taking over the science column on a rotating basis; later, longtime Book Review columnist Algis Budrys left to start his own magazine (see below), and will be replaced on a rotating basis by John Kessel and Orson Scott Card. New editor Kristine Kathryn Rusch, who took over the reins last year from longtime editor Ed Ferman, seems to be settling in nicely, and seems to be doing a first-rate job (to answer the cries of "Can she do it?" from last year—apparently, Yes).

The British magazine *Interzone* completed its second full year as a monthly publication. Circulation was down somewhat, by approximately 15 percent, although the magazine had another solid year in terms of literary quality—in fact, *Interzone* is one of the best science fiction magazines available today, and certainly one of the most reliable places to find quality work.

Two *new* SF magazines started in 1992, and one of them, a large-size full-color magazine called *Science Fiction Age*, edited by Scott Edelman, had one of the most successful launches of any new SF magazine in recent memory, achieving, according to one estimate, a circulation of more than 100,000 with its first issue. There is obviously money behind *Science Fiction Age*—it has high production values, is very slick-looking, is attracting the kind of upscale advertisers that rarely bother with SF magazines, and has been getting lots of prominent rack display, displayed right up near the cash register in many national bookstore chains; on the other hand, it must be a very expensive magazine to produce, which means they need a higher level of profitability than a digest magazine just to break even, and it takes very deep pockets indeed to *keep* a magazine out on display in those choice racks near the cash register, often as much as ten dollars per register *per store*, which can run into real money when you're talking about the big bookstore chains with thousands of franchises nationwide. So far, the gamble seems to be paying off for *Science Fiction Age,* and if they can manage to establish themselves solidly before their money runs out, they may become one of the most prominent and widely read SF magazines of the nineties—it is still too early to tell, though, with only three issues out to date; we may well have to wait until next year, or even longer, to determine the real outcome. Still, this could be the start of an important new market, in a field that can use all the short-fiction markets it can possibly get. It's way too early to get any definite feel for the editorial personality of *Science Fiction Age,* especially since this is something which often evolves and mutates over time anyway; so far, the issues have been split equally between fiction and nonfiction, which is a little too much nonfiction for *my* tastes—but hey, for all anyone knows, it could be the nonfiction that's selling the magazine! It's just too early to tell.

The other new magazine is *Tomorrow,* a considerably less upscale operation (not attracting many advertisers, so far, or getting any kind of national distribution), edited by Algis Budrys. *Tomorrow* published one issue late in 1992, but it was dated 1993—which for us pushes any consideration of material from it into next year. It's had a rocky launch so far; it started out being published by Pulphouse Publishing, but Budrys bought it from them late in 1992, and intends to publish it himself, although there will be a delay of several months between the first issue and the second. Unlike *Science Fiction Age,* there's clearly *not* a lot of money behind *Tomorrow*—but don't discount it; Budrys is a canny and experienced editor, and may well end up doing some very interesting things with this magazine, if it survives. At any rate, I wish it well, too—as I said above, the field can use all the short-fiction markets it can get.

As most of you probably know, I, Gardner Dozois, am also the editor of a prominent SF magazine, *Asimov's Science Fiction.* And that, as I've mentioned before, does pose a problem for me in compiling this summation, particularly the magazine-by-magazine review that follows. As the editor of *Asimov's,* I could be said to have a vested interest in the magazine's success, so that anything negative I said about another SF magazine (particularly another digest-sized magazine, my direct competition), could be perceived as an attempt to make my own magazine look good by tearing down the competition. Aware of this constraint, I've decided that nobody can complain if I only say *positive* things about the competition . . . and so, once again, I've limited myself to a listing of some of the worthwhile authors published by each.

Omni published good fiction this year by Terry Bisson, Tom Maddox, Harlan Ellison, Poul Anderson, Howard Waldrop, Jonathan Carroll and others. *Omni's* fiction editor is Ellen Datlow.

The Magazine of Fantasy & Science Fiction featured good work by Bradley Denton, Joe Haldeman, Robert Reed, Steven Utley, Marc Laidlaw, Pat Cadigan, Paul J. McAuley, Lisa Mason, Terry Bisson, and others. *F&SF*'s editor is Kristine Kathryn Rusch.

Asimov's Science Fiction published good work by Michael Swanwick, Connie Willis, Maureen F. McHugh, Nancy Kress, Mike Resnick, Pat Cadigan,

Frederik Pohl, Mary Rosenblum, Pamela Sargent, Lucius Shepard, Greg Egan, Tony Daniel, Ian R. MacLeod, and others. *Asimov's SF*'s editor is Gardner Dozois.

Analog featured good work by Geoffrey A. Landis, Vonda N. McIntyre, G. David Nordley, William E. Cochrane, Dean McLaughlin, Brian C. Coad, Ben Bova, and others. *Analog*'s longtime editor is Stanley Schmidt.

Amazing featured good work by L. Sprague de Camp, Pamela Sargent, Phillip C. Jennings, Ursula K. Le Guin, Brian Stableford, Avram Davidson, and others. *Amazing*'s editor is Kim Mohan.

Interzone published good work by Greg Egan, Ian McDonald, Gwenyth Jones, Eugene Byrne, Ian MacLeod, Diane Mapes, Lawrence Watt-Evans, Kim Stanley Robinson, David Langford, and others. *Interzone*'s editor is David Pringle.

Aboriginal Science Fiction featured good work by Patricia Anthony, Gregory Benford, Richard K. Lyon, Wendy Wheeler, Jamil Nasir, and others. The editor of *Aboriginal Science Fiction* is Charles C. Ryan.

Weird Tales published good work by S.P. Somtow, Tanith Lee, Avram Davidson, F. Paul Wilson, and others. *Weird Tales*'s editors are George H. Scithers and Darrell Schweitzer.

Pulphouse: A Fiction Magazine published good work by Kathe Koja, Parke Godwin, S.A. Stolnack, Suzy McKee Charnas, Tim Sullivan, Janet Kagan, Amy Bechtel, and others. *Pulphouse: A Fiction Magazine*'s editor was Dean Wesley Smith, but he is now acting as publisher and the editor is Jonathan E. Bond.

Science Fiction Age published only one issue this year, but it contained good work by Paul Di Filippo, Don Webb, and others. *Science Fiction Age*'s editor is Scott Edelman.

As usual, short SF continued to appear in many magazines outside genre boundaries. *Playboy* in particular continues to run a good deal of SF, under fiction editor Alice K. Turner; this year they featured good work by Robert Silverberg, Lucius Shepard, and John Varley, among others.

An interesting associational magazine started early in 1993, a hip (perhaps too self-consciously so) large-format national magazine called *Wired*, which seems to be devoted to exploring cutting-edge new technologies, especially computer networks, electronic media, and Virtual Reality. Although there's no science fiction as such published here, the magazine has a definite "Cyberpunk" feel to it, and the debut issue not only features an article by Bruce Sterling about the future of military technology, it also uses a blown-up *photo* of Bruce's face as its cover image! In spite of being so "creatively" laid out and typeset as to be nearly unreadable in spots, *Wired* is supposedly doing quite well in initial sales, and may be a success.

(Subscription addresses follow for those magazines hardest to find on the newsstands: *The Magazine of Fantasy & Science Fiction*, Mercury Press, Inc., Box 56, Cornwall, CT 06753, annual subscription—12 issues—$26 in U.S.; *Asimov's Science Fiction*, Dell Magazines Fiction Group, P.O. Box 5133, Harlan, IA, 51593-5133, $34.95 for 13 issues; *Interzone*, 217 Preston Drove, Brigh-

ton BN1 6FL, United Kingdom, $52 for an airmail one year—12 issues—
subscription; *Analog*, Dell Magazines Fiction Group, P.O. Box 5133, Harlan,
IA, 51593-5133, $34.95 for 13 issues; *Pulphouse: A Fiction Magazine*, P.O. Box
1227, Eugene, OR 97440, $39 per year (13 issues) in US; *Aboriginal Science
Fiction*, P.O. Box 2449, Woburn, MA 01888-0849, $18 for 4 issues in US;
Weird Tales, Terminus Publishing Company, P.O. Box 13418, Philadelphia,
PA 19101-3418, $16 for 4 issues in US; *Tomorrow*, The Unifont Company,
Inc., Box 6038, Evanston, IL 60204, $18 for 6 issues in US.)

It was a bad year in the semiprozine market, which continues to contract,
with more magazines lost this year in addition to the magazines lost *last* year.
Michael G. Adkisson's *New Pathways* seems to have finally died, or at least I've
seen no new issue from them since the one I reviewed here last year. The eclectic
Forbidden Lines went from bimonthly to quarterly sometime during 1992, and
Steve Pasechnick's promising *Strange Plasma* only published one issue this year,
and there are rumors that it is about to go under as well. The entertaining *Nova
Express*—edited by Lawrence Person, Glen Cox, and Dwight Brown—published
no issues during 1992, although they did produce an issue just before press time
in early 1993. *Science Fiction Review* evidently has died, as has *Iniquities*. An
issue of *Whispers* was again promised for this year, and once again failed to
appear. *Grue*, *2 AM*, *Deathrealm*, *Weirdbook*, *Midnight Graffiti* and *Tales of the
Unanticipated* all produced only single issues this year. Doug Fratz's *Quantum*
(formerly the long-running *Thrust*) announced that it would cease as an independent publication in 1992 and merge with *Science Fiction Eye*, which itself only
published one issue this year (although another issue did come out soon after
the beginning of 1993); allegedly, there is still one giant final issue of *Quantum*
yet to come. And *Marion Zimmer Bradley's Fantasy Magazine* remained unim-
pressive in quality.

On the (somewhat) more positive side, there continues to be a lively British
semiprozine scene, with several eclectic magazines such as *BBR*, *Nexus*, *Strange
Attractor*, *Scheherazade*, *Exuberance*, and a number of others struggling either
to be born or to stay alive long enough to produce another issue—we'll see how
the dust has settled by next year; some of these magazines are quite likely to be
already defunct. There's an interesting Canadian magazine called *On Spec* which
seems fairly reliably established and which has produced some interesting work
this year, and two worthwhile Australian magazines, *Aurealis* and *Eidolon*.
Cemetery Dance seems to have established itself as the most prominent of the
horror semiprozines, and is now readily available on many large newsstands.

Charles N. Brown's *Locus* and Andy Porter's *Science Fiction Chronicle* remain
your best bet among the semiprozines if you are looking for news and/or an
overview of what's happening in the genre. Stephen P. Brown's *Science Fiction
Eye* and *The New York Review of Science Fiction* (whose editorial staff includes
David G. Hartwell, Donald G. Keller, Robert Killheffer, and Gordon Van
Gelder) are the most fun to read of the criticalzines, the most highly opinionated,
the most ambitious, and also publish the most eclectic and furthest-ranging types
of material—*The New York Review of Science Fiction* has in addition established
itself as the most reliably published of these magazines, keeping to its twelve-

issue schedule once again this year. Another interesting criticalzine is the Damon Knight–edited *Monad*, whch put out its second edition this year.

(*Locus*, Locus Publications, Inc., P.O. Box 13305, Oakland, CA 94661, $38 for a one-year second-class subscription, 12 issues; *Science Fiction Chronicle*, Algol Press, P.O. Box 2730, Brooklyn, NY 11202-0056, $27 for one year, 12 issues, $33 first class; *Quantum* (formerly *Thrust*), Thrust Publications, 8217 Langport Terrace, Gaithersburg, MD 20877, $7 for 3 issues; *Science Fiction Eye*, P.O. Box 18539, Asheville, NC 28814, $10 for one year; *New Pathways*, MGA Services, P.O. Box 863994, Plano, TX 75086-3994, $25 for 6-issue subscription; *Nova Express*, White Car Publications, P.O. Box 27231, Austin, TX 78755-2231, $10 for a one-year (4-issue) subscription; *Strange Plasma*, Edgewood Press, P.O. Box 264, Cambridge, MA 02238, $8 for 3 issues; *Aurealis: The Australian Magazine of Fantasy and Science Fiction*, Chimaera Publications, P.O. Box 538, Mt. Waverley, Victoria 3149, Australia, $24 for a 4-issue (quarterly) subscription, "all money orders for overseas subscriptions should be in Australian dollars"; *BBR*, P.O. Box 625, Sheffield S1 3GY, United Kingdom, $18 for 4 issues; *The New York Review of Science Fiction*, Dragon Press, P.O. Box 78, Pleasantville, NY 10570, $25 per year; *Cemetery Dance*, CD Publications, P.O. Box 858, Edgewood, MD 21040, $15 for 4 issues (one year), $25 for 8 issues (two years); *Grue Magazine*, Hells Kitchen Productions, Box 370, Times Square Station, New York, NY 10108, $13 for 3 issues; *Midnight Graffiti*, P.O. Box 2546, Yucca Valley, CA 92286-2546, one year for $19.95; *Tales of the Unanticipated*, P.O. Box 8036, Lake Street Station, Minneapolis, MN 55408, $10 for three issues; *Eidolon*, Eidolon Publications, P.O. Box 225, North Perth, Western Australia 6006, $34 (Australian) for 4 issues overseas, payable to Richard Scriven; *Forbidden Lines*, P.O. Box 23, Chapel Hill, NC 27514, $12 for 4 issues (one year); *Monad*, Pulphouse Publishing, Box 1227, Eugene, OR 97440, $5 for single issues or $18 for four issues.)

This was a generally weak year for original anthologies—there were few outright stinkers, but even most of the best original anthologies of 1992 were a bit lackluster, with few really first-rate stories.

Universe 2 (Bantam Spectra), for instance, the second volume in the new series edited by Karen Haber and Robert Silverberg (a continuation of Terry Carr's old *Universe* series) is somewhat disappointing compared to 1990's *Universe 1*— this is still a solid anthology, and a good buy for the money, but (with the exception of the Kathe Koja story reprinted here) none of the stories in it are *exceptional* . . . entertaining, yes, good solid second-rank stuff, with few bad or even mediocre stories among them, but with nothing that's really of first-class quality, either; good work here by Joe Haldeman, Tony Daniel, Carolyn Gilman, Jamil Nasir, Deborah Wessell, Paula May, and others. *New Worlds* 2 (Gollancz), the second volume in the new British anthology series edited by David Garnett, is considerably weaker than last year's debut anthology, and all the more disappointing because 1991's *New Worlds* was such an outstanding anthology. As with *Universe* 2, there's nothing really first-rate here, although *New Worlds* 2 does feature good work by Ian McDonald, Jack Deighton, Stephen Baxter, and others. Unlike *Universe* 2, though, which at least maintains an even tone and a solid average level, there *is* a good deal of weak work in *New Worlds 2*, and some stuff that is just plain bad—I certainly could have done without the two pieces by Warwick Colvin Jnr. (which I gather is an in-joke pseudonym for one of the old *New Worlds* insiders), for instance, several of the other stories are annoyingly self-conscious and pretentious, and, with space at such a premium in an anthology which is only issued once a year (and which at the moment is Britain's *only* continuing SF anthology series), I can't help but wonder if it wasn't a mistake to devote so much of that space to two long outlines for never-to-be-written novels by the late Philip K. Dick; they're interesting, but I would rather have seen the space utilized for new stories, especially as there are so few professional British markets for short fiction these days.

Let's hope these two very important anthology series get back on track and produce stronger volumes next time around—especially *New Worlds*.

What Might Have Been Volume 4: Alternate Americas (Bantam Spectra), edited by Gregory Benford and Martin H. Greenberg, was somewhat weaker than previous volumes have been, perhaps because the theme for this one is too specialized (for the most part, it's a de facto *Alternate Columbus* anthology), and, as a result, too many of the stories are too similar to each other; still, a worthwhile anthology for the money, containing strong work, both original and reprint, from L. Sprague de Camp, Pamela Sargent, Robert Silverberg, A.A. Attanasio, Sheila Finch, and others. There were two issues of a promising new series of mixed original and reprint anthologies out this year, *Omni Best Science Fiction One* and *Omni Best Science Fiction Two*, both from Omni Books, and both edited by Ellen Datlow—Volume One contains good original work by Robert Silverberg, J.R. Dunn, Bruce McAllister, Elizabeth A. Lynn, and others; Volume Two contains good original work from Lucius Shepard, Pat Cadigan, Maggie Flinn, Elizabeth Hand, and others, and there is good reprint work from *Omni* in each volume. *L. Ron Hubbard Presents Writers of the Future Volume VIII* (Bridge), edited by Algis Budrys and Dave Wolverton, was, as usual, apprentice work by people who may—or may not—one day be writing at a really professional level, but who mostly are not as yet. Responding to my statement here last year that his *Synergy* series seemed to be dead, George Zebrowski tells me that the series is *not* dead, but will be published on an irregular basis, whenever he's assembled enough worthwhile material; there was no issue of *Synergy* out this year, for the second year in a row. The long-promised last edition of the Pulphouse hardback anthology series, *Pulphouse Twelve*, didn't appear this year either, and is now being promised for sometime in 1993.

There was a somewhat upscale shared-world anthology this year: *Murasaki* (Bantam Spectra), edited by Robert Silverberg. There is excellent material in *Murasaki*, by such people as Nancy Kress, Poul Anderson, Greg Bear, and others, but for once the cover line, "a novel in six parts," is accurate—none of the sections is really independent enough from the others to stand on its own feet as an individual story, which is why you find none of them reprinted here; this book—novel, anthology, whatever it is—contains some first-rate SF ideas and extrapolation, though, and is well worth a look.

Other shared-world anthologies this year included: *Tales of Riverworld* (Warner Questar), edited by Philip José Farmer and Martin H. Greenberg; *Wild Cards XI: Dealer's Choice* (Bantam), edited by George R. R. Martin; *Wild Cards: Card Sharks* (Bantam—listed as "Book One of a New Series"), edited by George R. R. Martin; *The Further Adventures of Batman 2: Featuring the Penguin* (Bantam Spectra), edited by Martin H. Greenberg; and *The Crafters, Book Two* (Ace), edited by Christopher Stasheff and Bill Fawcett.

Turning to the non-series anthologies, the best anthology of the year is probably *Alternate Presidents* (Tor), edited by Mike Resnick, a strong mixed reprint-and-original anthology featuring excellent work by Pat Cadigan, Eileen Gunn, Judith Moffett, Jack Chalker, Janet Kagan, Susan Shwartz, Lawrence Person, and others. *Alternate Kennedys* (Tor), edited by Mike Resnick, is also a strong anthology—featuring very good work by David Gerrold, Pat Cadigan, Barry N. Malzberg, Nancy Kress, Nicholas A. DiChario, Resnick himself, and others—but it suffers a bit from the same thing that afflicted *What Might Have Been Volume 4*: the theme is specialized enough—much more specialized than in *Alternate Presidents*—that many of the stories are too similar to each other, and others are driven to rather dubious extremes in order to try to avoid doing what everyone *else* is doing ("Suppose JFK and his brothers formed a rock group and were the big hits of the decade instead of the Beatles?"). Also unlike *Alternate Presidents*, which was solidly SF for the most part, there is a rather curious vein of fantasy that runs throughout this volume, wherein writers mix JFK and the other Kennedys with standard genre mermaids/leprechauns/wizards/druids, and so on—the result is rather queasy, and not often successful, although it does give one the uncomfortable feeling (perhaps not unintentionally on Resnick's part) that JFK himself is now a mythological figure, no less rare and fabulous than a unicorn. I prefer the stories here that work solidly and centrally with the kind of Alternate History that actually *might* have happened—and, fortunately, they make up the bulk of the book, and make this a very worthwhile anthology. Resnick's other 1992 science fiction anthology, *Whatdunits* (DAW), moves away from Alternate History and closer to the center of the field, with many of the stories dealing with aliens and distant worlds, but, unfortunately, it is also by far the weakest of Resnick's anthologies this year; the gimmick here is that various authors write science fiction mystery stories from plot ideas provided by Resnick himself, solving the mystery scenarios that he throws out to them, but very few of the writers rise adequately to the challenge, and most of the stories here are at best competent, making for a rather lackluster anthology. Much better is the British anthology *In Dreams* (Gollancz), edited by Paul J. McAuley and Kim Newman. This anthology "in celebration of the 7-inch single"—in other words, for the most part, it's a collection of SF and fantasy rock 'n roll stories—also suffers a bit from overspecialization, and contains several stories that wander so far off the ostensible theme that they might just as well be in some other anthology altogether, but it also features a brilliant story by Ian R. MacLeod, a first-rate jape by Jonathan Lethem and Lukas Jaeger, and good work by Ian McDonald, Lewis Shiner, Greg Egan, Lisa Tuttle, and Stephen Baxter, among others. Another interesting British anthology was a mixed science fiction/fantasy/horror/suspense anthology called *Narrow Houses* (Little Brown), edited by Peter

Crowther, which featured excellent to good work by Pat Cadigan, Brian Stableford, Ian McDonald, Ian Watson, and others. *The Ultimate Dinosaur* (Bantam Spectra), edited by Byron Preiss and Robert Silverberg, is a handsome book, but, like most of these big glossy Byron Preiss coffee-table volumes, it's more notable for the lavish artwork and the nonfiction articles included than for the fiction, although there is good work here by Connie Willis, L. Sprague de Camp, Paul Preuss, and others. *Ark of Ice* (Pottersfield Press), edited by Lesley Choyce, is this year's only "regional" SF anthology (*Future Boston* has still not come out), a mixed reprint/original anthology that purports to be "Canadian Futurefiction"—as usual with such anthologies, the rationale for selecting certain stories here is sometimes rather weak, but many of the stories are interesting, including good work by Garfield Reeves-Stevens, Phyllis Gotlieb, Eileen Kernaghan, and others, and I enjoyed it. I'm afraid I can't say the same thing for the most part about *Abortion Stories: Fiction on Fire* (MinRef Press), edited by Rick Lawler, but the majority of the stories here are not very good, and a few are both offensive *and* not very good, of the deliberately offensive watch-me-eat-my-own-snot variety. There was also an interesting mixed original/reprint anthology called *Life Among the Asteroids* (Ace), edited by Jerry Pournelle with John F. Carr.

Unusually—and encouragingly—there were several strong original fantasy anthologies this year. The strongest, and one of the strongest of the year in any genre (and certainly the strongest Greenberg anthology of 1992) was *After the King: Stories in Honor of J.R.R. Tolkien* (Tor), edited by Martin H. Greenberg. I'm sure that many Tolkien fans who bought this were disappointed to find none of the familiar Tolkien charcters or settings or plot materials used herein, but ignoring the whole J.R.R. Tolkien connection (which you might as well, since it is subjective to the point of being invisible), this is an interesting and very eclectic book that spans a wide range of different *kinds* of fantasy, and even includes a science fiction story or two; the best work here is by Robert Silverberg, John Brunner, Emma Bull, Gregory Benford, Judith Tarr, Terry Pratchett, and Jane Yolen, among others. Another good fantasy anthology, somewhat more specialized in theme than *After the King* but also showing a fairly wide range of moods and attacks, is *Grails: Quests, Visitations, and Other Occurrences* (Unnameable Press), edited by Richard Gilliam, Martin H. Greenberg, and Edward E. Kramer; not surprisingly, it's mostly Arthurian fantasy/Holy Grail Quest stuff here, but the tone varies nicely, and sometimes quite widely, from story to story—there's good work here by Neil Gaiman, S. P. Somtow, Pat Cadigan, Lee Hoffman, Robert Sampson, Gene Wolfe, Karl Edward Wagner, and others. *Aladdin: Master of the Lamp* (DAW), edited by Mike Resnick and Martin H. Greenberg also has some interesting high spots, although it may suffer more from uniformity of tone than *Grails* (at least most of the stories are *short*: 43 stories packed into a 351-page book); there's good work here by Maureen F. McHugh, Susan Casper, Pat Cadigan, Judith Tarr, Jane Yolen, Janet Kagan, Beth Meacham, and others. Also interesting were: *Christmas Bestiary* (DAW), edited by Rosalind M. Greenberg and Martin H. Greenberg; *The Magic of Christmas* (Roc), edited by John Silbersack and Christopher Schelling; and *Dragon Fantastic* (DAW), edited by Rosalind M. Greenberg and Martin H.

Greenberg. Starting in 1993, there will be an annual original fantasy anthology series called *Xanadu*, from Tor, edited by Jane Yolen, something I also find quite encouraging. (There were also a couple of British fantasy anthologies edited by Brian Stableford that I was unable to find this year; I'll catch up with them next year.)

I'm not following the horror field as closely as I used to, since it's now being covered by three separate Best of the Year anthologies, but there the big original anthologies seem to have been *MetaHorror* (Dell Abyss), edited by Dennis Etchison, a mixed original/reprint anthology called *Midnight Graffiti* (Warner), edited by Jessica Horsting and James Van Hise, and *Still Dead* (Ziesing), edited by John Skipp and Craig Spector.

This seemed to be a pretty strong year for novels, as far as literary quality is concerned, although the overall number of novels published declined somewhat as publishing cutbacks began to take hold, and will probably decline further in the future. According to *Locus*, there was an overall 8 percent decrease in the number of books published in 1992, with mass-market paperbacks down 16 percent, and mass-market paperback-originals down a whopping 19 percent; hardcover numbers remained steady, while the small-press market is actually growing. *Locus* estimates there were 239 new SF novels published last year (down from 1991's estimate of 308, and even from 1990's estimate of 281), 278 new fantasy novels published (down slightly from last year's estimate of 301), and 185 new horror novels (the same as last year's in spite of cutbacks in the horror market—*Locus* points out, though, that although adult horror novels have been cut back, young-adult horror novels have proliferated, taking up the slack). These figures can be used—and have been—to demonstrate that the number of *science fiction* books is in steady decline, with their rack space being eaten up by fantasy and horror novels, but there is a bit of subjectivity built into the figures, depending on *what* you choose to define as a *science fiction* novel—every year, there are a few novels listed as "fantasy" for which a case could be made that they are "actually" science fiction instead . . . and very probably vice versa as well! Nevertheless, slice that as you may, the fact remains that, in spite of cutbacks, there were still almost 700 new novels published this year in the related science fiction/fantasy/horror genres, not even counting those novels that were overlooked (as inevitably some always are), or which were published under some other aesthetic heading altogether (there is a novel on this year's Nebula Ballot, for instance, that was published completely out of genre, without a word about science fiction being mentioned on its dust jacket, and which therefore probably isn't included in these figures). But even if we accept the figure of "only" 700 new novels, even if we restricted ourselves to considering just the 200+ new science fiction novels alone, it has obviously become just about impossible for any one individual to read and evaluate *all* of them. With all of the reading I have to do at shorter lengths for *Asimov's* and for this anthology, I don't have the time to read all the novels anymore, and I'm not going to try to pretend here that I have done so—in fact, I haven't even come close.

So, then, as usual, I am going to limit myself here to mentioning that of the novels I *did* have time to read, I most enjoyed: *Red Mars*, Kim Stanley Robinson (Bantam Spectra); *Fools*, Pat Cadigan (Bantam Spectra); *China Mountain Zhang*, Maureen F. McHugh (Tor); *Doomsday Book*, Connie Willis (Bantam Spectra); *A Million Open Doors*, John Barnes (Tor); *Why Do Birds*, Damon Knight (Tor); *Worlds Enough and Time*, Joe Haldeman (Morrow); *A Deeper Sea*, Alexander Jablokov (Morrow/AvoNova); and *Steel Beach*, John Varley (Putnam).

Other novels that received a lot of attention and acclaim this year included: *A Fire Upon the Deep*, Vernor Vinge (Tor); *Mining the Oort*, Frederik Pohl (Del Rey); *Glass Houses*, Laura J. Mixon (Tor); *Aristoi*, Walter Jon Williams (Tor); *Anvil of Stars*, Greg Bear (Warner Questar); *The Broken Land*, Ian McDonald (Bantam Spectra); *Snow Crash*, Neal Stephenson (Bantam Spectra); *Time, Like an Ever-Rolling Stream*, Judith Moffett (St. Martin's Press); *Lord Kelvin's Machine*, James P. Blaylock (Arkham House); *Æstival Tide*, Elizabeth Hand (Bantam Spectra); *Count Geiger's Blues*, Michael Bishop (Tor); *Mars*, Ben Bova (Bantam Spectra); *Oracle*, Mike Resnick (Ace); *Transcendence*, Charles Sheffield (Del Rey); *High Aztech*, Ernest Hogan (Tor); *Chanur's Legacy*, C. J. Cherryh (DAW); *Last Call*, Tim Powers (Morrow); *Was*, Geoff Ryman (Knopf); *The Hollow Man*, Dan Simmons (Bantam Spectra); *Briar Rose*, Jane Yolen (Tor); *The Venom Trees of Sunga*, L. Sprague de Camp (Del Rey); *Labyrinth of Night*, Allen Steele (Ace); *The Remarkables*, Robert Reed (Bantam Spectra); *Bad Brains*, Kathe Koja (Dell Abyss); *Flying in Place*, Susan Palwick (Tor); *Use of Weapons*, Iain M. Banks (Bantam Spectra); *Ishmael*, Daniel Quinn (Bantam); *Cold as Ice*, Charles Sheffield (Tor); *Sideshow*, Sheri S. Tepper (Bantam Spectra); *Valentine*, S. P. Somtow (Tor); *The Memory of Earth*, Orson Scott Card (Tor); and *Destroying Angel*, Richard Paul Russo (Ace).

In spite of problems and corporate shakeups, it can be seen that Bantam Spectra had a strong year, as did Tor. Morrow is not as much of a presence on the list as it had been for the last couple of years, and I suspect that some of the books from Morrow that *did* get noticed this year were actually bought by ex-editor David G. Hartwell before he was fired; it remains to be seen if AvoNova, the replacement program for Morrow's SF line, can establish as strong a presence for itself.

There were several good first novels this year, although the most excitement was stirred up by Maureen F. McHugh's *China Mountain Zhang* and Susan Palwick's *Flying in Place*—particularly the McHugh, which attracted as much attention as any first novel has for a number of years. Other first novels included Steven Gould's *Jumper* (Tor), Don H. DeBrandt's *The Quicksilver Screen* (Del Rey), Charles Obendorf's *Sheltered Lives* (Bantam Spectra), Maya Kaathryn Bohnhoff's *The Meri* (Baen), and Poppy Z. Brite's *Lost Souls* (Delacorte Abyss).

Several young editors are to be congratulated on their willingness to take a chance with new writers, among them Ellen Key Harris of Del Rey, Patrick Nielsen Hayden of Tor, and Gordon Van Gelder of St. Martin's Press.

It should be an interesting horse race this year for the Hugo and the Nebula Awards, since several of the year's novels are stirring up unusual amounts of excitement and acclaim, especially Robinson's *Red Mars*, Willis's *Doomsday Book*, and Varley's *Steel Beach*. It will be intriguing to see which of these—if *any* of them—win what . . . but it's already shaping up as a strongly competitive year.

Associational items and obscurely published novels that might be of interest to SF readers this year included: Harvey Jacobs's *Beautiful Soup: A Novel for the 21st Century* ($12.95 from Celadon Press, 101 W. 12th St., New York, NY 10011); Carol Emshwiller's *Venus Rising* ($6 from Edgewood Press, P.O. Box 264, Cambridge, MA 02238); Neal Barrett, Jr.'s comic Mafia novel, *Pink Vodka Blues* (St. Martin's Press); and the publication of R. A. Lafferty's novel *More Than Melchisedech* in three separate volumes by United Mythologies Press: *Tales of Chicago*, *Tales of Midnight*, and *Argo* (each volume $19.95 plus $3 postage from United Mythologies Press, Box 390, Station A, Weston, Ont., Canada M9N 3N1).

It was another good year for short-story collections, and, once again, many of the best of them were published by small presses. The best collections of the year were: *Globalhead*, Bruce Sterling (Ziesing); the massive *The Collected Stories of Robert Silverberg, Volume 1: Secret Sharers* (Bantam Spectra); *Home by the Sea*, Pat Cadigan (WSFA Press); *Slightly Off Center*, Neal Barrett, Jr. (Swan Press); *Meeting in Infinity*, John Kessel (Arkham House); and *Speaking In Tongues*, Ian McDonald (Bantam Spectra). Also excellent were *And the Angels Sing*, Kate Wilhelm (St. Martin's Press); *When the Five Moons Rise*, Jack Vance (Underwood-Miller); *Iron Tears*, R. A. Lafferty (Edgewood Press); *Isaac Asimov: The Complete Stories, Volume 2* (Doubleday Foundation); *Will the Last Person to Leave the Planet Please Shut Off the Sun?*, Mike Resnick (Tor): *Kaeti on Tour*, Keith Roberts (Sirius Book Company); *Crosstime Traffic*, Lawrence Watt-Evans (Del Rey); and *The Sons of Noah & Other Stories*, Jack Cady (Broken Moon Press). *Young Wolfe*, Gene Wolfe (United Mythologies Press), will probably appeal mostly to really hardcore Wolfe fans and Wolfe completists, but is of considerable historic interest. *Kipling's Science Fiction* and *Kipling's Fantasy*, both from Tor and both edited by John Brunner, should help to reintroduce genre readers to one of the seminal authors in the development of both forms, and one who often reads as freshly and vividly today as he did eighty years ago. An interesting borderline collection, with some stories reminiscent of Magic Realism and some closer to the center of the field, is *Mrs. Vargas and the Dead Naturalist*, Kathleen Alcalá (CALYX Books). Noted without comment is *Geodesic Dreams*, Gardner Dozois (St. Martin's Press).

(Several of these small press publishers are small enough that there's little chance of finding these collections in bookstores, so I'll list mailing address for them here: Mark V. Ziesing, P.O. Box 76, Shingletown, CA 96088—$29.95 for *Globalhead*; Swan Press, P.O. Box 90006, Austin, TX 78709—$9.50 for *Slightly Off Center*; WSFA Press, P.O. Box 19951, Baltimore, MD 21211-0951—$49.95 for *Home by the Sea*; Arkham House, P.O. Box 546, Sauk City, WI 53583—$20.95 for *Meeting in Infinity*; Underwood-Miller, 708 Westover Drive, Lancaster, PA 17601, $29.95 for *When the Five Moons Rise*; Edgewood Press, P.O. Box 264, Cambridge, MA 02238—$10 plus $1.50 shipping and handling for *Iron Tears*; The Sirius Book Company, P.O. Box 122, Feltham,

Middlesex, England, UK—£13.95 for *Kaeti on Tour*; Broken Moon Press, P.O. Box 24585, Seattle, WA 98124-0585—$13.95 for *The Sons of Noah & Other Stories*; United Mythologies Press, Box 390, Station A, Weston, Ont., Canada M9N 3N1—$19.95 for *Young Wolfe*; CALYX Books, P.O. Box B, Corvallis, OR 97339—$9.95 for *Mrs. Vargas and The Dead Naturalist*.)

As you can see, small-press publishers continue to publish the bulk of the year's outstanding collections, although trade publishers such as Bantam Spectra and St. Martin's took up some of the slack this year. Those publishers who continue to publish hardcover collections are particularly courageous, as few hardcover collections these days ever sell a mass-market paperback edition, even those by relatively Big Names, a situation I find deplorable.

With the closing down of the *Author's Choice Monthly* line, with the *Short Story Paperback* line being put "on hold" for an indefinite period of time, with the drastic downscaling of the Axolotl novella line (with many announced individual titles cancelled), with the collapse of the proposed Axolotl/Bantam novella line, and with the death of the *Pulphouse: A Hardback Magazine* original anthology series, Pulphouse Publishing is just about out of the short-fiction business, with the exception of *Pulphouse: A Fiction Magazine*. And thus ends— in failure, alas—the most ambitious SF short-fiction publishing program of recent times. With the failure of the various *Pulphouse* lines, the failure of the Tor Doubles line, the canceling of the Axolotl/Bantam novella line, and the presumed failure of the British Legend novella line (At least, they have yet to follow up the initial releases with any *more* such books to date.), I'm afraid that short fiction in book form is going to become even *harder* to find in the science fiction genre than it already is, and collections, for the most part, will continue to be left to the small presses by most of the major trade publishers. A bleak prospect—the only bright spot here being that at least small-press collections are getting *noticed* more now than they were a few years ago, and are perhaps a bit more readily available now—mostly in SF specialty bookstores and in the more "literary" chain bookstores such as *Borders*—than they used to be.

Your best bets in the reprint anthology market in 1992, as is usually the case, were the various "Best of the Year" anthologies, and the annual Nebula Award anthology, *Nebula Awards 26* (Harcourt Brace Jovanovich), edited by James Morrow. Science fiction, which only two years ago was covered by three "Best" anthologies, is down to being covered by only one, the one you are holding in your hand at this moment. There are still three Best of the Year anthologies covering horror: Karl Edward Wagner's long-established *Year's Best Horror Stories* (DAW), now up to volume XX, a newer British series called *Best New Horror* (Carroll & Graf), edited by Ramsey Campbell and Stephen Jones, up to volume 3 this year, and the Ellen Datlow half of a mammoth volume covering both horror *and* fantasy, *The Year's Best Fantasy and Horror* (St. Martin's Press), edited by Ellen Datlow and Terri Windling, this year up to its Fifth Annual Collection. Fantasy, as distinguished from horror, is covered only by Terri Windling's half of the Datlow/Windling anthology—and at a time when the fantasy genre is expanding, too. I don't personally see why we need *three* "Best" anthologies covering horror when we only have one anthology covering science fiction and only *half* of an anthology covering fantasy—but the publishers certainly don't ask *my* opinion on these matters. Maybe next year someone will start another science fiction "Best" anthology, or a "Best" anthology devoted to fantasy alone.

Other good buys for the money this year were several "historical overview" type anthologies, the best of which was probably a massive overview of the horror field, *Foundations of Fear* (Tor), edited by David G. Hartwell. Other good values in this area included: the interesting although somewhat idiosyncratic *The Oxford Book of Science Fiction* (Oxford), edited by Tom Shippey; *Isaac Asimov Presents the Great SF Stories: 24* (DAW), edited by Isaac Asimov and Martin H. Greenberg; *Isaac Asimov Presents the Great SF Stories: 25* (DAW), edited by Isaac Asimov and Martin H. Greenberg; *The Mammoth Book of Fantastic Science Fiction Short Novels of the 1970s* (Robinson), edited by Isaac Asimov, Charles G. Waugh, and Martin H. Greenberg; *The Mammoth Book of Fantastic Fiction* (Carroll & Graf), edited by Isaac Asimov, Charles G. Waugh, and Martin H. Greenberg; *The Best of Astounding* (Carroll & Graf), edited by James Gunn; and a "Best" anthology drawn from the small-press field, *The Best of the Rest 1990* (Edgewood Press), edited by Stephen Pasechnick and Brian Youmans.

The best one-shot "theme" reprint anthology of the year was probably *Inside the Funhouse: 17 SF Stories About SF* (AvoNova), edited by Mike Resnick. When I heard about this one, I expected it to be pretty lightweight, but, in fact, several of the stories here are quite substantial in quality (notably Pohl and Kornbluth's "Mute Inglorious Tam," Edmond Hamilton's "The Pro," and Malzberg's "Corridors," among others), and none of the stories here are less than entertaining; if for nothing else, Resnick should be complimented for reprinting Philip K. Dick's "Waterspider," a rare story that features Poul Anderson as the main character! Also quite good, considerably better than the year's *original* Christmas anthologies, was *Christmas Stars* (Tor), edited by David G. Hartwell, which contained excellent stories by Connie Willis, Gene Wolfe, Jack McDevitt, Brian W. Aldiss, and others.

Also interesting were: *Bootcamp 3000* (Ace), edited by Gordon R. Dickson, Charles G. Waugh, and Martin H. Greenberg; and *Space Dogfights* (Ace), edited by Algis Budrys, Charles G. Waugh, and Martin H. Greenberg. Noted without comment are *Unicorns II* (Ace), edited by Jack Dann and Gardner Dozois, and *Isaac Asimov's Earth* (Ace), edited by Gardner Dozois and Sheila Williams.

This was a somewhat stronger year than average in the SF-oriented nonfiction SF reference book field, although once again, disappointingly, John Clute and Peter Nicholls's long-promised update of Nicholls's *The Science Fiction Encyclopedia* failed to appear (there are strong indications that it will really actually No Fooling appear next year, though; I've even seen a galley proof of my entry and as we go to press my editor swears he has actually touched a copy of the finished book). A new edition of *Twentieth-Century Science-Fiction Writers* (St. James Press), edited by Noelle Watson and Paul E. Schellinger, *was* released late in 1992, although I didn't catch up with it until early this year. It's a solid work, and a valuable reference tool, and certainly a better and more usable job than Gunn's *The New Encyclopedia of Science Fiction* from a few years back, but it too is plagued by frustrating omissions (you can understand how some of the newest writers can be overlooked, but how can a work published in 1992, the year when she won the Arthur C. Clarke Award, manage to overlook Pat Cadigan, for instance? Or overlook Nancy Kress, in the year when she won both the Hugo and the Nebula Awards? And there are many other omissions as well) and by irritating errors of fact—in my own entry, for instance, the one in which I can most easily check the facts, they insist on listing me as the editor of the *Full Spectrum* anthology series (much to the dismay of the *actual* editors, I'm sure!), even though I carefully corrected that mistake on the galleys. Nitpicking of this sort aside, *Twentieth-Century Science-Fiction Writers* is a valuable reference work, and certainly belongs in libraries, but it is not an entirely satisfactory replacement for Nicholls's 1979 *The Science Fiction Encyclopedia*, and the need for an update of the Nicholls book is still urgent, and growing more urgent every year. Elsewhere, your best bets for SF reference works this year were: *Science Fiction, Fantasy, & Horror: 1991* (Locus Press), edited by Charles N. Brown and William G. Contento; *Reginald's Science Fiction and Fantasy Awards, Second Edition* (Borgo Press), edited by Daryl F. Mallett and Robert Reginald; *Reference Guide to Science Fiction, Fantasy, and Horror* (Libraries Unlimited), edited by Michael Burgess; and *Science Fiction and Fantasy Literature II: A Checklist, 1975–1991* (Gale Research), edited by Robert Reginald. There were several books that might be of use to those interested in the craft of writing or in SF criticism, among them *The Profession of Science Fiction* (St. Martin's Press), edited by Maxim Jakubowski and Edward James; *Inside Science Fiction: Essays on Fantastic Literature* (Borgo Press), edited by James Gunn; *Strategies of Fantasy* (Indiana University Press), by Brian Attebery; *Fiction 2000: Cyberpunk and the Future of Narrative* (University of Georgia Press), edited by George Slusser and Tom Shippey; *Science Fiction and Fantasy Book Review Annual 1990* (Greenwood Press), edited by Robert A. Collins and Robert Latham; and *Victorian Fantasy Literature* (Edwin Mellen Press), by Karen Michalson. For those interested in science fiction in Other Lands, there was *Canadian Science Fiction and Fantasy* (Indiana University Press), by David Ketterer, and *Japanese Science Fiction: A View of a Changing Society* (Routledge), by Robert Matthew. And for those more interested in individual *authors*, there was a book-length interview with Michael Moorcock, *Michael Moorcock: Death Is No Obstacle* (Savoy), by Colin Greenland; a biography of Arthur C. Clarke, *Arthur C. Clarke: The Authorized Biography* (Contemporary), by Neil McAleer; and a book-length study of William Gibson, called, appropriately enough, *William Gibson* (Starmont House), by Lance Olsen.

Of the year's art books, by far the best was James Gurney's marvelous *Dinotopia* (Turner Publishing). Other artists in the field may paint dinosaurs better and more accurately than Gurney (Bob Walters, for instance, or Dougal Dixon), but Gurney here is unmatched for the imagination, creativity, and gentle whimsy that he brings to his wry and charming depiction of how human society might mingle *with* dinosaurs if the dinosaurs had not become extinct, and Gurney's control of technique here is painterly and masterful, even in the pieces that don't feature human-dinosaur interaction, such as the wonderfully evocative "Waterfall City." I wouldn't be at all surprised to see this book win Gurney a Hugo Award this year. Also worthwhile were: *John Berkey Painted Space* (Friedlander Publishing Group), John Berkey; *Virgil Finlay's Women of the Ages* (Underwood-Miller), Virgil Finlay; *The Fantasy Art Techniques of Tim Hildebrandt* (Paper Tiger), Tim Hildebrandt; *In the Garden of Unearthly Delights* (Paper Tiger), Josh Kirby; and *H.R. Giger's Necronomicon II* (Morpheus International), H.R. Giger.

In the general genre-related nonfiction field, the choice was also clear—the best general nonfiction book of the year was Bruce Sterling's compelling *The Hacker Crackdown: Law and Disorder on the Electronic Frontier* (Bantam). This isn't strictly *about* science fiction, although plenty of science fiction writers are mentioned prominently, but it will certainly be of absorbing interest to anyone who is intrigued by computers and computer crime, concerned with First Amendment issues involving the repression of free speech, or fascinated by speculations on what effect the rapidly evolving "electronic community" will have on the lifestyles and mores of a not-too-distant future society. Speaking of the "electronic community," some of that same territory is also explored in Arthur C. Clarke's *How the World Was One: Beyond the Global Village* (Bantam), another interesting speculation on how the communications revolution is about to change—and already *has* changed, in fact—our lives in every detail from the most mundane to the most profound.

In spite of the presence of several box-office blockbusters, 1992 seemed (to me, anyway) like a rather lackluster year for genre films. There were lots of sequels, and most of them demonstrated once again that *more* is usually *less*—a lesson that you would have thought that Hollywood had had plenty of time to learn by now. At any rate, *Batman Returns* was even more disappointing than the original *Batman*—and I didn't even like *that* all that much to begin with. *Alien³* was disappointing, by far the worst of the *Alien* movies (perhaps they should have used that screenplay by Bill Gibson *afterall*, eh?)—at least Sigourney Weaver got chomped (reputedly by request) and so doesn't have to worry about being stuck with doing another one of these . . . although after the lackluster box-office draw, that may not be too much of a possibility anyway. *Honey, I Blew Up the Kid* was also disappointing, lacking the naïve charm and energy of *Honey, I Shrunk the Kids*. In fact, "disappointing" is a good word for many of 1992's films, and is just as applicable for the same reasons when extended beyond strict genre boundaries: *Lethal Weapon 3*, for instance, was "disappointing," not even as good as the second movie in the sequence, let alone the first, and even *Home Alone 2*, although it made scads of money, was fundamentally just an overblown rerun of the tropes of the original movie, played with less energy and verve the second time around. Since this has been true of the vast majority of movie sequels since *Son of Kong*—if not long before—you'd think that the movie industry would have caught on by this point. Usually they don't even make all that much *money*—although every now and then a *Terminator 2* or a *Home*

Alone 2 makes a bizillion bucks, and then everyone goes sequel-crazy. I'm praying that there *won't* be a *Robin Hood: Prince of Thieves* 2. I might even be willing to make a small burnt offering to insure against it.

"Disappointing" isn't a word that applies only to *sequels*, of course. The bulk of the original genre films of 1992 were disappointing as well. *Toys* was stunningly beautiful and creative in its set-design and its costuming and photography, but as a *movie* it was dull, heavyhandedly preachy, and ponderously coy, full of thudding elephantine whimsy—too bad they didn't save some of that creativity for the *script*; even Robin Williams and Joan Cusack couldn't save this one. *Bram Stoker's Dracula* was handsome, glossy, glassy-eyed, and dead, like a stuffed panther in a museum case. *Prelude to a Kiss* was well-intentioned and well-acted, but ultimately rather glib and unsatisfactory, failing to come to grips with many of the more challenging aspects of its premise. Mel Gibson struggled manfully with the material in *Forever Young*, and did a credible job (especially in the scenes where he was interacting with the young boy), but leaky writing and holes in its plot logic you could fly a B-52 through without scraping the wingtips eventually scuttled the movie—interestingly, almost the identical thematic material was handed much more subtly and more satisfyingly in last year's much less expensive and much less hyped *Late for Dinner*. *Universal Soldier* was sort of like *Terminator 2* with everything that was *good* about that movie removed. *Freejack* had some good special effects, and some decent actors adrift in a rather muddled plotline. *The Lawnmower Man* had some good special effects—period. *Death Becomes Her* had some good jokes and some cute comicbook-grotesque special effects, but there was not really much *there* there, to paraphrase Dorothy Parker. *Buffy the Vampire Slayer* was dumb but energetic. *Encino Man* was dumb. I hated *Twin Peaks* enough on television that I couldn't bring myself to see *Twin Peaks· Fire Walk With Me*, so you're on your own there.

The best fantasy movie of 1992 in many respects was Disney's full-length animated feature *Aladdin*, which features some creative and (for Disney, anyway) unusually satirical animation and a funny and frentic over-the-top vocal performance by Robin Williams. (There were also some full-length animated features that *didn't* do all that well: *Cool World*, *Ferngully—The Last Rainforest*, and *Rock-A-Doodle*—proving that, in spite of the immense box-office draw of *Beauty and the Beast* and *Aladdin*, animated films aren't automatically the Road to Success.) *Thunderheart* was a well-acted intelligently scripted thriller with a strong, though subtly played, fantastic element drawn from American Indian mysticism. I myself didn't go to see *The Muppet Christmas Carol*, but it's gotten some good reviews and good word-of-mouth, and those who have seen it tell me that Michael Caine deserves some kind of special award for being able to give a serious and straight-faced performance as Scrooge while talking to felt pigs and frogs.

As usual, there were also tromping zombie legions of cheaply produced slasher/serial killer/exploding head movies, as well as some big-budget horror films such as *Sleepwalkers*, *Pet Semetary Two*, and *Hellraiser III: Hell on Earth*, and several entries in the new Killer Babysitter/Secretary/Roommate subgenre, such as *The*

Hand That Rocks the Cradle, but I've burnt out on horror movies (a low-budget sleeper called *Tremors* from a couple of years back was the last one I actually enjoyed), and am rarely able to force myself to sit through them any more, so you're on your own there, too.

My favorite movie of the year was Clint Eastwood's *Unforgiven*. I could justify a mention of it here by working up an elaborate rationale to the effect that its exactingly authentic portrayal of the *real* Wild West makes it as exotic as many an author's alien planet, and just as capable of delivering profound Culture Shock . . . but, fuck it, I'm not going to bother. It's a good movie. Go see it. I think you'll like it.

Most of the excitement about genre material this year actually seemed to be on television, anyway, to consideration of which we turn next.

The long-awaited and often-postponed Sci-Fi Channel, a cable channel devoted entirely to, well, "Sci-Fi," actually *did* debut this year, but we can't get it here in Philadelphia, so I'm unable to comment personally on it—from what I've read, though, and from what I've heard from others, it seems as if it's mostly another excuse to recycle the sort of films that they make fun of on "Mystery Science Theater 3000." Whether it'll ever be more than that, I don't know; I also don't have any really firm idea how it's doing financially, although one source said, vaguely, that it was doing "okay." We'll see.

Several genre-related shows came and went on television during 1992, the best of which was probably "The Young Indiana Jones Chronicles," which may get a new lease on life in 1993. "Scorch," "Nightmare Cafe," and "Fish Police" were not very good, and quickly went down the tubes. "Eerie, Indiana" also died, as, I think, did "Hi, Honey, I'm Home" and "Charlie Hoover." I *still* don't like "Dinosaurs" or "Quantum Leap," I'm tired of "The Simpsons," and the big new Cult Favorite, "The Ren and Stimpy Show," strikes me as overrated. "Star Trek: The Next Generation" is still probably the best science fiction show on television (and that includes the new SF series discussed below). The above-mentioned "Mystery Science Theater 3000" can be very funny indeed, although I get tired of it after a while and only rarely make it all the way through an episode. Fox's new animated series, "Batman," is surprisingly good and surprisingly intelligent, with some limited but effective animation, and good scripts— I actually like it *better* than the *Batman* theatrical movie and its sequel, if for no other reason than the fact that I don't have to keep thinking how completely wrong Michael Keaton is for the part while I'm watching it. "Northern Exposure" is still one of the top shows on television, although the writing has slipped in quality somewhat this year (possibly because network bigwigs, having noticed the show, are now busily trying to "improve" it—that's my guess, anyway), and still occasionally runs shows that have a fantastic element; Ed's old Indian ghost made a return appearance this year, for instance.

There was a *big* influx of new science fiction shows at the beginning of 1993— most of them will probably kill each other off, although it's probably too early to predict which of them will kill *which*. It's probably a fairly safe prediction that "Star Trek: Deep Space Nine" will survive—it *is* the best of the new lot of SF shows, and has the massive carry-over momentum generated by "Star Trek: The

Next Generation" going for it; if it can regularly pull a sizable proportion of the "Star Trek: TNG" viewing audience, that alone ought to ensure its survival for a while. Having said that it's the best of the new SF shows, I must also add that I find it somewhat disappointing overall—it is, so far, anyway, not as good as "Star Trek: TNG" has become (although it should be remembered that it took *that* show several seasons to really gather steam, and that the earlier episodes were actually rather weak), is on occasion slow almost to the point of being dull, and often somewhat flat. Part of the problem is that the cast does not feature anyone with the acting ability, or at least the theatrical presence, of the best actors from the "Star Trek: TNG" cast—the performances are often rather wooden, the most accomplished actor in the cast is given relatively little to do, and the most potentially interesting *character* is being portrayed by an actress who so far has yet to demonstrate her ability to act her way out of a paper Space Bag. So far only the actor who plays the Good Bad Guy (or Bad Good Guy, if you'd rather), Quark, is showing any sort of real flair or panache in his performance— something that "Star Trek: Deep Space Nine" could use a lot *more* of to divert you from the thought that, after all, it's just a show about a, like, you know, *space shopping mall.* Gee. Still, as I say, this one is likely to be around for a couple of seasons at the least—I'm not sure I'm as sanguine about the other new SF shows. I was predisposed to like "Babylon 5" because the genre people I know who work in Hollywood were sympathetic to it, and because of the widespread allegations that its scenario was ripped off by another production company (and, indeed, its back-story and setting are similar enough to those of "Star Trek: Deep Space Nine" that there are probably lawyers somewhere girding their loins right now to sue *some*body, one way or the other), but, when push came to shove, I found that I *didn't* like it very much afterall. The acting is even *more* wooden, if possible, than that in "Star Trek: Deep Space Nine," and the much-hyped computer-generated special effects are actually rather cheesy-looking, not nearly as good as the effects and production values on either "Star Trek: TNG" or "Star Trek: Deep Space Nine" (although probably a good deal *cheaper* to produce, which may count for something). I think that "Star Trek: Deep Space Nine" will probaby sink "Babylon 5," though—people certainly aren't going to watch *two* such similar shows, and "Star Trek: Deep Space Nine" is the slicker product, and comes with a built-in audience. I was even less impressed by "Space Rang- ers," which mostly wastes the wonderfully talented Linda Hunt, and which strikes me as "The A-Team" with spaceships—to be fair, I do know people who like this one, though. "Time Trax" is even worse, so bad, in fact, that I am hard pressed to find an adequate comparison for it—it's like "Knight Rider" with time- travelers, perhaps, although even that's not quite bad enough. By late February of 1993, it was being rumored that "Space Rangers" had already died, and I suspect that "Time Trax" will quickly follow it into oblivion, but don't worry, there are lots *more* SF shows coming up in the near future, including "Sea Quest," a "Cyberpunk" show called "Wild Palms," and perhaps, as a mid-season replacement, "Doors."

So, if any of these shows become wildly popular, will that then, as is sometimes claimed, generate vast new audiences for print science fiction? My answer is,

Probably Not. Oh, there will be *some* viewers who will be inspired by these shows to begin reading print science fiction, just as there were some who were inspired to do so by "Star Trek," *Star Wars*, and "Star Trek: The Next Generation"—but there won't be any significant *numbers* of them, if history is any guide. For the most part, viewers of those shows are only interested in reading print science fiction if it's *about* the shows that they like, i.e., a *Star Trek* novel; no significant spillover into the rest of the SF print genre has ever been demonstrated. What *is* likely to have a significant impact on the print SF genre is the flood of new TV-related tie-in books that will spill on to the newsstands if one of these shows becomes widely popular—already there's a multitude of *Star Trek: Deep Space Nine* novels being prepared, to join the armies of *Star Trek* and *Star Trek: The Next Generation* novels already on the racks, and if the other series are successful, we could conceivably see *Babylon 5* or *Time Trax* novels there in the near future, too. I don't begrudge viewers who enjoy these shows the right to read a novel based on one of them—what does make me grumpy occasionally, though, is that these kind of books tend to gobble up rack display space, something already in short supply, and therefore make it even harder for non-series, non-television/movie-related SF novels to get displayed. And *that* makes it even harder for a writer to *sell* an adult SF novel of quality, especially one that is "literary," or not part of a series or a "trilogy" or a sharecropper franchise. Why should publishers bother to buy such a risky item, or booksellers bother to display it, when the next *Star Trek: Deep Space Nine* novel is almost certainly going to sell considerably better? This is no one's fault, I guess, and I don't know what can be done about it . . . but it does cause me to cast a cynical eye on the claim that these TV shows, if successful, will be the salvation of the print SF genre. Yes, I think that a few of the viewers attracted by these shows *will* go on to reading Robert Heinlein or Connie Willis or William Gibson or Pat Cadigan—but that there will be enough of them to make up for the *negative* effects . . . I don't know. I'd like to think so, but, really, I doubt it.

The 50th World Science Fiction Convention, MagiCon, was held in Orlando, Florida, from September 2 to September 7, 1992, and drew an estimated attendance of 5900. The 1992 Hugo Awards, presented at MagiCon, were: Best Novel, *Barrayar*, by Lois McMaster Bujold; Best Novella, "Beggars in Spain," by Nancy Kress; Best Novelette, "Gold," by Isaac Asimov; Best Short Story, "A Walk in the Sun," by Geoffrey A. Landis; Best Non-Fiction, *The World of Charles Addams*, by Charles Addams; Best Professional Editor, Gardner Dozois; Best Professional Artist, Michael Whelan; Best Original Artwork, Michael Whelan for the cover for *The Summer Queen*; Best Dramatic Presentation, *Terminator 2*; Best Semiprozine, *Locus*; Best Fanzine, *Mimosa*, edited by Dick and Nicki Lynch; Best Fan Writer, David Langford; Best Fan Artist, Brad W. Foster; plus the John W. Campbell Award for Best New Writer to Ted Chiang.

The 1991 Nebula Awards, presented at a banquet at the Colony Square Hotel in Atlanta, Georgia, on April 25, 1992, were: Best Novel, *Stations of the Tide*, by Michael Swanwick; Best Novella, "Beggars in Spain," by Nancy Kress; Best

Novelette, "Guide Dog," by Mike Conner; Best Short Story, "Ma Qui," by Alan Brennert; plus a special Bradbury Award to *Terminator 2*.

The World Fantasy Awards, presented at the Eighteenth Annual World Fantasy Convention in Pine Mountain, Georgia, on November 1, 1992, were: Best Novel, *Boy's Life*, by Robert R. McCammon; Best Novella, "The Ragthorn," by Robert Holdstock and Garry Kilworth; Best Short Story, "The Somewhere Doors," by Fred Chappell; Best Collection, *The Ends of the Earth*, by Lucius Shepard; Best Anthology, *The Year's Best Fantasy and Horror: Fourth Annual Collection*, edited by Ellen Datlow and Terri Windling; Best Artist, Tim Hildebrandt; Special Award (Professional), George Scithers and Darrell Schweitzer for *Weird Tales*; Special Award (Non-Professional), W. Paul Ganley for *Weirdbook*, and a Life Achievement Award to Edd Cartier.

The 1992 Bram Stoker Awards, presented at the Parker Meridien Hotel in New York City by the Horror Writers of America, were: Best Novel, *Boy's Life*, by Robert R. McCammon; Best First Novel (tie), *The Cipher*, by Kathe Koja and *Prodigal*, by Melanie Tem; Best Collection, *Prayers to Broken Stones*, by Dan Simmons; Best Novella/Novelette, "The Beautiful Uncut Hair of Graves," by David Morrell; Best Short Story, "Lady Madonna," by Nancy Holder; Best Non-Fiction, *Clive Barker's Shadows in Eden*, edited by Stephen Jones; plus a Life Achievement Award to Gahan Wilson.

The 1991 John W. Campbell Memorial Award–winner was *Buddy Holly Is Alive and Well on Ganymede*, by Bradley Denton.

The 1991 Theodore Sturgeon Award was won by "Buffalo," by John Kessel.

The 1991 Philip K. Dick Memorial Award–winner was *King of Morning, Queen of Day*, by Ian McDonald.

The James Tiptree, Jr. Award was created in 1991 and the first award was given to *White Queen*, by Gwyneth Jones and to *A Woman of the Iron People*, by Eleanor Arnason. The 1992 James Tiptree, Jr. Award was given to *China Mountain Zhang*, by Maureen F. McHugh.

The 1991 Arthur C. Clarke award was won by *Synners*, by Pat Cadigan.

Death took a heavy toll from the science fiction field in 1992 and early 1993, claiming several of its most famous and beloved figures. Among the dead were: **Isaac Asimov**, 72, one of the original giants of science fiction's Golden Age, perhaps the most famous SF writer of the last half of the twentieth century, and certainly the most tireless and indefatigable science popularizer, author of the famous *Foundation* trilogy as well as *I, Robot*, *The Caves of Steel*, *The Naked Sun*, and literally hundreds of other books; **Fritz Leiber**, 81, another Golden Age giant and a seminal figure whose career spanned the entire development of the modern fields of science fiction, fantasy, and horror, all of which he influenced deeply, a multiple award winner, author of *Conjure Wife*, *The Wanderer*, *Our Lady of the Darkness*, and *The Big Time* (in my opinion, one of the ten best SF novels ever written); **Reginald Bretnor**, 80, the creator of the "Feghoot" and the "Papa Schimmelhorn" stories, as well as a respected academic who produced such works as *The Craft of Science Fiction*; **Keith Laumer**, 67, popular author of the long-running "Retief" series, as well as such novels as *Worlds of the Imperium*, *A Plague of Demons*, and the underrated *A Trace of Memory*; **Alan E. Nourse**, 63, veteran SF writer, author of *Trouble on Titan* and *Star Surgeon*, among many others; **Dwight V. Swain**, 76, longtime SF and fantasy writer; **Robert Sampson**, 65, a pulp-era author who in recent years had revitalized his career as a short-story writer with sales to many of the top markets; **Angela Carter**, 51, respected literary writer whose work was sometimes listed as a sort of "Magic Realism," author of *The War of Dreams*, *Nights at the Circus*, and many others; **Mary Norton**, 88, author of the renowned series of children's fantasy novels about the adventures of "The Borrowers," a miniature race that lives in hiding behind the scenes of our normal human world; **Gustav Hasford**, 45, author of *The Short-Timers*, *The Phantom Blooper*, and others; **Rosemary Sutcliff**, 71, historical novelist, author of the classic Arthurian novel *Sword at Sunset*; **Jack Sharkey**, 61, veteran SF author who was a popular writer for *Galaxy* in the fifties; **Daniel Da Cruz**, 69, author of *The Ayes of Texas* and other SF novels; **Kobo Abe**, 68, Japanese literary novelist who occasionally published some SF, such as *Inter Ice Age 4*; **Desmond W. Hall**, 82, former assistant editor of *Astounding*; **Joe Shuster**, 78, the co-creator of *Superman*; **George MacBeth**, 60, British poet, producer, and well-known figure in the British SF scene; **Millea Kenin**, 49, small-press publisher and writer; **William M. Gaines**, 70, publisher of *Mad* magazine; **Samuel S. Walker**, 65, founder and president of Walker Publishing; **Gerard K. O'Neill**, 69, physicist and highly influential advocate of space colonization, author of *The High Frontier*; **Gerald Feinberg**, 58, well-known physicist and longtime SF enthusiast; **Scott Meredith**, 69, founder and longtime head of one of the most successful literary agencies in the world; **Sidney Meredith**, 73, brother of Scott Meredith and co-founder of the Meredith Agency; **Gerry De La Ree**, well-known collector and publisher; **Vincent Miranda**, 46, longtime SF fan and academic, husband of SF writer Sarah Clemens, a friend; **Margo Skinner**, poet, wife of SF writer Fritz Leiber; **Horst Grimm**, 64, husband of SF writer Cherry Wilder; **Helen Silverberg**, 81, mother of SF writer Robert Silverberg; and **Mary Potter Bias**, 78, mother of SF figure Gay Haldeman.

GRIFFIN'S EGG

Michael Swanwick

Michael Swanwick made his debut in 1980, and has become one of the most popular and respected of all that decade's new writers. He has several times been a finalist for the Nebula Award, as well as for the World Fantasy Award and for the John W. Campbell Award, and has won the Theodore Sturgeon Award and the *Asimov's* Reader's Award poll. Last year, his critically acclaimed novel, *Stations of the Tide*, won him a Nebula Award as well. His other books include his first novel, *In the Drift*, which was published in 1985, and 1987s popular *Vacuum Flowers*. Aside from *Stations of the Tide*, his most recent books are a collection of his collaborative short work with other writers, *Slow Dancing Through Time*, and a collection of his solo short fiction, *Gravity's Angels*. Coming up is a new novel, tentatively entitled *The Iron Dragon's Daughter*. He's had stories in our Second, Third, Fourth, Sixth, and Seventh Annual Collections. Swanwick lives in Philadelphia with his wife, Marianne Porter, and their young son, Sean.

In the complex and powerful novella that follows, Swanwick takes us to the Moon, which, in Swanwick's hands, is a surprising place: a vast industrial park of bewildering scale and complexity, home to many top-secret, high-tech experimental projects, and home also to an intricate Lunar society with lifeways and customs of its own; a society that soon finds itself confronted with a bizarre and unsuspected menace, which could spell not only its own doom, but could inalterably change the whole human race . . . or wipe it out forever.

> The moon? It is a griffin's egg,
> Hatching to-morrow night.
> And how the little boys will watch
> With shouting and delight
> To see him break the shell and stretch
> And creep across the sky.
> The boys will laugh, The little girls,
> I fear, may hide and cry . . .
> —Vachel Lindsay

The sun cleared the mountains. Gunther Weil raised a hand in salute, then winced as the glare hit his eyes in the instant it took his helmet to polarize.

He was hauling fuel rods to Chatterjee Crater industrial park. The Chatterjee B reactor had gone critical forty hours before dawn, taking fifteen remotes and a microwave relay with it, and putting out a power surge that caused collateral damage to every factory in the park. Fortunately, the occasional meltdown was designed into the system. By the time the sun rose over the Rhaeticus highlands, a new reactor had been built and was ready to go online.

Gunther drove automatically, gauging his distance from Bootstrap by the amount of trash lining the Mare Vaporum road. Close by the city, discarded construction machinery and damaged assemblers sat in open-vacuum storage, awaiting possible salvage. Ten kilometers out, a pressurized van had exploded, scattering machine parts and giant worms of insulating foam across the landscape. At twenty-five kilometers, a poorly graded stretch of road had claimed any number of cargo skids and shattered running lights from passing traffic.

Forty kilometers out, though, the road was clear, a straight, clean gash in the dirt. Ignoring the voices at the back of his skull, the traffic chatter and automated safety messages that the truck routinely fed into his transceiver chip, he scrolled up the topographicals on the dash.

Right about here.

Gunther turned off the Mare Vaporum road and began laying tracks over virgin soil. "You've left your prescheduled route," the truck said. "Deviations from schedule may only be made with the recorded permission of your dispatcher."

"Yeah, well." Gunther's voice seemed loud in his helmet, the only physical sound in a babel of ghosts. He'd left the cabin unpressurized, and the insulated layers of his suit stilled even the conduction rumbling from the treads. "You and I both know that so long as I don't fall too far behind schedule, Beth Hamilton isn't going to care if I stray a little in between."

"You have exceeded this unit's linguistic capabilities."

"That's okay, don't let it bother you." Deftly he tied down the send switch on the truck radio with a twist of wire. The voices in his head abruptly died. He was completely isolated now.

"You said you wouldn't do that again." The words, broadcast directly to his trance chip, sounded as deep and resonant as the voice of God. "Generation Five policy expressly requires that all drivers maintain constant radio—"

"Don't whine. It's unattractive."

"You have exceeded this unit's linguistic—"

"Oh, shut up." Gunther ran a finger over the topographical maps, tracing the course he'd plotted the night before: Thirty kilometers over cherry soil, terrain no human or machine had ever crossed before, and then north on Murchison road. With luck he might even manage to be at Chatterjee early.

He drove into the lunar plain. Rocks sailed by to either side. Ahead, the mountains grew imperceptibly. Save for the treadmarks dwindling behind him, there was nothing from horizon to horizon to show that humanity had ever existed. The silence was perfect.

Gunther lived for moments like this. Entering that clean, desolate emptiness, he experienced a vast expansion of being, as if everything he saw, stars, plain, craters and all, were encompassed within himself. Bootstrap City was only a fading dream, a distant island on the gently rolling surface of a stone sea. Nobody will ever be first here again, he thought. Only me.

A memory floated up from his childhood. It was Christmas Eve and he was in his parents' car, on the way to midnight Mass. Snow was falling, thickly and windlessly, rendering all the familiar roads of Düsseldorf clean and pure under sheets of white. His father drove, and he himself leaned over the front seat to stare ahead in fascination into this peaceful, transformed world. The silence was perfect.

He felt touched by solitude and made holy.

The truck plowed through a rainbow of soft greys, submerged hues more hints than colors, as if something bright and festive held itself hidden just beneath a coating of dust. The sun was at his shoulder, and when he spun the front axle to avoid a boulder, the truck's shadow wheeled and reached for infinity. He drove reflexively, mesmerized by the austere beauty of the passing land.

At a thought, his peecee put music on his chip. "Stormy Weather" filled the universe.

He was coming down a long, almost imperceptible slope when the controls went dead in his hands. The truck powered down and coasted to a stop. "Goddamn you, you asshole machine!" he snarled. "What is it this time?"

"The land ahead is impassable."

Gunther slammed a fist on the dash, making the maps dance. The land ahead was smooth and sloping, any unruly tendencies tamed eons ago by the Mare Imbrium explosion. Sissy stuff. He kicked the door open and clambered down.

The truck had been stopped by a baby rille: a snakelike depression meandering across his intended route, looking for all the world like a dry streambed. He bounded to its edge. It was fifteen meters across, and three meters down at its deepest. Just shallow enough that it wouldn't show up on the topos. Gunther returned to the cab, slamming the door noiselessly behind him.

"Look. The sides aren't very steep. I've been down worse a hundred times. We'll just take it slow and easy, okay?"

"The land ahead is impassable," the truck said. "Please return to the originally scheduled course."

Wagner was on now. *Tannhäuser*. Impatiently, he thought it off.

"If you're so damned heuristic, then why won't you ever listen to reason?" He chewed his lip angrily, gave a quick shake of his head. "No, going back would put us way off schedule. The rille is bound to peter out in a few hundred meters. Let's just follow it until it does, then angle back to Murchison. We'll be at the park in no time."

Three hours later he finally hit the Murchison road. By then he was sweaty and smelly and his shoulders ached with tension. "Where are we?" he asked sourly. Then, before the truck could answer, "Cancel that." The soil had turned suddenly black. That would be the ejecta fantail from the Sony-Reinpfaltz mine. Their railgun was oriented almost due south in order to avoid the client factories, and so their tailings hit the road first. That meant he was getting close.

Murchison was little more than a confluence of truck treads, a dirt track crudely leveled and marked by blazes of orange paint on nearby boulders. In quick order Gunther passed through a series of landmarks: Harada Industrial fantail, Sea of Storms Macrofacturing fantail, Krupp funfzig fantail. He knew them all. G5 did the robotics for the lot.

A light flatbed carrying a shipped bulldozer sped past him, kicking up a spray of dust that fell as fast as pebbles. The remote driving it waved a spindly arm in greeting. He waved back automatically, and wondered if it was anybody he knew.

The land hereabouts was hacked and gouged, dirt and boulders shoved into careless heaps and hills, the occasional tool station or Oxytank Emergency Storage Platform chopped into a nearby bluff. A sign floated by: TOILET FLUSHING FACILITIES ½ KILOMETER. He made a face. Then he remembered that his radio was still off and slipped the loop of wire from it. Time to rejoin the real world. Immediately his dispatcher's voice, harsh and staticky, was relayed to his trance chip.

"—ofabitch! *Weil!* Where the fuck are you?"

"I'm right here, Beth. A little late, but right where I'm supposed to be."

"Sonofa—" The recording shut off, and Hamilton's voice came on, live and mean. "You'd better have a real good explanation for this one, honey."

"Oh, you know how it is." Gunther looked away from the road, off into the dusty jade highlands. He'd like to climb up into them and never come back. Perhaps he would find caves. Perhaps there were monsters: vacuum trolls and moondragons with metabolisms slow and patient, taking centuries to move one body's-length, hyperdense beings that could swim through stone as if it were water. He pictured them diving, following lines of magnetic force deep, deep into veins of diamond and plutonium, heads back and singing. "I picked up a hitchhiker, and we kind of got involved."

"Try telling that to E. Izmailova. She's mad as hornets at you."

"Who?"

"Izmailova. She's the new demolitions jock, shipped up here on a multi-corporate contract. Took a hopper in almost four hours ago, and she's been waiting for you and Siegfried ever since. I take it you've never met her?"

"No."

"Well, I have, and you'd better watch your step with her. She's exactly the kind of tough broad who won't be amused by your antics."

"Aw, come on, she's just another tech on a retainer, right? Not in my line of command. It's not like she can do anything to me."

"Dream on, babe. It wouldn't take much pull to get a fuckup like you sent down to Earth."

*   *   *

The sun was only a finger's breadth over the highlands by the time Chatterjee A loomed into sight. Gunther glanced at it every now and then, apprehensively. With his visor adjusted to the H-alpha wavelength, it was a blazing white sphere covered with slowly churning black specks: More granular than usual. Sunspot activity seemed high. He wondered that the Radiation Forecast Facility hadn't posted a surface advisory. The guys at the Observatory were usually right on top of things.

Chatterjee A, B, and C were a triad of simple craters just below Chladni, and while the smaller two were of minimal interest, Chatterjee A was the child of a meteor that had punched through the Imbrian basalts to as sweet a vein of aluminum ore as anything in the highlands. Being so convenient to Bootstrap made it one of management's darlings, and Gunther was not surprised to see that Kerr-McGee was going all out to get their reactor online again.

The park was crawling with walkers, stalkers, and assemblers. They were all over the blister-domed factories, the smelteries, loading docks, and vacuum garages. Constellations of blue sparks winked on and off as major industrial constructs were dismantled. Fleets of heavily loaded trucks fanned out into the lunar plain, churning up the dirt behind them. Fats Waller started to sing "The Joint is Jumping" and Gunther laughed.

He slowed to a crawl, swung wide to avoid a gas-plater that was being wrangled onto a loader, and cut up the Chatterjee B ramp road. A new landing pad had been blasted from the rock just below the lip, and a cluster of people stood about a hopper resting there. One human and eight remotes.

One of the remotes was speaking, making choppy little gestures with its arms. Several stood inert, identical as so many antique telephones, unclaimed by Earthside management but available should more advisors need to be called online.

Gunther unstrapped Siegfried from the roof of the cab and, control pad in one hand and cable spool in the other, walked him toward the hopper.

The human strode out to meet him. "You! What kept you?" E. Izmailova wore a jazzy red-and-orange Studio Volga boutique suit, in sharp contrast to his own company-issue suit with the G5 logo on the chest. He could not make out her face through the gold visor glass. But he could hear it in her voice: blazing eyes, thin lips.

"I had a flat tire." He found a good smooth chunk of rock and set down the cable spool, wriggling it to make sure it sat flush. "We got maybe five hundred yards of shielded cable. That enough for you?"

A short, tense nod.

"Okay." He unholstered his bolt gun. "Stand back." Kneeling, he anchored the spool to the rock. Then he ran a quick check of the unit's functions: "Do we know what it's like in there?"

A remote came to life, stepped forward and identified himself as Don Sakai, of G5's crisis management team. Gunther had worked with him before: a decent tough guy, but like most Canadians he had an exaggerated fear of nuclear energy. "Ms. Lang here, of Sony-Reinpfaltz, walked her unit in but the radiation was so strong she lost control after a preliminary scan." A second remote nodded confirmation, but the relay time to Toronto was just enough that Sakai missed it. "The remote just kept on walking." He coughed nervously, then added unnecessarily, "The autonomous circuits were too sensitive."

"Well, that's not going to be a problem with Siegfried. He's as dumb as a rock. On the evolutionary scale of machine intelligence he ranks closer to a crowbar than a computer." Two and a half seconds passed, and then Sakai laughed politely. Gunther nodded to Izmailova. "Walk me through this. Tell me what you want."

Izmailova stepped to his side, their suits pressing together briefly as she jacked a patch cord into his control pad. Vague shapes flickered across the outside of her visor like the shadows of dreams. "Does he know what he's doing?" she asked.

"Hey, I—"

"Shut up, Weil," Hamilton growled on a private circuit. Openly, she said, "He wouldn't be here if the company didn't have full confidence in his technical skills."

"I'm sure there's never been any question—" Sakai began. He lapsed into silence as Hamilton's words belatedly reached him.

"There's a device on the hopper," Izmailova said to Gunther. "Go pick it up."

He obeyed, reconfiguring Siegfried for a small, dense load. The unit bent low over the hopper, wrapping large, sensitive hands about the device. Gunther applied gentle pressure. Nothing happened. Heavy little bugger. Slowly, carefully, he upped the power. Siegfried straightened.

"Up the road, then down inside."

The reactor was unrecognizable, melted, twisted and folded in upon itself, a mound of slag with twisting pipes sprouting from the edges. There had been a coolant explosion early in the incident, and one wall of the crater was bright with sprayed metal. "Where is the radioactive material?" Sakai asked. Even though he was a third of a million kilometers away, he sounded tense and apprehensive.

"It's all radioactive," Izmailova said.

They waited. "I mean, you know. The fuel rods?"

"Right now, your fuel rods are probably three hundred meters down and still going. We are talking about fissionable material that has achieved critical mass. Very early in the process the rods will have all melted together in a sort of superhot puddle, capable of burning its way through rock. Picture it as a dense, heavy blob of wax, slowly working its way toward the lunar core."

"God, I love physics," Gunther said.

Izmailova's helmet turned toward him, abruptly blank. After a long pause, it switched on again and turned away. "The road down is clear at least. Take your unit all the way to the end. There's an exploratory shaft to one side there. Old one. I want to see if it's still open."

"Will the one device be enough?" Sakai asked. "To clean up the crater, I mean."

The woman's attention was fixed on Siegfried's progress. In a distracted tone she said, "Mr. Sakai, putting a chain across the access road would be enough to clean up this site. The crater walls would shield anyone working nearby from the gamma radiation, and it would take no effort at all to reroute hopper overflights so their passengers would not be exposed. Most of the biological danger of a reactor meltdown comes from alpha radiation emitted by particulate radioisotopes in the air or water. When concentrated in the body, alpha-emitters can do considerable damage; elsewhere, no. Alpha particles can be stopped by a sheet of paper. So long as you keep a reactor out of your ecosystem, it's as safe as any other large machine. Burying a destroyed reactor just because it is radioactive is unnecessary and, if you will forgive me for saying so, superstitious. But I don't make policy. I just blow things up."

"Is this the shaft you're looking for?" Gunther asked.

"Yes. Walk it down to the bottom. It's not far."

Gunther switched on Siegfried's chestlight, and sank a roller relay so the cable wouldn't snag. They went down. Finally Izmailova said, "Stop. That's far enough." He gently set the device down and then, at her direction, flicked the arming toggle. "That's done," Izmailova said. "Bring your unit back. I've given you an hour to put some distance between the crater and yourself." Gunther noticed that the remotes, on automatic, had already begun walking away.

"Um . . . I've still got fuel rods to load."

"Not today you don't. The new reactor has been taken back apart and hauled out of the blasting zone."

Gunther thought now of all the machinery being disassembled and re-moved from the industrial park, and was struck for the first time by the operation's sheer extravagances of scale. Normally only the most sensitive devices were removed from a blasting area. "Wait a minute. Just what kind of monster explosive are you planning to *use?*"

There was a self-conscious cockiness to Izmailova's stance. "Nothing I don't know how to handle. This is a diplomat-class device, the same design as saw action five years ago. Nearly one hundred individual applications without a single mechanical failure. That makes it the most reliable weapon in the history of warfare. You should feel privileged having the chance to work with one."

Gunther felt his flesh turn to ice. "Jesus Mother of God," he said. "You had me handling a briefcase nuke."

"Better get used to it. Westinghouse Lunar is putting these little babies into mass production. We'll be cracking open mountains with them, blasting roads through the highlands, smashing apart the rille walls to see what's inside." Her voice took on a visionary tone. "And that's just the beginning. There are plans for enrichment fields in Sinus Aestum. Explode a few bombs over the regolith, then extract plutonium from the dirt. We're going to be the fuel dump for the entire solar system."

His dismay must have shown in his stance, for Izmailova laughed. "Think of it as weapons for peace."

"You should've been there!" Gunther said. "It was unfuckabelievable. The one side of the crater just disappeared. It dissolved into nothing. Smashed to dust. And for a real long time everything *glowed!* Craters, machines, everything. My visor was so close to overload it started flickering. I thought it was going to burn out. It was nuts." He picked up his cards. "Who dealt this mess?"

Krishna grinned shyly and ducked his head. "I'm in."

Hiro scowled down at his cards. "I've just died and gone to Hell."

"Trade you," Anya said.

"No, I deserve to suffer."

They were in Noguchi Park by the edge of the central lake, seated on artfully scattered boulders that had been carved to look water-eroded. A knee-high forest of baby birches grew to one side, and somebody's toy sailboat floated near the impact cone at the center of the lake. Honeybees mazily browsed the clover.

"And then, just as the wall was crumbling, this crazy Russian bitch—"

Anya ditched a trey. "Watch what you say about crazy Russian bitches."

"—goes zooming up on her hopper . . ."

"I saw it on television," Hiro said. "We all did. It was news. This guy who works for Nissan told me the BBC gave it thirty seconds." He'd broken his nose in karate practice, when he'd flinched into his instructor's punch, and the contrast of square white bandage with shaggy black eyebrows gave him a surly, piratical appearance.

Gunther discarded one. "Hit me. Man, you didn't see anything. You didn't feel the ground shake afterward."

"Just what was Izmailova's connection with the Briefcase War?" Hiro asked. "Obviously not a courier. Was she in the supply end or strategic?"

Gunther shrugged.

"You do remember the Briefcase War?" Hiro said sarcastically. "Half of Earth's military elites taken out in a single day? The world pulled back from the brink of war by bold action? Suspected terrorists revealed as global heroes?"

Gunther remembered the Briefcase War quite well. He had been nineteen at the time, working on a Finlandia Geothermal project when the whole world had gone into spasm and very nearly destroyed itself. It had been a major factor in his decision to ship off the planet. "Can't we ever talk about anything but politics? I'm sick and tired of hearing about Armageddon."

"Hey, aren't you supposed to be meeting with Hamilton?" Anya asked suddenly.

He glanced up at the Earth. The east coast of South America was just crossing the dusk terminator. "Oh, hell, there's enough time to play out the hand."

Krishna won with three queens. The deal passed to Hiro. He shuffled quickly, and slapped the cards down with angry little punches of his arm.

"Okay," Anya said, "what's eating you?"

He looked up angrily, then down again and in a muffled voice, as if he had abruptly gone bashful as Krishna, said, "I'm shipping home."

"Home?"

"You mean to Earth?"

"Are you crazy? With everything about to go up in flames? *Why?*"

"Because I am so fucking tired of the Moon. It has to be the ugliest place in the universe."

"Ugly?" Anya looked elaborately about at the terraced gardens, the streams that began at the top level and fell in eight misty waterfalls before reaching the central pond to be recirculated again, the gracefully winding pathways. People strolled through great looping rosebushes and past towers of forsythia with the dreamlike skimming stride that made moonwalking so like motion underwater. Others popped in and out of the office tunnels, paused to watch the finches loop and fly, tended to beds of cucumbers. At the midlevel straw market, the tents where offduty hobby capitalists sold factory systems, grass baskets, orange glass paperweights and courses in postinterpretive dance and the meme analysis of Elizabethan poetry, were a jumble of brave silks, turquoise, scarlet, and aquamarine. "I think it looks nice. A little crowded, maybe, but that's the pioneer aesthetic."

"It looks like a shopping mall, but that's not what I'm talking about. It's—" He groped for words. "It's like—it's what we're doing to this world that bothers me. I mean, we're digging it up, scattering garbage about, ripping the mountains apart, and for what?"

"Money," Anya said. "Consumer goods, raw materials, a future for our children. What's wrong with that?"

"We're not building a future, we're building weapons."

"There's not so much as a handgun on the Moon. It's an intercorporate development zone. Weapons are illegal here."

"You know what I mean. All those bomber fuselages, detonation systems, and missile casings that get built here, and shipped to low Earth orbit. Let's not pretend we don't know what they're for."

"So?" Anya said sweetly. "We live in the real world, we're none of us naïve enough to believe you can have governments without armies. Why is it worse that these things are being built here rather than elsewhere?"

"It's the short-sighted, egocentric greed of what we're doing that gripes me! Have you peeked out on the surface lately and seen the way it's being ripped open, torn apart, and scattered about? There are still places where you can gaze upon a harsh beauty unchanged since the days our ancestors were swinging in trees. But we're trashing them. In a generation, two at most, there will be no more beauty to the Moon than there is to any other garbage dump."

"You've seen what Earthbound manufacturing has done to the environment," Anya said. "Moving it off the planet is a good thing, right?"

"Yes, but the Moon—"

"Doesn't even *have* an ecosphere. There's nothing here to harm."

They glared at each other. Finally Hiro said, "I don't want to talk about it," and sullenly picked up his cards.

Five or six hands later, a woman wandered up and plumped to the grass by Krishna's feet. Her eye shadow was vivid electric purple, and a crazy smile burned on her face. "Oh hi," Krishna said. "Does everyone here know Sally Chang? She's a research component of the Center for Self-Replicating Technologies, like me."

The others nodded. Gunther said, "Gunther Weil. Blue collar component of Generation Five."

She giggled.

Gunther blinked. "You're certainly in a good mood." He rapped the deck with his knuckles. "I'll stand."

"I'm on psilly," she said.

"One card."

"Psilocybin?" Gunther said. "I might be interested in some of that. Did you grow it or microfacture it? I have a couple of factories back in my room, maybe I could divert one if you'd like to license the software?"

Sally Chang shook her head, laughing helplessly. Tears ran down her cheeks.

"Well, when you come down we can talk about it." Gunther squinted at his cards. "This would make a great hand for chess."

"Nobody plays chess," Hiro said scornfully. "It's a game for computers."

Gunther took the pot with two pair. He shuffled, Krishna declined the cut, and he began dealing out cards. "So anyway, this crazy Russian lady—"

Out of nowhere, Chang howled. Wild gusts of laughter knocked her back on her heels and bent her forward again. The delight of discovery dancing in her eyes, she pointed a finger straight at Gunther. "You're a robot!" she cried.

"Beg pardon?"

"You're nothing but a robot," she repeated. "You're a machine, an automaton. Look at yourself! Nothing but stimulus-response. You have no free will at all. There's nothing there. You couldn't perform an original act to save your life."

"Oh yeah?" Gunther glanced around, looking for inspiration. A little boy—it might be Pyotr Nahfees, though it was hard to tell from here—was by the edge of the water, feeding scraps of shrimp loaf to the carp. "Suppose I pitched you into the lake? That would be an original act."

Laughing, she shook her head. "Typical primate behavior. A perceived threat is met with a display of mock aggression."

Gunther laughed.

"Then, when that fails, the primate falls back to a display of submission. Appeasal. The monkey demonstrates his harmlessness—you see?"

"Hey, this really isn't funny," Gunther said warningly. "In fact, it's kind of insulting."

"And so back to a display of aggression."

Gunther sighed and threw up both his hands. "How am I supposed to react? According to you, anything I say or do is wrong."

"Submission again. Back and forth, back and forth from aggression to submission and back again." She pumped her arm as if it were a piston. "Just like a little machine—you see? It's all automatic behavior."

"Hey, Kreesh—you're the neurobiowhatever here, right? Put in a good word for me. Get me out of this conversation."

Krishna reddened. He would not meet Gunther's eyes. "Ms. Chang is very highly regarded at the Center, you see. Anything she thinks about thinking is worth thinking about." The woman watched him avidly, eyes glistening, pupils small. "I think maybe what she means, though, is that we're all basically cruising through life. Like we're on autopilot. Not just you specifically, but all of us." He appealed to her directly. "Yes?"

"No, no, no, no." She shook her head. "Him specifically."

"I give up." Gunther put his cards down, and lay back on the granite slab so he could stare up through the roof glass at the waning Earth. When he closed his eyes, he could see Izmailova's hopper, rising. It was a skimpy device, little more than a platform-and-chair atop a cluster of four bottles of waste-gas propellant, and a set of smart legs. He saw it lofting up as the explosion blossomed, seeming briefly to hover high over the crater, like a hawk atop a thermal. Hands by side, the red-suited figure sat, watching with what seemed inhuman calm. In the reflected light she burned as bright as a star. In an appalling way, she was beautiful.

Sally Chang hugged her knees, rocking back and forth. She laughed and laughed.

Beth Hamilton was wired for telepresence. She flipped up one lens when Gunther entered her office, but kept on moving her arms and legs. Dreamy little ghost motions that would be picked up and magnified in a factory somewhere over the horizon. "You're late again," she said with no particular emphasis.

Most people would have experienced at least a twinge of reality sickness dealing with two separate surrounds at once. Hamilton was one of the rare few who could split her awareness between two disparate realities without loss of efficiency in either. "I called you in to discuss your future with Generation Five. Specifically, to discuss the possibility of your transfer to another plant."

"You mean Earthside."

"You see?" Hamilton said. "You're not as stupid as you like to make yourself out to be." She flipped the lens down again, stood very still, then lifted a metal-gauntleted hand and ran through a complex series of finger movements. "Well?"

"Well what?"

"Tokyo, Berlin, Buenos Aires—do any of these hold magic for you? How about Toronto? The right move now could be a big boost to your career."

"All I want is to stay here, do my job, and draw down my salary," Gunther said carefully. "I'm not looking for a shot at promotion, or a big raise, or a lateral career-track transfer. I'm happy right where I am."

"You've sure got a funny way of showing it." Hamilton powered down her gloves and slipped her hands free. She scratched her nose. To one side stood her work table, a polished cube of black granite. Her peecee rested there, alongside a spray of copper crystals. At her thought, it put Izmailova's voice onto Gunther's chip.

"It is with deepest regret that I must alert you to the unprofessional behavior of one of your personnel components," it began. Listening to the complaint, Gunther experienced a totally unexpected twinge of distress and, more, of resentment that Izmailova had dared judge him so harshly. He was careful not to let it show.

"Irresponsible, insubordinate, careless, and possessed of a bad attitude." He faked a grin. "She doesn't seem to like me much." Hamilton said nothing. "But this isn't enough to . . ." His voice trailed off. "Is it?"

"Normally, Weil, it would be. A demo jock isn't 'just a tech on retainer,' as you so quaintly put it; those government licenses aren't easy to get. And you may not be aware of it, but you have very poor efficiency ratings to begin with. Lots of potential, no follow-through. Frankly, you've been a disappointment. However, lucky for you, this Izmailova dame humiliated Don Sakai, and he's let us know that we're under no particular pressure to accommodate her."

"Izmailova humiliated Sakai?"

Hamilton stared at him. "Weil, you're oblivious, you know that?"

Then he remembered Izmailova's rant on nuclear energy. "Right, okay. I got it now."

"So here's your choice. I can write up a reprimand, and it goes into your permanent file, along with Izmailova's complaint. Or you can take a lateral Earthside, and I'll see to it that these little things aren't logged into the corporate system."

It wasn't much of a choice. But he put a good face on it. "In that case it looks like you're stuck with me."

"For the moment, Weil. For the moment."

He was back on the surface the next two days running. The first day he was once again hauling fuel rods to Chatterjee C. This time he kept to the road, and the reactor was refueled exactly on schedule. The second day he went all the way out to Triesnecker to pick up some old rods that had been in temporary storage for six months while the Kerr-McGee people argued over whether they should be reprocessed or dumped. Not a bad deal for him, because although the sunspot cycle was on the wane, there was a surface advisory in effect and he was drawing hazardous duty pay.

When he got there, a tech rep telepresenced in from somewhere in France to tell him to forget it. There'd been another meeting, and the decision had once again been delayed. He started back to Bootstrap with the new a capella version of *The Threepenny Opera* playing in his head. It sounded awfully sweet and reedy for his tastes, but that was what they were listening to up home.

Fifteen kilometers down the road, the UV meter on the dash *jumped.*

Gunther reached out to tap the meter with his finger. It did not respond. With a freezing sensation at the back of his neck, he glanced up at the roof of the cab and whispered, "Oh, no."

"The Radiation Forecast Facility has just intensified its surface warning to a Most Drastic status," the truck said calmly. "This is due to an unanticipated flare storm, onset immediately. Everyone currently on the surface is to proceed with all haste to shelter. Repeat: Proceed immediately to shelter."

"I'm eighty kilometers from—"

The truck was slowing to a stop. "Because this unit is not hardened, excessive fortuitous radiation may cause it to malfunction. To ensure the continued safe operation of this vehicle, all controls will be frozen in manual mode and this unit will now shut off."

With the release of the truck's masking functions, Gunther's head filled with overlapping voices. Static washed through them, making nonsense of what they were trying to say:

astic   Stus-Repeat: *   ***l! This is**eth. Th** *   **ail, are you there? C
S**face**d***ory ha** *   h*** just i**ue**a M**   o***on, good **ddy, gi
een***grad***to M**t   t D***tic**dvis*****G   ve ***a hoo** **ko, S
Dra**ic Stat**. A** u   et off t***surface**Go   abra, **ng**i-ge**yo**
nits *nd perso*****are   ddamn **u, are yo* lis   asses *****groun***ig
to find shelt***imm   tening? Find s**lter. D   ht*ow. **don't wan**to
ediatel*. Maxim*m *x   on' t try to **t **ck to   h*** you've st*yed*be
posu** **enty min**e   Bootstrap.***o f**, it'll   **n**to turn**** the l
s.***nd ***lter i**ed* *   fry you.***ten, t**re * *   *ght***ho el*** i**out t
*tely. Thi**is t** recor *   ** thr***factorie**n** *   here?**ome**n ri**t n
ded*voice of**he Radi   **r fr***your pre***t   ow. Ev**y**e! Any**dy
ati***Forecast Faci*it   l***t**n. A*e you *ist   *now w***e Mikha** i
y.**u**to an unpr**i**   en**g, you***ofoff? Wei *   ** C'mon,*Misha, don*
** sol** flare,***e su* *   *sk*pf A**is**ne, Ni** *   t**ou get coy *n us. So
face adv**o***has been   **, an**Luna**M***os   u** us with ***r voice,
upgrade***o Most Dras   t**ct**al. Weil!**et me   he**? W***ot **rd Ez

"Beth! The nearest shelter is back at Weisskopf—that's half an hour at top speed and I've got an advisory here of twenty minutes. Tell me what to do!"

But the first sleet of hard particles was coming in too hard to make out anything more. A hand, his apparently, floated forward and flicked off the radio relay. The voices in his head died.

The crackling static went on and on. The truck sat motionless, half an hour from nowhere, invisible death sizzling and popping down through the cab roof. He put his helmet and gloves on, double-checked their seals, and unlatched the door.

It slammed open. Pages from the op manual flew away, and a glove went tumbling gaily across the surface, chasing the pink fuzzy-dice that Eurydice had given him that last night in Sweden. A handful of wheat biscuits in an open tin on the dash turned to powder and were gone, drawing the tin after them. Explosive decompression. He'd forgotten to depressurize. Gunther froze in dismayed astonishment at having made so basic—so dangerous—a mistake.

Then he was on the surface, head tilted back, staring up at the sun. It was angry with sunspots, and one enormous and unpredicted solar flare.

I'm going to die, he thought.

For a long, paralyzing instant, he tasted the chill certainty of that thought. He was going to die. He knew that for a fact, knew it more surely than he had ever known anything before.

In his mind, he could see Death sweeping across the lunar plain toward him. Death was a black wall, featureless, that stretched to infinity in every direction. It sliced the universe in half. On this side were life, warmth, craters and flowers, dreams, mining robots, thought, everything that Gunther knew or could imagine. On the other side . . . something? Nothing? The wall gave no hint. It was unreadable, enigmatic, absolute. But it was bearing down on him. It was so close now that he could almost reach out and touch it. Soon it would be here. He would pass through, and then he would know.

With a start he broke free of that thought, and jumped for the cab. He scrabbled up its side. His trance chip hissing, rattling and crackling, he yanked the magnetic straps holding Siegfried in place, grabbed the spool and control pad, and jumped over the edge.

He landed jarringly, fell to his knees, and rolled under the trailer. There was enough shielding wrapped around the fuel rods to stop any amount of hard radiation—no matter what its source. It would shelter him as well from the sun as from his cargo. The trance chip fell silent, and he felt his jaws relaxing from a clenched tension.

Safe.

It was dark beneath the trailer, and he had time to think. Even kicking his rebreather up to full, and offlining all his suit peripherals, he didn't have enough oxygen to sit out the storm. So okay. He had to get to a shelter. Weisskopf was closest, only fifteen kilometers away and there was a shelter in the G5 assembly plant there. That would be his goal.

Working by feel, he found the steel supporting struts, and used Siegfried's magnetic straps to attach himself to the underside of the trailer. It was clumsy, difficult work, but at last he hung face-down over the road. He fingered the walker's controls, and sat Siegfried up.

Twelve excruciating minutes later, he finally managed to get Siegfried down from the roof unbroken. The interior wasn't intended to hold anything half so big. To get the walker in he had first to cut the door free, and then rip the chair out of the cab. Discarding both items by the roadside, he squeezed Siegfried in. The walker bent over double, reconfigured, reconfigured again, and finally managed to fit itself into the space. Gently, delicately, Siegfried took the controls and shifted into first.

With a bump, the truck started to move.

It was a hellish trip. The truck, never fast to begin with, wallowed down the road like a cast-iron pig. Siegfried's optics were bent over the controls, and couldn't be raised without jerking the walker's hands free. He couldn't look ahead without stopping the truck first.

He navigated by watching the road pass under him. To a crude degree he could align the truck with the treadmarks scrolling by. Whenever he wandered off the track, he worked Siegfried's hand controls to veer the truck back, so that it drifted slowly from side to side, zig-zagging its way down the road.

Shadows bumping and leaping, the road flowed toward Gunther with dangerous monotony. He jiggled and vibrated in his makeshift sling. After a while his neck hurt with the effort of holding his head back to watch the glaring road disappearing into shadow by the front axle, and his eyes ached from the crawling repetitiveness of what they saw.

The truck kicked up dust in passing, and the smaller particles carried enough of a static charge to cling to his suit. At irregular intervals he swiped at the fine grey film on his visor with his glove, smearing it into long, thin streaks.

He began to hallucinate. They were mild visuals, oblong patches of colored light that moved in his vision and went away when he shook his head and firmly closed his eyes for a concentrated moment. But every moment's release from the pressure of vision tempted him to keep his eyes closed longer, and that he could not afford to do.

It put him in mind of the last time he had seen his mother, and what she had said then. That the worst part of being a widow was that every day her life began anew, no better than the day before, the pain still fresh, her husband's absence a physical fact she was no closer to accepting than ever. It was like being dead, she said, in that nothing ever changed.

Ah God, he thought, this isn't worth doing. Then a rock the size of his head came bounding toward his helmet. Frantic hands jerked at the controls, and Siegfried skewed the truck wildly, so that the rock jumped away and missed him. Which put an end to *that* line of thought.

He cued his peecee. *Saint James' Infirmary* came on. It didn't help.

Come on, you bastard, he thought. You can do it. His arms and shoulders ached, and his back too, when he gave it any thought. Perversely enough, one of his legs had gone to sleep. At the angle he had to hold his head to watch the road, his mouth tended to hang open. After a while, a quivering motion alerted him that a small puddle of saliva had gathered in the curve of his faceplate. He was drooling. He closed his mouth, swallowing back his spit, and stared forward. A minute later he found that he was doing it again.

Slowly, miserably, he drove toward Weisskopf.

The G5 Weisskopf plant was typical of its kind: A white blister-dome to moderate temperature swings over the long lunar day, a microwave relay tower to bring in supervisory presence, and a hundred semiautonomous units to do the work.

Gunther overshot the access road, wheeled back to catch it, and ran the truck right up to the side of the factory. He had Siegfried switch off the engine, and then let the control pad fall to the ground. For well over a minute he simply hung there, eyes closed, savoring the end of motion. Then he kicked free of the straps, and crawled out from under the trailer.

Static scatting and stuttering inside his head, he stumbled into the factory.

In the muted light that filtered through the dome covering, the factory was dim as an undersea cavern. His helmet light seemed to distort as much as it illumined. Machines loomed closer in the center of its glare, swelling up as if seen through a fisheye lens. He turned it off, and waited for his eyes to adjust.

After a bit, he could see the robot assemblers, slender as ghosts, moving with unearthly delicacy. The flare storm had activated them. They swayed like seaweed, lightly out of sync with each other. Arms raised, they danced in time to random radio input.

On the assembly lines lay the remains of half-built robots, looking flayed and eviscerated. Their careful frettings of copper and silver nerves had been exposed to view and randomly operated upon. A long arm jointed down, electric fire at its tip, and made a metal torso twitch.

They were blind mechanisms, most of them, powerful things bolted to the floor in assembly logic paths. But there were mobile units as well, overseers and jacks-of-all-trades, weaving drunkenly through the factory with sun-maddened eye.

A sudden motion made Gunther turn just in time to see a metal puncher swivel toward him, slam down an enormous arm and put a hole in the floor by his feet. He felt the shock through his soles.

He danced back. The machine followed him, the diamond-tipped punch sliding nervously in and out of its sheath, its movements as trembling and dainty as a newborn colt's.

"Easy there, baby," Gunther whispered. To the far end of the factory, green arrows supergraffixed on the crater wall pointed to an iron door. The shelter. Gunther backed away from the punch, edging into a service aisle between two rows of machines that rippled like grass in the wind.

The punch press rolled forward on its trundle. Then, confused by that field of motion, it stopped, hesitantly scanning the ranks of robots. Gunther froze.

At last, slowly, lumberingly, the metal puncher turned away.

Gunther ran. Static roared in his head. Grey shadows swam among the distant machines, like sharks, sometimes coming closer, sometimes receding. The static loudened. Up and down the factory welding arcs winked on at the assembler tips, like tiny stars. Ducking, running, spinning, he reached the shelter and seized the airlock door. Even through his glove, the handle felt cold.

He turned it.

The airlock was small and round. He squeezed through the door and fit himself into the inadequate space within, making himself as small as possible. He yanked the door shut.

Darkness.

He switched his helmet lamp back on. The reflected glare slammed at his eyes, far too intense for such a confined area. Folded knees-to-chin into the roundness of the lock he felt a wry comradeship with Siegfried back in the truck.

The inner lock controls were simplicity itself. The door hinged inward, so that air pressure held it shut. There was a yank bar which, when pulled, would bleed oxygen into the airlock. When pressure equalized, the inner door would open easily. He yanked the bar.

The floor vibrated as something heavy went by.

The shelter was small, just large enough to hold a cot, a chemical toilet and a rebreather with spare oxytanks. A single overhead unit provided light and heat. For comfort there was a blanket. For amusement, there were pocket-sized editions of the Bible and the Koran, placed there by impossibly distant missionary societies. Even empty, there was not much space in the shelter.

It wasn't empty.

A woman, frowning and holding up a protective hand, cringed from his helmet lamp. "Turn that thing off," she said.

He obeyed. In the soft light that ensued he saw: stark white flattop, pink scalp visible through the sides. High cheekbones. Eyelids lifted slightly, like wings, by carefully sculpted eye shadow. Dark lips, full mouth. He had to admire the character it took to make up a face so carefully, only to hide it beneath a helmet. Then he saw her red and orange Studio Volga suit.

It was Izmailova.

To cover his embarrassment, he took his time removing his gloves and helmet. Izmailova moved her own helmet from the cot to make room, and he sat down beside her. Extending a hand, he stiffly said, "We've met before. My name is—"

"I know. It's written on your suit."

"Oh yeah. Right."

For an uncomfortably long moment, neither spoke. At last Izmailova cleared her throat and briskly said, "This is ridiculous. There's no reason we should—"

CLANG.

Their heads jerked toward the door in unison. The sound was harsh, loud, metallic. Gunther slammed his helmet on, grabbed for his gloves. Izmailova, also suiting up as rapidly as she could, tensely subvocalized into her trance chip: "What is it?"

Methodically snapping his wrist latches shut one by one, Gunther said, "I think it's a metal punch." Then, because the helmet muffled his words, he repeated them over the chip.

CLANG. This second time, they were waiting for the sound. Now there could be no doubt. Something was trying to break open the outer airlock door.

"A what?!"

"Might be a hammer of some type, or a blacksmith unit. Just be thankful it's not a laser jig." He held up his hands before him. "Give me a safety check."

She turned his wrists one way, back, took his helmet in her hands and gave it a twist to test its seal. "You pass." She held up her own wrists. "But what is it trying to do?"

Her gloves were sealed perfectly. One helmet dog had a bit of give in it, but not enough to breach integrity. He shrugged. "It's deranged—it could want anything. It might even be trying to repair a weak hinge."

CLANG.

"It's trying to get in here!"

"That's another possibility, yes."

Izmailova's voice rose slightly. "But even scrambled, there can't possibly be any programs in its memory to make it do that. How can random input make it act this way?"

"It doesn't work like that. You're thinking of the kind of robotics they had when you were a kid. These units are state of the art: They don't manipulate instructions, they manipulate concepts. See, that makes them more flexible. You don't have to program in every little step when you want one to do something new. You just give it a goal—"

CLANG.

"—like, to Disassemble a Rotary Drill. It's got a bank of available skills, like Cutting and Unbolting and Gross Manipulation, which it then fits together in various configurations until it has a path that will bring it to the goal." He was talking for the sake of talking now, talking to keep himself from panic. "Which normally works out fine. But when one of these things malfunctions, it does so on the conceptual level. See? So that—"

"So that it decides we're rotary drills that need to be disassembled."

"Uh . . . yeah."

CLANG.

"So what do we do when it gets in here?" They had both involuntarily risen to their feet, and stood facing the door. There was not much space, and what little there was they filled. Gunther was acutely aware that there was not enough room here to either fight or flee.

"I don't know about you," he said, "but I'm going to hit that sucker over the head with the toilet."

She turned to look at him.

CLA— The noise was cut in half by a breathy, whooshing explosion. Abrupt, total silence. "It's through the outer door," Gunther said flatly.

They waited.

Much later, Izmailova said, "Is it possible it's gone away?"

"I don't know." Gunther undogged his helmet, knelt and put an ear to the floor. The stone was almost painfully cold. "Maybe the explosion damaged it." He could hear the faint vibrations of the assemblers, the heavier rumblings of machines roving the factory floor. None of it sounded close. He silently counted to a hundred. Nothing. He counted to a hundred again.

Finally he straightened. "It's gone."

They both sat down. Izmailova took off her helmet, and Gunther clumsily began undoing his gloves. He fumbled at the latches. "Look at me." He laughed shakily. "I'm all thumbs. I can't even handle this, I'm so unnerved."

"Let me help you with that." Izmailova flipped up the latches, tugged at his glove. It came free. "Where's your other hand?"

Then, somehow, they were each removing the other's suit, tugging at the latches, undoing the seals. They began slowly but sped up with each latch undogged, until they were yanking and pulling with frantic haste. Gunther opened up the front of Izmailova's suit, revealing a red silk camisole. He slid his hands beneath it, and pushed the cloth up over her breasts. Her nipples were hard. He let her breasts fill his hands and squeezed.

Izmailova made a low, groaning sound in the back of her throat. She had Gunther's suit open. Now she pushed down his leggings and reached within to seize his cock. He was already erect. She tugged it out and impatiently shoved him down on the cot. Then she was kneeling on top of him and guiding him inside her.

Her mouth met his, warm and moist.

Half in and half out of their suits, they made love. Gunther managed to struggle one arm free, and reached within Izmailova's suit to run a hand up her long back and over the back of her head. The short hairs of her buzz cut stung and tickled his palm.

She rode him roughly, her flesh slippery with sweat against his. "Are you coming yet?" she murmured. "Are you coming yet? Tell me when you're about to come." She bit his shoulder, the side of his neck, his chin, his lower lip. Her nails dug into his flesh.

"Now," he whispered. Possibly he only subvocalized it, and she caught it on her trance chip. But then she clutched him tighter than ever, as if she were trying to crack his ribs, and her whole body shuddered with orgasm. Then he came too, riding her passion down into spiraling desperation, ecstasy and release.

It was better than anything he had ever experienced before.

Afterward, they finally kicked free of their suits. They shoved and pushed the things off the cot. Gunther pulled the blanket out from beneath them, and with Izmailova's help wrapped it about the both of them. They lay together, relaxed, not speaking.

He listened to her breathe for a while. The noise was soft. When she turned her face toward him, he could feel it, a warm little tickle in the hollow of his throat. The smell of her permeated the room. This stranger beside him.

Gunther felt weary, warm, at ease. "How long have you been here?" he asked. "Not here in the shelter, I mean, but . . ."

"Five days."

"That little." He smiled. "Welcome to the Moon, Ms. Izmailova."

"Ekatarina," she said sleepily. "Call me Ekatarina."

Whooping, they soared high and south, over Herschel. The Ptolemaeus road bent and doubled below them, winding out of sight, always returning. "This is great!" Hiro crowed. "This is—I should've talked you into taking me out here a year ago."

Gunther checked his bearings and throttled down, sinking eastward. The other two hoppers, slaved to his own, followed in tight formation. Two days had passed since the flare storm and Gunther, still on mandatory recoop, had promised to guide his friends into the highlands as soon as the surface advisory was dropped. "We're coming in now. Better triplecheck your safety harnesses. You doing okay back there, Kreesh?"

"I am quite comfortable, yes."

Then they were down on the Seething Bay Company landing pad.

Hiro was the second down and the first on the surface. He bounded about like a collie off its leash, chasing upslope and down, looking for new vantage points. "I can't believe I'm here! I work out this way every day, but you know what? This is the first time I've actually been out here. Physically, I mean."

"Watch your footing," Gunther warned. "This isn't like telepresence—if you break a leg, it'll be up to Krishna and me to carry you out."

"I trust you. Man, anybody who can get caught out in a flare storm, and end up nailing—"

"Hey, watch your language, okay?"

"Everybody's heard the story. I mean, we all thought you were dead, and then they found the two of you *asleep*. They'll be talking about it a hundred years from now." Hiro was practically choking on his laughter. "You're a legend!"

"Just give it a rest." To change the subject, Gunther said, "I can't believe you want to take a photo of this mess." The Seething Bay operation was a strip mine. Robot bulldozers scooped up the regolith and fed it to a processing plant that rested on enormous skids. They were after the thorium here, and the output was small enough that it could be transported to the breeder reactor by hopper. There was no need for a railgun and the tailings were piled in artificial mountains in the wake of the factory.

"Don't be ridiculous." Hiro swept an arm southward, toward Ptolemaeus. "There!" The crater wall caught the sun, while the lowest parts of the surrounding land were still in shadow. The gentle slopes seemed to tower; the crater itself was a cathedral, blazing white.

"Where is your camera?" Krishna asked.

"Don't need one. I'll just take the data down on my helmet."

"I'm not too clear on this mosaic project of yours," Gunther said. "Explain to me one more time how it's supposed to work."

"Anya came up with it. She's renting an assembler to cut hexagonal floor tiles in black, white, and fourteen intermediate shades of grey. I provide the pictures. We choose the one we like best, scan it in black and white, screen for values of intensity, and then have the assembler lay the floor, one tile per pixel. It'll look great—come by tomorrow and see."

"Yeah, I'll do that."

Chattering like a squirrel, Hiro led them away from the edge of the mine. They bounded westward, across the slope.

Krishna's voice came over Gunther's trance chip. It was an old groundrat trick. The chips had an effective transmission radius of fifteen yards—you could turn off the radio and talk chip-to-chip, if you were close enough. "You sound troubled, my friend."

He listened for a second carrier tone, heard nothing. Hiro was out of range. "It's Izmailova. I sort of—"

"Fell in love with her."

"How'd you know that?"

They were spaced out across the rising slope, Hiro in the lead. For a time neither spoke. There was a calm, confidential quality to that shared silence, like the anonymous stillness of the confessional. "Please don't take this wrong," Krishna said.

"Take what wrong?"

"Gunther, if you take two sexually compatible people, place them in close proximity, isolate them and scare the hell out of them, they will fall in love. That's a given. It's a survival mechanism, something that was wired into your basic makeup long before you were born. When billions of years of evolution say it's bonding time, your brain doesn't have much choice but to obey."

"Hey, come on over here!" Hiro cried over the radio. "You've got to see this."

"We're coming," Gunther said. Then, over his chip, "You make me out to be one of Sally Chang's machines."

"In some ways we *are* machines. That's not so bad. We feel thirsty when we need water, adrenaline pumps into the bloodstream when we need an extra boost of aggressive energy. You can't fight your own nature. What would be the point of it?"

"Yeah, but . . ."

"Is this great or what?" Hiro was clambering over a boulder field. "It just goes on and on. And look up there!" Upslope, they saw that what they were climbing over was the spillage from a narrow cleft entirely filled with boulders. They were huge, as big as hoppers, some of them large as prefab oxysheds. "Hey, Krishna, I been meaning to ask you—just what is it that you do out there at the Center?"

"I can't talk about it."

"Aw, come on." Hiro lifted a rock the size of his head to his shoulder and shoved it away, like a shot-putter. The rock soared slowly, landed far down-slope in a white explosion of dust. "You're among friends here. You can trust us."

Krishna shook his head. Sunlight flashed from the visor. "You don't know what you're asking."

Hiro hoisted a second rock, bigger than the first. Gunther knew him in this mood, nasty-faced and grinning. "My point exactly. The two of us know zip about neurobiology. You could spent the next ten hours lecturing us, and we couldn't catch enough to compromise security." Another burst of dust.

"You don't understand. The Center for Self-Replicating Technologies is here for a reason. The lab work could be done back on Earth for a fraction of what a lunar facility costs. Our sponsors only move projects here that they're genuinely afraid of."

"So what *can* you tell us about? Just the open stuff, the video magazine stuff. Nothing secret."

"Well . . . okay." Now it was Krishna's turn. He picked up a small rock, wound up like a baseball player and threw. It dwindled and disappeared in the distance. A puff of white sprouted from the surface. "You know Sally Chang? She has just finished mapping the neurotransmitter functions."

They waited. When Krishna added nothing further, Hiro dryly said, "Wow."

"Details, Kreesh. Some of us aren't so fast to see the universe in a grain of sand as you are."

"It should be obvious. We've had a complete genetic map of the brain for almost a decade. Now add to that Sally Chang's chemical map, and it's analogous to being given the keys to the library. No, better than that. Imagine that you've spent your entire life within an enormous library filled with books in a language you neither read nor speak, and that you've just found the dictionary and a picture reader."

"So what are you saying? That we'll have complete understanding of how the brain operates?"

"We'll have complete *control* over how the brain operates. With chemical therapy, it will be possible to make anyone think or feel anything we want. We will have an immediate cure for all nontraumatic mental illness. We'll be able to fine-tune aggression, passion, creativity—bring them up, damp them down, it'll be all the same. You can see why our sponsors are so afraid of what our research might produce."

"Not really, no. The world could use more sanity," Gunther said.

"I agree. But who defines sanity? Many governments consider political dissent grounds for mental incarceration. This would open the doors of the brain, allowing it to be examined from the outside. For the first time, it would be possible to discover unexpressed rebellion. Modes of thought could be outlawed. The potential for abuse is not inconsiderable.

"Consider also the military applications. This knowledge combined with some of the new nanoweaponry might produce a berserker gas, allowing you to turn the enemy's armies upon their own populace. Or, easier, to throw them into a psychotic frenzy and let them turn on themselves. Cities could be pacified by rendering the citizenry catatonic. A secondary, internal reality could then be created, allowing the conqueror to use the masses as slave labor. The possibilities are endless."

They digested this in silence. At last Hiro said, "Jeez, Krishna, if that's the open goods, what the hell kind of stuff do you have to hide?"

"I can't tell you."

A minute later, Hiro was haring off again. At the foot of a nearby hill he found an immense boulder standing atilt on its small end. He danced about, trying to get good shots past it without catching his own footprints in them.

"So what's the problem?" Krishna said over his chip.

"The problem is, I can't arrange to see her. Ekatarina. I've left messages, but she won't answer them. And you know how it is in Bootstrap—it takes a real effort to avoid somebody who wants to see you. But she's managed it."

Krishna said nothing.

"All I want to know is, just what's going on here?"

"She's avoiding you."

"But why? I fell in love and she didn't, is that what you're telling me? I mean, is that a crock or what?"

"Without hearing her side of the story, I can't really say how she feels. But the odds are excellent she fell every bit as hard as you did. The difference is that you think it's a good idea, and she doesn't. So of course she's avoiding you. Contact would just make it more difficult for her to master her feelings for you."

"Shit!"

An unexpected touch of wryness entered Krishna's voice. "What do you want? A minute ago you were complaining that I think you're a machine. Now you're unhappy that Izmailova thinks she's not."

"Hey, you guys! Come over here. I've found the perfect shot. You've got to see this."

They turned to see Hiro waving at them from the hilltop. "I thought you were leaving," Gunther grumbled. "You said you were sick of the Moon, and going away and never coming back. So how come you're upgrading your digs all of a sudden?"

"That was yesterday! Today, I'm a pioneer, a builder of worlds, a founder of dynasties!"

"This is getting tedious. What does it take to get a straight answer out of you?"

Hiro bounded high and struck a pose, arms wide and a little ridiculous. He staggered a bit on landing. "Anya and I are getting married!"

Gunther and Krishna looked at each other, blank visor to blank visor. Forcing enthusiasm into his voice, Gunther said, "Hey, no shit? Really! Congratu—"

A scream of static howled up from nowhere. Gunther winced and cut down the gain. "My stupid radio is—"

One of the other two—they had moved together and he couldn't tell them apart at this distance—was pointing upward. Gunther tilted back his head, to look at the Earth. For a second he wasn't sure what he was looking for. Then he saw it: a diamond pinprick of light in the middle of the night. It was like a small, bright hole in reality, somewhere in continental Asia. "What the hell is *that?*" he asked.

Softly, Hiro said, "I think it's Vladivostok."

By the time they were back over the Sinus Medii, that first light had reddened and faded away, and two more had blossomed. The news jockey at the Observatory was working overtime splicing together reports from the major news feeds into a montage of rumor and fear. The radio was full of talk about hits on Seoul and Buenos Aires. Those seemed certain. Strikes against Panama, Iraq, Denver, and Cairo were disputed. A stealth missile had flown low over Hokkaido and been deflected into the Sea of Japan. The Swiss Orbitals had lost some factories to fragmentation satellites. There was no agreement as to the source aggressor, and though most suspicions trended in one direction, Tokyo denied everything.

Gunther was most impressed by the sound feed from a British video essayist, who said that it did not matter who had fired the first shot, or why. "Who shall we blame? The Southern Alliance, Tokyo, General Kim, or possibly some Grey terrorist group that nobody has ever heard of before? In a world whose weapons were wired to hair triggers, the question is irrelevant. When the first device exploded, it activated autonomous programs which launched what is officially labeled 'a measured response.' Gorshov himself could not have prevented it. His tactical programs chose this week's three most likely aggressors—at least two of which were certainly innocent—and launched a response. Human beings had no say over it.

"Those three nations in turn had their own reflexive 'measured responses.' The results of which we are just beginning to learn. Now we will pause for five days, while all concerned parties negotiate. How do we know this? Abstracts of all major defense programs are available on any public data net. They are no secret. Openness is in fact what deterrence is all about.

"We have five days to avert a war that literally nobody wants. The question is, in five days can the military and political powers seize control of their own defense programming? Will they? Given the pain and anger involved, the traditional hatreds, national chauvinism, and the natural reactions of those who number loved ones among the already dead, can those in charge overcome their own natures in time to pull back from final and total war? Our best informed guess is no. No, they cannot.

"Good night, and may God have mercy on us all."

They flew northward in silence. Even when the broadcast cut off in midword, nobody spoke. It was the end of the world, and there was nothing they could say that did not shrink to insignificance before that fact. They simply headed home.

The land about Bootstrap was dotted with graffiti, great block letters traced out in boulders: KARL OPS—EINDHOVEN '49 and LOUISE MCTIGHE ALBUQUERQUE NM. An enormous eye in a pyramid. ARSENAL WORLD RUGBY CHAMPS with a crown over it. CORNPONE. Pi Lambda Phi. MOTORHEADS. A giant with a club. Coming down over them, Gunther reflected that they all referred to places and things in the world overhead, not a one of them indigenous to the Moon. What had always seemed pointless now struck him as unspeakably sad.

It was only a short walk from the hopper pad to the vacuum garage. They didn't bother to summon a jitney.

The garage seemed strangely unfamiliar to Gunther now, though he had passed through it a thousand times. It seemed to float in its own mystery, as if everything had been removed and replaced by its exact double, rendering it different and somehow unknowable. Row upon row of parked vehicles were slanted by type within the painted lines. Ceiling lights strained to reach the floor, and could not.

"Boy, is this place still!" Hiro's voice seemed unnaturally loud.

It was true. In all the cavernous reaches of the garage, not a single remote or robot service unit stirred. Not so much as a pressure-leak sniffer moved.

"Must be because of the news," Gunther muttered. He found he was not ready to speak of the war directly. To the back of the garage, five airlocks stood all in a row. Above them a warm, yellow strip of window shone in the rock. In the room beyond, he could see the overseer moving about.

Hiro waved an arm, and the small figure within leaned forward to wave back. They trudged to the nearest lock and waited.

Nothing happened.

After a few minutes, they stepped back and away from the lock to peer up through the window. The overseer was still there, moving unhurriedly. "Hey!" Hiro shouted over open frequency. "You up there! Are you on the job?"

The man smiled, nodded and waved again.

"Then open the goddamned door!" Hiro strode forward, and with a final, nodding wave, the overseer bent over his controls.

"Uh, Hiro," Gunther said, "there's something odd about . . . ."

The door exploded open.

It slammed open so hard and fast the door was half torn off its hinges. The air within blasted out like a charge from a cannon. For a moment the garage was filled with loose tools, parts of vacuum suits and shreds of cloth. A wrench struck Gunther a glancing blow on his arm, spinning him around and knocking him to the floor.

He stared up in shock. Bits and pieces of things hung suspended for a long, surreal instant. Then, the air fled, they began to slowly shower down.

He got up awkwardly, massaging his arm through the suit. "Hiro, are you all right? Kreesh?"

"Oh my God," Krishna said.

Gunther spun around. He saw Krishna crouched in the shadow of a flatbed, over something that could not possibly be Hiro, because it bent the wrong way. He walked through shimmering unreality and knelt beside Krishna. He stared down at Hiro's corpse.

Hiro had been standing directly before the door when the overseer opened it without depressurizing the corridor within first. He had caught the blast straight on. It had lifted him and smashed him against the side of a flatbed, snapping his spine and shattering his helmet visor with the backlash. He must have died instantaneously.

"Who's there?" a woman said.

A jitney had entered the garage without Gunther's noticing it. He looked up in time to see a second enter, and then a third. People began piling out. Soon there were some twenty individuals advancing across the garage. They broke into two groups. One headed straight toward the locks and the smaller group advanced on Gunther and his friends. It looked for all the world like a military operation. "Who's there?" the woman repeated.

Gunther lifted his friend's corpse in his arms and stood. "It's Hiro," he said flatly. "Hiro."

They floated forward cautiously, a semicircle of blank-visored suits like so many kachinas. He could make out the corporate logos. Mitsubishi. Westinghouse. Holst Orbital. Izmailova's red-and-orange suit was among them, and a vivid Mondrian pattern he didn't recognize. The woman spoke again, tensely, warily. "Tell me how you're feeling, Hiro."

It was Beth Hamilton.

"That's not Hiro," Krishna said. "It's Gunther. *That's* Hiro. That he's carrying. We were out in the highlands and—" His voice cracked and collapsed in confusion.

"Is that you, Krishna?" someone asked. "There's a touch of luck. Send him up front, we're going to need him when we get in." Somebody else slapped an arm over Krishna's shoulders and led him away.

Over the radio, a clear voice spoke to the overseer. "Dmitri, is that you? It's Signe. You remember me, don't you, Dmitri? Signe Ohmstede. I'm your friend."

"Sure I remember you, Signe. I remember you. How could I ever forget my friend? Sure I do."

"Oh, good. I'm so happy. Listen carefully, Dmitri. Everything's fine."

Indignantly, Gunther chinned his radio to send. "The hell it is! That fool up there—!"

A burly man in a Westinghouse suit grabbed Gunther's bad arm and shook him. "Shut the fuck *up!*" he growled. "This is serious, damn you. We don't have the time to baby you."

Hamilton shoved between them. "For God's sake, Posner, he's just seen—" She stopped. "Let me take care of him. I'll get him calmed down. Just give us half an hour, okay?"

The others traded glances, nodded, and turned away.

To Gunther's surprise, Ekatarina spoke over his trance chip. "I'm sorry Gunther," she murmured. Then she was gone.

He was still holding Hiro's corpse. He found himself staring down at his friend's ruined face. The flesh was bruised and as puffy-looking as an over-boiled hot dog. He couldn't look away.

"Come on." Beth gave him a little shove to get him going. "Put the body in the back of that pick-up and give us a drive out to the cliff."

At Hamilton's insistence, Gunther drove. He found it helped, having some-thing to do. Hands afloat on the steering wheel, he stared ahead looking for the Mausoleum road cut-off. His eyes felt scratchy, and inhumanly dry.

"There was a preemptive strike against us," Hamilton said. "Sabotage. We're just now starting to put the pieces together. Nobody knew you were out on the surface or we would've sent somebody out to meet you. It's all been something of a shambles here."

He drove on in silence, cushioned and protected by all those miles of hard vacuum wrapped about him. He could feel the presence of Hiro's corpse in the back of the truck, a constant psychic itch between his shoulder blades. But so long as he didn't speak, he was safe; he could hold himself aloof from the universe that held the pain. It couldn't touch him. He waited, but Beth didn't add anything to what she'd already said.

Finally he said, "Sabotage?"

"A software meltdown at the radio station. Explosions at all the railguns. Three guys from Microspacecraft Applications bought it when the Boitsovij Kot railgun blew. I suppose it was inevitable. All the military industry up here, it's not surprising somebody would want to knock us out of the equation. But that's not all. Something's happened to the people in Bootstrap. Some-thing really horrible. I was out at the Observatory when it happened. The newsjay called back to see if there was any backup software to get the station going again, and she got nothing but gibberish. Crazy stuff. I mean, *really* crazy. We had to disconnect the Observatory's remotes, because the operators were . . ." She was crying now, softly and insistently, and it was a minute before she could speak again. "Some sort of biological weapon. That's all we know."

"We're here."

As he pulled up to the foot of the Mausoleum cliff, it occurred to Gunther that they hadn't thought to bring a drilling rig. Then he counted ten black niches in the rockface, and realized that somebody had been thinking ahead.

"The only people who weren't hit were those who were working at the Center or the Observatory, or out on the surface. Maybe a hundred of us all told."

They walked around to the back of the pick-up. Gunther waited, but

Hamilton didn't offer to carry the body. For some reason that made him feel angry and resentful. He unlatched the gate, hopped up on the treads, and hoisted the suited corpse. "Let's get this over with."

Before today, only six people had ever died on the Moon. They walked past the caves in which their bodies awaited eternity. Gunther knew their names by heart: Heisse, Yasuda, Spehalski, Dubinin, Mikami, Castillo. And now Hiro. It seemed incomprehensible that the day should ever come when there would be too many dead to know them all by name.

Daisies and tiger lilies had been scattered before the vaults in such profusion that he couldn't help crushing some underfoot.

The entered the first empty niche, and he laid Hiro down upon a stone table cut into the rock. In the halo of his helmet lamp the body looked piteously twisted and uncomfortable. Gunther found that he was crying, large hot tears that crawled down his face and got into his mouth when he inhaled. He cut off the radio until he had managed to blink the tears away. "Shit." He wiped a hand across his helmet. "I suppose we ought to say something."

Hamilton took his hand and squeezed.

"I've never seen him as happy as he was today. He was going to get married. He was jumping around, laughing and talking about raising a family. And now he's dead, and I don't even know what his religion was." A thought occurred to him, and he turned helplessly toward Hamilton. "What are we going to tell Anya?"

"She's got problems of her own. Come on, say a prayer and let's go. You'll run out of oxygen."

"Yeah, okay." He bowed his head. *"The Lord is my shepherd, I shall not want. . . ."*

Back at Bootstrap, the surface party had seized the airlocks and led the overseer away from the controls. The man from Westinghouse, Posner, looked down on them from the observation window. "Don't crack your suits," he warned. "Keep them sealed tight at all times. Whatever hit the bastards here is still around. Might be in the water, might be in the air. One whiff and you're out of here! You got that?"

"Yeah, yeah," Gunther grumbled. "Keep your shirt on."

Posner's hand froze on the controls. "Let's get serious here. I'm not letting you in until you acknowledge the gravity of the situation. This isn't a picnic outing. If you're not prepared to help, we don't need you. Is that understood?"

"We understand completely, and we'll cooperate to the fullest," Hamilton said quickly. *"Won't we*, Weil?"

He nodded miserably.

Only the one lock had been breached, and there were five more sets of pressurized doors between it and the bulk of Bootstrap's air. The city's designers had been cautious.

Overseen by Posner, they passed through the corridors, locks and changing rooms and up the cargo escalators. Finally they emerged into the city interior.

They stood blinking on the lip of Hell.

At first, it was impossible to pinpoint any source for the pervasive sense of wrongness gnawing at the edge of consciousness. The parks were dotted with people, the fill lights at the juncture of crater walls and canopy were bright, and the waterfalls still fell gracefully from terrace to terrace. Button quail bobbed comically in the grass.

Then small details intruded. A man staggered about the fourth level, head jerking, arms waving stiffly. A plump woman waddled by, pulling an empty cart made from a wheeled microfactory stand, quacking like a duck. Someone sat in the kneehigh forest by Noguchi Park, tearing out the trees one by one.

But it was the still figures that were on examination more profoundly disturbing. Here a man lay half in and half out of a tunnel entrance, as unselfconscious as a dog. There, three women stood in extreme postures of lassitude, bordering on despair. Everywhere, people did not touch or speak or show in any way that they were aware of one other. They shared an absolute and universal isolation.

"What shall—" Something slammed onto Gunther's back. He was knocked forward, off his feet. Tumbling, he became aware that fists were striking him, again and again, and then that a lean man was kneeling atop his chest, hysterically shouting, "Don't do it! Don't do it!"

Hamilton seized the man's shoulders and pulled him away. Gunther got to his knees. He looked into the face of madness: eyes round and fearful, expression full of panic. The man was terrified of Gunther.

With an abrupt wrench, the man broke free. He ran as if pursued by demons. Hamilton stared after him. "You okay?" she asked.

"Yeah, sure." Gunther adjusted his tool harness. "Let's see if we can find the others."

They walked toward the lake, staring about at the self-absorbed figures scattered about the grass. Nobody attempted to speak to them. A woman ran by, barefooted. Her arms were filled with flowers. "Hey!" Hamilton called after her. She smiled fleetingly over her shoulder, but did not slow. Gunther knew her vaguely, an executive supervisor for Martin Marietta.

"Is *every*body here crazy?" he asked.

"Sure looks that way."

The woman had reached the shore and was flinging the blossoms into the water with great sweeps of her arm. They littered the surface.

"Damned waste." Gunther had come to Bootstrap before the flowers; he knew the effort involved getting permission to plant them and rewriting the city's ecologics. A man in a blue-striped Krupp suit was running along the verge of the lake.

The woman, flowers gone, threw herself into the water.

At first it appeared she'd suddenly decided to take a dip. But from the struggling, floundering way she thrashed deeper into the water it was clear that she could not swim.

In the time it took Gunther to realize this, Hamilton had leaped forward, running for the lake. Belatedly, he started after her. But the man in the

Krupp suit was ahead of them both. He splashed in after the woman. An outstretched hand seized her shoulder and then he fell, pulling her under. She was red-faced and choking when he emerged again, arm across her chest.

By then Gunther and Beth were wading into the lake, and together they three got the woman to shore. When she was released, the woman calmly turned and walked away, as if nothing had happened.

"Gone for more flowers," the Krupp component explained. "This is the third time fair Ophelia there's tried to drown herself. She's not the only one. I've been hanging around, hauling 'em out when they stumble in."

"Do you know where everybody else is? Is there anyone in charge? Somebody giving out orders?"

"Do you need any help?" Gunther asked.

The Krupp man shrugged. "I'm fine. No idea where the others are, though. My friends were going on to the second level when I decided I ought to stay here. If you see them, you might tell 'em I'd appreciate hearing back from them. Three guys in Krupp suits."

"We'll do that," Gunther said.

Hamilton was already walking away.

On a step just beneath the top of the stairs sprawled one of Gunther's fellow G5 components. "Sidney," he said carefully. "How's it going?"

Sidney giggled. "I'm making the effort, if that's what you mean. I don't see that the 'how' of it makes much difference."

"Okay."

"A better way of phrasing that might be to ask why I'm not at work." He stood, and in a very natural manner accompanied Gunther up the steps. "Obviously I can't be two places at once. You wouldn't want to perform major surgery in your own absence, would you?" He giggled again. "It's an oxymoron. Like horses: those classically beautiful Praxitelesian bodies excreting these long surreal turds."

"Okay."

"I've always admired them for squeezing so much art into a single image."

"Sidney," Hamilton said. "We're looking for our friends. Three people in blue-striped work suits."

"I've seen them. I know just where they went." His eyes were cool and vacant; they didn't seem to focus on anything in particular.

"Can you lead us to them?"

"Even a flower recognizes its own face." A gracefully winding gravel path led through private garden plots and croquet malls. They followed him down it.

There were not many people on the second terrace; with the fall of madness, most seemed to have retreated into the caves. Those few who remained either ignored or cringed away from them. Gunther found himself staring obsessively into their faces, trying to analyze the deficiency he felt in each. Fear nested in their eyes, and the appalled awareness that some terrible thing had happened to them coupled with a complete ignorance of its nature.

"God, these people!"

Hamilton grunted.

He felt he was walking through a dream. Sounds were muted by his suit, and colors less intense seen through his helmet visor. It was as if he had been subtly removed from the world, there and not-there simultaneously, an impression that strengthened with each new face that looked straight through him with mad, unseeing indifference.

Sidney turned a corner, broke into a trot and jogged into a tunnel entrance. Gunther ran after him. At the mouth of the tunnel, he paused to let his helmet adjust to the new light levels. When it cleared he saw Sidney dart down a side passage. He followed.

At the intersection of passages, he looked and saw no trace of their guide. Sidney had disappeared. "Did you see which way he went?" he asked Hamilton over the radio. There was no answer. "Beth?"

He started down the corridor, halted, and turned back. These things went deep. He could wander around in them forever. He went back out to the terraces. Hamilton was nowhere to be seen.

For lack of any better plan, he followed the path. Just beyond an ornamental holly bush he was pulled up short by a vision straight out of William Blake.

The man had discarded shirt and sandals, and wore only a pair of shorts. He squatted atop a boulder, alert, patient, eating a tomato. A steel pipe slanted across his knees like a staff or scepter, and he had woven a crown of sorts from platinum wire with a fortune's worth of hyperconductor chips dangling over his forehead. He looked every inch a kingly animal.

He stared at Gunther, calm and unblinking.

Gunther shivered. The man seemed less human than anthropoid, crafty in its way, but unthinking. He felt as if he were staring across the eons at Grandfather Ape, crouched on the edge of awareness. An involuntary thrill of superstitious awe seized him. Was this what happened when the higher mental functions were scraped away? Did Archetype lie just beneath the skin, waiting for the opportunity to emerge?

"I'm looking for my friend," he said. "A woman in a G5 suit like mine? Have you seen her? She was looking for three—" He stopped. The man was staring at him blankly. "Oh, never mind."

He turned away and walked on.

After a time, he lost all sense of continuity. Existence fragmented into unconnected images: A man bent almost double, leering and squeezing a yellow rubber duckie. A woman leaping up like a jack-in-the-box from behind an air monitor, shrieking and flapping her arms. An old friend sprawled on the ground, crying, with a broken leg. When he tried to help her, she scrabbled away from him in fear. He couldn't get near her without doing more harm. "Stay here," he said, "I'll find help." Five minutes later he realized that he was lost, with not the slightest notion of how to find his way back to her again. He came to the stairs leading back down to the bottom level. There was no reason to go down them. There was no reason not to. He went down.

He had just reached the bottom of the stairs when someone in a lavender boutique suit hurried by.

Gunther chinned on his helmet radio.

"Hello!" The lavender suit glanced back at him, its visor a plate of obsidian, but did not turn back. "Do you know where everyone's gone? I'm totally lost. How can I find out what I should be doing?" The lavender suit ducked into a tunnel.

Faintly, a voice answered, "Try the city manager's office."

The city manager's office was a tight little cubby an eighth of a kilometer deep within the tangled maze of administrative and service tunnels. It had never been very important in the scheme of things. The city manager's prime duties were keeping the air and water replenished and scheduling airlock inspections, functions any computer could handle better than a man had they dared trust them to a machine. The room had probably never been as crowded as it was now. Dozens of people suited for full vacuum spilled out into the hall, anxiously listening to Ekatarina confer with the city's Crisis Management Program. Gunther pushed in as close as he could; even so, he could barely see her.

"—the locks, the farms and utilities, and we've locked away all the remotes. What comes next?"

Ekatarina's peecee hung from her work harness, amplifying the CMP's silent voice. "Now that elementary control has been established, second priority must go to the industrial sector. The factories must be locked down. The reactors must be put to sleep. There is not sufficient human supervisory presence to keep them running. The factories have mothballing programs available upon request.

"Third, the farms cannot tolerate neglect. Fifteen minutes without oxygen, and all the tilapia will die. The calimari are even more delicate. Three experienced agricultural components must be assigned immediately. Double that number, if you only have inexperienced components. Advisory software is available. What are your resources?"

"Let me get back to you on that. What else?"

"What about the people?" a man asked belligerently. "What the hell are you worrying about factories for, when our people are in the state they're in?"

Izmailova looked up sharply. "You're one of Chang's research components, aren't you? Why are you here? Isn't there enough for you to do?" She looked about, as if abruptly awakened from sleep. "All of you! What are you waiting for?"

"You can't put us off that easily! Who made you the little brass-plated general? We don't have to take orders from you."

The bystanders shuffled uncomfortably, not leaving, waiting to take their cue from each other. Their suits were as good as identical in this crush, their helmets blank and expressionless. They looked like so many ambulatory eggs.

The crowd's mood balanced on the instant, ready to fall into acceptance or anger with a featherweight's push. Gunther raised an arm. "General!" he said loudly. "Private Weil here! I'm awaiting my orders. Tell me what to do."

Laughter rippled through the room, and the tension eased. Ekatarina said, "Take whoever's nearest you, and start clearing the afflicted out of the administrative areas. Guide them out toward the open, where they won't be so likely to hurt themselves. Whenever you get a room or corridor emptied, lock it up tight. Got that?"

"Yes, ma'am." He tapped the suit nearest him, and its helmet dipped in a curt nod. But when they turned to leave, their way was blocked by the crush of bodies.

"You!" Ekatarina jabbed a finger. "Go to the farmlocks and foam them shut; I don't want any chance of getting them contaminated. Anyone with experience running factories—that's most of us, I think—should find a remote and get to work shutting the things down. The CMP will help direct you. If you have nothing else to do, buddy up and work at clearing out the corridors. I'll call a general meeting when we've put together a more comprehensive plan of action." She paused. "What have I left out?"

Surprisingly, the CMP answered her: "There are twenty-three children in the city, two of them seven-year-old prelegals and the rest five years of age or younger, offspring of registered-permanent lunar components. Standing directives are that children be given special care and protection. The third-level chapel can be converted to a care center. Word should be spread that as they are found, the children are to be brought there. Assign one reliable individual to oversee them."

"My God, yes." She turned to the belligerent man from the Center, and snapped, "Do it."

He hesitated, then saluted ironically and turned to go.

That broke the logjam. The crowd began to disperse. Gunther and his co-worker—it turned out to be Liza Nagenda, another ground-rat like himself—set to work.

In after years Gunther was to remember this period as a time when his life entered a dark tunnel. For long, nightmarish hours he and Liza shuffled from office to storage room, struggling to move the afflicted out of the corporate areas and into the light.

The afflicted did not cooperate.

The first few rooms they entered were empty. In the fourth, a distraught-looking woman was furiously going through drawers and files and flinging their contents away. Trash covered the floor. "It's in here somewhere," she said frantically.

"What's in there, darling?" Gunther said soothingly. He had to speak loudly so he could be heard through his helmet. "What are you looking for?"

She tilted her head up with a smile of impish delight. Using both hands, she smoothed back her hair, elbows high, pushing it straight over her skull, then tucking in stray strands behind her ears. "It doesn't matter, because I'm sure to find it now. Two scarabs appear, and between them the blazing disk of the sun, that's a good omen, not to mention being an analogy for sex. I've had sex, all the sex anyone could want, buggered behind the outhouse by the lizard king when I was nine. What did I care? I had wings then and thought that I could fly."

Gunther edged a little closer. "You're not making any sense at all."

"You know, Tolstoy said there was a green stick in the woods behind his house that once found would cause all men to love one another. I believe in that green stick as a basic principle of physical existence. The universe exists in a matrix of four dimensions which we can perceive and seven which we cannot, which is why we experience peace and brotherhood as a seven-dimensional green stick phenomenon."

"You've got to listen to me."

"Why? You gonna tell me Hitler is dead? I don't believe in that kind of crap."

"Oh hell," Nagenda said. "You can't reason with a flick. Just grab her arms and we'll chuck her out."

It wasn't that easy, though. The woman was afraid of them. Whenever they approached her, she slipped fearfully away. If they moved slowly, they could not corner her, and when they both rushed her, she leapt up over a desk and then down into the kneehole. Nagenda grabbed her legs and pulled. The woman wailed, and clutched at the knees of Nagenda's suit. "Get offa me," Liza snarled. "Gunther, get this crazy woman off my damn legs."

"Don't kill me!" the woman screamed. "I've always voted twice—you know I did. I told them you were a gangster, but I was wrong. Don't take the oxygen out of my lungs!"

They got the woman out of the office, then lost her again when Gunther turned to lock the door. She went fluttering down the corridor with Nagenda in hot pursuit. Then she dove into another office, and they had to start all over again.

It took over an hour to drive the woman from the corridors and release her into the park. The next three went quickly enough by contrast. The one after that was difficult again, and the fifth turned out to be the first woman they had encountered, wandered back to look for her office. When they'd brought her to the open again, Liza Nagenda said, "That's four flicks down and three thousand eight hundred fifty-eight to go."

"Look—" Gunther began. And then Krishna's voice sounded over his trance chip, stiffly and with exaggerated clarity. "Everyone is to go to the central lake immediately for an organizational meeting. Repeat: Go to the lake immediately. Go to the lake now." He was obviously speaking over a jury-rigged transmitter. The sound was bad and his voice boomed and popped on the chip.

"All right, okay, I got that," Liza said. "You can shut up now."

"Please go to the lake immediately. Everyone is to go directly to the central—"

"Sheesh."

By the time they got out to the parklands again, the open areas were thick with people. Not just the suited figures of the survivors, either. All the afflicted were emerging from the caves and corridors of Bootstrap. They walked blindly, uncertainly, toward the lake, as if newly called from the grave. The ground level was filling with people.

"Sonofabitch," Gunther said wonderingly.

"Gunther?" Nagenda asked. "What's going on?"

"It's the trance chips! Sonofabitch, all we had to do was speak to them over the chips. They'll do whatever the voice in their heads tells them to do."

The land about the lake was so crowded that Gunther had trouble spotting any other suits. Then he saw a suited figure standing on the edge of the second level waving broadly. He waved back and headed for the stairs.

By the time he got to level two, a solid group of the unafflicted had gathered. More and more came up, drawn by the concentration of suits. Finally Ekatarina spoke over the open channel of her suit radio.

"There's no reason to wait for us all to gather. I think everyone is close enough to hear me. Sit down, take a little rest, you've all earned it." People eased down on the grass. Some sprawled on their backs or stomachs, fully suited. Most just sat.

"By a fortunate accident, we've discovered a means of controlling our afflicted friends." There was light applause. "But there are still many problems before us, and they won't all be solved so easily. We've all seen the obvious. Now I must tell you of worse. If the war on Earth goes full thermonuclear, we will be completely and totally cut off, possibly for decades."

A murmur passed through the crowd.

"What does this mean? Beyond the immediate inconveniences—no luxuries, no more silk shirts, no new seed stock, no new videos, no way home for those of us who hadn't already decided to stay—we will be losing much that we require for survival. All our microfacturing capability comes from the Swiss Orbitals. Our water reserves are sufficient for a year, but we lose minute quantities of water vapor to rust and corrosion and to the vacuum every time somebody goes in or out an airlock, and those quantities are necessary for our existence.

"But we can survive. We can process raw hydrogen and oxygen from the regolith, and burn them to produce water. We already make our own air. We can do without most nanoelectronics. We can thrive and prosper and grow, even if Earth . . . even if the worst happens. But to do so we'll need our full manufacturing capability, and full supervisory capability as well. We must not only restore our factories, but find a way to restore our people. There'll be work and more for all of us in the days ahead."

Nagenda touched helmets with Gunther and muttered, "What a crock."

"Come on, I want to hear this."

"Fortunately, the Crisis Management Program has contingency plans for exactly this situation. According to its records, which may be incomplete, I have more military command experience than any other functional. Does anyone wish to challenge this?" She waited, but nobody said anything. " We will go to a quasimilitary structure for the duration of the emergency. This is strictly for organizational purposes. There will be no privileges afforded the officers, and the military structure will be dismantled *immediately* upon resolution of our present problems. That's paramount."

She glanced down at her peecee. "To that purpose, I am establishing beneath me a triumvirate of subordinate officers, consisting of Carlos Diaz-Rodrigues, Miiko Ezumi, and Will Posner. Beneath them will be nine officers, each responsible for a cadre of no more than ten individuals."

She read out names. Gunther was assigned to Cadre Four, Beth Hamilton's group. Then Ekatarina said, "We're all tired. The gang back at the Center have rigged up a decontamination procedure, a kitchen and sleeping spaces of sorts. Cadres One, Two, and Three will put in four more hours here, then pull down a full eight hours sleep. Cadres Four through Nine may return now to the Center for a meal and four hours rest." She stopped. "That's it. Go get some shut-eye."

A ragged cheer arose, fell flat, and died. Gunther stood. Liza Nagenda gave him a friendly squeeze on the butt and when he started to the right yanked his arm and pointed him left, toward the service escalators. With easy familiarity, she slid an arm around his waist.

He'd known guys who'd slept with Liza Nagenda, and they all agreed that she was bad news, possessive, hysterical, ludicrously emotional. But what the hell. It was easier than not.

They trudged off.

There was too much to do. They worked to exhaustion—it was not enough. They rigged a system of narrow-band radio transmissions for the CMP and ran a microwave patch back to the Center, so it could direct their efforts more efficiently—it was not enough. They organized and rearranged constantly. But the load was too great and accidents inevitably happened.

Half the surviving railguns—small units used to deliver raw and semi-processed materials over the highlands and across the bay—were badly damaged when the noonday sun buckled their aluminum rails; the sunscreens had not been put in place in time. An unknown number of robot bulldozers had wandered off from the strip mines and were presumably lost. It was hard to guess how many because the inventory records were scrambled. None of the food stored in Bootstrap could be trusted; the Center's meals had to be harvested direct from the farms and taken out through the emergency locks. An inexperienced farmer mishandled her remote, and ten aquaculture tanks boiled out into vacuum geysering nine thousand fingerlings across the surface. On Posner's orders, the remote handler rigs were hastily packed and moved to the Center. When uncrated, most were found to have damaged rocker arms.

There were small victories. On his second shift, Gunther found fourteen bales of cotton in vacuum storage and set an assembler to sewing futons for the Center. That meant an end to sleeping on bare floors and made him a local hero for the rest of that day. There were not enough toilets in the Center;

Diaz-Rodrigues ordered the flare storm shelters in the factories stripped of theirs. Huriel Garza discovered a talent for cooking with limited resources.

But they were losing ground. The afflicted were unpredictable, and they were everywhere. A demented systems analyst, obeying the voices in his head, dumped several barrels of lubricating oil in the lake. The water filters clogged, and the streams had to be shut down for repairs. A doctor somehow managed to strangle herself with her own diagnostic harness. The city's ecologics were badly stressed by random vandalism.

Finally somebody thought to rig up a voice loop for continuous transmission. "I am calm," it said. "I am tranquil. I do not want to do anything. I am happy where I am."

Gunther was working with Liza Nagenda trying to get the streams going again when the loop came on. He looked up and saw an uncanny quiet spread over Bootstrap. Up and down the terraces, the flicks stood in postures of complete and utter impassivity. The only movement came from the small number of suits scurrying like beetles among the newly catatonic.

Liza put her hands on her hips. "Terrific. Now we've got to *feed* them."

"Hey, cut me some slack, okay? This is the first good news I've heard since I don't know when."

"It's not good anything, sweetbuns. It's just more of the same."

She was right. Relieved as he was, Gunther knew it. One hopeless task has been traded for another.

He was wearily suiting up for his third day when Hamilton stopped him and said, "Weil! You know any electrical engineering?"

"Not really, no. I mean, I can do the wiring for a truck, or maybe rig up a microwave relay, stuff like that, but . . ."

"It'll have to do. Drop what you're on, and help Krishna set up a system for controlling the flicks. Some way we can handle them individually."

They set up shop in Krishna's old lab. The remnants of old security standards still lingered, and nobody had been allowed to sleep there. Consequently, the room was wonderfully neat and clean, all crafted-in-orbit laboratory equipment with smooth, anonymous surfaces. It was a throwback to a time before clutter and madness had taken over. If it weren't for the new-tunnel smell, the raw tang of cut rock the air carried, it would be possible to pretend nothing had happened.

Gunther stood in a telepresence rig, directing a remote through Bootstrap's apartments. They were like so many unconnected cells of chaos. He entered one and found the words BUDDHA = COSMIC INERTIA scrawled on its wall with what looked to be human feces. A woman sat on the futon tearing handfuls of batting from it and flinging them in the air. Cotton covered the room like a fresh snowfall. The next apartment was empty and clean, and a microfactory sat gleaming on a ledge. "I hereby nationalize you in the name of the People's Provisional Republic of Bootstrap, and of the oppressed masses everywhere," he said dryly. The remote gingerly picked it up. "You done with that chip diagram yet?"

"It will not be long now," Krishna said.

They were building a prototype controller. The idea was to code each peecee, so the CMP could identify and speak to its owner individually. By stepping down the voltage, they could limit the peecee's transmission range to a meter and a half so that each afflicted person could be given individualized orders. The existing chips, however, were high-strung Swiss Orbital thoroughbreds, and couldn't handle oddball power yields. They had to be replaced.

"I don't see how you can expect to get any useful work out of these guys, though. I mean, what we need are supervisors. You can't hope to get coherent thought out of them."

Bent low over his peecee, Krishna did not answer at first. Then he said, "Do you know how a yogi stops his heart? We looked into that when I was in grad school. We asked Yogi Premanand if he would stop his heart while wired up to our instruments, and he graciously consented. We had all the latest brain scanners, but it turned out the most interesting results were recorded by the EKG.

"We found that the yogi's heart did not as we had expected slow down, but rather went faster and faster, until it reached its physical limits and began to fibrillate. He had not slowed his heart; he had sped it up. It did not stop, but went into spasm.

"After our tests, I asked him if he had known these facts. He said no, that they were most interesting. He was polite about it, but clearly did not think our findings very significant."

"So you're saying . . . ?"

"The problem with schizophrenics is that they have too much going on in their heads. Too many voices. Too many ideas. They can't focus their attention on a single chain of thought. But it would be a mistake to think them incapable of complex reasoning. In fact, they're thinking brilliantly. Their brains are simply operating at such peak efficiencies that they can't organize their thoughts coherently.

"What the trance chip does is to provide one more voice, but a louder, more insistent one. That's why they obey it. It breaks through that noise, provides a focus, serves as a matrix along which thought can crystallize."

The remote unlocked the door into a conference room deep in the administrative tunnels. Eight microfactories waited in a neat row atop the conference table. It added the ninth, turned, and left, locking the door behind it. "You know," Gunther said, "all these elaborate precautions may be unnecessary. Whatever was used on Bootstrap may not be in the air anymore. It may never have *been* in the air. It could've been in the water or something."

"Oh, it's there all right, in the millions. We're dealing with an airborne schizomimetic engine. It's designed to hang around in the air indefinitely."

"A schizomimetic engine? What the hell is that?"

In a distracted monotone, Krishna said, "A schizomimetic engine is a strategic nonlethal weapon with high psychological impact. It not only incapacitates its target vectors, but places a disproportionately heavy burden on the enemy's manpower and material support caring for the victims. Due to the particular quality of the effect, it has a profoundly demoralizing influence on those exposed to the victims, especially those involved in their care. Thus, it is particularly desirable as a strategic weapon." He might have been quoting from an operations manual.

Gunther pondered that. "Calling the meeting over the chips wasn't a mistake, was it? You knew it would work. You knew they would obey a voice speaking inside their heads."

"Yes."

"This shit was brewed up at the Center, wasn't it? This is the stuff that you couldn't talk about."

"Some of it."

Gunther powered down his rig and flipped up the lens. "God damn you, Krishna! God damn you straight to Hell, you stupid fucker!"

Krishna looked up from his work, bewildered. "Have I said something wrong?"

"No! No, you haven't said a damned thing wrong—you've just driven four thousand people out of their fucking minds, is all! Wake up and take a good look at what you maniacs have done with your weapons research!"

"It wasn't weapons research," Krishna said mildly. He drew a long, involuted line on the schematic. "But when pure research is funded by the military, the military will seek out military applications for the research. That's just the way it is."

"What's the difference? It happened. You're responsible."

Now Krishna actually set his peecee aside. He spoke with uncharacteristic fire. "Gunther, we *need* this information. Do you realize that we are trying to run a technological civilization with a brain that was evolved in the neolithic? I am perfectly serious. We're all trapped in the old hunter-gatherer programs, and they are of no use to us anymore. Take a look at what's happening on Earth. They're hip-deep in a war that nobody meant to start and nobody wants to fight and it's even money that nobody can stop. The type of thinking that put us in this corner is not to our benefit. It has to change. And that's what we are working toward—taming the human brain. Harnessing it. Reining it in.

"Granted, our research has been turned against us. But what's one more weapon among so many? If neuroprogrammers hadn't been available, something else would have been used. Mustard gas maybe, or plutonium dust. For that matter, they could've just blown a hole in the canopy and let us all strangle."

"That's self-justifying bullshit, Krishna! Nothing can excuse what you've done."

Quietly, but with conviction, Krishna said, "You will never convince me that our research is not the most important work we could possibly be doing today. We must seize control of this monster within our skulls. We must change our ways of thinking." His voice dropped. "The sad thing is that we cannot change unless we survive. But in order to survive, we must first change."

They worked in silence after that.

Gunther awoke from restless dreams to find that the sleep shift was only half over. Liza was snoring. Careful not to wake her, he pulled his clothes on and padded barefoot out of his niche and down the hall. The light was on in the common room and he heard voices.

Ekatarina looked up when he entered. Her face was pale and drawn. Faint circles had formed under her eyes. She was alone.

"Oh, hi. I was just talking with the CMP." She thought off her peecee. "Have a seat."

He pulled up a chair and hunched down over the table. Confronted by her, he found it took a slight but noticeable effort to draw his breath. "So. How are things going?"

"They'll be trying out your controllers soon. The first batch of chips ought to be coming out of the factories in an hour or so. I thought I'd stay up to see how they work out."

"It's that bad, then?" Ekatarina shook her head, would not look at him. "Hey, come on, here you are waiting up on the results, and I can see how tired you are. There must be a lot riding on this thing."

"More than you know," she said bleakly. "I've just been going over the numbers. Things are worse than you can imagine."

He reached out and took her cold, bloodless hand. She squeezed him so tightly it hurt. Their eyes met and he saw in hers all the fear and wonder he felt.

Wordlessly, they stood.

"I'm niching alone," Ekatarina said. She had not let go of his hand, held it so tightly, in fact, that it seemed she would never let it go.

Gunther let her lead him away.

They made love, and talked quietly about inconsequential things, and made love again. Gunther had thought she would nod off immediately after the first time, but she was too full of nervous energy for that.

"Tell me when you're about to come," she murmured. "Tell me when you're coming."

He stopped moving. "Why do you always say that?"

Ekatarina looked up at him dazedly, and he repeated the question. Then she laughed a deep, throaty laugh. "Because I'm frigid."

"Hah?"

She took his hand, and brushed her cheek against it. Then she ducked her head, continuing the motion across her neck and up the side of her scalp. He felt the short, prickly hair against his palm and then, behind her ear, two bumps under the skin where biochips had been implanted. One of those would be her trance chip and the other . . . "It's a prosthetic," she explained.

Her eyes were grey and solemn. "It hooks into the pleasure centers. When I need to, I can turn on my orgasm at a thought. That way we can always come at the same time." She moved her hips slowly beneath him as she spoke.

"But that means you don't really need to have any kind of sexual stimulation at all, do you? You can trigger an orgasm at will. While you're riding on a bus. Or behind a desk. You could just turn that thing on and come for hours at a time."

She looked amused. "I'll tell you a secret. When it was new, I used to do stunts like that. Everybody does. One outgrows that sort of thing quickly."

With more than a touch of stung pride, Gunther said, "Then what am I doing here? If you've got that thing, what the hell do you need me for?" He started to draw away from her.

She pulled him down atop her again. "You're kind of comforting," she said. "In an argumentative way. Come here."

He got back to his futon and began gathering up the pieces of his suit. Liza sat up sleepily and gawked at him. "So," she said. "It's like that, is it?"

"Yeah, well. I kind of left something unfinished. An old relationship." Warily, he extended a hand. "No hard feelings, huh?"

Ignoring his hand, she stood, naked and angry. "You got the nerve to stand there without even wiping my smile off your dick first and say no hard feelings? Asshole!"

"Aw, come on now, Liza, it's not like that."

"Like hell it's not! You got a shot at that white-assed Russian ice queen, and I'm history. Don't think I don't know all about her."

"I was hoping we could still be, you know, friends."

"Nice trick, shithead." She balled her fist and hit him hard in the center of his chest. Tears began to form in her eyes. "You just slink away. I'm tired of looking at you."

He left.

But did not sleep. Ekatarina was awake and ebullient over the first reports coming in on the new controller system. "They're working!" she cried. "They're working!" She'd pulled on a silk camisole, and strode back and forth excitedly, naked to the waist. Her pubic hair was a white flame, with almost invisible trails of smaller hairs reaching for her navel and caressing the sweet insides of her thighs. Tired as he was, Gunther felt new desire for her. In a weary, washed-out way, he was happy.

"Whooh!" She kissed him hard, not sexually, and called up the CMP. "Rerun all our earlier projections. We're putting our afflicted components back to work. Adjust all work schedules."

"As you direct."

"How does this change our long-range prospects?"

The program was silent for several seconds, processing. Then it said, "You are about to enter a necessary but very dangerous stage of recovery. You are going from a low-prospects high-stability situation to a high-prospects high-instability one. With leisure your unafflicted components will quickly grow dissatisfied with your government."

"What happens if I just step down?"

"Prospects worsen drastically."

Ekatarina ducked her head. "All right, what's likely to be our most pressing new problem?"

"The unafflicted components will demand to know more about the war on Earth. They'll want the media feeds restored immediately."

"I could rig up a receiver easily enough," Gunther volunteered. "Nothing fancy, but . . ."

"Don't you dare!"

"Hah? Why not?"

"Gunther, let me put it to you this way: What two nationalities are most heavily represented here?"

"Well, I guess that would be Russia and—oh."

"Oh is right. For the time being, I think it's best if nobody knows for sure who's supposed to be enemies with whom." She asked the CMP, "How should I respond?"

"Until the situation stabilizes, you have no choice but distraction. Keep their minds occupied. Hunt down the saboteurs and then organize war crime trials."

"That's out. No witch hunts, no scapegoats, no trials. We're all in this together."

Emotionlessly, the CMP said, "Violence is the left hand of government. You are rash to dismiss its potentials without serious thought."

"I won't discuss it."

"Very well. If you wish to postpone the use of force for the present, you could hold a hunt for the weapon used on Bootstrap. Locating and identifying it would involve everyone's energies without necessarily implicating anybody. It would also be widely interpreted as meaning an eventual cure was possible, thus boosting the general morale without your actually lying."

Tiredly, as if this were something she had gone over many times already, she said, "Is there really no hope of curing them?"

"Anything is possible. In light of present resources, though, it cannot be considered likely."

Ekatarina thought the peecee off, dismissing the CMP. She sighed. "Maybe that's what we ought to do. Donkey up a hunt for the weapon. We ought to be able to do something with that notion."

Puzzled, Gunther said, "But it was one of Chang's weapons, wasn't it? A schizomimetic engine, right?"

"Where did you hear that?" she demanded sharply.

"Well, Krishna said . . . he didn't act like . . . I thought it was public knowledge."

Ekatarina's face hardened. "Program!" she thought.

The CMP came back to life. "Ready."

"Locate Krishna Narasimhan, unafflicted, Cadre Five. I want to speak with him immediately." Ekatarina snatched up her panties and shorts, and furiously began dressing. "Where are my damned sandals? Program! Tell him to meet me in the common room. Right away."

"Received."

To Gunther's surprise, it took over an hour for Ekatarina to browbeat Krishna into submission. Finally, though, the young research component went to a lockbox, identified himself to it, and unsealed the storage areas. "It's not all that secure," he said apologetically. "If our sponsors knew how often we just left everything open so we could get in and out, they'd—well, never mind."

He lifted a flat, palm-sized metal rectangle from a cabinet. "This is the most likely means of delivery. It's an aerosol bomb. The biological agents are loaded *here*, and it's triggered by snapping this back *here*. It's got enough pressure in it to spew the agents fifty feet straight up. Air currents do the rest." He tossed it to Gunther who stared down at the thing in horror. "Don't worry, it's not armed."

He slid out a slim drawer holding row upon gleaming row of slim chrome cylinders. "These contain the engines themselves. They're off-the-shelf nano-weaponry. State of the art stuff, I guess." He ran a fingertip over them. "We've programmed each to produce a different mix of neurotransmitters. Dopamine, phencyclidine, norepinephrine, acetylcholine, met-enkephalin, substance P, serotonin—there's a hefty slice of Heaven in here, and—" he tapped an empty space—"right here is our missing bit of Hell." He frowned, and muttered, "That's curious. Why are there *two* cylinders missing?"

"What's that?" Ekatarina said. "I didn't catch what you just said."

"Oh, nothing important. Um, listen, it might help if I yanked a few biological pathways charts and showed you the chemical underpinnings of these things."

"Never mind that. Just keep it sweet and simple. Tell us about these schizomimetic engines."

It took over an hour to explain.

The engines were molecule-sized chemical factories, much like the assemblers in a microfactory. They had been provided by the military, in the hope Chang's group would come up with a misting weapon that could be sprayed in an army's path to cause them to change their loyalty. Gunther dozed off briefly while Krishna was explaining why that was impossible, and woke up sometime after the tiny engines had made their way into the brain.

"It's really a false schizophrenia," Krishna explained. "True schizophrenia is a beautifully complicated mechanism. What these engines create is more like a bargain-basement knockoff. They seize control of the brain chemistry, and start pumping out dopamine and a few other neuromediators. It's not an actual disorder, *per se*. They just keep the brain hopping." He coughed. "You see."

"Okay," Ekatarina said. "Okay. You say you can reprogram these things. How?"

"We use what are technically called messenger engines. They're like neuromodulators—they tell the schizomimetic engines what to do." He slid open another drawer, and in a flat voice said, "They're gone."

"Let's keep to the topic, if we may. We'll worry about your inventory later. Tell us about these messenger engines. Can you brew up a lot of them, to tell the schizomimetics to turn themselves off?"

"No, for two reasons. First, these molecules were hand-crafted in the Swiss Orbitals; we don't have the industrial plant to create them. Secondly, you can't tell the schizomimetics to turn themselves off. They don't *have* off switches. They're more like catalysts than actual machines. You can reconfigure them to produce different chemicals, but . . ." He stopped, and a distant look came into his eyes. "Damn." He grabbed up his peecee, and a chemical pathways chart appeared on one wall. Then beside it, a listing of major neurofunctions. Then another chart covered with scrawled behavioral symbols. More and more data slammed up on the wall.

"Uh, Krishna . . . ?"

"Oh, go away," he snapped. "This is important."

"You think you might be able to come up with a cure?"

"Cure? No. Something better. Much better."

Ekatarina and Gunther looked at each other. Then she said, "Do you need anything? Can I assign anyone to help you?"

"I need the messenger engines. Find them for me."

"How? How do we find them? Where do we look?"

"Sally Chang," Krishna said impatiently. "She must have them. Nobody else had access." He snatched up a light pen, and began scrawling crabbed formulae on the wall.

"I'll get her for you. Program! Tell—"

"Chang's a flick," Gunther reminded her. "She was caught by the aerosol bomb." Which she must surely have set herself. A neat way of disposing of evidence that might've led to whatever government was running her. She'd have been the first to go mad.

Ekatarina pinched her nose, wincing. "I've been awake too long," she said. "All right, I understand. Krishna, from now on you're assigned permanently to research. The CMP will notify your cadre leader. Let me know if you need any support. Find me a way to turn this damned weapon off." Ignoring the way he shrugged her off, she said to Gunther, "I'm yanking you from Cadre Four. From now on, you report directly to me. I want you to find Chang. Find her, and find those messenger engines."

Gunther was bone-weary. He couldn't remember when he'd last had a good eight hours' sleep. But he managed what he hoped was a confident grin. "Received."

A madwoman should not have been able to hide herself. Sally Chang could. Nobody should have been able to evade the CMP's notice, now that it was hooked into a growing number of afflicted individuals. Sally Chang did. The

CMP informed Gunther that none of the flicks were aware of Chang's whereabouts. It accepted a directive to have them all glance about for her once every hour until she was found.

In the west tunnels, walls had been torn out to create a space as large as any factory interior. The remotes had been returned, and were now manned by almost two hundred flicks spaced so that they did not impinge upon each other's fields of instruction. Gunther walked by them, through the CMP's whispering voices: "Are all bulldozers accounted for? If so . . . Clear away any malfunctioning machines; they can be placed . . . for vacuum-welded dust on the upper surfaces of the rails . . . reduction temperature, then look to see that the oxygen feed is compatible . . ." At the far end a single suit sat in a chair, overseer unit in its lap.

"How's it going?" Gunther asked.

"Absolutely top-notch." He recognized Takayuni's voice. They'd worked in the Flammaprion microwave relay station together. "Most of the factories are up and running, and we're well on our way to having the railguns operative too. You wouldn't believe the kind of efficiencies we're getting here."

"Good, huh?"

Takayuni grinned; Gunther could hear it in his voice. "Industrious little buggers!"

Takayuni hadn't seen Chang. Gunther moved on.

Some hours later he found himself sitting wearily in Noguchi Park, looking at the torn-up dirt where the kneehigh forest had been. Not a seedling had been spared; the silver birch was extinct as a lunar species. Dead carp floated belly-up in the oil-slicked central lake; a chain-link fence circled it now, to keep out the flicks. There hadn't been the time yet to begin cleaning up the litter, and when he looked about, he saw trash everywhere. It was sad. It reminded him of Earth.

He knew it was time to get going, but he couldn't. His head sagged, touched his chest, and jerked up. Time had passed.

A flicker of motion made him turn. Somebody in a pastel lavender boutique suit hurried by. The woman who had directed him to the city controller's office the other day. "Hello!" he called. "I found everybody just where you said. Thanks. I was starting to get a little spooked."

The lavender suit turned to look at him. Sunlight glinted on black glass. A still, long minute later, she said, "Don't mention it," and started away.

"I'm looking for Sally Chang. Do you know her? Have you seen her? She's a flick, kind of a little woman, flamboyant, used to favor bright clothes, electric makeup, that sort of thing."

"I'm afraid I can't help you." Lavender was carrying three oxytanks in her arms. "You might try the straw market, though. Lots of bright clothes there." She ducked into a tunnel opening and disappeared within.

Gunther stared after her distractedly, then shook his head. He felt so very, very tired.

*   *   *

The straw market looked as though it had been through a storm. The tents had been torn down, the stands knocked over, the goods looted. Shards of orange and green glass crunched underfoot. Yet a rack of Italian scarves worth a year's salary stood untouched amid the rubble. It made no sense at all.

Up and down the market, flicks were industriously cleaning up. They stooped and lifted and swept. One of them was being beaten by a suit.

Gunther blinked. He could not react to it as a real event. The woman cringed under the blows, shrieking wildly and scuttling away from them. One of the tents had been re-erected, and within the shadow of its rainbow silks, four other suits lounged against the bar. Not a one of them moved to help the woman.

"Hey!" Gunther shouted. He felt hideously self-conscious, as if he'd been abruptly thrust into the middle of a play without memorized lines or any idea of the plot or notion of what his role in it was. "Stop that!"

The suit turned toward him. It held the woman's slim arm captive in one gloved hand. "Go away," a male voice growled over the radio.

"What do you think you're doing? Who are you?" The man wore a Westinghouse suit, one of a dozen or so among the unafflicted. But Gunther recognized a brown, kidney-shaped scorch mark on the abdomen panel. "Posner—is that you? Let that woman go."

"She's not a woman," Posner said. "Hell, look at her—she's not even human. She's a flick."

Gunther set his helmet to record. "I'm taping this," he warned. "You hit that woman again, and Ekatarina will see it all. I promise."

Posner released the woman. She stood dazed for a second or two, and then the voice from her peecee reasserted control. She bent to pick up a broom, and returned to work.

Switching off his helmet, Gunther said, "Okay. What did she do?"

Indignantly, Posner extended a foot. He pointed sternly down at it. "She peed all over my boot!"

The suits in the tent had been watching with interest. Now they roared. "Your own fault, Will!" one of them called out. "I told you you weren't scheduling in enough time for personal hygiene."

"Don't worry about a little moisture. It'll boil off next time you hit vacuum!"

But Gunther was not listening. He stared at the flick Posner had been mistreating and wondered why he hadn't recognized Anya earlier. Her mouth was pursed, her face squinched up tight with worry, as if there were a key in the back of her head that had been wound three times too many. Her shoulders cringed forward now, too. But still.

"I'm sorry, Anya," he said. "Hiro is dead. There wasn't anything we could do."

She went on sweeping, oblivious, unhappy.

*   *   *

He caught the shift's last jitney back to the Center. It felt good to be home
again. Miiko Ezumi had decided to loot the outlying factories of their oxygen
and water surpluses, then carved a shower room from the rock. There was a
long line for only three minutes' use, and no soap, but nobody complained.
Some people pooled their time, showering two and three together. Those
waiting their turns joked rowdily.

Gunther washed, grabbed some clean shorts and a Glavkosmos tee-shirt,
and padded down the hall. He hesitated outside the common room, listening
to the gang sitting around the table, discussing the more colorful flicks they'd
encountered.

"Have you seen the Mouse Hunter?"

"Oh yeah, and Ophelia!"

"The Pope!"

"The Duck Lady!"

"Everybody knows the Duck Lady!"

They were laughing and happy. A warm sense of community flowed from
the room, what Gunther's father would have in his sloppy-sentimental way
called *Gemütlichkeit*. Gunther stepped within.

Liza Nagenda looked up, all gums and teeth, and froze. Her jaw snapped
shut. "Well, if it isn't Izmailova's personal spy!"

"What?" The accusation took Gunther's breath away. He looked helplessly
about the room. Nobody would meet his eye. They had all fallen silent.

Liza's face was grey with anger. "You heard me! It was you that ratted on
Krishna, wasn't it?"

"Now that's way out of line! You've got a lot of fucking gall if—" He
controlled himself with an effort. There was no sense in matching her hysteria
with his own. "It's none of your business what my relationship with Izmailova
is or is not." He looked around the table. "Not that any of you deserve to
know, but Krishna's working on a cure. If anything I said or did helped put
him back in the lab, well then, so be it."

She smirked. "So what's your excuse for snitching on Will Posner?"

"I never—"

"We all heard the story! You told him you were going to run straight to
your precious Izmailova with your little helmet vids."

"Now, Liza," Takayuni began. She slapped him away.

"Do you know what Posner was doing?" Gunther shook a finger in Liza's
face. "Hah? Do you? He was beating a woman—Anya! He was beating Anya
right out in the open!"

"So what? He's one of us, isn't he? Not a zoned-out, dead-eyed, ranting,
drooling *flick*!"

"You bitch!" Outraged, Gunther lunged at Liza across the table. "I'll kill
you, I swear it!" People jerked back from him, rushed forward, a chaos of
motion. Posner thrust himself in Gunther's way, arms spread, jaw set and
manly. Gunther punched him in the face. Posner looked surprised, and fell

back. Gunther's hand stung, but he felt strangely good anyway; if everyone else was crazy, then why not him?

"You just try it!" Liza shrieked. "I knew you were that type all along!"

Takayuni grabbed Liza away one way. Hamilton seized Gunther and yanked him the other. Two of Posner's friends were holding him back as well.

"I've had about all I can take from you!" Gunther shouted. "You cheap cunt!"

"Listen to him! Listen what he calls me!"

Screaming, they were shoved out opposing doors.

"It's all right, Gunther." Beth had flung him into the first niche they'd come to. He slumped against a wall, shaking, and closed his eyes. "It's all right now."

But it wasn't. Gunther was suddenly struck with the realization that with the exception of Ekatarina he no longer had any friends. Not real friends, close friends. How could this have happened? It was as if everyone had been turned into werewolves. Those who weren't actually mad were still monsters. "I don't understand."

Hamilton sighed. "What don't you understand, Weil?"

"The way people—the way we all treat the flicks. When Posner was beating Anya, there were four other suits standing nearby, and not a one of them so much as lifted a finger to stop him. Not one! And I felt it too, there's no use pretending I'm superior to the rest of them. I wanted to walk on and pretend I hadn't seen a thing. What's happened to us?"

Hamilton shrugged. Her hair was short and dark about her plain round face. "I went to a pretty expensive school when I was a kid. One year we had one of those exercises that're supposed to be personally enriching. You know? A life experience. We were divided into two groups—Prisoners and Guards. The Prisoners couldn't leave their assigned areas without permission from a guard, the Guards got better lunches, stuff like that. Very simple set of rules. I was a Guard.

"Almost immediately, we started to bully the Prisoners. We pushed 'em around, yelled at 'em, kept 'em in line. What was amazing was that the Prisoners let us do it. They outnumbered us five to one. We didn't even have authority for the things we did. But not a one of them complained. Not a one of them stood up and said no, you can't do this. They played the game.

"At the end of the month, the project was dismantled and we had some study seminars on what we'd learned: the roots of fascism, and so on. Read some Hannah Arendt. And then it was all over. Except that my best girlfriend never spoke to me again. I couldn't blame her, either. Not after what I'd done.

"What did I really learn? That people will play whatever role you put them in. They'll do it without knowing that that's what they're doing. Take a minority, tell them they're special, and make them guards—they'll start playing Guard."

"So what's the answer? How do we keep from getting caught up in the roles we play?"

"Damned if I know, Weil. Damned if I know."

Ekatarina had moved her niche to the far end of a new tunnel. Hers was the only room the tunnel served, and consequently she had a lot of privacy. As Gunther stepped in, a staticky voice swam into focus on his trance chip. ". . . reported shock. In Cairo, government officials pledged . . ." It cut off.

"Hey! You've restored—" He stopped. If radio reception had been restored, he'd have known. It would have been the talk of the Center. Which meant that radio contact had never really been completely broken. It was simply being controlled by the CMP.

Ekatarina looked up at him. She'd been crying, but she'd stopped. "The Swiss Orbitals are gone!" she whispered. "They hit them with everything from softbombs to brilliant pebbles. They dusted the shipyards."

The scope of all those deaths obscured what she was saying for a second. He sank down beside her. "But that means—"

"There's no spacecraft that can reach us, yes. Unless there's a ship in transit, we're stranded here."

He took her in his arms. She was cold and shivering. Her skin felt clammy and mottled with gooseflesh. "How long has it been since you've had any sleep?" he asked sharply.

"I can't—"

"You're wired, aren't you?"

"I can't afford to sleep. Not now. Later."

"Ekatarina. The energy you get from wire isn't free. It's only borrowed from your body. When you come down, it all comes due. If you wire yourself up too tightly, you'll crash yourself right into a coma."

"I haven't been—" She stalled, and a confused, uncertain look entered her eyes. "Maybe you're right. I could probably use a little rest."

The CMP came to life. "Cadre Nine is building a radio receiver. Ezumi gave them the go-ahead."

"Shit!" Ekatarina sat bolt upright. "Can we stop it?"

"Moving against a universally popular project would cost you credibility you cannot afford to lose."

"Okay, so how can we minimize the—"

"Ekatarina," Gunther said. "Sleep, remember?"

"In a sec, babe." She patted the futon. "You just lie down and wait for me. I'll have this wrapped up before you can nod off." She kissed him gently, lingeringly. "All right?"

"Yeah, sure." He lay down and closed his eyes, just for a second.

When he awoke, it was time to go on shift, and Ekatarina was gone.

It was only the fifth day since Vladivostok. But everything was so utterly changed that times before then seemed like memories of another world. In a previous life I was Gunther Weil, he thought. I lived and worked and had a few laughs. Life was pretty good then.

He was still looking for Sally Chang, though with dwindling hope. Now, whenever he talked to suits he'd ask if they needed his help. Increasingly, they did not.

The third-level chapel was a shallow bowl facing the terrace wall. Tiger lilies grew about the chancel area at the bottom, and turquoise lizards skittered over the rock. The children were playing a ball in the chancel. Gunther stood at the top, chatting with a sad-voiced Ryohei Iomato.

The children put away the ball and began to dance. They were playing London Bridge. Gunther watched them with a smile. From above they were so many spots of color, a flower unfolding and closing in on itself. Slowly, the smile faded. They were dancing too well. Not one of the children moved out of step, lost her place, or walked away sulking. Their expressions were intense, self-absorbed, inhuman. Gunther had to turn away.

"The CMP controls them," Iomato said. "I don't have much to do, really. I go through the vids and pick out games for them to play, songs to sing, little exercises to keep them healthy. Sometimes I have them draw."

"My God, how can you stand it?"

Iomato sighed. "My old man was an alcoholic. He had a pretty rough life, and at some point he started drinking to blot out the pain. You know what?"

"It didn't work."

"Yah. Made him even more miserable. So then he had twice the reason to get drunk. He kept on trying, though, I've got to give him that. He wasn't the sort of man to give up on something he believed in just because it wasn't working the way it should."

Gunther said nothing.

"I think that memory is the only thing keeping me from just taking off my helmet and joining them."

The Corporate Video Center was a narrow run of offices in the farthest tunnel reaches, where raw footage for adverts and incidental business use was processed before being squirted to better-equipped vid centers on Earth. Gunther passed from office to office, slapping off flatscreens left flickering since the disaster.

It was unnerving going through the normally busy rooms and finding no one. The desks and cluttered work stations had been abandoned in purposeful disarray, as though their operators had merely stepped out for a break and would be back momentarily. Gunther found himself spinning around to confront his shadow, and flinching at unexpected noises. With each machine he turned off, the silence at his back grew. It was twice as lonely as being out on the surface.

He doused a last light and stepped into the gloomy hall. Two suits with interwoven H-and-A logos loomed up out of the shadows. He jumped in shock. They were empty, of course—there were no Hyundai Aerospace components among the unafflicted. Someone had simply left these suits here in temporary storage before the madness.

The suits grabbed him.

"Hey!" He shouted in terror as they seized him by the arms and lifted him off his feet. One of them hooked the peecee from his harness and snapped it off. Before he knew what was happening he'd been swept down a short flight of stairs and through a doorway.

"Mr. Weil."

He was in a high-ceilinged room carved into the rock to hold airhandling equipment that hadn't been constructed yet. A high string of temporary work lamps provided dim light. To the far side of the room a suit sat behind a desk, flanked by two more, standing. They all wore Hyundai Aerospace suits. There was no way he could identify them.

The suits that had brought him in crossed their arms.

"What's going on here?" Gunther asked. "Who are you?"

"You are the last person we'd tell that to." He couldn't tell which one had spoken. The voice came over his radio, made sexless and impersonal by an electronic filter. "Mr. Weil, you stand accused of crimes against your fellow citizens. Do you have anything to say in your defense?"

"What?" Gunther looked at the suits before him and to either side. They were perfectly identical, indistinguishable from each other, and he was suddenly afraid of what the people within might feel free to do, armored as they were in anonymity. "Listen, you've got no right to do this. There's a governmental structure in place, if you've got any complaints against me."

"Not everyone is pleased with Izmailova's government," the judge said.

"But she controls the CMP, and we could not run Bootstrap without the CMP controlling the flicks," a second added.

"We simply have to work around her." Perhaps it was the judge; perhaps it was yet another of the suits. Gunther couldn't tell.

"Do you wish to speak on your own behalf?"

"What exactly am I charged with?" Gunther asked desperately. "Okay, maybe I've done something wrong, I'll entertain that possibility. But maybe you just don't understand my situation. Have you considered that?"

Silence.

"I mean, just what are you angry about? Is it Posner? Because I'm not sorry about that. I won't apologize. You can't mistreat people just because they're sick. They're still people, like anybody else. They have their rights."

Silence.

"But if you think I'm some kind of a spy or something, that I'm running around and ratting on people to Ek—to Izmailova, well that's simply not true. I mean, I talk to her, I'm not about to pretend I don't, but I'm not her spy or anything. She doesn't have any spies. She doesn't need any! She's just trying to hold things together, that's all.

"Jesus, you don't know what she's gone through for you! You haven't seen how much it takes out of her! She'd like nothing better than to quit. But she has to hang in there because—" An eerie dark electronic gabble rose up on his radio, and he stopped as he realized that they were laughing at him.

"Does anyone else wish to speak?"

One of Gunther's abductors stepped forward. "Your honor, this man says that flicks are human. He overlooks the fact that they cannot live without our support and direction. Their continued well-being is bought at the price of our unceasing labor. He stands condemned out of his own mouth. I petition the court to make the punishment fit the crime."

The judge looked to the right, to the left. His two companions nodded, and stepped back into the void. The desk had been set up at the mouth of what was to be the air intake duct. Gunther had just time enough to realize this when they reappeared, leading someone in a G5 suit identical to his own.

"We could kill you, Mr. Weil," the artificial voice crackled. "But that would be wasteful. Every hand, every mind is needed. We must all pull together in our time of need."

The G5 stood alone and motionless in the center of the room.

"Watch."

Two of the Hyundai suits stepped up to the G5 suit. Four hands converged on the helmet seals. With practiced efficiency, they flicked the latches and lifted the helmet. It happened so swiftly the occupant could not have stopped it if he'd tried.

Beneath the helmet was the fearful, confused face of a flick.

"Sanity is a privilege, Mr. Weil, not a right. You are guilty as charged. However, we are not cruel men. *This once* we will let you off with a warning. But these are desperate times. At your next offense—be it only so minor a thing as reporting this encounter to the Little General—we may be forced to dispense with the formality of a hearing." The judge paused. "Do I make myself clear?"

Reluctantly, Gunther nodded.

"Then you may leave."

On the way out, one of the suits handed him back his peecee.

Five people. He was sure there weren't any more involved than that. Maybe one or two more, but that was it. Posner had to be hip-deep in this thing, he was certain of that. It shouldn't be too hard to figure out the others.

He didn't dare take the chance.

At shift's end he found Ekatarina already asleep. She looked haggard and unhealthy. He knelt by her, and gently brushed her cheek with the back of one hand.

Her eyelids fluttered open.

"Oh, hey. I didn't mean to wake you. Just go back to sleep, huh?"

She smiled. "You're sweet, Gunther, but I was only taking a nap anyway. I've got to be up in another fifteen minutes." Her eyes closed again. "You're the only one I can really trust anymore. Everybody's lying to me, feeding me misinformation, keeping silent when there's something I need to know. You're the only one I can count on to tell me things."

You have enemies, he thought. They call you the Little General, and they don't like how you run things. They're not ready to move against you directly, but they have plans. And they're ruthless.

Aloud, he said, "Go back to sleep."

"They're all against me," she murmured. "Bastard sons of bitches."

The next day he spent going through the service spaces for the new airhandling system. He found a solitary flick's nest made of shredded vacuum suits, but after consultation with the CMP concluded that nobody had lived there for days. There was no trace of Sally Chang.

If it had been harrowing going through the sealed areas before his trial, it was far worse today. Ekatarina's enemies had infected him with fear. Reason told him they were not waiting for him, that he had nothing to worry about until he displeased them again. But the hindbrain did not listen.

Time crawled. When he finally emerged into daylight at the end of his shift, he felt light-headedly out of phase with reality from the hours of isolation. At first he noticed nothing out of the ordinary. Then his suit radio was full of voices, and people were hurrying about every which way. There was a happy buzz in the air. Somebody was singing.

He snagged a passing suit and asked, "What's going on?"

"Haven't you heard? The war is over. They've made peace. And there's a ship coming in!"

The *Lake Geneva* had maintained television silence through most of the long flight to the Moon for fear of long-range beam weapons. With peace, however, they opened direct transmission to Bootstrap.

Ezumi's people had the flicks sew together an enormous cotton square and hack away some trailing vines so they could hang it high on the shadowed side of the crater. Then, with the fill lights off, the video image was projected. Swiss spacejacks tumbled before the camera, grinning, all denim and red cowboy hats. They were talking about their escape from the hunter-seeker missiles, brash young voices running one over the other.

The top officers were assembled beneath the cotton square. Gunther recognized their suits. Ekatarina's voice boomed from newly erected loudspeakers. "When are you coming in? We have to make sure the spaceport field is clear. How many hours?"

Holding up five fingers, a blond woman said, "Forty-five!"

"No, forty-three!"

"Nothing like that!"

"*Almost* forty-five!"

Again Ekatarina's voice cut into the tumult. "What's it like in the orbitals? We heard they were destroyed."

"Yes, destroyed!"

"Very bad, very bad, it'll take years to—"

"But most of the people are—"

"We were given six orbits warning; most went down in lifting bodies, there was a big evacuation."

"Many died, though. It was very bad."

Just below the officers, a suit had been directing several flicks as they assembled a camera platform. Now it waved broadly, and the flicks stepped away. In the *Lake Geneva* somebody shouted, and several heads turned to stare at an offscreen television monitor. The suit turned the camera, giving them a slow, panoramic scan.

One of the spacejacks said, "What's it like there? I see that some of you are wearing space suits, and the rest are not. Why is that?"

Ekatarina took a deep breath. "There have been some changes here."

There was one hell of a party at the Center when the Swiss arrived. Sleep schedules were juggled, and save for a skeleton crew overseeing the flicks, everyone turned out to welcome the dozen newcomers to the Moon. They danced to skiffle, and drank vacuum-distilled vodka. Everyone had stories to tell, rumors to swap, opinions on the likelihood that the peace would hold.

Gunther wandered away midway through the party. The Swiss depressed him. They all seemed so young and fresh and eager. He felt battered and cynical in their presence. He wanted to grab them by the shoulders and shake them awake.

Depressed, he wandered through the locked-down laboratories. Where the Viral Computer Project had been, he saw Ekatarina and the captain of the *Lake Geneva* conferring over a stack of crated bioflops. They bent low over Ekatarina's peecee, listening to the CMP.

"Have you considered nationalizing your industries?" the captain asked. "That would give us the plant needed to build the New City. Then, with a few hardwired utilities, Bootstrap could be managed without anyone having to set foot inside it."

Gunther was too distant to hear the CMP's reaction, but he saw both women laugh. "Well," said Ekatarina. "At the very least we will have to renegotiate terms with the parent corporations. With only one ship functional, people can't be easily replaced. Physical presence has become a valuable commodity. We'd be fools not to take advantage of it."

He passed on, deeper into shadow, wandering aimlessly. Eventually, there was a light ahead, and he heard voices. One was Krishna's, but spoken faster and more forcefully than he was used to hearing it. Curious, he stopped just outside the door.

Krishna was in the center of the lab. Before him, Beth Hamilton stood nodding humbly. "Yes, sir," she said. "I'll do that. Yes." Dumbfounded, Gunther realized that Krishna was giving her orders.

Krishna glanced up. "Weil! You're just the man I was about to come looking for."

"I am?"

"Come in here, don't dawdle." Krishna smiled and beckoned, and Gunther had no choice but to obey. Krishna looked like a young god now. The force of his spirit danced in his eyes like fire. It was strange that Gunther had never noticed before how tall he was. "Tell me where Sally Chang is."

"I don't—I mean, I can't, I—" He stopped and swallowed. "I think Chang must be dead." Then, "Krishna? What's happened to you?"

"He's finished his research," Beth said.

"I rewrote my personality from top to bottom," Krishna said. "I'm not half-crippled with shyness anymore—have you noticed?" He put a hand on Gunther's shoulder, and it was reassuring, warm, comforting. "Gunther, I won't tell you what it took to scrape together enough messenger engines from traces of old experiments to try this out on myself. But it works. We've got a treatment that among other things will serve as a universal cure for everyone in Bootstrap. But to do that, we need the messenger engines, and they're not here. Now tell me why you think Sally Chang is dead."

"Well, uh, I've been searching for her for four days. And the CMP has been looking too. You've been holed up here all the time, so maybe you don't know the flicks as well as the rest of us do. But they're not very big on planning. The likelihood one of them could actively evade detection that long is practically zilch. The only thing I can think is that somehow she made it to the surface before the effects hit her, got into a truck and told it to drive as far as her oxygen would take her."

Krishna shook his head and said, "No. It is simply not consistent with Sally Chang's character. With all the best will in the world, I cannot picture her killing herself." He slid open a drawer: row upon row of gleaming cannisters. "This may help. Do you remember when I said there were *two* cannisters of mimetic engines missing, not just the schizomimetic?"

"Vaguely."

"I've been too busy to worry about it, but wasn't that odd? Why would Chang have taken a cannister and not used it?"

"What was in the second cannister?" Hamilton asked.

"Paranoia," Krishna said. "Or rather a good enough chemical analog. Now, paranoia is a rare disability, but a fascinating one. It's characterized by an elaborate but internally consistent delusional system. The paranoid patient functions well intellectually, and is less fragmented than a schizophrenic. Her emotional and social responses are closer to normal. She's capable of concerted effort. In a time of turmoil, it's quite possible that a paranoid individual could elude our detection."

"Okay, let's get this straight," Hamilton said. "War breaks out on Earth. Chang gets her orders, keys in the software bombs, and goes to Bootstrap with a cannister full of madness and a little syringe of paranoia—no, it doesn't work. It all falls apart."

"How so?"

"Paranoia wouldn't inoculate her against schizophrenia. How does she protect herself from her own aerosols?"

Gunther stood transfixed. "Lavender!"

*   *   *

They caught up with Sally Chang on the topmost terrace of Bootstrap. The top level was undeveloped. Someday—so the corporate brochures promised—fallow deer would graze at the edge of limpid pools, and otters frolic in the streams. But the soil hadn't been built up yet, the worms brought in or the bacteria seeded. There were only sand, machines, and a few unhappy opportunistic weeds.

Chang's camp was to one side of a streamhead, beneath a fill light. She started to her feet at their approach, glanced quickly to the side and decided to brazen it out.

A sign reading EMERGENCY CANOPY MAINTENANCE STATION had been welded to a strut supporting the stream's valve stem. Under it were a short stacked pyramid of oxytanks and an aluminum storage crate the size of a coffin. "Very clever," Beth muttered over Gunther's trance chip. "She sleeps in the storage crate, and anybody stumbling across her thinks it's just spare equipment."

The lavender suit raised an arm and casually said, "Hiya, guys. How can I help you?"

Krishna strode forward and took her hands. "Sally, it's me—Krishna!"

"Oh, thank God!" She slumped in his arms. "I've been so afraid."

"You're all right now."

"I thought you were an Invader at first, when I saw you coming up. I'm so hungry—I haven't eaten since I don't know when." She clutched at the sleeve of Krishna's suit. "You do know about the Invaders, don't you?"

"Maybe you'd better bring me up to date."

They began walking toward the stairs. Krishna gestured quickly to Gunther and then toward Chang's worksuit harness. A cannister the size of a hip flask hung there. Gunther reached over and plucked it off. The messenger engines! He held them in his hand.

To the other side, Beth Hamilton plucked up the near-full cylinder of paranoia-inducing engines and made it disappear.

Sally Chang, deep in the explication of her reasonings, did not notice. ". . . obeyed my orders, of course. But they made no sense. I worried and worried about that until finally I realized what was really going on. A wolf caught in a trap will gnaw off its leg to get free. I began to look for the wolf. What kind of enemy justified such extreme actions? Certainly nothing human."

"Sally," Krishna said, "I want you to entertain the notion that the conspiracy—for want of a better word—may be more deeply rooted than you suspect. That the problem is not an external enemy, but the workings of our own brain. Specifically that the Invaders are an artifact of the psychotomimetics you injected into yourself back when this all began."

"No. No, there's too much evidence. It all fits together! The Invaders needed a way to disguise themselves both physically, which was accomplished by the vacuum suits, and psychologically, which was achieved by the general madness. Thus, they can move undetected among us. Would a human enemy have converted all of Bootstrap to slave labor? Unthinkable! They can read our minds like a book. If we hadn't protected ourselves with the schizomimetics, they'd be able to extract all our knowledge, all our military research secrets . . ."

Listening, Gunther couldn't help imagining what Liza Nagenda would say to all of this wild talk. At the thought of her, his jaw clenched. Just like one of Chang's machines, he realized, and couldn't help being amused at his own expense.

Ekatarina was waiting at the bottom of the stairs. Her hands trembled noticeably, and there was a slight quaver in her voice when she said, "What's all this the CMP tells me about messenger engines? Krishna's supposed to have come up with a cure of some kind?"

"We've got them," Gunther said quietly, happily. He held up the cannister. "It's over now, we can heal our friends."

"Let me see," Ekatarina said. She took the cannister from his hand.

"No, wait!" Hamilton cried, too late. Behind her, Krishna was arguing with Sally Chang about her interpretations of recent happenings. Neither had noticed yet that those in front had stopped.

"Stand back." Ekatarina took two quick steps backward. Edgily, she added, "I don't mean to be difficult. But we're going to sort this all out, and until we do, I don't want anybody too close to me. That includes you too, Gunther."

Flicks began gathering. By ones and twos they wandered up the lawn, and then by the dozen. By the time it was clear that Ekatarina had called them up via the CMP, Krishna, Chang, and Hamilton were separated from her and Gunther by a wall of people.

Chang stood very still. Somewhere behind her unseen face, she was revising her theories to include this new event. Suddenly, her hands slapped at her suit, grabbing for the missing cannisters. She looked at Krishna and with a trill of horror said, "You're one of them!"

"Of course I'm not—" Krishna began. But she was turning, stumbling, fleeing back up the steps.

"Let her go," Ekatarina ordered. "We've got more serious things to talk about." Two flicks scurried up, lugging a small industrial kiln between them. They set it down, and a third plugged in an electric cable. The interior began to glow. "This cannister is all you've got, isn't it? If I were to autoclave it, there wouldn't be any hope of replacing its contents."

"Izmailova, listen," Krishna said.

"I am listening. Talk."

Krishna explained, while Izmailova listened with arms folded and shoulders tilted skeptically. When he was done, she shook her head. "It's a noble folly, but folly is all it is. You want to reshape our minds into something alien to the course of human evolution. To turn the seat of thought into a jet pilot's couch. This is your idea of a solution? Forget it. Once this particular box is opened, there'll be no putting its contents back in again. And you haven't advanced any convincing arguments for opening it."

"But the people in Bootstrap!" Gunther objected. "They—"

She cut him off. "Gunther, nobody *likes* what's happened to them. But if the rest of us must give up our humanity to pay for a speculative and ethically dubious rehabilitation . . . well, the price is simply too high. Mad or not, they're at least human now."

"Am I inhuman?" Krishna asked. "If you tickle me, do I not laugh?"

"You're in no position to judge. You've rewired your neurons and you're stoned on the novelty. What tests have you run on yourself? How thoroughly have you mapped out your deviations from human norms? Where are your figures?" These were purely rhetorical questions; the kind of analyses she meant took weeks to run. "Even if you check out completely human—and I don't concede you will!—who's to say what the long-range consequences are? What's to stop us from drifting, step by incremental step, into madness? Who decides what madness is? Who programs the programmers? No, this is impossible. I won't gamble with our minds." Defensively, almost angrily, she repeated, "I won't gamble with our minds."

"Ekatarina," Gunther said gently, "how long have you been up? Listen to yourself. The wire is doing your thinking for you."

She waved a hand dismissively, without responding.

"Just as a practical matter," Hamilton said, "how do you expect to run Bootstrap without it? The setup is turning us all into baby fascists. You say you're worried about madness—what will we be like a year from now?"

"The CMP assures me—"

"The CMP is only a program!" Hamilton cried. "No matter how much interactivity it has, it's not flexible. It has no hope. It cannot judge a new thing. It can only enforce old decisions, old values, old habits, old fears."

Abruptly Ekatarina snapped. *"Get out of my face!"* she screamed. "Stop it, stop it, stop it! I won't listen to any more."

"Ekatarina—" Gunther began.

But her hand had tightened on the cannister. Her knees bent as she began a slow genuflection to the kiln. Gunther could see that she had stopped listening. Drugs and responsibility had done this to her, speeding her up and bewildering her with conflicting demands, until she stood trembling on the brink of collapse. A good night's sleep might have restored her, made her capable of being reasoned with. But there was no time. Words would not stop her now. And she was too far distant for him to reach before she destroyed the engines. In that instant he felt such a strong outwelling of emotion toward her as would be impossible to describe.

"Ekatarina," he said. "I love you."

She half-turned her head toward him and in a distracted, somewhat irritated tone said, "What are you—"

He lifted the bolt gun from his work harness, leveled it, and fired.

Ekatarina's helmet shattered.

She fell.

"I should have shot to just breach the helmet. That would have stopped her. But I didn't think I was a good enough shot. I aimed right for the center of her head."

"Hush," Hamilton said. "You did what you had to. Stop tormenting yourself. Talk about more practical things."

He shook his head, still groggy. For the longest time, he had been kept on beta endorphins, unable to feel a thing, unable to care. It was like being swathed in cotton batting. Nothing could reach him. Nothing could hurt him. "How long have I been out of it?"

"A day."

"A day!" He looked about the austere room. Bland rock walls and laboratory equipment with smooth, noncommital surfaces. To the far end, Krishna and Chang were hunched over a swipeboard, arguing happily and impatiently overwriting each other's scrawls. A Swiss spacejack came in and spoke to their backs. Krishna nodded distractedly, not looking up. "I thought it was much longer."

"Long enough. We've already salvaged everyone connected with Sally Chang's group, and gotten a good start on the rest. Pretty soon it will be time to decide how you want yourself rewritten."

He shook his head, feeling dead. "I don't think I'll bother, Beth. I just don't have the stomach for it."

"We'll give you the stomach."

"Naw, I don't . . ." He felt a black nausea come welling up again. It was cyclic; it returned every time he was beginning to think he'd finally put it down. "I don't want the fact that I killed Ekatarina washed away in a warm flood of self-satisfaction. The idea disgusts me."

"We don't want that either." Posner led a delegation of seven into the lab. Krishna and Chang rose to face them, and the group broke into swirling halves. "There's been enough of that. It's time we all started taking responsibility for the consequences of—" Everyone was talking at once. Hamilton made a face.

"Started taking responsibility for—"

Voices rose.

"We can't talk here," she said. "Take me out on the surface."

They drove with the cabin pressurized, due west on the Seething Bay road. Ahead, the sun was almost touching the weary walls of Sömmering crater. Shadow crept down from the mountains and cratertops, yearning toward the radiantly lit Sinus Medii. Gunther found it achingly beautiful. He did not want to respond to it, but the harsh lines echoed the lonely hurt within him in a way that he found oddly comforting.

Hamilton touched her peecee. "Putting on the Ritz" filled their heads.

"What if Ekatarina was right?" he said sadly. "What if we're giving up everything that makes us human? The prospect of being turned into some kind of big-domed emotionless superman doesn't appeal to me much."

Hamilton shook her head. "I asked Krishna about that, and he said No. He said it was like . . . were you ever nearsighted?"

"Sure, as a kid."

"Then you'll understand. He said it was like the first time you came out of the doctor's office after being lased. How everything seemed clear and vivid and distinct. What had once been a blur that you called 'tree' resolved itself into a thousand individual and distinct leaves. The world was filled with unexpected detail. There were things on the horizon that you'd never seen before. Like that."

"Oh." He stared ahead. The disk of the sun was almost touching Sömmering. "There's no point in going any farther."

He powered down the truck.

Beth Hamilton looked uncomfortable. She cleared her throat and with brusque energy said, "Gunther, look. I had you bring me out here for a reason. I want to propose a merger of resources."

"A what?"

"Marriage."

It took Gunther a second to absorb what she had said. "Aw, no . . . I don't . . ."

"I'm serious. Gunther, I know you think I've been hard on you, but that's only because I saw a lot of potential in you, and that you were doing nothing with it. Well, things have changed. Give me a say in your rewrite, and I'll do the same for you."

He shook his head. "This is just too weird for me."

"It's too late to use that as an excuse. Ekatarina was right—we're sitting on top of something very dangerous, the most dangerous opportunity humanity faces today. It's out of the bag, though. Word has gotten out. Earth is horrified and fascinated. They'll be watching us. Briefly, very briefly, we can control this thing. We can help to shape it now, while it's small. Five years from now, it will be out of our hands.

"You have a good mind, Gunther, and it's about to get better. I think we agree on what kind of a world we want to make. I want you on my side."

"I don't know what to say."

"You want true love? You got it. We can make the sex as sweet or nasty as you like. Nothing easier. You want me quieter, louder, gentler, more assured? We can negotiate. Let's see if we can come to terms."

He said nothing.

Hamilton eased back in the seat. After a time, she said, "You know? I've never watched a lunar sunset before. I don't get out on the surface much."

"We'll have to change that," Gunther said.

Hamilton stared hard into his face. Then she smiled. She wriggled closer to him. Clumsily, he put an arm over her shoulder. It seemed to be what was expected of him. He coughed into his hand, then pointed a finger. "There it goes."

Lunar sunset was a simple thing. The crater wall touched the bottom of the solar disk. Shadows leaped from the slopes and raced across the lowlands. Soon half the sun was gone. Smoothly, without distortion, it dwindled. A last brilliant sliver of light burned atop the rock, then ceased to be. In the instant before the windshield adjusted and the stars appeared, the universe filled with darkness.

The air in the cab cooled. The panels snapped and popped with the sudden shift in temperature.

Now Hamilton was nuzzling the side of his neck. Her skin was slightly tacky to the touch, and exuded a faint but distinct odor. She ran her tongue up the line of his chin and poked it in his ear. Her hand fumbled with the latches of his suit.

Gunther experienced no arousal at all, only a mild distaste that bordered on disgust. This was horrible, a defilement of all he had felt for Ekatarina.

But it was a chore he had to get through. Hamilton was right. All his life his hindbrain had been in control, driving him with emotions chemically derived and randomly applied. He had been lashed to the steed of consciousness and forced to ride it wherever it went, and that nightmare gallop had brought him only pain and confusion. Now that he had control of the reins, he could make this horse go where he wanted.

He was not sure what he would demand from his reprogramming. Contentment, perhaps. Sex and passion, almost certainly. But not love. He was done with the romantic illusion. It was time to grow up.

He squeezed Beth's shoulder. One more day, he thought, and it won't matter. I'll feel whatever is best for me to feel. Beth raised her mouth to his. Her lips parted. He could smell her breath.

They kissed.

EVEN THE QUEEN

Connie Willis

Connie Willis lives in Greeley, Colorado, with her family. She first attracted attention as a writer in the late '70s with a number of outstanding stories for the now-defunct magazine *Galileo*, and went on to establish herself as one of the most popular and critically acclaimed writers of the 1980s. She won two Nebula Awards in 1982, one for her superb novelette "Fire Watch," and one for her poignant short story "A Letter from the Clearys." A few months later, "Fire Watch" went on to win her a Hugo Award as well. In 1989, her powerful novella "The Last of the Winnebagos" won both the Nebula and the Hugo, and she won another Nebula in 1990 for her novelette "At the Rialto." Her books include the novels *Water Witch* and *Light Raid*, written in collaboration with Cynthia Felice, *Fire Watch*, a collection of her short fiction, and the outstanding *Lincoln's Dreams*, her first solo novel. Her most recent book is a major new solo novel, *Doomsday Book*, and a new collection, *Impossible Things*, will be published soon. She has had stories in our First, Second, Fourth, Sixth, Seventh, Eighth, and Ninth Annual Collections.

Here she provides a wry and controversial examination of a technological change so sweeping and fundamental that it affects every woman on Earth . . .

The phone sang as I was looking over the defense's motion to dismiss. "It's the universal ring," my law clerk Bysshe said, reaching for it. "It's probably the defendant. They don't let you use signatures from jail."

"No, it's not," I said. "It's my mother."

"Oh." Bysshe reached for the receiver. "Why isn't she using her signature?"

"Because she knows I don't want to talk to her. She must have found out what Perdita's done."

"Your daughter Perdita?" he asked, holding the receiver against his chest. "The one with the little girl?"

"No, that's Viola. Perdita's my younger daughter. The one with no sense."

"What's she done?"

"She's joined the Cyclists."

Bysshe looked enquiringly blank, but I was not in the mood to enlighten him. Or in the mood to talk to Mother. "I know exactly what Mother will say," I said. "She'll ask me why I didn't tell her, and then she'll demand to know what I'm going to do about it, and there is nothing I *can* do about it, or I obviously would have done it already."

Bysshe looked bewildered. "Do you want me to tell her you're in court?"

"No." I reached for the receiver. "I'll have to talk to her sooner or later." I took it from him. "Hello, Mother," I said.

"Traci," Mother said dramatically, "Perdita has become a Cyclist."

"I know."

"Why didn't you tell me?"

"I thought Perdita should tell you herself."

"Perdita!" She snorted. "She wouldn't tell me. She knows what I'd have to say about it. I suppose you told Karen."

"Karen's not here. She's in Iraq." The only good thing about this whole debacle was that thanks to Iraq's eagerness to show it was a responsible world community member and its previous penchant for self-destruction, my mother-in-law was in the one place on the planet where the phone service was bad enough that I could claim I'd tried to call her but couldn't get through, and she'd have to believe me.

The Liberation has freed us from all sorts of indignities and scourges, including Iraq's Saddams, but mothers-in-law aren't one of them, and I was almost happy with Perdita for her excellent timing. When I didn't want to kill her.

"What's Karen doing in Iraq?" Mother asked.

"Negotiating a Palestinian homeland."

"And meanwhile her granddaughter is ruining her life," she said irrelevantly. "Did you tell Viola?"

"I *told* you, Mother. I thought Perdita should tell all of you herself."

"Well, she didn't. And this morning one of my patients, Carol Chen, called me and demanded to know what I was keeping from her. I had no idea what she was talking about."

"How did Carol Chen find out?"

"From her daughter, who almost joined the Cyclists last year. *Her* family talked her out of it," she said accusingly. "Carol was convinced the medical community had discovered some terrible side-effect of ammenerol and were covering it up. I cannot believe you didn't tell me, Traci."

And I cannot believe I didn't have Bysshe tell her I was in court, I thought. "I told you, Mother. I thought it was Perdita's place to tell you. After all, it's her decision."

"Oh, Traci!" Mother said. "You cannot mean that!"

In the first fine flush of freedom after the Liberation, I had entertained hopes that it would change everything—that it would somehow do away with inequality and matriarchal dominance and those humorless women determined to eliminate the word "manhole" and third-person singular pronouns from the language.

Of course it didn't. Men still make more money, "herstory" is still a blight on the semantic landscape, and my mother can still say, "Oh, *Traci!*" in a tone that reduces me to pre-adolescence.

"Her decision!" Mother said. "Do you mean to tell me you plan to stand idly by and allow your daughter to make the mistake of her life?"

"What can I do? She's twenty-two years old and of sound mind."

"If she were of sound mind she wouldn't be doing this. Didn't you try to talk her out of it?"

"Of course I did, Mother."

"And?"

"And I didn't succeed. She's determined to become a Cyclist."

"Well, there must be something we can do. Get an injunction or hire a deprogrammer or sue the Cyclists for brainwashing. You're a judge, there must be some law you can invoke—"

"The law is called personal sovereignty, Mother, and since it was what made the Liberation possible in the first place, it can hardly be used against Perdita. Her decision meets all the criteria for a case of personal sovereignty: it's a personal decision, it was made by a sovereign adult, it affects no one else—"

"What about my practice? Carol Chen is convinced shunts cause cancer."

"Any effect on your practice is considered an indirect effect. Like secondary smoke. It doesn't apply. Mother, whether we like it or not, Perdita has a perfect right to do this, and we don't have any right to interfere. A free society has to be based on respecting others' opinions and leaving each other alone. We have to respect Perdita's right to make her own decisions."

All of which was true. It was too bad I hadn't said any of it to Perdita when she called. What I had said, in a tone that sounded exactly like my mother's, was "Oh, Per*di*ta!"

"This is all your fault, you know," Mother said. "I *told* you you shouldn't have let her get that tattoo over her shunt. And don't tell me it's a free society. What good is a free society when it allows my granddaughter to ruin her life?" She hung up.

I handed the receiver back to Bysshe.

"I really liked what you said about respecting your daughter's right to make her own decisions," he said. He held out my robe. "And about not interfering in her life."

"I want you to research the precedents on deprogramming for me," I said, sliding my arms into the sleeves. "And find out if the Cyclists have been charged with any free-choice violations—brainwashing, intimidation, coercion."

The phone sang, another universal. "Hello, who's calling?" Bysshe said cautiously. His voice became suddenly friendlier. "Just a minute." He put his hand over the receiver. "It's your daughter Viola."

I took the receiver. "Hello, Viola."

"I just talked to Grandma," she said. "You will not believe what Perdita's done now. She's joined the Cyclists."

"I know," I said.

"You *know?* And you didn't tell me? I can't believe this. You never tell me anything."

"I thought Perdita should tell you herself," I said tiredly.

"Are you kidding? She never tells me anything either. That time she had eyebrow implants she didn't tell me for three weeks, and when she got the laser tattoo she didn't tell me at all. *Twidge* told me. You should have called me. Did you tell Grandma Karen?"

"She's in Baghdad," I said.

"I know," Viola said. "I called her."

"Oh, Viola, you didn't!"

"Unlike you, Mom, I believe in telling members of our family about matters that concern them."

"What did she say?" I asked, a kind of numbness settling over me now that the shock had worn off.

"I couldn't get through to her. The phone service over there is terrible. I got somebody who didn't speak English, and then I got cut off, and when I tried again they said the whole city was down."

Thank you, I breathed silently. Thank you, thank you, thank you.

"Grandma Karen has a right to know, Mother. Think of the effect this could have on Twidge. She thinks Perdita's wonderful. When Perdita got the eyebrow implants, Twidge glued LED's to hers, and I almost never got them off. What if Twidge decides to join the Cyclists, too?"

"Twidge is only nine. By the time she's supposed to get her shunt, Perdita will have long since quit." I hope, I added silently. Perdita had had the tattoo for a year and a half now and showed no signs of tiring of it. "Besides, Twidge has more sense."

"It's true. Oh, Mother, how *could* Perdita do this? Didn't you tell her about how awful it was?"

"Yes," I said. "And inconvenient. And unpleasant and unbalancing and painful. None of it made the slightest impact on her. She told me she thought it would be fun."

Bysshe was pointing to his watch and mouthing, "Time for court."

"Fun!" Viola said. "When she saw what I went through that time? Honestly, Mother, sometimes I think she's completely brain-dead. Can't you have her declared incompetent and locked up or something?"

"No," I said, trying to zip up my robe with one hand. "Viola, I have to go. I'm late for court. I'm afraid there's nothing we can do to stop her. She's a rational adult."

"Rational!" Viola said. "Her eyebrows light up, Mother. She has Custer's Last Stand lased on her arm."

I handed the phone to Bysshe. "Tell Viola I'll talk to her tomorrow." I zipped up my robe. "And then call Baghdad and see how long they expect the phones to be out." I started into the courtroom. "And if there are any more universal calls, make sure they're local before you answer."

Bysshe couldn't get through to Baghdad, which I took as a good sign, and my mother-in-law didn't call. Mother did, in the afternoon, to ask if lobotomies were legal.

She called again the next day. I was in the middle of my Personal Sovereignty class, explaining the inherent right of citizens in a free society to make complete jackasses of themselves. They weren't buying it.

"I think it's your mother," Bysshe whispered to me as he handed me the phone. "She's still using the universal. But it's local. I checked."

"Hello, Mother," I said.

"It's all arranged," Mother said. "We're having lunch with Perdita at McGregor's. It's on the corner of Twelfth Street and Larimer."

"I'm in the middle of class," I said.

"I know. I won't keep you. I just wanted to tell you not to worry. I've taken care of everything."

I didn't like the sound of that. "What have you done?"

"Invited Perdita to lunch with us. I told you. At McGregor's."

"Who is 'us,' Mother?"

"Just the family," she said innocently. "You and Viola."

Well, at least she hadn't brought in the deprogrammer. Yet. "What are you up to, Mother?"

"Perdita said the same thing. Can't a grandmother ask her granddaughters to lunch? Be there at twelve-thirty."

"Bysshe and I have a court calendar meeting at three."

"Oh, we'll be done by then. And bring Bysshe with you. He can provide a man's point of view."

She hung up.

"You'll have to go to lunch with me, Bysshe," I said. "Sorry."

"Why? What's going to happen at lunch?"

"I have no idea."

On the way over to McGregor's, Bysshe told me what he'd found out about the Cyclists. "They're not a cult. There's no religious connection. They seem to have grown out of a pre-Liberation women's group," he said, looking at his notes, "although there are also links to the pro-choice movement, the University of Wisconsin, and the Museum of Modern Art."

"What?"

"They call their group leaders 'docents.' Their philosophy seems to be a mix of pre-Liberation radical feminism and the environmental primitivism of the eighties. They're floratarians and they don't wear shoes."

"Or shunts," I said. We pulled up in front of McGregor's and got out of the car. "Any mind control convictions?" I asked hopefully.

"No. A bunch of suits against individual members, all of which they won."

"On grounds of personal sovereignty."

"Yeah. And a criminal one by a member whose family tried to deprogram her. The deprogrammer was sentenced to twenty years, and the family got twelve."

"Be sure to tell Mother about that one," I said, and opened the door to McGregor's.

It was one of those restaurants with a morning glory vine twining around the *maître d'*'s desk and garden plots between the tables.

"Perdita suggested it," Mother said, guiding Bysshe and me past the onions to our table. "She told me a lot of the Cyclists are floratarians."

"Is she here?" I asked, sidestepping a cucumber frame.

"Not yet." She pointed past a rose arbor. "There's our table."

Our table was a wicker affair under a mulberry tree. Viola and Twidge were seated on the far side next to a trellis of runner beans, looking at menus.

"What are you doing here, Twidge?" I asked. "Why aren't you in school?"

"I am," she said, holding up her LCD slate. "I'm remoting today."

"I thought she should be part of this discussion," Viola said. "After all, she'll be getting her shunt soon."

"My friend Kensy says she isn't going to get one, like Perdita," Twidge said.

"I'm sure Kensy will change her mind when the time comes," Mother said. "Perdita will change hers, too. Bysshe, why don't you sit next to Viola?"

Bysshe slid obediently past the trellis and sat down in the wicker chair at the far end of the table. Twidge reached across Viola and handed him a menu. "This is a great restaurant," she said. "You don't have to wear shoes." She held up a bare foot to illustrate. "And if you get hungry while you're waiting, you can just pick something." She twisted around in her chair, picked two of the green beans, gave one to Bysshe, and bit into the other one. "I bet she doesn't. Kensy says a shunt hurts worse than braces."

"It doesn't hurt as much as not having one," Viola said, shooting me a Now-Do-You-See-What-My-Sister's-Caused? look.

"Traci, why don't you sit across from Viola?" Mother said to me. "And we'll put Perdita next to you when she comes."

"If she comes," Viola said.

"I told her one o'clock," Mother said, sitting down at the near end. "So we'd have a chance to plan our strategy before she gets here. I talked to Carol Chen—"

"Her daughter nearly joined the Cyclists last year," I explained to Bysshe and Viola.

"*She* said they had a family gathering, like this, and simply talked to her daughter, and she decided she didn't want to be a Cyclist after all." She looked around the table. "So I thought we'd do the same thing with Perdita. I think we should start by explaining the significance of the Liberation and the days of dark oppression that preceded it—"

"*I* think," Viola interrupted, "we should try to talk her into just going off the ammenerol for a few months instead of having the shunt removed. If she comes. Which she won't."

"Why not?"

"Would you? I mean, it's like the Inquisition. Her sitting here while all of us 'explain' at her. Perdita may be crazy, but she's not stupid."

"It's hardly the Inquisition," Mother said. She looked anxiously past me toward the door. "I'm sure Perdita—" She stopped, stood up, and plunged off suddenly through the asparagus.

I turned around, half-expecting Perdita with light-up lips or a full-body tattoo, but I couldn't see through the leaves. I pushed at the branches.

"Is it Perdita?" Viola said, leaning forward.

I peered around the mulberry bush. "Oh, my God," I said.

It was my mother-in-law, wearing a black abayah and a silk yarmulke. She swept toward us through a pumpkin patch, robes billowing and eyes flashing. Mother hurried in her wake of trampled radishes, looking daggers at me.

I turned them on Viola. "It's your grandmother Karen," I said accusingly. "You told me you didn't get through to her."

"I didn't," she said. "Twidge, sit up straight. And put your slate down."

There was an ominous rustling in the rose arbor, as of leaves shrinking back in terror, and my mother-in-law arrived.

"Karen!" I said, trying to sound pleased. "What on earth are you doing here? I thought you were in Baghdad."

"I came back as soon as I got Viola's message," she said, glaring at everyone in turn. "Who's this?" she demanded, pointing at Bysshe. "Viola's new livein?"

"No!" Bysshe said, looking horrified.

"This is my law clerk, Mother," I said. "Bysshe Adams-Hardy."

"Twidge, why aren't you in school?"

"I *am*," Twidge said. "I'm remoting." She held up her slate. "See? Math."

"I see," she said, turning to glower at me. "It's a serious enough matter to require my great-grandchild's being pulled out of school *and* the hiring of legal assistance, and yet you didn't deem it important enough to notify *me*. Of course, you *never* tell me anything, Traci."

She swirled herself into the end chair, sending leaves and sweet pea blossoms flying, and decapitating the broccoli centerpiece. "I didn't get Viola's cry for help until yesterday. Viola, you should never leave messages with Hassim. His English is virtually nonexistent. I had to get him to hum me your ring. I recognized your signature, but the phones were out, so I flew home. In the middle of negotiations, I might add."

"How *are* negotiations going, Grandma Karen?" Viola asked.

"They *were* going extremely well. The Israelis have given the Palestinians half of Jerusalem, and they've agreed to time-share the Golan Heights." She turned to glare momentarily at me. "*They* know the importance of communication." She turned back to Viola. "So why are they picking on you, Viola? Don't they like your new livein?"

"I am *not* her livein," Bysshe protested.

I have often wondered how on earth my mother-in-law became a mediator and what she does in all those negotiation sessions with Serbs and Catholics and North and South Koreans and Protestants and Croats. She takes sides, jumps to conclusions, misinterprets everything you say, refuses to listen. And yet she talked South Africa into a Mandelan government and would probably get the Palestinians to observe Yom Kippur. Maybe she just bullies everyone into submission. Or maybe they have to band together to protect themselves against her.

Bysshe was still protesting."I never even met Viola till today. I've only talked to her on the phone a couple of times."

"You must have done something," Karen said to Viola. "They're obviously out for your blood."

"Not mine," Viola said. "Perdita's. She's joined the Cyclists."

"The Cyclists? I left the West Bank negotiations because you don't approve of Perdita joining a biking club? How am I supposed to explain this to the president of Iraq? She will *not* understand, and neither do I. A biking club!"

"The Cyclists do not ride bicycles," Mother said.

"They menstruate," Twidge said.

There was a dead silence of at least a minute, and I thought, it's finally happened. My mother-in-law and I are actually going to be on the same side of a family argument.

"All this fuss is over Perdita's having her shunt removed?" Karen said finally. "She's of age, isn't she? And this is obviously a case where personal sovereignty applies. You should know that, Traci. After all, you're a judge."

I should have known it was too good to be true.

"You mean you approve of her setting back the Liberation twenty years?" Mother said.

"I hardly think it's that serious," Karen said. "There are anti-shunt groups in the Middle East, too, you know, but no one takes them seriously. Not even the Iraqis, and they still wear the veil."

"Perdita is taking them seriously."

Karen dismissed Perdita with a wave of her black sleeve. "They're a trend, a fad. Like microskirts. Or those dreadful electronic eyebrows. A few women wear silly fashions like that for a little while, but you don't see women as a whole giving up pants or going back to wearing hats."

"But Perdita. . . ." Viola said.

"If Perdita wants to have her period, I say let her. Women functioned perfectly well without shunts for thousands of years."

Mother brought her fist down on the table. "Women also functioned *perfectly well* with concubinage, cholera, and corsets," she said, emphasizing each word with her fist. "But that is no reason to take them on voluntarily, and I have no intention of allowing Perdita—"

"Speaking of Perdita, where is the poor child?" Karen said.

"She'll be here any minute," Mother said. "I invited her to lunch so we could discuss this with her."

"Ha!" Karen said. "So you could browbeat her into changing her mind, you mean. Well, I have no intention of collaborating with you. *I* intend to listen to the poor thing's point of view with interest and an open mind. Respect, that's the key word, and one you all seem to have forgotten. Respect and common courtesy."

A barefoot young woman wearing a flowered smock and a red scarf tied around her left arm came up to the table with a sheaf of pink folders.

"It's about time," Karen said, snatching one of the folders away from her. "Your service here is dreadful. I've been sitting here ten minutes." She snapped the folder open. "I don't suppose you have Scotch."

"My name is Evangeline," the young woman said. "I'm Perdita's docent." She took the folder away from Karen. "She wasn't able to join you for lunch, but she asked me to come in her place and explain the Cyclist philosophy to you."

She sat down in the wicker chair next to me.

"The Cyclists are dedicated to freedom," she said. "Freedom from artificiality, freedom from body-controlling drugs and hormones, freedom from the male patriarchy that attempts to impose them on us. As you probably already know, we do not wear shunts."

She pointed to the red scarf around her arm. "Instead, we wear this as a badge of our freedom and our femaleness. I'm wearing it today to announce that my time of fertility has come."

"We had that, too," Mother said, "only we wore it on the back of our skirts."

I laughed.

The docent glared at me. "Male domination of women's bodies began long before the so-called 'Liberation,' with government regulation of abortion and fetal rights, scientific control of fertility, and finally the development of ammenerol, which eliminated the reproductive cycle altogether. This was all part of a carefully planned takeover of women's bodies, and by extension, their identities, by the male patriarchal regime."

"What an interesting point of view!" Karen said enthusiastically.

It certainly was. In point of fact, ammenerol hadn't been invented to eliminate menstruation at all. It had been developed for shrinking malignant tumors, and its uterine lining-absorbing properties had only been discovered by accident.

"Are you trying to tell us," Mother said, "that men *forced* shunts on women?! We had to *fight* everyone to get it approved by the FDA!"

It was true. What surrogate mothers and anti-abortionists and the fetal rights issue had failed to do in uniting women, the prospect of not having to menstruate did. Women had organized rallies, petitioned, elected senators, passed amendments, been excommunicated, and gone to jail, all in the name of Liberation.

"Men were *against* it," Mother said, getting rather red in the face. "And the religious right and the maxipad manufacturers, and the Catholic church—"

"They knew they'd have to allow women priests," Viola said.

"Which they did," I said.

"The Liberation hasn't freed you," the docent said loudly. "Except from the natural rhythms of your life, the very wellspring of your femaleness."

She leaned over and picked a daisy that was growing under the table. "We in the Cyclists celebrate the onset of our menses and rejoice in our bodies," she said, holding the daisy up. "Whenever a Cyclist comes into blossom, as we call it, she is honored with flowers and poems and songs. Then we join hands and tell what we like best about our menses."

"Water retention," I said.

"Or lying in bed with a heating pad for three days a month," Mother said.

"I think I like the anxiety attacks best," Viola said. "When I went off the ammenerol, so I could have Twidge, I'd have these days where I was convinced the space station was going to fall on me."

A middle-aged woman in overalls and a straw hat had come over while Viola was talking and was standing next to Mother's chair. "I had these mood swings," she said. "One minute I'd feel cheerful and the next like Lizzie Borden."

"Who's Lizzie Borden?" Twidge asked.

"She killed her parents," Bysshe said. "With an ax."

Karen and the docent glared at both of them. "Aren't you supposed to be working on your math, Twidge?" Karen said.

"I've always wondered if Lizzie Borden had PMS," Viola said, "and that was why—"

"No," Mother said. "It was having to live before tampons and ibuprofen. An obvious case of justifiable homicide."

"I hardly think this sort of levity is helpful," Karen said, glowering at everyone.

"Are you our waitress?" I asked the straw-hatted woman hastily.

"Yes," she said, producing a slate from her overalls pocket.

"Do you serve wine?" I asked.

"Yes. Dandelion, cowslip, and primrose."

"We'll take them all," I said.

"A bottle of each?"

"For now. Unless you have them in kegs."

"Our specials today are watermelon salad and *choufleur gratinée*," she said, smiling at everyone. Karen and the docent did not smile back. "You hand-pick your own cauliflower from the patch up front. The floratarian special is sautéed lily buds with marigold butter."

There was a temporary truce while everyone ordered. "I'll have the sweet peas," the docent said, "and a glass of rose water."

Bysshe leaned over to Viola. "I'm sorry I sounded so horrified when your grandmother asked if I was your livein," he said.

"That's okay," Viola said. "Grandma Karen can be pretty scary."

"I just didn't want you to think I didn't like you. I do. Like you, I mean."

"Don't they have soyburgers?" Twidge asked.

As soon as the waitress left, the docent began passing out the pink folders she'd brought with her. "These will explain the working philosophy of the Cyclists," she said, handing me one, "along with practical information on the menstrual cycle." She handed Twidge one.

"It looks just like those books we used to get in junior high," Mother said, looking at hers. " 'A Special Gift,' they were called, and they had all these pictures of girls with pink ribbons in their hair, playing tennis and smiling. Blatant misrepresentation."

She was right. There was even the same drawing of the fallopian tubes I remembered from my middle school movie, a drawing that had always reminded me of *Alien* in the early stages.

"Oh, yuck," Twidge said. "This is disgusting."

"Do your math," Karen said.

Bysshe looked sick. "Did women really *do* this stuff?"

The wine arrived, and I poured everyone a large glass. The docent pursed her lips disapprovingly and shook her head. "The Cyclists do not use the artificial stimulants or hormones that the male patriarchy has forced on women to render them docile and subservient."

"How long do you menstruate?" Twidge asked.

"Forever," Mother said.

"Four to six days," the docent said. "It's there in the booklet."

"No, I mean, your whole life or what?"

"A woman has her menarche at twelve years old on the average and ceases menstruating at age fifty-five."

"I had my first period at eleven," the waitress said, setting a bouquet down in front of me. "At school."

"I had my last one on the day the FDA approved *ammenerol*," Mother said.

"Three hundred and sixty-five divided by twenty-eight," Twidge said, writing on her slate. "Times forty-three years." She looked up. "That's five hundred and fifty-nine periods."

"That can't be right," Mother said, taking the slate away from her. "It's at least five thousand."

"And they all start on the day you leave on a trip," Viola said.

"Or get married," the waitress said.

Mother began writing on the slate.

I took advantage of the ceasefire to pour everyone some more dandelion wine.

Mother looked up from the slate. "Do you realize with a period of five days, you'd be menstruating for nearly three thousand days? That's over eight solid years."

"And in between there's PMS," the waitress said, delivering flowers.

"What's PMS?" Twidge asked.

"Pre-menstrual syndrome was the name the male medical establishment fabricated for the natural variation in hormonal levels that signal the onset of menstruation," the docent said. "This mild and entirely normal fluctuation was exaggerated by men into a debility." She looked at Karen for confirmation.

"I used to cut my hair," Karen said.

The docent looked uneasy.

"Once I chopped off one whole side," Karen went on. "Bob had to hide the scissors every month. And the car keys. I'd start to cry every time I hit a red light."

"Did you swell up?" Mother asked, pouring Karen another glass of dandelion wine.

"I looked just like Orson Welles."

"Who's Orson Welles?" Twidge asked.

"Your comments reflect the self-loathing thrust on you by the patriarchy," the docent said. "Men have brainwashed women into thinking menstruation is evil and unclean. Women even called their menses 'the curse' because they accepted men's judgment."

"I called it the curse because I thought a witch must have laid a curse on me," Viola said. "Like in 'Sleeping Beauty.' "

Everyone looked at her.

"Well, I did," she said. "It was the only reason I could think of for such an awful thing happening to me." She handed the folder back to the docent. "It still is."

"I think you were awfully brave," Bysshe said to Viola, "going off the ammenerol to have Twidge."

"It was awful," Viola said. "You can't imagine."

Mother sighed. "When I got my period, I asked my mother if Annette had it, too."

"Who's Annette?" Twidge said.

"A Mouseketeer," Mother said and added, at Twidge's uncomprehending look, "on TV."

"High-rez," Viola said.

"The Mickey Mouse Club," Mother said.

"There was a high-rezzer called the Mickey Mouse Club?" Twidge said incredulously.

"They were days of dark oppression in many ways," I said.

Mother glared at me. "Annette was every young girl's ideal," she said to Twidge. "Her hair was curly, she had actual breasts, her pleated skirt was always pressed, and I could not imagine that she could have anything so *messy* and undignified. Mr. Disney would never have allowed it. And if Annette didn't have one, I wasn't going to have one either. So I asked my mother—"

"What did she say?" Twidge cut in.

"She said every woman had periods," Mother said. "So I asked her, 'Even the Queen of England?' and she said, 'Even the Queen.' "

"Really?" Twidge said. "But she's so *old!*"

"She isn't having it now," the docent said irritatedly. "I told you, menopause occurs at age fifty-five."

"And then you have hot flashes," Karen said, "and osteoporosis and so much hair on your upper lip you look like Mark Twain."

"Who's—" Twidge said.

"You are simply reiterating negative male propaganda," the docent interrupted, looking very red in the face.

"You know what I've always wondered?" Karen said, leaning conspiratorially close to Mother. "If Maggie Thatcher's menopause was responsible for the Falklands War."

"Who's Maggie Thatcher?" Twidge said.

The docent, who was now as red in the face as her scarf, stood up. "It is clear there is no point in trying to talk to you. You've all been completely brainwashed by the male patriarchy." She began grabbing up her folders. "You're blind, all of you! You don't even see that you're victims of a male conspiracy to deprive you of your biological identity, of your very woman-hood. The Liberation wasn't a liberation at all. It was only another kind of slavery!"

"Even if that were true," I said, "even if it had been a conspiracy to bring us under male domination, it would have been worth it."

"She's right, you know," Karen said to Mother. "Traci's absolutely right. There are some things worth giving up anything for, even your freedom, and getting rid of your period is definitely one of them."

"Victims!" the docent shouted. "You've been stripped of your femininity, and you don't even care!" She stomped out, destroying several squash and a row of gladiolas in the process.

"You know what I hated most before the Liberation?" Karen said, pouring the last of the dandelion wine into her glass. "Sanitary belts."

"And those cardboard tampon applicators," Mother said.

"I'm never going to join the Cyclists," Twidge said.

"Good," I said.

"Can I have dessert?"

I called the waitress over, and Twidge ordered sugared violets. "Anyone else want dessert?" I asked. "Or more primrose wine?"

"I think it's wonderful the way you're trying to help your sister," Bysshe said, leaning close to Viola.

"And those Modess ads," Mother said. "You remember, with those glamorous women in satin brocade evening dresses and long white gloves, and below the picture was written, 'Modess, because. . . .' I thought Modess was a perfume."

Karen giggled. "I thought it was a brand of *champagne!*"

"I don't think we'd better have any more wine," I said.

The phone started singing the minute I got to my chambers the next morning, the universal ring.

"Karen went back to Iraq, didn't she?" I asked Bysshe.

"Yeah," he said. "Viola said there was some snag over whether to put Disneyland on the West Bank or not."

"When did Viola call?"

Bysshe looked sheepish. "I had breakfast with her and Twidge this morning."

"Oh." I picked up the phone. "It's probably Mother with a plan to kidnap Perdita. Hello?"

"This is Evangeline, Perdita's docent," the voice on the phone said. "I hope you're happy. You've bullied Perdita into surrendering to the enslaving male patriarchy."

"I have?" I said.

"You've obviously employed mind control, and I want you to know we intend to file charges." She hung up. The phone rang again immediately, another universal.

"What is the good of signatures when no one ever uses them?" I said and picked up the phone.

"Hi, Mom," Perdita said. "I thought you'd want to know I've changed my mind about joining the Cyclists."

"Really?" I said, trying not to sound jubilant.

"I found out they wear this red scarf thing on their arm. It covers up Sitting Bull's horse."

"That is a problem," I said.

"Well, that's not all. My docent told me about your lunch. Did Grandma Karen really tell you you were right?"

"Yes."

"Gosh! I didn't believe that part. Well, anyway, my docent said you wouldn't listen to her about how great menstruating is, that you all kept talking about the negative aspects of it, like bloating and cramps and crabbiness, and I said, 'What are cramps?' and she said, 'Menstrual bleeding frequently causes headaches and discomfort,' and I said, 'Bleeding?!? Nobody ever said anything about bleeding!' Why didn't you tell me there was blood involved, Mother?"

I had, but I felt it wiser to keep silent.

"And you didn't say a word about its being painful. And all the hormone fluctuations! Anybody'd have to be crazy to want to go through that when they didn't have to! How did you stand it before the Liberation?"

"They were days of dark oppression," I said.

"I *guess*! Well, anyway, I quit and now my docent is really mad. But I told her it was a case of personal sovereignty, and she has to respect my decision. I'm still going to become a floratarian, though, and I *don't* want you to try to talk me out of it."

"I wouldn't dream of it," I said.

"You know, this whole thing is really your fault, Mom! If you'd told me about the pain part in the first place, none of this would have happened. Viola's right! You never tell us *anything*!"

THE ROUND-EYED BARBARIANS

L. Sprague de Camp

L. Sprague de Camp is a seminal figure, one whose career spans almost the entire development of modern fantasy and SF. For the fantasy magazine *Unknown* in the early 1940s, he helped create a whole new modern style of fantasy writing—funny, whimsical, and irreverent—of which he is still the most prominent practitioner. His most famous books include *Lest Darkness Fall*, *The Incompleat Enchanter* (with Fletcher Pratt), *The Glory that Was*, *The Hand of Zei*, *Land of Unreason* (with Pratt), *The Tower of Zanid*, and *Rogue Queen*. His short fiction has been collected in *The Continent Makers*, *A Gun for Dinosaur*, *Tales From Gavagan's Bar* (with Fletcher Pratt), *The Purple Pterodactyls*, and *The Best of L. Sprague de Camp*. He has also written many acclaimed historical novels (*The Bronze God of Rhodes*, *An Elephant for Aristotle*) and nonfiction books (*Lost Continents*, *The Ancient Engineers*), including some critical studies of importance to the genre, such as *Lovecraft: A Biography* and *Dark Valley Destiny: The Life of Robert E. Howard*. His most recent book is *The Honorable Barbarian*. In the last year or so he's been writing a new sequence of tales about the adventures of Reginald Rivers, the hero of his famous story "A Gun for Dinosaur," which will be assembled in the upcoming collection *Rivers in Time*. He lives in Texas with his wife, writer Catherine Crook de Camp.

In the typically sly and witty story that follows, he takes us sideways in time for a look at cultures in conflict, and a bitingly satiric version of how things *might* have been . . .

Ho Youwen, General of the Advanced Imperial Eastern Force, to the esteemed Li Ganjing, Director of the Eastern Continent Section of the Barbarian Relations Bureau of the External Affairs Department of the Overseas Branch of His Imperial Majesty's government. Health, prosperity, and many sons!

Dear old friend: This person thinks that, besides his formal report on the affair of the round-eyed barbarians, which will follow in the next dispatch, you would also like a personal letter to furnish background for this turn on events. It is all very well for officials of the Upper Mandarinate to sneer at barbarian thoughts and deeds as of no interest to representatives of mighty Zhongguo.* True, barbarians' customs are often strange and disgusting, their

---

*In the Pinyin transcription of Chinese, *zh* stands for the sound of the *j* in *journal*.

beliefs outlandish, their manners appalling, and their emotions childish. But to be realistic, barbarous tribes and nations also include many dangerously vigorous and ingenious people. It was just such a toplofty attitude that in the days of the Sung led to the Mongol plague and the subjection of civilization to the rule of barbarian hordes for a century.

The same shortsightedness threatened a century ago, when Zheng-tung was the Son of Heaven. A cabal of scholars and soldiers sought to end the voyages of exploration and tribute gathering begun by the great Zheng Ho. These misguided persons sought to stop all foreign contacts. They held that, since the Middle Kingdom had everything needed by civilization, such contacts would only have adverse effects.

Luckily the cabal was defeated; the work of exploration and of scientific development initiated under the accursed Mongols was continued. Hence the exploration and conquest of this Eastern Continent has proceeded in an orderly manner. The red-skinned barbarians, realizing the futility of opposing the advance of civilization with weapons of wood and stone, have been offered the benefits of our superior culture. Many take advantage of this opportunity and, in another few centuries, may have raised themselves almost to the level of civilized human beings.

But to return to the round-eyed barbarians. One day this summer, this person was reconnoitering the eastern side of the Lower Mountains, in an area not yet brought under the benevolent sway of the Son of Heaven. I led a company of Hitchiti infantry, armed with our new breech-loading rifles. A scout reported the approach of a force of redskin warriors of the Ochuse tribe, who dwell on the shores of the great water to the south. Signal drums and gongs alerted my detachment.

A *shi* later this force debouched from the trail. First came a scattering of redskins, from their paint evidently the Ochuse. After them rode a horseman in a steel helmet, cuirass, and other pieces of plate armor. After him came hundreds of round-eyed men afoot, less impressively armored, in the garb of Yuropian barbarians, wherewith the voyages of Admiral Xing have familiarized us. Their loins were covered with short, bulging breeches, below which they either went barelegged or wore a kind of skintight trouser on each leg. They bore pikes, crossbows, and firearms of primitive types, obsolete in the Celestial Empire for a century. My redskin spies had warned me of the incursions of such people along the coast of this continent, but these were the first such intruders whom I had personally seen.

Behind them, threading their way through the forest, I glimpsed many other redskins, men and women bowed beneath the weight of the burdens they bore. Farther back yet, barely visible amid the towering trees, came a troop of armored horsemen and other men leading unsaddled horses.

At the sight of my group, taking cover behind rocks, bushes, and hummocks, the newcomers halted. The armored man in the lead swung off his horse with a clank of armor and handed the reins to another round-eye, who led the animal to the rear. The armored round-eye was handed a pole, and another man afoot joined him in front of the array. This was a lean man in a long black robe; through my telescope I saw that he was clean-shaven.

The armored man drove the butt of his pole into the soil. From the upper end of this pole hung a flag; but since the day was still, there was no wind to flutter this banner. All I could see was that it bore a pattern of red and yellow.

The armored man then shouted in his native gibberish. Through my telescope I saw that he was of medium size, with a sun-browned skin, sharp, beak-nosed features, and a full black beard. This, I perceived, must be one of those round-eyed barbarians inhabiting the Far Western Peninsula, called Yuropa by its natives, of which Admiral Xing informed us on his return from those lands in the reign of Hung Wu. The other round-eyes crowded up behind him.

When the armored man finished his proclamation, the other round-eye, the black-robed one, raised his hands and uttered another unintelligible speech. I called to the scout Falaya nearby:

"O scout, you know the Ochuse tongue. Find out what this be all about!"

Falaya stood up and shouted in the tongue of the coastal redskins. Presently one of the Ochuse conferred with the armored man and shouted back. This translating back and forth, as you can imagine, proved a lengthy, tedious business. Mankind were better off if all men spake the tongue of Zhongguo, which is after all the speech of civilization. At length Falaya turned to me, saying in broken Zhongguo:

"O General, he say man in armor say he claim all this land in name of his king, Felipe of Espanya."

Somewhat astonished, I told Falaya: "Ask this bold fellow, who claims lands belonging to the Son of Heaven, who he be?"

After the usual pause for translation from Zhongguo to Ochuse and from Ochuse to the armored man's Yuropian dialect, the reply came back:

"He say he Captain Tristan de Luna y Arellano, and who be we?"

This person gave Falaya the needed information, adding: "And by whose leave, barbarian, do you trespass on the lands of the Son of Heaven and, moreover, claim parts of it in the name of some tribal chieftain in the Far Western Peninsula?"

I know not how literally my words were translated, but they seemed to arouse the armored round-eye to a frenzy. He began to shout a reply; but the black-robed one laid a hand on his arm. I could not hear what they said at that distance—not that I could have understood their blather anyway. But black-robe seemed to be urging negotiation.

At last the armored round-eye fell silent and signaled black-robe to speak. The result, translated sentence by sentence, was a lengthy homily. It reminded me of the endless sermons of that loquacious bonze, Brother Xiaojin, whom we sent home last year. He could put a hungry tiger to sleep with his endless disquisitions on the wisdom of the compassionate Buddha.

This fellow, the black-robed one, advanced an astonishing claim: that his master, a Yuropian high priest called a *papa*, had divided the world between two Yuropian rulers, the kings of Espanya and Portugar; and this part had gone to the King of Espanya. There was more, about how the Yuropian god had commanded all men to love one another; and if we would but accept his theological doctrines, we were all assured of endless bliss in his Yuropian Heaven. If we refused to swallow these myths, we should all be slain by the Yuropians' weapons and then suffer eternal torment in the Yuropian Hell, a fearsome afterworld reminding me of the more eccentric afterlife concepts of the Tibetan Buddhists.

Although this person knows better than to laugh under such serious circumstances, I could not suppress a burst of mirth. I sent back the message that his *papa* seemed very free in giving away other peoples' countries and that in any case all men came naturally under the dominion of the Son of Heaven.

As for his theology, I was satisfied that I must have done something right in a previous incarnation to have earned my present rank as a reward. I would try by correct action and keeping my *karma* clean at least to maintain this status, compared to which round-eyed barbarians were less than worms beneath my feet. They must have committed grave offenses in previous lives to have been born into such a lowly estate.

At this the armored man altogether lost control of himself and screamed orders. His redskins spread out to the flanks, nocking their arrows, whilst a couple of hundred other round-eyes formed a double line facing us and readying their primitive firearms. These operated by means of lengths of cord, treated to burn slowly; I have seen specimens of similar weapons in the Imperial War Museum.

One round-eye passed down the line with a bucket of glowing coals, wherein each of the invaders dipped the end of his cord until it was alight. Then he clamped it to the mechanism of his gun. Meanwhile those armed with crossbows cocked them. The leader shouted some more, and my scout reported:

"He say we surrender or die, sir!"

I replied with a vulgarism expressing my disdain for such primitive insolence. The armored man shouted again, whereupon the other round-eyes discharged their weapons. After the first rank had fired and begun the lengthy business of reloading, the second rank stepped forth between them and fired in their turn. On their flanks, the redskins shot arrows.

The guns made loud reports and tremendous puffs of smoke, whilst their musket balls and crossbow bolts whistled past us. Since my people were well under cover, and those of the second rank had fired blindly, because of the curtain of smoke before them, we sustained no casualties save a few flesh wounds among my Hitchiti from the arrows.

When the pall of smoke had somewhat dissipated, I said: "Fire!"

Our rifles opened up, and a number of trespassers, both round-eyed and red-skinned, fell.

"Reload!" I said, and then: "Fire!"

The round-eyes were still struggling to reload, which with firearms of that archaic type is a protracted process. As I later learned, such a gunner does well to get off twenty shots in one *ko*, whereas a well-trained soldier can fire one of our breech-loaders a hundred times in that interval, if he run not out of cartridges.

At our third volley, the intruders' redskins fled. Half the round-eyes were down; but the leader was still erect, shouting commands and defiance. I told the captain of my force:

"Choose a sharpshooter and order him to wound that armored man in the leg. I wish him alive, and also a redskin who can speak his language."

So it was done. At the fall of the leader, the other round-eyes joined the redskins in flight: first a few here and there, then all of them. Some dropped their guns to run faster. Behind them the redskin porters also dropped their loads and fled, while the horsemen cantered off with their armor jingling. I did not command a pursuit, knowing that in these forests of immense trees the pursued can easily slip away and the pursuer as easily get lost. My Hitchiti broke from cover and raced away to collect the scalps of the fallen foes.

Later, when I had donned my official robe instead of my filthy uniform, and my peacock-feather hat in place of the steel cap, I commanded that the wounded Yuropian leader be brought to my tent, along with his redskin interpreter and our own Ochuse-speaking scout. I also sent men to retrieve the baggage dropped by the fleeing porters.

This Tristan de Luna appeared at the entrance to my tent with a pair of my redskins gripping his arms. His armor had been shed, and his garb was ordinary Yuropian, with the puffed trunks and below them the skintight trousers of their kind. He sweated heavily in the heat, limped on his bandaged leg, and supported himself by a tree branch he had somehow obtained, whittled down to a walking stick.

Now that I had a closer look at the man, I saw that he was older than I had thought. His curly black hair and beard were, like mine, beginning to show gray. But his stance was still erect and his movements youthfully springy, save for his wounded leg.

As he neared, I became aware that the man had not bathed lately, if ever. Not to put too fine a point on it, he stank. I then attributed this to the exigencies of travel, but my redskin spies inform me that this is usual with Yuropians. Not only have they a naturally stronger bodily odor than normal folk; but also the Yuropian religion discourages cleanliness. Most adhere to Christianity, whereas the other major western creeds, Islam and Judaism, value bathing and cleanliness. Christians suspected of going over to either of these other faiths are burned alive, as the more warlike redskin tribes do to captive foes. Therefore among Christians, cleanliness arouses suspicion of conversion to one of those other cults, which are completely outlawed in Espanya.

At the entrance Captain Tristan wrenched loose an arm, placed his hand over his heart, and made a low bow. This gesture, evidently meant as a polite greeting, overbalanced him in his crippled state. He staggered and would have fallen had not the two redskins caught him. He did not go to his knees and touch his forehead to the carpet, but one must make allowances for barbarians who have never been taught civilized manners; the full *ko-tou* would have been difficult for him in any way.

At least this barbarian had evidently decided on a more urbane approach. His translated words were:

"Sir, now that I perceive you more closely, it appears that you come from the Great Khan of Cathay. Be this true?"

Yuropians had evidently not kept up with events in the Middle Kingdom. I told Tristan: "Two centuries past, your impression might have been apt. But we sons of Han expelled the Khans long ago and restored the Celestial Empire to the proper Sons of Heaven, now reigning as the glorious Ming. The Khans were but barbarian usurpers from the Gobi. Whence came you?"

He said: "From the land that the deceased Captain Ponce discovered and named *la Florida*. He thought it an island, but unbroken land appears to extend far to the north thereof, and also to the west to Mexico." After a pause he continued:

"Then be we in truth in the Indes? When that Italian Colón returned from his voyages, half a century ago, he insisted that he had reached them, or at least come to a chain of islands to the east of them, whence another day's sail would have brought him to the Spice Islands.

"But a ship of that fellow Magallanes returned to Espanya thirty-odd years ago. The captain thereof, Delcano, asserted that far to the west of these lands lies an ocean so vast as to require three or four months to sail across, and that the lands of the Great Khan lie beyond it. But this Delcano was a Basque and therefore not to be implicitly trusted. If this be the true Indes, that were greatly to the advantage of my sovran."

I told him: "Your Captain Delcano is quite correct. In any case, the Eastern Continent whereon we now stand is wide enough to take a well-mounted man, with remounts, as long to ride across as your Magallanes found the Eastern Ocean. It has nought to do with the land of India, which is even farther than the Celestial Empire. And now, what is all this nonsense about claiming this land for some Yuropian chieftain?"

The man muttered: "So huge a world!" Then followed another harangue, essentially repeating what the black-robed man had said before the shooting began.

"I could better explain it," said Tristan, "if your men had not slain our holy father. I myself have small knowledge of letters and history. But what have you done with my woman?"

"Woman? We have no captive women. There were a couple of female bodies in the woods behind your battle line. I suppose they were struck by our fire before all your redskins fled. What woman claim you to have had?"

"The daughter of a chief of the Nanipacana," said he. "We fell in love and eloped."

To straighten this out took further questions, since there be nought in Zhongguo exactly corresponding to these concepts, save perhaps in Li Po's poetry. But, like Captain Tristan, I am no literary man, familiar with such things. Besides, the mating habits of barbarians afford endless amusement.

Tristan said that he and the woman had not only fled secretly, defying the wrath of the woman's father, but had also caused the black-robed one to conduct a rite over their union, according to his customs rendering it permanent and unbreakable. I later learned that Tristan already had a wife somewhere, notwithstanding that Yuropians are supposed to be monogamous. But that is no affair of ours.

"Sir," said Tristan, "could you let me have something to eat? We are all half-starved, for the Indians" (as the Espanyans ridiculously call the redskins, although these live halfway round the world from the true Indians) "along the route had fled, taking all their food supplies with them before we arrived. Those *cabrones*—"

Falaya could not translate that word, but questioning revealed that it meant a eunuch. Notwithstanding the high rank of the eunuchs of the Imperial Court, the term is a deadly insult among round-eyes.

Whilst this person was getting Captain Tristan's meaning straightened out, a Hitchiti of my personal guard thrust his head into the tent. "O General!" he cried. "Our scouts report a large force of Nanipacana approaching, in full war paint."

"Kwanyin save us!" I exclaimed, rising. "Sound the alarms!"

This time things went more smoothly despite the war paint. The new force was led by Chief Imathla, with whom I had had dealings and so knew personally. I had been trying to persuade him voluntarily to place himself under the protection of the Son of Heaven, to save us the necessity of conquering him. So, when Imathla thrust his spear into the ground and laid his skull-cracker beside it, I signaled him to advance.

When he and I returned to my headquarters tent, the round-eye Tristan still stood there, leaning on his walking stick and with his free hand hungrily gnawing an ear of maize. At the sight of him, Chief Imathla burst into a tirade. Had he had his weapons to hand, I would not have wagered a brass cash on Tristan's life. The round-eye shouted back. When the polemics ran down, I said to Falaya:

"Ask whether this speech refers to the chief's daughter."

At length Falaya reported: "He say aye, it does. This round-eye carry off his daughter, delight of his age, and chief set out in pursuit. When his war party near this place, they come upon daughter Mihilayo wandering, lost, in forest, with some Piachi whom Espanyans enslave and now flee back home. From her chief learn that round-eye and his men fight great general and lose. He say he happy to see scoundrel captive, and he know some excellent tortures to dispose of him."

Tristan, to whom his own interpreter had been feeding a translation, visibly paled beneath his swarthy skin at the mention of torture. Then he squared his shoulders, raised his chin, and assumed an attitude of defiance, as captive redskin warriors are wont to do at the prospect of being burned alive by their foes. I could not help a twinge of admiration for his courage, barbarian though he was. He asked:

"Where be she now?"

Imathla replied: "Know that she is safe under her father's protection. Where that be is no affair of yours."

"She is my lawful wedded wife! That is whose affair it be! Fetch her here!"

I suggested: "That might be a sensible thought, O Chief, to unravel this knot."

"Never!" said Imathla. "You know not, O General, the depths of evil of these palefaces. Before they passed through our tribal lands, they had descended upon the Piachi tribe, whom they enslaved to furnish porters for their supplies. When some Piachi defied the palefaces' commands, the invaders seized them, chopped off their hands and feet, and cast them out to die. Others they strung up by the hands and affixed weights to their feet until they expired, or forced water down their throats until they burst inside."

"Why should they go to so much trouble? If one wishes to kill a man, it is quicker and easier to shoot him or chop off his head."

"They have a passion for that pretty yellow metal that we get in ornaments by trade from other tribes. They would not believe that there were no hidden stores of this metal, and they thought that by such treatment they could force the Piachi to reveal its whereabouts. Of course the Piachi are not Nanipacana and so not real human beings, or we should have felt obliged to avenge them.

"Twenty years ago the accursed Ernando de Soto came through, treating those who gainsaid him in this same ferocious manner. He also brought strange diseases amongst the tribes, whereof over half of us perished. Had our towns been still fully populated, O General, you would not have found it so easy to pass amongst us unscathed."

The round-eye was hopping up and down on his unwounded leg, indicating an eagerness to say his say. I told Falaya to give Tristan my permission. The barbarian shouted:

"These savages are too stupid and ignorant to appreciate the benefits we offer! They refuse to understand that by accepting our religion they may live to serve us, as is only right for such lowly folk, in return for the boons we bestow. Then, after death, they shall enjoy an eternity of pleasures in Heaven, praising the true God."

"Is that all you do in this Heaven?" I asked.

"What more is needed? We sit on clouds, play the *arpa*, and sing the praises of God."

"Forever?"

"Aye, forever."

This person commented: "Your Yuropian God must get bored with incessant flattery. Our gods are more rational; they are busy keeping records and otherwise carrying out their duties in the Heavenly bureaucracy."

When this had been translated, Tristan gave a contemptuous snort. But he forbore to argue theology, for which I doubt whether either of us had enough book knowledge. I regretted that the bonze Xiao-jin was no longer with us, having set out to return to his monastery in civilization. He would have argued spiritual matters with the barbarian all day and all the following night. Tristan said:

"I still demand my wife! I rescued her when two of my colonists would have raped her and then slain her for her golden earrings."

"All the demands in the world will not get the poor thing," said Chief Imathla. "She is well quit of you."

"Then fetch her here and let her choose her own fate!" cried Tristan.

"Ridiculous!" cried Imathla. Those twain began shouting again, until I roared them to silence. I said: "Come, honorable Chief, tell me: Is the woman where we can reach her?"

"She is under the protection of my personal guard," growled Imathla.

"Well, am I to understand that you wish her to be happy?"

"Aye, O General. That is my dearest wish, since her mother died of one of those diseases these accursed palefaces brought into our land."

"Then why not fetch her here, set the alternatives before her, and let her decide? If after that she be not happy, the fault will not be yours."

Imathla growled a bit, but after further argument I talked him round. The fact that he was alone in my tent, with rifle-bearing Hitchiti standing by, may have influenced his decision.

So Imathla put his head out the tent and called to one of his warriors. After some converse in Nanipacana, the warrior set off at a run. Whilst we waited, I caused tea to be brewed and offered to our guests. Imathla drank his, while Tristan took a mouthful, made a face, and returned the cup to the Hitchiti who had brought it.

At length the warrior returned, leading a young Nanipacana female. When she entered the tent, Tristan limped forward and seized her in an embrace. He performed that gesture of affection used by Yuropians and Arabs, of pressing the lips against the esteemed one.

Then Tristan placed his hands on the woman's shoulders and held her at arm's length. He said something sharply to her; she replied, and they argued. It sounded as if he were making some demand and she refusing. I asked Falaya for a translation.

"O General," he said, "he say she must cover self; she say no cover, too hot."

Mihilayo was clad in the normal garb of these southern redskins in hot weather, namely: naked save for a pair of golden earrings and reticular designs painted on her body and limbs. Yuropians, coming I suspect from a cooler climate, regard such exposure as improper.

A heated argument followed amongst the three: the woman Mihilayo, the round-eye Captain Tristan, and the Chieftain Imathla. Mihilayo and Imathla spake in Nanipacana, whilst Mihilayo and Tristan conversed in the tongue of Espanya, which she spake albeit somewhat brokenly. Tristan and Imathla, having no tongue in common, had to communicate through the interpreters.

At last Imathla said to me: "My daughter wishes to know if you, O General, need a wife."

The question so surprised me that for a few heartbeats I was unable to reply. At last I said:

"I have my Number One wife back at Fort Tai-ze. But she has long nagged me to take a second wife, to relieve her of some of the burdens of domesticity. Besides, she says that she is too old to enjoy the act of love any more, whereas I am still fully able. Suppose I did take Mihilayo as proposed; how would that sit with you?"

Imathla grinned. "I should deem it a splendid idea, giving me access to the General's ear, and high standing amongst the tribes."

"Does your daughter truly wish this?"

"She assures me that indeed she does."

"How about that previous indissoluble marriage to Captain Tristan?"

"Oh, she says that is easy. His Yuropian mumbo-jumbo means nought to her. If there be any doubt on that score, the answer is simple. Slay him and make her a widow, free to wed whom she likes under any nation's customs."

According to what I hear, she was not quite correct, since it is said that in India they burn widows alive. A wasteful custom, I should say. But I saw no point in correcting the woman.

When Tristan's interpreter had given him the gist of this dialogue, the round-eye uttered a scream of rage. Wrenching loose from his guards—for he was a powerful man—he limped forward, gripping his walking stick in both hands and raising it over his head. I know not whom he meant to bludgeon first: Mihilayo, Imathla, or me. Before he got within hitting distance, however, one of my guards fired his rifle at close range. With a howl of frustrated fury, Tristan fell back on my Tang-dynasty rug, writhed a little, and fell still. He was dead from a bullet that entered his ribs below the heart, came out his back, and punched a hole in the canvas behind him.

I questioned Imathla about Nanipacana marriage customs. He told me that when a man and a woman moved into the same hut, that was deemed a marriage. There were none of the processions, music, gifts, fireworks, and so forth that solemnize a wedding in civilization. Imathla said in Nanipacana that he gave Mihilayo to me, and that was that.

Later I asked my new bride why she had chosen me in lieu of her round-eye lover. That, she said, was simple. When she saw the power that Captain Tristan commanded by his thunder sticks and his armor and weapons of this Yuropian metal, she decided that he would make a suitable spouse and protector of her and their children. When she observed that I commanded even greater power, by my superior thunder sticks and my well-trained army, she decided that I should be an even more effective protector. Besides, the union would confer honor on her family, clan, and tribe. She added that Tristan stank; although redskins, as a result of smearing their bodies with animal fats to protect themselves against insect bites, are also fairly rank.

Such a foresightedly practical outlook makes me hopeful of eventually

raising the redskins to our level of civilization. About the emotional Yuropians I am more doubtful.

Now I am back in Fort Tai-ze with two wives. My Number One carped
about my taking a Number Two whom she had never seen, let alone chosen
for me; but that died down. A more vexing problem is acting as judge when
the two women daily disagree over some detail of household management.
Although Mihilayo is fast becoming fluent in the language of civilization, I
fear she does not fully accept her position as subordinate to the Number
One. She also tries to elicit from me more frequent love-making than is easy
for a man of middle age.

On the other hand, ere we parted, Chief Imathla declared his allegiance
to the Son of Heaven and placed the Nanipacana beneath our benevolent
protection.

With this letter I shall send samples of the guns and armor of the round-
eyes, to see whether they have features that might usefully be copied and
improved upon by our makers of armaments. I doubt that this be the case;
for in these techniques the men of Espanya seem to be about where we of
Zhongguo were a century and a half ago.

I regret the death of Captain Tristan de Luna, fool though he was. Had
he lived, I should have brought him back to Tai-ze. I should have questioned
him about conditions in Yuropa and amongst the men of Espanya who have
landed along the coasts of the Eastern Continent and begun to subdue and
enslave the redskins. If he proved reticent, I have ample means to loosen his
tongue.

But how typically barbarian to make such an unseemly fracas over so trivial
a matter as affection for a woman! As I said at the start, their customs are
strange, their beliefs outlandish, and their emotions childish. Let us thank
the divine bureaucrats that we, at least, are truly civilized!

DUST

Greg Egan

Born in 1961, Greg Egan lives in Australia, and is certainly in the running for the title of "Hottest New Writer" of the nineties to date, along with other newcomers such as Ian R. MacLeod, Maureen F. McHugh, Mary Rosenblum, Stephen Baxter, and Tony Daniel. Egan has been very impressive *and* very prolific in the early '90s, seeming to turn up almost everywhere with high-quality stories. He is a frequent contributor to *Interzone* and *Isaac Asimov's Science Fiction Magazine*, and has made sales to *Pulphouse, Analog, Aurealis, Eidolon,* and elsewhere. Several of his stories have appeared in various "Best of the Year" series, including this one; in fact, he placed *two* stories in *both* our Eighth and Ninth Annual Collections, the first author ever to do that back-to-back in consecutive volumes. His first novel, *Quarantine*, has just appeared, and it was sold as part of a package deal that includes a second novel and a collection of his short fiction—a pretty high-powered deal for such a new writer. He may well turn out to be one of the Big Names of the next decade.

Here he gives us an unsettling and brilliantly original study of just what it is that makes us *human* . . .

I open my eyes, blinking at the room's unexpected brightness, then lazily reach out to place one hand in a patch of sunlight spilling onto the bed from a gap between the curtains. Dust motes drift across the shaft of light, appearing for all the world to be conjured into, and out of, existence—evoking a childhood memory of the last time I found this illusion so compelling, so hypnotic. I feel utterly refreshed—and utterly disinclined to give up my present state of comfort. I don't know why I've slept so late, and I don't care. I spread my fingers on the sun-warmed sheet, and think about drifting back to sleep.

Something's troubling me, though. A dream? I pause and try to dredge up some trace of it, without much hope; unless I'm catapulted awake by a nightmare, my dreams tend to be evanescent. And yet—

I leap out of bed, crouch down on the carpet, fists to my eyes, face against my knees, lips moving soundlessly. The shock of realization is a palpable thing: a red lesion behind my eyes, pulsing with blood. Like . . . the aftermath of a hammer blow to the thumb—and tinged with the very same mixture of surprise, anger, humiliation, and idiot bewilderment. Another childhood memory: *I held a nail to the wood, yes—but only to camouflage my true intention. I was curious about everything, including pain. I'd seen my father injure himself this way—but I knew that I needed firsthand experience to understand what he'd been through. And I was sure that it would be worth it, right up to the very last moment—*

I rock back and forth, on the verge of laughter, trying to keep my mind blank, waiting for the panic to subside. And eventually, it does—laced by one simple, perfectly coherent thought: *I don't want to be here.*

For a moment, this conclusion seems unassailable, but then a countervailing voice rises up in me: *I'm not going to quit. Not again. I swore to myself that I wouldn't . . . and there are a hundred good reasons not to—*

Such as?

For a start, I can't afford it—

No? Who can't afford it?

I whisper, "I know *exactly* how much this cost, you bastard. And I honestly don't give a shit. *I'm not going through with it.*"

There's no reply. I clench my teeth, uncover my eyes, look around the room. Away from the few dazzling patches of direct sunshine, everything glows softly in the diffuse light: the matte-white brick walls, the imitation (imitation) mahogany desk; even the Dalí and Giger posters look harmless, domesticated. The simulation is perfect—or rather, finer-grained than my "visual" acuity, and hence indistinguishable from reality—as no doubt it was the other four times. Certainly, none of the other Copies complained about a lack of verisimilitude in their environments. In fact, they never said anything very coherent; they just ranted abuse, whined about their plight, and then terminated themselves—all within fifteen (subjective) minutes of gaining consciousness.

And me? What ever made me—him—think that I won't do the same? How am I different from Copy number four? Three years older. More stubborn? More determined? More desperate for success? I *was*, for sure . . . back when I was still thinking of myself as the one who'd stay real, the one who'd sit outside and watch the whole experiment from a safe distance.

Suddenly I wonder: What makes me so sure that I'm *not* outside? I laugh weakly. I don't remember anything after the scan, which is a bad sign, but I was overwrought, and I'd spent so long psyching myself up for "this" . . .

Get it over with.

I mutter the password, "Bremsstrahlung"—and my last faint hope vanishes, as a black-on-white square about a meter wide, covered in icons, appears in midair in front of me.

I give the interface window an angry thump; it resists me as if it were solid, and firmly anchored. *As if I were solid, too.* I don't really need any more convincing, but I grip the top edge and lift myself right off the floor. I regret this; the realistic cluster of effects of exertion—down to the plausible twinge in my right elbow—pin me to this "body," anchor me to this "place," in exactly the way I should be doing everything I can to avoid.

Okay. Swallow it: *I'm a Copy.* My memories may be those of a human being, but *I* will never inhabit a real body "again." Never inhabit *the real world* again . . . unless my cheapskate original scrapes up the money for a telepresence robot—in which case I could blunder around like the slowest, clumsiest, most neurologically impaired cripple. *My model-of-a-brain runs seventeen times slower than the real thing.* Yeah, sure, technology will catch up one day—and seventeen times faster for me than for him. In the mean-time? I rot in this prison, jumping through hoops, carrying out his precious research—while he lives in my apartment, spends my money, sleeps with Elizabeth. . . .

I close my eyes, dizzy and confused; I lean against the cool surface of the interface.

"His" research? I'm just as curious as him, aren't I? I wanted this; I did this to myself. Nobody forced me. I knew exactly what the drawbacks would be, but I thought I'd have the strength of will (this time, at last) to transcend them, to devote myself, monklike, to the purpose for which I'd been brought into being—content in the knowledge that my other self was as unconstrained as ever.

Past tense. Yes, I made the decision—but I never really faced up to the consequences. *Arrogant, self-deluding shit.* It was only the knowledge that "I" would continue, free, on the outside, that gave me the "courage" to go ahead—but that's no longer true, for *me.*

Ninety-eight percent of Copies made are of the very old, and the terminally ill. People for whom it's the last resort—most of whom have spent millions beforehand, exhausting all the traditional medical options. And despite the fact that they have no other choice, 15 percent decide upon awakening—usually in a matter of hours—that they just can't hack it.

And of those who are young and healthy, those who are merely curious, those who know they have a perfectly viable, living, breathing body outside?

The bail-out rate has been, so far, one hundred percent.

I stand in the middle of the room, swearing softly for several minutes, trying to prepare myself—although I know that the longer I leave it, the harder it will become. I stare at the floating interface; its dreamlike, hallucina-tory quality helps, slightly. I rarely remember my dreams, and I won't remem-ber this one—but there's no tragedy in that, is there?

I don't want to be here.

I don't want to be *this.*

And to think I used to find it so often disappointing, waking up yet again as the *real* Paul Durham: self-centered dilettante, spoiled by a medium-sized inheritance, too wealthy to gain any sense of purpose from the ordinary human struggle to survive—but insufficiently brain-dead to devote his life to the accumulation of ever more money and power. No status-symbol luxuries for Durham: no yachts, no mansions, no bioenhancements. He indulged other urges; threw his money in another direction entirely.

And I don't know, anymore, what he thinks it's done for *him*—but I know what it's done to *me.*

I suddenly realize that I'm still stark naked. Habit—if no conceivable propriety—suggests that I should put on some clothes, but I resist the urge. One or two perfectly innocent, perfectly ordinary actions like that, and I'll find I'm taking myself seriously, thinking of myself as real.

I pace the bedroom, grasp the cool metal of the doorknob a couple of times, but manage to keep myself from turning it. *There's no point even starting to explore this world.*

I can't resist peeking out the window, though. The view of the city is flawless—every building, every cyclist, every tree, is utterly convincing— and so it should be: it's a recording, not a simulation. Essentially photo-graphic—give or take a little computerized touching up and filling in—and totally predetermined. What's more, only a tiny part of it is "physically" accessible to me; I can see the harbor in the distance, but if I tried to go for a stroll down to the water's edge . . .

Enough. Just get it over with.

I prod a menu icon labeled UTILITIES; it spawns another window in front of the first. The function I'm seeking is buried several menus deep— but for all that I thought I'd convinced myself that I wouldn't want to use it, I brushed up on the details just a week ago, and I know exactly where to look. For all my self-deception, for all that I tried to relate only to *the one who'd stay outside*, deep down, I must have understood full well that I had two separate futures to worry about.

I finally reach the EMERGENCIES menu, which includes a cheerful icon of a cartoon figure suspended from a parachute. *Bailing out* is what they call it—but I don't find that too cloyingly euphemistic; after all, I can't commit "suicide" when I'm not legally human. In fact, the law requires that a bail-out option be available, without reference to anything so troublesome as the "rights" of the Copy; this stipulation arises solely from the ratification of certain purely technical, international software standards.

I prod the icon; it comes to life, and recites a warning spiel. I scarcely pay attention. Then it says, "Are you absolutely sure that you wish to shut down this Copy of Paul Durham?"

Nothing to it. Program A asks Program B to confirm its request for orderly termination. Packets of data are exchanged.

"Yes, I'm sure."

A metal box, painted red, appears at my feet. I open it, take out the parachute, strap it on.

Then I close my eyes and say, "Listen, you selfish, conceited, arrogant turd: How many times do you need to be told? I'll skip the personal angst; you've heard it all before—and ignored it all before. But when are you going to stop wasting your time, your money, your energy . . . when are you going to stop wasting your *life* . . . on something which you just don't have the strength to carry through? After all the evidence to the contrary, do you honestly still believe that you're brave enough, or crazy enough, to be your own guinea pig? Well, I've got news for you: *You're not.*"

With my eyes still closed, I grip the release lever.

I'm nothing: a dream, a soon-to-be-forgotten dream.

My fingernails need cutting; they dig painfully into the skin of my palm.

Have I never, in a dream, feared the extinction of waking? Maybe I have—but a dream is not a life. If the only way I can reclaim my body, reclaim my world, is to wake and forget—

I pull the lever.

After a few seconds, I emit a constricted sob—a sound more of confusion than any kind of emotion—and open my eyes.

The lever has come away in my hand.

I stare dumbly at this metaphor for . . . what? A bug in the termination software? Some kind of hardware glitch?

Feeling—at last—truly dreamlike, I unstrap the parachute, and unfasten the neatly packaged bundle.

Inside, there is no illusion of silk, or Kevlar, or whatever else there might plausibly have been. Just a sheet of paper. A note.

> *Dear Paul,*
>
> *The night after the scan was completed, I looked back over the whole preparatory stage of the project, and did a great deal of soul searching. And I came to the conclusion that—right up to the very last moment—my attitude was poisoned with ambivalence.*
>
> *With hindsight, I very quickly came to realize just how foolish my qualms were—but that was too late for you. I couldn't afford to ditch you, and have myself scanned yet again. So, what could I do?*
>
> *This: I put your awakening on hold for a while, and tracked down someone who could make a few alterations to the virtual environment utilities. I know, that wasn't strictly legal . . . but you know how important it is to me that you—that we—succeed this time.*
>
> *I trust you'll understand, and I'm confident that you'll accept the situation with dignity and equanimity.*
>
> *Best wishes,*
Paul

I sink to my knees, still holding the note, staring at it in disbelief. *He can't have done this. He can't have been so callous.*

No? Who am I kidding? Too weak to be so cruel to anyone else—perhaps. Too weak to go through with this in person—certainly. But as for making a Copy, and then—once its future was no longer *his* future, no longer anything for *him* to fear—taking away its power to escape . . .

It rings so true that I hang my head in shame.

Then I drop the note, raise my head, and bellow with all the strength in my non-existent lungs:

"DURHAM! YOU *PRICK!*"

※   ※   ※

I think about smashing furniture. Instead, I take a long, hot shower. In part, to calm myself; in part, as an act of petty vengeance: I may not be adding to the cheapskate's water bill, but he can damn well pay for twenty virtual minutes of gratuitous hydrodynamic calculations. I scrutinize the droplets and rivulets of water on my skin, searching for some small but visible anomaly at the boundary between my body—computed down to subcellular resolution—and the rest of the simulation, which is modeled much more crudely. If there are any discrepancies, though, they're too subtle for me to detect.

I dress—I'm just not comfortable naked—and eat a late breakfast. The muesli tastes exactly like muesli, the toast exactly like toast, but I know there's a certain amount of cheating going on with both taste and aroma. The detailed effects of chewing, and the actions of saliva, are being faked from empirical rules, not generated from first principles; there are no individual molecules being dissolved from the food and torn apart by enzymes—just a rough set of evolving nutrient concentration values, associated with each microscopic "parcel" of saliva. Eventually, these will lead to plausible increases in the concentrations of amino acids, various carbohydrates, and other substances all the way down to humble sodium and chloride ions, in similar "parcels" of gastric juices . . . which in turn will act as input data to the models of my intestinal villus cells. From there, into the bloodstream.

The coffee makes me feel alert, but also slightly detached—as always. Neurons, of course, are modeled with the greatest care of all, and whatever receptors to caffeine and its metabolites were present on each individual neuron in my original's brain at the time of the scan, my model-of-a-brain should incorporate every one of them—in a simplified, but functionally equivalent, form.

I close my eyes and try to imagine the physical reality behind all this: a cubic meter of silent, motionless optical crystal, configured as a cluster of over a billion individual processors, one of a few hundred identical units in a basement vault . . . somewhere on the planet. I don't even know what city I'm in; the scan was made in Sydney, but the model's implementation would have been contracted out by the local node to the lowest bidder at the time.

I take a sharp vegetable knife from the kitchen drawer, and drive the point a short way into my forearm. I flick a few drops of blood onto the table— and wonder exactly which software is now responsible for the stuff. Will the blood cells "die off" slowly—or have they already been surrendered to the extrasomatic general-physics model, far too unsophisticated to represent them, let alone keep them "alive"?

If I tried to slit my wrists, when exactly would he intervene? I gaze at my distorted reflection in the blade. Maybe he'd let me die, and then run the whole model again from scratch, simply leaving out the knife. After all, I reran all the earlier Copies hundreds of times, tampering with various aspects of their surroundings, trying in vain to find some cheap trick that would keep them from wanting to bail out. It must be a measure of sheer stubbornness that it took me—him—so long to admit defeat and rewrite the rules.

I put down the knife. I don't want to perform that experiment. Not yet.

I go exploring, although I don't know what I'm hoping to find. Outside my own apartment, everything is slightly less than convincing; the architecture of the building is reproduced faithfully enough, down to the ugly plastic pot-plants, but every corridor is deserted, and every door to every other apartment is sealed shut—concealing, literally, nothing. I kick one door, as hard as I can; the wood seems to give slightly, but when I examine the surface, the paint isn't even marked. The model will admit to no damage here, and the laws of physics can screw themselves.

There are people and cyclists on the street—all purely recorded. They're solid rather than ghostly, but it's an eerie kind of solidity; unstoppable, unswayable, they're like infinitely strong, infinitely disinterested robots. I hitch a ride on one frail old woman's back for a while; she carries me down the street, heedlessly. Her clothes, her skin, even her hair, all feel the same to me: hard as steel. Not cold, though. Neutral.

This street isn't meant to serve as anything but three-dimensional wallpaper; when Copies interact with each other, they often use cheap, recorded environments full of purely decorative crowds. Plazas, parks, open-air cafés; all very reassuring, no doubt, when you're fighting off a sense of isolation and claustrophobia. There are only about three thousand Copies in existence—a small population, split into even smaller, mutually antagonistic, cliques—and they can only receive realistic external visitors if they have friends or relatives willing to slow down their mental processes by a factor of seventeen. Most dutiful next-of-kin, I gather, prefer to exchange video recordings. Who wants to spend an afternoon with great-grandfather, when it burns up half a week of your life? Durham, of course, has removed all of my communications facilities; he can't have me blowing the whistle on him and ruining everything.

When I reach the corner of the block, the visual illusion of the city continues, far into the distance, but when I try to step forward onto the road, the concrete pavement under my feet starts acting like a treadmill, sliding backward at precisely the rate needed to keep me motionless, whatever pace I adopt. I back off and try leaping over this region, but my horizontal velocity dissipates—without the slightest pretense of any "physical" justification—and I land squarely in the middle of the treadmill.

The people of the recording, of course, cross the border with ease. One man walks straight at me; I stand my ground, and find myself pushed into a zone of increasing viscosity, the air around me becoming painfully unyielding before I slip free to one side. The software impeding me is, clearly, a set of clumsy patches which aims to cover every contingency—but which might not in fact be complete. The sense that discovering a way to breach this barrier would somehow "liberate" me is compelling—but completely irrational. Even if I did find a flaw in the program which enabled me to break through, I doubt I'd gain anything but decreasingly realistic surroundings. The recording can only contain complete information for points of view within a certain, finite zone; all there is to "escape to" is a range of coordinates where my view of the city would be full of distortions and omissions, and would eventually fade to black.

I step back from the corner, half dispirited, half amused. What did I expect to find? A big door at the edge of the model, marked EXIT, through which I could walk out into reality? Stairs leading metaphorically down to some boiler room representation of the underpinnings of this world, where I could throw a few switches and blow it all apart? Hardly. I have no right to be dissatisfied with my surroundings; they're precisely what I ordered.

It's early afternoon on a perfect spring day; I close my eyes and lift my face to the sun. Whatever I believe intellectually, there's no denying that I'm beginning to feel a purely physical sense of integrity, of identity. My skin soaks up the warmth of the sunlight. I stretch the muscles in my arms, my shoulders, my back; the sensation is perfectly ordinary, perfectly familiar—and yet I feel that I'm reaching out from the self "in my skull" to the rest of me, binding it all together, staking some kind of claim. I feel the stirrings of an erection. *Existence is beginning to seduce me.* This body doesn't want to evaporate. This body doesn't want to bail out. It doesn't much care that there's another—"more real"—version of itself elsewhere. It wants to retain its wholeness. It wants to *endure*.

And this may be a travesty of life, now—but there's always the chance of improvement. Maybe I can persuade Durham to restore my communications facilities; that would be a start. And when I get bored with holovision libraries; news systems; databases; and, if any of them deign to meet me, the ghosts of the senile rich? I could have myself suspended until processor speeds catch up with reality—when people will be able to visit without slow-down, and telepresence robots might actually be worth inhabiting.

I open my eyes, and shiver. I don't know what I want anymore—the chance to bail out, to declare this bad dream *over* . . . or the chance of virtual immortality—but I have to accept that there's only one way that I'm going to be given a choice.

I say quietly, "I won't be your guinea pig. A collaborator, yes. An equal partner. If you want cooperation, if you want meaningful data, then you're going to have to treat me like a *colleague*, not a piece of fucking apparatus. Understood?"

A window opens up in front of me. I'm shaken by the sight, not of his ugly face, but of the room behind him. It's only my study—and I wandered through the virtual equivalent, disinterested, just minutes ago—but this is still my first glimpse of the real world, in real time. I move closer to the window, in the hope of seeing if there's anyone else in the room with him—*Elizabeth?*—but the image is two-dimensional, the perspective doesn't change.

He emits a brief, high-pitched squeak, then waits with visible impatience while a second, smaller window gives me a slowed-down replay.

"Of course it's understood. That was always my intention. I'm just glad you've finally come to your senses and decided to stop sulking. We can begin whenever you're ready."

I try to look at things objectively.

Every Copy is already an experiment—in perception, cognition, the nature of consciousness. A sub-cellular mathematical model of a specific human body is a spectacular feat of medical imaging and computing technology—but it's certainly not itself a human being. A lump of gallium arsenic phosphide awash with laser light is not a member of *Homo sapiens*— so a Copy manifestly isn't "human" in the current sense of the word.

The real question is: What does a Copy have *in common with* human beings? Information-theoretically? Psychologically? Metaphysically?

And from these similarities and differences, what can be revealed?

The Strong AI Hypothesis declares that consciousness is a property of certain algorithms, independent of their implementation. A computer which manipulates data in essentially the same way as an organic brain must possess essentially the same mental states.

Opponents point out that when you model a hurricane, nobody gets wet. When you model a fusion power plant, no energy is produced. When you model digestion and metabolism, no nutrients are consumed—no *real digestion* takes place. So when you model the human brain, why should you expect *real thought* to occur?

It depends, of course, on what you mean by "real thought." How do you characterize and compare the hypothetical mental states of two systems which are, physically, radically dissimilar? Pick the right parameters, and you can get whatever answer you like. If consciousness is defined purely in terms of physiological events—actual neurotransmitter molecules crossing synapses between real neurons—then those who oppose the Strong AI Hypothesis win, effortlessly. A hurricane requires real wind and actual drops of rain. If consciousness is defined, instead, in information-processing terms—*this* set of input data evokes *that* set of output data (and, perhaps, a certain kind of internal representation)—then the Strong AI Hypothesis is almost a tautology.

Personally, I'm no longer in a position to quibble. *Cogito ergo sum.* But if I can't doubt my own consciousness, I can't expect my testimony—the output of a mere computer program—to persuade the confirmed skeptics. Even if I passionately insisted that my inherited memories of experiencing biological consciousness were qualitatively indistinguishable from my present condition, the listener would be free to treat this outburst as nothing but a computer's (eminently reasonable) prediction of what my original *would have said*, had he experienced exactly the same sensory input as my model-of-a-brain has received (and thus been tricked into believing that he was nothing but a Copy). The skeptics would say that comprehensive modeling of *mental states that might have been* does not require any "real thought" to have taken place.

Unless you *are* a Copy, the debate is unresolvable. For *me*, though—and for anyone willing to grant me the same presumption of consciousness that they grant their fellow humans—the debate is almost irrelevant. The real point is that there are questions about the nature of this condition which a Copy is infinitely better placed to explore than any human being.

I sit in my study, in my favorite armchair (although I'm not at all convinced that the texture of the surface has been accurately reproduced). Durham appears on my terminal—which is otherwise still dysfunctional. It's odd, but I'm already beginning to think of him as a bossy little *djinn* trapped inside the screen, rather than a vast, omnipotent deity striding the halls of Reality, pulling all the strings. Perhaps the pitch of his voice has something to do with it.

Squeak. Slow-motion replay: "Experiment one, trial zero. Baseline data. Time resolution one millisecond—system standard. Just count to ten, at one-second intervals, as near as you can judge it. Okay?"

I nod, irritated. I planned all this myself, I don't need step-by-step instructions. His image vanishes; during the experiments, there can't be any cues from real time.

I count. Already, I'm proving something: my subjective time, I'm sure, will differ from his by a factor very close to the ratio of model time to real time. Of course, that's been known ever since the first Copies were made—and even then, it was precisely what everyone had been expecting—but from my current perspective, I can no longer think of it as a "trivial" result.

The *djinn* returns. Staring at his face makes it harder, not easier, to believe that we have so much in common. My image of myself—to the extent that such a thing existed—was never much like my true appearance—and now, in defense of sanity, is moving even further away.

Squeak. "Okay. Experiment one, trial number one. Time resolution five milliseconds. Are you ready?"

"Yes."

He vanishes. I count: "One. Two. Three. Four. Five. Six. Seven. Eight. Nine. Ten."

Squeak. "Anything to report?"

I shrug. "No. I mean, I can't help feeling slightly apprehensive, just knowing that you're screwing around with my . . . infrastructure. But apart from that, nothing."

His eyes no longer glaze over while he's waiting for the speeded-up version of my reply; either he's gained a degree of self-discipline—or, more likely, he's interposed some smart editing software to conceal his boredom.

Squeak. "Don't worry about apprehension. We're running a control, remember?"

I'd rather not. Durham has cloned me, and he's feeding exactly the same sensorium to my clone, but he's only making changes in the model's time resolution for one of us. A perfectly reasonable thing to do—indeed, an essential part of the experiment—but it's still something I'd prefer not to dwell on.

Squeak. "Trial number two. Time resolution ten milliseconds."

I count to ten. The easiest thing in the world—when you're made of flesh, when you're made of matter, when the quarks and the electrons just do what comes naturally. I'm not built of quarks and electrons, though. I'm not even built of photons—I'm comprised of the data *represented by* the presence or absence of pulses of light, not the light itself.

A human being is embodied in a system of continuously interacting matter—ultimately, fields of fundamental particles, which seem to me incapable of being anything other than themselves. *I* am embodied in a vast set of finite, digital representations of numbers. Representations which are purely conventions. Numbers which certainly *can be* interpreted as describing aspects of a model of a human body sitting in a room . . . but it's hard to see that meaning as intrinsic, as *necessary*. Numbers whose values are recomputed—according to reasonable, but only approximately "physical," equations—for equally spaced successive values of the model's notional time.

Squeak. "Trial number three. Time resolution twenty milliseconds."

"One. Two. Three."

So, when do *I* experience existence? During the computation of these variables—or in the brief interludes when they sit in memory, unchanging, doing nothing but *representing* an instant of my life? When both stages are taking place a thousand times a subjective second, it hardly seems to matter, but very soon—

Squeak. "Trial number four. Time resolution fifty milliseconds."

Am I the data? The process that generates it? The relationships between the numbers? *All of the above?*

"One hundred milliseconds."

I listen to my voice as I count—as if half expecting to begin to notice the encroachment of silence, to start perceiving the gaps in myself.

"Two hundred milliseconds."

A fifth of a second. "One. Two." Am I strobing in and out of existence now, at five subjective hertz? "Three. Four. Sorry, I just—" An intense wave of nausea passes through me, but I fight it down. "Five. Six. Seven. Eight. Nine. Ten."

The *djinn* emits a brief, solicitous squeak. "Do you want a break?"

"No. I'm fine. Go ahead." I glance around the sun-dappled room, and laugh. *What will he do if the control and the subject just gave two different replies?* I try to recall my plans for such a contingency, but I can't remember them—and I don't much care. It's *his* problem now, not mine.

Squeak. "Trial number seven. Time resolution five hundred milliseconds."

I count—and the truth is, I feel no different. A little uneasy, yes—but factoring out any metaphysical squeamishness, everything about my experience remains the same. And "of course" it does—because nothing is being omitted, in the long run. My model-of-a-brain is only being fully described at half-second (model time) intervals—but each description still includes the effects of everything that "would have happened" in between. Perhaps not quite as accurately as if the complete cycle of calculations was being carried out on a finer time scale—but that's irrelevant. Even at millisecond resolution, my models-of-neurons behave only roughly like their originals—just as any one person's neurons behave only roughly like anyone else's. Neurons aren't precision components, and they don't need to be; brains are the most fault-tolerant machines in the world.

"One thousand milliseconds."

What's more, the equations controlling the model are far too complex to solve in a single step, so in the process of calculating the solutions, vast arrays of partial results are being generated and discarded along the way. These partial results *imply*—even if they don't directly *represent*—events taking place within the gaps between successive complete descriptions. So in a sense, the intermediate states are still being described—albeit in a drastically recoded form.

"Two thousand milliseconds."

"One. *Two*. Three. *Four*."

If I seem to speak (and hear myself speak) every number, it's because the effects of having said "three" (and having heard myself say it) are implicit in the details of calculating how my brain evolves from the time when I've just said "two" to the time when I've just said "four."

"Five thousand milliseconds."

"One. Two. Three. Four. *Five*."

In any case, is it so much stranger to hear words that I've never "really" spoken, than it has been to hear *anything at all* since I woke? Millisecond sampling is far too coarse to resolve the full range of audible tones. Sound isn't represented in this world by fluctuations in air pressure values—which couldn't change fast enough—but in terms of audio power spectra: profiles of intensity versus frequency. Twenty kilohertz is just a number here, a label; nothing can actually *oscillate* at that rate. Real ears analyze pressure waves into components of various pitch; mine are fed the pre-existing power spectrum values directly, plucked out of the non-existent air by a crude patch in the model.

"Ten thousand milliseconds."

"One. Two. Three."

My sense of continuity remains as compelling as ever. Is this experience arising in retrospect from the final, complete description of my brain . . . or is it emerging from the partial calculations as they're being performed? What would happen if someone shut down the whole computer, right now?

I don't know what that *means*, though. In any terms but my own, I don't know when "right now" *is*.

"Eight. Nine. Ten."

Squeak. "How are you feeling?"

Slightly giddy—but I shrug and say, "The same as always." And basically, it's true. Aside from the unsettling effects of contemplating what might or might not have been happening to me, I can't claim to have experienced anything out of the ordinary. No altered states of consciousness, no hallucinations, no memory loss, no diminution of self-awareness, no real disorientation. "Tell me—was I the control, or the subject?"

Squeak. He grins. "I can't answer that, Paul—I'm still speaking to both of you. I'll tell you one thing, though: the two of you are still identical. There were some very small, transitory discrepancies, but they've died away completely now—and whenever the two of you were in comparable representations, all firing patterns of more than a couple of neurons were the same."

I'm curiously disappointed by this—*and my clone must be, too*—although I have no good reason to be surprised.

I say, "What did you expect? Solve the same set of equations two different ways, and of course you get the same results—give or take some minor differences in round-off errors along the way. You *must*. It's a mathematical certainty."

Squeak. "Oh, I agree. However much we change the details of the way the model is computed, the state of the subject's brain—whenever he has one—and everything he says and does—in whatever convoluted representation—*must* match the control. Any other result would be unthinkable." He writes with his finger on the window:

$$(1 + 2) + 3 = 1 + (2 + 3)$$

I nod. "So why bother with this stage at all? I *know*—I wanted to be rigorous, I wanted to establish solid foundations. All that naive *Principia* stuff. But the truth is, it's a waste of resources. Why not skip the bleeding obvious, and get on with the kind of experiment where the answer isn't a foregone conclusion?"

Squeak. He frowns. "I didn't realize you'd grown so cynical, so quickly. AI isn't a branch of pure mathematics; it's an empirical science. Assumptions have to be tested. Confirming the so-called 'obvious' isn't such a dishonorable thing, is it? Anyway, if it's all so straightforward, what do you have to fear?"

I shake my head. "I'm not afraid; I just want to get it over with. Go ahead. Prove whatever you think you have to prove, and then we can move on."

Squeak. "That's the plan. But I think we should both get some rest now. I'll enable your communications—for incoming data only." He turns away, reaches off-screen, hits a few keys on a second terminal.

Then he turns back to me, smiling—and I know exactly what he's going to say.

Squeak. "By the way, I just deleted one of you. Couldn't afford to keep you both running, when all you're going to do is laze around."

I smile back at him, although something inside me is screaming. "Which one did you terminate?"

Squeak. "What difference does it make? I told you, they were identical. And you're still here, aren't you? Whoever you are. Whichever you *were*."

*   *   *

Three weeks have passed outside since the day of the scan, but it doesn't take me long to catch up with the state of the world; most of the fine details have been rendered irrelevant by subsequent events, and much of the ebb and flow has simply canceled itself out. Israel and Palestine came close to war again, over alleged water treaty violations on both sides—but a joint peace rally brought more than a million people onto the glassy plain that used to be Jerusalem, and the governments were forced to back down. Former US President Martin Sandover is still fighting extradition to Palau, to face charges arising from his role in the bloody *coup d'état* of thirty-five; the Supreme Court finally reversed a long-standing ruling which had granted him immunity from all foreign laws, and for a day or two things looked promising— but then his legal team apparently discovered a whole new set of delaying tactics. In Canberra, another leadership challenge has come and gone, with the Prime Minister undeposed. One journalist described this as *high drama*; I guess you had to be there. Inflation has fallen half a percent; unemployment has risen by the same amount.

I scan through the old news reports rapidly, skimming over articles and fast-forwarding scenes that I probably would have studied scrupulously, had they been "fresh." I feel a curious sense of resentment, at having "missed" so much—it's all here in front of me, *now*, but that's not the same at all.

And yet, shouldn't I be relieved that I didn't waste my time on so much ephemeral detail? The very fact that I'm now disinterested only goes to show how little of it really mattered, in the long run.

Then again, what does? People don't inhabit geological time. People inhabit hours and days; they have to care about things on that time scale.

People inhabit hours and days. *I* don't.

I plug into real time holovision, and watch a sitcom flash by in less than two minutes, the soundtrack an incomprehensible squeal. A game show. A war movie. The evening news. It's as if I'm in deep space, rushing back toward the Earth through a sea of Doppler-shifted broadcasts—and this image is strangely comforting: my situation isn't so bizarre, after all, if *real people* could find themselves in much the same relationship with the world as I am. Nobody would claim that Doppler shift or time dilation could render some- one less than human.

Dusk falls over the recorded city. I eat a microwaved soya protein stew— wondering if there's any good reason now, moral or otherwise, to continue to be a vegetarian.

I listen to music until well after midnight. Tsang Chao, Michael Nyman, Philip Glass. It makes no difference that each note "really" lasts seventeen times as long as it should, or that the audio ROM sitting in the player "really" possesses no microstructure, or that the "sound" itself is being fed into my model-of-a-brain by a computerized sleight-of-hand that bears no resem- blance to the ordinary process of hearing. The climax of Glass's *Mishima* still seizes me like a grappling hook through the heart.

If the computations behind *all this* were performed over millennia, by people flicking abacus beads, would I still feel exactly the same? It's outrageous to admit it—but the answer has to be *yes*.

What does that say about real time, and real space?

I lie in bed, wondering: *Do I still want to wake from this dream?* The question remains academic, though; I still don't have any choice.

"I'd like to talk to Elizabeth."

Squeak. "That's not possible."

"Not possible? Why don't you just ask her?"

Squeak. "I can't do that, Paul. She doesn't even know you exist."

I stare at the screen. "But . . . I was going to tell her! As soon as I had a Copy who survived, I was going to tell her everything, explain everything—"

Squeak. The *djinn* says drily, "Or so we thought."

"I don't believe it! Your life's great ambition is finally being fulfilled—and you can't even share it with the one woman . . . ."

Squeak. His face turns to stone. "I really don't wish to discuss this. Can we get on with the experiment, please?"

"Oh, sure. Don't let me hold things up. I almost forgot: you turned forty-five while I slept, didn't you? Many happy returns—but I'd better not waste too much time on congratulations. I don't want you dying of old age in the middle of the conversation."

Squeak. "Ah, but you're wrong. I took some short cuts while you slept—shut down ninety percent of the model, cheated on most of the rest. You got six hours' sleep in ten hours' real time. Not a bad job, I thought."

"You had no right to do that!"

Squeak. "Be practical. Ask yourself what you'd have done in my place."

"It's not a *joke!*" I can sense the streak of paranoia in my anger; I struggle to find a rational excuse. "The experiment is worthless if you're going to intervene at random. Precise, controlled changes—that's the whole point. You have to promise me you won't do it again."

Squeak. "You're the one who was complaining about waste. Someone has to think about conserving our dwindling resources."

"Promise me!"

Squeak. He shrugs. "All right. You have my word: no more ad hoc intervention."

Conserving our dwindling resources? What will he do, when he can no longer afford to keep me running? Store me until he can raise the money to start me up again, of course. In the long term, set up a trust fund; it would only have to earn enough to run me part time, at first: keep me in touch with the world, stave off excessive culture shock. Eventually, computing technology is sure to transcend the current hurdles, and once again enter a phase of plummeting costs and increasing speed.

Of course, all these reassuring plans were made by a man with two futures. *Will he really want to keep an old Copy running, when he could save his money for a death-bed scan, and "his own" immortality?* I don't know. And I may not be sure if I *want* to survive—but I wish the choice could be *mine*.

We start the second experiment. I do my best to concentrate, although I'm angry and distracted—and very nearly convinced that my dutiful introspection is pointless. Until the model itself is changed—not just the detailed way it's computed—it remains a mathematical certainty that the subject and the control will end up with identical brains. If the subject claims to have experienced anything out of the ordinary, then *so will the control*—proving that the effect was spurious.

And yet, I still can't shrug off any of this as "trivial." Durham was right about one thing: there's no dishonor in confirming the obvious—and when it's as bizarre, as counterintuitive as this, the only way to believe it is to experience it firsthand.

This time, the model will be described at the standard resolution of one millisecond, throughout—but the order in which the states are computed will be varied.

Squeak. "Experiment two, trial number one. Reverse order."

I count, "One. Two. Three." After an initial leap into the future, I'm now traveling backward through real time. I wish I could view an external event on the terminal—some entropic cliché like a vase being smashed—and dwell on the fact that it was *me*, not the image, that was being rewound . . . but that would betray the difference between subject and control. Unless the control was shown an artificially reversed version of the same thing? Reversed how, though, if the vase was destroyed in real time? The control would have to be run separately, after the event. Ah, but even the *subject* would have to see a delayed version, because computing his real-time-first but model-time-final state would require information on all his model-time-earlier perceptions of the broken vase.

"Eight. Nine. Ten." Another imperceptible leap into the future, and the *djinn* reappears.

Squeak. "Trial number two. Odd numbered states, then even."

In external terms, I will count to ten . . . then forget having done so, and count again.

And from *my* point of view? As I count, once only, the external world—even if I can't see it—is flickering back and forth between two separate regions of time, which have been chopped up into seventeen-millisecond portions, and interleaved.

So which of us is *right*? Relativity may insist upon equal status for all reference frames . . . but the coordinate transformations it describes are smooth—possibly extreme, but always continuous. One observer's spacetime can be stretched and deformed in the eyes of another—but it can't be sliced like a loaf of bread, and then shuffled like a deck of cards.

"Every tenth state, in ten sets."

If I insisted on being parochial, I'd have to claim that the outside world was now rapidly cycling through fragments of time drawn from ten distinct periods. The trouble is, this allegedly shuddering universe is home to all the processes that implement me, and they *must*—in some objective, absolute sense—be running smoothly, bound together in unbroken causal flow, or I wouldn't even exist. My perspective is artificial, a contrivance relying on an underlying, continuous reality.

"Every twentieth state, in twenty sets."

Nineteen episodes of amnesia, nineteen new beginnings. How can I swallow such a convoluted explanation for ten perfectly ordinary seconds of my life?

"Every hundredth state, in one hundred sets."

I've lost any real feeling for what's happening to me. I just count.

"Pseudo-random ordering of states."

"One. Two. Three."

Now I am dust. Uncorrelated moments scattered throughout real time. Yet the pattern of my awareness remains perfectly intact: it finds itself, assembles itself from these scrambled fragments. I've been taken apart like a jigsaw puzzle—but my dissection and shuffling are transparent to me. On their *own* terms, the pieces remain connected.

How? Through the fact that every state reflects its entire model-time past? Is the jigsaw analogy wrong—am I more like the fragments of a hologram? But in each millisecond snapshot, do I recall and review all that's gone before? Of course not! In each snapshot, I *do* nothing. In the computations between them, then? Computations that drag me into the past and the future at random—wildly adding and subtracting experience, until it all cancels out in the end—or rather, all adds up to the very same effect as ten subjective seconds of continuity.

"Eight. Nine. Ten."

Squeak. "You're sweating."

"Both of me?"

Squeak. He laughs. "What do you think?"

"Do me a favor. The experiment is over. Shut down one of me—control or subject, I don't care."

Squeak. "Done."

"Now there's no need to conceal anything, is there? So run the pseudo-random effect on me again—and stay on-line. This time, *you* count to ten."

Squeak. He shakes his head. "Can't do it, Paul. Think about it: You can't be computed non-sequentially when past perceptions aren't known."

Of course; the broken vase problem all over again. I say, "Record yourself, then, and use that."

He seems to find the request amusing, but he indulges me; he even slows down the recording, so it lasts ten of my own seconds. I watch his blurred lips and jaws, listen to the drone of white noise.

Squeak. "Happy now?"

"You did scramble *me*, and not the recording?"

Squeak. "Of course. Your wish is my command."

"Yeah? Then do it again."

He grimaces, but obliges.

"Now, scramble *the recording*."

It looks just the same. Of course.

"Again."

Squeak. "What's the point of all this?"

"Just do it."

I'm convinced that I'm on the verge of a profound insight—arising, not from any revelatory aberration in my mental processes, but from the "obvious," "inevitable" fact that the wildest permutations of the relationship between model time and real time leave me perfectly intact. I've accepted the near certainty of this, tacitly, for twenty years—but the experience is provocative in a way that the abstract understanding never could be.

It needs to be pushed further, though. The truth has to be shaken out of me.

"When do we move on to the next stage?"

Squeak. "Why so keen all of a sudden?"

"Nothing's changed. I just want to get it over and done with."

Squeak. "Well, lining up all the other machines is taking some delicate negotiations. The network allocation software isn't designed to accommodate whims about geography. It's a bit like going to a bank and asking to deposit some money . . . at a certain location in a particular computer's memory. Basically, people think I'm crazy."

I feel a momentary pang of empathy, recalling my own anticipation of these difficulties. *Empathy verging on identification.* I smother it, though; we're two utterly different people now, with different problems and different goals, and the stupidest thing I could do would be to forget that.

Squeak. "I could suspend you while I finalize the arrangements, save you the boredom, if that's what you want."

I have a lot to think about, and not just the implications of the last experiment. If he gets into the habit of shutting me down at every opportunity, I'll "soon" find myself faced with decisions that I'm not prepared to make.

"Thanks. But I'd rather wait."

I walk around the block a few times, to stretch my legs and switch off my mind. I can't dwell on the knowledge of what I am, every waking moment; if I did, I'd soon go mad. There's no doubt that the familiar streetscape helps me forget my bizarre nature, lets me take myself for granted and run on autopilot for a while.

It's hard to separate fact from rumor, but apparently even the gigarich tend to live in relatively mundane surroundings, favoring realism over power fantasies. A few models-of-psychotics have reportedly set themselves up as dictators in opulent palaces, waited on hand and foot, but most Copies have aimed for an illusion of continuity. If you desperately want to convince yourself that you *are* the same person as your memories suggest, the worst thing to do would be to swan around a virtual antiquity (with mod cons), pretending to be Cleopatra or Ramses II.

I certainly don't believe that I "am" my original, but . . . why do I believe that I exist *at all?* What gives me my sense of identity? Continuity. Consistency. Once I would have dragged in *cause and effect,* but I'm not sure that I still can. The cause and effect that underlies me bears no resemblance whatsoever to the pattern of my experience—not now, and least of all when the software was dragging me back and forth through time. I can't deny that the computer which runs me is obeying the real-time physical laws—and I'm sure that, to a real-time observer, those laws would provide a completely satisfactory explanation for every pulse of laser light that constitutes my world, my flesh, my being. And yet . . . if it makes *no perceptible difference to me* whether I'm a biological creature, embodied in real cells built of real proteins built of real atoms built of real electrons and quarks . . . or a randomly time-scrambled set of descriptions of a crude model-of-a-brain . . . then surely *the pattern* is all, and cause and effect are irrelevant. The whole experience might just as well have arisen by chance.

Is that conceivable? Suppose an intentionally haywire computer sat for a thousand years or more, twitching from state to state in the sway of nothing but electrical noise. *Might it embody consciousness?*

In real time, the answer is: *Probably not*—the chance of any kind of coherence arising at random being so small. Real time, though, is only one possible reference frame; what about all the others? If the states the machine passed through can be re-ordered in time arbitrarily (with some states omitted—perhaps *most* omitted, if need be) then who knows what kind of elaborate order might emerge from the chaos?

Is that fatuous? As absurd, as empty, as claiming that every large-enough quantity of rock—contiguous or not—contains Michelangelo's *David*, and every warehouse full of paint and canvas contains the complete works of Rembrandt and Picasso—not in any mere latent form, awaiting some skilful forger to physically rearrange them, but *solely by virtue of the potential redefinition of the coordinates of space-time?*

For a statue or a painting, yes, it's a hollow claim—where is the observer who perceives the paint to be in contact with the canvas, the stone figure to be suitably delineated by air?

If the pattern in question is *not* an isolated object, though, but *a self-contained world*, complete with at least one observer to join up the dots . . .

There's no doubt that it's possible. *I've done it.* I've assembled myself and my world—effortlessly—from the dust of randomly scattered states, from apparent noise in real time. Specially contrived noise, admittedly—but given enough of the real thing, there's no reason to believe that some subset of it wouldn't include patterns, embody relationships, as complex and coherent as the ones which underly me.

I return to the apartment, fighting off a sense of giddiness and unreality. *Do I still want to bail out?* No. *No!* I still wish that he'd never created me—but how can I declare that I'd happily wake and forget myself—wake and "reclaim" my life—when already I've come to an insight that he never would have reached himself?

The *djinn* looks tired and frayed; all the begging and bribery he must have been through to set this up seems to have taken its toll.

Squeak. "Experiment three, trial zero. Baseline data. All computations performed by processor cluster number four six two, Hitachi Supercomputer Facility, Tokyo."

"One. Two. Three." *Nice to know where I am, at last. Never visited Japan before.* "Four. Five. Six." *And in my own terms, I still haven't. The view out the window is Sydney, not Tokyo. Why should I defer to external descriptions?* "Seven. Eight. Nine. Ten."

Squeak. "Trial number one. Model partitioned into five hundred sections, run on five hundred processor clusters, distributed globally."

I count. *Five hundred clusters.* Five only for the crudely modeled external world; all the rest are allocated to my body—and most to the brain, of course. I lift my hand to my eyes—and the information flow that grants me motor control and sight now traverses tens of thousands of kilometers of optical cable. This introduces no perceptible delays; each part of me simply hibernates when necessary, waiting for the requisite feedback from around the world. Moderately distributed processing is one thing, but *this* is pure lunacy, computationally and economically. I must be costing at least a hundred times as much as usual—not quite five hundred, since each cluster's capacity is only being partly used—and my model-time to real-time factor must be more like fifty than seventeen.

Squeak. "Trial number two. One thousand sections, one thousand clusters."

Brain the size of a planet—and here I am, counting to ten. I recall the perennial—naïve and paranoid—fear that all the networked computers of the world might one day spontaneously give birth to a global hypermind—but I am, almost certainly, the first planet-sized intelligence on Earth. I don't feel much like a digital Gaia, though. I feel like an ordinary human being sitting in an ordinary armchair.

Squeak. "Trial number three. Model partitioned into fifty sections and twenty time sets, implemented on one thousand clusters."

"One. Two. Three." I try to imagine the outside world in my terms, but it's almost impossible. Not only am I scattered across the globe, but widely separated machines are simultaneously computing different moments of model-time. Is the distance from Tokyo to New York now the length of my *corpus callosum?* Has the planet been shrunk to the size of my skull—and banished from time altogether, except for the fifty points that contribute to my notion of the present?

Such a pathological transformation seems nonsensical—but in some hypothetical space traveler's eyes, the whole planet is virtually frozen in time and flat as a pancake. Relativity declares that this point of view is perfectly valid—but mine is not. Relativity permits continuous deformation, but no cutting and pasting. *Why?* Because it must allow for *cause and effect.* Influences must be localized, traveling from point to point at a finite velocity; chop up space-time and rearrange it, and the causal structure would fall apart.

What if you're an observer, though, who has no *causal structure?* A self-aware pattern appearing by chance in the random twitches of a noise machine, your time coordinate dancing back and forth through causally respectable "real time"? Why should you be declared a second-class being, with no right to see the universe your way? What fundamental difference is there between so-called cause and effect, and any other internally consistent pattern of perceptions?

Squeak. "Trial number four. Model partitioned into fifty sections; sections and states pseudo-randomly allocated to one thousand clusters."

"One. Two. Three."

I stop counting, stretch my arms wide, stand. I wheel around once, to examine the room, checking that it's still intact, complete. Then I whisper, "This is dust. *All* dust. This room, this moment, is scattered across the planet, scattered across five hundred seconds or more—*and yet it remains whole*. Don't you see what that means?"

The *djinn* reappears, frowning, but I don't give him a chance to chastise me.

"Listen! If I can assemble myself, this room—if I can construct my own coherent space-time out of nothing but scattered fragments—*then what makes you think that you're not doing the very same thing?*

"Imagine . . . a universe completely without structure, without topology. No space, no time; just a set of random events. I'd call them 'isolated,' but that's not the right word; there's simply *no such thing as distance*. Perhaps I shouldn't even say 'random,' since that makes it sound like there's some kind of natural order in which to consider them, one by one, and find them random—but there isn't.

"What *are* these events? We'd describe them as points in space-time, and assign them coordinates—times and places—but if that's not permitted, what's left? Values of all the fundamental particle fields? Maybe even that's assuming too much. Let's just say that each event is a collection of numbers.

"Now, if the pattern that is *me* could pick itself out from the background noise of all the other events taking place on this planet . . . then why shouldn't the pattern we think of as 'the universe' assemble itself, find itself, in exactly the same way?"

The *djinn*'s expression hovers between alarm and irritation.

Squeak. "Paul . . . I don't see the point of any of this. Space-time is a construct; the *real* universe is nothing but a sea of disconnected events . . . it's all just metaphysical waffle. An unfalsifiable hypothesis. What explanatory value does it have? What difference would it make?"

"*What difference?* We perceive—we *inhabit*—one arrangement of the set of events. But why should that arrangement be *unique*? There's no reason to believe that the pattern we've found is the only coherent way of ordering the dust. There must be billions of other universes coexisting with us, made of the very same stuff—just differently arranged. If *I* can perceive events thousands of kilometers and hundreds of seconds apart to be side-by-side and simultaneous, there could be worlds, and creatures, built up from what we'd think of as points in space-time scattered all over the galaxy, all over the universe. We're one possible solution to a giant cosmic anagram . . . but it would be ludicrous to think that we're the only one."

Squeak. "So where are all the left-over letters? If this primordial alphabet soup really is random, don't you think it's highly unlikely that we could structure the whole thing?"

That throws me, but only for a moment. "We *haven't* structured the whole thing. The universe *is* random, at the quantum level. Macroscopically, the pattern seems to be perfect; microscopically, it decays into uncertainty. We've swept the residue of randomness down to the lowest level. The anagram analogy's flawed; the building blocks are more like random pixels than random letters. Given a sufficient number of random pixels, you could construct virtually any image you liked—but under close inspection, the randomness would be revealed."

Squeak. "None of this is testable. How would we ever observe a planet whose constituent parts were scattered across the universe? Let alone communicate with its hypothetical inhabitants? I don't doubt that what you're saying has a certain—purely mathematical—validity: grind the universe down to a fine enough level, and I'm sure the dust could be rearranged in other ways that make as much sense as the original. If these rearranged worlds are inaccessible, though, it's all angels on the heads of pins."

"How can you say that? I've *been* rearranged! I've *visited* another world!"

Squeak. "If you did, it was an artificial world; created, not discovered."

"Found a pattern, created a pattern . . . there's no real difference."

Squeak. "Paul, you know that everything you experienced was due to the way your model was programmed; there's no need to invoke *other worlds*. The state of your brain at every moment can be explained completely in terms of *this* arrangement of time and space."

"Of course! Your pattern hasn't been violated; the computers did exactly what was expected of them. That doesn't make my perspective any less valid, though. Stop thinking of explanations, causes and effects; there are only *patterns*. The scattered events that formed my experience had an internal consistency every bit as real as the consistency in the actions of the computers. And perhaps the computers didn't provide all of it."

Squeak. "What do you mean?"

"The gaps, in experiment one. What filled them in? What was I made of, when the processors weren't describing me? Well . . . it's a big universe. Plenty of dust to *be me*, in between descriptions. Plenty of events—nothing to do with your computers, maybe nothing to do with your planet or your epoch—out of which to construct ten seconds of experience, consistent with everything that had gone before—and everything yet to come."

Squeak. The *djinn* looks seriously worried now. "Paul, listen: you're a Copy in a virtual environment under computer control. Nothing more, nothing less. These experiments prove that your internal sense of space and time is invariant—as expected. But your states are *computed*, your memories *have to be* what they would have been without manipulation. You haven't visited any other worlds, you haven't built yourself out of fragments of distant galaxies."

I laugh. "Your stupidity is . . . surreal. What the fuck did you *create me for*, if you're not even going to *listen* to me? We've stumbled onto something of cosmic importance! Forget about farting around with the details of neural models; we have to devote all our resources to exploring this further. We've had a glimpse of the truth behind . . . *everything*: space, time, the laws of physics. You can't shrug that off by saying that my states were *inevitable*."

Squeak. "Control and subject are still identical."

I scream with exasperation. "Of *course* they are, you moron! That's the whole point! Like acceleration and gravity in General Relativity, it's the equivalent experience of two different observers that blows the old paradigm apart."

Squeak. The *djinn* mutters, dismayed, "Elizabeth said this would happen. She said it was only a matter of time before you'd lose touch."

I stare at him. "*Elizabeth?* You said you hadn't even told her!"

Squeak. "Well, I have. I didn't let you know, because I didn't think you'd want to hear her reaction."

"Which was?"

Squeak. "She wanted to shut you down. She said I was . . . seriously disturbed, to even think about doing this. She said she'd find help for me."

"Yeah? Well, what would *she* know? Ignore her!"

Squeak. He frowns apologetically, an expression I recognize from the inside, and my guts turn to ice. "Paul, maybe I should pause you, while I think things over. Elizabeth *does* care about me, more than I realized. I should talk it through with her again."

"No. Oh, shit, no." *He won't restart me from this point. Even if he doesn't abandon the project, he'll go back to the scan, and try something different, to keep me in line. Maybe he won't perform the first experiments at all—the ones which gave me this insight. The ones which made me who I am.*

Squeak. "Only temporarily. I promise. Trust me."

"Paul. Please."

He reaches off-screen.

"*No!*"

There's a hand gripping my forearm. I try to shake it off, but my arm barely moves, and a terrible aching starts up in my shoulder. I open my eyes, close them again in pain. I try again. On the fifth or sixth attempt, I manage to see a face through washed-out brightness and tears.

Elizabeth.

She holds a cup to my lips. I take a sip, splutter and choke, but then force some of the thin sweet liquid down.

She says, "You'll be okay soon. Just don't try to move too quickly."

"Why are you here?" I cough, shake my head, wish I hadn't. I'm touched, but confused. Why did my original lie, and claim that she wanted to shut me down, when in fact she was sympathetic enough to go through the arduous process of visiting me?

I'm lying on something like a dentist's couch, in an unfamiliar room. I'm in a hospital gown; there's a drip in my right arm, and a catheter in my urethra. I glance up to see an interface helmet, a bulky hemisphere of magnetic axon current inducers, suspended from a gantry, not far above my head. Fair enough, I suppose, to construct a simulated meeting place that looks like the room that her real body must be in; putting me in the couch, though, and giving me all the symptoms of a waking visitor, seems a little extreme.

I tap the couch with my left hand. "What's the point of all this? You want me to know exactly what you're going through? Okay. I'm grateful. And it's good to see you." I shudder with relief, and delayed shock. "Fantastic, to tell the truth." I laugh weakly. "I honestly thought he was going to wipe me out. The man's a complete lunatic. Believe me, you're talking to his better half."

She's perched on a stool beside me. "Paul. Try to listen carefully to what I'm going to say. You'll start to reintegrate the suppressed memories gradually, on your own, but it'll help if I talk you through it all first. To start with, you're not a Copy. You're flesh and blood."

I stare at her. "What kind of sadistic joke is that? Do you know how hard it was, how long it took me, to come to terms with the truth?"

She shakes her head. "It's not a joke. I know you don't remember yet, but after you made the scan that was going to run as Copy number five, you finally told me what you were doing. And I persuaded you not to run it—until you'd tried another experiment: putting yourself in its place. Finding out, first hand, what *it* would be forced to go through.

"And you agreed. You entered the virtual environment which the Copy would have inhabited—with your memories since the day of the scan suppressed, so you had no way of knowing that you were only a visitor."

Her face betrays no hint of deception—but software can smooth that out. "I don't believe you. How can I *be* the original? I *spoke to* the original. What am I supposed to believe? *He* was the Copy?"

She sighs, but says patiently, "Of course not. That would hardly spare the Copy any trauma, would it? The scan was never run. *I* controlled the puppet that played your 'original'—software provided the vocabulary signature and body language, but I pulled the strings."

I shake my head, and whisper, "Bremsstrahlung." No interface window appears. I grip the couch and close my eyes, then laugh. "You say I agreed to this? What kind of masochist would do that? I'm going out of my mind! *I don't know what I am!*"

She takes hold of my arm again. "Of course you're still disoriented—but trust me, it won't last long. And you *know* why you agreed. You were sick of Copies bailing out on you. One way or another, you have to come to terms with their experience. Spending a few days believing you were a Copy would make or break the project: you'd either end up truly prepared, at last, to give rise to a Copy who'd be able to cope with its fate—or you'd gain enough sympathy for their plight to stop creating them."

A technician comes into the room and removes my drip and catheter. I prop myself up and look out through the windows of the room's swing doors; I can see half a dozen people in the corridor. I bellow wordlessly at the top of my lungs; they all turn to stare in my direction. The technician says, mildly, "Your penis might sting for an hour or two."

I slump back onto the couch and turn to Elizabeth. "You wouldn't pay for reactive crowds. *I* wouldn't pay for reactive crowds. Looks like you're telling the truth."

People, glorious *people*: thousands of strangers, meeting my eyes with suspicion or puzzlement, stepping out of my way on the street—or, more often, clearly, consciously refusing to. I'll never feel alone in a crowd again; I remember what *true* invisibility is like.

The freedom of the city is so sweet. I walked the streets of Sydney for a full day, exploring every ugly shopping arcade, every piss-stinking litter-strewn park and alley, until, with aching feet, I squeezed my way home through the evening rush-hour, to watch the real-time news.

There is no room for doubt: I am not in a virtual environment. Nobody in the world could have reason to spend so much money, simply to deceive me.

When Elizabeth asks if my memories are back, I nod and say, of course. She doesn't grill me on the details. In fact, having gone over her story so many times in my head, I can almost imagine the stages: my qualms after the fifth scan, repeatedly putting off running the model, confessing to Elizabeth about the project, accepting her challenge to experience for myself just what my Copies were suffering.

And if the suppressed memories haven't actually integrated, well, I've checked the literature, and there's a 2.5 percent risk of that happening.

I have an account from the database service which shows that I consulted the very same articles before.

I reread and replayed the news reports that I accessed from inside; I found no discrepancies. In fact, I've been reading a great deal of history, geography, and astronomy, and although I'm surprised now and then by details that I'd never learnt before, I can't say that I've come across anything that definitely contradicts my prior understanding.

Everything is consistent. Everything is explicable.

I still can't stop wondering, though, what might happen to a Copy who's shut down, and never run again. A normal human death is one thing—woven into a much vaster tapestry, it's a process that makes perfect sense. From the internal point of view of a Copy whose model is simply *halted*, though, there is no explanation whatsoever for this "death"—just an edge where the pattern abruptly ends.

If a Copy could assemble itself from dust scattered across the world, and bridge the gaps in its existence with dust from across the universe, why should it ever come to an *inconsistent* end? Why shouldn't the pattern keep on finding itself? Or find, perhaps, a *larger* pattern into which it could merge?

Perhaps it's pointless to aspire to know the truth. If I *was* a Copy, and "found" this world, this arrangement of dust, then the seam will be, *must* be, flawless. For the patterns to merge, both "explanations" must be equally true. If I was a Copy, then it's also true that I was the flesh-and-blood Paul Durham, believing he was a Copy.

Once I had two futures. Now I have two pasts.

Elizabeth asked me yesterday what decision I'd reached: to abandon my life's obsession, or to forge ahead, now that I know firsthand what's involved. My answer disappointed her, and I'm not sure if I'll ever see her again.

In this world.

Today, I'm going to be scanned for the sixth time. I can't give up now. *I* can't discover the truth—but that doesn't mean that nobody *else* can. If I make a Copy, run him for a few virtual days, then terminate him abruptly . . . then *he*, at least, will know if his pattern of experience continues. Again, there will be an "explanation"; again, the "new" flesh-and-blood Paul Durham will have an extra past. Inheriting my memories, perhaps he will repeat the whole process again.

And again. And *again*. Although the seams will always be perfect, the "explanations" will necessarily grow ever more "contrived," less convincing, and the dust hypothesis will become ever more compelling.

I lie in bed in the predawn light, waiting for sunrise, staring into the future down this corridor of mirrors.

One thing nags at me. I could swear I had a dream—an elaborate fable, conveying some kind of insight—but my dreams are evanescent, and I don't expect to remember what it was.

TWO GUYS FROM THE FUTURE

Terry Bisson

Here's a wild, woolly, and funny take on the classic time-travel story, in which two fast-talking guys from the future arrive with an Offer You Can't Refuse . . .

Terry Bisson is the author of a number of critically acclaimed novels such as *Fire on the Mountain*, *Wyrldmaker*, the popular *Talking Man*, which was a finalist for the World Fantasy Award in 1986, and, most recently, *Voyage to the Red Planet*. In 1991, his famous story "Bears Discover Fire" won the Nebula Award, the Hugo Award, the Theodore Sturgeon Award, and the *Asimov's* Reader's Award—the only story ever to sweep them all. Upcoming is a collection, *Bears Discover Fire and Other Stories*. He lives with his family in Brooklyn, New York.

"We are two guys from the future."

"Yeah, right. Now get the hell out of here!"

"Don't shoot! Is that a gun?"

That gave me pause; it was a flashlight. There were two of them. They both wore shimmery suits. The short one was kind of cute. The tall one did all the talking.

"Lady, we are serious guys from the future," he said. "This is not a hard-on."

"You mean a put-on," I said. "Now kindly get the hell out of here."

"We are here on a missionary position to all mankind," he said. "No shit is fixing to hang loose any someday now."

"Break loose," I said. "Hey, are you guys talking about nuclear war?"

"We are not allowed to say," the cute one said.

"The bottom line is, we have come to salvage the art works of your posteriors," the tall one said.

"Save the art and let the world go. Not a bad idea," I said. "But, *mira*, it's midnight and the gallery's closed. Come back *en la mañana*."

"*¡Qué bueno! No hay mas necesidad que hablar en inglés*," the tall one said. "Nothing worse than trying to communicate in a dead language," he went on in Spanish. "But how did you know?"

"Just a guess," I said, also in Spanish, and we spoke in the mother tongue from then on. "If you really are two guys from the future, you can come back in the future, like tomorrow after we open, right?"

"Too much danger of Timeslip," he said. "We have to come and go between midnight and four A.M., when we won't interfere with your world. Plus we're from far in the future, not just tomorrow. We are here to save art works that will otherwise be lost in the coming holocaust by sending them through a Chronoslot to our century in what is, to you, the distant future."

"I got that picture," I said. "But you're talking to the wrong girl. I don't own this art gallery. I'm just an artist."

"Artists wear uniforms in your century?"

"Okay, so I'm moonlighting as a security guard."

"Then it's your boss we need to talk to. Get him here tomorrow at midnight, okay?"

"He's a her," I said. "Besides, *mira*, how do I know you really are, on the level, two guys from the future?"

"You saw us suddenly materialize in the middle of the room, didn't you?"

"Okay, so I may have been dozing. You try working two jobs."

"But you noticed how bad our *inglés* was. And how about these outfits?"

"A lot of people in New York speak worse *inglés* than you," I said. "And here on the Lower East Side, funny suits don't prove anything." Then I remembered a science-fiction story I had once heard about. (I never actually *read* science fiction.)

"You did *what?*" said Borogove, the gallery owner, the next morning when I told her about the two guys from the future.

"I lit a match and held it to his sleeve."

"Girl, you're lucky he didn't shoot you."

"He wasn't carrying a gun. I could tell. Those shimmery suits are pretty tight. Anyway, when I saw that the cloth didn't burn, I decided I believed their story."

"There's all sorts of material that doesn't burn," Borogove said. "And if they're really two guys from the future who have come back to save the great art of our century, how come they didn't take anything?"

She looked around the gallery, which was filled with giant plastic breasts and buttocks, the work of her dead ex-husband, "Bucky" Borogove. She seemed disappointed that all of them were still hanging.

"Beats me," I said. "They insist on talking to the gallery owner. Maybe you have to sign for it or something."

"Hmmmmm. There have been several mysterious disappearances of great art lately. That's why I hired you; it was one of the conditions in Bucky's will. In fact, I'm still not sure this isn't one of his posthumous publicity stunts. What time are these guys from the future supposed to show up?"

"Midnight."

"Hmmmmm. Well, don't tell anyone about this. I'll join you at midnight, like MacBeth on the tower."

"Hamlet," I said. "And tomorrow's my night off. My boyfriend is taking me to the cockfights."

"I'll pay you time and a half," she said. "I may need you there to translate. My *español* is a little rusty."

Girls don't go to cockfights and I don't have a boyfriend. How could I? There aren't any single men in New York. I just didn't want Borogove to think I was easy.

But in fact, I wouldn't have missed it for the world.

I was standing beside her in the gallery at midnight when a column of air in the center of the room began to shimmer and glow and . . . but you've seen *Star Trek*. There they were. I decided to call the tall one Stretch and the cute one Shorty.

"*Bienvenidos* to our century," said Borogove, in Spanish, "and to the Borogove Gallery." Her Spanish was more than a little rusty; turned out she had done a month in Cuernavaca in 1964. "We are described in *Art Talk* magazine as " 'the traffic control center of the Downtown Art Renaissance.' "

"We are two guys from the future," Stretch said, in Spanish this time. He held out his arm.

"You don't have to prove anything," said Borogove. "I can tell by the way you arrived here that you're not from our world. But if you like, you could show me some future money."

"We're not allowed to carry cash," said Shorty.

"Too much danger of Timeslip," explained Stretch. "In fact, the only reason we're here at all is because of a special exemption in the Chronolaws, allowing us to save great art works that otherwise would be destroyed in the coming holocaust."

"Oh dear. What coming holocaust?"

"We're not allowed to say," said Shorty. It seemed to be the only thing he was allowed to say. But I liked the way that no matter who he was talking to, he kept stealing looks at me.

"Don't worry about it," said Stretch, looking at his watch. "It doesn't happen for quite a while. We're buying the art early to keep the prices down. Next month our time (last year, yours) we bought two Harings and a Ledesma right around the corner."

"Bought?" said Borogove. "Those paintings were reported stolen."

Stretch shrugged. "That's between the gallery owners and their insurance companies. But we are not thieves. In fact . . ."

"What about the people?" I asked.

"You stay out of this," Borogove whispered, in *inglés*. "You're just here to translate."

I ignored her. "You know, in this coming holocaust thing. What happens to the people?"

"We're not allowed to save people," said Shorty.

"No big deal," said Stretch. "People all die anyway. Only great art is forever. Well, almost forever."

"And Bucky made the short list!" said Borogove. "That son of a bitch. But I'm not surprised. If self-promotion can—"

"Bucky?" Stretch looked confused.

"Bucky Borogove. My late ex-husband. The artist whose work is hanging all around us here. The art you came to save for future generations."

"Oh, no," said Stretch. He looked around at the giant tits and asses hanging on the walls. "We can't take this stuff. It would never fit through the Chronoslot anyway. We came to give you time to get rid of it. We're here for the early works of Teresa Algarín Rosado, the Puerto Rican neoretro-maximinimalist. You will hang her show next week, and we'll come back and pick up the paintings we want."

"I beg your pardon!" said Borogove. "Nobody tells me who will or will not hang in this gallery. Not even guys from the future. Besides, who's ever heard of this Rosado?"

"I didn't mean to be rude," said Stretch. "It's just that we already know what will happen. Besides, we've already deposited three hundred thousand dollars in your account first thing tomorrow."

"Well, in that case . . ." Borogove seemed mollified. "But who is she? Do you have her phone number? Does she even have a phone? A lot of artists . . ."

"How many paintings are you going to buy?" I asked.

"You stay out of this!" she whispered, in *inglés*.

"But I am Teresa Algarín Rosado," I said.

I quit my job as a security guard. A few nights later I was in my apartment when I noticed a shimmering by the sink. The air began to glow and . . . but you've seen *Star Trek*. I barely had time to pull on my jeans. I was painting and I usually work in a T-shirt and underpants.

"Remember me, one of the two guys from the future?" Shorty said, in Spanish, as soon as he had fully appeared.

"So you can talk," I said, in Spanish also. "Where's your *compañero*?"

"It's his night off. He's got a date."

"And you're working?"

"It's my night off, too. I just—uh—uh . . ." He blushed.

"Couldn't get a date," I said. "It's all right. I'm about ready to knock off anyway. There's a Bud in the refrigerator. Get me one too."

"You always work at midnight? Can I call you Teresa?"

"Please do. Just finishing a couple of canvases. This is my big chance. My own show. I want everything to be just right. What are you looking for?"

"A bud?"

"A Bud is a *cerveza*," I said. "The top twists off. To the left. Are you sure you guys are from the future and not the past?" (Or just the country, I thought to myself.)

"We travel to many different time zones," he said.

"Must be exciting. Do you get to watch them throw the Christians to the lions?"

"We don't go there, it's all statues," he said. "Statues won't fit through the Chronoslot. You might have noticed, Stretch and I broke quite a few before we quit trying."

"Stretch?"

"My partner. Oh, and call me Shorty."

It was my first positive illustration of the power of the past over the future.

"So what kind of art do you like?" I asked while we got comfortable on the couch.

"I don't like any of it, but I guess paintings are best; you can turn them flat. Say, this is pretty good *cerveza*. Do you have any roll and rock?"

I thought he meant the beer but he meant the music. I also had a joint, left over from a more interesting decade.

"Your century is my favorite," Shorty said. Soon he said he was ready for another petal.

"Bud," I said. "In the fridge."

"The *cerveza* in your century is very good," he called out from the kitchen.

"Let me ask you two questions," I said from the couch.

"Sure."

"Do you have a wife or a girlfriend back there, or up there, in the future?"

"Are you kidding?" he said. "There are no single girls in the future. What's your second question?"

"Do you look as cute out of that shimmery suit as you do in it?"

"There's one missing," said Borogove, checking off her list as the workmen unloaded the last of my paintings from the rented panel truck and carried them in the front door of the gallery. Other workmen were taking Bucky's giant tits and asses out the back door.

"This is all of it," I said. "Everything I've ever painted. I even borrowed back two paintings that I had traded for rent."

Borogove consulted her list. "According to the two guys from the future, three of your early paintings are in the Museo de Arte Inmortal del Mundo in 2255: 'Tres Dolores,' 'De Mon Mouse,' and 'La Rosa del Futuro.' Those are the three they want."

"Let me see that list," I said.

"It's just the titles. They have a catalog with pictures of what they want, but they wouldn't show it to me. Too much danger of Timesplits."

"Slips," I said. We looked through the stacked canvases again. I am partial to portraits. "De Mon Mouse" was an oil painting of the super in my building, a rasta who always wore Mickey Mouse T-shirts. He had a collection of two. "Tres Dolores" was a mother, daughter, and grandmother I had known on Avenue B; it was a pose faked up from photographs—a sort of tampering with time in itself, now that I thought of it.

But "La Rosa del Futuro"? "Never heard of it," I said.

Borogove waved the list. "It's on here. Which means it's in their catalog."

"Which means it survives the holocaust," I said.

"Which means they pick it up at midnight, after the opening Wednesday night," she said.

"Which means I must paint it between now and then."

"Which means you've got four days."

"This is crazy, Borogove."

"Call me Mimsy," she said. "And don't worry about it. Just get to work."

"There's pickled herring in the *nevera*," I said, in Spanish.

"I thought you were Puerto Rican," said Shorty.

"I am, but my ex-boyfriend was Jewish, and that stuff keeps forever."

"I thought there were no single men in New York."

"Exactly the problem," I said. "His wife was Jewish too."

"You're sure I'm not keeping you from your work?" said Shorty.

"What work?" I said forlornly. I had been staring at a blank canvas since 10:00 P.M. "I still have one painting to finish for the show, and I haven't even started it."

"Which one?"

" 'La Rosa del Futuro,' " I said. I had the title pinned to the top corner of the frame. Maybe that was what was blocking me. I wadded it up and threw it at the wall. It only went halfway across the room.

"I think that's the most famous one," he said. "So you know it gets done. Is there a blossom . . ."

"A Bud," I said. "In the door of the fridge."

"Maybe what you need," he said, with that shy, sly, futuristic smile I was growing to like, "is a little rest."

After our little rest, which wasn't so little, and wasn't exactly a rest, I asked him, "Do you do this often?"

"This?"

"Go to bed with girls from the past. What if I'm your great-great-grand-mother or something?"

"I had it checked out," he said. "She's living in the Bronx."

"So you do! You bastard! You do this all the time."

"Teresa! *Mi corazón!* Never before. It's strictly not allowed. I could lose my job! It's just that when I saw those little . . ."

"Those little what?"

He blushed. "Those little hands and feet. I fell in love."

It was my turn to blush. He had won my heart, a guy from the future, forever.

"So if you love me so much, why don't you take me back to the future with you?" I asked, after another little rest.

"Then who would paint all the paintings you are supposed to paint over the next thirty years? Teresa, you don't understand how famous you are going to be. Even I have heard of Picasso, Michelangelo, and the great Algarín— and art is not my thing. If something happened to you, the Timeslip would throw off the whole history of art."

"Oh. How about that." I couldn't seem to stop smiling. "So why don't you stay here with me."

"I've thought about it," he said. "But if I stayed here, I wouldn't be around to come back here and meet you in the first place. And if I had stayed here, we would know about it anyway, since there would be some evidence of it. See how complicated Time is? I'm just a delivery guy and it gives me a headache. I need another leaf."

"Bud," I said. "You know where they are."

He went into the kitchen for a *cerveza* and I called out after him: "So you're going to go back to the future and let me die in the coming holocaust?"

"Die? Holocaust?"

"The one you're not allowed to tell me about. The nuclear war."

"Oh, that. Stretch is just trying to alarm you. It's not a war. It's a warehouse fire."

"All this *mischigosch* for a warehouse fire?"

"It's cheaper to go back and get the stuff than to avoid the fire," he said. "It all has to do with Timeslip insurance or something."

The phone rang. "How's it going?"

"It's two in the morning, Borogove!" I said, in *inglés*.

"Please, Teresa, call me Mimsy. Is it finished?"

"I'm working on it," I lied. "Go to sleep."

"Who was that?" Shorty asked, in Spanish. "*La Gordita?*"

"Don't be cruel," I said, pulling on my T-shirt and underpants. "You go to sleep, too. I have to get back to work"

"Okay, but wake me up by four. If I oversleep and get stuck here—"

"If you had overslept we would already know about it, wouldn't we?" I said, sarcastically. But he was already snoring.

"I can't put it off for a week!" said Borogove the next day at the gallery. "Everybody who's anybody in the downtown art scene is going to be here tomorrow night."

"But . . ."

"Teresa, I've already ordered the wine."

"But . . ."

"Teresa, I've already ordered the cheese. Plus, remember, whatever we sell beyond the three paintings they're coming for is gravy. *Comprende?*"

"*En inglés*, Borogove," I said. "But what if I don't finish this painting in time?"

"Teresa, I insist, you must call me Mimsy. If you weren't going to finish it, they would have arranged a later pickup date, since they already know what will happen. For god's sake, girl, quit worrying. Go home and get to work! You have until tomorrow night."

"But I don't even know where to start!"

"Don't you artists have any imagination? Make something up!"

I had never been blocked before. It's not like constipation; when you're constipated you can work sitting down.

I padded and paced like a caged lion, staring at my blank canvas as if I were trying to get up the appetite to eat it. By 11:30 I had started it and painted it out six times. It just didn't feel right.

Just as the clock was striking midnight, a column of air near the sink began to shimmer and . . . but you've seen *Star Trek*. Shorty appeared by the sink, one hand behind his back.

"Am I glad to see you!" I said. "I need a clue."

"A clue?"

"This painting. 'La Rosa del Futuro.' Your catalog from the future has a picture of it. Let me see it."

"Copy your own painting?" Shorty said. "That would cause a Timeslip for sure."

"I won't copy it!" I said. "I just need a clue. I'll just glance at it."

"Same thing. Besides, Stretch carries the catalog. I'm just his helper."

"Okay, then just *tell* me, what's it a picture of?"

"I don't know, Teresa . . ."

"How can you say you love me if you won't even break the rules to help me?"

"No, I mean I *really* don't know. Like I said, art is not my thing. I'm just a delivery guy. Besides—" he blushed. "You know what my thing is."

"Well, my thing *is* art," I said. "And I'm going to lose the chance of a lifetime—hell, of more than that, of artistic *inmortalidad*—if I don't come up with something pretty soon."

"Teresa, quit worrying," he said. "The painting's so famous even I've heard of it. There's no way it can *not* happen. Meanwhile, let's don't spend our last . . ."

"Our what? Our last what? Why are you standing there with your hand behind your back?"

He pulled out a rose. "Don't you understand? This Chronolink closes forever after the pickup tonight. I don't know where my next job will take me, but it won't be here."

"So what's the rose for?"

"To remember our . . . our . . ." He burst into tears.

Girls cry hard and fast and it's over. Guys from the future are more sentimental, and Shorty cried himself to sleep. After comforting him as best I could, I pulled on my T-shirt and underpants and found a clean brush and started pacing again. I left him snoring on the bed, a short brown Adonis without even a fig leaf.

"Wake me up at four," he mumbled, then went back to sleep.

I looked at the *rosa* he had brought. The roses of the future had soft thorns; that was encouraging. I laid it on the pillow next to his cheek and that was when it came to me, in the form of a whole picture, which is how it always comes to me when it finally does. (And it always does.)

When I'm painting and it's going well, I forget everything. It seemed like only minutes before the phone rang.

"Well? How's it going?"

"Borogove, it's almost four in the morning."

"No, it's not, it's four in the afternoon. You've been working all night and all day, Teresa, I can tell. But you really have to call me Mimsy."

"I can't talk now," I said. "I have a live model. Sort of."

"I thought you didn't work from live models."

"This time I am."

"Whatever. Don't let me bother you while you're working; I can tell you're getting somewhere. The opening is at seven. I'm sending a van for you at six."

"Make it a limo, Mimsy," I said. "We're making art history."

"It's beautiful," Borogove said, as I unveiled "La Rosa del Futuro" for her. "But who's the model? He looks vaguely familiar."

"He's been around the art world for years and years," I said.

The gallery was packed. The show was a huge success. "La Rosa," "De Mon Mouse" and "Los Tres" were already marked SOLD, and SOLD stickers went up on my other paintings at the rate of one every twenty minutes. Everybody wanted to meet me. I had left Shorty directions and cab fare by the bed, and at 11:30 he showed up wearing only my old boyfriend's trench coat, saying that his shimmery suit had disappeared into thin air while he was pulling it on.

I wasn't surprised. We were in the middle of a Timeslip, after all.

"Who's the barefoot guy in the fabulous Burberry?" Borogove asked. "He looks vaguely familiar."

"He's been around the art world for ever and ever," I said.

Shorty was looking jet-lagged. He was staring dazedly at the wine and cheese and I signaled to one of the caterers to show him where the beer was kept, in the back room.

At 11:55, Borogove threw everybody else out and turned down the lights. At midnight, right on time, a glowing column of air appeared in the center of the room, then gradually took on the shape of . . . but you've seen *Star Trek*. It was Stretch, and he was alone.

"We are—uh—a guy from the future," Stretch said, starting in English and finishing *en español*. He was wobbling a little.

"I could have sworn there were two of you guys," said Borogove. "Or did I make that up?" she whispered to me, in *inglés*.

"Could be a Timeslip," said Stretch. He looked confused himself, then brightened. "No problem though! Happens all the time. This is a light pickup. Only three paintings!"

"We have all three right here," said Borogove. "Teresa, why don't you do the honors. I'll check them off as you hand them to this guy from the future."

I handed him "De Mon Mouse." Then "Los Tres Dolores." He slipped them both through a dark slot that appeared in the air.

"Whoops," Stretch said, his knees wobbling. "Feel that? Slight aftershock."

Shorty had wandered in from the back room with a Bud in his hand. In nothing but a raincoat, he looked very disoriented.

"This is my boyfriend, Shorty," I said. He and Stretch stared at each other blankly and I felt the fabric of space/time tremble just for a moment. Then it was over.

"Of course!" said Stretch. "Of course, I'd recognize you anywhere."

"Huh? Oh." Shorty looked at the painting I was holding, the last of the three. "La Rosa del Futuro." It was a full length nude of a short brown Adonis, asleep on his back without even a fig leaf, a rose placed tenderly on the pillow by his cheek. The paint was still tacky but I suspected that by the time it arrived in the future it would be dry.

"Reminds me of the day I met Mona Lisa," said Stretch. "How many times have I seen this painting, and now I meet the guy! Must feel weird to have the world's most famous, you know . . ." He winked toward Shorty's crotch.

"I don't know about weird," said Shorty. "Something definitely feels funny."

"Let's get on with this," I said. I handed Stretch the painting and he pushed it through the slot, and Shorty and I lived happily ever after. For a while. More or less. . . .

But you've seen *I Love Lucy*.

THE MOUNTAIN TO MOHAMMED

Nancy Kress

Born in Buffalo, New York, Nancy Kress now lives in Brockport, New York. She began selling her elegant and incisive stories in the mid-seventies, and has since become a frequent contributor to *Asimov's*, *F & SF*, *Omni*, and elsewhere. Her books include the novels *The Prince of Morning Bells*, *The Golden Grove*, *The White Pipes*, *An Alien Light*, and *Brain Rose*, and the collection *Trinity and Other Stories*. Her most recent book is the novel version of her Hugo- and Nebula-winning story, *Beggars in Spain*. She has also won a Nebula Award for her story "Out Of All Them Bright Stars." She has had stories in our Second, Third, Sixth, Seventh, Eighth, and Ninth Annual Collections.

In the all-too-plausible story that follows, she takes us to a crowded and impoverished future society for a look at how sometimes following your conscience can cost you all that you have . . .

> *"A person gives money to the physician.*
> *Maybe he will be healed.*
> *Maybe he will not be healed."*
> *—The Talmud*

When the security buzzer sounded, Dr. Jesse Randall was playing *go* against his computer. Haruo Kaneko, his roommate at Downstate Medical, had taught him the game. So far nineteen shiny black and white stones lay on the grid under the scanner field. Jesse frowned; the computer had a clear shot at surrounding an empty space in two moves, and he couldn't see how to stop it. The buzzer made him jump.

Anne? But she was on duty at the hospital until one. Or maybe he remembered her rotation wrong. . . .

Eagerly he crossed the small living room to the security screen. It wasn't Anne. Three stories below a man stood on the street, staring into the monitor. He was slight and fair, dressed in jeans and frayed jacket with a knit cap pulled low on his head. The bottoms of his ears were red with cold.

"Yes?" Jesse said.

"Dr. Randall?" The voice was low and rough.

"Yes."

"Could you come down here a minute to talk to me?"

"About what?"

"Something that needs talkin' about. It's personal. Mike sent me."

A thrill ran through Jesse. This was it, then. He kept his voice neutral. "I'll be right down."

He turned off the monitor system, removed the memory disk, and carried it into the bedroom, where he passed it several times over a magnet. In a gym bag he packed his medical equipment: antiseptics, antibiotics, sutures, clamps, syringes, electromed scanner, as much equipment as would fit. Once, shoving it all in, he laughed. He dressed in a warm pea coat bought second-hand at the Army-Navy store and put the gun, also bought second-hand, in the coat pocket. Although of course the other man would be carrying. But Jesse liked the feel of it, a slightly heavy drag on his right side. He replaced the disk in the security system and locked the door. The computer was still pretending to consider its move for *go*, although of course it had near-instantaneous decision capacity.

"Where to?"

The slight man didn't answer. He strode purposefully away from the building, and Jesse realized he shouldn't have said anything. He followed the man down the street, carrying the gym bag in his left hand.

Fog had drifted in from the harbor. Boston smelled wet and grey, of rotting piers and dead fish and garbage. Even here, in the Morningside Security Enclave, where that part of the apartment maintenance fees left over from security went to keep the streets clean. Yellow lights gleamed through the gloom, stacked twelve stories high but crammed close together; even insurables couldn't afford to heat much space.

Where they were going there wouldn't be any heat at all.

Jesse followed the slight man down the subway steps. The guy paid for both of them, a piece of quixotic dignity that made Jesse smile. Under the lights he got a better look: The man was older than he'd thought, with webbed lines around the eyes and long, thin lips over very bad teeth. Probably hadn't ever had dental coverage in his life. What had been in his genescan? God, what a system.

"What do I call you?" he said as they waited on the platform. He kept his voice low, just in case.

"Kenny."

"All right, Kenny," Jesse said, and smiled. Kenny didn't smile back. Jesse told himself it was ridiculous to feel hurt; this wasn't a social visit. He stared at the tracks until the subway came.

At this hour the only other riders were three hard-looking men, two black and one white, and an even harder-looking Hispanic girl in a low-cut red dress. After a minute Jesse realized she was under the control of one of the black men sitting at the other end of the car. Jesse was careful not to look at her again. He couldn't help being curious, though. She looked healthy. All four of them looked healthy, as did Kenny, except for his teeth. Maybe none of them were uninsurable; maybe they just couldn't find a job. Or didn't want one. It wasn't his place to judge.

That was the whole point of doing this, wasn't it?

The other two times had gone as easy as Mike said they would. A deltoid suture on a young girl wounded in a knife fight, and burn treatment for a baby scalded by a pot of boiling water knocked off a stove. Both times the families had been so grateful, so respectful. They knew the risk Jesse was taking. After he'd treated the baby and left antibiotics and analgesics on the pathetic excuse for a kitchen counter, a board laid across the non-functional radiator, the young Hispanic mother had grabbed his hand and covered it with kisses. Embarrassed, he'd turned to smile at her husband, wanting to say something, wanting to make clear he wasn't just another sporadic do-gooder who happened to have a medical degree.

"I think the system stinks. The insurance companies should never have been allowed to deny health coverage on the basis of genescans for potential disease, and employers should never have been allowed to keep costs down by health-based hiring. If this were a civilized country, we'd have national health care by now!"

The Hispanic had stared back at him, blank-faced.

"Some of us are trying to do better," Jesse said.

It was the same thing Mike—Dr. Michael Cassidy—had said to Jesse and Anne at the end of a long drunken evening celebrating the halfway point in all their residencies. Although, in retrospect, it seemed to Jesse that Mike hadn't drunk very much. Nor had he actually said very much outright. It was all implication, probing masked as casual philosophy. But Anne had understood, and refused instantly. "God, Mike, you could be dismissed from the hospital! The regulations forbid residents from exposing the hospital to the threat of an uninsured malpractice suit. There's no money."

Mike had smiled and twirled his glasses between fingers as long as a pianist's. "Doctors are free to treat whomever they wish, at their own risk, even uninsurables. *Carter v. Sunderland.*"

"Not while a hospital is paying their malpractice insurance as residents, if the hospital exercises its right to so forbid. *Janisson v. Lechchevko.*"

Mike laughed easily. "Then forget it, both of you. It's just conversation."

Anne said, "But do you personally risk—"

"It's not right," Jesse cut in—couldn't she see that Mike wouldn't want to incriminate himself on a thing like this?—"that so much of the population can't get insurance. Every year they add more genescan pre-tendency barriers, and the poor slobs haven't even got the diseases yet!"

His voice had risen. Anne glanced nervously around the bar. Her profile was lovely, a serene curving line that reminded Jesse of those Korean screens in the expensive shops on Commonwealth Avenue. And she had lovely legs, lovely breasts, lovely everything. Maybe, he'd thought, now that they were neighbors in the Morningside Enclave. . . .

"Another round," Mike had answered.

Unlike the father of the burned baby, who never had answered Jesse at all. To cover his slight embarrassment—the mother had been so effusive—Jesse gazed around the cramped apartment. On the wall were photographs in cheap plastic frames of people with masses of black hair, all lying in bed. Jesse had read about this: It was a sort of mute, powerless protest. The subjects had all been photographed on their death beds. One of them was a beautiful girl, her eyes closed and her hand flung lightly over her head, as if asleep. The Hispanic followed Jesse's gaze and lowered his eyes.

"Nice," Jesse said. "Good photos. I didn't know you people were so good with a camera."

Still nothing.

Later, it occurred to Jesse that maybe the guy hadn't understood English.

The subway stopped with a long screech of equipment too old, too poorly maintained. There was no money. Boston, like the rest of the country, was broke. For a second Jesse thought the brakes weren't going to catch at all and his heart skipped, but Kenny showed no emotion and so Jesse tried not to, either. The car finally stopped. Kenny rose and Jesse followed him.

They were somewhere in Dorchester. Three men walked quickly toward them and Jesse's right hand crept toward his pocket. "This him?" one said to Kenny.

"Yeah," Kenny said. "Dr. Randall," and Jesse relaxed.

It made sense, really. Two men walking through this neighborhood probably wasn't a good idea. Five was better. Mike's organization must know what it was doing.

The men walked quickly. The neighborhood was better than Jesse had imagined: small row houses, every third or fourth one with a bit of frozen lawn in the front. A few even had flowerboxes. But the windows were barred, and over all hung the grey fog, the dank cold, the pervasive smell of garbage.

The house they entered had no flowerbox. The steel front door, triple-locked, opened directly into a living room furnished with a sagging sofa, a TV, and an ancient daybed whose foamcast headboard flaked like dandruff. On the daybed lay a child, her eyes bright with fever.

Sofa, TV, headboard vanished. Jesse felt his professional self take over, a sensation as clean and fresh as plunging into cool water. He knelt by the bed and smiled. The girl, who looked about nine or ten, didn't smile back. She had a long, sallow, sullen face, but the long brown hair on the pillow was beautiful: clean, lustrous, and well-tended.

"It's her belly," said one of the men who had met them at the subway. Jesse glanced up at the note in his voice, and realized that he must be the child's father. The man's hand trembled as he pulled the sheet from the girl's lower body. Her abdomen was swollen and tender.

"How long has she been this way?"

"Since yesterday," Kenny said, when the father didn't answer.

"Nausea? Vomiting?"

"Yeah. She can't keep nothing down."

Jesse's hands palpated gently. The girl screamed.

Appendicitis. He just hoped to hell peritonitis hadn't set in. He didn't want to deal with peritonitis. Not here.

"Bring in all the lamps you have, with the brightest watt bulbs. Boil water—" He looked up. The room was very cold. "Does the stove work?"

The father nodded. He looked pale. Jesse smiled and said, "I don't think it's anything we can't cure, with a little luck here." The man didn't answer.

Jesse opened his bag, his mind racing. Laser knife, sterile clamps, scaramine—he could do it even without nursing assistance provided there was no peritonitis. But only if . . . the girl moaned and turned her face away. There were tears in her eyes. Jesse looked at the man with the same long, sallow face and brown hair. "You her father?"

The man nodded.

"I need to see her genescan."

The man clenched both fists at his side. Oh, God, if he didn't *have* the official printout . . . sometimes, Jesse had read, uninsurables burned them. One woman, furious at the paper that would forever keep her out of the middle class, had mailed hers, smeared with feces, and packaged with a plasticine explosive, to the president. There had been headlines, columns, petitions . . . and nothing had changed. A country fighting for its very economic survival didn't hesitate to expend front-line troops. If there was no genescan for this child, Jesse couldn't use scaramine, that miracle immune-system booster, to which about 15 percent of the population had a fatal reaction. Without scaramine, under these operating conditions, the chances of post-operative infection were considerably higher. If she couldn't take scaramine. . . .

The father handed Jesse the laminated print-out, with the deeply embossed seal in the upper corner. Jesse scanned it quickly. The necessary RB antioncogene on the eleventh chromosome was present. The girl was not potentially allergic to scaramine. Her name was Rosamund.

"Okay, Rose," Jesse said gently. "I'm going to help you. In just a little while you're going to feel so much better. . . ." He slipped the needle with anesthetic into her arm. She jumped and screamed, but within a minute she was out.

Jesse stripped away the bedclothes, despite the cold, and told the men how to boil them. He spread Betadine over her distended abdomen and poised the laser knife to cut.

The hallmark of his parents' life had been caution. *Don't fall, now! Drive carefully! Don't talk to strangers!* Born during the Depression—the other one—they invested only in Treasury bonds and their own one-sixth acre of suburban real estate. When the marching in Selma and Washington had turned to killing in Detroit and Kent State, they shook their heads sagely: *See? We said so. No good comes of getting involved in things that don't concern you.* Jesse's father had held the same job for thirty years; his mother considered it immoral to buy anything not on sale. They waited until she was over forty to have Jesse, their only child.

At sixteen, Jesse had despised them; at twenty-four, pitied them; at twenty-eight, his present age, loved them with a despairing gratitude not completely free of contempt. They had missed so much, dared so little. They lived now in Florida, retired and happy and smug. "The pension"—they called it that, as if it were a famous diamond or a well-loved estate—was inflated by Collapse prices into providing a one-bedroom bungalow with beige carpets and a pool. In the pool's placid, artificially blue waters, the Randalls beheld chlorined visions of triumph. "Even after we retired," Jesse's mother told him proudly, "we didn't have to go backward."

"That's what comes from thrift, son," his father always added. "And hard work. No reason these deadbeats today couldn't do the same thing."

Jesse looked around their tiny yard at the plastic ducks lined up like headstones, the fanatically trimmed hedge, the blue-and-white striped awning, and his arms made curious beating motions, as if they were lashed to his side. "Nice, Mom. Nice."

"You know it," she said, and winked roguishly. Jesse had looked away before she could see his embarrassment. Boston had loomed large in his mind, compelling and vivid and hectic as an exotic disease.

There was no peritonitis. Jesse sliced free the spoiled bit of tissue that had been Rosamund's appendix. As he closed with quick, sure movements, he heard a click. A camera. He couldn't look away, but out of a sudden rush of euphoria he said to whoever was taking the picture, "Not one for the gallery this time. This one's going to *live*."

When the incision was closed, Jesse administered a massive dose of scaramine. Carefully he instructed Kenny and the girl's father about the medication, the little girl's diet, the procedures to maintain asepsis which, since they were bound to be inadequate, made the scaramine so necessary. "I'm on duty the next thirty-six hours at the hospital. I'll return Wednesday night, you'll either have to come get me or give me the address, I'll take a taxi and—"

The father drew in a quick, shaky breath like a sob. Jesse turned to him. "She's got a strong fighting chance, this procedure isn't—" A woman exploded from a back room, shrieking.

"No, no, noooooo. . . ." She tried to throw herself on the patient. Jesse lunged for her, but Kenny was quicker. He grabbed her around the waist, pinning her arms to her sides. She fought him, wailing and screaming, as he dragged her back through the door. "Murderer, baby killer, nooooooo—"

"My wife," the father finally said. "She doesn't . . . doesn't understand."

Probably doctors were devils to her, Jesse thought. Gods who denied people the healing they could have offered. Poor bastards. He felt a surge of quiet pride that he could teach them different.

The father went on looking at Rosamund, now sleeping peacefully. Jesse couldn't see the other man's eyes.

Back home at the apartment, he popped open a beer. He felt fine. Was it too late to call Anne?

It was—the computer clock said 2:00 A.M. She'd already be sacked out. In seven more hours his own thirty-six-hour rotation started, but he couldn't sleep.

He sat down at the computer. The machine hadn't moved to surround his empty square after all. It must have something else in mind. Smiling, sipping at his beer, Jesse sat down to match wits with the Korean computer in the ancient Japanese game in the waning Boston night.

Two days later, he went back to check on Rosamund. The rowhouse was deserted, boards nailed diagonally across the window. Jesse's heart began to pound. He was afraid to ask information of the neighbors; men in dark clothes kept going in and out of the house next door, their eyes cold. Jesse went back to the hospital and waited. He couldn't think what else to do.

Four rotations later the deputy sheriff waited for him outside the building, unable to pass the security monitors until Jesse came home.

COMMONWEALTH OF MASSACHUSETTS
SUFFOLK COUNTY   SUPERIOR COURT
   To Jesse Robert Randall of Morningside Security Enclave, Building 16, Apartment 3C, Boston, within our county of Suffolk. Whereas Steven & Rose Gocek of Boston within our County of Suffolk have begun an action of Tort against you returnable in the Superior Court holden at Boston within our County of Suffolk on October 18, 2004, in which action damages are claimed in the sum of $2,000,000 as follows:

TORT AND/OR CONTRACT FOR MALPRACTICE

as will more fully appear from the declaration to be filed in said Court when and if said action is entered therein:

   WE COMMAND YOU, if you intend to make any defense of said action, that on said date or within such further time as the law allows you cause your written appearance to be entered and your written answer or other lawful pleadings to be filed in the office of the Clerk of the Court to which said writ is returnable, and that you defend against said action according to law.

   Hereof fail not at your peril, as otherwise said judgment may be entered against you in said action without further notice.

   Witness, Lawrence F. Monastersky, Esquire, at Boston, the fourth day of March in the year of our Lord two thousand four.

                                        Alice P. McCarren
                                        Clerk

Jesse looked up from the paper. The deputy sheriff, a soft-bodied man with small, light eyes, looked steadily back.

"But what . . . what happened?"

The deputy looked out over Jesse's left shoulder, a gesture meaning he wasn't officially saying what he was saying. "The kid died. The one they say you treated."

"Died? Of what? But I went back. . . ." He stopped, filled with sudden sickening uncertainty about how much he was admitting.

The deputy went on staring over his shoulder. "You want my advice, Doc? Get yourself a lawyer."

Doctor, lawyer, Indian chief, Jesse thought suddenly, inanely. The inanity somehow brought it all home. He was being sued. For malpractice. By an uninsurable. Now. Here. Him, Jesse Randall. Who had been only trying to help.

"Cold for this time of year," the deputy remarked. "They're dying of cold and malnutrition down there, in Roxbury and Dorchester and Southie. Even the goddamn weather can't give us a break."

Jesse couldn't answer. A wind off the harbor fluttered the paper in his hand.

"These are the facts," the lawyer said. He looked tired, a small man in a dusty office lined with second-hand law books. "The hospital purchased malpractice coverage for its staff, including residents. In doing so, it entered into a contract with certain obligations and exclusions for each side. If a specific incident falls under these exclusions, the contract is not in force with regard to that incident. One such exclusion is that residents will not be covered if they treat uninsured persons unless such treatment occurs within the hospital setting or the resident has reasonable grounds to assume that such a person is insured. Those are not the circumstances you described to me."

"No," Jesse said. He had the sensation that the law books were falling off the top shelves, slowly but inexorably, like small green and brown glaciers. Outside, he had the same sensation about the tops of buildings.

"Therefore, you are not covered by any malpractice insurance. Another set of facts: Over the last five years jury decisions in malpractice cases have averaged 85 percent in favor of plaintiffs. Insurance companies and legislatures are made up of insurables, Dr. Randall. However, juries are still drawn by lot from the general citizenry. Most of the educated general citizenry finds ways to get out of jury duty. They always did. Juries are likely to be 65 percent or more uninsurables. It's the last place the havenots still wield much real power, and they use it."

"You're saying I'm dead," Jesse said numbly. "They'll find me guilty."

The little lawyer looked pained. "Not 'dead,' Doctor. Convicted—most probably. But conviction isn't death. Not even professional death. The hospital may or may not dismiss you—they have that right—but you can still finish your training elsewhere. And malpractice suits, however they go, are not of themselves grounds for denial of a medical license. You can still be a doctor."

"Treating who?" Jesse cried. He threw up his hands. The books fell slightly faster. "If I'm convicted I'll have to declare bankruptcy—there's no way I could pay a jury settlement like that! And even if I found another residency at some third-rate hospital in Podunk, no decent practitioner would ever accept me as a partner. I'd have to practice alone, without money to set up more than a hole-in-the-corner office among God-knows-*who* . . . and even that's assuming I can find a hospital that will let me finish. All because I wanted to help people who are getting shit on!"

The lawyer took off his glasses and rubbed the lenses thoughtfully with a tissue. "Maybe," he said, "they're shitting back."

"What?"

"You haven't asked about the specific charges, Doctor."

"Malpractice! The brat died!"

The lawyer said, "Of massive scaramine allergic reaction."

The anger leeched out of Jesse. He went very quiet.

"She was allergic to scaramine," the lawyer said. "You failed to ascertain that. A basic medical question."

"I—" The words wouldn't come out. He saw again the laminated gene-scan chart, the detailed analysis of chromosome 11. A camera clicking, recording that he was there. The hysterical woman, the mother, exploding from the back room: *noooooooooo*. . . . The father standing frozen, his eyes downcast.

It wasn't possible.

Nobody would kill their own child. Not to discredit one of the fortunate ones, the haves, the insurables, the employables. . . . No one would do that.

The lawyer was watching him carefully, glasses in hand.

Jesse said, "Dr. Michael Cassidy—" and stopped.

"Dr. Cassidy what?" the lawyer said.

But all Jesse could see, suddenly, was the row of plastic ducks in his parents' Florida yard, lined up as precisely as headstones, garish hideous yellow as they marched undeviatingly wherever it was they were going.

"No," Mike Cassidy said. "I didn't send him."

They stood in the hospital parking lot. Snow blew from the east. Cassidy wrapped both arms around himself and rocked back and forth. "He didn't come from us."

"He said he did!"

"I know. But he didn't. His group must have heard we were helping illegally, gotten your name from somebody—"

"But why?" Jesse shouted. "Why frame me? Why kill a child just to frame *me*? I'm nothing!"

Cassidy's face spasmed. Jesse saw that his horror at Jesse's position was real, his sympathy genuine, and both useless. There was nothing Cassidy could do.

"I don't know," Cassidy whispered. And then, "Are you going to name me at your malpractice trial?"

Jesse turned away without answering, into the wind.

Chief of Surgery Jonathan Eberhart called him into his office just before Jesse started his rotation. Before, not after. That was enough to tell him everything. He was getting very good at discovering the whole from a single clue.

"Sit down, Doctor," Eberhart said. His voice, normally austere, held unwilling compassion. Jesse heard it, and forced himself not to shudder.

"I'll stand."

"This is very difficult," Eberhart said, "but I think you already see our position. It's not one any of us would have chosen, but it's what we have. This hospital operates at a staggering deficit. Most patients cannot begin to cover the costs of modern technological health care. State and federal governments are both strapped with enormous debt. Without insurance companies and the private philanthropical support of a few rich families, we would not be able to open our doors to anyone at all. If we lose our insurance rating we—"

"I'm out on my ass," Jesse said. "Right?"

Eberhart looked out the window. It was snowing. Once Jesse, driving through Oceanview Security Enclave to pick up a date, had seen Eberhart building a snowman with two small children, probably his grandchildren. Even rolling lopsided globes of cold, Eberhart had had dignity.

"Yes, Doctor. I'm sorry. As I understand it, the facts of your case are not in legal dispute. Your residency here is terminated."

"Thank you," Jesse said, an odd formality suddenly replacing his crudeness. "For everything."

Eberhart neither answered nor turned around. His shoulders, framed in the grey window, slumped forward. He might, Jesse thought, have had a sudden advanced case of osteoporosis. For which, of course, he would be fully insured.

He packed the computer last, fitting each piece carefully into its original packing. Maybe that would raise the price that Second Thoughts was willing to give him: *Look, almost new, still in the original box.* At the last minute he decided to keep the playing pieces for *go*, shoving them into the suitcase with his clothes and medical equipment. Only this suitcase would go with him.

When the packing was done, he walked up two flights and rang Anne's bell. Her rotation ended a half hour ago. Maybe she wouldn't be asleep yet.

She answered the door in a loose blue robe, toothbrush in hand. "Jesse, hi, I'm afraid I'm really beat—"

He no longer believed in indirection. "Would you have dinner with me tomorrow night?"

"Oh, I'm sorry, I can't," Anne said. She shifted her weight so one bare foot stood on top of the other, a gesture so childish it had to be embarrassment. Her toenails were shiny and smooth.

"After your next rotation?" Jesse said. He didn't smile.

"I don't know when I—"

"The one after that?"

Anne was silent. She looked down at her toothbrush. A thin pristine line of toothpaste snaked over the bristles.

"Okay," Jesse said, without expression. "I just wanted to be sure."

"Jesse—" Anne called after him, but he didn't turn around. He could already tell from her voice that she didn't really have anything more to say. If he had turned it would have been only for the sake of a last look at her toes, polished and shiny as *go* stones, and there really didn't seem to be any point in looking.

He moved into a cheap hotel on Boylston Street, into a room the size of a supply closet with triple locks on the door and bars on the window, where his money would go far. Every morning he took the subway to the Copley Square library, rented a computer cubicle, and wrote letters to hospitals across the country. He also answered classified ads in the *New England Journal of Medicine*, those that offered practice out-of-country where a license was not crucial, or low-paying medical research positions not too many people might want, or supervised assistantships. In the afternoons he walked the grubby streets of Dorchester, looking for Kenny. The lawyer representing Mr. and Mrs. Steven Gocek, parents of the dead Rosamund, would give him no addresses. Neither would his own lawyer, he of the collapsing books and desperate clientele, in whom Jesse had already lost all faith.

He never saw Kenny on the cold streets.

The last week of March, an unseasonable warm wind blew from the south, and kept up. Crocuses and daffodils pushed up between the sagging buildings. Children appeared, chasing each other across the garbage-laden streets, crying raucously. Rejections came from hospitals, employers. Jesse had still not told his parents what had happened. Twice in April he picked up a public phone, and twice he saw again the plastic ducks marching across the artificial lawn, and something inside him slammed shut so hard not even the phone number could escape.

One sunny day in May he walked in the Public Garden. The city still maintained it fairly well; foreign tourist traffic made it profitable. Jesse counted the number of well-dressed foreigners versus the number of ragged street Bostonians. The ratio equaled the survival rate for uninsured diabetics.

"Hey, mister, help me! Please!"

A terrified boy, ten or eleven, grabbed Jesse's hand and pointed. At the bottom of a grassy knoll an elderly man lay crumpled on the ground, his face twisted.

"My grandpa! He just grabbed his chest and fell down! Do something! Please!"

Jesse could smell the boy's fear, a stink like rich loam. He walked over to the old man. Breathing stopped, no pulse, color still pink. . . .

No.

This man was an uninsured. Like Kenny, like Steven Gocek. Like Rosamund.

"Grandpa!" the child wailed. "Grandpa!"

Jesse knelt. He started mouth-to-mouth. The old man smelled of sweat, of old flesh. No blood moved through the body. "Breathe, dammit, breathe," Jesse heard someone say, and then realized it was him. *Breathe*, you old fart, you uninsured deadbeat, you stinking ingrate, breathe—"

The old man breathed.

He sent the boy for more adults. The child took off at a dead run, returning twenty minutes later with uncles, father, cousins, aunts, most of whom spoke some language Jesse couldn't identify. In that twenty minutes none of the well-dressed tourists in the Garden approached Jesse, standing guard beside the old man, who breathed carefully and moaned softly, stretched full-length on the grass. The tourists glanced at him and then away, their faces tightening.

The tribe of family carried the old man away on a homemade stretcher. Jesse put his hand on the arm of one of the young men. "Insurance? Hospital?"

The man spat onto the grass.

Jesse walked beside the stretcher, monitoring the old man until he was in his own bed. He told the child what to do for him, since no one else seemed to understand. Later that day he went back, carrying his medical bag, and gave them the last of his hospital supply of nitroglycerin. The oldest woman, who had been too busy issuing orders about the stretcher to pay Jesse any attention before, stopped dead and jabbered in her own tongue.

"You a doctor?" the child translated. The tip of his ear, Jesse noticed, was missing. Congenital? Accident? Ritual mutilation? The ear had healed clean.

"Yeah," Jesse said. "A doctor."

The old woman chattered some more and disappeared behind a door. Jesse gazed at the walls. There were no deathbed photos. As he was leaving, the woman returned with ten incredibly dirty dollar bills.

"Doctor," she said, her accent harsh, and when she smiled Jesse saw that all her top teeth and most of her bottom ones were missing, the gum swollen with what might have been early signs of scurvy.

"Doctor," she said again.

He moved out of the hotel just as the last of his money ran out. The old man's wife, Androula Malakassas, found him a room in somebody else's rambling, dilapidated boardinghouse. The house was noisy at all hours, but the room was clean and large. Androula's cousin brought home an old, multi-positional dentist chair, probably stolen, and Jesse used that for both examining and operating table. Medical substances—antibiotics, chemotherapy, IV drugs—which he had thought of as the hardest need to fill outside of controlled channels, turned out to be the easiest. On reflection, he realized this shouldn't have surprised him.

In July he delivered his first breech birth, a primapara whose labor was so long and painful and bloody he thought at one point he'd lose both mother and baby. He lost neither, although the new mother cursed him in Spanish and spit at him. She was too weak for the saliva to go far. Holding the warm-assed, nine-pound baby boy, Jesse had heard a camera click. He cursed too, but feebly; the sharp thrill of pleasure that pierced from throat to bowels was too strong.

In August he lost three patients in a row, all to conditions that would have needed elaborate, costly equipment and procedures: renal failure, aortic aneurysm, narcotic overdose. He went to all three funerals. At each one the family and friends cleared a little space for him, in which he stood surrounded by respect and resentment. When a knife fight broke out at the funeral of the aneurysm, the family hustled Jesse away from the danger, but not so far away that he couldn't treat the loser.

In September a Chinese family, recent immigrants, moved into Androula's sprawling boarding house. The woman wept all day. The man roamed Boston, looking for work. There was a grandfather who spoke a little English, having learned it in Peking during the brief period of American industrial expansion into the Pacific Rim before the Chinese government convulsed and the American economy collapsed. The grandfather played *go*. On evenings when no one wanted Jesse, he sat with Lin Shujen and moved the polished white and black stones over the grid, seeking to enclose empty spaces without losing any pieces. Mr. Lin took a long time to consider each move.

In October, a week before Jesse's trial, his mother died. Jesse's father sent him money to fly home for the funeral, the first money Jesse had accepted from his family since he'd finally told them he had left the hospital. After the funeral Jesse sat in the living room of his father's Florida house and listened to the elderly mourners recall their youths in the vanished prosperity of the '50s and '60s.

"Plenty of jobs then for people who're willing to work."

"Still plenty of jobs. Just nobody's willing any more."

"Want everything handed to them. If you ask me, this collapse'll prove to be a good thing in the long run. Weed out the weaklings and the lazy."

"It was the sixties we got off on the wrong track, with Lyndon Johnson and all the welfare programs—"

They didn't look at Jesse. He had no idea what his father had said to them about him.

Back in Boston, stinking under Indian summer heat, people thronged his room. Fractures, cancers, allergies, pregnancies, punctures, deficiencies, imbalances. They were resentful that he'd gone away for five days. He should be here; they needed him. He was the doctor.

* * *

The first day of his trial, Jesse saw Kenny standing on the courthouse steps. Kenny wore a cheap blue suit with loafers and white socks. Jesse stood very still, then walked over to the other man. Kenny tensed.

"I'm not going to hit you," Jesse said.

Kenny watched him, chin lowered, slight body balanced on the balls of his feet. A fighter's stance.

"I want to ask something," Jesse said. "It won't affect the trial. I just want to know. Why'd you do it? Why did *they*? I know the little girl's true genescan showed 98 percent risk of leukemia death within three years, but even so—how could you?"

Kenny scrutinized him carefully. Jesse saw that Kenny thought Jesse might be wired. Even before Kenny answered, Jesse knew what he'd hear. "I don't know what you're talking about, man."

"You couldn't get inside the system. Any of you. So you brought me out. If Mohammed won't go to the mountain—"

"You don't make no sense," Kenny said.

"Was it worth it? To you? To them? Was it?"

Kenny walked away, up the courthouse steps. At the top waited the Goceks, who were suing Jesse for two million dollars he didn't have and wasn't insured for, and that they knew damn well they wouldn't collect. On the wall of their house, wherever it was, probably hung Rosamund's deathbed picture, a little girl with a plain, sallow face and beautiful hair.

Jesse saw his lawyer trudge up the courthouse steps, carrying his briefcase. Another lawyer, with an equally shabby briefcase, climbed in parallel several feet away. Between the two men the courthouse steps made a white empty space.

Jesse climbed, too, hoping to hell this wouldn't take too long. He had an infected compound femoral fracture, a birth with potential erythroblastosis fetalis, and an elderly phlebitis, all waiting. He was especially concerned about the infected fracture, which needed careful monitoring because the man's genescan showed a tendency toward weak T-cell production. The guy was a day laborer, foul-mouthed and ignorant and brave, with a wife and two kids. He'd broken his leg working illegal construction. Jesse was determined to give him at least a fighting chance.

THE COMING OF VERTUMNUS

Ian Watson

One of the most brilliant innovators to enter SF in many years, Ian Watson writes fiction that is typified by its vivid and highly original conceptualization. He sold his first story in 1969, and attracted widespread critical attention in 1973 with his first novel, *The Embedding*. His novel *The Jonah Kit* won the British Science Fiction Award and the British Science Fiction Association Award in 1976 and 1977, respectively. Watson's other books include *Alien Embassy, Miracle Visitors, The Martian Inca, Under Heaven's Bridge* (coauthored with Michael Bishop), *Chekhov's Journey, Deathhunter, The Gardens of Delight, Queenmagic, Kingmagic, The Book of the River, The Book of the Stars,* and *The Book of Being,* the collections *The Very Slow Time Machine, Sunstroke, Slow Birds,* and *Evil Water*. As editor, his books include the anthologies *Pictures at an Exhibition, Changes* (coedited with Michael Bishop), and *Afterlives* (coedited with Pamela Sargent). His most recent books are the collection *Stalin's Teardrops* and the novel *The Flies of Memory*. He has had stories in our First and Fifth Annual Collections. Watson lives with his wife and daughter in a small village in Northhamptonshire, England.

In the complex, suspenseful, and deliciously paranoid novella that follows, Watson demonstrates, with typical ingenuity and inventiveness, that the best conspiracies are those that go *way* back . . .

Do you know the *Portrait of Jacopo Strada*, which Titian painted in 1567 or so?

Bathed in golden light, this painting shows us a rich connoisseur displaying a nude female statuette which is perhaps eighteen inches high. Oh yes, full-bearded Signor Strada is prosperous—in his black velvet doublet, his cerise satin shirt, and his ermine cloak. He holds that voluptuous little Venus well away from an unseen spectator. He gazes at that spectator almost shiftily. Strada is exposing his Venus to view, yet he's also withholding her proprietorially so as to whet the appetite.

With her feet supported on his open right hand, and her back resting across his left palm, the sculpted woman likewise leans away as if in complicity with Strada. How carefully his fingers wrap around her. One finger eclipses a breast. Another teases her neck. Not that her charms aren't on display. *Her* hands are held high, brushing her shoulders. Her big-navelled belly and mons veneris are on full show. A slight crossing of her knees hints at a helpless, lascivious reticence.

She arouses the desire to acquire and to handle her, a yearning that is at once an artistic and an erotic passion. Almost, she seems to be a homunculus—a tiny woman bred within an alchemist's vessel by the likes of a Paracelsus, who had died only some twenty-five years previously.

I chose this portrait of Jacopo Strada as the cover for my book, *Aesthetic Concupiscence*. My first chapter was devoted to an analysis of the implications of this particular painting . . .

Jacopo Strada was an antiquary who spent many years in the employ of the Habsburg court, first at Vienna and then at Prague, as Keeper of Antiquities. He procured and catalogued gems and coins as well as classical statuary.

Coins were important to the Habsburg Holy Roman Emperors, because coins bore the portraits of monarchs. A collection of coins was a visible genealogy of God-anointed rulers. Back on Christmas Day in the year 800 the Pope had crowned Charlemagne as the first "Emperor of the Romans." The Church had decided it no longer quite had the clout to run Europe politically as well as spiritually. This imperial concoction—at times heroic, at other times hiccuping along—lasted until 1806. That was when the last Holy Roman Emperor, Francis II, abdicated without successor so as to thwart Napoleon from grabbing the title. By then, as they say, the Emperor presided over piecemeal acres which were neither an empire, nor Roman, nor holy. Of course, effectively the Habsburg dynasty had hijacked the title of Emperor, which was supposed to be elective.

History has tended to view the Habsburg court of Rudolph II at Prague in the late 1570s and 80s as wonky, wacky, and weird: an excellent watering hole for any passing nut-cases, such as alchemists, hermetic occultists, or astrologers—who of course, back then, were regarded as "scientists." Not that true science wasn't well represented, too! Revered astronomer Tycho Brahe burst his bladder with fatal result at Rudolph's court, due to that Emperor's eccentric insistence that no one might be excused from table till his Caesarian Majesty had finished revelling.

Botanists were very busy classifying plants there, and naturalists were taxonomizing exotic wildlife (of which many specimens graced Rudolph's zoo)—just as Strada himself tried to impose order and methodology upon ancient Venuses.

Strada resigned and quit Prague in 1579, perhaps in irritation that his aesthetic criteria held less sway over Rudolph than those of another adviser on the Imperial art collection—namely *Giuseppe Archimboldo* . . .

My troubles began when I received a phone call at Central St. Martin's School of Art in Charing Cross Road, where I lectured part-time in History of the Same. The caller was one John Lascelles. He introduced himself as the UK personal assistant to Thomas Rumbold Wright. Oil magnate and art collector, no less. Lascelles's voice had a youthfully engaging, though slightly prissy timbre.

Was I the Jill Donaldson who had written *Aesthetic Concupiscence?* I who had featured scintillatingly on *Art Debate at Eight* on Channel 4 TV? Mr Wright would very much like to meet me. He had a proposition to make. Might a car be sent for me, to whisk me the eighty-odd miles from London to the North Cotswolds?

What sort of proposition?

Across my mind there flashed a bizarre image of myself as a diminutive Venus sprawling in this oil billionaire's acquisitive, satin-shirted arms. For of course in my book I had cleverly put the stiletto-tipped boot into all such as he, who contributed to the obscene lunacy of art prices.

Maybe Thomas Rumbold Wright was seeking a peculiar form of recompense for my ego-puncturing stiletto stabs, since he—capricious bachelor—was certainly mentioned once in my book . . .

"What sort of proposition?"

"I've no idea," said Lascelles, boyishly protesting innocence.

I waited. However, Lascelles was very good at silences, whereas I am not.

"Surely you must have *some* idea, Mr. Lascelles?"

"Mr Wright will tell you, Ms. Donaldson."

Why not? Why not indeed? I had always revelled in paradoxes, and it must be quite paradoxical—not to mention constituting a delicious piece of fieldwork—for Jill Donaldson to accept an invitation from Thomas R. Wright, lavisher of untold millions upon old canvases.

One of my prime paradoxes—in my "Stratagems of Deceit" chapter—involved a comparison between the consumption of sensual fine art, and of visual pornography. I perpetrated an iconography of the latter based upon interviews I conducted with "glamour" photographers on the job. No, I *didn't* see it as my mission to deconstruct male-oriented sexism. Not a bit of it. That would be banal. I came to praise porn, not to bury it. Those sumptuous nudes in oils of yore were the buoyant, respectable porn of their day. What we needed nowadays, I enthused—tongue in cheek, several tongues in cheek indeed—were issues of *Penthouse* magazine entirely painted by latterday Masters, with tits by the Titians of today, vulvas by Veroneses, pubes by populist Poussins . . . Ha!

I was buying a little flat in upper Bloomsbury, with the assistance of Big Brother Robert who was a bank manager in Oxford. Plump sanctimonious Bob regarded this scrap of property as a good investment. Indeed, but for his support, I could hardly have coped. Crowded with books and prints, on which I squandered too much, Chez Donaldson was already distinctly cramped. I *could* hold a party in it—so long as I only invited a dozen people and we spilled on to the landing.

Even amidst slump and eco-puritanism, London property prices still bore a passing resemblance to Impressionist price-tags. Perhaps eco-puritanism actually *sustained* high prices, since it seemed that one ought to be penalized for wishing to live fairly centrally in a city, contributing to the sewage burden and resources and power demand of megalopolis, and whatnot.

Well, we were definitely into an era of radical repressiveness. The Eco bandwagon was rolling. Was one's lifestyle environmentally friendly, third-world friendly, future friendly? The no-smoking, no-car, no-red-meat, no-frilly-knickers, sackcloth-and-ashes straitjacket was tightening; and while I might have seemed to be on that side ethically as regards the conspicuous squandering of megamillions on paintings, I simply did not buy the package. Perhaps the fact that I smoked cigarettes—oh penalized sin!—accounted in part for my antipathy to the Goody-Goodies. Hence my naughtiness in exalting (tongues in cheek) such a symptom of unreconstructed consciousness as porn. Paradox, paradox. I did like to *provoke*.

How many lovers had such a tearaway as myself had by the age of thirty-one? Just three, in fact; one of them another woman, a painting student.

Peter, Annie, and Phil. No one at the moment. I wasn't exactly outrageous in private life.

Peter had been the prankster, the mercurial one. For his "God of the Deep" exhibition he wired fish skeletons into the contours of bizarre Gothic cathedrals, which he displayed in tanks of water. Goldfish were the congregations—was this art, or a joke? Several less savoury anarchistic exploits finally disenchanted me with Peter—about the time I decided definitively that I really was an art historian and a critic (though of capricious spirit).

Sending a Mercedes, with darkened windows, to collect me could have wiped out my street cred. Personally, I regarded this *as a Happening*.

Mind you, I did experience a twinge of doubt—along the lines that maybe I ought to phone someone (Phil? Annie? Definitely not Peter . . .) to confide where I was being taken, just in case "something *happens* to me . . ." I didn't do so, yet the spice of supposed danger added a certain frisson.

When my doorbell rang, the radio was bemoaning the death of coral reefs, blanched leprous by the extinction of the symbiotic algae in them. This was sad, of course, *tragic*; yet I didn't intend to scourge myself personally, as the participants in the programme seemed to feel was appropriate.

The driver proved to be a Dutchman called Kees, pronounced Case, who "did things" for Rumby—as he referred to Thomas Rumbold Wright. Athletic-looking and bearded, courteous and affable, Case wore jeans, Reeboks, and an open-necked checked shirt. No uniform or peaked cap for this driver, who opened the front door of the Merc so that I should sit next to him companionably, not behind in splendid isolation. Case radiated the easy negligence of a cultured bodyguard-if-need-be. I was dressed in similar informal style, being determined not to doll myself up in awe for the grand encounter—though I refused to wear trainers with designer names on them.

Although Wright maintained a corporate headquarters in Texas, he personally favoured his European bastion, Bexford Hall. This had recently been extended by the addition of a mini-mock-Tudor castle wing to house his art in even higher security. The *Sunday Times* colour supplement had featured photos of this jail of art. (Did it come complete with a dungeon, I wondered?)

The mid-June weather was chilly and blustery—either typical British summer caprice or a Greenhouse spasm, depending on your ideology.

As we were heading out towards the motorway, we soon passed one of those hoardings featuring a giant poster of Archimboldo's portrait of Rudolph II as an assembly of fruits, vegetables, and flowers. Ripe pear nose; flushed round cheeks of peach and apple; cherry and mulberry eyes; spiky chestnut husk of a chin; corn-ear brows, and so on, and so on.

The Emperor Rudolph as Vertumnus, Roman god of fruit trees, of growth and transformation. Who cared about that particular snippet of art historical info? Across the portrait's chest splashed the Eco message, *WE ARE ALL PART OF NATURE.* This was part of that massive and highly successful Green propaganda campaign exploiting Archimboldo's "nature-heads"—a campaign which absolutely caught the eye in the most persuasive style.

These posters had been adorning Europe and America and wherever else for the best part of two years now. Indeed, they'd become such a radiant emblem of eco-consciousness, such a part of the mental landscape, that I doubted they would *ever* disappear from our streets. People even wore minia-tures as badges—as though true humanity involved becoming a garlanded bundle of fruit and veg, with a cauliflower brain, perhaps.

Case slowed and stared at that hoarding.

"Rudolph the red-nosed," I commented.

Somewhat to my surprise, Case replied, "Ah, and Rudolph loved Archim-boldo's jokes so much that he made him into a Count! Sense of humour's sadly missing these days, don't you think?"

My driver must have been boning up on his art history. The Green poster campaign was certainly accompanied by no background info about the artist whose images they were ripping off—or perhaps one ought to say "recuperat-ing" for the present day . . . rather as an ad agency might exploit the Mona Lisa to promote tampons. (*Why is she smiling . . . ?*)

"Those paintings weren't *just* jokes," I demurred.

"No, and neither are those posters." Case seemed to loathe those, as though he would like to tear them all down. He speeded up, and soon we reached the motorway.

Under the driving mirror—where idiots used to hang woolly dice, and where nowadays people often hung plastic apples or pears, either sincerely or else in an attempt to immunize their vehicles against ecovandals—there dangled a little model . . . of a rather complex-looking space station. The model was made of silver, or was at least silver-plated. It swung to and fro as we drove. At times, when I glanced that way, I confused rear-view mirror with model so that it appeared as if a gleaming futuristic craft was pursuing us up the M40, banking and yawing behind us.

Down where my left hand rested I found power-controls for the passenger seat. So I raised the leather throne—yes indeed, I was sitting on a dead animal's hide, and no wonder the windows were semi-opaque from outside. I lowered the seat and reclined it. I extruded and recessed the lumbar support.

Now that I'd discovered this box of tricks, I just couldn't settle on the most restful position for myself. Supposing the seat had been inflexible, there'd have been no problem. Excessive tech, perhaps? I felt fidgety.

"Do you mind if I smoke?" I asked Case.

"Rumby smokes in this car," was his answer, which didn't quite confide his own personal feelings, unless the implication was that these were largely irrelevant amongst Wright's entourage.

Case ignored the 60-mile-an-hour fuel-efficiency speed limit, though he drove very safely in this cushioned tank of a car. He always kept an eye open well ahead and well behind as if conscious of possible interception, by a police patrol, or—who knows?—by Green vigilante kidnappers.

Bexford Hall was in the triangle between Stow-on-the-Wold, Broadway, and Winchcombe, set in a wooded river valley cutting through the rolling, breezy, sheep-grazed uplands.

The house was invisible from the leafy side road, being masked by the high, wire-tipped stone boundary wall in good repair, and then by trees. Case opened wrought iron gates electronically from the car—apparently the head gardener and family lived in the high-pitched gatehouse alongside—and we purred up a winding drive.

Lawns with topiary hedges fronted the mullion-windowed house. Built of soft golden limestone around a courtyard, Chez Wright somewhat resembled a civilian castle even before his addition of the bastioned, bastard-architectural art wing. A helicopter stood on a concrete apron. A Porsche, a Jaguar, and various lesser beasts were parked in a row on gravel. A satellite dish graced the rear slate-tiled roof, from which Tudor chimneys rose.

The sun blinked through, though clouds still scudded.

And so—catching a glimpse en route of several people at computer consoles, scrutinizing what were probably oil prices—we passed through to John Lascelles' office, where the casual piles of glossy art books mainly caught my eye.

Having delivered me, Case left to "do things" . . .

Lascelles was tall, willowy, and melancholy. He favoured dark mauve corduroy trousers and a multipocketed purple shirt loaded with many pens, not to mention a clip-on walkie-talkie. On account of the ecclesiastical hues I imagined him as a sort of secular court chaplain to Wright. His smile was a pursed, wistful affair, though there was that boyish lilt to his voice which had misled me on the phone. His silences were the truer self.

He poured coffee for me from a percolator; then he radioed news of my arrival. It seemed that people communicated by personal radio in the house. In reply he received a crackly splutter of Texan which I hardly caught.

Lascelles sat and scrutinized me while I drank and smoked a cigarette; on his littered desk I'd noted an ashtray with a cheroot stub crushed in it.

Lascelles steepled his hands. He was cataloguing me: a new person collected—at least potentially—by his non-royal master, as he himself must once have been collected.

Woman. Thirty-one. Mesomorphic build; though not exactly chunky. Small high breasts. Tight curly brown hair cropped quite short. Violet vampiric lipstick. Passably callipygian ass.

Then in bustled *Rumby*—as I simply had to think of the man thereafter.

Rumby was a roly-poly fellow attired in crumpled bronze slacks and a floppy buff shirt with lots of pockets for pens, calculator, radio. He wore scruffy trainers, though I didn't suppose that he jogged around his estate. His white complexion said otherwise. His face was quizzically owlish, with large spectacles—frames of mottled amber—magnifying his eyes into brown orbs; and his thinning feathery hair was rebellious.

He beamed, almost tangibly projecting *energy*. He pressed my flesh quickly. He drew me along in his slipstream from Lascelles' office down a walnut-panelled corridor. We entered a marble-floored domed hall which housed gleaming spotlit models. Some in perspex cases, others hanging. Not models of oil-rigs, oh no. Models of a Moon base, of spacecraft, of space stations.

Was Rumby a little boy at heart? Was this his den? Did he play with these toys?

"What do you think about space?" he asked me.

Mischief urged me to be contrary, yet I told him the truth.

"Personally," I assured him, "I think that if we cop out of space now, as looks highly likely, then we'll be locked up here on Mother Earth for ever after eating a diet of beans and being repressively good with 'Keep off the Grass' signs everywhere. Oh dear, we mustn't mess up Mars by going there the way we messed up Earth! Mess up Mars, for Christ's sake? It's *dead* to start with—a desert of rust. I think if we can grab all those clean resources and free energy in space, we'd be crazy to hide in our shell instead. But there's neopuritanism for you."

Rumby rubbed his hands. "And if Green propaganda loses us our launch window of the next fifty years or so, then we've lost forever because we'll have spent all our spunk. I knew you'd be *simpatico*, Jill. I've read *Aesthetic Concubines* twice."

"*Concupiscence*, actually," I reminded him.

"Let's call it *Concubines*. That's easier to say."

Already my life and mind were being mutated by Rumby . . .

"So how did you extrapolate my views on space from a book on the art market?" I asked.

He tapped his brow. "I picked up on your anti-repressive streak and the perverse way you think. Am I right?"

"Didn't you regard my book as a bit, well, rude?"

"I don't intend to take things personally when the future of the human race is at stake. It is, you know. It is. Green pressures are going to nix everyone's space budget. Do you know they're pressing to limit the number of rocket launches to a measly dozen per year *world-wide* because of the exhaust gases? And all those would have to be Earth-Resources-relevant. Loony-tune environ-*mentalists*! There's a *religious* fervour spreading like clap in a cathouse. It's screwing the world's brains." How colourfully he phrased things. Was he trying to throw me off balance? Maybe he was oblivious to other people's opinions. I gazed blandly at him.

"Jill," he confided, "I'm part of a pro-space pressure group of industrialists called The Star Club. We've commissioned surveys. Do you know, in one recent poll forty-five per cent of those questioned said that they'd happily give up quote all the benefits of 'science' if they could live in a more natural world without radioactivity? Can you believe such scuzzbrains? We *know* how fast this Eco gangrene is spreading. How do we disinfect it? Do we use rational scientific argument? You might as well reason with a hippo in heat."

"Actually, I don't see how this involves me . . ."

"*We'll* need to use some tricks. So, come and view the Wright Collection."

He took me through a security-coded steel door into his climate-controlled sanctum of masterpieces.

Room after room. Rubens. Goya. Titian. And other lesser luminaries . . .
. . . till we came to the door of an inner sanctum.

I half expected to find the Mona Lisa herself within. But no . . .

On an easel sat . . . a totally pornographic, piscine portrait. A figure made of many fishes (along with a few crustaceans).

A female figure.

A spread-legged naked woman, red lobster dildo clutched in one octopus-hand, frigging herself. A slippery, slithery, lubricious Venus composed of eels and catfish and trout and a score of other species. Prawn labia, with legs and feelers as pubic hair . . . The long suckery fingers of her other octopus-hand teased a pearl nipple . . .

The painting just had to be by Archimboldo. It was very clever and, mm, persuasive. It also oozed lust and perversity.

"So how do you like her?" asked Rumby.

"That lobster's rather a nippy notion," I said.

"It isn't a lobster," he corrected me. "It's a cooked freshwater crayfish."

"She's, well, fairly destabilizing if you happen to drool over all those 'We are part of Nature' posters."

"Right! And Archimboldo painted a *dozen* such porn portraits for private consumption by crazy Emperor Rudolph."

"He *did*?" This was astonishing news.

"I've laid hands on them all, though they aren't all here."

Rumby directed me to a table where a portfolio lay. Opening this, I turned over a dozen large glossy colour reproductions—of masturbating men made of mushrooms and autumnal fruits, men with large hairy nuts and spurting seed; of licking lesbian ladies composed of marrows and lettuce leaves . . .

"You researched all the background bio on Strada, Jill. Nobody knows what sort of things our friend Archy might have been painting between 1576 and 1587 before he went back home to Milan, hmm?"

"I thought he was busy arranging festivals for Rudolph. Masques and tournaments and processions."

"That isn't *all* he was arranging. Rudy was fairly nutty."

"Oh, I don't know if that's quite fair to Rudolph . . ."

"What, to keep a chained lion in the hall? To sleep in a different bed every night? His mania for exotica! Esoterica! Erotica! A pushover for any passing magician. Bizarre foibles. Loopy as King Ludo of Bavaria—yet with *real power*. The power to indulge himself—secretly—in orgies and weird erotica, there in vast Ratzen Castle in Prague."

I wondered about the provenance of these hitherto unknown paintings.

To which, Rumby gave a very plausible answer.

When the Swedes under the command of von Wrangel sacked Prague in 1648 as their contribution to the Thirty Years' War, they pillaged the imperial collections. Thus a sheaf of Archimboldos ended up in Skoklosters Castle at Bålsta in Sweden.

"Skoklosters *Slott*. Kind of evocative name, huh?"

When Queen Christina converted to Catholicism in 1654 and abdicated the Swedish throne, she took many of those looted art treasures with her to Rome itself—with the exception of so-called *German* art, which she despised. In her eyes, Archimboldo was part of German art.

However, in the view of her catechist (who was a subtle priest), those locked-away *porn* paintings were a different kettle of fish. The Vatican should take charge of those and keep them *sub rosa*. Painters were never fingered by the Inquisition, unlike authors of the written word. Bonfires of merely lewd material were never an issue in an era when clerics often liked a fuck. Nevertheless, such paintings might serve as a handy blackmail tool against Habsburg Emperors who felt tempted to act too leniently towards Protestants in their domains. A blot on the Habsburg scutcheon, suggesting a strain of lunacy.

The cardinal-diplomat to whom the paintings were consigned deposited them for safe keeping in the crypt at a certain enclosed convent of his patronage. There, as it happened, they remained until discovered by a private collector in the 1890s. By then the convent had fallen on hard times. Our collector relieved the holy mothers of the embarrassing secret heritage in return for a substantial donation . . .

"It's a watertight story," concluded Rumby, blinking owlishly at me. "Of course it's also a complete lie . . ."

The dirty dozen Archimboldos were forgeries perpetrated in Holland within the past couple of years, to Rumby's specifications, by a would-be surrealist.

I stared at the fishy masturbatress, fascinated.

"They're fine forgeries," he enthused. "Painted on antique oak board precisely eleven millimetres thick. Two base layers of white lead, chalk, and charcoal slack . . ." He expatiated with the enthusiasm of a petrochemist conducting an assay of crude. The accuracy of the lipid and protein components. The pigments consisting of azurite, yellow lead, malachite . . . Mr Oil seemed to know rather a lot about such aspects of oil painting.

He waved his hand impatiently. "Point is, it'll stand up under X-ray, infrared, most sorts of analysis. This is perfectionist forgery with serious money behind it. Oh yes, sponsored exhibition in Europe, book, prints, postcards, media scandal . . . ! These naughty Archies are going to fuck all those Green Fascists in the eyeballs. Here's their patron saint with his pants down. Here's what red-nosed Rudy really got off on. Nobody'll be able to gaze dewy-eyed at those posters any more, drooling about the sanctity of nature. *This* is nature—red in dildo and labia. A fish-fuck. Their big image campaign will blow up in their faces—ludicrously, obscenely. Can you beat the power of an image? Why yes, you *can*— with an anti-image! We'll have done something really positive to save the space budget. You'll write the intro to the art book, Jenny, in your inimitable style. Scholarly—but provocative."

"I will?"

"Yes, because I'll pay you three quarters of a million dollars."

A flea-bite to Rumby, really . . .

The budget for this whole escapade was probably ten times that. Or more. Would that represent the output of one single oil well for a year? A month . . . ? I really had no idea.

Aside from our crusade for space, smearing egg conspicuously on the face of the ecofreaks might materially assist Rumby's daily business and prove to be a sound investment, since he profited so handsomely by pumping out the planet's non-renewable resources.

"*And* because you want to sock Green Fascism, Jill. And on account of how this is so splendidly, provocatively perverse."

Was he right, or was he right?

He was certainly different from the kind of man I'd expected to meet.

Obviously I mustn't spill the beans in the near future. *Consequently* the bulk of my fee would be held on deposit in my name in a Zurich bank, but would only become accessible to me five years after publication of *Archimboldo Erotico* . . .

Until then I would need to lead roughly the same life as usual—plus the need to defend my latest opus amongst my peers and on TV and in magazines and wherever else. Rumby—or Chaplain Lascelles—would certainly strive to ensure a media circus, if none such burgeoned of its own accord. I would be Rumby's front woman.

I liked the *three quarters* of a million aspect. This showed that Rumby had subtlety. One million would have been a blatant bribe.

I also liked Rumby himself.

I had indeed been collected.

And that 750K (as Brother Bob would count it) wasn't by any means the only consideration. *I approved.*

As to my fallback position, should the scheme be—ahem—rumbled . . . well, pranks question mundane reality in a revolutionary manner, don't they just?

That was a line from Peter, which I half believed—though not enough to stage a diversion in the National Gallery by stripping my blouse off, as he had wished, while Peter glued a distempery canine turd to Gainsborough's painting, *White Dogs*, so as to question "conventions." I'd balked at *that* proposed escapade of Peter's ten years previously.

This was a political prank—a blow against an insidious, powerful kind of repression; almost, even, a blow for art.

Thus, my defence.

I took a copy of the erotic portfolio back with me to Bloomsbury to gaze at for a few days; and to keep safely locked up when I wasn't looking at it. Just as well that Phil wasn't involved in my immediate life these days, though we still saw each other casually. I'm sure Phil's antennae would have twitched if he had still been sleeping with a strangely furtive me. Being art critic for the *Sunday Times* had seemed to imbue him with the passions of an investigative journalist. Just as soon as *Archimboldo Erotico* burst upon the scene, no doubt he would be in touch . . . I would need to tell lies to a former lover and ensure that "in touch" remained a phrase without physical substance. Already I could envision his injured, acquisitive expression as he rebuked me for not leaking this great art scoop to him personally. ("But why not, Jill? Didn't we share a great deal? I must say I think it's damned queer that you didn't breathe a word about this! Very *peculiar*, in fact. It makes me positively *suspicious* . . . This isn't some kind of *revenge* on your part, is it? But why, *why?*")

And what would Annie think? She was painting in Cornwall in a women's artistic commune, and her last letter had been friendly . . . If I hadn't offended her with my porn paradoxes, then attaching my name to a glossy volume of fish-frigs and spurting phallic mushrooms oughtn't to make too much difference, unless she had become radically repressive of late . . .

In other words, I was wondering to what extent this escapade would cause a hindwards reconstruction of my own life on account of the duplicity in which I'd be engaging.

And what about the *future*—in five years time—when I passed GO and became three quarters of a dollar millionairess? What would I *do* with all that money? Decamp to Italy? Quit the London grime and buy a farmhouse near Florence?

In the meantime I wouldn't be able to confide the truth to any intimate friend. I wouldn't be able to afford intimacy. I might become some pursed-smile equivalent of Chaplain Lascelles, though on a longer leash.

Maybe Rumby had accurately calculated that he was getting a bargain.

To be sure, the shape of my immediate future all somewhat depended on the impact of the book, the exhibition, the extent of the hoo-ha . . . Personally, I'd give the book as much impact as I could. After all, I did like to provoke.

I returned to Bexford House a week later, to stay two nights and to sort through Rumby's stock of material about Archimboldo, Rudolph, and the Prague Court. I have a good reading knowledge of German, French, and Italian, though I'm not conversationally fluent in those tongues. Any book I needed to take away with me was photocopied in its entirety by Lascelles on a high-speed, auto-page-turning machine. Pop in a book—within five minutes out popped its twin, collated and bound. The machine cost twenty thousand dollars.

A week after that, Case drove me to the docklands airport for a rather lux commuter flight with him to Amsterdam, where I examined all the other Archimboldo "originals"; although I didn't meet the forger himself, nor did I even learn his name. The paintings were stored in three locations: in the apartment of Rumby's chosen printer, Wim Van Ewyck, in that of the gallery owner who would host the show, Geert de Lugt, and in a locked room of the Galerij Bosch itself. In the event of premature catastrophe, the entire corpus of controversial work (minus the fishy masturbatress at Bexford House) wouldn't be wiped out en masse.

Presumably the printer didn't need to be in on the conspiracy. What about the gallery owner? Maybe; maybe not . . . *This*, as Case impressed on me, was a subject which shouldn't even be aluded to—nor did Mijnheer de Lugt so much as hint.

The other eleven Archimboldos were even more stunning at full size in the frame than in colour reproduction. And also more . . . appalling?

I returned to Bloomsbury to write twenty large pages of introduction. Less would have been skimpy; more would have been excessive. Since I was being fastidiously attentive to every nuance of the text, the writing took me almost three weeks, with five or six drafts. ("Put some feeling into it," Rumby had counselled. "Smear some vaginal jelly on the words.")

The task done, I phoned Bexford Hall. Case drove the Merc to London the same evening to courier the pages personally. Next day, Rumby phoned to pronounce himself quite delighted. He only suggested a few micro-changes. We were rolling. Our exhibition would open in the Galerij Bosch on the first of September, coinciding with publication of the book.

And of course I must attend the private showing on the last day of August—the vernissage, as it were. (I did hope the varnish was totally dry!)

While in Amsterdam, our party—consisting of Rumby and Case and Lascelles and myself—the Grand Hotel Krasnopolsky because that hotel boasted a Japanese restaurant, and Rumby was a bit of a pig for raw fish. I wasn't complaining.

We arrived a day early in case Rumby had any last-minute thoughts about the layout of the show, or Case about its security aspects. So the morning of the thirty-first saw us at the Galerij Bosch, which fronted a tree-lined canal not far from where dozens of antique shops clustered on the route to the big art museums.

The high neck gable of the building, ornamented with two bounteous sculpted classical maidens amidst cascades of fruits and vegetables—shades of Archimboldo, indeed!—incorporated a hoisting beam, though I doubted that any crated paintings had entered the loft of the gallery by that particular route for a long time. Venetian blinds were currently blanking the three adjacent ground-floor windows—the uprights and transoms of which were backed by discreet steel bars, as Case pointed out; and already Mijnheer de Lugt, a tall blond man with a bulbous nose, had three muscular fellows lounging about in the large, spot-lit exhibition room. One in a demure blue security uniform—he was golden-skinned and moon-faced, obviously of Indonesian ancestry. The other chunky Germanic types wore light suits and trainers.

A high pile of copies of *Archimboldo Erotico* stood in one corner for presentation that evening to the guests: the media people, museum directors, cultural mandarins and mavericks. Particularly the media people.

And my heart quailed.

Despite all the gloss, mightn't someone promptly *denounce* this exhibition? We were in liberal Holland, where the obscenity in itself would not offend. Yet wouldn't someone cry "Hoax!"?

Worse, mightn't some inspired avant-garde type perhaps enthusiastically *applaud* this exhibition as an ambitious jape?

De Lugt seemed a tad apprehensive beneath a suave exterior. He blew that snozzle of his a number of times without obvious reason, as though determined to be squeaky-clean.

"Ms. Donaldson, would you sign a copy of the book for me as a souvenir?" he asked. When I had obliged, he scrutinized my signature as if the scrawly autograph might be a forgery.

Maybe I was simply being paranoid. But I was damn glad of this dry run amongst the exhibits.

Case conferred with the security trio quietly in Dutch. They smiled; they nodded.

The wet run that evening—lubricated by champagne to celebrate the resurrection of long-lost works of a bizarre master, and contemporary of Rabelais— went off quite as well as could be expected.

A young red-haired woman in a severe black cocktail dress walked out along with her escort in shock and rage. She had been wearing an Archimboldo eco-badge as her only form of jewellery, with the word *Ark* printed upon it.

A fat bluff bearded fellow in a dinner jacket, with an enormous spotted cravat instead of bow tie, got drunk and began guffawing. Tears streamed down his hairy cheeks till Case discreetly persuaded him to step outside for an airing.

Rumby was bombarded by questions, to which he would grin and reply, "It's all in the book. Take a copy!" One of the great art finds, yes. Casts quite a new light on Archimboldo, that emotionally complex man.

So why had Mr. Wright sprung this surprise on the art world by way of a private gallery? Rather than lending these paintings to some major public museum?

"Ah now, do you really suppose your big museum would have leapt at the chance of showing such *controversial* material, Ladies and Gentlemen? Some big city museum with its reputation to think about? Of course, I'll be perfectly delighted to loan this collection out in future . . ."

I was quizzed too. Me, in my new purple velvet couturier pant-suit.

Geert De Lugt smiled and nodded approvingly, confidently. Naturally Rumby would have paid him handsomely for use of his gallery, yet I was becoming convinced that Mijnheer De Lugt himself was innocent of the deception. He had merely had stage nerves earlier.

We stayed in Amsterdam for another five days. Press and media duly obliged with publicity, and I appeared on Dutch and German TV, both with Rumby and without him. So many people flocked to the Galerij Bosch that our Security boys had to limit admittance to thirty people at any one time, while a couple of tolerant police hung about outside. Our book sold like hot cakes to the visitors; and by now it was in the bookshops too. ("At this rate," joked Rumby, "we'll be making a fucking *profit*.")

During spare hours, I wandered round town with Case. Rumby mainly stayed in his suite at the Krasnapolsky in phone and fax contact with Bexford and Texas, munching sushi. I nursed a fancy that Chaplain Lascelles might perhaps lugubriously be visiting the Red Light District to let his hair and his pants down, but he certainly wasn't getting high on any dope. Me, I preferred the flea-market on Waterlooplein, where I picked up a black lace shawl and a slightly frayed Khasmiri rug for the flat back in Bloomsbury.

I noticed a certain item of graffiti on numerous walls: *Onze Wereld is onze Ark*.

"Our world is our Ark," translated Case.

Sometimes there was only the word *Ark* on its own writ even larger in spray-paint. I couldn't but recall the badge worn by that pissed-off woman at the party in the gallery. Pissed-off? No . . . *mortally offended*. Obviously, *Ark* was a passionate, punning, mispronounced allusion to . . . who else but Emperor Rudolph's court jester?

When I mentioned this graffito to Rumby, he almost growled with glee.

"Ha! So what do you do in this fucking *ark* of theirs? You hide, anchored by gravity—till you've squandered all your major resources, then you can't get to anyplace else. Sucks to arks."

We all flew back to England on the Sunday. At seven A.M. on the Monday the phone bullied me awake.

Lascelles was calling.

Late on the Sunday night, a van had mounted the pavement outside Galerij Bosch. The driver grabbed a waiting motorbike and sped off. Almost at once the van exploded devastatingly, demolishing the whole frontage of the building. As well as explosives, there'd been a hell of a lot of jellied petrol and phosphorus in that van. Fireworks, indeed! The gallery was engulfed in flames. So were part of the street and a couple of trees. Even the canal caught fire, and a nearby houseboat blazed, though the occupants had been called away by some ruse. The two security guards who were in the gallery on night shift died.

And of course all the Archimboldos had been burnt, though that seemed a minor aspect to me right then . . .

Case was coming pronto to pick me up. Rumby wanted us to talk face to face before the media swarmed.

Two hours later, I was at Bexford Hall.

Rumby, Lascelles, Case, and I met together in a book-lined upstairs study, furnished with buff leather armchairs upon a russet Persian carpet. The single large window, composed of stone mullions, seemed somewhat at odds with the Italianate plasterwork ceiling which featured scrolls and roses, with cherubs and putti supporting the boss of an electrified chandelier. Maybe Rumby had bought this ceiling in from some other house because it was the right size, and he liked it. The room smelled of cheroots, and soon of my Marlboro too.

"Let's dismiss the financial side right away," commenced Rumby. "The paintings weren't insured. So I'm not obliged to make any kind of claim. Hell, do I need to? The book will be the only record—and your fee stays secure, Jill. Now, is it to our disadvantage that the paintings themselves no longer exist? Might someone hint that *we* ourselves arranged the torching of the gallery before independent art experts could stick their fingers in the pie? I think two tragic deaths say no to that. Those poor guys had no chance. T. Rumbold Wright isn't known for assassinations. So, ghastly as this is, it could be to our advantage—especially if it smears the ecofreaks, the covenanters of the Ark."

What a slur on the ecofreaks that they might destroy newly discovered masterpieces of art for ideological reasons in a desperate effort to keep the artist pure for exploitation by themselves. When people saw any Archimboldo badge or poster now, they might think, *Ho-ho* . . . I was thinking about the two dead guards.

Lascelles had been liaising with Holland.

"The Dutch police are puzzled," he summarized. "Is this an outburst of art-terrorism? A few years ago some people revived a group called the SKG—so-called 'City Art Guerillas' who caused street and gallery trouble. They never killed anyone. Even if the couple on that houseboat were kept out of harm's way to make the attackers seem more benign, De Lugt's two guards were just slaughtered . . .

"Then what about these Ark people? The loony fringe of the Dutch Eco movement *have* gone in for destructive industrial sabotage—but again, they haven't caused any deaths. This is more like the work of the German Red Column, though it seems they haven't operated in Holland recently. Why do so now? And why hit the gallery?"

"To hurt a noted Capitalist, in the only way they could think of?" asked Rumby. "No, I don't buy that. It's got to be the Ecofreaks."

"The ecology movement is very respectable in Holland."

Rumby grinned wolfishly. "Mightn't be, soon."

"Ecology is government policy there."

How much more newsworthy the destruction made those naughty paintings! How convenient that they were now beyond the reach of sceptical specialists.

"I don't suppose," said I, "one of your *allies* in the Star Club might conceivably have arranged this attack?"

Drop a ton of lead into a pond.

"Future of the human race," I added weakly. "Big motivation."

Rumby wrestled a cheroot from his coat of many pockets and lit it. "You can forget that idea. Let's consider *safety*. Your safety, Jill."

I suppose he couldn't avoid making this sound like a threat, however benevolently intentioned—or making it seem as if he wished to keep my free spirit incommunicado during the crisis . . .

"Someone has bombed and murdered ruthlessly," said Rumby. "*I'm* safe here."

"Yes, you are," Case assured him.

"But you, Jill, you live in some little scumbag flat in any old street in London. I'd like to invite you to stay here at Bexford for a week or two until things clarify."

"Actually, I can't," I told him, with silly stubbornness. "I have a couple of lectures to give at St. Martin's on Thursday."

"Screw them. Cancel them."

"And it isn't exactly a scumbag flat."

"Sorry—you know what I mean."

"At least until there's a communiqué," Lascelles suggested to me. "Then we'll know what we're dealing with. It's only sensible."

"Don't be *proud*," said Rumby. He puffed. The cherubs above collected a tiny little bit more nicotine on their innocent hands. "Please."

And some more nicotine from me too.

"You don't need to feed some goddam *cat*, do you?" asked Rumby.

"No . . ." In fact I loathed cats—selfish, treacherous creatures—but Rumby probably wouldn't have cared one way or the other.

In the event, I stayed at Bexford. Until Wednesday afternoon. No news emerged from Holland of any communiqué.

Could the attackers not have *known* about those two guards inside the gallery? So now they were ashamed, and politically reluctant, to claim credit?

Unlikely. You don't assemble a vanload of explosives and napalm and phosphorus, make sure there's a getaway motorbike waiting, and bail out the occupants of a nearby houseboat, without checking everything else about the target too.

Lascelles was stonewalling queries from the media. ("Mr. Wright is shocked. He grieves at the two deaths. He has no other comment at present . . .") Stubbornly, I insisted on being driven back to Bloomsbury.

My little flat had been burgled. My CD player and my TV were missing. Entry was by way of the fire escape door, which had been smashed off its none too sturdy hinges. Otherwise, there wasn't much damage or mess.

I hadn't wished Case to escort me upstairs; thus he had already driven away. Of course I *could* have reached him on the Merc's car phone. Yet this was so ordinary a burglary that I simply phoned the police. Then I thumbed the Yellow Pages for an emergency repair service which was willing to turn up within the next six hours.

The constable who visited me presently was a West Indian. A couple of other nearby flats had also been broken into the day before for electrical goods, so he said. Was I aware of this? He seemed to be pitching his questions towards eliciting whether I might perhaps have robbed myself so as to claim insurance.

"Fairly *neat* break-in, Miss, all things considered."

"Except for the door."

"You're lucky. Some people find excrement spread all over their homes."

"Did that happen in the other flats that were burgled?"

"Not on this occasion. So you reported this just as soon as you came back from—?"

"From the Cotswolds."

"Nice part of the country, I hear. Were you there long?"

"Three days."

"Visiting friends?"

"My employer." Now why did I have to say *that?*

Blurt, blurt.

"Oh, so you live here, but your boss is in the Cotswolds?"

"He isn't exactly my boss. He was consulting me."

The constable raised his eyebrow suggestively.

Obviously he believed in keeping the suspect off balance.

"You do have a lot of expensive books here, Miss," was his next tack.

Yes, rows of glossy art books. Why hadn't those been stolen—apart from the fact that they weighed a ton?

"I don't suppose the burglars were interested in art," I suggested.

He pulled out a *Botticelli,* with library markings on the spine, from the shelf.

"This is from a college library," he observed.

"I teach there. I lecture about art."

"I thought you said you were a *consultant* . . ."

By the time he left, I was half-convinced that I had burgled myself, that I habitually thieved from libraries, and that I was a call-girl who had been supplying sexual favours to Mr. X out in the country. Would these suspicions be entered in the police computer? Did I have the energy to do anything about this? No, it was all so . . . tentative. Did I want to seem paranoid?

Bert the Builder finally turned up and fixed the door for a hundred and thirteen pounds . . . which of course the insurance would be covering. Otherwise the job would have cost just sixty, cash.

I did manage to look over my lecture notes—on Titian and Veronese. I microwaved a madras beef curry with pilau rice; and went to bed, fed up.

The phone rang.

It was Phil. He'd been calling my number for days.

These weird long-lost Archimboldos! Why hadn't I told him anything? And the terrorist attack! What had happened? Could he come round?

"Sorry, Phil, but I've just had my CD and TV nicked. And the helpful visiting constable thinks I'm a hooker."

I was glad of the excuse of the burglary.

Towards mid-morning my phone started ringing, and a couple of Press sleuths turned up in person, pursuing the art bombing story; but I stonewalled, and escaped in the direction of St. Martin's where, fortunately, no reporters lurked.

At four in the afternoon I stepped out from the factory-like frontage of the art school into a Charing Cross Road aswarm with tourists. Beneath a grey overcast the fumy air was warm. A sallow Middle Eastern youth in checked shirt and jeans promptly handed me a leaflet advertising some English Language Academy.

"I already speak English," I informed the tout. He frowned momentarily as if he didn't understand. No points to the Academy.

"Then you learn *cheaper*," he suggested, pursuing me along the pavement.

"Do not bother that lady," interrupted a tall blond young man dressed in a lightweight off-white jacket and slacks.

"No, it's all right," I assured my would-be protector.

"It is not all right. Any trash is on our streets. They are not safe."

He waved, and a taxi pulled up almost immediately. The young man opened the door, plunged his hand inside his jacket, and showed me a small pistol hidden in his palm. Was he some urban vigilante crusader pledged to rescue damsels from offensive encounters? I just didn't understand what was happening.

"Get in quickly," he said, "or I will shoot you dead."

Help, I mouthed at the Arab, or whatever.

In vain.

I did as Prince Charming suggested. Did *anyone* notice me being abducted? Or only see a handsome young man hand me enthusiastically into that taxi?

The driver didn't look round.

"Keep quiet," said the young man. "Put these glasses on." He handed me glasses black as night equipped with side-blinkers, such as someone with a rare hypersensitive eye ailment might wear. Only, these were utterly dark; I couldn't see a thing through them.

We drove for what seemed like half an hour. Eventually we drew up—and waited, perhaps so that passers-by might have time to pass on by—before my abductor assisted me from the cab. Quickly he guided me arm in arm up some steps. A door closed behind us. Traffic noise grew mute.

We mounted a broad flight of stairs, and entered an echoing room—

where I was pressured into a straight-backed armchair. Immediately one hand pressed under my nose, and another on my jaw, to force my mouth open.

"Drink!"

Liquid poured down my throat—some sweet concoction masking a bitter undertaste. I gagged and spluttered but had no choice except to swallow.

What had I drunk? What had I drunk?

"I need to see the eyes," said a sombre, if somewhat slobbery voice. "The truth is in the eyes." The accent was Germanic.

A hand removed my glasses.

I found myself in a drawing room with a dusty varnished floor and double oak doors. A small chandelier of dull lustres shone. Thick blue brocade curtains cloaked tall windows, which in any event appeared to be shuttered. A dustsheet covered what I took to be a baby grand piano. An oblong of less faded rose-and-lily wallpaper, over a marble fireplace, showed where some painting had hung.

On a chaise longue sat a slim elegant grizzle-haired man of perhaps sixty kitted out in a well-tailored grey suit. A walking cane was pressed between his knees. His hands opened and closed slowly to reveal the chased silver handle. A second middle-aged man stood near him: stouter, bald, wearing a long purple velvet robe with fur trimmings which at first I thought was some exotic dressing gown. This man's face was jowly and pouchy. He looked like Goering on a bad day. His eyes were eerie: bulgy, yet bright as if he was on cocaine.

My abductor had stationed himself directly behind me.

On a walnut table lay a copy of *Archimboldo Erotico*, open at my introduction.

Shit.

"My apologies," said the seated gent, "for the manner of your coming here, Miss Donaldson." He gestured at the book. "But you owe me a profound apology—and restitution. Your libels must be corrected."

The fellow in the robe moved closer, to stare at me. His fingers wiggled.

"What libels?" I asked, rather deeply scared. These people had to be nutters, possessed by some zany fanatical motive. Well-heeled, well-groomed nutters were maybe the really dangerous sort. *What had I drunk? A slow poison? Would I soon be begging for the antidote?*

"Libels against a certain Holy Roman Emperor, Miss Donaldson. Thus, libels against the Habsburg dynasty . . . which may yet be the salvation of Europe, and of the world. Very *untimely* libels." The gent raised his cane and slashed it to and fro as if decapitating daisies. "I am sure you will see reason to denounce your fabrications publicly . . ."

"What fabrications?"

He stood up smoothly and brought his cane down savagely upon my book, though his expression remained suave and polite. I jerked, imagining that cane striking me instead.

"These! These obscenities were never painted by Rudolph's court artist!"

"But," I murmured, "the looting of Prague . . . Skoklosters Castle . . . Queen Christina's chaplain . . ."

He sighed. "Lies. All lies. And I do not quite know why. Let us discuss art and history, Miss Donaldson."

"She is deceitful," said the fellow in the robe, always peering at me. "She has a guilty conscience."

"Who are you?" I asked. "The local mind-reader?"

The stout man smiled unctuously.

"Herr Voss is my occultist," explained the gent.

"Oculist? You mean, optician?"

"My *occultist!* My pansophist. The holder of the keys to the Unknown. And *my* name happens to be Heinrich von Habsburg, Miss Donaldson . . ."

"Oh . . . ," I said.

"I shall not burden your brain with genealogy, except to say that I am the living heir to the Holy Roman throne."

Genealogy indeed. "I thought," said I, "that your Roman throne couldn't be inherited by virtue of blood—"

He cut me short. "You misunderstand divine right. What the Electors bestowed wasn't rightly theirs, but God's, to give. God finally vested this title in the Habsburg family. Let us discuss *art* instead. And *sacred history.*"

This, His Royal Heinrich proceeded to do, while the keeper of the keys contemplated me and my guard hovered behind me.

Rudolph and his father Maximilian before him had been astute, benevolent rulers, who aimed to heal discord in Christian Europe by uniting it under Habsburg rule. They lived noble and honourable lives, as did Count Giuseppe Archimboldo. His supposed fantasias possessed a precise political and metaphysical significance in the context of the Holy Roman throne. The aesthetic harmony of natural elements in the *Vertumnus* and in the other portrait heads bespoke the harmony which would bless Europe under the benificent leadership of the House of Austria . . .

Jawohl, I thought.

Ever-present, like the elements themselves, the Habsburgs would rule both microcosm and macrocosm—both the political world, and nature too. Archimboldo's cycle of the seasons, depicted as Habsburg heads wrought of Wintry, Vernal, Summery, and Autumnal ingredients, confided that Habsburg rule would extend eternally through time in one everlasting season. Under the secular and spiritual guidance of those descendants of Hercules, the House of Habsburg, the Golden Age would return to a united Europe.

Right on.

In due course of time, this happy culmination had almost come to pass. The "Great King," as predicted, nay, propagandized by Nostradamus, loomed on the horizon.

When the Habsburgs united with the House of Lorraine, and when Marie Antoinette became Queen of France, the House of Habsburg-Lorraine was within a generation of dominion over Europe—had the French Revolution not intervened.

What a pity.

Throughout the nineteenth century the House attempted to regroup. However, the upheavals attending the end of the First World War toppled the Habsburgs from power, ushering in chaos . . .

Shame.

Now all Europe was revived and reuniting, and its citizens were ever more aware that the microcosm of Man and the macrocosm of Nature were a unity.

Yet lacking, as yet, a *head.*

A Holy Roman Imperial head.

Early restoration of the monarchy in Hungary was one possible ace card, though other cards were also tucked up the imperial sleeve . . .

Archimboldo's symbolic portraits were holy ikons of this golden dream, especially in view of their ecoinjection into the European psyche. Those paintings were programming the people with a subconscious expectation, a hope, a longing, a secret sense of destiny, which a restored Habsburg Holy Roman Empire would fulfill.

"Now do you see why your obscenities are such a libelous blasphemy, Miss Donaldson?"

Good God.

"Do you mean to tell me that *you're* behind the Archimboldo eco-campaign?" I asked His Imperial Heinrich.

"The power of symbols," remarked Voss, "is very great. Symbols are my speciality."

Apparently they weren't going to tell me whether they simply hoped to exploit an existing, serendipitous media campaign—or whether some loyal Habsburg mole had actively persuaded the ecofreaks to plaster what were effectively Habsburg heads—in fruit and veg, and flowers and leaves—all over Europe and America.

"You broke into my flat," I accused the man behind me. "Looking for some dirt that doesn't exist because the erotic paintings are genuine!"

Blondie slapped me sharply across the head.

"Martin! You know that is unnecessary!" H. von H. held up his hand prohibitively—for the moment, at least.

"You broke my door down," I muttered over my shoulder, thinking myself reprieved, "and you stole my CD and TV just to make the thing look plausible. I bet you burgled those other flats in the neighbourhood too as a deception."

Martin, on his *own?* Surely not . . . There must have been others involved. The taxi driver . . . and whoever else . . .

"Actually, we broke your door *after* the burglary," boasted Martin. "We *entered* with more circumspection."

Voss smiled in a predatory fashion. "With secret keys, as it were."

Others. Others . . .

They had blown up the Galerij Bosch! They had burned those two guards to death . . .

I shrank.

"I see that the magnitude of this is beginning to dawn on your butterfly mind," said the Habsburg. "A united Europe must be saved from *pollution*. Ecological pollution, of course—a Holy Roman Emperor is as a force of nature. But moral pollution too."

"How about racial?" I queried.

"I'm an aristocrat, not a barbarian," remarked Heinrich. "The Nazis were contemptible. Yet plainly we cannot have Moslems—Turkish *heathens*—involved in the affairs of Holy Europe. We cannot have those who besieged our Vienna in 1683 succeeding now by the back door."

Oh, the grievances of centuries long past . . . Rumby and his science Star Club suddenly seemed like such Johnnies-Come-Lately indeed.

Science . . . versus imperial *magic* . . . with ecomysticism in the middle . . .

"I just can't believe you're employing a frigging *magician* to gain the throne of Europe!"

"*Language*, Miss Donaldson!" snapped the Habsburg. "You are corrupt."

Voss smoothed his robe as though I had mussed it.

"You're a creature of your time, Miss Donaldson," said H. von H. "Whereas I am a creation of the centuries."

"Would that be *The Centuries of Nostradamus*?" Yes, that was the title of that volume of astrological rigmarole.

"I mustn't forget that you're educated, by the lights of today. Tell me, what do you suppose the *Centuries* of the title refer to?"

"Well, years. A long time, the future."

"Quite wrong. There simply happen to be a hundred quatrains—verses of four lines—in each section. You're only half educated. And thus you blunder. How much did your American art collector pay you for writing that introduction?"

Obviously Rumby would have paid me *something* . . . I wouldn't have written those pages for nothing . . .

"Three thousand dollars," I improvised.

"That doesn't sound very much, considering the evil intent. Is Mr Wright being hoaxed *too*?"

Again, he slammed the cane on to my book.

An astonishing flash of agony seared across my back. I squealed and twisted round—but Martin was holding no cane.

He was holding nothing at all. With a grin, Martin displayed his empty paws for me. Voss giggled, and when I looked at him he winked.

It was as though that open volume was some voodoo doll of myself which the Habsburg had just chastised.

The Habsburg lashed at my words again, and I cried out, for the sudden pain was intense—yet I knew there would be no mark on me.

Voss licked his lips. "Symbolic resonances, Miss Donaldson. The power of symbolic actions."

What drug had been in that liquid I swallowed? I didn't *feel* disoriented—save for nerves and dread—yet I must be in some very strange state of mind to account for my suggestibility to pain.

"We can continue thus for a while, Miss Donaldson." Heinrich raised his cane again.

"Wait."

Was three quarters of a million dollars enough to compensate for being given the third degree right now by crazy, ruthless *murderers*—who could torture me symbolically, but effectively?

I experienced an absurd vision of myself attempting to tell the West Indian detective-constable that actually my flat had been broken into by agents of a Holy Roman Emperor who hoped to take over Europe—and that I was seeking police protection because the Habsburgs could hurt me agonizingly by whipping my words . . .

Was I mad, or was I mad?

The room seemed luminous, glowing with an inner light. Every detail of furniture or drapery was intensely *actual*. I thought that my sense of reality had never been stronger.

"Okay," I admitted, "the paintings were all forgeries. They were done in Holland, but I honestly don't know who by. I never met him. I never learned his name. Rumby—Mr. Wright—hates the ecology lobby because they hate space exploration, and he thinks that's our only hope. I have a friend at the *Sunday Times*. I'll tell him everything—about how the paintings were a prank. They'll love to print that! Wright will have egg on his face."

"What a treacherous modern creature you are," the Habsburg said with casual contempt; and I squirmed with shame and fear.

"Just watch for next weekend's paper," I promised.

"At this moment," said Voss, "she believes she is going to do what she says—and of course she knows that our Martin can find her, if she breaks her word . . ."

He peered.

"Ah: she's relieved that *you* cannot reach her from a distance with the whipping cane.

"And she wonders whether Martin would really kill her, and thus lose us her testimony . . ."

No, he *wasn't* reading my mind. He wasn't! He was reading my face, my muscles. He could do so because everything was so real.

More peering.

"She feels a paradoxical affection for her friend . . . *Rumby*. Solidarity, as well as greed. Yes, a definite loyalty." If only I hadn't called him Rumby. If only I'd just called him Wright. It was all in the words. Voss wasn't reading my actual thoughts.

"So therefore," H. von H. said to Voss, "she must be retrained in her loyalties."

What did he mean? What did he mean?

"She must be conditioned by potent symbols, Voss."

"Just so, Excellency."

"Thus she will not wish to betray us. Enlighten her, Voss. Show her the real depth of history, from where we come. Your juice will be deep in her now."

Numbness crept over me, as Voss loomed closer. The sheer pressure of his approach was paralyzing me.

"Wait," I managed to squeak.

"Wait?" echoed H. von H. "Oh, I have waited long enough already. My family has waited long enough. Through the French Revolution, through the Communist intermezzo . . . The Holy Roman Empire *will* revive at this present cusp of history—for it has always remained in being, at least as a state of mind. And *mind* is what matters, Miss Donaldson—as Rudolph knew, contrary to your pornographic lies! Ah yes, my ancestor avidly sought the symbolic key to the ideal world. Practitioners of the symbolic, hermetic arts visited him in Prague Castle—though he lacked the loyal services of a Voss . . ."

The Habsburg slid his cane under the dustsheet of the piano, and whisked the cloth off. Seating himself on the stool, he threw open the lid of the baby grand with a crash. His slim, manicured fingers started to play plangent, mournful Debussyish chords in which I could almost feel myself begin to drown.

Voss crooned to me—or sang—in some dialect of German . . . and I couldn't move a muscle. Surely I was shrinking—or else the drawing room was expanding. Or both. Voss was becoming vast.

I was a little child again—yet not a child, but rather a miniature of myself. When I was on the brink of puberty, lying in bed just prior to drifting off to sleep, this same distortion of the senses used to happen to me.

The music lamented.

And Voss crooned my lullaby.

A bearded man in black velvet and cerise satin held my nude paralyzed body in his hands. He held the *whole* of me in his hands—for I was tiny now, the height of his forearm.

Draped over his shoulders was a lavish ermine cloak.

I was stiff, unmoving.

He placed me in a niche, ran his fingertip down my belly, and traced the cleft between my thighs.

He stepped back.

Then he left.

I was in a great gloomy vaulted chamber housing massive cupboards and strongboxes. The slit windows in the thick stone wall were grated so as to deter any slim catburglars. Stacked several deep around a broad shelf, and likewise below, were mythological and Biblical oil paintings: Tintorettos, Titians, by the look of them . . . Neither the lighting nor the decor were at all in the spirit of any latter-day museum. Here was art as treasure—well and truly locked up.

Days and nights passed.

Weeks of static solitude until I was going crazy. I would have welcomed any change whatever, any newcomer. My thoughts looped around a circuit of Strada, death in Amsterdam, Habsburgs, with the latter assuming ever more significance—and necessity—with each mental swing.

Eventually the door opened, and in walked a figure who made the room shine. For his face and hair were made of a hundred springtime flowers, his collar of white daisies, and his clothes of a hundred lush leaves.

He stood and gazed at me through floral eyes, and with his rosebud lips he smiled faintly.

He simply went away.

A season passed, appalling in its sheer duration. I saw daisies like stars before my eyes, in an unending afterimage.

Then in walked glowing Summer. His eyes were ripe cherries. His teeth were little peas. Plums and berries tangled in his harvest-hair; and his garment was of woven straw.

And he too smiled, and went away in turn.

And another season passed . . .

. . . till rubicund Autumn made his appearance. He was a more elderly fellow with an oaten beard, a fat pear of a nose, mushroom ears, clusters of grapes instead of locks of hair. His chin was a pomegranate. He wore an overripe burst fig as an earring. He winked lecherously, and departed even as I tried to cry out to him through rigid lips, to stay.

For next came Winter, old and gnarled, scabbed and scarred, his nose a stump of rotted branch, his skin of fissured bark, his lips of jutting bracket-fungus.

Winter stayed for a longer grumbly time, though he no more reached to touch me than had his predecessors. His departure—the apparent end of this cycle of seasons—plunged me into despair. I was as cold as marble.

Until one day the door opened yet again, and golden light bathed my prison chamber.

Vertumnus himself advanced—the fruitful God, his cheeks of ripe apple and peach, head crowned with fruit and grain, his chest a mighty pumpkin. His cherry and blackberry eyes glinted.

Rudolph!

He reached for me. Oh to be embraced by him! To be warmed.

He lifted my paralyzed naked body from its dusty niche.

The crash which propelled me back into the drawing room might almost have been caused by his dropping me and letting me shatter.

For a moment I thought that this was indeed so.

Yet it was my trance which had been shattered.

A policeman was in the room. An armed policeman, crouching. He panned his gun around. Plainly I was the only other person present.

The crash must have been that of those double oak doors flying open as he burst in.

Footsteps thumped, elsewhere in the house.

Voices called.

"Empty!"

"Empty!"

Several other officers spilled into the room.

"You all right, Miss?"

I could move my limbs—which were clothed exactly as earlier on, in jeans and maroon paisley sweater. I wasn't tiny and naked, after all. I stared around. No sign of von Habsburg or Voss or Martin.

"You all right, Miss? Do you understand me?"

I nodded slowly. I still felt feeble.

"She was just sitting here all on her own," commented the officer, putting his pistol away. "So what's happening?" he demanded of me.

How did they know I was here?

"I was . . . forced into a taxi," I said. "I was brought here, then given some drug."

"What sort of drug? *Why?*"

"It made me . . . dream."

"Who brought you here?"

"A man called Martin . . ."

He's the Habsburg Emperor's hit-man . . . The drug was concocted by a magician . . .

How could I tell them such things? How could I explain about Rudolph Vertumnus . . . ? (And how could I *deny* Vertumnus, who had almost rekindled me . . . ?)

"They were trying to get me to deny things I wrote about the painter Archimboldo . . ."

"About a *painter?*"

I tried to explain about the pictures, the bombing in Amsterdam, and how my flat had been burgled. My explanation slid away of its own accord—for the sake of sheer plausibility, and out of logical necessity!—from any Habsburg connexion, and into the ecofreak channel.

The officer frowned. "You're suggesting that the Greens who bombed that gallery also kidnapped you? There's no one here now."

"They must have seen you coming and run away. I'm quite confused."

"Hmm," said the officer. "Come in, Sir," he called.

In walked Phil: chunky, dapper Phil, velvet jacketed and suede-shoed, his rich glossy brown hair brushed back in elegant waves, as ever.

It was Phil who had seen me pushed into the taxi; he who had noticed the gleam of gun from right across the street where he had been loitering with intent outside a bookshop, waiting for me to emerge from St. Martin's so that he could bump into me. He'd managed to grab another taxi and follow. He'd seen me hustled into that house in North London, wearing those black "goggles." It took about an hour for him to stir up the armed posse—an hour, during which four seasons had passed before my eyes.

The fact that Phil and I were long-term "friends" and that he turned out to be a "journalist"—of sorts—irked the police. The abduction—by persons unknown, to a vacant house, where I simply sat waiting patiently—began to seem distinctly stage-managed . . . for the sake of publicity. Nor—given the Amsterdam connection—did my mention of drugs help matters. Calling out armed police was a serious matter.

We were both obliged to answer questions until late in the evening before we could leave the police station; and even then it seemed as if we ourselves might still be charged with some offence. However, those deaths in Amsterdam lent a greater credence to what I said. Maybe there was something serious behind this incident . . .

I, of course, was "confused." Thus, early on, I was given a blood test, about which the police made no further comment; there couldn't have been any evidence of hash or acid in my system.

I needed to stay "confused" until I could get to talk to Rumby.

Peeved Phil, of course, insisted on talking to me over late dinner in a pizzeria—we were both starving by then.

I lied quite a lot; and refrained from any mention of Habsburgs or the Star Club. The Archimboldo paintings had all been genuine. Rumby was an upfront person. Euro Ecofreaks must have bombed the gallery. Must have abducted me. Blondie Martin; elderly man, name unknown; stout man, name of Voss, who wore a strange costume. German speakers. Just the same as I'd told the police, five or six times over. The kidnappers had tried to persuade me to denounce what I had written because my words were an insult to Archimboldo, emblem of the Greens. They had drugged me into a stupor—from which I recovered with surprising swiftness. Rescue had come too soon for much else to transpire . . .

Phil and I were sharing a tuna, anchovy, and prawn ensemble on a crispy base, and drinking red wine.

"It's quite some story, Jill. Almost front-page stuff."

"I doubt it."

"The Eco connection! Bombing, abduction . . . I'd like to run this by Freddy on the news desk."

"You're an art critic, Phil—and so am I. I don't want some cockeyed blather in the papers."

"Jill," he reproached me, "I've just spent *all evening* in a police station on account of you."

"I'm grateful you did what you did, Phil. Let's stop it there."

"For Christ's sake, you could still be in danger! Or . . . *aren't you*, after all? Was this a publicity stunt? Was it staged by *Wright*? You're in deep, but you want out now? Why would he stage such a stunt? If he did . . . what really happened in Amsterdam?"

Dear God, how his antennae were twitching. "No, no, no. It couldn't be a stunt because the only witness to it was *you*, and that was quite by chance!"

"By chance," he mused . . . as though maybe I might have spied him from an upper window in St. Martin's and promptly phoned for a kidnapper.

"Look, Phil, I'm confused. I'm tired. I need *sleep.*"

Into the pizzeria stepped a stout, bald man wearing a dark blue suit. He flourished a silver-tipped walking stick. Goering on a night out. His bulgy eyes fixed on mine. He swished the stick, and I screamed with pain, jerking against the table, spilling both our wines.

"Jill!"

Phil managed to divert the red tide with his paper napkin at the same time as he reached out towards me. Other customers stared agog, and the manager hastened in our direction. Were we engaged in some vicious quarrel? Wine dripped on to the floor tiles.

Voss had vanished. I slumped back.

"Sorry," I said to the manager. "I had a bad cramp."

The manager waved a waiter to minister to the mess. Other diners resumed munching their pizzas.

"Whatever happened?" whispered Phil.

"A cramp. Just a cramp."

Could one of those Habsburgers have trailed us to the police station and hung around outside for hours, keeping watch till we emerged?

Had I truly seen Voss, or only someone who resembled him? Someone whose appearance and whose action triggered that pain reflex? That agonizing hallucination . . .

Phil took me back to the flat in a taxi. I had no choice but to let him come up with me—in case the place was infested.

It wasn't. Then it took half an hour to get rid of my friend, no matter how much tiredness I claimed. By the time I phoned Rumby's private number it was after eleven.

Him, I did start to tell about the Habsburgs.

He was brevity itself. "Say no more," my rich protector cut in. *My Rumby Daddy.* "Stay there. I'm sending Case *now.* He'll phone from the car just as soon as he's outside your place. Make quite sure you see it's him before you open your door."

I dozed off soundly in the Merc. When I arrived at Bexford, Rumby had waited up to quiz me and pump me—attended by Case, and a somewhat weary Lascelles.

I got to bed around four . . .

. . . leaving Rumby aiming to do some serious phoning. Had Big Daddy been breaking out the benzedrine? Not exactly. Rumby always enjoyed a few hours advantage over us local mortals. So as to stay more in synch with American time-zones he habitually rose very late of a morning. A night shift duo always manned the computer consoles and transatlantic satellite link. In that sense, Bexford never really closed down.

I'd already gathered that *crisis* was somewhat of a staff of life around

Rumby—who seemed to cook up his own personal supply of benzedrine internally. During my previous two-day sojourn, there'd been the incident of the microlite aircraft. Thanks to a Cotswold Air Carnival, microlites were overflying Bexford at a few hundred feet now and then. Rumby took exception and had Lascelles trying to take out a legal injunction against the organizers.

Simultaneously, there'd been the business of the starlings. Affronted by those microlite pterodactyls, and seeking a new air-base for their sorties, a horde of the quarrelsome birds took up residence on the satellite dish. Their weight or their shit might distort bits of information worth millions. What to do? After taking counsel from an avian welfare organization, Rumby despatched his helicopter to collect a heap of French *pétard* firecrackers from Heathrow to string underneath the gutters. So my stay had been punctuated by random explosive farts . . .

I woke at noon, and Rumby joined me for breakfast in the big old kitchen—antiquity retrofitted with stainless steel and ceramic hobs. A large TV set was tuned to CNN, and an ecologist was inveighing about rocket exhausts and the ozone holes.

"Each single shuttle launch releases a hundred and sixty-three *thousand* kilograms of hydrogen chloride that converts into an atmospheric mist of hydrochloric acid! So now they're kindly promising to change the oxidizer of the fuel—the ammonium perchlorate that produces this vast cloud of pollution—to ammonium *nitrate* instead—"

As soon as I finished my croissant, Rumby scuttled the cooks—a couple of local women—out to pick herbs and vegetables. He blinked at me a few times.

"Any more sightings of flowerpot men? Or Habsburgs?" he enquired.

"That isn't funny, Rumby. It happened."

He nodded. "I'm afraid you've been given a ringbinder, Jill."

"Come again?"

"I've been talking to one of my best chemists over in Texas. Sally has a busy mind. Knows a lot about pharmaceuticals." He consulted scribbles in a notebook. "The ring in question's a molecular structure called an indole ring . . . These rings *bind* to synapses in the brain. Hence, ring-binder. They're psychotomimetic—they mimic psychoses. Your little pets will proba-bly stay in place a long time instead of breaking down. Seems there's a lot of covert designer drug work going on right now, aimed at cooking up chemicals to manipulate people's beliefs. Sally had heard rumours of one drug code-named *Confusion*—and another one called *Persuasion*, which seems to fit the bill here. It's the only explanation for the hallucination—which came from within you, of course, once you were given the appropriate prod."

"I do realize I was hallucinating the . . . flowerpot men. You mean this can continue . . . indefinitely?"

"You flashed on for a full encore in that pizza parlour, right? Whiplash!

Any fraught scenes in future involving old Archy could do the same. Media interviews, that sort of thing—if you disobey the Habsburg view of Archy. Though I guess you mustn't spill the beans about them publicly."

"They told me so. How did I get away with telling *you* last night?"

"They were interrupted before they'd finished influencing you." He grinned. "I guess I might be high enough in the hierarchy of your loyalties to outrank their partial hold on you. Media or Press people wouldn't be, so you'd be advised to follow the Habsburg party line with them. Maybe you could resist at a cost."

"Of what?"

"Pain, inflicted by your own mind. Distortions of reality. That's what Sally says. That's the word on these new ring-binders. They bind you."

The more I thought about this, the less I liked it.

"How many people know about these persuader drugs?" I asked him carefully.

"They haven't exactly featured in *Newsweek*. I gather they're a bit experimental. Sally has an ear for rumours. She's part of my research division. Runs a search-team scanning the chemistry journals. Whatever catches the eye. Any tips of future icebergs. New petrochemical applications, mainly." He spoke as if icebergs started out fully submerged, then gradually revealed themselves. "She helped dig up data on the correct paint chemistry for the Archies."

How frank he was being.

Apparently. And how glib.

"So how would a Habsburg *magician* get his paws on prototype persuader drugs?" I demanded.

Rumby looked rueful. "Hell, maybe he *is* a magician! Alchemy precedes chemistry, don't they say?"

"In the same sense that Icarus precedes a jumbo jet?"

One of the cooks returned bearing an obese marrow.

Impulse took me to the kitchen garden, to brood on my own. The sun had finally burned through persistent haze to brighten the rows of cabbages, majestic cauliflowers, and artichokes, the rhubarb, the leeks. An ancient brick wall backed this domain, trusses of tomatoes ranged along it. Rooks cawed in the elms beyond, prancing about those raggedy sticknests that seemed like diseases of the branches.

Had the old gent whom I'd met really been Heinrich von Habsburg? A Holy Roman Emperor waiting in the wings to step on the world stage? Merely because he told me so, in *persuasive* circumstances?

What if that trio in the drawing room had really been *ecofreaks* masquerading as Habsburgs, pulling the wool over my eyes, trying to bamboozle me into confession?

Did puritanical ecofreaks have the wit to stage such a show?

How much more likely that the Star Club, with its presumed access to cutting-edge psychochemistry—and a penchant for dirty tricks?—was responsible for the charade, and for my drugging!

Whether Rumby himself knew so, or not.

Wipe me out as a reliable witness to my own part in the prank? Eliminate me, by giving me an ongoing nervous breakdown?

Would that invalidate what I'd written?

Ah no. The slur would be upon ecologists . . .

And maybe, at the same time, *test* that persuader drug? Give it a field-trial on a highly suitable test subject, namely myself? The Club's subsequent aim might be try similar *persuasion* on influential ecofreaks to alter their opinions or to make them seem crazy . . .

In my case, of course, they wouldn't wish to turn me into an eco-groupie . . . Thus the Habsburg connection could have seemed like a fertile ploy.

Was there a genuine, elderly Heinrich von Habsburg somewhere in Germany or Austria? Oh, doubtless there would be . . .

The vegetable garden began slithering, pulsing, throbbing. Ripe striped marrows thumped upon the ground, great green gonads. Tomatoes tumesced. Leeks were waxy white candles with green flames writhing high. Celery burst from earth, spraying feathery leaves. Sprouts jangled. Cauliflowers were naked brains.

The garden was trying to transform itself, to assemble itself into some giant sprawled potent body—of cauli brain, leek fingers, marrow organs, green leaf flesh . . .

I squealed and fled back towards the kitchen itself.

Then halted, like a hunted animal.

I couldn't go inside—where Rumby and Case and Lascelles plotted . . . the downfall of Nature, the rape of the planets, the bleeding of oil from Earth's veins to burn into choking smoke.

Behind me, the vegetable jungle had stilled. Its metamorphosis had halted, reversed.

If I thought harmoniously, not perversely, I was safe.

Yet my mind was churning, and reality was unstuck.

In my perception one conspiracy overlayed another. One scheming plot, another scheming plot. Therefore one reality overlayed another reality with hideous persuasiveness. Where had I just been, but in a *vegetable plot*?

I couldn't go into that house, to which I had fled for safety only the night before. For from inside Bexford Hall invisible tendrils arched out across the sky, bouncing up and down out of space, linking Rumby to star crusaders who were playing with my mind—and to whom he might be reporting my condition even now, guilefully or innocently.

On the screen of the sky I spied a future world of Confusion and Persuasion, where devoted fanatics manipulated moods chemically so that Nature became a multifold *creature* evoking horror—since it might absorb one into itself, mind-meltingly, one's keen consciousness dimming into pulsing, orgasmic dreams; and from which one could only flee in silver ships, out to the empty serenity of space where no universally linked weeds infested the floating rocks, no bulging tomato haemorrhoids the asteroids . . .

Or else conjuring up a positive lust for vital vegetative unity!

I slapped myself, trying to summon a Habsburger whiplash of pain to jerk me out of this bizarre dual vision.

I must go indoors. To sanity. And beyond.

The ring-binder was clamping more and more of me; and my mind was at war. I was scripting my own hallucinations from the impetus of ecofreak ideology, exaggerated absurdly, and from the myth of the Holy Roman Empire . . . I was dreaming, wide awake.

And Case stood, watching me.

"You okay, Jill?"

I nodded. I shouldn't tell him the truth. There was no truth any more; there was only potent imagery, subject to interpretation.

Certain bedrock facts existed: the bombing, the deaths in Amsterdam, my abduction . . . Event-*images*: that's what those were. The interpretation was another matter, dependent upon what one believed—just as art was forever being reinterpreted in the context of a new epoch; and even history too.

Persuasion—and Confusion too?—had torn me loose from my moorings, so that interpretations cascaded about me simultaneously, synchronously. I had become a battlefield between world-views, which different parts of my mind were animating.

With dread, I sensed something stirring which perhaps had lain dormant ever since humanity split from Nature—ever since true consciousness of self had dawned as a sport, a freak, a biological accident . . .

"You sure, Jill?"

You. I. Myself. *Me.*

The independent thinking entity, named Jill Donaldson.

I wasn't thinking quite so independently any longer. An illusion of Self— that productive illusion upon which civilization itself had been founded— was floundering.

"Quite sure," said I.

I, I, I. Ich. Io. Ego.

And Jilldonaldson hastened past him into the kitchen, where one of the cooks was hollowing out the marrow. The big TV set, tuned to CNN, scooping signals bounced from space, shimmered. The colours bled and reformed. The pixel pixies danced a new jig.

The countenance of Vertumnus gazed forth from that screen, he of the laughing lips, the ripe rubicund cheeks of peach and apple, the pear-nose, the golden ears of corn that were his brows. Oh the flashing hilarity of his berry-eyes. Oh those laughing lips.

With several nods of his head he gestured Jill elsewhere.

Jill adopted a pan-face.

She walked through the corridors of the house, to the front porch. She stepped out on to the gravel drive.

Ignition keys were in the red Porsche.

Jill ought to be safe with Annie in a colony of women. Rudolph Vertumnus was a male, wasn't he?

A hop through Cheltenham, then whoosh by motorway to Exeter and on down into Cornwall. She would burn fuel but keep an eye out for police patrols. Be at Polmerrin by dusk . . .

The Porsche wasn't even approaching Cheltenham when the car phone burbled, inevitably.

She had been counting on a call.

A stolen bright red Porsche would be a little obvious on the motorway. So she had her excuse lined up. She was going to visit her brother—in Oxford, in roughly the opposite direction. She'd be back at Bexford that evening. Brother Bob was a banker. Let Rumby worry that she was going to blab to him to protect her 750K investment, about which she no longer cared a hoot. Let Case and some co-driver hare after her fruitlessly towards Oxford in the Merc.

The voice wasn't Case's. Or Lascelles'. Or even Rumby's.

She nearly jerked the Porsche off the road.

The voice was that of Voss.

"Can you hear me, Fräulein Donaldson?"

Hands shaking, legs trembling, she guided the car into a gateway opening on to a huge field of close-cut golden stubble girt by a hawthorn hedge. A Volvo hooted in protest as it swung by. A rabbit fled.

"How did you find me, Voss—?" she gasped. Horrid perspectives loomed. "They told you! They know you!"

The caller chuckled.

"I'm merely the voice of *Vertumnus*, Fräulein. My image is everywhere these days, so why shouldn't I be everywhere too? Are you perhaps worried about the collapse of your precious Ego, Fraulein?"

How persuasive his voice was. "This has all happened before, you know. The God of the Bible ruled the medieval world, but when He went into eclipse *Humanity* seized His sceptre. Ah, that exalted Renaissance Ego! How puffed up it was! By the time of Rudolph, that same Ego was already collapsing. Its confidence had failed. A new unity was needed—a bio-cosmic social unity. The Holy Roman Emperor Rudolph sought to be the *head* of society— hence the painting of so many regal *heads* by the artist you have libelled. Those biological, botanical heads."

"I already know this," she said.

"He would be the head—and the people, the limbs, the organs. Of one body! In the new world now a-dawning life will be a unity again. The Emperor will be the head—but not a separate, egotistic head. Nor will the limbs and organs be separate individualists."

"You're telling me what I know!" Aye, and *what she most feared*—namely the loss of Self. Its extinction. And what she most feared might well *win*; for what is feared is potent.

"Who are you? What are you?" she cried into the phone—already suspecting that Voss's voice, the voice of Vertumnus, might well be in her own wayward head, either ring-bound or else planted there by alchemical potion.

She slammed the hand-set down on to its cradle by the gearshift lever, thumbed the windows fully open, and lit a cigarette to calm herself. Whispers of smoke drifted out towards the shorn field.

A mat of golden stubble cloaked the broad shoulders of the land. A ghostly pattern emerged across the great network of dry stalks: a coat of arms. The hedge was merely green braiding. Her car was a shiny red bug parked on the shoulder of a giant sprawling being.

Angrily she pitched her cigarette through the passenger window towards the field, wishing that it might start a fire, though really the straw was far too short to combust.

She drove on; and when the phone seemed to burble again, she ignored it.

She smoked. She threw out half-burned cigarettes till the pack was empty, but no smoke ever plumed upwards far behind her.

Half way through Cheltenham, in slow-moving traffic, she passed a great billboard flaunting Rudolph Vertumnus. *WE ARE ALL PART OF NA-TURE*, proclaimed the all too familiar text.

Evidently unseen by other drivers and pedestrians, the fruity Emperor shouldered his way out of the poster. A pumpkin-belly that she had never seen before reared into view. And marrow-legs, from between which auber-gine testicles and a carrot cock dangled. Vertumnus towered over the other cars and vans behind her, bestriding the roadway. His carrot swelled enor-mously.

Raphanidosis: ancient Greek word. To be fucked by a giant radish. To be radished, ravished.

Vertumnus was coming.

A red light changed to green, and she was able to slip onward before the giant could advance to unpeel the roof of the Porsche and lift her out, homunculus-like, from her container.

Even in the heart of the city, a chthonic entity was coming to life. A liberated, incarnated deity was being born.

No one else but Jill saw it as yet.

Yet everyone knew it from ten thousand posters and badges—wearing its varied seasonal faces. Everyone knew Vertumnus by now, deity of change and transformation; for change was in the air, as ripe Autumn matured. The death of Self was on the horizon.

When she reached the motorway, those triple lanes cutting far ahead through the landscape opened up yawning perspectives of time rather than of space.

Deep time, in which there'd been no conscious mind present at all, only vegetable and animal existence. Hence, the blankness of the road . . .

Soon, a new psychic era might dawn in which the sovereign virtue of the conscious Self faded as humanity re-entered Nature once again—willing the demise of dissective, alienating logics and sciences, altering the mind-set, hypnotizing itself into a communal empathy with the world, whose potent figurehead wasn't any vague, cloudy Gaea, but rather her son Vertumnus. Every eating of his body—of fruits and nuts and vegetables and fishes— would be a vividly persuasive communion. His royal representative would reign in Budapest, or in Prague, or Vienna. His figurehead.

The phone burbled, and this time Jill did answer as she swung along the endless tongue of tarmac, and through time.

"Jill, don't hang up." *Rumby*. "I know why you've skipped out. And you must believe it ain't my fault."

What was he talking about?

"I've been the well-meaning patsy in this business. I've been the Gorby."

"Who was *he*?" she asked mischievously. Here was a message from a different era.

"I'm fairly sure by now that my goddam Star Club *was* behind the bombing *and* the ring-binder. Didn't trust me to be *thorough* enough. The whole Archy situation was really a lot more serious than even I saw. Those damn posters were really imprinting people on some deep-down level—not just surface propaganda. These are power-images. Fucking servosymbols—"

"You're only *fairly* sure?" she asked.

"What tipped you off? Was it something *Case* said? Or Johnny Lascelles? Something Johnny let slip? I mean, why did you skip?"

Something Case or Lascelles had let slip . . . ? So Rumby was becoming a tad paranoid about his own staff in case they were serving two masters— Rumby himself, and some other rich gent in that secret Star Club of theirs . . . A gent whom she had perhaps met in that drawing room in North London; who had caned her at a distance . . .

"Come back, Jill, and tell me all you know. I'm serious! I need to know."

Oh yes, she could recognize the authentic tones of paranoia . . .

"Sorry about taking the Porsche," she said.

"Never mind the fucking car. Where are you, Jill?"

She remembered.

"I'm going to Oxford to see my brother. He's a bank manager."

She hung up, and ignored repeated calls.

Polmerrin lay in a wooded little valley within a couple of miles of the rocky, wind-whipped North Cornwall coastline. Sheltered by the steep plunge of land and by oakwood, the once-derelict hamlet of cottages now housed studios and craft workshops, accompanied by a dozen satellite caravans. Pottery, jewellery, painting, sculpting, candle-making . . .

Kids played. Women worked. A few male companions lent an enlightened hand. Someone was tootling a flute, and a buzzard circled high overhead. A kingfisher flashed to and fro along a stream, one soggy bank of which was edged by alder buckthorn. Some brimstone butterflies still fluttered, reluctant to succumb to worn-out wings and cooling nights. The sunset was brimstone too: sulphur and orange peel. A few arty tourists were departing.

Immediately Jill realized that she had come to the wrong place entirely. She ought to have fled to some high-tech airport hotel with gleaming glass elevators—an inorganic, air-conditioned, sealed machine resembling a space station in the void.

She was too tired to reverse her route.

Red-haired Annie embraced Jill, in surprise and joy. She kissed Jill, hugged her.

Freckled Annie was wearing one of those Indian cotton dresses—in green hues—with tiny mirrors sewn into it; and she'd put some extra flesh upon her once-lithe frame, though not to the extent of positive plumpness. She had also put on slim, scrutinizing glasses. Pewter rings adorned several fingers, with scarab and spider motifs.

One former barn was now a refectory, to which she led a dazed Jill to drink lemonade.

"How long has it been, Jilly? Four years? You'll stay with me, of course. So what's *happening*?" She frowned. "I did hear about your book—and that awful bombing. I still listen to the radio all day long while I'm painting—"

"Jill's drugged," said Jill. "Vertumnus is reborn. And the Holy Roman Empire is returning."

Annie scrutinized her with concern. "Holy shit." She considered. "You'd better not tell any of the others. There are kids here. Folks might worry."

They whispered, as once they had whispered confidences.

"Do you know the *Portrait of Jacopo Strada*?" Jill began. She found she could still speak about herself in the first person, historically.

Presently there were indeed kids and mothers and a medley of other women, and a few men in the refectory too, sharing an early supper of spiced beans and rice and salad and textured vegetable protein, Madras style, while Vivaldi played from a tape-deck. The beams of the barn were painted black, and murals of fabulous creatures relieved the whiteness of the plaster: a phoenix, a unicorn, a minotaur, each within a mazelike Celtic surround, so that it seemed as if so many heraldic shields were poised around the walls. Tourists would enjoy cream teas in here of an afternoon.

Sulphur and copper had cleared from a sky that was now deeply leaden-blue, fast darkening. Venus and Jupiter both shone. A shooting star streaked across the vault of void; or was that a failed satellite burning up?

Annie shared a studio with Rosy and Meg, who would be playing chess that evening in the recreation barn beside the refectory. The whole ground floor of the reconditioned cottage was studio. Meg's work was meticulous neo-medieval miniatures featuring eerie freaks rather than anyone comely. Rosy specialized in acrylic studies of transparent hourglass buildings set within forests, or in crystalline deserts, and crowded with disembodied heads instead of sand.

Annie *used* to paint swirling, luminous abstracts. Now she specialized in large acrylic canvasses of bloom within bloom within bloom, vortexes that sucked the gaze down into a central focus from which an eye always gazed out: a cat's, a bird's, a person's. Her pictures were like strange, exploded, organic cameras.

Jill looked; Jill admired. The paintings looked at her. Obviously there was a thematic empathy between the three women who used this studio.

"The conscious mind is going into eclipse," Jill remarked, and Annie smiled hesitantly.

"That's a great title. I might use it."

A polished wooden stairway led up to a landing with three bedrooms.

Annie's wide bed was of brass, with a floral duvet. Marguerites, daisies, buttercups.

In the morning when Jill awoke, the flowers had migrated from the duvet.

Annie's face, her neck, her shoulders were petals and stalks. Her skin was of white and pink blossoms. Her ear was a tulip, her nose was the bud of a lily, and her hair a fountain of red nasturtiums.

Jill reached to peel off some of the petals, but the flowers were flesh, and Annie awoke with a squeak of protest. Her open eyes were black nightshades with white blossom pupils.

And Jilldonaldson, whose name was dissolving, was the first to see such a transformation as would soon possess many men and women who regarded one another in a suitable light as part of Nature.

Jilldona stepped from the brass bed, towards the window, and pulled the curtains aside.

The valley was thick with mist. Yet a red light strobed the blur of vision. Spinning, this flashed from the roof of a police car parked beside the Porsche. Shapeless wraiths danced in its dipped headlight beams. One officer was scanning the vague, evasive cottages. A second walked around the Porsche, peered into it, then opened the passenger door.

"Hey," said Annie, "why did you tweak me?"

Annie's flesh was much as the night before, except that Jill continued to see a faint veil of flowers, an imprint of petals.

"Jill just wanted a cigarette," said Jill.

"I quit a couple of years ago," Annie reminded her. "Tobacco costs too much. Anyway, *you* didn't smoke last night."

"Jill forgot to. Fuzz are down there. Fuzz make Jill want a fag."

"That braggartly car—we ought to have driven it miles away! Miles and miles." Yet Annie didn't sound totally convinced that sheltering this visitor might be the best idea.

Jilldona pulled on her paisley sweater and jeans, and descended. Annie's paintings eyed her brightly as she passed by, recording her within their petal-ringed pupils.

She walked over to the police, one of whom asked:

"You wouldn't be a Miss Jill Donaldson, by any chance?" The burr of his Cornish accent . . .

"Names melt," she told her questioner. "The mind submerges in a unity of being. Have the Habsburgs sent you?" she asked. "Or was it the Star Club?"

One officer removed the ignition key from the Porsche and locked the car.

The other steered her by the arm into the back of the strobing vehicle. She could see no flowers on these policemen. However, a pair of wax strawberries dangled discretely from the driving mirror like blood-bright testicles.

For Hannah Shapero

A LONG NIGHT'S VIGIL
AT THE TEMPLE

Robert Silverberg

Here's one man's moving crisis of faith and conscience, played out against the lush and richly evocative background of a society so far in the future that our familiar everyday world, everything we see around us, all our history and culture, everything we are, is a fading distant memory, blurred almost to nothing by time, all but forgotten. Even in this unimaginably distant future age, though, *some* things don't change—like the eternal question, What Is Truth? . . .

Robert Silverberg is one of the most famous SF writers of modern times, with dozens of novels, anthologies, and collections to his credit. Silverberg has won five Nebula Awards and four Hugo Awards. His novels include *Dying Inside, Lord Valentine's Castle, The Book of Skulls, Downward to the Earth, Tower of Glass, The World Inside, Born with the Dead, Shadrach in the Furnace, Tom O'Bedlam, Star of Gypsies,* and *At Winter's End.* His collections include *Unfamiliar Territory, Capricorn Games, Majipoor Chronicles, The Best of Robert Silverberg, At the Con-glomeroid Cocktail Party,* and *Beyond the Safe Zone.* His most recent books are two novel-length expansions of famous Isaac Asimov stories, *Nightfall* and *The Ugly Little Boy,* the solo novels *The Face of the Waters* and *Kingdoms of the Wall,* and a massive retrospective collection, *The Collected Stories of Robert Silverberg, Volume One: Secret Sharers.* For many years he edited the prestigious anthology series *New Dimensions,* and has recently, along with his wife, Karen Haber, taken over the editing of the *Universe* anthology series. His stories have appeared in all nine previous editions of *The Year's Best Science Fiction,* a record unmatched by anyone else. He lives in Oakland, California.

The moment of total darkness was about to arrive. The Warder Diriente stepped forward onto the portico of the temple, as he had done every night for the past thirty years, to perform the evening invocation. He was wearing, as always, his bright crimson warder's cassock and the tall double-peaked hat of his office, which had seemed so comical to him when he had first seen his father wearing it long ago, but which he now regarded, when he thought of it at all, as simply an article of clothing. There was a bronze thurible in his left hand and in the right he held a tapering, narrow-necked green vessel, sleek and satisfying to the touch, the fine celadon ware that only the craftsmen of Murrha Island were capable of producing.

The night was clear and mild, a gentle summer evening, with the high, sharp sound of tree-frogs in the air and the occasional bright flash of golden light from the lantern of a glitterfly. Far below, in the valley where the sprawling imperial city of Citherione lay, the myriad lights of the far-off residential districts were starting to come on, and they looked like glitterfly gleams also, wavering and winking, an illusion born of great distance.

It was half an hour's journey by groundwagon from the closest districts of the city to the temple. The Warder had not been down there in months. Once he had gone there more frequently, but now that he was old the city had become an alien place to him, dirty, strange-smelling, discordant. The big stone temple, massive and solid in its niche on the hillside, with the great tawny mountain wall rising steeply behind it, was all that he needed these days: the daily round of prayer and observance and study, the company of good friends, a little work in the garden, a decent bottle of wine with dinner, perhaps some quiet music late at night. A comfortable, amiably reclusive life, untroubled by anguished questions of philosophy or urgent challenges of professional struggle.

His profession had been decided for him before his birth: the post of temple warder was hereditary. It had been in his family for twelve generations. He was the eldest son; his elevation to the wardership was a certainty throughout all his childhood, and Diriente had prepared himself unquestioningly for the post from the first. Of course, somewhere along the way he had lost whatever faith he might once have had in the tenets of the creed he served, and that had been a problem for him for a time, but he had come to terms with that a long while back.

The temple portico was a broad marble slab running the entire length of the building along its western face, the face that looked toward the city. Below the portico's high rim, extending outward from it like a fan, was a sloping lawn thick as green velvet—a hundred centuries of dedicated garden-ers had tended it with love—bordered by groves of ornamental flowering shrubs. Along the north side of the temple garden was a stream that sprang from some point high up on the mountain and flowed swiftly downward into the far-off valley. There were service areas just alongside and behind the temple—a garbage dump, a little cemetery, cottages for the temple staff—and back of those lay a tangle of wilderness forming a transitional zone between the open sloping flank of the mountain on which the temple had been constructed and the high wall of rock that rose to the rear of the site.

Warders were supposed to be in some semblance of a state of grace, that receptivity to the infinite which irreverent novices speak of as "cosmic connection," when they performed the evening invocation. Diriente doubted that he really did achieve the full degree of rapport, or even that such rapport was possible; but he did manage a certain degree of concentration that seemed acceptable enough to him. His technique of attaining it was to focus his attention on the ancient scarred face of the moon, if it was a night when the moon was visible, and otherwise to look toward the Pole Star. Moon or stars, either would do: the essential thing was to turn his spirit outward toward the realm where the great powers of the Upper World resided. It usually took him only a moment or two to attune himself properly for the rite. He had had plenty of practice, after all.

This night as he looked starward—there was no moon—and began to feel the familiar, faintly prickly sensation of contact awakening in him, the giddy feeling that he was climbing his own spinal column and gliding through his forehead into space, he was startled by an unusual interruption. A husky figure came jogging up out of the garden toward the temple and planted itself right below him at the portico's edge.

"Diriente?" he called. "Listen, Diriente, you have to come and look at something that I've found."

It was Mericalis, the temple custodian. The Warder, his concentration shattered, felt a sharp jolt of anger and surprise. Mericalis should have had more sense than that.

Testily the Warder indicated the thurible and the celadon vessel.

"Oh," Mericalis said, sounding unrepentant. "You aren't finished yet, then?"

"No, I'm not. I was only just starting, as a matter of fact. And you shouldn't be bothering me just this minute."

"Yes, yes, I know that. But this is important. Look, I'm sorry I broke in on you, but I had a damned good reason for it. Get your ceremony done with quickly, will you, Diriente? And then I want you to come with me. Right away."

Mericalis offered no other explanation. The Warder demanded none. It would only be a further distraction, and he was distracted enough as it was.

He attempted with no more than partial success to regain some measure of calmness.

"I'll finish as soon as you let me," he told the custodian irritably.

"Yes. Do. I'll wait for you down here."

The Warder nodded brusquely. Mericalis disappeared back into the shadows below the portico.

So. Then. Starting over from the beginning. The Warder drew his breath in deeply and closed his eyes a moment and waited until the effects of the intrusion had begun to ebb. After a time the jangling in his mind eased. Then once more he turned his attention to his task, looking up, finding the Pole Star with practiced ease and fixing his eyes upon it. From that direction, ten thousand years ago, the three Visitants had come to Earth to rescue mankind from great peril; or so the Scriptures maintained. Perhaps it actually had happened. There was no reason to think that it hadn't and some to think that it had.

He focused the entire intensity of his being on the Upper World, casting his soul skyward into the dark terrible gulfs between the galaxies. It was a willed feat of the imagination for him: with conscious effort he pictured himself roving the stars, a disembodied attenuated intelligence gliding like a bright needle through the black airless infinities.

The Warder often felt as though there once had been a time when making that leap had not required an effort of will: that in the days when he was new to his priestly office he had simply stepped forth and looked upward, and everything else had followed as a matter of course. The light of the Pole Star had penetrated his soul and he had gone out easily, effortlessly, on a direct course toward the star of the Three. Was it so? He couldn't remember. He had been Warder for so long. He had performed the evening invocation some ten thousand times at least. Everything was formula and rote by now. It was difficult now to believe that his mind had ever been capable of ascending in one joyous bound into those blazing depths of endless night, or that he had ever seriously thought that looking at the stars and dumping good wine into a stone channel might have some real and undeniable redemptive power. The best he could hope for these days was some flicker—some quivering little stab—of the old ecstasy, while he stood each night beneath the heavens in all their glory. And even that flicker, that tiny stab, was suspect, a probable counterfeit, an act of willful self-delusion.

The stars were beautiful, at any rate. He was grateful for that one blessing. His faith in the literal existence of the Visitants and their onetime presence on the Earth might be gone, but not his awareness of the immensity of the universe, the smallness of Man, the majesty of the great vault of night.

Standing poised and steady, head thrust back, face turned toward the heavens, he began to swing the thurible, sending a cloud of pungent incense swirling into the sky. He elevated the sleek green porcelain vessel, offering it to the three cardinal points, east and west and zenith. The reflexes of his professionalism had hold of him now: he was fully into the ceremony, as deeply as his skepticism would allow him ever to get. In the grasp of the moment he would let no doubts intrude. They would come back to him quickly enough, just afterward.

Solemnly now he spoke the Holy Names:

"Oberith . . . Aulimiath . . . Vonubius."

He allowed himself to believe that he had made contact.

He summoned up the image of the Three before him, the angular alien figures shimmering with spectral light. He told them, as he had told them so many times before, how grateful the world was for all that they had done for the people of Earth long ago, and how eager Earth was for their swift return from their present sojourn in the distant heavens.

For the moment the Warder's mind actually did seem free of all questions of belief and unbelief. Had the Three in fact existed? Had they truly come to Earth in its time of need? Did they rise up to the stars again in a fiery chariot when their work was done, vowing to return some day and gather up all the peoples of the world in their great benevolence? The Warder had no idea. When he was young he believed every word of the Scriptures, like everyone else; then, he was not sure exactly when, he stopped believing. But that made no conspicuous difference to the daily conduct of his life. He was the Warder of the high temple; he had certain functions to perform; he was a servant of the people. That was all that mattered.

The ritual was the same every evening. According to generally accepted belief it hadn't changed in thousands of years, going back to the very night of the Visitants' departure from Earth, though the Warder was privately skeptical of that, as he was of so many other matters. Things change with time; distortions enter any system of belief; of that he was certain. Even so, he outwardly maintained the fiction that there had been no alterations in any aspect of the liturgy, because he was aware that the people preferred to think that that was the case. The people were profoundly conservative in their ways; and he was here to serve the people. That was the family tradition: we are Warders, and that means we serve.

The invocation was at its climax, the moment of the offering. Softly the Warder spoke the prayer of the Second Advent, the point of the entire exercise, expressing the hope that the Three would not long delay their return to the world. The words rolled from him quickly, perfunctorily, as though they were syllables in some lost language, holding no meaning for him. Then he called the Names a second time, with the same theatrical solemnity as before. He lifted the porcelain vessel high, inverted it, and allowed the golden wine that it contained to pour into the stone channel that ran down the hill toward the temple pond. That was the last of it, the finale of the rite. Behind him, at that moment, the temple's hydraulus-player, a thin hatchet-faced man sitting patiently in the darkness beside the stream, struck from his instrument the three great thunderous chords that concluded the service.

At this point any worshipers who had happened to have remained at the temple this late would have fallen to their knees and cried out in joy and hope while making the sign of the Second Advent. But there were no worshipers on hand this evening, only a few members of the temple staff, who, like the Warder, were going about the business of shutting the place down for the night. In the moment of the breaking of the contact the Warder stood by himself, very much conscious of the solitude of his spirit and the futility of his profession as he felt the crashing wave of his unbelief come sweeping back in upon him. The pain lasted only an instant; and then he was himself again.

Out of the shadows then came Mericalis once more, broad-shouldered, insistent, rising before the Warder like a specter he had conjured up himself.

"You're done? Ready to go?"

The Warder glared at him. "Why are you in such a hurry? Do you mind if I put the sacred implements away first?"

"Go right ahead," the custodian said, shrugging. "Take all the time you want, Diriente." There was an unfamiliar edge on his voice.

The Warder chose to ignore it. He re-entered the temple and placed the thurible and the porcelain wine-vessel in their niche just within the door. He closed the wrought-iron grillwork cover of the niche and locked it, and quickly muttered the prayer that ended his day's duties. He put aside his tall hat and hung his cassock on its peg. Underneath it he wore a simple linen surplice, belted with a worn strip of leather.

He stepped back outside. The members of the temple staff were drifting off into the night, heading down by torchlight to their cottages along the temple's northern side. Their laughter rose on the soft air. The Warder envied them their youth, their gaiety, their assurance that the world was as they thought it was.

Mericalis, still waiting for him beside a flowering bayerno bush just below the thick marble rim of the portico, beckoned to him.

"Where are we going?" The Warder asked, as they set out briskly together across the lawn.

"You'll see."

"You're being very damned mysterious."

"Yes. I suppose I am."

Mericalis was leading him around the temple's northwestern corner to the back of the building, where the rough road began that by a series of steep switchbacks ascended the face of the hill against which the temple had been built. He carried a small automatic torch, a mere wand of amber light. On this moonless evening the torch seemed more powerful than it really was.

As they went past the garbage dump Mericalis said, "I really am sorry I broke in on you just as you were about to do the invocation. I did actually think you were done with it already."

"That doesn't make any difference now."

"I felt bad, though. I know how important that rite is to you."

"Do you?" the Warder said, not knowing what to make of the custodian's remark.

The Warder had never discussed his loss of faith with anyone, not even Mericalis, who over the years had become perhaps his closest friend, closer to him than any of the temple's priests. But he doubted that it was much of a secret. Faith shines in a man's face like the full moon breaking through the mists on a winter night. The Warder was able to see it in others, that special glow. He suspected that they were unable to see it in him.

The custodian was a purely secular man. His task was to maintain the structural integrity of the temple, which, after all, had been in constant service for ten thousand years and by now was perpetually in precarious condition, massive and sturdy though it was. Mericalis knew all the weak places in the walls, the subtle flaws in the buttresses, the shifting slabs in the floor, the defects of the drains. He was something of an archaeologist as well, and could discourse learnedly on the various stages of the ancient building's complex history, the details of the different reconstructions, the stratigraphic boundaries marking one configuration of the temple off from another, showing how it had been built and rebuilt over the centuries. Of religious feeling, Mericalis seemed to have none at all: it was the temple that he loved, not the creed that it served.

They were well beyond the garbage dump now, moving along the narrow unpaved road that ran up toward the summit of the mountain. The Warder found his breath coming short as the grade grew more steep.

He had rarely had occasion to use this road. There were old altars higher up on the mountain, remnants of a primitive fire-rite that had become obsolete many hundreds of years before, during the Samtharid Interregnum. But they held no interest for him. Mericalis, pursuing his antiquarian studies, probably went up there frequently, the Warder supposed, and now he must have made some startling discovery amidst the charred ancient stones, something bizarre and troublesome enough to justify breaking in on him during the invocation. A scene of human sacrifice? The tomb of some prehistoric king? This mountain had been holy land a long time, going back, so it was said, even into the days before the old civilization of machines and miracles had collapsed. What strangeness had Mericalis found?

But their goal didn't seem to lie above them on the mountain. Instead of continuing to ascend, the custodian turned abruptly off the road when they were still only a fairly short distance behind the temple and began pushing his way vigorously into a tangle of underbrush. The Warder, frowning, followed. By this time he knew better than to waste his breath asking questions. He stumbled onward, devoting all his energy to the job of maintaining his footing. In the deep darkness of the night, with Mericalis' little torch the only illumination, he was hard pressed to keep from tripping over hidden roots or vines.

After about twenty paces of tough going they came to a place where a second road—a crude little path, really—unexpectedly presented itself. This one, to the Warder's surprise, curved back down the slope in the direction of the temple, but instead of returning them to the service area on the northern side it carried them around toward the opposite end of the building, into a zone which the Warder long had thought was inaccessible because of the thickness of the vegetation. They were behind the temple's southeastern corner now, perhaps a hundred paces from the rear wall of the building itself. In all his years here the Warder had never seen the temple from this angle. Its great oblong bulk reared up against the sky, black on black, a zone of intense starless darkness against a star-speckled black backdrop.

There was a clearing here in the scrub. A roughly circular pit lay in the center of it, about as wide across as the length of a man's arm. It seemed recently dug, from the fresh look of the mound of tailings behind it.

Mericalis walked over to the opening and poked the head of his torch into it. The Warder, coming up alongside him, stared downward. Despite the inadequacy of the light he was able to see that the pit was actually the mouth of a subterranean passageway which sloped off at a sharp angle, heading toward the temple.

"What's all this?" the Warder asked.

"An unauthorized excavation. Some treasure-hunters have been at work back here."

The Warder's eyes opened wide. "Trying to tunnel into the temple, you mean?"

"Apparently so," said Mericalis. "Looking for a back way into the vaults."

He stepped down a little way into the pit, paused, and looked back, beckoning impatiently to the Warder. "Come on, Diriente. You need to see what's here."

The Warder stayed where he was.

"You seriously want me to go down there? The two of us crawling around in an underground tunnel in the dark?"

"Yes. Absolutely."

"I'm an old man, Mericalis."

"Not all that old. And it's a very capably built little passageway. You can manage it."

Still the Warder held back. "And what if the men who dug it come back and find us while we're in there?"

"They won't," said Mericalis. "I promise you that."

"How can you be so sure?"

"Trust me, Diriente."

"I'd feel better if we had a couple of the younger priests with us, all the same."

The custodian shook his head. "Once you've seen what I'm going to show you, you'll be glad that there's no one here but you and me to see it. Come on, now. Are you going to follow me or aren't you?"

Uneasily the Warder entered the opening. The newly broken ground was soft and moist beneath his sandaled feet. The smell of the earth rose to his nostrils, rich, loamy, powerful. Mericalis was five or six paces ahead of him and moving quickly along without glancing back. The Warder found that he had to crouch and shuffle to keep from hitting his head on the narrow tunnel's low roof. And yet the tunnel was well made, just as the custodian had said. It descended at a sharp angle until it was perhaps twice the height of a man below the ground, and then leveled out. It was nicely squared off at the sides and bolstered every ten paces by timbers. Months of painstaking work must have been required for all this. The Warder felt a sickly sense of violation. To think that thieves had managed to work back here undisturbed all this time! And had they reached the vaults? The temple wasn't actually a single building, but many, of different eras, each built upon the foundation of its predecessor. Layer beneath layer of inaccessible chambers, some of them thousands of years old, were believed to occupy the area underneath the main ceremonial hall of the present-day temple. The temple possessed considerable treasure, precious stones, ingots of rare metals, works of art: gifts of forgotten monarchs, hidden away down there in those old vaults long ago and scarcely if ever looked at since. It was believed that there were tombs in the building's depths, too, the burial places of ancient kings, priests, heroes. But no one ever tried to explore the deeper vaults. The stairs leading down to them were hopelessly blocked with debris, so that not even Mericalis could distinguish between what might once have been a staircase and what was part of the building's foundation. Getting down to the lower strata would be impossible without ripping up the present-day floors and driving broad shafts through the upper basements, and no one dared to try that: such excavation might weaken the entire structure and bring the building crashing down. As for tunneling into the deep levels from outside—well, no one in the Warder's memory had ever proposed doing that, either, and he doubted that the Grand Assize of the Temple would permit such a project to be carried out even if application were made. There was no imaginable spiritual benefit to be gained from rooting about in the foundations of the holy building, and not much scientific value in it either, considering how many other relicts of Earth's former civilizations, still unexcavated after all this time, were on hand everywhere to keep the archaeologists busy.

But if the diggers had been thieves, not archaeologists—

No wonder Mericalis had come running up to him in the midst of the invocation!

"How did you find this?" the Warder asked, as they moved farther in. The air here was dank and close, and the going was very slow.

"It was one of the priests that found it, actually. One of the younger ones, and no, I won't tell you his name, Diriente. He came around back here a few days ago with a certain young priestess to enjoy a little moment or two of privacy and they practically fell right into it. They explored it to a point about as far as we are now and realized it was something highly suspicious, and they came and told me about it."

"But you didn't tell me."

"No," Mericalis said. "I didn't. It seemed purely a custodial affair then. There was no need to get you involved in it. Someone had been digging around behind the temple, yes. Very likely for quite some time. Coming in by night, maybe, working very, very patiently, hauling away the tailings and dumping them in the woods, pushing closer and closer to the wall of the building, no doubt with the intent of smashing through into one of the deep chambers and carrying off the vast wealth that's supposedly stored down there. My plan was to investigate the tunnel myself, find out just what had been going on here, and then to bring the city police in to deal with it. You would have been notified at that point, of course."

"So you haven't taken it to the police yet, then?"

"No," said Mericalis. "I haven't."

"But why not?"

"I don't think there's anyone for them to arrest, that's why. Look here, Diriente."

He took the Warder by the arm and tugged him forward so that the Warder was standing in front of him. Then he reached his arm under the Warder's and flashed the torch into the passageway just ahead of them.

The Warder gasped.

Two men in rough work clothes were sprawled on the tunnel floor, half buried beneath debris that had fallen from overhead. The Warder could see shovels and picks jutting out from the mound of fallen earth beside them. A third man—no, this one was a woman—lay a short distance away. A sickening odor of decay rose from the scene.

"Are they dead?" the Warder asked quietly.

"Do you need to ask?"

"Killed by a rockfall, you think?"

"That's how it looks, doesn't it? These two were the diggers. The girl was their lookout, I suspect, posted at the mouth of the tunnel. She's armed: you see? Two guns and a dagger. They must have called her in here to see something unusual, and just then the roof fell in on them all." Mericalis stepped over the slender body and picked his way through the rubble beyond it, going a few paces deeper into the passageway.

"Come over here and I'll show you what I think happened."

"What if the roof collapses again?"

"I don't think it will," Mericalis said.

"If it can collapse once, it can collapse again," said the Warder, shivering a little now despite the muggy warmth of the tunnel. "Right on our heads. Shouldn't we get out of here while we can?"

The custodian ignored him. "Look here, now: what do you make of this?" He aimed the torch to one side, holding it at a ninety-degree angle to the direction of the tunnel. The Warder squinted into the darkness. He saw what looked like a thick stone lintel which had fallen from the tunnel vault and was lying tipped up on end. There were archaic-looking inscriptions carved in it, runes of some sort. Behind it was an opening, a gaping oval of darkness in the darkness, that appeared to be the mouth of a second tunnel running crosswise to the one they were in. Mericalis leaned over the fallen lintel and flashed his beam beyond it. A tunnel, yes. But constructed in a manner very different from that of the one they had been following. The walls were of narrow stone blocks, carefully laid edge to edge; the roof of the tunnel was a long stone vault, supported by pointed arches. The craftsmanship was very fine. The joints had an archaic look.

"How old is this?" the Warder asked.

"Old. Do you recognize those runes on the lintel? They're proterohistoric stuff. This tunnel's as ancient as the temple itself, most likely. Part of the original sacred complex. The thieves couldn't have known it was here. As they were digging their way toward the temple they intersected it by accident. They yelled for the girl to come in and look—or maybe they wanted her to help them pull the lintel loose. Which they proceeded to do, and the weak place where the two tunnels met gave way, and the roof of their own tunnel came crashing down on them. For which I for one feel no great sorrow, I have to admit."

"Do you have any idea where this other tunnel goes?"

"To the temple," said Mericalis. "Or under it, rather, into the earliest foundation. It leads straight toward the deepest vaults."

"Are you sure?"

"I've been inside already. Come."

There was no question now of retreating. The Warder, following close along behind Mericalis, stared at the finely crafted masonry of the tunnel in awe.

Now and again he saw runic inscriptions, unreadable, mysterious, carved in the stone floor. When they had gone about twenty paces yet another stone-vaulted passageway presented itself, forking off to the left. The custodian went past it without a glance. "There are all sorts of tunnels down here," Mericalis said. "But this is the one we want. So far as I've been able to determine at this point, it's the only one that enters the temple." The Warder saw that Mericalis had left a marker that glowed by the reflected light of his torch, high up on the wall of the passage they were following, and he supposed that there were other markers farther on to serve as guides for them. "We're in a processional hypogeum," the custodian explained. "Probably it was just about at ground level, ten thousand years ago, but over the centuries it was buried by construction debris from the later temples, and other trash of various sorts. There was a whole maze of other stone-walled processional chambers around it, leading originally to sacrificial sites and open-air altars. The tunnel we just passed was one of them. It's blocked a little way onward. I spent two days in here going down one false trail after another. Until I came through this way, and—behold, Diriente!"

Mericalis waved his torch grandly about. By the pale splash of light that came from its tip the Warder saw that the sides of the tunnel expanded outward here, spreading to the right and the left to form a great looming wall of superbly dressed stone, with one small dark aperture down at the lower left side. They had reached the rear face of the temple. The Warder trembled. He had an oppressive sense of the thickness of the soil above him, the vast weight pressing down, the temple itself rising in all its intricacy of strata above him. He was at the foundation of foundations. Once all this had been in the open: ten thousand years ago, when the Visitants still walked the Earth.

"You've been inside?" the Warder asked hoarsely.

"Of course," said Mericalis. "You have to crawl the first part of the way. Take care to breathe shallowly: there's plenty of dust."

The air here was hot and musty and dry, ancient air, lifeless air. The Warder choked and gagged on it. On hands and knees, head down, he crept along behind Mericalis. Several times, overcome by he knew not what, he closed his eyes and waited until a spasm of dizziness had passed.

"You can stand now," the custodian told him.

They were in a large square stone chamber. The walls were rough-hewn and totally without ornament. The room was empty except for three long, narrow coffers of unpolished white marble side by side at the far end.

"Steady yourself, old friend," Mericalis said. "And then come and see who we have here."

They crossed the room. The coffers were covered with a thick sheet of some transparent yellowish material that looked much like glass, but in fact was some other substance that the Warder could not identify.

An icy shiver ran through the Warder as he peered through the coverings.

There was a skeleton in each coffer, lying face upward: the glistening fleshless bones of some strange long-shanked creature, manlike in size and general outline, but different in every detail. Their heads bore curving bony crests; their shoulders were crested also; their knees were double ones; they had spikelike protrusions at their ankles. Ribs, pelvises, fingers, toes—everything strange, everything unfamiliar. These were the bodies of alien beings.

Mericalis said, "My guess is that the very tall one in the center is Vonubius. That's probably Aulimiath on the right and the other one has to be Oberith, then."

The Warder looked up at him sharply. "What are you saying?"

"This is obviously a sepulcher. Those are sarcophagi. These are three skeletons of aliens that we're looking at here. They've been very carefully preserved and buried in a large and obviously significant chamber on the deepest and therefore oldest level of the Temple of the Visitants, in a room that once was reached by a grand processional passageway. Who else do you think they would be?"

"The Visitants went up into the heavens when their work on Earth was done," said the Warder hollowly. "They ascended on a ship of fire and returned to their star."

"You believe that?" Mericalis asked, chuckling.

"It says so in the Scriptures."

"I know that it does. Do you believe it, though?"

"What does it matter what I believe?" The Warder stared again at the three elongated alien skeletons. "The historical outlines aren't questioned by anybody. The world was in a crisis—in collapse. There was war everywhere. In the midst of it all, three ambassadors from another solar system arrived and saw what was going on, and they used their superior abilities to put things to rights. Once a stable new world order had emerged, they took off for the stars again. The story turns up in approximately the same form in every society's myths and folk-tales, all over the Earth. There's got to be some truth to it."

"I don't doubt that there is," said Mericalis. "And there they are, the three wise men from afar. The Scriptures have the story a little garbled, apparently. Instead of going back to their native star, promising to return and redeem us at some new time of trouble, they died while still on Earth and were buried underneath the temple of the cult that sprang up around them. So there isn't going to be any Second Advent, I'd tend to think. And if there ever is, it may not be a friendly one. They didn't die natural deaths, you'll notice. If you'll take a careful look you'll see that the heads of all three were severed violently from their trunks."

"What?"

"Look closely," Mericalis said.

"There's a break in the vertebrae, yes. But that could have been—"

"It's the same sort of break in all three. I've seen the skeletons of executed men before, Diriente. We've dug up dozens of them around the old gibbet down the hill. These three were decapitated. Believe me."

"No."

"They were martyrs. They were put to death by their loving admirers and devoted worshipers, the citizens of Earth."

"No. No. No. No."

"Why are you so stunned, Diriente? Does it shock you, that such a dreadful thing could have happened on our lovely green planet? Have you been squirreled up in your nest on this hillside so long that you've forgotten everything you once knew about human nature? Or is it the unfortunate evidence that the Scriptural story is wrong that bothers you?

You don't believe in the Second Advent anyway, do you?"

"How do you know I don't?"

"Please, Diriente."

The Warder was silent. His mind was aswirl with confusions.

After a time he said, "These could be any three aliens at all."

"Yes. I suppose they could. But we know of only three beings from space that ever came to this planet: the ones who we call the Visitants. This is the temple of the faith that sprang up around them. Somebody went to great trouble to bury these three underneath it. I have difficulty believing that these would be three *different* alien beings."

Stubbornly the Warder said, "How do you know that these things are genuine skeletons? They might be idols of some sort."

"Idols in the form of skeletons? *Decapitated* skeletons, at that?" Mericalis laughed. "I suppose we could test them chemically to see if they're real, if you like. But they look real enough to me."

"The Visitants were like gods. They *were* gods, compared with us. Certainly they were regarded as divine—or at least as the ministers and ambassadors of the Divine Being—when they were here. Why would they have been killed? Who would have dared to lay a hand on them?"

"Who can say? Maybe they didn't seem as divine as all that in the days when they walked among us," Mericalis suggested.

"But the Scriptures say—"

"The Scriptures, yes. Written how long after the fact? The Visitants may not have been so readily recognized as holy beings originally. They might simply have seemed threatening, maybe—dangerous—tyrannical. A menace to free will, to man's innate right to make trouble for himself. It was a time of anarchy, remember. Maybe there were those who didn't *want* order restored. I don't know. Even if they *were* seen as godly, Diriente: remember that there's an ancient tradition on this planet of killing one's gods. It goes back a long, long way. Study your prehistoric cults. You dig down deep enough, you find a murdered god somewhere at the bottom of almost all of them."

The Warder fell into silence again. He was unable to take his eyes from those bony-crested skulls, those strange-angled empty eye sockets.

"Well," Mericalis said, "there you have them, at any rate: three skeletons of what appear to be beings from another world that somebody just happened to bury underneath your temple a very long time ago. I thought you ought to know about them."

"Yes. Thank you."

"You have to decide what to do about them, now."

"Yes," the Warder said. "I know that."

"We could always seal the passageway up again, I suppose, and not say a word about this to anyone. Which would avoid all sorts of uncomfortable complications, wouldn't it? It strikes me as a real crime against knowledge, doing something like that, but if you thought that we should—"

"Who knows about this so far?"

"You. Me. No one else."

"What about the priest and priestess who found the excavation pit?"

"They came right to me and told me about it. They hadn't gone very far inside, no more than five or six paces. Why should they have gone any farther?"

"They might have," the Warder said.

"They didn't. They had no torch and they had their minds on other things. All they did was look a little way in, just far enough to see that something unusual was going on. They hadn't even gone far enough to find the thieves. But they didn't say a thing about dead bodies in the tunnel. They'd certainly have told me about them, if they had come upon them. And they'd have looked a whole lot shakier, too."

"The thieves didn't come in here either?"

"It doesn't seem that way to me. I don't think they got any farther than the place where they pulled that lintel out of the passage wall. They're dead, in any case."

"But what if they did get this far? And what if there was someone else with them, someone who managed to escape when the tunnel caved in? Someone who might be out there right now telling all his friends what he saw in this room?"

Mericalis shook his head. "There's no reason to think that. And I could see, when I first came down this passage and into the sepulchral chamber, that nobody had been through here in more years than we can imagine. There'd have been tracks in the dust, and there weren't any. This place has gone undisturbed a very long time. Long enough for the whole story of how the Visitants died to be forgotten and covered over with a nice pretty myth about their ascent into the heavens on a pillar of fire."

The Warder considered that for a moment.

"All right," he said finally. "Go back outside, Mericalis."

"And leave you here alone?"

"Leave me here alone, yes."

Uneasily Mericalis said, "What are you up to, Diriente?"

"I want to sit here all by myself and think and pray, that's all."

"Do I have to believe that?"

"Yes. You do."

"If you go wandering around down here you'll end up trapped in some unknown passageway and most likely we'll never be able to find you again."

"I'm not going to wander around anywhere. I told you what I'm going to do. I'm going to sit right here, in this very room. You've brought me face to face with the dead bodies of the murdered gods of the religion that I'm supposed to serve, and I need to think about what that means. That's all. Go away, Mericalis. This is something I have to do all by myself. You'll only be a distraction. Come back for me at dawn and I promise you that you'll find me sitting exactly where I am now."

"There's only one torch. I'll need it if I'm going to be able to find my way out of the tunnel. And that means I have to leave you in the dark."

"I realize that, Mericalis."

"But—"

"Go," the Warder said. "Don't worry about me. I can stand a few hours of darkness. I'm not a child. Go," he said again. "Just go, will you? Now."

He couldn't deny that he was frightened. He was well along in years; by temperament he was a sedentary man; it was totally against his nature to be spending a night in a place like this, far beneath the ground, where the air managed to seem both dusty-dry and sticky-moist at the same time, and the sharp, pungent odor of immense antiquity jabbed painfully at his nostrils. How different it was from his pleasant little room, surrounded by his books, his jug of wine, his familiar furnishings! In the total darkness he was free to imagine the presence of all manner of disagreeable creatures of the depths creeping about him, white eyeless toads and fleshless chittering lizards and slow, contemplative spiders lowering themselves silently on thick silken cords from invisible recesses of the stone ceiling. He stood in the center of the room and it seemed to him that he saw a sleek fat serpent, pallid and gleaming, with blind blue eyes bright as sapphires, issue from a pit in the floor and rise up before him, hissing and bobbing and swaying as it made ready to strike. But the Warder knew that it was only a trick of the darkness. There was no pit; there was no serpent.

He perspired freely. His light robe was drenched and clung to him like a shroud. With every breath it seemed to him that he was pulling clusters of cobwebs into his lungs. The darkness was so intense it hammered at his fixed, rigidly staring eyes until he was forced to shut them. He heard inexplicable sounds coming from the walls, a grinding hum and a steady unhurried ticking and a trickling sound, as of sand tumbling through hidden inner spaces. There were menacing vibrations and tremors, and strange twanging hums, making him fear that the temple itself, angered by this intrusion into its bowels, was preparing to bring itself down upon him. What I hear is only the echoes of Mericalis' footfalls, the Warder told himself. The sounds that he makes as he retraces his way down the tunnel toward the exit.

After a time he arose and felt his way across the room toward the coffers in the corner, clinging to the rough stones of the wall to guide himself. Somehow he missed his direction, for the corner was empty when he reached it, and as he continued past it his inquiring fingers found themselves pressing into what surely was the opening that led to the tunnel. He stood quietly for a moment in the utter darkness, trying to remember the layout of the funeral chamber, certain that the coffers must have been in the corner he had gone to and unable to understand why he had not found them. He thought of doubling back his path and looking again. But perhaps he was disoriented; perhaps he had gone in precisely the opposite direction from the one he supposed he had taken. He kept going, past the opening, along the wall on the other side. To the other corner. No coffers here. He turned right, still clinging to the wall. A step at a time, imagining yawning pits opening beneath his feet. His knee bumped into something. He had reached the coffers, yes.

He knelt. Grasped the rim of the nearest one, leaned forward, looked down into it.

To his surprise he was able to see a little now, to make out the harsh, angular lines of the skeleton it contained. How was that possible? Perhaps his eyes were growing accustomed to the darkness. No, that wasn't it. A nimbus of light seemed to surround the coffer. A faint reddish glow had begun to rise from it and with the aid of that unexpected illumination he could actually see the outlines of the elongated shape within.

An illusion? Probably. Hallucination, even. This was the strangest moment of his life, and anything was to be expected, anything at all. There is magic here, the Warder found himself thinking, and then he caught himself up in amazement and wonder that he should have so quickly tumbled into the abyss of the irrational. He was a prosaic man. He had no belief in magic. And yet—and yet—

The glow grew more intense. The skeleton blazed in the darkness. With eerie clarity he saw the alien crests and spines, the gnarled alien vertebrae, everything sending up a strange crimson fire to make its aspect plain to him. The empty eye sockets seemed alive with fierce intelligence.

"Who are you?" the Warder asked, almost belligerently. "Where did you come from? Why did you ever poke your noses into our affairs? Did you even *have* noses?" He felt strangely giddy. The closeness of the air, perhaps. Not enough oxygen. He laughed, too loudly, too long. "Oberith, is that who you are? Aulimiath? And that's Vonubius in the center box, yes? The tallest one, the leader of the mission."

His body shook with sudden anguish. Waves of fear and bewilderment swept over him. His own crude joking had frightened him. He began to sob.

The thought that he might be in the presence of the actual remains of the actual Three filled him with confusion and dismay. He had come over the years to think of the tale of the Advent as no more than a myth—the gods who came from the stars—and now he was stunned by this evidence that they had been real, that they once were tangible creatures who had walked and eaten and breathed and made water—and had been capable of dying, of being killed. He had reached a point long ago of not believing that. This discovery required him to reevaluate everything. Did it trivialize the religion he served into mere history? No—no, he thought; the existence here in this room of these bones elevated history into miracle, into myth. They truly had come. And had served, and had departed: not to the stars, but to the realm of death. From which they would return in the due course of time, and in their resurrection would bring the redemption that had been promised, the forgiveness for the crime that had been committed against them.

Was that it? Was that the proper way to interpret the things this room held?

He didn't know. He realized that he knew nothing at all.

The Warder shivered and trembled. He wrapped his arms around himself and held himself tight.

He fought to regain some measure of control over himself.

"No," he said sternly. "It can't be. You aren't them. I don't believe that those are your names."

From the coffers no answer came.

"You could be any three aliens at all," the Warder told them fiercely. "Who just happened to come to Earth, just dropped in one afternoon to see what might be here. And lived to regret it. Am I right?"

Still silence. The Warder, crouching down against the nearest coffer with his cheek pressed against the dry cold stone, shivered and trembled.

"Speak to me," he begged. "What do I have to do to get you to speak to me? Do you want me to pray? All right, then, I'll pray, if that's what you want."

In the special voice that he used for the evening invocation he intoned the three Holy Names:

"Oberith . . . Aulimiath . . . Vonubius."

There was no reply.

Bitterly he said, "You don't know your names, do you? Or are you just too stubborn to answer to them?"

He glowered into the darkness.

"Why are you here?" he asked them, furious now. "Why did Mericalis have to discover you? Oh, damn him, why did he ever have to tell me about you?"

Again there was no answer; but now he felt a strange thing beginning to occur. Serpentine columns of light were rising from the three coffers. They flickered and danced like tongues of cold fire before him, commanding him to be still and pay heed. The Warder pressed his hands against his forehead and bowed his head and let everything drain from his mind, so that he was no more than an empty shell crouching in the darkness of the room. And as he knelt there things began to change around him, the walls of the chamber melted and dropped away, and he found himself transported upward and outward until he was standing outside, in the clear sweet air, under the golden warmth of the sun.

The day was bright, warm, springlike, a splendid day, a day to cherish. But there were ugly dissonances. The Warder heard shouts to his right, to his left—harsh voices everywhere, angry outcries.

"There they are! Get them! Get them!"

Three slender grotesque figures came into view, half again as tall as a man, big-eyed, long-limbed, strange of shape, moving swiftly but with somber dignity, as though they were floating rather than striding, keeping just ahead of their pursuers. The Warder understood that these were the Three in their final moments, that they have been harried and hunted all this lovely day across the sweet meadows of this lush green valley. Now there is nowhere further for them to go, they are trapped in a cul-de-sac against the flank of the mountain, the army of their enemies is closing in and all hope of escape is impossible.

Now the Warder heard savage triumphant screams. Saw reddened, swollen, wrathful faces. Weapons bristling in the air, clubs, truncheons, pitchforks, hatchets. Wild eyes, distended lips, clenched fists furiously shaken. And on a little mound facing their attackers are the Three, standing close together, offering no resistance, seemingly at peace. They appear perplexed by what is happening, perhaps, or perhaps not—how can he tell? What do their alien expressions mean? But almost certainly they are not angry. Anger is not an emotion that can pertain to them in any way. They have a look about them that seems to indicate that they had expected this. *Forgive them, for they know not what they do.* A moment of hesitation: the mob suddenly uneasy at the last, frightened, even, uncertain of the risks in what they are doing. Then the hesitation was overcome, the people surged forward like a single berserk creature, there was the flash of steel in the sunlight—

The vision abruptly ended. He was within the stone chamber again. The light was gone. The air about him was dry and stale, not sweet and mild. The tomb was dark and empty.

The Warder felt stunned by what he had seen, and shamed. A sense of almost suicidal guilt overwhelmed him. Blindly he rushed back and forth across the dark room, frenzied, manic, buffeting himself against the unseen walls. Then, exhausted, he paused for a moment to gasp for breath and stared into the darkness at the place where he thought the coffers were situated. He would break through those transparent coverings, he told himself, and snatch up the three strange skulls and carry them out into the bright light of day, and he would call the people together and show them what he has brought forth from the depths of the Earth, brandishing the skulls in their faces, and he would cry out to them, "Here are your gods. This is what you did to them. All your beliefs were founded on a lie." And then he would hurl himself from the mountain.

No.

He will not. How can he crush their hopes that way? And having done it, what good would his death achieve?

And yet—to allow the lie to endure and persist—

"What am I going to do about you?" the Warder asked the skeletons in their coffers. "What am I going to tell the people?" His voice rose to a wild screech. It echoed and reechoed from the stone walls of the room, reverberating in his throbbing skull. "The *people!* The *people!* *The people!*"

"Speak to me!" the Warder cried. "Tell me what I'm supposed to do!"

Silence. Silence. Silence. They would give him no answers.

He laughed at his own helplessness. Then he wept for a time, until his eyes were raw and his throat ached from his sobbing. He fell to his knees once more beside one of the coffers. "Who are you?" he asked, in nothing more than a whisper. "Can you really be Vonubius?"

And this time imagines that he hears a mocking answer: *I am who I am. Go in peace, my son.*

Peace? Where? How?

At last, a long while later, he began to grow calm once more, and thought that this time he might be able to remain that way. He saw that he was being ridiculous—the old Warder, running to and fro in a stone chamber underground, crying out like a lunatic, praying to gods in whom he didn't believe, holding conversations with skeletons. Gradually his churning soul moved away from the desperate turbulence into which it had fallen, the manic frenzy, the childish anger. There was no reddish glow, no. His over-wrought mind had conjured up some tormented fantasy for him. Darkness still prevailed in the chamber. He was unable to see a thing. Before him, he knew, were three ancient stone boxes containing age-old dry bones, the earthly remains of unearthly creatures long dead.

He was calm, yes. But there seemed no way even now to hide from his despair. These relics, he knew, called his whole life into question. The whole ugly truth of it stood unanswerably revealed. He had served a false creed, knowingly offering people the empty hope that they would be redeemed by benevolent gods. Night after night standing up there on the portico, invoking the Three, praying for their swift return to this troubled planet. Whereas in truth they had never left Earth at all. Had perished, in fact, at the hands of the very people they had come here—so he supposed—to redeem.

What now? the Warder asked himself. Reveal the truth? Display the bodies of the Three to the dismayed, astounded faithful, as he had imagined himself doing just a short time ago? Would he do any such thing? Could he? *Your beliefs were founded on a lie*, he pictured himself telling them. How could he do that? But it was the truth. Small wonder that I lost my own faith long ago, he thought. He had known the truth before he ever knew he knew it. It was the truth that he had sworn to serve, first and always. Was that not so? But there was so much that he did not understand—could not understand, perhaps.

He looked in the direction of the skeletons, and a host of new questions formed in his mind.

"Why did you want to come to us?" he asked, not angrily now, but in a curious tranquillity of spirit. "Why did you choose to serve us as you did? Why did you allow us to destroy you, since surely it was in your power to prevent it?"

Powerful questions. The Warder had no answers to them. But yet who knew what miracles might grow from the asking of them. Yes. Yes. Miracles! True faiths can arise from the ruined fragments of false ones, was that not so?

He was so very tired. It had been such a long night.

Gradually he slipped downward until he was lying completely prone, face pillowed in his arms. It seemed to him that the gentle light of morning was entering the chamber, that the long vigil was over at last. How could that be, light reaching him underground? He chose not to pursue the question.

He lay quietly, waiting. And then he heard footsteps. Mericalis was returning. The night was over indeed.

"Diriente? Diriente, are you all right?"

"Help me up," the Warder says. "I'm not accustomed to spending my nights lying on stone floors."

The custodian flashes his torch around the room as if he expects it to have changed in some fashion since he last saw it.

"Well?" he says, finally.

"Let's get out of here, shall we?"

"You're all right?"

"Yes, yes, I'm all right!"

"I was very worried. I know you said you wanted to be alone, but I couldn't help thinking—"

"Thinking can be very dangerous," says the Warder coolly. "I don't recommend it."

"I want to tell you, Diriente, that I've decided that what I suggested last night is the best idea. The evidence in this room could blow the Church to pieces. We ought to seal the place up and forget we ever were in here."

"No," says the Warder.

"We aren't required to reveal what we've found to anybody. My job is simply to keep the temple building from falling down. Yours is to perform the rituals of the faith."

"And if the faith is a false one, Mericalis?"

"We don't know that it is."

"We have our suspicions, don't we?"

"To say that the Three never returned safely to the stars is heresy, isn't it, Diriente? Do you want to be responsible for spreading heresy?"

"My responsibility is to promote the truth," says the Warder. "It always has been."

"Poor Diriente. What have I done to you?"

"Don't waste your pity on me, Mericalis. I don't need it. Just help me find my way out of here, all right? All right?"

"Yes," the custodian says. "Whatever you say."

The passageway is much shorter and less intricate on the way out than it seemed to be when they entered. Neither of them speaks a word as they traverse it. Mericalis trudges quickly forward, never once looking back. The Warder, following briskly along behind, moves with a vigor he hasn't felt in years. His mind is hard at work: he occupies himself with what he will say later in the day, first to the temple staff, then to the worshipers who come that day, and then, perhaps, to the emperor and all his court, down in the great city below the mountain. His words will fall upon their ears like the crack of thunder at the mountaintop; and then let whatever happen that may. *Brothers and Sisters, I announce unto you a great joy*, is how he intends to begin. *The Second Advent is upon us. For behold, I can show you the Three themselves. They are with us now, nor have they ever left us—*

THE HAMMER OF GOD

Arthur C. Clarke

Arthur C. Clarke is perhaps the most famous modern science fiction writer in the world, seriously rivaled for that title only by the late Isaac Asimov and Robert A. Heinlein. Clarke is probably most widely known for his work on Stanley Kubrick's film *2001: A Space Odyssey*, but he is also renowned as a novelist, short-story writer, and as a writer of nonfiction, usually on technological subjects such as spaceflight. He has won three Nebula Awards, three Hugo Awards, the British Science Fiction Award, the John W. Campbell Memorial Award, and a Grandmaster Nebula for Life Achievement. His best-known books include the novels *Childhood's End, The City and the Stars, The Deep Range, Rendezvous with Rama, A Fall of Moondust, 2001: A Space Odyssey, 2010: Odyssey Two, 2061: Odyssey Three, The Songs of Distant Earth*, and *The Fountains of Paradise*, and the collections *The Nine Billion Names of God, Tales of Ten Worlds*, and *The Sentinel*. He has also written many nonfiction books on scientific topics, the best known of which are probably *Profiles of the Future* and *The Wind from the Sun*. Clarke is generally considered to be the man who first came up with the idea of the communications satellite. His most recent works are the novel *The Garden of Rama* (written with Gentry Lee) and the nonfiction book *How the World Was One*. Upcoming is a novel version of this story, *The Hammer of God*. Born in Somerset, England, Clarke now lives in Sri Lanka.

The incisive and elegant story that follows was first published in *Time* magazine, which, to my knowledge, is the only science fiction story and only the second work of fiction of any sort ever published by *Time*, an indication of Clarke's stature. It covers some ground that will be familiar to long-time Clarke readers, but it handles its themes with classical purity and grace. With marvelous economy and precision, it manages to pack enough content into a very short story to last many an author for an entire four-hundred-page novel. Its quietness is deceptive too, for in Clarke's typically cool, calm, understated fashion, it ultimately delivers quite an emotional punch—as well as carrying a message vital for the survival of the human race, and perhaps of all life on Earth.

It came in vertically, punching a hole 10 km wide through the atmosphere, generating temperatures so high that the air itself started to burn. When it hit the ground near the Gulf of Mexico, rock turned to liquid and spread outward in mountainous waves, not freezing until it had formed a crater 200 km across.

That was only the beginning of disaster: now the real tragedy began. Nitric oxides rained from the air, turning the sea to acid. Clouds of soot from incinerated forests darkened the sky, hiding the sun for months. Worldwide, the temperature dropped precipitously, killing off most of the plants and animals that had survived the initial cataclysm. Though some species would linger on for millenniums, the reign of the great reptiles was finally over.

The clock of evolution had been reset; the countdown to Man had begun. The date was, very approximately, 65 million B.C.

Captain Robert Singh never tired of walking in the forest with his little son Toby. It was, of course, a tamed and gentle forest, guaranteed to be free of dangerous animals, but it made an exciting contrast to the rolling sand dunes of their last environment in the Saudi desert—and the one before that, on Australia's Great Barrier Reef. But when the Skylift Service had moved the house this time, something had gone wrong with the food-recycling system. Though the electronic menus had fail-safe backups, there had been a curious metallic taste to some of the items coming out of the synthesizer recently.

"What's that, Daddy?" asked the four-year-old, pointing to a small hairy face peering at them through a screen of leaves.

"Er, some kind of monkey. We'll ask the Brain when we get home."

"Can I play with it?"

"I don't think that's a good idea. It could bite. And it probably has fleas. Your robotoys are much nicer."

"But . . ."

Captain Singh knew what would happen next: he had run this sequence a dozen times. Toby would begin to cry, the monkey would disappear, he would comfort the child as he carried him back to the house . . .

But that had been twenty years ago and a quarter-billion kilometers away. The playback came to an end; sound, vision, the scent of unknown flowers and the gentle touch of the wind slowly faded. Suddenly, he was back in this cabin aboard the orbital tug *Goliath*, commanding the 100-person team of Operation ATLAS, the most critical mission in the history of space exploration. Toby, and the stepmothers and stepfathers of his extended family, remained behind on a distant world which Singh could never revisit. Decades in space—and neglect of the mandatory zero-G exercises—had so weakened him that he could now walk only on the Moon and Mars. Gravity had exiled him from the planet of his birth.

"One hour to rendezvous, captain," said the quiet but insistent voice of David, as *Goliath*'s central computer had been inevitably named. "Active mode, as requested. Time to come back to the real world."

Goliath's human commander felt a wave of sadness sweep over him as the final image from his lost past dissolved into a featureless, simmering mist of white noise. Too swift a transition from one reality to another was a good recipe for schizophrenia, and Captain Singh always eased the shock with the most soothing sound he knew: waves falling gently on a beach, with sea gulls crying in the distance. It was yet another memory of a life he had lost, and of a peaceful past that had now been replaced by a fearful present.

For a few more moments, he delayed facing his awesome responsibility. Then he sighed and removed the neural-input cap that fitted snugly over his skull and had enabled him to call up his distant past. Like all spacers, Captain Singh belonged to the "Bald Is Beautiful" school, if only because wigs were a nuisance in zero gravity. The social historians were still staggered by the fact that one invention, the portable "Brainman," could make bare heads the norm within a single decade. Not even quick-change skin coloring, or the lens-corrective laser shaping which had abolished eyeglasses, had made such an impact upon style and fashion.

"Captain," said David. "I know you're there. Or do you want me to take over?"

It was an old joke, inspired by all the insane computers in the fiction and movies of the early electronic age. David had a surprisingly good sense of humor: he was, after all, a Legal Person (Nonhuman) under the famous Hundredth Amendment, and shared—or surpassed—almost all the attributes of his creators. But there were whole sensory and emotional areas which he could not enter. It had been felt unnecessary to equip him with smell or taste, though it would have been easy to do so. And all his attempts at telling dirty stories were such disastrous failures that he had abandoned the genre.

"All right, David," replied the captain. "I'm still in charge." He removed the mask from his eyes, and turned reluctantly toward the viewport. There, hanging in space before him, was Kali.

It looked harmless enough: just another small asteroid, shaped so exactly like a peanut that the resemblance was almost comical. A few large impact craters, and hundreds of tiny ones, were scattered at random over its charcoal-gray surface. There were no visual clues to give any sense of scale, but Singh knew its dimensions by heart: 1,295 m maximum length, 456 m minimum width. Kali would fit easily into many city parks.

No wonder that, even now, most of humankind could still not believe that this modest asteroid was the instrument of doom. Or, as the Chrislamic Fundamentalists were calling it, "the Hammer of God."

The sudden rise of Chrislam had been traumatic equally to Rome and Mecca. Christianity was already reeling from John Paul XXV's eloquent but belated plea for contraception and the irrefutable proof in the New Dead Sea Scrolls that the Jesus of the Gospels was a composite of at least three persons. Meanwhile the Muslim world had lost much of its economic power when the Cold Fusion breakthrough, after the fiasco of its premature announcement, had brought the Oil Age to a sudden end. The time had been ripe for a new religion embodying, as even its severest critics admitted, the best elements of two ancient ones.

The Prophet Fatima Magdalene (née Ruby Goldenburg) had attracted almost 100 million adherents before her spectacular—and, some maintained, self-contrived—martyrdom. Thanks to the brilliant use of neural programming to give previews of Paradise during its ceremonies, Chrislam had grown explosively, though it was still far outnumbered by its parent religions.

Inevitably, after the Prophet's death the movement split into rival factions, each upholding *the* True Faith. The most fanatical was a fundamentalist group calling itself "the Reborn," which claimed to be in direct contact with God (or at least Her Archangels) via the listening post they had established in the silent zone on the far side of the Moon, shielded from the radio racket of Earth by 3,000 km of solid rock.

Now Kali filled the main viewscreen. No magnification was needed, for *Goliath* was hovering only 200 m above its ancient, battered surface. Two crew members had already landed, with the traditional "One small step for a man"—even though walking was impossible on this almost zero-gravity worldlet.

"Deploying radio beacon. We've got it anchored securely. Now Kali won't be able to hide from us."

It was a feeble joke, not meriting the laughter it aroused from the dozen officers on the bridge. Ever since rendezvous, there had been a subtle change in the crew's morale, with unpredictable swings between gloom and juvenile humor. The ship's physician had already prescribed tranquilizers for one mild case of manic-depressive symptoms. It would grow worse in the long weeks ahead, when there would be little to do but wait.

The first waiting period had already begun. Back on Earth, giant radio telescopes were tuned to receive the pulses from the beacon. Although Kali's orbit had already been calculated with the greatest possible accuracy, there was still a slim chance that the asteroid might pass harmlessly by. The radio measuring rod would settle the matter, for better or worse.

It was a long two hours before the verdict came, and David relayed it to the crew.

"Spaceguard reports that the probability of impact on Earth is 99.9%. Operation ATLAS will begin immediately."

The task of the mythological Atlas was to hold up the heavens and prevent them from crashing down upon Earth. The ATLAS booster that *Goliath* carried as an external payload had a more modest goal: keeping at bay only a small piece of the sky.

It was the size of a small house, weighed 9,000 tons and was moving at 50,000 km/ h. As it passed over the Grand Teton National Park, one alert tourist photographed the incandescent fireball and its long vapor trail. In less than two minutes, it had sliced through the Earth's atmosphere and returned to space.

The slightest change of orbit during the billions of years it had been circling the sun might have sent the asteroid crashing upon any of the world's great cities with an explosive force five times that of the bomb that destroyed Hiroshima.

The date was Aug. 10, 1972.

* * *

Spaceguard had been one of the last projects of the legendary NASA, at the close of the 20th century. Its initial objective had been modest enough: to make as complete a survey as possible of the asteroids and comets that crossed the orbit of Earth—and to determine if any were a potential threat.

With a total budget seldom exceeding $10 million a year, a worldwide network of telescopes, most of them operated by skilled amateurs, had been established by the year 2000. Sixty-one years later, the spectacular return of Halley's Comet encouraged more funding, and the great 2079 fireball, luckily impacting in mid-Atlantic, gave Spaceguard additional prestige. By the end of the century, it had located more than 1 million asteroids, and the survey was believed to be 90% complete. However, it would have to be continued indefinitely: there was always a chance that some intruder might come rushing in from the uncharted outer reaches of the solar system.

As had Kali, which had been detected in late 2212 as it fell sunward past the orbit of Jupiter. Fortunately humankind had not been wholly unprepared, thanks to the fact that Senator George Ledstone (Independent, West America) had chaired an influential finance committee almost a generation earlier.

The Senator had one public eccentricity and, he cheerfully admitted, one secret vice. He always wore massive horn-rimmed eyeglasses (nonfunctional, of course) because they had an intimidating effect on uncooperative witnesses, few of whom had ever encountered such a novelty. His "secret vice," perfectly well known to everyone, was rifle shooting on a standard Olympic range, set up in the tunnels of a long-abandoned missile silo near Mount Cheyenne. Ever since the demilitarization of Planet Earth (much accelerated by the famous slogan "Guns Are the Crutches of the Impotent"), such activities had been frowned upon, though not actively discouraged.

There was no doubt that Senator Ledstone was an original; it seemed to run in the family. His grandmother had been a colonel in the dreaded Beverly Hills Militia, whose skirmishes with the L.A. Irregulars had spawned endless psychodramas in every medium, from old-fashioned ballet to direct brain stimulation. And his grandfather had been one of the most notorious bootleggers of the 21st century. Before he was killed in a shoot-out with the Canadian Medicops during an ingenious attempt to smuggle a kiloton of tobacco up Niagara Falls, it was estimated that "Smokey" had been responsible for at least 20 million deaths.

Ledstone was quite unrepentant about his grandfather, whose sensational demise had triggered the repeal of the late U.S.'s third, and most disastrous, attempt at Prohibition. He argued that responsible adults should be allowed to commit suicide in any way they pleased—by alcohol, cocaine or even tobacco—as long as they did not kill innocent bystanders during the process.

When the proposed budget for Spaceguard Phase 2 was first presented to him, Senator Ledstone had been outraged by the idea of throwing billions of dollars into space. It was true that the global economy was in good shape; since the almost simultaneous collapse of communism and capitalism, the skillful application of chaos theory by World Bank mathematicians had broken the old cycle of booms and busts and averted (so far) the Final Depression predicted by many pessimists. Nonetheless, the Senator argued that the money could be much better spent on Earth—especially on his favorite project, reconstructing what was left of California after the Superquake.

When Ledstone had twice vetoed Spaceguard Phase 2, everyone agreed that no one on Earth would make him change his mind. They had reckoned without someone from Mars.

The Red Planet was no longer quite so red, though the process of greening it had barely begun. Concentrating on the problems of survival, the colonists (they hated the word and were already saying proudly "we Martians") had little energy left over for art or science. But the lightning flash of genius strikes where it will, and the greatest theoretical physicist of the century was born under the bubble domes of Port Lowell.

Like Einstein, to whom he was often compared, Carlos Mendoza was an excellent musician; he owned the only saxophone on Mars and was a skilled performer on that antique instrument. He could have received his Nobel Prize on Mars, as everyone expected, but he loved surprises and practical jokes. Thus he appeared in Stockholm looking like a knight in high-tech armor, wearing one of the powered exoskeletons developed for paraplegics. With this mechanical assistance, he could function almost unhandicapped in an environment that would otherwise have quickly killed him.

Needless to say, when the ceremony was over, Carlos was bombarded with invitations to scientific and social functions. Among the few he was able to accept was an appearance before the World Budget Committee, where Senator Ledstone closely questioned him about his opinion of Project Spaceguard.

"I live on a world which still bears the scars of a thousand meteor impacts, some of them *hundreds* of kilometers across," said Professor Mendoza. "Once they were equally common on Earth, but wind and rain—something we don't have yet on Mars, though we're working on it!—have worn them away."

Senator Ledstone: "The Spaceguarders are always pointing to signs of asteroid impacts on Earth. How seriously should we take their warnings?"

Professor Mendoza: "Very seriously, Mr. Chairman. Sooner or later, there's bound to be another major impact."

Senator Ledstone was impressed, and indeed charmed, by the young scientist, but not yet convinced. What changed his mind was not a matter of logic but of emotion. On his way to London, Carlos Mendoza was killed in a bizarre accident when the control system of his exoskeleton malfunctioned. Deeply moved, Ledstone immediately dropped his opposition to Spaceguard, approving construction of two powerful orbiting tugs, *Goliath* and *Titan*, to be kept permanently patrolling on opposite sides of the sun. And when he was a very old man, he said to one of his aides, "They tell me we'll soon be able to take Mendoza's brain out of that tank of liquid nitrogen, and talk to it through a computer interface. I wonder what he's been thinking about, all these years . . ."

*   *   *

Assembled on Phobos, the inner satellite of Mars, ATLAS was little more than a set of rocket engines attached to propellant tanks holding 100,000 tons of hydrogen. Though its fusion drive could generate far less thrust than the primitive missile that had carried Yuri Gagarin into space, it could run continuously not merely for minutes but for weeks. Even so, the effect on the asteroid would be trivial, a velocity change of a few centimeters per second. Yet that might be sufficient to deflect Kali from its fatal orbit during the months while it was still falling earthward.

Now that ATLAS's propellant tanks, control systems and thrusters had been securely mounted on Kali, it looked as if some lunatic had built an oil refinery on an asteroid. Captain Singh was exhausted, as were all the crew members, after days of assembly and checking. Yet he felt a warm glow of achievement: they had done everything that was expected of them, the countdown was going smoothly, and the rest was up to ATLAS.

He would have been far less relaxed had he known of the ABSOLUTE PRIORITY message racing toward him by tight infrared beam from ASTROPOL headquarters in Geneva. It would not reach *Goliath* for another 30 minutes. And by then it would be much too late.

At about T minus 30 minutes, *Goliath* had drawn away from Kali to stand well clear of the jet with which ATLAS would try to nudge it from its present course. "Like a mouse pushing an elephant," one media person had described the operation. But in the frictionless vacuum of space, where momentum could never be lost, even one mousepower would be enough if applied early and over a sufficient length of time.

The group of officers waiting quietly on the bridge did not expect to see anything spectacular: the plasma jet of the ATLAS drive would be far too hot to produce much visible radiation. Only the telemetry would confirm that ignition had started and that Kali was no longer an implacable juggernaut, wholly beyond the control of humanity.

There was a brief round of cheering and a gentle patter of applause as the string of zeros on the accelerometer display began to change. The feeling on the bridge was one of relief rather than exultation. Though Kali was stirring, it would be days and weeks before victory was assured.

And then, unbelievably, the numbers dropped back to zero. Seconds later, three simultaneous audio alarms sounded. All eyes were suddenly fixed on Kali and the ATLAS booster which should be nudging it from its present course. The sight was heartbreaking: the great propellant tanks were opening up like flowers in a time-lapse movie, spilling out the thousands of tons of reaction mass that might have saved the Earth. Wisps of vapor drifted across the face of the asteroid, veiling its cratered surface with an evanescent atmosphere.

Then Kali continued along its path, heading inexorably toward a fiery collision with the Earth.

* * *

Captain Singh was alone in the large, well-appointed cabin that had been his home for longer than any other place in the solar system. He was still dazed but was trying to make his peace with the universe.

He had lost, finally and forever, all that he loved on Earth. With the decline of the nuclear family, he had known many deep attachments, and it had been hard to decide who should be the mothers of the two children he was permitted. A phrase from an old American novel (he had forgotten the author) kept coming into his mind: "Remember them as they were—and write them off." The fact that he himself was perfectly safe somehow made him feel worse; *Goliath* was in no danger whatsoever, and still had all the propellant it needed to rejoin the shaken survivors of humanity on the Moon or Mars.

Well, he had many friendships—and one that was much more than that—on Mars; this was where his future must lie. He was only 102, with decades of active life ahead of him. But some of the crew had loved ones on the Moon; he would have to put *Goliath*'s destination to the vote.

Ship's Orders had never covered a situation like this.

I still don't understand," said the chief engineer, "why that explosive cord wasn't detected on the preflight check-out."

"Because that Reborn fanatic could have hidden it easily—and no one would have dreamed of looking for such a thing. Pity ASTROPOL didn't catch him while he was still on Phobos."

"But *why* did they do it? I can't believe that even Chrislamic crazies would want to destroy the Earth."

"You can't argue with their logic—if you accept their premises. God, Allah, is testing us, and we mustn't interfere. If Kali misses, fine. If it doesn't, well, that's part of Her bigger plan. Maybe we've messed up Earth so badly that it's time to start over. Remember that old saying of Tsiolkovski's: 'Earth is the cradle of humankind, but you cannot live in the cradle forever.' Kali could be a sign that it's time to leave."

The captain held up his hand for silence.

"The only important question now is, Moon or Mars? They'll both need us. I don't want to influence you" (that was hardly true; everyone knew where he wanted to go), "so I'd like your views first."

The first ballot was Mars 6, Moon 6, Don't know 1, captain abstaining.

Each side was trying to convert the single "Don't know" when David spoke.

"There is an alternative."

"What do you mean?" Captain Singh demanded, rather brusquely.

"It seems obvious. Even though ATLAS is destroyed, we still have a chance of saving the Earth. According to my calculations, *Goliath* has just enough propellant to deflect Kali—if we start thrusting against it immediately. But the longer we wait, the less the probability of success."

There was a moment of stunned silence on the bridge as everyone asked the question, "Why didn't I think of that?" and quickly arrived at the answer.

David had kept his head, if one could use so inappropriate a phrase, while all the humans around him were in a state of shock. There were some compensations in being a Legal Person (Nonhuman). Though David could not know love, neither could he know fear. He would continue to think logically, even to the edge of doom.

With any luck, thought Captain Singh, this is my last broadcast to Earth. I'm tired of being a hero, and a slightly premature one at that. Many things could still go wrong, as indeed they already have . . .

"This is Captain Singh, space tug *Goliath*. First of all, let me say how glad we are that the Elders of Chrislam have identified the saboteurs and handed them over to ASTROPOL.

"We are now 50 days from Earth, and we have a slight problem. This one, I hasten to add, will not affect our new attempt to deflect Kali into a safe orbit. I note that the news media are calling this deflection Operation Deliverance. We like the name, and hope to live up to it, but we still cannot be absolutely certain of success. David, who appreciates all the goodwill messages he has received, estimates that the probability of Kali impacting Earth is still 10% . . .

"We had intended to keep just enough propellant reserve to leave Kali shortly before encounter and go into a safer orbit, where our sister ship *Titan* could rendezvous with us. But that option is now closed. While *Goliath* was pushing against Kali at maximum drive, we broke through a weak point in the crust. The ship wasn't damaged, but we're stuck! All attempts to break away have failed.

"We're not worried, and it may even be a blessing in disguise. Now we'll use the *whole* of our remaining propellant to give one final nudge. Perhaps that will be the last drop that's needed to do the job.

"So we'll ride Kali past Earth, and wave to you from a comfortable distance, in just 50 days."

It would be the longest 50 days in the history of the world.

Now the huge crescent of the Moon spanned the sky, the jagged mountain peaks along the terminator burning with the fierce light of the lunar dawn. But the dusty plains still untouched by the sun were not completely dark; they were glowing faintly in the light reflected from Earth's clouds and continents. And scattered here and there across that once dead landscape were the glowing fireflies that marked the first permanent settlements humankind had built beyond the home planet. Captain Singh could easily locate Clavius Base, Port Armstrong, Plato City. He could even see the necklace of faint lights along the Translunar Railroad, bringing its precious cargo of water from the ice mines at the South Pole.

Earth was now only five hours away.

*   *   *

Kali entered Earth's atmosphere soon after local midnight, 200 km above Hawaii. Instantly, the gigantic fireball brought a false dawn to the Pacific, awakening the wildlife on its myriad islands. But few humans had been asleep this night of nights, except those who had sought the oblivion of drugs.

Over New Zealand, the heat of the orbiting furnace ignited forests and melted the snow on mountaintops, triggering avalanches into the valleys beneath. But the human race had been very, very lucky: the main thermal impact as Kali passed the Earth was on the Antarctic, the continent that could best absorb it. Even Kali could not strip away all the kilometers of polar ice, but it set in motion the Great Thaw that would change coastlines all around the world.

No one who survived hearing it could ever describe the sound of Kali's passage; none of the recordings were more than feeble echoes. The video coverage, of course, was superb, and would be watched in awe for generations to come. But nothing could ever compare with the fearsome reality.

Two minutes after it had sliced into the atmosphere, Kali reentered space. Its closest approach to Earth had been 60 km. In that two minutes, it took 100,000 lives and did $1 trillion worth of damage.

Goliath had been protected from the fireball by the massive shield of Kali itself; the sheets of incandescent plasma streamed harmlessly overhead. But when the asteroid smashed into Earth's blanket of air at more than 100 times the speed of sound, the colossal drag forces mounted swiftly to five, 10, 20 gravities—and peaked at a level far beyond anything that machines or flesh could withstand.

Now indeed Kali's orbit had been drastically changed; never again would it come near Earth. On its next return to the inner solar system, the swifter spacecraft of a later age would visit the crumpled wreckage of *Goliath* and bear reverently homeward the bodies of those who had saved the world.

Until the next encounter.

GROWNUPS

Ian R. MacLeod

New British writer Ian R. MacLeod has been one of the most talked-about young
writers of the '90s, publishing a slew of strong stories in the first three years of the
decade in *Interzone, Isaac Asimov's Science Fiction Magazine, Weird Tales, Amazing,* and *The Magazine of Fantasy & Science Fiction,* among other markets. Several
of those stories made the cut for one or another of the various "Best of the Year"
anthologies, including appearances here in our Eight and Ninth Annual Collections.
In 1990, in fact, he appeared in *three* different Best of the Year anthologies with
three different stories, certainly a rare distinction. He has yet to produce a novel, but
it is being eagerly awaited by genre insiders, and as he has recently given up his day
job to write full-time; perhaps we won't have long to wait. MacLeod is in his early
thirties, and lives with his wife and baby daughter in the West Midlands of England.

In the disquieting story that follows, he takes us to a world that's very like our
own—except for all the ways that count the *most*—to relate one of the most bizarre
coming-of-age stories ever written.

Bobby finally got around to asking Mum where babies came from on the
evening of his seventh birthday. It had been hot all day, and the grownups
and a few of the older children who had come to his party were still outside
on the lawn. He could hear their talk and evening birdsong through his open
window as Mum closed the curtains. She leaned down to kiss his forehead.
She'd been drinking since the first guests arrived before lunch and her breath
smelt like windfall apples. Now seemed as a good a time as any. As she
turned towards the door, he asked his question. It came out as a whisper,
but she heard, and frowned for a moment before she smiled.

"You children always want to know too soon," she said. "I was the same,
believe me, Bobby. But you must be patient. You really must."

Bobby knew enough about grownups to realize that it was unwise to push
too hard. So he forced himself to yawn and blink slowly so she would think
he was truly sleepy. She patted his hand.

After his door had clicked shut, after her footsteps had padded down the
stairs, Bobby slid out of bed. Ignoring the presents piled in the corner by the
closet—robots with sparking eyes, doll soldiers, and submarines—he peered
from the window. They lived at the edge of town, where rooftops dwindled

to green hills and the silver curl of the river. He watched Mum emerge from the French windows onto the wide lawn below. She stopped to say something to Dad as he sat lazing in a deckchair with the other men, a beercan propped against his crotch. Then she took a taper from the urn beside the barbecue and touched it to the coals. She proceeded to light the lanterns hanging from the boughs of the cherry trees.

The whole garden filled with stars. After she had lit the last lantern, Mum put the taper to her mouth and extinguished it with her tongue. Then she rejoined the women gossiping on the white wrought iron chairs. The remaining children were all leaving for home. Cars were starting up, turning out from the shaded drive. Bobby heard his brother Tony call goodnight to the grownups and thunder up the stairs. He tensed in case Tony should decide to look in on him before he went to bed, but relaxed after the toilet had flushed and Tony's bedroom door had slammed. It was almost night. Bobby knew that his window would show as no more than a darker square against the wall of the house. He widened the parting in the curtain.

He loved to watch the grownups when they thought they were alone. It was a different world. One day, Mum had told him often enough, one day, sweet little Bobby, you'll understand it all, touching his skin as she spoke with papery fingers. But give it time, my darling one, give it time. Being a grownup is more wonderful than you children could ever imagine. More wonderful. Yes, my darling. Kissing him on the forehead and each eye and then his mouth, the way she did when she got especially tender.

Bobby gazed down at the grownups. They had that loose look that came when the wine and the beer had gone down well and there was more to come, when the night was warm and the stars mirrored the lanterns. Dad raised his can from his crotch to his lips. One of the men beside him made a joke and the beer spluttered down Dad's chin, gleaming for a moment before he wiped it away. The men always talked like this, loud between bursts of silence, whilst the women's voices—laughing serious sad—brushed soft against the night. Over by the trellis archway that led by the garbage cans to the front, half a dozen uncles sat in the specially wide deckchairs that Dad kept for them behind the mower in the shed.

Bobby couldn't help staring at the uncles. They were all grossly fat. There was Uncle Stan, Uncle Harold, and, of course, his own Uncle Lew. Bobby saw with a certain pride that Lew was the biggest. His tie was loose and his best shirt strained like a full sail across his belly. Like all the uncles, Lew lived alone, but Dad or the father of one of the other families Lew was uncle to was always ready to take the car down on a Saturday morning, paint the windows of his house, or see to the lawn. In many ways, Bobby thought, it was an ideal life. People respected uncles. Even more than their girth required, they stepped aside from them in the street. But at the same time, his parents were often edgy when Lew was around, uncharacteristically eager to please. Sometimes late in the night, Bobby had heard the unmistakable clatter of his van on the gravel out front, Mum and Dad's voices whispering softly excited in the hall. Gazing at Lew, seated with the other uncles, Bobby

remembered how he had dragged him to the moist folds of his belly, rumbling
Won't You Just Look At This Sweet Kid? His yeasty aroma came back like
the aftertaste of bad cooking.

Someone turned the record player on in the lounge. Sibilant music drifted
like smoke. Some of the grownups began to dance. Women in white dresses
blossomed as they turned, and the men were darkly quick. The music and
the sigh of their movement brushed against the humid night, coaxed the
glow of the lanterns, silvered the rooftops and the stars.

The dancing quickened, seeking a faster rhythm inside the slow beat.
Bobby's eyes fizzed with sleep. He thought he saw grownups floating heartbeat
on heartbeat above the lawn. Soon they were leaping over the lanterned
cherry trees, flying, pressing close to his window with smiles and waves,
beckoning him to join them. Come out and play, Bobby, out here amid the
stars. The men darted like eels, the women did high kicks across the rooftop,
their dresses billowing coral frills over their heads. The uncles bobbed around
the chimney like huge balloons.

When Bobby awoke, the lanterns were out. There was only darkness,
summer chill.

As he crawled back to bed, a sudden sound made him freeze. Deep and
feral, some kind of agony that was neither pain nor grief, it started loud then
came down by notches to a stuttering sob. Bobby unfroze when it ended and
hauled the blankets up to his chin. Through the bedroom wall, he could
hear the faint mutter of Dad's voice, Mum's half-questioning reply. Then
Uncle Lew saying goodnight. Slow footsteps down the stairs. The front door
slam. Clatter of an engine coming to life.

Sigh of gravel.

Silence.

Bobby stood at the far bank of the river. His hands clenched and unclenched.
Three years had passed. He was now ten; his brother Tony was sixteen.

Tony was out on the river, atop the oildrum raft that he and the other kids
of his age had been building all summer. The wide sweep that cut between
the fields and the gasometers into town had narrowed in the drought heat.
Tony was angling a pole through the sucking silt to get to the deeper current.
He was absorbed, alone; he hadn't noticed Bobby standing on the fissured
mud of the bank. Earlier in the summer, there would have been a crowd of
Tony's friends out there, shouting and diving, sitting with their heels clutched
in brown hands, chasing Bobby away with shouts or grabbing him with
terrible threats that usually ended in a simple ducking or just laughter, some
in cutoff shorts, their backs freckled pink from peeling sunburn, some sleekly
naked, those odd dark patches of hair showing under their arms and bellies.
Maggie Brown, with a barking voice you could hear half a mile off, Pete
Thorn, who kept pigeons and always seemed to watch, never said anything,
maybe Johnnie Redhead and his sidekicks, even Trev Lee, if his hay fever,
asthma, and psoriasis hadn't kept him inside, or maybe the twin McDonald
sisters, whom no one could tell apart.

Now Tony was alone.

"Hey!" Bobby yelled, not wanting to break into his brother's isolation, but knowing he had to. "Hey, Tony!"

Tony poled once more toward the current. The drums shook, tensed against their bindings, then inched toward the main sweep of the river.

"Hey, Tony, Mum says you've got to come home right *now*."

"All right, *all right*."

Tony let go of the pole, jumped down into the water. It came just below his naked waist. He waded out clumsily, falling on hands and knees. He crouched to wash himself clean in a cool eddy where the water met the shore, then shook like a dog. He grabbed his shorts from the branch of a dead willow and hauled them on.

"Why didn't you just come?" Bobby asked. "You must have known it was time. The doc's waiting at home to give you your tests."

Tony slicked back his hair. They both stared at the ground. The river still dripped from Tony's chin, made tiny craters in the sand. Bobby noticed that Tony hadn't shaved, which was a bad sign in itself. Out on the river, the raft suddenly bobbed free, floating high on the quick current.

Tony shook his head. "Never did that when *I* was on it. Seemed like a great idea, you know? Then you spend the whole summer trying to pole out of the mud."

Around them, the bank was littered with the spoor of summer habitation. The blackened ruin of a bonfire, stones laid out in the shape of a skull, junkfood wrappers, an old flap of canvas propped up like a tent, ringpull cans and cigarette butts, a solitary shoe. Bobby had his own friends—his own special places—and he came to this spot rarely and on sufferance. But still, he loved his brother, and was old enough to have some idea of how it must feel to leave childhood behind. But he told himself that most of it had gone already. Tony was the last; Pete and Maggie and the McDonald twins had grown up. Almost all the others too. That left just Trev Lee, who had locked himself in the bathroom and swallowed a bottle of bleach whilst his parents hammered at the door.

Tony made a movement that looked as though it might end in a hug. But he slapped Bobby's head instead, almost hard enough to hurt. They always acted tough with each other; it was too late now to start changing the rules.

They followed the path through the still heat of the woods to the main road. It was midday. The shimmering tarmac cut between yellow fields toward town. Occasionally, a car or truck would appear in the distance, floating silent on heat ghosts before the roar and the smell suddenly broke past them, whipping dust into their faces. Bobby gazed at stalking pylons, ragged fences, the litter-strewn edges of the countryside; it was the map of his own childhood. It was Tony's too—but Tony only stared at the verge. It was plain that he was tired of living on the cliff-edge of growing up.

Tony looked half a grownup already, graceful, clumsy, self-absorbed. He hadn't been his true self through all this later part of the summer, or at least not since Joan Trackett had grown up. Joan had a fierce crop of hair and protruding eyes; she had come to the area with her parents about six years before. Bobby knew that she and Tony had been having sex since at least last winter and maybe before. He'd actually stumbled across them one day in spring, lying on a dumped mattress in the east fields up beyond the garbage dump, hidden amid the bracken in a corner that the farmer hadn't bothered to plough. Tony had chased him away, alternately gripping the open waistband of his jeans and waving his fists. But that evening Tony had let Bobby play with his collection of model cars, which was a big concession, even though Bobby knew that Tony had mostly lost interest in them already. They had sat together in Tony's bedroom that smelled of peppermint and socks. I guess you know what Joan and I were doing, he had said. Bobby nodded, circling a black V8 limo with a missing tire around the whorls and dustballs of the carpet. It's no big deal, Tony said, picking at a scab on his chin. But his eyes had gone blank with puzzlement, as though he couldn't remember something important.

Bobby looked up at Tony as they walked along the road. He was going to miss his big brother. He even wanted to say it, although he knew he wouldn't be able to find the words. Maybe he'd catch up with him again when he turned grownup himself, but that seemed a long way off. At least five summers.

The fields ended. The road led into Avenues, Drives, and Crofts that meandered a hundred different ways toward home.

The doctor's red station wagon was parked under the shade of the poplar in their drive.

"You *don't* make people wait," Mum said, her breath short with impatience, shooing them both quickly down the hallway into the kitchen. "I'm disappointed in you, Tony. You too, Bobby. You're both old enough to know better." She opened the fridge and took out a tumbler of bitter milk. "And Tony, you didn't drink this at breakfast."

"Mum, does it matter? I'll be a grownup soon anyway."

Mum placed it on the scrubbed table. "Just drink it."

Tony drank. He wiped his chin and banged down the glass.

"Well, off you go," Mum said.

He headed up the stairs.

Doctor Halstead was waiting for Tony up in the spare room. He'd been coming around to test him every Tuesday since Mum and Dad received the brown envelope from school, arriving punctually at twelve thirty, taking best-china coffee with Mum in the lounge afterward. There was no mystery about the tests. Once or twice, Bobby had seen the syringes and the blood analysis equipment spread out on the candlewick bedspread through the open door. Tony had told him what it was like, how the doc stuck a big needle in your arm to take some blood. It hurt some, but not much. He had shown Bobby the sunset bruises on his arm with that perverse pride that kids display over any wound.

Doctor Halstead came down half an hour later, looking stern and noncommittal. Tony followed in his wake. He shushed Bobby and tried to listen to

Mum's conversation with the doc over coffee in the lounge by standing by the door in the hall. But grownups had a way of talking that made it difficult to follow, lowering their voices at the crucial moment, clinking their cups. Bobby imagined them stifling their laughter behind the closed door, deliberately uttering meaningless fragments they knew the kids would hear. He found the thought oddly reassuring.

Tony grew up on the Thursday of that same week. He and Bobby had spent the afternoon together down at Monument Park. They had climbed the whispering boughs of one of the big elm trees along the avenue and sat with their legs dangling, trying to spit on the heads of the grownups passing below.

"Will you tell me what it's like?" Bobby had asked when his mouth finally went dry.

"What?" Tony looked vague. He picked up a spider that crawled onto his wrist and rolled it between finger and thumb.

"About being a grownup. Talk to me afterward. I want . . . I want to know."

"Yeah, yeah. We're still brothers, right?"

"You've got it. And—"

"—Hey, shush!"

Three young grownups were heading their way, a man, a woman, and an uncle. Bobby supposed they were courting—they had their arms around each other in that vaguely passionless way that grownups had, their faces absent, staring at the sky and the trees without seeing. He began to salivate.

"Bombs away."

Bobby missed with his lob, but Tony hawked up a green one and scored a gleaming hit on the crown of the woman's head. The grownups walked on, stupidly oblivious.

It was a fine afternoon. They climbed higher still, skinning their palms and knees on the greenish bark, feeling the tree sway beneath them like a dancer. From up here, the park shimmered, you could see everything; the lake, the glittering greenhouses, grownups lazing on the grass, two fat kids from Tony's year lobbing stones at a convoy of ducks. Bobby grinned and threw back his head. Here, you could feel the hot sky around you, taste the clouds like white candy.

"You *will* tell me what it's like to be a grownup?" he asked again.

But Tony suddenly looked pale and afraid, holding onto the trembling boughs. "Let's climb down," he said.

When Bobby thought back, he guessed that that was the beginning.

Mum took one look at Tony when they got home and called Doctor Halstead. He was quick in coming. On Mum's instructions, Bobby also phoned Dad at the office, feeling terribly grownup and responsible as he asked to be put through in the middle of a meeting.

Tony was sitting on the sofa in the lounge, rocking to and fro, starting to moan. Dad and the doc carried him to the spare bedroom. Mum followed them up the stairs, then pulled the door tightly shut. Bobby waited downstairs in the kitchen and watched the shadows creep across the scrubbed table. Occasionally, there were footsteps upstairs, the rumble of voices, the hiss of a tap.

He had to fix his own tea from leftovers in the fridge. Later, somehow all the house lights got turned on. Everything was hard and bright like a fierce lantern, shapes burned through to the filaments beneath. Bobby's head was swimming. He was someone else, thinking, this is my house, my brother, knowing at the same time that it couldn't be true. Upstairs, he could hear someone's voice screaming, saying My God No.

Mum came down after ten. She was wearing some kind of plastic apron that was wet where she'd wiped it clean.

"Bobby, you've got to go to bed." She reached to grab his arm and pull him from the sofa.

Bobby held back for a moment. "What's happening to Tony, Mum? Is he okay?"

"Of course he's *okay*. It's nothing to get excited about. It happens to us all, it . . ." Anger came into her face. "Will you just get upstairs to bed, Bobby? You shouldn't be up this late anyway. Not tonight, not any night."

Mum followed Bobby up the stairs. She waited to open the door of the spare room until he'd gone into the bathroom. Bobby found there was no hot water, no towels; he had to dry his hand on squares of toilet paper, and the flush was slow to clear, as though something was blocking it.

He sprinted across the dangerous space of the landing and into bed. He tried to sleep.

In the morning there was the smell of toast. Bobby came down the stairs slowly, testing each step.

"So, you're up," Mum said, lifting the kettle from the burner as it began to boil.

It was eight thirty by the clock over the fridge; a little late, but everything was as brisk and sleepy as any other morning. Dad stared at the sports pages, eating his cornflakes. Bobby sat down opposite him at the table, lifted the big cereal packet that promised a scale model if you collected enough coupons. That used to drive Tony wild, how the offer always changed before you had enough. Bobby shook some flakes into a bowl.

"How's Tony?" he asked, tipping out milk.

"Tony's fine," Dad said. Then he swallowed and looked up from the paper—a rare event in itself. "He's just resting, Son. Upstairs in his own room, his own bed."

"Yes, darling." Mum's voice came from behind. Bobby felt her hands on his shoulders, kneading softly. "It's such a happy day for your Dad and me. Tony's a grownup now. Isn't that wonderful?" The fingers tightened, released.

"That doesn't mean *you* don't go to school," Dad added. He gave his paper a shake, rearranged it across the teapot and the marmalade jar.

"But be sure to tell Miss Gibson what's happened." Mum's voice faded to the back of the kitchen. The fridge door smacked open. "She'll want to know why you're late for register." Bottles jingled. Mum wafted close again. She came around to the side of the table and placed a tumbler filled with white fluid beside him. The bitter milk. "We know you're still young," she said. "But there's no harm, and now seems as good a time as any." Her fingers turned a loose button on her blouse. "Try it, darling, it's not so bad."

What happens if I don't. . . . Bobby glanced quickly at Mum, at Dad. What happens if . . . through the kitchen window, the sky was summer grey, the clouds casting the soft warm light that he loved more than sunlight, that brought out the green in the trees and made everything seem closer and more real. What happens . . . Bobby picked up the tumbler in both hands, drank it down in breathless gulps, the way he'd seen Tony do so often in the past.

"Good lad," Mum sighed after he'd finished. She was behind him again, her fingers trailing his neck. Bobby took a breath, suppressed a shudder. This bitter milk tasted just as Tony always said it did: disgusting.

"Can I see Tony now, before I go to school?"

Mum hesitated. Dad looked up again from his newspaper. Bobby knew what it would be like later, the cards, the flowers, the house lost in strangers. This was his best chance to speak to his brother.

"Okay," Mum said. "But not for long."

Tony was sitting up in bed, the TV Mum and Dad usually kept in their own bedroom propped on the dressing table. Having the TV was a special sign of illness; Bobby had had it twice himself, once with chicken pox, and then with mumps. The feeling of luxury had almost made the discomfort worthwhile.

"I just thought I'd see how you were," Bobby said.

"What?" Tony lifted the remote control from the bedspread, pressed the red button to kill the sound. It was a reluctant gesture that Bobby recognized from Dad.

"How are you feeling?"

"I'm fine, Bobby."

"Did it hurt?"

"Yes . . . Not really." Tony shrugged. "What do you want me to say? You'll find out soon enough, Bobby."

"Don't you remember yesterday? You said you'd tell me everything."

"Of course I remember, but I'm just here in bed . . . watching the TV. You can see what it's like." He spread his arms. "Come here, Bobby."

Bobby stepped forward.

Tony grinned. "Come on, little brother."

Bobby leaned forward over the bed, let Tony clasp him in his arms. It was odd to feel his brother this way, the soft plates of muscle, the ridges of chest and arm. They'd held each other often enough before, but only in the wrestling bouts that Bobby launched into when he had nothing better to do, certain that he'd end up bruised and kicking, pinned down and forced to submit. But now the big hands were patting his back. Tony was talking over his shoulder.

"I'll sort through all the toys in the next day or so. You can keep all the best stuff to play with. Like we said yesterday, we're still brothers, right?" He leaned Bobby back, looked into his eyes. "Right?"

Bobby had had enough of grownup promises to know what they meant. Grownups were always going to get this and fix that, build wendy houses on the lawn, take you to the zoo, staple the broken strap on your satchel—favors that never happened, things they got angry about if you ever mentioned them again.

"All the best toys. Right?"

"Right," Bobby said. He turned for the door, then hesitated. "Will you tell me one thing?"

"What?"

"Where babies come from."

Tony hesitated, but not unduly; grownups always thought before they spoke. "They come from the bellies of uncles, Bobby. A big slit opens and they tumble out. It's no secret, it's a natural fact."

Bobby nodded, wondering why he'd been so afraid to ask. "I thought so . . . thanks."

"Any time," Tony said, and turned up the TV.

"Thanks again." Bobby closed the door behind him.

Tony finished school officially at the end of that term. But there were no awards, no speeches, no bunting over the school gates. Like the other new grownups, he just stopped attending, went in one evening when it was quiet to clear out his locker, as though the whole thing embarrassed him. Bobby told himself that was one thing he'd do differently when his time came. He'd spent most of his life at school, and he wasn't going to pass it by that easily. Grownups just seemed to let things *go*. It had been the same with Dad, when he moved from the factory to the admin offices in town, suddenly ignoring men he'd shared every lunchtime with and talked about for years as though they were friends.

Tony sold his bicycle through the classified pages to a kid from across town who would have perhaps a year's use of it before he too grew up. He found a temporary job at the local supermarket. He and Dad came home at about the same time each evening, the same bitter work smell coming off their bodies. Over dinner, Mum would ask them how everything had gone and the talk would lie flat between them, drowned by the weak distractions of the food.

For Tony, as for everyone, the early years of being a grownup were a busy time socially. He went out almost every night, dressed in his new grownup clothes and smelling of soap and aftershave. Mum said he looked swell. Bobby knew the places in town he went to by reputation. He had passed them regularly and caught the smell of cigarettes and booze, the drift of breathless air and sudden laughter. There were strict rules against children entering. If he was with Mum, she would snatch his hand and hurry him on. But she and Dad were happy for Tony to spend his nights in these places now that he was a grownup, indulging in the ritual dance that led to courtship, marriage, and a fresh uncle in the family. On the few occasions that Tony wasn't out late, Dad took him for driving lessons, performing endless three-point turns on the tree-lined estate roads.

Bobby would sit with his homework spread on the dining room table as Mum saw to things that didn't need seeing to. There was a distracting stiffness about her actions that was difficult to watch, difficult not to. Bobby guessed that although Tony was still living at home and she was pleased that he'd taken to grownup life, she was also missing him, missing the kid he used to be. It didn't require a great leap of imagination for Bobby to see things that way; he missed Tony himself. The arguments, the fights, the sharing and the not-sharing, all lost with the unspoken secret of being children together, of finding everything frightening, funny, and new.

In the spring, Tony passed his driving test and got a proper job at the supermarket as trainee manager. There was a girl called Marion who worked at the checkout. She had skin trouble like permanent sunburn and never looked at you when she spoke. Bobby already knew that Tony was seeing her in the bars at night. He sometimes answered the phone by mistake when she rang, her slow voice saying Is Your Brother Around as Tony came down the stairs from his room looking annoyed. The whole thing was supposed to be a secret, until suddenly Tony started bringing Marion home in the second-hand coupe he'd purchased from the dealers on Main Street.

Tony and Marion spent the evenings of their courtship sitting in the lounge with Mum and Dad, watching the TV. When Bobby asked why, Tony said that they had to stay in on account of their saving for a little house. He said it with the strange fatalism of grownups. They often talked about the future as though it was already there.

Sometimes a strange uncle would come around. Dad always turned the TV off as soon as he heard the bell. The uncles were generally fresh-faced and young, their voices high and uneasy. If they came a second time, they usually brought Bobby an unsuitable present, making a big show of hiding it behind their wide backs.

Then Uncle Lew began to visit more often. Bobby overheard Mum and Dad talking about how good it would be, keeping the same uncle in the family, even if Lew was a little old for our Tony.

Looking down at him over his cheeks, Lew would ruffle Bobby's hair with his soft fingers.

"And how are you, young man?"

Bobby said he was fine.

"And what is it you're going to be this week?" This was Lew's standard question, a joke of sorts that stemmed from some occasion when Bobby had reputedly changed his mind about his grownup career three or four times in a day.

Bobby paused. He felt an obligation to be original.

"Maybe an archaeologist," he said.

Lew chuckled. Tony and Marion moved off the settee to make room for him, sitting on the floor with Bobby.

After a year and a half of courtship, the local paper that his brother had used to sell his bicycle finally announced that Tony, Marion, and Uncle Lew were marrying. Everyone said it was a happy match. Marion showed Bobby the ring. It looked big and bright from a distance, but, close-up he saw that the diamond was tiny, centered in a much larger stub of metal that was cut to make it glitter.

Some evenings, Dad would fetch some beers for himself, Tony, and Uncle Lew, and let Bobby sip the end of a can to try the flat dark taste. Like most other grownup things, it was a disappointment.

So Tony married Marion. And he never did get around to telling Bobby how it felt to be a grownup. The priest in the church beside the crematorium spoke of the bringing together of families and of how having Uncle Lew for a new generation was a strengthened commitment. Dad swayed in the front pew from nerves and the three whiskies he'd sunk beforehand. Uncle Lew wore the suit he always wore at weddings, battered victim of too much strain on the buttons, too many spilled buffets. There were photos of the families, photos of the bridesmaids, photos of Lew smiling with his arms around the shoulders of the two newlyweds. Photograph the whole bloody lot, Dad said, I want to see where the money went.

The reception took place at home on the lawn. Having decided to find out what it was like to get drunk, Bobby lost his taste for the warm white wine after one glass. He hovered at the border of the garden. It was an undeniably pretty scene, the awnings, the dresses, the flowers. For once, the boundaries between grownups and children seemed to dissolve. Only Bobby remained outside. People raised their glasses and smiled, drunken uncles swayed awkwardly between the trestle tables. Darkness carried the smell of the car exhaust and the dry fields beyond the houses. Bobby remembered the time when he had watched from his window and the music had beaten smoky wings, when the grownups had flown over the cherry trees that now seemed so small.

The headlights of the rented limousine swept out of the darkness. Everyone ran to the drive to see Tony and Marion duck into the leather interior. Uncle Lew squeezed in behind them, off with the newlyweds to some secret place. Neighbors who hadn't been invited came out onto their drives to watch, arms folded against the non-existent chill, smiling. Marion threw her bouquet. It tumbled high over the trees and the rooftops, up through the stars. Grownups oohed and ahhed. The petals bled into the darkness. It dropped back down as a dead thing of grey and plastic. Bobby caught it without thinking; a better, cleaner catch than anything he'd ever managed in the playing fields at school. Everyone laughed—that a kid should do that!—and he blushed furiously. Then the car pulled away, low at the back from the weight of the three passengers and their luggage. The taillights dwindled, were cut out by the bend in the road. Dad swayed and shouted something, his breath reeking. People went inside and the party lingered on, drawing to its stale conclusion.

Uncle Lew had Tony and Marion's first child a year later. Mum took

Bobby to see the baby at his house when he came out of the hospital a few days after the birth. Uncle Lew lived in town, up on the hill on the far side of the river. Mum was nervous about gradient parking and always used the big pay and display down by the library. From there, you had to cut through the terraced houses, then up the narrowly winding streets that formed the oldest part of town. The houses were mostly grey pebbledash with deepset windows, yellowed lace curtains, and steps leading though steep gardens. The hill always seemed steeper than it probably was to Bobby; he hated visiting.

Uncle Lew was grinning, sitting in his usual big chair by the bay window. The baby was a mewing thing. It smelled of soap and sick. Marion was taking the drugs to make her lactate, and everything was apparently going well. Bobby peered at the baby lying cradled in her arms. He tried to offer her the red plastic rattle Mum had made him buy. Everyone smiled at that. Then there was tea and rock cakes that Bobby managed to avoid. Uncle Lew's house was always dustlessly neat, but it had a smell of neglect that seemed to emanate from behind the old-fashioned green cupboards in the kitchen. Bobby guessed that the house was simply too big for him; too many rooms.

"Are you still going to be an archaeologist?" Uncle Lew asked, leaning forward from his big chair to take both of Bobby's hands. He was wearing a dressing gown with neatly pressed pajamas underneath but for a moment the buttons parted and Bobby glimpsed wounded flesh.

The room went smilingly silent; he was obviously expected to say more than simply no or yes. "I'd like to grow up," he said, "before I decide."

The grownups all laughed. Then the baby started to cry. Grateful for the distraction, Bobby went out through the kitchen and into the grey garden, where someone's father had left a fork and spade on the crazy paving, the job of lifting out the weeds half-done. Bobby was still young enough to pretend that he wanted to play.

Then adolescence came. It was a perplexing time for Bobby, a grimy anteroom leading to the sudden glories of growing up. He watched the hair grow on his body, felt his face inflame with pimples, heard his voice change to an improbable whine before finally settling on an octave that left him sounding forever like someone else. The grownups themselves always kept their bodies covered, their personal actions impenetrably discreet. Even in the lessons and the chats, the slide-illuminated talks in the nudging darkness of the school assembly hall, Bobby sensed that the teachers were disgusted by what happened to children's bodies, and by the openness with which it did so. The *things* older children got up to, messy tricks that nature made them perform. Periods. Masturbation. *Sex*. The teachers mouthed the words like an improbable disease. Mum and Dad both said Yes they remembered, they knew exactly how it was . . . but they didn't want to touch him any longer, acted awkwardly when he was in the room, did and said things that reminded him of how they were with Tony in his later childhood years.

Bobby's first experience of sex was with May Barton, one afternoon when a crowd of school friends had cycled out to the meadows beyond town. The other children had headed back down to the road whilst Bobby was fixing a broken spoke on his back wheel. When he turned around, May was there alone. It was, he realized afterward, a situation she'd deliberately engineered. She said Let's do it, Bobby. Squinting, her head on one side. You haven't done it before, have you? Not waiting for an answer, she knelt down in the high clover and pulled her dress up over her head. Her red hair tumbled over her freckled shoulders. She asked Bobby to touch her breasts. Go on, you must have seen other boys doing this. Which he had. But still he was curious to touch her body, to find her nipples hardening in his palms. For a moment she seemed different in the wide space of the meadow, stranger almost than a grownup, even though she was just a girl. Here, she said, Bobby, and here. Down on the curving river, a big barge with faded awnings seemed not to be moving. A tractor was slicing a field from green to brown, the chatter of its engine lost on the warm wind. The town shimmered. Rooftops reached along the road. His hand traveled down her belly, explored the slippery heat of her arousal as her own fingers began to part the buttons of his shirt and jeans, did things that only his own hands had done before. He remembered the slide shows at school, the teacher's bored, disgusted voice, the fat kids sniggering more than anyone at the back, as though the whole thing had nothing to do with them.

May Barton lay down. Bobby had seen the drawings and slides, watched the mice and rabbits in the room at the back of the biology class. He knew what to do. The clover felt cool and green on his elbows and knees. She felt cool too, strangely uncomfortable, like wrestling with someone who didn't want to fight. A beetle was climbing a blade of grass at her shoulder. When she began to shudder, it flicked its wings and vanished.

After that, Bobby tried sex with several of the other girls in the neighborhood, although he tended to return most often to May. They experimented with the variations you were supposed to be able to do, found that most of them were uncomfortable and improbable, but generally not impossible.

Mum caught Bobby and May having sex one afternoon in the fourth year summer holidays when a canceled committee meeting brought her home early. Peeling off her long white cotton gloves as she entered the lounge, she found them naked in the curtained twilight, curled together like two spoons. She just clicked her tongue, turned and walked back out into the hall, her eyes blank, as if she'd just realized she'd left something in the car. She never mentioned the incident afterward—which was tactful, but to Bobby also seemed unreal, as though the act of sex had made him and May Barton momentarily invisible.

There was a sequel to this incident when Bobby returned home one evening without his key. He went through the gate round the back, to find the French windows open. He'd expected lights on in the kitchen, the murmur of the TV in the lounge. But everything was quiet. He climbed the stairs. Up on the landing, where the heat of the day still lingered, mewing sounds came from his parents' bedroom. The door was ajar. He pushed it

wide—one of those things you do without ever being able to explain why—
and walked in. It was difficult to make out the partnership of the knotted
limbs. Dad seemed to be astride Uncle Lew, Mum half underneath. The
sounds they made were another language. Somehow, they sensed his presence. Legs and arms untwined like dropped coils of rope.

It all happened very quickly. Mum got up and snatched her dressing gown
from the bedside table. On the bed, Dad scratched at his groin and Uncle
Lew made a wide cross with his forearms to cover his womanly breasts.

"It's okay," Bobby said, taking a step back toward the door, taking another.
The room reeked of mushrooms. Mum still hadn't done up her dressing
gown and Bobby could see her breasts swaying as she walked, the dark triangle
beneath her belly. She looked little different from all the girls Bobby had
seen. Through the hot waves of his embarrassment, he felt a twinge of sadness
and familiarity.

"It's okay," he said again, and closed the door.

He never mentioned the incident. But it helped him understand Mum's
reasons for not saying anything about finding him in the lounge with May.
There were plenty of words for sex, ornate words and soft words and words
that came out angry, words for what the kids got up to and special words too
for the complex congress that grownups indulged in. But you couldn't use
any of them as you used other words; a space of silence surrounded them,
walled them into a dark place that was all their own.

Bobby grew. He found to his surprise that he was one of the older kids at
school, towering over the chirping freshmen with their new blazers, having
sex with May and the other girls, taking three-hour exams at the ends of
term, worrying about growing up. He remembered that this had seemed a
strange undersea world when Tony had inhabited it; now that he had reached
it himself, this last outpost of childhood, it hardly seemed less so.

The strangeness was shared by all the children of his age. It served to bring
them together. Bobby remembered that it had been the same for Tony's
generation. Older kids tended to forget who had dumped on whom in junior
high school, the betrayals and the fights behind the bicycle sheds. Now,
every experience had a sell-by date, even if the date itself wasn't clear.

In the winter term, when Bobby was fifteen, the children all experienced
a kind of growing up in reverse, an intensification of childhood. There was
never any hurry to get home after school. A crowd of them would head into
the bare dripping woods or sit on the steps of the monument in the park.
Sometimes they would gather at Albee's Quick Restaurant and Take Away
next to the bridge. It was like another world outside, beyond the steamed
windows, grownups drifting past in cars or on foot, greying the air with breath
and motor exhaust. Inside, lights gleamed on red seats and cheap wood
paneling, the air smelled of wet shoes and coffee, thinned occasionally by a
cold draft and the broken tinkle of the bell as a new arrival joined the throng.

"I won't go through with it," May Barton said one afternoon when the
sidewalks outside were thick with slush that was forecasted to freeze to razored
puddles overnight.

No one needed to ask what she meant.

"Jesus, it was disgusting!"

May stared into her coffee. That afternoon in biology they had seen the last in a series of films entitled The Miracle Of Life. Half way through, the pink and black cartoons had switched over to scenes that purported to come from real life. They had watched a baby tumble wet onto the green sheet from an uncle's open belly, discreet angles of grownups making love. That had been bad enough—I mean, we didn't *ask* to see this stuff!—but the last five minutes had included shots of a boy and a girl in the process of growing up. The soundtrack had been discreet, but every child in the classroom had felt the screams.

The voice-over told them things they had read a hundred times in the school biology textbooks that automatically fell open at the relevant pages. Chapter thirteen—unlucky for some, as many a schoolroom wit had quipped. How the male's testicles and scrotal sac contracted back inside the body, hauled up on some fleshy block and tackle. How the female's ovaries made their peristaltic voyage along the fallopian tubes to nestle down in the useless womb, close to the equally useless cervix. A messy story that had visited them all in their dreams.

"Where the hell am *I* supposed to be when all this is going on?" someone asked. "I'm certainly not going to be *there*."

Silence fell around the corner table in Albee's. Every kid had their own bad memory. An older brother or sister who had had a hard time growing up, bloodied sheets in the laundry bin, a door left open at the wrong moment. The espresso machine puttered. Albee sighed and wiped the counter. His beer belly strained at a grey undershirt—he was almost fat enough to be an uncle. Almost, but not quite. Every kid could tell the difference. It was in the way they smelled, the way they moved. Albee wasn't an uncle—he was just turning to fat, some ordinary guy with a wife and kids back at home, and an uncle of his own with a lawn that needed mowing and crazy paving with the weeds growing through. He was just getting through life, earning a living of sorts behind his counter, putting up with Bobby and the rest of the kids from school as long as they had enough money to buy coffee.

Harry, who was a fat kid, suggested they all go down to the bowling alley. But no one else was keen. Harry was managing to keep up a jollity that the other children had lost. They all assumed that he and his friend Jonathan were the most likely candidates in their year to grow into uncles. The complicated hormonal triggers threw the dice in their favor. And it was a well-known fact that uncles had it easy, that growing up for them was a slow process, like putting on weight. But for everyone, even for Harry, the facts of life were closing in. After Christmas, at the start of the new term, their parents would all receive the brown envelopes telling them that the doctor would be around once a week.

The cafe door opened and closed, letting in the raw evening air as the kids began to drift away. A bus halted at the newsstand opposite, grownup faces framed at the windows, top deck and bottom, ordinary and absorbed. When it pulled away, streetlight and shadow filled the space behind. Underneath everything, Bobby thought, lies pain, uncertainty, and blood. He took a pull at the coffee he'd been nursing the last half hour. It had grown a skin and tasted cold, almost as bitter as the milk Mum made him drink every morning.

He and May were the last to leave Albee's. The shop windows were filled with promises of Christmas. Colors and lights streamed over the slushy pavement. The cars were inching headlight to brakelight down Main Street, out of town. Bobby and May leaned on the parapet of the bridge. The lights of the houses on the hill where Uncle Lew lived were mirrored in the sliding water. May was wearing mittens, a scarf, a beret, her red hair tucked out of sight, just her nose and eyes showing.

"When I was eight or nine," she said, "Mum and Dad took me on holiday to the coast. It was windy and sunny. I had a big brother then. His name was Tom. We were both kids and he used to give me piggy backs, sometimes tickle me till I almost peed. We loved to explore the dunes. Had a whole world there to ourselves. One morning we were sliding down this big slope of sand, laughing and climbing all the way up again. Then Tom doubled up at the bottom, and I thought he must have caught himself on a hidden rock or something. I shouted Are You Okay, but all he did was groan."

"He was growing up?"

May nodded. "The doc at home had said it was fine to go away, but I realized what was happening. I said You Stay There, which was stupid really, and I shot off to get someone. The sand kept sliding under my sandals. It was a nightmare, running through treacle. I ran right into Dad's arms. He'd gone looking for us. I don't know why, perhaps it's something grownups can sense. He found someone else to ring the ambulance and we went back down the beach to see Tom. The tide was coming in and I was worried it might reach him . . ."

She paused. Darkness was flowing beneath the river arches. "When we got back, he was all twisted, and I knew he couldn't be alive, no one could hold themselves that way. The blood was in the sand, sticking to his legs. Those black flies you always get on a beach were swarming."

Bobby began, "That doesn't . . ." but he pulled the rest of the chilly sentence back into his lungs.

May turned to him. She pulled the scarf down to her chin. Looking at her lips, the glint of her teeth inside, Bobby remembered the sweet hot things they had done together. He marveled at how close you could get to someone and still feel alone.

"We're always early developers in our family," May said. "Tom was the first in his class. I suppose I'll be the same."

"Maybe it's better . . . get it over with."

"I suppose everyone thinks that it'll happen first to some kid in another class, someone you hardly know. Then to a few others. Perhaps a friend, someone you can visit afterward and find out you've got nothing to say but that it's no big deal after all. Everything will always be *fine*."

"There's still a long—"

"—How long? What difference is a month more or less?" She was angry, close to tears. But beneath, her face was closed off from him. "You had an elder brother who survived, Bobby. Was he ever the same?"

Bobby shrugged. The answer was obvious, all around them. Grownups were *grownups*. They drove cars, fought wars, dressed in boring and uncomfortable clothes, built roads, bought newspapers every morning that told them the same thing, drank alcohol without getting merry from it, pulled hard on the toilet door to make sure it was shut before they did their business.

"Tony was all right," he said. "He's still all right. We were never that great together anyway—just brothers. I don't think it's the physical changes that count . . . or even that that's at the heart of it. . . ." He didn't know what the hell else to say.

"I'm happy as I *am*," May said. "I'm a kid. I feel like a kid. If I change, I'll cease to be *me*. Who wants that?" She took off her mitten, wiped her nose on the back of her hand. "So I'm not going through with it."

Bobby stared at her. It was like saying you weren't going through with death because you didn't like the sound of it. "It can't be *that* bad, May. Most kids get through all right. Think of all the grownups . . . Jesus, think of your own parents."

"Look, Bobby. I know growing up hurts. I know it's dangerous. *I* should know, shouldn't I? That's not what I care about. What I care about is losing *me*, the person I am and want to be. . . . You just don't believe me, do you? I'm *not* going through with it, I'll stay a kid. I don't care who I say it to, because they'll just think I'm acting funny, but Bobby, I thought *you* might believe me. There *has* to be a way out."

"You can. . . ." Bobby said. But already she was walking away.

The envelopes were handed out at school. A doctor started to call at Bobby's house, and at the houses of all his friends. Next day there was always a show of bravado as they compared the bruises on their arms. The first child to grow up was a boy named Arthur Mumford, whose sole previous claim to fame was the ability to play popular tunes by squelching his armpits. In that way that the inevitable always has, it happened suddenly and without warning. One Tuesday in February, just five weeks after the doctor had started to call at their houses, Arthur didn't turn up for registration. A girl two years below had spotted the doctor's car outside his house on her paper round the evening before. Word was around the whole school by lunchtime.

There was an unmistakable air of disappointment. When he wasn't performing his party piece, Arthur was a quiet boy: he was tall, and stooped from embarrassment at his height. He seldom spoke. But it wasn't just that it should happen first to someone as ordinary as Arthur—I mean, it has to happen to all of us sooner or later, right? But none of the children felt as excited—or even as afraid—as they had expected. When it had happened to kids in the senior years, it had seemed like something big, seeing a kid they'd known suddenly walking along Main Street in grownup clothes with the dazed expression that always came to new grownups, ignoring old school friends, looking for work, ducking into bars. They had speculated excitedly about who would go next, prayed that it would be one of the school bullies. But now that it was their turn, the whole thing felt like a joke that had been played too many times. Arthur Mumford was just an empty desk, a few belongings that needed picking up.

In the spring, at least half a dozen of the children in Bobby's year had grown up. The hot weather seemed to speed things up. Sitting by the dry fountain outside the Municipal Offices one afternoon, watching the litter and the grownups scurry by, a friend of Bobby's named Michele suddenly dropped her can of drink and coiled up in a screaming ball. The children and the passing grownups all fluttered uselessly as she rolled around on the sidewalk until a doctor who happened to be walking by forced her to sit up on the rim of the fountain and take deep slow breaths. Yes, she's growing up, he snapped, glowering at the onlookers, then down at his watch. I suggest someone call her parents or get a car. Michele was gasping through tears and obviously in agony, but the doctor's manner suggested that she was making far too much of the whole thing. A car arrived soon enough, and Michele was bundled into the back. Bobby never saw her again.

He had similar, although less dramatic, partings with other friends. One day, you'd be meeting them at the bus stop to go to the skating rink. The next, you would hear that they had grown up. You might see them around town, heading out of a shop as you were going in, but they would simply smile and nod, or make a point of saying Hello Bobby just to show that they remembered your name. Everything was changing. That whole summer was autumnal, filled with a sense of loss. In their own grownup way, even the parents of the remaining children were affected. Although there would inevitably be little time left for their children to enjoy such things, they became suddenly generous with presents, finding the cash that had previously been missing for a new bike, a train set, or even a pony.

May and Bobby still spent afternoons together, but more often now they would just sit in the kitchen at May's house, May by turns gloomy and animated, Bobby laughing with her or—increasingly against his feelings— trying to act reassuring and grownup. They usually had the house to themselves. In recognition of the dwindling classes, the teachers were allowing any number of so-called study periods, and both of May's parents worked days and overtime in the evenings to keep up with the mortgage on their clumsy mock-tudor house.

One afternoon, when they were drinking orange juice mixed with sweet sherry filched from the liquor cabinet and wondering if they dared to get drunk, May got up and went to the fridge. Bobby thought she was getting more orange juice, but instead she produced the plastic flask that contained her bitter milk. She laughed at his expression as she unscrewed the childproof cap and put the flask to her lips, gulping it down as though it tasted good. Abstractly, Bobby noticed that her parents used a brand-name product. His own parents always bought the supermarket's own.

"Try it," she said.

"What?"

"Go on."

Bobby took the flask and sipped. He was vaguely curious to find out whether May's bitter milk was any less unpleasant than the cheaper stuff he was used to. It wasn't. Just different, thicker. He forced himself to swallow.

"You don't just *drink* this, do you?" he asked, wondering for the first time whether her attitude wasn't becoming something more than simply odd.

"Of course I don't," she said. "But I could if I liked. You see, it's *not* bitter milk."

Bobby stared at her.

"Look."

May opened the fridge again, took out a carton of ordinary pasteurized milk. She put it on the counter, then reached high inside a kitchen cabinet, her blouse briefly raising at the back to show the ridges of her lower spine that Bobby so enjoyed touching. She took down a can of flour, a plastic lemon dispenser, and a bottle of white wine vinegar.

"The flour stops it from curdling," she said, "and ordinary vinegar doesn't work. It took me days to get it right." She tipped some milk into a tumbler, stirred in the other ingredients. "I used to measure everything out, but now I can do it just anyhow."

She handed him the tumbler. "Go on."

Bobby tasted. It was quite revolting, almost as bad as the brand-name bitter milk.

"You see?"

Bobby put the glass down, swallowing back a welcome flood of saliva to weaken the aftertaste. Yes, he saw—or at least, he was *beginning* to see.

"I haven't been drinking bitter milk for a month now. Mum buys it, I tip it down the sink when she's not here and do my bit of chemistry. It's that simple. . . ." She was smiling, then suddenly blinking back tears. ". . . that easy. . . . Of course, it doesn't taste exactly the same, but when was the last time your parents tried tasting bitter milk?"

"Look, May . . . don't you think this is dangerous?"

"Why?" She tilted her head, wiped a stray trickle from her cheek. "What exactly is going to happen to me? You tell me that."

Bobby was forced to shrug. Bitter milk was for children, like cod liver oil. Grownups avoided the stuff, but it was good for you, it *helped*.

"I'm *not* going to grow up, Bobby," she said. "I told you I wasn't joking."

"Do you really think that's going to make any difference?"

"Who knows?" she said. She gave him a sudden hug, her lips wet and close to his ear. "Now let's go upstairs."

Weeks later, Bobby got a phone call from May one evening at home. Mum called him down from his bedroom, holding the receiver as though it might bite.

He took it.

"It's me, Bobby."

"Yeah." He waited for the lounge door to close. "What is it?"

"Jesus, I think it's started. Mum and Dad are out at a steak bar and I'm getting these terrible pains."

The fake bitter milk. The receiver went slick in his hand.

"It can't be. You can't be sure."

"If I was sure I wouldn't be . . . look, Bobby, can you come around?" She gave a gasp. "There it is again. You really must. I can't do this alone."

"You gotta ring the hospital."

"No."

"You—"

"*No!*"

Bobby gazed at the telephone directories that Mum stacked on a shelf beneath the phone as though they were proper books. He remembered that night with Tony, the lights on everywhere, burning though everything as though it wasn't real. He swallowed. The TV was still loud in the lounge.

"Okay," he said. "God knows what I'm supposed to tell Mum and Dad. Give me half an hour."

His excuse was a poor one, but his parents took it anyway. He didn't care what they believed; he'd never felt as shaky in his life.

He cycled through the housing development. The air rushed against his face, drowning him in that special feeling that came from warm nights. May must have been watching for him from a window. She was at the door when he scooted down the drive.

"Jesus, Bobby, I'm bleeding."

"I can't see anything."

She pushed her hand beneath the waistband of her dress, then held it out. "Look. Do you believe me now?"

Bobby swallowed, then nodded.

She was alone in the house. Her parents were out. Bobby helped her up the stairs. He found an old plastic raincoat to spread across the bed, and helped her to get clean. The blood was clotted and fibrous, then watery thin. It didn't seem like an ordinary wound.

When the first panic was over, he pushed her jumbled clothes off the bedside chair and slumped down. May's cheeks were flushed and rosy. For all her talk about not wanting to grow up, he reckoned that he probably looked worse than she did at that moment. What was all this about? Had she *ever* had a brother named Tom? One who died? She'd lived in another development then. Other than asking, there was no way of knowing. "I think I'd better go and phone—"

"—Don't!" She forced a smile and reached out a hand toward him. "*Don't.*"

Bobby hesitated, then took her hand.

"Look, it's stopped now anyway. Perhaps it was a false alarm."

"Yeah," Bobby said, "False alarm," although he was virtually sure there was no such thing. You either grew up or you didn't.

"I feel okay now," she said. "Really, I do."

"That's good," Bobby said.

May was still smiling. She seemed genuinely relieved. "Kiss me, Bobby," she said.

Her eyes were strange. She smelled strange. Like the river, like the rain. He kissed her, softly on the warmth of her cheek; the way you might kiss a grownup. He leaned back from the bed and kept hold of her hand.

They talked.

Bobby got back home close to midnight. His parents had gone up to bed, but, as he crossed the darkened landing, he sensed that they were both awake and listening beyond the bedroom door. Next morning, nothing was said, and May was at school with the rest of what remained of their class. The teachers had mostly given up on formal lessons, getting the children instead to clear out stockrooms or tape the spines of elderly textbooks. He watched May as she drifted through the chalk-clouded air, the sunlight from the tall windows blazing her hair. Neither grownup nor yet quite a kid, she moved between the desks with unconscious grace.

That lunchtime, she told Bobby that she was fine. But Yes, she was still bleeding a bit. I have to keep going to the little girl's room. I've gone through two pairs of underpants, flushed them away. It's a real nuisance, Bobby, she added, above the clatter in the dining hall, as though it was nothing, like hay fever or a cold sore. Her face was clear and bright, glowing through the freckles and the smell of communal cooking. He nodded, finding that it was easier to believe than to question. May smiled. And you *will* come see me tonight, won't you, Bobby? We'll be on our own. Again, Bobby found himself nodding.

He announced to Mum and Dad after dinner that evening that he was going out again. He told them that he was working on a school play that was bound to take up a lot of his time.

Mum and Dad nodded. Bobby tried not to study them too closely, although he was curious to gauge their reaction.

"Okay," Mum said. "But make sure you change the batteries on your lamps if you're going to cycle anywhere after dark." She glanced at Dad, who nodded and returned to his paper.

"You know I'm careful like that." Bobby tried to keep the wariness out of his voice. He suspected that they saw straight through him and knew that he was lying. He'd been in this kind of situation before. That was an odd thing about grownups: you could tell them the truth and they'd fly into a rage. Other times, such as this, when you had to lie, they said nothing at all.

May was waiting at the door again that evening. As she had promised, her parents were out. He kissed her briefly in the warm light of the hall. Her lips were soft against his, responding with a pressure that he knew would open at the slightest sign from him. She smelled even more rainy than before. There was something else too, something that was both new and familiar. Just as her arms started to encircle his back, he stepped back, his heart suddenly pounding.

He looked at her. "Christ, May, what are you wearing?"

"This." She gave a twirl. The whole effect was odd, yet hard to place for a moment. A tartanish pleated dress. A white blouse. A dull necklace. Her hair pulled back in a tight bun. And her eyes, her mouth, her whole face . . . looked like it had been sketched on, the outlines emphasized, the details ignored. Then he licked his lips and knew what it was; the same smell and taste that came from Mum on nights when she leaned over his bed and said, you will be good while we're out, won't you, my darling, jewelry glimmering like starlight around her neck and at the lobes of her ears. May was wearing makeup. She was dressed like a grownup.

For a second, the thought that May had somehow managed to get through the whole messy process of growing up since leaving school that afternoon came to him. Then he saw the laughter in her eyes and he knew that it couldn't be true.

"What do you think, Bobby?"

"I don't know why grownups wear that stuff. It isn't comfortable, it doesn't even look good. What does it feel like?"

"Strange," May said. "It changes you inside. Come upstairs. I'll show you."

May led him up the stairs and beyond a door he had never been through before. Even though they were out, her parents' bedroom smelled strongly of grownup, especially the closet, where the dark lines of suits swung gently on their hangers. Bobby was reasonably tall for his age, as tall as many grownups, May's father included.

The suit trousers itched his legs and the waist was loose, but not so loose as to fall down. He knotted a tie over a white shirt, pulled on the jacket. May got some oily stuff from the dresser, worked it into his hair and combed it smooth. Then she stood beside him as he studied himself in the mirror. Dark and purposeful, two strange grownups gazed back. He glanced down at himself, hardly believing that it was true. He pulled a serious face back at the mirror, the sort you might see behind the counter at a bank. Then he started to chuckle. And May began to laugh. It was so inconceivably easy. They were doubled over, their bellies aching. They held each other tight. They just couldn't stop.

An hour later, May closed the front door and turned the dead bolt. Heels clipping the pavement, they walked to the bus stop. Perhaps in deference to their new status as grownups, the next bus into town came exactly when it was due. They traveled on the top deck, which was almost empty apart from a gaggle of cleaning ladies at the back. They were busy talking, and the driver hadn't even bothered to look up when he gave them two straight adult fares (don't say please, May had whispered as the tall lights of the 175 had pulled into the stop, grownups don't do that kind of thing). Dressed in his strange grownup clothes, his back spreading huge inside the jacket shoulder pads, Bobby felt confident anyway. Like May said, the grownup clothes changed you inside.

They got off outside Albee's Quick Restaurant and Take Away. For some reason, May wanted to try visiting a place where they were actually known.

Bobby was too far gone with excitement to argue about taking an unnecessary extra risk. Her manner was smooth; he doubted if anyone else would have noticed the wildness in her eyes beneath the makeup. Rather than dodge the cars across the road, they waited for a big gap and walked slowly, sedately. The lights of Albee's glowed out to greet them. They opened the door to grownup laughter, the smell of smoke and grownup sweat. People nodded and smiled, then moved to let them through. Albee grinned at them from the bar, eager to please, the way the teachers were at school when the principal came unexpectedly into class. He said Good evening Sir and What'll it be. Bobby heard his own voice say something calm and easy in reply. He raked a stool back for May and she sat down, tucking her dress neatly under her thighs. He glanced around as drinks were served, half expecting the other grownups to float up from their chairs, to begin to fly. They'd been here after school a hundred times, but this was a different world.

It was the same on a dozen other nights, whenever they hit on an excuse that they had the nerve to use on their unquestioning parents. Albee's, they found, was much further from the true heart of the grownup world than they'd imagined. They found hotel bars where real fountains tinkled and the drinks were served chilled on paper coasters that stuck to the bottom of the glass. There were loud pubs where you could hardly stand up for the yellow-lit crush and getting served was an evening's endeavor. There were restaurants where you were offered bowls brimming with crackers and salted nuts just to sit and read the crisply printed menus and say Well Thanks, But It Doesn't Look As Though Our Friends Are Coming And The Baby Sitter You Know. . . . Places they had seen day in and day out through their whole lives were changed by the darkness, the hot charge of car fumes, buzzing street lights, glittering smiles, the smell of perfume, changed beyond recognition to whispering palaces of crystal and velvet.

After changing at May's house back into his sweatshirt and sneakers, Bobby would come home late, creeping down the hall in the bizarre ritual of pretending not to disturb his parents, whom he was certain would be listening open-eyed in the darkness from the first unavoidable creak of the front door. In the kitchen, he checked for new bottles of bitter milk. By the light of the open fridge door, he tipped the fluid down the sink, chased it away with a quick turn of the hot water faucet—which was quieter than the cold—and replaced it with a fresh mixture of spirit vinegar, lemon juice, milk, and flour.

The summer holidays came. Bobby and May spent all their time together, evenings and days. Lying naked in the woods on the soft prickle of dry leaves, looking up at the green latticed sky. Bobby reached again toward May. He ran his hand down the curve of her belly. It was soft and sweet and hard, like an apple. Her breath quickened. He rolled onto his side, lowered his head to lick at her breasts. More than ever before, her nipples swelled amazingly to his tongue. But after a moment her back stiffened.

"Just kiss me here," she said, "my mouth," gently cupping his head in her hands and drawing it up. "Don't suck at me today, Bobby. I feel too tender."

Bobby acquiesced to the wonderful sense of her around him, filling the sky and the woods. She'd been sensitive about some of the things he did before, often complaining about tenderness and pain a few days before she started her bleeding. But the bleeding hadn't happened for weeks, months.

They still went out some nights, visiting the grownup places, living their unbelievable lie. Sometimes as he left the house, or coming back late with his head spinning from the drink and the things they'd done, Bobby would look up and see Mum's face pale at the bedroom window. But he said nothing. And nothing was ever said. It was an elaborate dance, back to back, Mum and Dad displaying no knowledge or denial, each moment at the kitchen table and the rare occasions when they shared the lounge passing without question. A deception without deceit.

The places they went to changed. From the smart rooms lapped with deep carpets and chrome they glided on a downward flight path through urine-reeking doorways. This was where the young grownups went, people they recognized as kids from assembly at school just a few years before. Bars where the fermented light only deepened the darkness, where the fat uncles sat alone as evening began, looking at the men and the women as the crowds thickened, looking away.

Bobby and May made friends, people who either didn't notice what they were or didn't care. Hands raised and waving through the chaos and empty glasses. Hey Bobby, May, over here, sit yourselves right down here. Place for the old butt. Jokes to be told, lips licked, lewd eyes rolled, skirt hems pulled firmly down then allowed to roll far up again. Glimpses of things that shouldn't be seen. They were good at pretending to be grownups by now, almost better than the grownups themselves. For the purposes of the night, Bobby was in town from a university in the city, studying whatever came into his head. May was deadly serious or laughing, saying my God, you wouldn't believe the crap I have to put up with at the office, the factory, the shop. Playing it to a tee. And I'm truly glad to be here and now with you all before it starts again in the morning.

Time broke in beery waves. The account at the bank that Bobby had been nurturing for some unspecified grownup need sunk to an all-time low. But it could have been worse—they were a popular couple, almost as much in demand as the unattached fat uncles when a few drinks had gone down. They hardly ever had to put in for a round.

The best part was when they came close to discovery. A neighbor who probably shouldn't have been there in the first place, a family friend, a teacher. Then once it was Bobby's brother Tony. Late, and he had his arms around a fat uncle, his face sheened with sweat. He was grinning and whispering wet lips close to his ear. There was a woman with them too, her hands straying quick and hard over both of their bodies. It wasn't Marion.

"Let's go," Bobby said. There was a limit to how far you could take a risk. But May would have none of it. She stared straight at Tony through the swaying bodies, challenging him to notice.

For a moment, his eyes were on them, his expression drifting back from lust. Bobby covered his hand with his mouth, feeling the grownup clothes and confidence dissolve around him, the schoolkid inside screaming to get out. Tony made to speak, but there was no chance of hearing. In another moment, he vanished into the mass of the crowd.

Now that the danger had passed, it was the best time of all; catching Tony out in a way that he could never explain. Laughter bursting inside them, they ran out into the sudden cool of the night. May held onto him and her lips were over his face, breathless and trembling from the sudden heightening of the risk. He held tight to her, swaying, not caring about the cars, the grownups stumbling by, pulling her close, feeling the taut rounded swell of her full breasts and belly that excited him so.

"Do you want to be like them?" she whispered. "Want to be a fool and a grownup?"

"Never." He leaned back and shouted it at the stars. "Never!"

Arm in arm, they swayed down the pavement toward the bus stop. Incredibly, Tuesday was coming around again tomorrow; Doc Halstead would be pulling up the drive at home at about eleven, washing his hands one more time and saying How Are You My Man before taking best-china coffee with Mum in the lounge, whispering things he could never quite hear. May's eyes were eager, gleaming with the town lights, drinking it all in. More than him, she hated this world and loved it. Sometimes, when things were swirling, she reminded him of a true grownup. It all seemed far away from that evening in town after biology, leaning on the bridge alone after leaving Albee's and gazing down at the river, May saying I won't go through with it, Bobby, I'm not just some kid acting funny. As though something as easy as fooling around with the bitter milk could make that much of a difference.

Doctor Halstead arrived next morning only minutes after Bobby had finished breakfast and dressed. In the spare bedroom, he spread out his rubber and steel. He dried his hands and held the big syringe up to the light before leaning down.

Bobby smeared the fresh bead of blood over the bruises on his forearm, then licked the salt off his fingertips.

Doctor Halstead was watching the readouts. The paper feed gave a burp and chattered out a thin strip like a supermarket receipt. The doc tore it off, looked at it for a moment, and tutted before screwing it into a ball. He pressed a button that flattened the dials, pressed another to make them drift up again.

"Is everything okay?"

"Everything's fine."

The printer chattered again. He tore it off. "You've still got some way to go."

"How many weeks?"

"If I had a dollar for every time I've been asked that question. . . ."

"Don't you *know*?"

He handed Bobby the printout. Faint figures and percentages. The machine needed a new ribbon.

"Us grownups don't know everything. I know it seems that way."

"Most of my friends have gone." He didn't want to mention May, although he guessed Mum had told him anyway. "How long can it go on for?"

"As long as it takes."

"What if nothing happens?"

"Something always happens."

He gave Bobby a smile.

Bobby and May went out again that night. A place they'd never tried before, a few stops out of town, with a spluttering neon sign, a shack motel at the back, and a dusty parking area for the big container rigs. The inside was huge, with bare boards and patches of linoleum, games machines lining the walls, too big to fill with anything but smoke and patches of yellowed silence on even the busiest of nights. Being a Wednesday, and the grownups' pay packets being thin until the weekend, it was quiet. They sat alone in the smoggy space for most of the evening. They didn't know anyone, and for once it seemed that no one wanted to know them. Bobby kept thinking of the way Doctor Halstead had checked the readouts, checked them again. And he knew May had her own weekly test the following afternoon. It wasn't going to be one of their better nights. May looked pale. She went out to the ladies room far more often than their slow consumption of the cheap bottled beer would explain. Once, when she came back and leaned forward to tell him something, he realized that the rain had gone from her breath. He smelled vomit.

At about ten, a fat uncle crossed the room, taking a drunken detour around the chairs.

"Haven't seen you two here before," he said, his belly swaying above the table, close to their faces. "I've got a contract delivering groceries from here to the city and back. Every other day, I'm here."

"We must have missed you."

He squinted down at them, still swaying but now seeming less than drunk. For places like here, Bobby and May wore casual clothes. Bobby dressed the way Dad did for evenings at home, in an open-collared striped shirt and trousers that looked as though they had started out as part of a work suit. May hadn't put on much makeup, which she said she hated anyway. Bobby wondered if they were growing complacent, if this fat uncle hadn't seen what all the other grownups had apparently failed to notice.

"Mind if I . . ." The uncle reached for a chair and turned it around, sat down with his legs wide and his arms and belly propped against the backrest. "Where are you from anyway?"

Bobby and May exchanged secret smiles. Now they were in their element, back in the territory of the university in the city, the office, the shop, the grownup places that had developed a life of their own through frequent re-telling.

It was pleasant to talk to an uncle on equal terms for a change, away from the pawings and twittering of other grownups which usually surrounded them. Bobby felt that he had a lot of questions to ask, but the biggest one was answered immediately by this uncle's cautious but friendly manner, by the way he spoke of his job and the problems he was having trying to find an apartment. In all the obvious ways, he was just like any other young grownup. He bought them a drink. It seemed polite to buy him one in return, then—what the hell—a chaser. Soon, they were laughing. People were watching, smiling but keeping their distance across the ranks of empty tables.

Bobby knew what was happening, but he was curious to see how far it would go. He saw a plump hand stray to May's arm—still covered by a long sleeved shirt to hide the bruises—then up to her shoulder. He saw the way she reacted by not doing anything.

"You don't know how lonely it gets," the uncle said, leaning forward, his arm around Bobby's back too, his hand reaching down. "Always on the road. I stay here, you know. Most Wednesdays. A lot of them sleep out in the cab. But they pay you for it and I like to lie on something soft. Just out the back." He nodded. "Through that door, the way you came in, left past the kitchens."

"Will you show us?" May asked, looking at Bobby. "I think we'd like to see."

The motel room was small. Someone had tried to do it up years before, but the print had rubbed off the wallpaper by the door and above the green bed. The curtains had shrunk, and Bobby could still see the parking lot and the lights of the road. A sliding door led to a toilet and the sound of a dripping tap.

The fat uncle sat down. The bed squealed. Bobby and May remained standing, but if the uncle saw their nervousness he didn't comment. He seemed more relaxed now, easy with the drink and the certainty of what they were going to do. He unlaced his boots and peeled off his socks, twiddling his toes with a sigh that reminded Bobby of Dad at the end of a hard day. He was wearing a sweatshirt that had once said something. He pulled it off over his head with his hands on the waistband, the way a girl might do, threw it onto the rug beside his feet. He had an undershirt on underneath. The hems were unraveling, but he and it looked clean enough, and he smelt a lot better than Uncle Lew did at close quarters, like unbaked dough. He pulled the undershirt off too. His breasts were much bigger than May's. There was hardly any hair under his arms. Bobby stared at the bruised scar that began under his ribcage and vanished beneath the wide band of his jeans, slightly moist where it threatened to part.

"You're going to stay dressed, are you?" he said with a grin. He scratched himself and the springs squealed some more. "This goddamn bed's a problem."

"We'd like to watch," May said. "For now, if that's okay with you."

"That's great by me. I'm not fussy . . . I mean . . ." he stood up and stepped out of his trousers and underpants in one movement. "Well, you know what I mean."

Under the huge flap of his belly, Bobby couldn't see much of what lay beneath. Just darkness and hair. Every night, he thought, a million times throughout the world, this is going on. Yet he couldn't believe it, couldn't even believe it about his parents with Uncle Lew, even though he'd seen them once on that hot afternoon.

"Tell you what," the uncle said. "It's been a long day. I think you'd both appreciate it if yours truly freshened up a bit." He went over to Bobby, brushed the fine hairs at the back of his neck with soft fingers. "I won't be a mo. You two sort yourselves out, eh?"

He waddled off into the bathroom, slid the door shut behind him. They heard the toilet seat bang down, a sigh, and the whisper of moving flesh. Then a prolonged fart. A pause. A splash. Then another.

May looked at Bobby. Her face reddened. She covered her mouth to block the laughter. Bobby's chest heaved. He covered his mouth too. He couldn't help it: the joke was incredibly strong. Signaling to Bobby, tears brimming in her eyes, May stooped to pick up the sweatshirt, the shoes, the undershirt. Bobby gathered the jeans. There were more clothes heaped in a corner. They took those too, easing the door open as quietly as they could before the laughter rolled them over like a high wind.

They sprinted madly across the parking lot, down the road, into the night.

Next morning, the sky was drab. It seemed to Bobby like the start of the end of summer, the first of the grey veils that would eventually thicken to autumn. Downstairs, Mum was humming. He went first into the kitchen, not that he wanted to see her, but he needed to re-establish the charade of them ignoring his nights away from the house. One day, he was sure, it would break, she'd have a letter from the police, the doctor, the owner of some bar, a fact that couldn't be ignored.

"It's you," she said. Uncharacteristically, she kissed him. He'd been taller than her for a year or two, she didn't need to bend down, but it still felt that way. "Do you want anything from the supermarket? I'm off in a few minutes."

Bobby glanced at the list she kept on the wipe-clean plastic board above the stove. Wash pow, toilet pap, marg, lemon juice, wine vinegar. He looked at her face, but it was clear and innocent.

"Aren't you going to go into the dining room? See what's waiting?"

"Waiting?"

"Your birthday, Bobby." She gave him a laugh and a quick, stiff hug. "I asked you what you wanted weeks ago and you never said. So I hope you like it. I've kept the receipt—you boys are so difficult."

"Yeah." He hadn't exactly forgotten, he'd simply been pushing the thing back in his mind, the way you do with exams and visits from the doctor, hoping that if you make yourself forget, then the rest of the world will forget, too.

He was seventeen and still a kid. It was at least one birthday too many. He opened the cards first, shaking each envelope carefully to see if there was any money. Some of them had pictures of archaic countryside and inappropriate verses, the sort that grownups gave to each other. One or two people had made the effort to find a child's card, but there wasn't much of a market for seventeen year olds. The most enterprising had combined stick-ons for 1 and 7. Bobby moved to the presents, using his toast knife to slit the tape, trying not to damage any of the wrapping paper, which Mum liked to iron and re-use. Although she hadn't spoken, he was conscious that she was standing watching at the door. Fighting the sinking feeling of discovering books on subjects that didn't interest him, accessories for hobbies he didn't pursue, model cars for a collection he'd given up years ago, he tried to display excitement and surprise.

Mum and Dad's present was a pair of binoculars, something he'd coveted when he was thirteen for reasons he couldn't now remember. He gazed at the marmalade jar in close up, through the window at the individual leaves of the nearest cherry tree in the garden.

"We thought you'd find them useful when you grew up too," Mum said, putting her arms around him.

"It's great," he said. In truth, he liked the smell of the case—leather, oil and glass—more than the binoculars themselves. But he knew that wasn't the point. And then he remembered why he'd so wanted a pair of binoculars, how he'd used to love looking up at the stars.

"Actually, I've lots of stuff to get at the supermarket, Bobby. Dad's taking a half day and we're going to have a party for you. Everyone's coming. Isn't that great?"

Bobby went with Mum to the supermarket. They drove into town past places he and May had visited at night. Even though the sky was clearing to sun, they looked flat and grey. Wandering the supermarket aisles, Mum insisted that Bobby choose whatever he want. He settled at random for iced fancies, pâté, green-veined cheese. Tony came out from his office behind a window of silvered glass, a name badge on his lapel and his hair starting to recede. He clapped Bobby's shoulder and said he'd never have believed it, seventeen, my own little brother. They chatted awkwardly for a while in the chill drift of the frozen meats. Even though there was a longer line, they chose Marion's checkout. She was back working at the supermarket part time now that their kid had started nursery school. It wasn't until Bobby saw her blandly cheerless face that he remembered that night with Tony and the other uncle in the bar. He wondered if she knew, if she cared.

There were cars in the driveway at home and spilling along the cul de sac, little kids with names he couldn't remember running on the lawn. The weather had turned bright and hot. Dad had fished out all the deckchairs as soon as he got home, the ordinary ones and the specials he kept for uncles. People kept coming up to Bobby and then running out of things to say. He couldn't remember whether they'd given him cards or presents, what to thank them for. Uncle Lew was in a good mood, the facets of one of the best wine glasses trembling sparks across his rounded face.

"Well, Bobby," he said, easing himself down in his special deckchair. He was starting to look old, ugly. Too many years, too many happy events. He was nothing like the fresh fat uncle at the motel. "And what are you going to be when you grow up?"

Bobby shrugged. He had grown sick of thinking up lies to please people.

The canvas of Lew's deckchair was wheezing and slightly torn. Bobby hoped that he'd stay a kid long enough to see him fall through.

"Well, get yourself a nice girlfriend," he said. "It means a lot to me that I'm uncle to your Momma and Poppa *and* to Tony and Marion too." He sucked at his wine. "But that's all up to you."

Looking back up the lawn toward the house, Bobby saw May and her parents emerging into the sunlight from the open French windows. May looked drab and tired. Her belly was big, her ankles swollen.

She waddled over to them, sweat gleaming on her cheeks.

"Hello, Bobby." She leaned over to let Uncle Lew give her a hug. He put his lips to her ear. She wriggled and smiled before she pulled away.

"Hello, May."

She was wearing a cheap print, something that fell in folds like a tent.

"This whole party is a surprise, isn't it? Your Mum insisted that I didn't say anything when she told me last week. Here. Happy birthday."

She gave him a package. He opened it. Five minutes later, he couldn't remember what it contained.

Dad banged the trestle table and people gathered around on the lawn as he made a speech about how he could hardly believe the way the years had flown, saying the usual things that grownups always said about themselves when it was a child's birthday. He raised his glass. A toast. Bobby. Everyone intoned his name. *Bobby.* The sun retreated toward the rooftops and the trees, filling the estate with evening, the weary smell of cooking. Those grownups who hadn't been able to skip work arrived in their work clothes. Neighbors drifted in.

May came over to Bobby again, her face flushed with the drink and the sun.

"Did the doc come over to see you today?" he asked, for want of anything better. The hilarious intimacy of the things they had done in the night suddenly belonged to a world even more distant than that of the grownups.

"Nothing happened," she said, spearing a piece of herring on the paper plate she carried with a plastic fork. "Nothing ever happens." She took a bite of the herring, then pulled a face. "Disgusting. God knows how the grownups enjoy this shit."

Bobby grinned, recognizing the May he knew. "Let's go somewhere. No one will notice."

She shrugged yes and propped her plate on the concrete bird bath. They went through the back gate, squeezed between the bumpers on the driveway, and out along the road.

"Do you still think you'll never grow up?" Bobby asked.

May shook her head. "What about you?"

"I suppose it's got to happen. We're not fooling anyone, are we, going out, not drinking the milk? I'm sure Mum and Dad know. They just don't seem to care. I mean, we can't be the first kids in the history of the world to have stumbled on this secret. Well, it can't *be* a secret, can it?"

"How about we climb up to the meadows?" May said. "The town looks good from up there."

"Have you ever read *Peter Pan?*" Bobby asked as they walked up the dirt road between the allotments and the saw mill. "He never grew up. Lived in a wonderful land and learned how to fly." He held open the kissing gate that led into the fields. May had to squeeze through. The grass was high and slivered with seed, whispering under a deepening sky. "When I was young," he said, "on evenings like this, I used to look out of my bedroom window and watch the grownups. I thought that they could fly."

"Who do you think can fly now?"

"No one. We're all the same."

They stopped to catch their breath and look down at the haze below. Hills, trees, and houses, the wind carrying the chime of an ice-cream van, the river stealing silver from the sky. He felt pain spread through him, then dissolve without finding focus.

May took his hand. "Remember when we came up here alone that time, years ago?" She drew it toward her breast, then down. "You touched me here, and here. We had sex. You'd never done it before." She let his hand fall. Bobby felt no interest. May no longer smelled of rain, and he was relieved that he didn't have to turn her down.

The pain came again, more strongly this time. He swayed. The shimmering air cleared, and for one moment there was a barge on the river, a tractor slicing a field from green to brown, a hawk circling high overhead, May smiling, sweet and young, as she said Let's Do It, Bobby, pulling her dress up over her head. He blinked.

"Are you okay?"

"I'm fine," he said, leaning briefly against her, feeling the thickness of her arms.

"I think we'd better go back."

Down the hill, the pain began to localize. First circling in his spine, then gradually shifting orbit toward his belly. It came and went. When it was there, it was so unbelievable that he put it aside in the moments of recession. Had to be a bad dream. The trees swayed with the rush of twilight, pulling him forward, drawing him back.

Progress was slow. Night came somewhere along the way. Helped by May, he staggered from lamppost to lamppost, dreading the darkness between. People stared, or asked if everything was okay before hurrying on. He tasted rust in his mouth. He spat on the pavement, wiped his hand. It came away black.

"Nearly there," May said, half-holding him around his searing belly.

He looked up and saw houses he recognized, the mailbox that was the nearest one to home. His belly was crawling. He remembered how that mailbox had been a marker of his suffering one day years before when he'd been desperate to get home and pee, and, another time, walking back from school when his shoes were new and tight. Then the pain rocked him, blocking his sight. True pain, hard as flint, soft as drowning. He tried to laugh. That made it worse and better. Bobby knew that this was just the start, an early phase of the contractions.

He couldn't remember how they reached home. There were hands and voices, furious dialings of the phone. Bobby couldn't get upstairs and didn't want to mess up the settee by lying on it. But the grownups insisted, pushed him down, and then someone found a plastic sheet and tucked it under him in between the worst of the waves. He thrashed around, seeing the TV, the mantelpiece, the fibers of the carpet, the light burning at his eyes. I'm not here, he told himself, this isn't real. Then the biggest, darkest wave yet began to reach him.

Wings of pain settled over him. For a moment without time, Bobby dreamed that he was flying.

Bobby awoke in a chilly white room. There was a door, dim figures moving beyond the frosted glass. He was still floating, hardly conscious of his own body. The whiteness of the room hurt his eyes. He closed them, opened them again. Now it was night. Yellow light spilled through the glass. The figures moving beyond had globular heads, no necks, tapering bodies.

One of the figures paused. The door opened. The silence cracked like a broken seal. He could suddenly hear voices, the clatter of trolleys. He was conscious of the hard flatness of the bed against his back, coils of tubing descending into his arm from steel racks. His throat hurt. His mouth tasted faintly of liquorice. The air smelled the way the bathroom cabinet did at home. Of soap and aspirins.

"Your eyes are open. Bobby, can you see?"

The shape at the door blocked the light. It was hard to make it out. Then it stepped forward, and he saw the soft curve of May's cheek, the glimmer of her eye.

"Can you speak?"

"No," he said.

May turned on a light over the bed and sat down with a heavy sigh. He tried to track her by moving his eyes, but after the brief glimpse of her face, all he could see was the dimpled curve of her elbow.

"This is the hospital?"

"Yes. You've grown up."

The hospital. Growing up. They must have taken him here from home. Which meant that it had been a difficult change.

May said, "You're lucky to be alive."

Alive. Yes. Alive. He waited for a rush of some feeling or other—relief, gratitude, achievement, pride. There was nothing, just this white room, the fact of his existence.

"What happens now?" he asked.

"Your parents will want to see you."

"Where are they?"

"At home. It's been *days*, Bobby."

"Then why . . ." the taste of liquorice went gritty in his mouth. He swallowed it back. "Why are you here, May?"

"I'm having tests, Bobby. I just thought I'd look in."

"Thanks."

"There's no need to thank me. I won't forget the times we had."

Times. We. Had. Bobby put the words together, then let them fall apart.

"Yes," he said.

"Well." May stood up.

Now he could see her. Her hair was cut short, sitting oddly where her fat cheeks met her ears. Her breasts hung loose inside a T-shirt. Along with everything else about her, they seemed to have grown, but the nipples had gone flat and she'd given up wearing a bra. She shrugged and spread her arms. He caught a waft of her scent: she needed a wash. It was sickly but somehow appealing, like the old cheese that you found at the back of the fridge and needed to eat right away.

"Sometimes it happens," she said.

"Yes," Bobby said. "The bitter milk."

"No one knows really, do they? Life's a mystery."

Is it? Bobby couldn't be bothered to argue.

"Will you change your name?" he asked. "Move to another town?"

"Maybe. It's a slow process. I'm really not an uncle yet, you know."

Still a child. Bobby gazed at her uncomfortably, trying to see it in her eyes, finding with relief that the child wasn't there.

"What's it like?" May asked.

"What?"

"Being a grownup."

"Does anyone ask a child what it's like to be a child?"

"I suppose not."

His head ached, his voice was fading. He blinked slowly. He didn't want to say more. What else was there to say? He remembered waiting stupidly as his brother Tony sat up in bed watching TV that first morning after he'd grown up. Waiting as though there was an answer. But growing up was just part of the process of living, which he realized now was mostly about dying.

May reached out to touch his face. The fingers lingered for a moment, bringing a strange warmth. Their odor was incredibly strong to Bobby. But it was sweet now, like the waft from the open door of a bakery. It hit the back of his palate and then ricocheted down his spine. He wondered vaguely if he was going to get an erection and killed the thought as best he could; he hated the idea of appearing vulnerable to May. After all, she was still half a child.

"You'd better be going," he said.

May backed away. "You're right." She reached for the handle of the door, clumsily, without looking.

"Goodbye, May," Bobby said.

She stood for a moment in the open doorway. For a moment, the light fell kindly on her face and she was beautiful. Then she stepped back and all her youth was gone.

"Goodbye, Bobby," she said, and glanced down at her wristwatch. "I've got things to do. I really must fly."

GRAVES

Joe Haldeman

Shakespeare said it best, as usual: "To sleep: perchance to dream: ay, there's the rub . . ." as amply demonstrated by the chilling story that follows.

Born in Oklahoma City, Oklahoma, Joe Haldeman received a B.S. in physics and astronomy from the University of Maryland, and did postgraduate work in mathematics and computer science. But his plans for a career in science were cut short by the U.S. Army, which sent him to Vietnam in 1968 as a combat engineer. Seriously wounded in action, Haldeman returned home in 1969 and began to write. He sold his first story to *Galaxy* in 1969, and by 1976 had garnered both the Nebula Award and the Hugo Award for his famous novel *The Forever War*, one of the landmark books of the '70s. He took another Hugo Award in 1977 for his story "Tricentennial," won the Rhysling Award in 1983 for the best science-fiction poem of the year (although usually thought of primarily as a "hard-science" writer, Haldeman is, in fact, also an accomplished poet, and has sold poetry to most of the major professional markets in the genre), and won both the Nebula and the Hugo Award in 1991 for the novella version of "The Hemingway Hoax." His other books include a mainstream novel, *War Year*, the SF novels *Mindbridge*, *All My Sins Remembered*, *There Is No Darkness* (written with his brother, SF writer Jack C. Haldeman II), *Worlds*, *Worlds Apart*, *Buying Time*, and *The Hemingway Hoax*, the "techno-thriller" *Tool of the Trade*, the collections *Infinite Dreams* and *Dealing in Futures*, and, as editor, the anthologies *Study War No More*, *Cosmic Laughter*, and *Nebula Award Stories Seventeen*. His most recent book is the SF novel *Worlds Enough and Time*, and upcoming is a major new mainstream novel, *1969*. He has had stories in our First, Third, and Eighth Annual Collections. Haldeman lives part of the year in Boston, where he teaches writing at M.I.T., and the rest of the year in Florida, where he and his wife, Gay, make their home.

I have this persistent sleep disorder that makes life difficult for me, but still I want to keep it. Boy, do I want to keep it. It goes back twenty years, to Vietnam. To Graves.

Dead bodies turn from bad to worse real fast in the jungle. You've got a few hours before rigor mortis makes them hard to handle, hard to stuff in a bag. By that time, they start to turn greenish, if they started out white or yellow, where you can see the skin. It's mostly bugs by then, usually ants. Then they go to black and start to smell.

They swell up and burst.

You'd think the ants and roaches and beetles and millipedes would make short work of them after that, but they don't. Just when they get to looking and smelling the worst, the bugs sort of lose interest, get fastidious, send out for pizza. Except for the flies. Laying eggs.

The funny thing is, unless some big animal got to it and tore it up, even after a week or so, you've still got something more than a skeleton, even a sort of a face. No eyes, though. Every now and then, we'd get one like that. Not too often, since soldiers usually don't die alone and sit there for that long, but sometimes. We called them "dry ones." Still damp underneath, of course, and inside, but kind of like a sunburned mummy otherwise.

You tell people what you do at Graves Registration, "Graves," and it sounds like about the worst job the army has to offer. It isn't. You just stand there all day and open body bags, figure out which parts maybe belong to which dog tag—not that it's usually that important—sew them up more or less with a big needle, account for all the wallets and jewelry, steal the dope out of their pockets, box them up, seal the casket, do the paperwork. When you have enough boxes, you truck them out to the airfield. The first week maybe is pretty bad. But after a hundred or so, after you get use to the smell and the god-awful feel of them, you get to thinking that opening a body bag is a lot better than ending up inside one. They put Graves in safe places.

Since I'd had a couple years of college, premed, I got some of the more interesting jobs. Captain French, who was the pathologist actually in charge of the outfit, always took me with him out into the field when he had to examine a corpse in situ, which happened only maybe once a month. I got to wear a .45 in a shoulder holster, tough guy. Never fired it, never got shot at, except the one time.

That was a hell of a time. It's funny what gets to you, stays with you.

Usually when we had an in situ, it was a forensic matter, like an officer they suspected had been fragged or otherwise terminated by his own men. We'd take pictures and interview some people, and then Frenchy would bring the stiff back for autopsy, see whether the bullets were American or Vietnamese. (Not that that would be conclusive either way. The Vietcong stole our weapons, and our guys used the North Vietnamese AK-47s, when we could get our hands on them. More reliable than the M-16, and a better cartridge for killing. Both sides proved that over and over.) Usually Frenchy would send a report up to Division, and that would be it. Once he had to testify at a court-martial. The kid was guilty, but just got life. The officer was a real prick.

Anyhow, we got the call to come look at this in situ corpse about five in the afternoon. Frenchy tried to put it off until the next day, since if it got dark, we'd have to spend the night. The guy he was talking to was a major, though, and obviously proud of it, so it was no use arguing. I threw some C's and beer and a couple canteens into two rucksacks that already had blankets and air mattresses tied on the bottom. Box of .45 ammo and a couple hand grenades. Went and got a jeep while Frenchy got his stuff together and made sure Doc Carter was sober enough to count the stiffs as they came in. (Doc Carter was the one supposed to be in charge, but he didn't much care for the work.)

Drove us out to the pad, and lo and behold, there was a chopper waiting, blades idling. Should've started to smell a rat then. We don't get real high priority, and it's not easy to get a chopper to go anywhere so close to sundown. They even helped us stow our gear. Up, up and away.

I never flew enough in helicopters to make it routine. Kontum looked almost pretty in the low sun, golden red. I had to sit between two flame-throwers, though, which didn't make me feel too secure. The door gunner was smoking. The flamethrower tanks were stenciled NO SMOKING.

We went fast and low out toward the mountains to the west. I was hoping we'd wind up at one of the big fire bases up there, figuring I'd sleep better with a few hundred men around. But no such luck. When the chopper started to slow down, the blades' whir deepening to a whuck-whuck-whuck, there was no clearing as far as the eye could see. Thick jungle canopy everywhere. Then a wisp of purple smoke showed us a helicopter-sized hole in the leaves. The pilot brought us down an inch at a time, nicking twigs. I was very much aware of the flamethrowers. If he clipped a large branch, we'd be so much pot roast.

When we touched down, four guys in a big hurry unloaded our gear and the flamethrowers and a couple cases of ammo. They put two wounded guys and one client on board and shooed the helicopter away. Yeah, it would sort of broadcast your position. One of them told us to wait; he'd go get the major.

"I don't like this at all," Frenchy said.

"Me neither," I said. "Let's go home."

"Any outfit that's got a major and two flamethrowers is planning to fight a real war." He pulled his .45 out and looked at it as if he'd never seen one before. "Which end of this do you think the bullets come out of?"

"Shit," I advised, and rummaged through the rucksack for a beer. I gave Frenchy one, and he put it in his side pocket.

A machine gun opened up off to our right. Frenchy and I grabbed the dirt. Three grenade blasts. Somebody yelled for them to cut that out. Guy yelled back he thought he saw something. Machine gun started up again. We tried to get a little lower.

Up walks this old guy, thirties, looking annoyed. The major.

"You men get up. What's wrong with you?" He was playin' games.

Frenchy got up, dusting himself off. We had the only clean fatigues in twenty miles. "Captain French, Graves Registration."

"Oh," he said, not visibly impressed. "Secure your gear and follow me." He drifted off like a mighty ship of the jungle. Frenchy rolled his eyes, and we hoisted our rucksacks and followed him. I wasn't sure whether "secure your gear" meant bring your stuff or leave it behind, but Budweiser could get to be a real collector's item in the boonies, and there were a lot of collectors out here.

We walked too far. I mean a couple hundred yards. That meant they were really spread out thin. I didn't look forward to spending the night. The goddamned machine gun started up again. The major looked annoyed and shouted, "Sergeant, will you please control your men?" and the sergeant told the machine gunner to shut the fuck up, and the machine gunner told the sergeant there was a fuckin' gook out there, and then somebody popped a big one, like a Claymore, and then everybody was shooting every which way. Frenchy and I got real horizontal. I heard a bullet whip by over my head. The major was leaning against a tree, looking bored, shouting, "Cease firing, cease firing!" The shooting dwindled down like popcorn getting done. The major looked over at us and said, "Come on. While there's still light." He led us into a small clearing, elephant grass pretty well trampled down. I guess everybody had had his turn to look at the corpse.

It wasn't a real gruesome body, as bodies go, but it was odd-looking, even for a dry one. Moldy, like someone had dusted flour over it. Naked and probably male, though incomplete: all the soft parts were gone. Tall; one of our Montagnard allies rather than an ethnic Vietnamese. Emaciated, dry skin taut over ribs. Probably old, though it doesn't take long for these people to get old. Lying on its back, mouth wide open, a familiar posture. Empty eye sockets staring skyward. Arms flung out in supplication, loosely, long past rigor mortis.

Teeth chipped and filed to points, probably some Montagnard tribal custom. I'd never seen it before, but we didn't "do" many natives.

Frenchy knelt down and reached for it, then stopped. "Checked for booby traps?"

"No," the major said. "Figure that's your job." Frenchy looked at me with an expression that said it was my job.

Both officers stood back a respectful distance while I felt under the corpse. Sometimes they pull the pin on a hand grenade and slip it under the body so that the body's weight keeps the arming lever in place. You turn it over, and *Tomato Surprise!*

I always worry less about a hand grenade than about the various weird serpents and bugs that might enjoy living underneath a decomposing corpse. Vietnam has its share of snakes and scorpions and megapedes.

I was lucky this time; nothing but maggots. I flicked them off my hand and watched the major turn a little green. People are funny. What does he think is going to happen to him when he dies? Everything has to eat. And he was sure as hell going to die if he didn't start keeping his head down. I remember that thought, but didn't think of it then as a prophecy.

They came over. "What do you make of it, Doctor?"

"I don't think we can cure him." Frenchy was getting annoyed at this cherry bomb. "What else do you want to know?"

"Isn't it a little . . . *odd* to find something like this in the middle of nowhere?"

"Naw. Country's full of corpses." He knelt down and studied the face, wiggling the head by its chin. "We keep it up, you'll be able to walk from the Mekong to the DMZ without stepping on anything but corpses."

"But he's been castrated!"

"Birds." He toed the body over, busy white crawlers running from the light. "Just some old geezer who walked out into the woods naked and fell over dead. Could happen back in the World. Old people do funny things."

"I thought maybe he'd been tortured by the VC or something."

"God knows. It could happen." The body eased back into its original position with a creepy creaking sound, like leather. Its mouth had closed halfway. "If you want to put 'evidence of VC torture' in your report, your body count, I'll initial it."

"What do you mean by that, Captain?"

"Exactly what I said." He kept staring at the major while he flipped a cigarette into his mouth and fired it up. Nonfilter Camels; you'd think a guy who worked with corpses all day long would be less anxious to turn into one. "I'm just trying to get along."

"You believe I want you to falsify—"

Now, "falsify" is a strange word for a last word. The enemy had set up a heavy machine gun on the other side of the clearing, and we were the closest targets. A round struck the major in the small of his back, we found on later examination. At the time, it was just an explosion of blood and guts, and he went down with his legs flopping every which way, barfing, then loud death rattle. Frenchy was on the ground in a ball, holding his left hand, going, "Shit shit shit." He'd lost the last joint of his little finger. Painful, but not serious enough, as it turned out, to get him back to the World.

I myself was horizontal and aspiring to be subterranean. I managed to get my pistol out and cocked, but realized I didn't want to do anything that might draw attention to us. The machine gun was spraying back and forth over us at about knee height. Maybe they couldn't see us; maybe they thought we were dead. I was scared shitless.

"Frenchy," I stage-whispered, "we've got to get outa here." He was trying to wrap his finger up in a standard first-aid-pack gauze bandage, much too large. "Get back to the trees."

"After you, asshole. We wouldn't get halfway." He worked his pistol out of the holster, but couldn't cock it, his left hand clamping the bandage and slippery with blood. I armed it for him and handed it back. "These are going to do a hell of a lot of good. How are you with grenades?"

"Shit. How you think I wound up in Graves?" In basic training, they'd put me on KP whenever they went out for live grenade practice. In school, I was always the last person when they chose up sides for baseball, for the same reason—though, to my knowledge, a baseball wouldn't kill you if you couldn't throw far enough. "I couldn't get one halfway there." The tree line was about sixty yards away.

"Neither could I, with this hand." He was a lefty.

Behind us came the "poink" sound of a sixty-millimeter mortar, and in a couple of seconds, there was a gray-smoke explosion between us and the tree line. The machine gun stopped, and somebody behind us yelled, "Add twenty!"

At the tree line, we could hear some shouting in Vietnamese, and a clanking of metal. "They're gonna bug out," Frenchy said. "Let's di-di."

We got up and ran, and somebody did fire a couple of bursts at us, probably an AK-47, but he missed, and then there were a series of poinks and a series of explosions pretty close to where the gun had been.

We rushed back to the LZ and found the command group, about the time the firing started up again. There was a first lieutenant in charge, and when things slowed down enough for us to tell him what had happened to the major, he expressed neither surprise nor grief. The man had been an observer from Battalion, and had assumed command when their captain was killed that morning. He'd take our word for it that the guy was dead—that was one thing we were trained observers in—and not send a squad out for him until the fighting had died down and it was light again.

We inherited the major's hole, which was nice and deep, and in his rucksack found a dozen cans and jars of real food and a flask of scotch. So, as the battle raged through the night, we munched pâté on Ritz crackers, pickled herring in sour-cream sauce, little Polish sausages on party rye with real French mustard. We drank all the scotch and saved the beer for breakfast.

For hours the lieutenant called in for artillery and air support, but to no avail. Later we found out that the enemy had launched coordinated attacks on all the local airfields and Special Forces camps, and every camp that held POWs. We were much lower priority.

Then, about three in the morning, Snoopy came over. Snoopy was a big C-130 cargo plane that carried nothing but ammunition and Gatling guns; they said it could fly over a football field and put a round into every square inch. Anyhow, it saturated the perimeter with fire, and the enemy stopped shooting. Frenchy and I went to sleep.

At first light, we went out to help round up the KIAs. There were only four dead, counting the major, but the major was an astounding sight, at least in context.

He looked sort of like a cadaver left over from a teaching autopsy. His shirt had been opened and his pants pulled down to his thighs, and the entire thoracic and abdominal cavities had been ripped open and emptied of everything soft, everything from esophagus to testicles, rib cage like blood-streaked fingers sticking rigid out of sagging skin, and there wasn't a sign of any of the guts anywhere, just a lot of dried blood.

Nobody had heard anything. There was a machine-gun position not twenty yards away, and they'd been straining their ears all night. All they'd heard was flies.

Maybe an animal feeding very quietly. The body hadn't been opened with a scalpel or a knife; the skin had been torn by teeth or claws—but seemingly systematically, throat to balls.

And the dry one was gone. Him with the pointed teeth.

There is one rational explanation. Modern warfare is partly mindfuck, and we aren't the only ones who do it, dropping unlucky cards, invoking magic and superstition. The Vietnamese knew how squeamish Americans were, and would mutilate bodies in clever ways. They could also move very quietly. The dry one? They might have spirited him away just to fuck with us. Show what they could do under our noses.

And as for the dry one's odd mummified appearance, the mold, there might be an explanation. I found out that the Montagnards in that area don't bury their dead; they put them in a coffin made from a hollowed-out log and leave them aboveground. So maybe he was just the victim of a grave robber. I thought the nearest village was miles away, like twenty miles, but I could have been wrong. Or the body could have been carried that distance for some obscure purpose—maybe the VC set it out on the trail to make the Americans stop in a good place to be ambushed.

That's probably it. But for twenty years now, several nights a week, I wake up sweating with a terrible image in my mind. I've gone out with a flashlight, and there it is, the dry one, scooping steaming entrails from the major's body, tearing them with its sharp teeth, staring into my light with black empty sockets, unconcerned. I reach for my pistol, and it's never there. The creature stands up, shiny with blood, and takes a step toward me—for a year or so, that was it; I would wake up. Then it was two steps, and then three. After twenty years it has covered half the distance and its dripping hands are raising from its sides.

The doctor gives me tranquilizers. I don't take them. They might help me stay asleep.

THE GLOWING CLOUD

Steven Utley

Steven Utley's fiction has appeared in *The Magazine of Fantasy & Science Fiction*, *Universe*, *Galaxy*, *Amazing*, *Vertex*, *Stellar*, *Shayol*, and elsewhere. He was one of the best-known new writers of the '70s, both for his solo work and for some strong work in collaboration with fellow Texan Howard Waldrop, but fell silent at the end of the decade and wasn't seen in print again for more than ten years. In the last few years he's made a strong comeback, though, becoming a frequent contributor to *Asimov's Science Fiction* magazine, as well as selling again to *The Magazine of Fantasy & Science Fiction* and elsewhere. In 1992 alone, Utley published at least three other stories that would have been considered good enough for inclusion in this anthology in another year—in *addition* to the vivid and suspenseful novella that follows. In it, Utley takes us to the troubled island of Martinique in 1902, in company with a somewhat reluctant time traveler on a desperate mission, with the fate of history itself in the balance—a mission that he must rush to complete before he is destroyed by one of the greatest natural disasters of all time: the awesome eruption of Mount Pelée on the morning of May 8th, 1902 . . .

Steven Utley is the coeditor, with Geo. W. Proctor , of the anthology *Lone Star Universe*, the first—and possibly the only—anthology of SF stories by Texans. Utley lives in Austin, Texas.

He could see no moon, no stars. The sky was black where it curved to meet the western horizon, and to the east it was roiling and opaque and glowed red about the summit of a burning mountain. He was descending to a landing at a point on the slope well below the crater but overlooking the narrow crescent of illumination that defined the town.

This part felt like a dream. He could feel the tingling, not-unpleasant burn of the drug behind his eyes and in his fingertips and teeth. His saliva tasted metallic. It's the drug, he told himself, a hallucination induced by the drug, but he had never quite convinced himself of this on any previous occasion, and couldn't now. He came down slowly, at a shallow angle. He could see not only what he reasonably would have expected to see from a great height at night, but also to a great depth. He saw, imagined, what nobody had ever seen: the planet in cross-section, with the green, unsubmerged peaks of the Windward and Leeward islands stretching across the Caribbean's blue, map-flat expanse from Puerto Rico to a Rand-McNally–colored South America complete with place names. There were latitude and longitude lines as well. Two of these intersected several kilometers west of his position, and in one corner of the intersection was a neat notation, *14°45', 61°15'*. East of the islands, the world had been sawn in half. Its mechanisms were exposed, rendered with textbook definition and shading from the blue-black of the outermost layer of atmosphere to the yellow-white of the nickel-iron core. The scale was skewed, emphasizing the massive conical bases of the Windwards, particularly that of the island to which he was being drawn. To the east of the archipelago, the edge of one plate of oceanic crust slipped under another. They ground and scraped and warmed, and masses of molten stuff the size of major planetoids burned their way up through the island's, so to speak, basement and went shooting out through the, so to speak, roof. The magma beneath the crust was done in incandescent yellow but darkened through streaky orange to primary red as it made its way to the surface. He thought the view as impressive now as when he had first seen it, years before, in school, in a geo holo.

Adding to the dreaminess was a time-lapse effect. Medlin sank through a leafy canopy, disturbing it no more than a moonbeam, and alighted on firm ground. Trees cut off his view of the town. All he could see of the volcano now was a red-tinged dark sky. He could see it better, in fact, than he could see his own nimbused hand. Yet, even as he watched, the sky lightened, pinkish-brown cumulous masses of volcanic smoke raced across the sky, and shafts of sunlight speared down through gaps in the treetops. He was standing in the middle of an unpaved road in the heart of a tropical forest.

As he solidified, he became aware of other, less pleasant details.

The air was full of white specks that looked like snowflakes but stung like nettles when they hit bare skin. He took a breath, and the moisture in his mouth evaporated. A second breath made the lining of his throat sear and pucker. A paroxysm of coughing bent him double, and frightening thoughts filled his head.

Perhaps he had mistimed his arrival.

Perhaps he didn't have the better part of a week after all.

Perhaps he had arrived instead at the climactic moment.

But he did not shrivel, did not burst and stew in his own juices, did not become a charcoal mannequin. He lived, and felt as though he were coughing himself inside out, and reached with one hand to steady himself against a huge tree garlanded with lianas and orchids. The bole was warm to his fingertips, almost hot. He pulled a handkerchief from his pocket and covered his mouth and nose. That made breathing easier—a little easier.

Watery-eyed and puffy-lidded, he rested against the tree, and at almost the same moment, he realized two things: one, he was not alone; two, Ranke was not present.

The road was barely more than a trail of wheel ruts through the jungle. It branched above a fast, swollen creek, one fork veering to his left, the other plunging straight down the creek bank into water full of uprooted trees and other vegetation. Coming off the creek was a powerful smell of rotten eggs and dead animals. Strung in a ragged line beside it were two hundred men, women, and children. They were staring gloomily at the water. Medlin immediately knew them for what they were. He had seen their like thirty-six hours before, subjective time, in the Low Countries in 1940. As a consequence of that experience, he was convinced that it was impossible to mistake even small numbers of refugees for any other group one might encounter anywhere. These were, with a single exception, dark-skinned people. The men wore straw hats, loose trousers, and shirts. The women wore madras scarves, white blouses, long skirts. They carried little more than their infants.

The exception among them was a late-middle-aged white man dressed in a cassock. He was the only one wearing shoes. He started so violently when he noticed Medlin that Medlin thought the priest must somehow have detected the luminous vapor that clung to him. His alarm did not entirely fade as the man strode forward with a belligerent expression on his face: even as reason asserted itself—the envelope of charged particles which Medlin saw as a nimbus about himself was as imperceptible as water vapor to denizens—he retreated two steps backward and thrust his hand into his coat pocket to feel the butt of the revolver there. The priest had enormous ropey hands and looked very fit for his age. Behind his wire-rimmed glasses was the fixed squint of someone who had spent a great many daylight hours hatless in the sun. He slightly knitted the muscles between his thick eyebrows, and the squint transformed into a scowl that told Medlin, here is a clergyman used to getting his way with the laity. The priest said, in snappish French, "Do not waste your time trying to persuade us to return! We are not going back!"

Behind him, several of the men put on scowls of their own. Medlin mustered all the sunny good nature he had in him at the moment and said, "I beg your pardon, Father. I have no intention of persuading you to go back. In fact, I have no idea what you are talking about."

The priest looked past him in obvious expectation of seeing others. Finding no one, he relaxed his expression somewhat.

"With that accent," he said, "you are a foreigner."

"I am an American traveler."

"Ah! An American!" The priest half-turned for a moment to give the refugees a reassuring smile and nod. The men's scowls yielded to the same disconsolate looks as before. "Americans are the only other people on this island who have shown any good sense so far! Accept my most sincere apologies. I am Father Hayot. When I saw you, I thought that the governor must have sent you after us."

"I myself have never met the governor." One played these things by ear.

Father Hayot's face wrinkled into a relief-map of righteous anger. Up close, he was even more formidable. He had eyes like musketballs. "My parishioners and I are from Le Prêcheur, a village to the north. Yesterday, while Governor Mouttet was safe in his residency in Fort-de-France, where the mountain cannot possibly harm him, *we* were fleeing for our lives. The lava destroyed everything, homes, crops—even the statue of the Virgin. Then, when we reached St. Pierre, the governor telegraphed the military commandant to confine us to the town hall compound, as though we were criminals! We would be there even now if I had not persuaded the guard to let us go."

Medlin thought it generally good policy to listen sympathetically to denizens, so he said, "But why would the governor have you confined?"

"He is too concerned with elections. He must feel a few poor refugees will cause a panic that will drive people from the polls!"

The volcano made a sound like something clearing its throat. Medlin would not have imagined it possible for the villagers to look any unhappier than they did already. They surprised him.

"They believe the mountain is the chimney of a gigantic blacksmith shop—God's or the Devil's, they are unsure." Father Hayot's expression was both patronizing and exasperated. "I have been with them for many years now, and still, *still*, I cannot make them understand the vital difference between Christian faith and paganistic belief."

Medlin had never understood the difference himself, but did not say so. Instead, he asked, "Where does this trail lead?"

"Over the ridge to Morne Rouge if you follow it east. Straight to the coast road if you go west." Suspicion suddenly clouded the priest's face again. "Do you mean to say that you do not know where you are?"

Medlin put on a rueful smile. "I know that I am standing next to a live volcano. Obviously, I *am* lost. I am not even sure what day it is."

Dismayed but disarmed, the priest clucked reproachfully. "Today is Saturday."

Five days, Medlin thought, relieved. Five whole days and nights.

"If you have been lost out here on the mountainside," Father Hayot went on, "you are indeed most fortunate to be alive and unharmed. This is dangerous country even under normal conditions. Serpents. Wild pigs." He lowered his voice, and there was a fresh element of bitterness in it. "Sometimes I think there are no true Christians here in this countryside. People here may have a priest, may say prayers to the Virgin, but in their hearts they believe in magic and the world of ghosts. They listen to the *quimboi-seurs*—the wizards, who kill whomever they meet and use human bones in their evil work. You must be very careful whom you meet in the jungle."

"I have a companion who seems to be lost, too. Perhaps you have seen him. He is a white man."

"We have passed few people at all since we left the coast road. Probably your lost companion has gone on to St. Pierre. But, were I you, I do not think I would follow him there. The situation has become very bad since just yesterday morning. No one knows what to do. Worse, no one seems to care. My parishioners want to return to their homes, whatever is left of them, but we are cut off by the torrent. The river is impassable all the way to the sea. I am trying to convince them to let me lead them inland. There is a convent at Morne Rouge where they can find shelter. You should come with us."

Medlin made himself look as though he were mulling over the suggestion. He actually was pondering his next move, but it involved finding Ranke and getting on with the business at hand, not running from volcanoes. Ranke's absence was nothing to get too alarmed about, yet. He could simply be late. Passengers sometimes got momentarily misplaced. Experienced travelers and passengers sometimes arrived not even approximately simultaneously. More disturbing than Ranke's missing a rendezvous by minutes or hours was the idea of his missing it by kilometers. He could have arrived on the opposite side of the island, or far out to sea. Damn all islands anyway. He could have come down close to the heart of the volcano's red glow. Not that it had to be anything melodramatic. He could have landed right on target, right on schedule, but clumsily, and broken his neck.

Medlin almost wished that, then admonished himself. Ought to have offered Ranke a hand to hold, he thought, and immediately recoiled from the idea. Holding hands was not essential, and it was no guarantee of anything, either. Some passengers found it reassuring. There was nothing travelers wanted more than calm passengers, but Christ-all-bleeding-mighty, *Ranke*. Not one to take anybody's hand, unless maybe to break a finger. His problem—Medlin's problem, now—was not that he needed reassurance or that he was even afraid of time-travel, but that he was no good at it.

Still, as long as he had stood close to Medlin, within the circle marked on the floor with strips of duct tape, he should have gone wherever Medlin went. Only he hadn't, and Medlin would eventually have to explain why not. It could go very badly indeed if the guy stayed lost. "Agent Ranke and I disliked each other," Medlin could hear himself explaining, "and it was unpleasant for us to stand close together, so perhaps he unconsciously pushed himself away at a crucial moment," and, "Perhaps," he could hear someone on the board of inquiry retorting, "unconsciously or otherwise, you may have pushed Agent Ranke away," and "Well," he could hear himself concluding lamely, "Agent Ranke was there one moment and not there the next."

Damn damn damn damn damn damn *damn*.

And then there was Garrick. At least the fugitive was near, or traces of her, anyway, scattered on the thick midday air, perceptible but ungraspable. Ranke was much, much better at this stuff. What for Ranke would have been a big neon arrow pointing directly toward Garrick was a film of cobwebs to Medlin.

It was enough to fill Medlin with a glum resolve. He said, "Thank you for your concern, Father, but I must locate my companion. We have important business in St. Pierre."

Father Hayot used his lips to make an soft, unpleasant, unpriestly sound, disgusted and dismissive. "Everyone," he growled, "has *important business* in that wicked place. Little Paris of the West Indies. Little Paris! A more appropriate name would be Little Sodom, or Little Gomorrah, especially if the lava should destroy it! Judgment is going to fall on those Pierrotins—a judgment of fire for their sinfulness and stupidity! The attitude among them is that my parishioners are foolish country people, and that Americans are cowards. Most of your countrymen have already sailed away."

"Still, I must go there."

"Then may God go with you, my son."

Father Hayot regarded him with unanticipated kindliness as he said that, and Medlin marveled at his own luck in being the one thing on Earth today, an American, for which this cantankerous priest evidently had positive feelings. He said, "Good luck to you as well, Father," and started walking away. The refugees hardly bothered looking at him as he passed.

"There is no luck," the priest called after him, "there is only God's mercy. And God's mercy is bigger than any mountain."

Medlin didn't look back, but gave a friendly wave, as though taking the priest's word for it. As soon as the villagers were out of sight around the bend in the road, he paused, shakily took a pint flask of distilled water from the left pocket of his coat, and drank half. First meetings with denizens always left him sweating and dry-mouthed.

He came eventually to the edge of the jungle. Beyond the trees was a field of cane stubble and, beyond that, other fields ranked in tiers extending all the way down to the sea, three or four miles away. In some of the fields were rippling stands of cane and little moving specks that were canecutters hard at their work. Off to the south lay the town, a quarter-moon by day as well as by night, its outline dictated by the natural amphitheater in which it lay. Medlin walked out from under the trees and went some distance before he thought to turn and take a look at the volcano.

He had to crane his head back to see it. Half-obscured by haze, the volcano's rocky collar was surely some distance away, and yet the steep green slope beneath the crater seemed to loom directly above him. It was as though a jungle had been stood on end and a great sooty smoky fire lighted at the higher end. No open sky was visible to the north; the smoke rolled away to infinity. The sight was hypnotic. He turned his back on it with no small effort of will and struck out along the margin of the cane stubble.

He headed south when he reached the coast road. To his right, the land sloped down into a calm sea. On his left, the road was edged with tropical trees. Set among them at intervals were stone crucifixes and shrines dedicated to the Virgin. On a slight rise near the northern point of the crescent, he paused for a first good look at his destination. While he surveyed the town, he took another drink from his flask, almost draining it, and ate his one nutrition bar, a dense, chewy foodstick a little larger than his thumb.

Between the crescent's horns, the waterfront stretched along a thin, scalloped beach of black sand. Crowded together along its entire length were wharves, warehouses, and, undoubtedly, establishments for the entertainment of sailors. A main thoroughfare ran the length of the crescent, about a mile. Numerous intersecting streets crept up from the waterfront to the base of the wooded slope behind the town, a distance of a quarter of a mile. There were one-storied buildings with tin awnings behind the quayside, and blocks of two-, even three-storied buildings. Most of the substantial-looking structures had walls of yellow stone and tiled roofs; the ash-coated tiles were faded pink. Here and there was something more impressive. Medlin saw a lighthouse, a twin-towered cathedral, and what appeared to be a fort or prison. But for the jungle and the volcano, he felt that he could have been looking at any small French Mediterranean seaport.

The town seemed peaceful to the point of stultification. Everyone in it could have been dead already, suffocated by ash. Then he saw distant figures unhurriedly moving about in the streets, comporting themselves as though there were not an active volcano in the world. At the water's edge, on a broad, sloping square dominated by the lighthouse, roustabouts worked like tiny ants. The roadstead was full of ships. The island shelved off at such a steep angle that even big ships were able to anchor close to shore.

On the outskirts of town, soldiers were dragging dead animals from a cart and flinging them into a pit beside the road. Mounds of freshly turned dirt lined both sides of the road; this activity had been going on for some time. Only the soldiers seemed remotely interested in their work, and that only to the point of quite clearly disliking it. Mass animal burials could have been the commonest sight on the island for all the attention paid by civilian passersby.

Medlin entered the town behind a tall black woman who strode along purposefully with a wooden tray of fruits and vegetables balanced on her head. He estimated that she could not have been carrying much under sixty pounds. Watching the play of muscles in her dusky calves made him feel flabby. Trotting along sometimes in front and sometimes beside or behind the woman was a miniature edition of her, with a miniature edition of her burden.

The streets were filled with black, brown, and yellow people, with a sprinkling of white. The falling ash muffled every sound, and voices blended together into a soft background burble. The predominant speech was, to Medlin's ear, like French come through Africa.

It quickly became obvious to him that the situation was not only as bad as Father Hayot had said, but becoming steadily worse. Groups of people stood about who seemed to have no place to go, no idea of what to do. These, too, had that unmistakable look of refugees; the authorities must have stopped confining them, but had not decided as yet what else to do with them. Livestock wandered loose. They seemed to be dropping dead faster than the soldiers could haul away the carcasses. Asphyxiated birds lay everywhere. The fountains were fouled with black mud.

Yet commerce was gamely trying to flourish. Ash bedraggled flowers in the vendor's stalls and made foodstuffs look grayish and unappetizing. The variety was more impressive than either the quality or the quantities—there were bananas, oranges, pineapples, tomatoes, breadfruit, sapodillas. Apart from the vendors' manifest irritation at continually having to brush grit from their wares, few people evidenced much concern about the volcano. Many did not even seem interested. Everyone joked and haggled, harangued and gossiped.

He rested on a stone bench under the mango and tamarind trees edging the lighthouse square. Shipping brokers, all of them Caucasian, stood about conversing among themselves while black and brown roustabouts manhandled casks and hogsheads onto lighter barges and yelled to one another in their mutant-French creole. Unmindful of hazards, children chased one another among the barrels. The scene was surreal: sweating workers, tropical trees, blistering pseudo-snowflakes swirling in the air. The concentration of rum, sugar, fruit-tree, and waterfront aromas almost masked the stench of sulphur.

Garrick, too, was on the heavy air. She fluctuated between the almost-there and the almost-not-there. Now she was just beyond touch, just out of sight and hearing, and now she was across the world, on the moon, passing the orbit of Neptune. She was an object removed from its proper matrix, like Medlin, anomalous, leaving, wherever she went, a trail of disturbance like gossamer, like insects' breathing, like prickles of sensation in a long-amputated limb. Medlin could sense the achronicity but could not follow the trail. His forte was exploiting weak spots in time. Garrick was an itch he could not locate.

He was very hungry as well. His empty stomach seemed to be devouring itself. He sucked the last few drops of distilled water from his canteen and patted the pockets of his coat in the silly hope that he had somehow overlooked a second foodstick until now. There were only the revolver and fake identity papers. If currency had been issued, Ranke had it. Probably it had not been issued at all. No one had thought or, rather, Thomas, the agency chief, had not figured, that Medlin would have to stay long enough to need money. Thomas' credo was "Get in, get it done, get out."

He fantasized about using the revolver to hold up women carrying trays of fruits and vegetables on their heads, then reminded himself he had gone without food or water for two days in Trincomalee that time. Ranke will show up any second now, he thought. We'll grab Garrick and get the hell out of here before sundown.

He waited. The longshoremen went on loading cargo onto lighters, and the children kept playing among the barrels and hogsheads. A cool breeze blew across the square, bringing some relief from heat and bad smells. No one paid any attention to Medlin. He was just a lover of magnificent sunsets, or a drunk. By sundown, the shipping brokers and the laborers and most of the children had gone. The sky stayed red over the volcano, and the streets neither cleared nor quietened. The day's commerce was simply replaced by the evening's.

Medlin ground his fist into his palm and stood up. He did not want to move, but the last place he wanted to stay, besides *here* in general, was *here* in particular, on the waterfront at night on a Saturday. No burning mountain or ashfall was going to discourage people in a place like this from getting themselves roughed up, possibly robbed, possibly rubbed out.

He took a step away from the bench and started to fall. The ground was not where his foot expected it. He went down hard on one knee and thought for a second that he had stepped into an unseen hole. But the ground itself was moving. The bench collapsed behind him—it was a simple stone slab set on uprights—and from the direction of the landing came a sound like the grinding of millstones. He heard a child's shrill, brief scream.

Casks and hogsheads were rolling down the slope and piling up at the water's edge. In the dim light, two or three children ran past him, flat-out, in terror. Their short, harsh breaths were like sobs.

He saw what had happened: a toppling barrel had crushed a small boy. The child was so skinny, so shabbily dressed, that he looked like a small pile of sticks and rags on the paving stones. Amazingly, he hadn't been instantly killed—Medlin, as he started to kneel, heard a wheeze and a bubbling exhalation above the slosh of waves and the human commotion all along the waterfront. He thought better of kneeling and looked around anxiously. It was against regulations to call undue attention to oneself or to become involved with denizens any more than was essential to the completion of a mission. During the past week, subjective time, he had seen enough in Belgium to think himself inured to the sight of the dead. He knew that everyone in this town was going to die. But no one had told him there would be mashed children beforehand.

Human figures were running back and forth on the square above the jumble at the water's edge. Voices filled the night. He heard shrieks of fright, shrieks of laughter, as if, he thought, suddenly enraged, everybody in town were saying, To think that such a little shake really frightened us! A uniformed white man ran toward him. Medlin could not tell by the flickering light of the man's torch whether he was a policeman or a military officer, but then he turned and bawled out an order, and five or six colonial soldiers appeared. One of them carried a stretcher fashioned from poles and canvas sacking.

"Quickly, quickly," the officer gasped. The injured boy wheezed and exhaled wetly. He did not inhale again. The officer pushed aside the soldier with the stretcher and knelt, checked for a pulse, rose shaking his head. He told two of his men to take the body away and the rest to search for other possible victims in the wreckage at the water's edge. The soldiers scattered across the landing.

"It is really too bad," the officer said to Medlin, "but these little black wharf children are as thick as rats. I wonder that more of them are not hurt or killed every day." He had a roman nose of fabulous dimension. Its shadow hid his mouth as he spoke. "Did you see the accident, Monsieur?"

"No. I only heard a scream."

"You are—"

"An American."

"You are from the embassy, or one of the ships in the harbor?"

Medlin said, "Yes," as though he were actually answering the question.

"Then I must advise you to return. That tremor has caused more than the death of this child tonight."

"Just one damned thing after another."

"Quite so, Monsieur. It is terrible." The officer touched the bill of his cap with a forefinger and went to rejoin his men.

Medlin turned and lost himself in the crowd. He let it carry him where it would. Some portion of it carried him straight onto a street filled with raucousness and ripe smells. There were many sailors. They walked in small groups in the middle of the street—there was no horse or wheel traffic here, and the sidewalks, barely wide enough to deserve that name, had accordingly been reserved as seating or standing space for those too google-eyed to walk. Every doorway on both sides of the street was an illumined hole that spewed human noises, inarticulate cries and shouts, eruptions of laughter and singing, and a continuous rumbling thunder of conversation. Moving remoralike in the wake or on the flank of this or that group of men, trying to look as though he belonged, Medlin heard snatches of French, the local creole, English, Dutch, Italian, Spanish, Portuguese, other languages he could not begin to identify. On second-floor balconies above the doorways more or less dark-skinned women stood leaning on iron railings or sat on cane chairs. A few gazed down upon the promenade with grave humor in their expressions. One woman gave Medlin an especially unnerving look, not of cool, professional invitation but of contemptuous expectation, not daring him to come up to see her sometime but merely holding him to the low standard of male behavior of her experience. She gripped the railing as if she could tear it apart with her hands. Her expression became doubly contemptuous when she realized that he was not going to oblige her. It gave him the creeps. Then she shifted her attention to someone else in the street. It struck Medlin first that her presentation could not net her very many customers, and next that she might only be waiting for one more. She was a knife waiting to fly out of its sheath at somebody.

Most of the women were exuberant and lascivious. They called down to the sailors, issued impossible ribald challenges, and the least-inhibited among them pantomimed fellatio or parted their robes to expose their breasts. There were breasts of every size, shape, and shade. The sailors roared approval and roared answers to the challenges and trooped indoors, roaring still.

Not all propositions were made from balconies. Medlin suddenly found his path blocked by an ancient, gnomish woman whose head barely came to his breastbone. She had a face as rough as a coconut and a grip like a blacksmith's. With her bony hand tight on his elbow, she began tugging him in the direction of one of the buildings. As she tugged, she spoke to him so fast that he did not think he caught as much as one word in three.

Still, her meaning was clear. He saw now that he was being drawn toward not a doorway but the narrow alley between two buildings. Just around the corner, the woman seemed to be saying, and up the stairs, I have the most beautiful young girl for you. Medlin planted his feet on the cobblestones and tried to jerk his elbow free. The woman weighed nothing. He lifted her off the ground when he moved his arm, but he could not shake her loose. Even as he swung her around she continued to babble at him. A girl for you,

Monsieur, just this way, come, see, you will like her very much. He felt a little stir of panic, cursed aloud, and broke away with a blow to the woman's wrist. She gave a cry and skipped away shaking her hand in the air as though it had caught fire. She did no more, however, than glare at him for a few seconds while she rubbed her wrist; then she was looking around for the next customer.

Next victim is more like it, Medlin thought as he moved on. No light fell in the alley toward which she had pulled him. It was a perfect place to get one's skull bashed in.

The crowd on what he was starting to think of as the Rue Syphilis sometimes flowed smoothly and swiftly, sometimes lurched along as though pulled by the ambulatory drunks in its ranks. It expanded and contracted, broke apart, reformed, spun off men through the beckoning doorways, drew them out when they had been depleted. Then, abruptly, the saloons and brothels were behind him, and, no less abruptly, the character of the crowd changed. The sailors and other commerce-minded individuals blew away like chaff. In their place were disoriented-looking townspeople.

Medlin's knee hurt. He found a place where he could sit, rest, watch, and not get tripped over by people as they ran about. After a while, he realized that many of them seemed to be moving with a purpose now. Thinking that perhaps they knew something he didn't, he went with them. They quietened as they moved farther from the waterfront. With their footfalls muffled by ash, they walked, Medlin among them, like phantoms through the chaos of winding, unlevel streets, until they reached the gate of a cemetery. Beyond the graveyard was the twin-towered cathedral he had noticed that afternoon, and, surrounding this, a great, dense, milling mob of men, women, and children. They were very quiet—extraordinarily, eerily quiet, he thought. Uniformed men, again, either policeman or soldiers, tried to clear the area. Probably they had been at it for some time, but the crowd ignored them. Abruptly, the uniformed men gave up on persuasion and began to shove. The crowd answered with a surly collective complaint as it was prodded and pushed. For all of the commotion, nobody seemed to go anywhere. The crowd resisted efforts to get it to move through the expedient of pretending to move, withdrawing at right angles to the direction of any concerted drive made by its would-be herders, closing in behind them. Medlin had seen— only on the real-time news, of course—crowds and crowd-managers lose patience with each other, and he thought, Just what I *need*, to get caught in a riot. But there was no riot. Some faces were petulant. That was all. No one seemed angry or even frightened, and this, Medlin reflected, amazed, with the big spark-spitter itself just to the north, looking very much indeed like God's chimney or the Devil's whirlpool bath. Perhaps the big statue of the Virgin that stood before the cathedral was exerting its pacifistic effect on everyone.

Whatever she was doing and however good she was, he did not believe that she could keep it up indefinitely. He had a sudden sense of tectonic activity kilometers below. He could feel it through the soles of his shoes.

Again he saw, or imagined, cold, heavy Atlantic Ocean bottom being sub-
ducted by Caribbean Sea bottom, becoming less cold, less heavy, rising
under pressure and full of gas through weak spots in overlying rock, up into
the back of the island's throat. Some bubble broke there, like a god's belch.
Shutters rattled nearby. An invisible hand gave him a shove. He waited for
something more, and all around him the people stirred, nervous as antelope.
He began to walk, with a deliberation dictated by his knee. He found an
arched doorway where he would not get caught in a stampede if there was
going to be one. He sagged against the wall and waited.

Some minutes later, as he catalogued his personal miseries, a thick, black
cloud settled. It got everyone's attention immediately, like an eyeful of pep-
per. Blinded and choking, Medlin staggered and collided with a wall. People
blundered by, tripping, screaming. Animals bleated their anguish. Somebody
stepped all over him. He tried to get out of the way, was engulfed in bodies,
found himself barely able to breathe or keep his feet on the ground. The
mob came to a shuddering, uncoordinated halt as it piled around him. The
doorway was a *cul-de-sac*. The human mass encasing Medlin collapsed onto
itself as first somebody went down and then everybody else fell. Medlin
kicked free of arms and legs, found himself trapped in a corner. He curled
into a ball, screwed his eyes tightly shut, and pressed his handkerchief hard
against his face. The fumes still reached him. *I'm going to die here.*

But he didn't die there. Ten minutes later, or an hour—he couldn't guess
how long—he heard bells toll midnight and looked up with smarting eyes.
The terrible cloud was dissipating. He made out indistinct moving figures,
then, blurrily, the walls of the surrounding buildings. By the time his vision
cleared, the mob had evaporated like the cloud, leaving the ground covered
with debris. Not far from him lay a woman. Everything about her was gray
with ash, her skin and clothing, her open eyes.

Coughing and aching, he left her there.

He was resting on a wooden bench set under a tin awning when the
volcano showed that it was not finished for the night. There was a brilliant
flash; a split-second later, the sound of a tremendous explosion. Purple
lightning strobes defined a vast, airborne pile of soot above the summit, and
made the world glow a lurid magenta. Out of the cloud spun and tumbled
bits of junk like cut-rate meteors, with masses of sparks at their heads and
streamers of smoke out behind. These pyrotechnics were accompanied by a
rising, falling, unending roar.

From somewhere behind him came the sound of laughter.

The streets were filling with people again. Still more people were pushing
back the shutters from upstairs bedroom windows and leaning out to watch
the fireworks. They pointed and waved torches and whooped and oohed.

First Garrick goes crazy, Medlin thought, now everyone in the French
West Indies. . . .

There was a pattering like hail on the awning. Someone in the street let
out a howl of surprise and pain. The howl became a chorus, and the crowd
vanished. Bedroom shutters slammed closed.

The precipitate was pumice. Most of the particles were very small, no bigger than grains of sand, but there were fragments as big as golf balls in the gritty drizzle. They bounced and smoked on the pavement and clacked deafeningly on the tin awning.

The street was empty when the fall let up about a quarter of an hour later. The town seemed to have lost consciousness. Medlin found more substantial shelter, in another arched doorway, and crouched there feeling sorry for himself, wondering what the hell else he was supposed to do, and waiting for daylight. He would have prayed for it had he known how.

He dozed off in a squatting position. When he awoke, his bruised knee was stiff and throbbing. As he hauled himself up, two men strolled by in the street. They looked like any other two Pierrotins he had seen till now, save for the faint, luminous vapor that clung to them.

Nothing had been said to him about other travelers.

It was useless hiding—the two men noticed Medlin's nimbus at once; in the shadows beneath the doorway, he must have looked equally spooklike to them—so he gave them a sheepish grin and said, in English, "Feet've gone to sleep," and felt like a complete idiot.

They conferred, standing side by side and not taking their eyes off him, one of them bending slightly at the waist to speak quietly to his companion. The man on the right was small, flat-faced, with a stub nose and no lips. Whatever half-thought-out request for assistance Medlin had in mind, he stifled. Beyond the fact that *it wasn't done*, he was too taken aback by the flat-faced man's expression of annoyance to ask for help. The flat-faced man shook his head in answer to something his companion said, and they both turned and walked away, deliberately, without haste.

Nothing ventured, Medlin told himself, and called out, "Wait!"

The other man glanced back over his shoulder and gave him a half-apologetic look, a helpless shrug, but kept walking. Soon, even the strangers' fox-fire was lost to sight.

Swell, Medlin thought, as if my plate wasn't full enough, there're strangers in town, and they're stuck-up! He had no idea who they were, where they came from; just one more goddamn thing wrong. He had been unhappy about this mission to begin with. Now he hated it. If it had been up to him, he would have let go then and there and gone home. He cursed Thomas for sending him. He cursed Ranke for being no good at traveling and making it necessary that Thomas send Medlin. He cursed Garrick for making trouble for everybody.

He must have dozed again against the wall. The next thing he knew, it was dawn, Sunday morning, someone was pulling at his sleeve. He could hear church bells ringing and, closer, a child's voice saying, "Monsieur! Monsieur!"

He looked down and saw a boy standing next to him. The boy was dressed in shorts and a baggy shirt. By the light of the filmy sunrise, he looked to be about twelve years old and could have been the twin of the boy Medlin had seen lying mangled on the waterfront. Had that really been only last night?

"You are Monsieur Medlin?"

He was too stunned to answer.

"The lady wishes you to have this," and the boy handed him a folded newspaper.

Medlin took it, asked, "What lady? Who gave you this?"

"A white lady."

"Where did you talk to her?"

The boy looked over his shoulder, toward the entrance to the square. "Just there, on the Avenue Victor Hugo."

"Show me!" Medlin stuffed the newspaper into his pocket and urged the boy to run.

The Avenue Victor Hugo was the main thoroughfare. Though the sun had yet to peek over the highland behind the town, the street was packed. People rose early enough in the tropics anyway, Medlin knew, but the people he saw now looked as though they were up late rather than early. They looked the way he felt, unrested and dirty. No one in the town could have slept much with all the fireworks. There were numerous white faces among the darker ones, none of them the right face. But Garrick did waft on the dirty air. He tried to hold on to her. It was like trying to grab a small wind-borne scrap of paper.

"Crazy woman," he muttered, "crazy goddamn old woman!"

He whipped out the newspaper and opened it furiously. It was a broadsheet called *Les Colonies*, dated Samedi 3 May 1902. A banner proclaimed this to be an extraordinary edition. There were no photographs or other illustrations.

Written in dark pencil in the upper righthand corner, above the logo, was, *See Mme Boislaville—G.*

The boy was still at his side. Medlin said, "Do you know where I can find a Madame Boislaville?"

The boy nodded happily and said, "She is my aunt," and set off at a trot down the Avenue Victor Hugo. Medlin called him back and said that he had hurt his leg and could only hobble. The boy led him at a more considerate pace onto a side street. Medlin found himself surrounded by food shops and cafes. Only a few shopkeepers had taken down their shutters today, and they were being overwhelmed by impatient-looking customers. The babble here had a hard, argumentative edge to it.

Halfway down the street, the boy stopped before a yellow two-storied building with blue trim. Its shutters were closed. The boy pounded on the door with his small brown fist.

The voice within was a woman's. Medlin didn't have to understand the words to get the meaning: Go away! The boy pleaded. There was silence from behind the door for a moment, then the sound of a bolt being drawn. The door opened wide enough for one eye to peer out.

Remembering his manners, Medlin said, "Madame Boislaville, I presume," and gave her the merest suggestion of a bow.

The space between door and jamb widened. Madame Boislaville was tall, limber-looking, mocha-colored, of indeterminate age. She could have been twenty-five or forty. She said, "You are the friend of Madame Garrick?"

"Yes. My name is Medlin. Your nephew here—"

She looked down at the boy sharply. He was almost squirming. He said, in French rather than creole, so that Medlin would understand, "Madame Garrick promised that I would be paid to bring this gentleman here."

"And Madame Garrick," the woman retorted, also in French, "undoubtedly paid you herself, Symphar. You wicked boy, go home to your poor mother. She must have work for you to do. Or perhaps she will just give you a good beating. Go!"

Foiled, wicked Symphar ran away.

"Come inside quickly, Monsieur." Madame waved him in with urgent gestures and slammed the bolt behind her with obvious relief. It took Medlin's eyes a few seconds to adjust to the gloom, and then he saw that he was in a cramped and dimly lit cafe. Garrick had been here. As palpable as shadow, her trace enveloped him. She had been here *recently*, had lingered here, had touched or been touched by Madame's hands, had . . . had what? He looked around, not quite hopeful or expectant, not quite fearful, not quite knowing how he might feel if he were to see her. Chairs sat legs-up on tables. The only person in the room besides Madame and himself was a mulatto girl who stood by a curtained doorway that separated the serving area from the rear of the building. She looked about as old as the boy. She was eyeing him watchfully. Then a stooped, ancient woman holding a ratty broom appeared behind her and made to put an arm around her—protectively, he thought, until the child evaded the embrace and darted behind the bar. The woman muttered harshly and glared at Medlin as though something were all his fault. She began scratching in a corner with her broom.

Madame had cleared off a table and invited him to sit. He could not help sighing as he did so.

She said, "Are you hungry, thirsty? Would you care to rest?"

"I am very thirsty."

"I have just the thing for it." She turned and clapped her hands and called out a name, Elizabeth. The girl popped up behind the bar, listened to brief instructions, disappeared again. There was a clink of glass, and she emerged around the end of the bar carrying a small filled tray. She kept Madame between Medlin and herself as she set the tray on the table. She was as wary as a half-feral cat, ready to bolt at the first hint of danger from any direction. Her gaze was steady and expressionless, and he could tell from the way she held her head that she was listening with one ear for the old woman. He could only guess the nature of that disagreement. It occurred to him that because he was white, male, and a grown-up, she probably believed him capable of anything. He gave her what he intended as a friendly smile. She responded by scurrying away into some back room.

Madame filled a glass with clear liquid, added syrup from a little pitcher and a bit of lime peel, and gave the mixture a quick stir. She set the glass before him with an air of supreme confidence in the efficacy of its contents. He took a cautious sip. It was basically rum, and went down pleasantly. He took a second sip. It went down very pleasantly indeed, washing away the taste of sulphur, soothing his throat.

Go easy on this stuff, he warned himself. His tolerance for alcohol was low. He made a heartfelt sound of delight and gratitude for his hostess.

She looked pleased by it and said, "Your friend has arranged for your food and lodging here. She paid me for a week in advance, paid for everything. Now sit and rest. I will have a hot bath prepared for you while you eat," and with that she turned and spoke in rapid-fire creole first to the girl and then to the old woman. The girl nodded obediently and disappeared.

The old woman shook her head and went on fussing in the corner. When Madame spoke to her again, with somewhat of an edge in her voice, the old woman turned and made a short reply. They began to argue as though they had been at it for years and could take up their dispute wherever they had left off last time. His eyes had adjusted to the light in the place, and he thought that he detected a slight but certain resemblance between the women. The older one could have been the younger one's mother or grandmother. Whatever their argument was really about, he realized all at once that he had become part of it, for the old woman was gesturing at him with her broom as she screamed at Madame. Madame pointed in his direction as well, and then enumerated unguessable points on her long fingers. He found being argued about in a language he couldn't understand more than a little scary.

At length, the old woman was in such a fury that she left words behind. She gargled a cry, dropped the broom, raked the air over her head with two bird-claw hands, and stormed into the back. A moment later, the girl came out in a hurry, carrying another tray.

Medlin said, "I am sorry, I have come at a bad time," and reluctantly started to get up.

Madame held up her hand. He settled hopefully back into the chair. "Do not trouble yourself about that old woman," she said. "She is a superstitious country woman, very ignorant. She thinks all whites have the evil eye." The way she said it suggested to him that she herself thought some whites might have the evil eye. "She came here when the mountain began to erupt. She thinks whites are to blame."

The girl had placed the second tray on the table. From it, Madame set warm bread and a bowl of steaming gumbo before him. He put his faith in inoculations and tasted the gumbo. It was delicious. He said so at once.

Madame smiled for the first time. She had a big, pleasant smile. Medlin found himself thinking that much of the best of African, European, Asian, and Amerindian faces had collected in her features.

"There is not much food here now," she said. "This ash, *aiee*, it ruins everything! We did not open for business today because we have nothing to serve—only enough for ourselves and you. I did not believe Madame Garrick. She said there would be shortages because of the mountain."

She seemed about to leave him to eat in peace. He said, "An extraordinary person, my friend. When did you see her last?"

"It was two mornings ago, Friday, just after the mountain began to erupt."

"Did she say where I may find her?"

"She said that she would call for you here."

"Anything else?"

"She asked if I have relatives living elsewhere on the island. I told her that everyone on Martinique is related, except for the freshest arrival from France. Even then, I told her, they say it is only a matter of time."

Medlin laughed along with her. "What did she say to that?"

"Oh, she laughed, Monsieur, she laughed the most wonderful laugh."

She smiled at the memory of that, and Medlin thought, Garrick, you old charmer. Then Madame became serious.

"But then," she said, "she told me that if I have relatives in the south, I should give some thought to visiting them. She told me that the mountain is going to destroy the town.

"Do you believe her?"

"I do not know. The mountain has not erupted since anyone can remember. It made some harmless puffs of smoke many years ago, when my grandmothers were young girls. But I do not know what to believe now. If you will excuse me, Monsieur," and she moved away with a rustle of skirts.

When he had finished eating, she reappeared and led him to a small, steam-filled room built onto the back of the house. Covered storage jars and other earthenware were ranked against the walls. There was a small hearth for heating water in one corner. The girl was pouring water from a large pan into a metal bathtub that sat in the middle of the floor.

"Here are towels and a sponge and some soap," Madame said, indicating each thing with a palm-up wave as she named it, "and here is a robe. If you will leave your garments outside the door, I shall clean them. It is a sin to work on Sunday, but you must have clean clothes." She paused and stepped out of the way to let the girl pass with her empty kettle. "Do you require anything else, Monsieur?

Medlin looked at her, was about to say no, said nothing. She was standing at the door, watching him, the fingertips of her right hand resting lightly against her sternum above the slope of her bosom. It was not a provocative stance, and yet he thought he saw something in it that was not a welcome and not a challenge, but only a look of expectation. Men always required something else. He could not help thinking of the whore on the Rue Syphilis, and it shocked him.

"No," he managed to say, "nothing else," and waited too long before adding, "a good long quiet soak is all I need, thank you," and felt like a complete idiot for the second time since he had arrived in town, "thank you very much."

"You are welcome, Monsieur."

Medlin stared at the door after she had closed it behind herself. Had he read those signals right? Had she been offering to let him—? Christ, no, surely not. If washing clothes on Sunday was a sin, what did that make—?

No, surely not, surely not.

A cheap cloth curtain covered the single window. He drew it aside and looked out onto an unpaved courtyard with a small fountain. There was a vegetable garden in one corner of the yard, and what he took to be a cooking shed against the near wall. Some dead birds lay on the ground opposite. Everything looked dingy. Flecks of ash still turned in the air.

He let the curtain drop, and his fingers came away dirty. Ash seeping in through the space between window frame and curtain had collected moisture from the humid air in the room and settled on everything in a gritty paste.

Medlin peeled himself to the skin. First taking care to empty the pockets of his coat, he neatly folded his outer garments, rolled his shirt and underwear into a bundle, and set them outside the door along with his tired-looking shoes. Then he eased himself into the tub. He had always believed that bathing was the benchmark of civilization. But for the thin scum of ash collecting on the surface of his bath water and the sediments of fine volcanic matter on the bottom of the tub, this could have been the best bath he had ever taken. Excepting that time when he and—what *was* her name? His thoughts abruptly veered back to the vision of Madame Boislaville standing at the door, waiting for him to say it, if she had in fact been waiting for him to say something.

You're imagining stuff, he told himself. One glimpse of the nightlife in Little Sodom, Little Gomorrah, and you think every woman in town's for rent.

But, he asked himself, *did* Garrick pay her to do *that*, too?

What the hell, Med, Garrick's crazy. She really *is* crazy, really *has* to be crazy to be doing what she's doing, really is capable of anything, but this Boislaville woman's a *denizen* for chrissake, be like screwing a ghost for chrissake, be like, and he forced the Madames Garrick and Boislaville from his mind for the moment and let the water claim him.

When he began to doze, he got out of the tub, dried off, and put on the robe. It was clean but worn. It felt tight across his shoulders. His hostess evidently heard him thumping around, for now came a discreet knock at the door, and she said, "Monsieur enjoyed his bath?"

He peered around the edge of the door at her and could not read her expression. There was in her voice no note of anything except professional solicitude. He began to feel ashamed of himself, and it confused him. She was only a denizen.

"It was the most pleasant bath I have ever taken," he told her.

She gave a slight nod and led him upstairs to a small room with a cot, a table, and a chair. On the table was a metal washbasin containing a pitcher and a block of soap the size of a half-brick. There was a porcelain chamber pot beneath the cot. The door had no lock. She nodded at both shuttered windows.

"More dust gets in with the shutters closed than light gets in with the shutters opened."

Small wonder, Medlin thought. There was no glass in the windows, an ideal arrangement for the tropics unless there happened to be a nearby volcano pumping out schmutz.

The woman made a furrow in the thin layer of ash on the tabletop and showed him her gray fingertip. "It is impossible to keep house. I had the girl clean here just this morning. I shall bring your clothes as soon as they are clean."

"Thank you."

The room was an oven. As soon as Madame left, he opened the shutters of both windows in the, as it turned out, vain hope of getting some air to blow through. The windows faced north and west, and from them he could look out on the street in front of the Boislaville establishment and also see the volcano and roadstead. The volcano seemed to doze fitfully. The sea looked lead-gray and sluggish.

Garrick, he thought, Garrick, what *are* you up to?

Garrick had never been one to do anything just for the sake of doing it.

Medlin sat on the sill and unfolded the newspaper again. By the poor light of the ash-veiled day he began to read, impatiently at first, then more intently and with deepening disbelief.

> Yesterday the people of St. Pierre were treated to a grandiose spectacle in the majesty of the smoking volcano. While at St. Pierre the admirers of the beautiful could not take their eyes from the smoke of the volcano and the ensuing falls of cinder, timid people were committing their souls to God.
>
> It would seem that many signs ought really to have warned us that Mount Pelée was in a state of serious eruption. There have been slight earthquake shocks this noon. The rivers are in overflow. The need now is for the people outside St. Pierre to seek the shelter of the town. Citizens of St. Pierre! It is your duty to give these people succor and comfort.
>
> Because of the situation in the hinterland, the excursion to Mount Pelée which had been organized for tomorrow morning will not leave St. Pierre, the crater being absolutely inaccessible. Those who were to have joined the party will be notified when it will be found practical to carry out the original plan.

There was a burst of complaint from the street below. He looked down to see a fistfight in front of a shop two doors away. No one moved to stop it. An aproned man with an alarmed expression stood to one side, making pushing gestures with his hands and volubly exhorting everyone to go away. The bystanders ignored him. Most of them watched the fight. Perhaps half a dozen separated from the crowd and coalesced into a discrete group that moved with stunning suddenness into a vegetable shop across the street. Medlin saw no signals exchanged, no indication that the people knew one another; looting was an idea whose moment had come. There were shouts and crashes. The group emerged and turned into its constituent strangers, who ran away clutching handfuls of vegetables as though they were trophies.

The idea caught on. Other shops were raided. Some raiders began to tear shutters off the closed shops. Medlin noticed a couple of men look speculatively at him and at Madame Boislaville's closed shutters. One of the men took a step forward, and Medlin slipped a hand into the pocket of the robe, wrapped his fingers around the butt of the revolver, wondered if he could actually bring himself to use it on anyone except Garrick.

Another thought intruded on that one: could he do even that?

Now a squad of soldiers appeared. It was met by distraught shopkeepers, who jabbered in creole and French and pointed accusingly at individual onlookers. One of the accused, a burly mulatto, answered by raising a yam to his mouth, biting into it defiantly, and chewing with exaggerated gusto. The lieutenant was distracted by shopkeepers' hands on his lapels. The enlisted men behind him clutched their rifles, looking uneasy.

Medlin started to close the shutter, then stared. From the volcano an enormous black cloud was spreading across the sky. He watched, alarmed, as stuff began to rain from the cloud's underside. From the corner of his eye, he glimpsed an object flashing downward at terrific speed. An instant later— before he could turn his head—the object struck the eaves of a nearby roof, shattering tiles and spraying the street with ceramic shrapnel. Below his window, accusations broke off in yelps and screeches. He slammed the shutter and rushed to close the other. He listened unhappily for a time, sitting on the cot, yawning in spite of himself. Finally, he stretched out and fell asleep so fast that it was like blacking out. The last thing he heard was the sound of church bells punctuating the clatter of falling pumice.

Heat and the rotten-egg smell woke him. He limped dazedly to the window and cracked the shutter. It was just as hot and smelled just as bad outside, but the view was impressive. Sunset made the vast poisonous cloud hanging over the volcano a thing of beauty. He started to return to the cot when he saw his coat hanging on a peg set into the wall. His trousers and shirt hung over the back of the chair, and there was a bundle on the table that had to be his underwear. His shoes were by the door; they still looked tired. Medlin removed the trousers and shirt, dragged the chair over to the door, and wedged the back under the handle.

He slept poorly and rose early. Madame had arisen even earlier and came tapping at the door as he was washing his face. She apologized profusely and repetitiously for the breakfast she brought. The ash was in everything, she said. The bread was stale, the fruit was speckled. There was no cream for the coffee, which tasted of sulphur anyway.

He thanked her all the same. He ate and drank and then resignedly opened the shutters to meet the new day. This Monday morning, the volcano had crowned itself with wisps of dirty white smoke. Most people in the street had handkerchiefs tied over their lower faces. It reminded him irresistibly of Tokyo and Mexico City.

The old woman was almost directly below his window, stirring up ash on the sidewalk with her remnant of a broom. She was absorbed in her work until a carriage drew up at the curb; Medlin caught some infinitesimal, unseeable, untouchable, but undeniable portion of Garrick's being. A glimmering arm appeared at the window of the cab and rested on the sill. The shimmering hand beckoned. Oblivious to the glow but radiating her own suspicion, the woman shuffled over to the carriage. Words were spoken, and she suddenly turned to look up at him. There was no mistaking the hatred in her expression. She nodded to the person in the cab and disappeared through the door below.

Medlin shook the ash out of his coat and shoes and rushed downstairs, catching the old woman as she was still sullenly conveying her message to Madame.

"Please excuse my hurry," he said as he dashed past, "but I must go!" The carriage was covered with ash. Both the driver and the horse were red-eyed and miserable. The cab door was flung open invitingly, and it did not surprise Medlin, as he stepped up to climb in, to see Garrick waiting for him. Still, he paused, and hung half in and half out while his face grew hot and the muscles in his forehead contracted into a frown. Garrick was dressed in white and had a stylish hat on her head. She was so old and faded that, but for the pale blue band of her hat and the glimmer around her, she would have been achromatic. One hand, as gnarled as mangrove roots, curled around the handle of a wooden walking stick. Her other hand was drawn into a knobby fist like the head of a shillelagh. Poking from the fist was a small revolver. The muzzle was negligently trained on Medlin's midriff.

Garrick grinned, and skin around her eyes crinkled like parchment. The rest of her face was smooth and taut. Her skin looked shrinkwrapped over the pointed chin and nose and the high, sharp cheekbones. She said, "It's good to see you, Med. How was World War Two?"

"Garrick," Medlin said tonelessly, eyeing the revolver, and then after a second added, "is a gun necessary?"

"It depends. How sure are you of your own loyalties?"

"At the moment . . ."

"Just to be on the safe side, why don't I trouble you for the gun you're carrying? Lean in just a bit." Garrick let go of the walking stick, slipped her hand into the pocket of Medlin's coat, withdrew his revolver by the barrel, gingerly, as though it were a dead mouse. "Why do men always have to have such big guns?" she said, as she put it and her own weapon into a handbag. "Now come on in."

Medlin stepped in as she told the driver to proceed to the Morne d'Orange. The driver addressed his horse, there was the soft *swick* of a whip cutting the air, and the carriage began to move. Its wheels made no sound on the ash carpet and had trouble getting sufficient traction. The vehicle skidded alarmingly as it negotiated a turn.

Garrick settled back in her seat and looked along her shoulder. Her expression became mock-concerned. "You look like your feelings've really been hurt."

Medlin exhaled with some vehemence. "Until now," he said, his voice threatening to shake, "I was sure it was all a mistake, that everything'd be okay once you went back and explained. Now . . ."

"Well," she said, "I guess there's nothing like having a friend point a gun at you to make you have serious doubts about the relationship."

"How are you feeling?"

Now her expression became mock-surprised. "Is that their line? I'm this senile and dazed old dear who's wandered off in time? Or is it that I've been under a lot of stress and gone harpo?"

"Haven't you?"

"Haven't I which?"

"Either, hell, I don't know!"

"If I'd done one or the other—gone senile, gone crazy—would I be able to *say*, one way or another? I guess if you really pressed me for an answer, I'd say I've just gone fishing."

Medlin licked his gritty lips. "They say you stole two dozen ampoules of the drug."

"Oh," she said happily, "I stole the drugs, all right. But I wouldn't put too much faith in anything else they told you. They're really just mad because I took my ball and went home. In their present state of mind, maybe I should say, in their future state of mind, they're liable to accuse me of anything. Was I hard to find?"

"After you checked out everything the library has on volcanoes, Martinique, and *fin de siècle*? Took us about thirty minutes to decide you'd come here and weren't just throwing us off the track. Took me most of a day to locate the hole you came through, but, then, I was dead tired. I'd just brought Witts back from watching Hitler roll up Europe. Otherwise . . . an earthmover leaves fainter tracks than you did."

"Ah. Well, you can't've had much time to familiarize yourself with the situation here." Garrick cocked an eyebrow. "By the way, where'd you tell me Ranke is?"

"I didn't."

"Well, tell me now."

"Why should I know where he is?"

"Now don't be coy," she said, looking more amused, "it doesn't become you. We both know you're the only one who could've come after me here. But you're mush inside." Her colorless eyes locked with Medlin's and dared him either to deny the accusation or to look away. "So they had to send Ranke, too. I don't think he's arrived yet. Timing's never been his strong suit, but I've never known him to just not show up at all."

"He could've come to grief."

"Mm, I wouldn't bet on it. You'll bring him through, sooner or later. You're good at what you do. You damn well ought to be. I trained you."

"You trained Ranke, too."

Garrick laughed. It was no wonder Madame Boislaville had been charmed; notwithstanding the circumstances, Medlin still thought she had the pleasantest laugh he had ever heard. "And won't my face be red if he nails me! But, listen, just in case he does, you better get used to the idea of having him around, because you won't be going anywhere without him from now on. They have a *plan*, dear heart, and they're not going to let it get fouled up by anybody's mavericking. They *trust* Ranke. He's the kind of person they use to keep an eye on all the other kinds of people they use. By the way, how do you like Madame Boislaville's?"

"Best dive I've ever been in."

"Don't be a snob. I'll have you know that Madame Boislaville runs a good, clean establishment—as clean as any place can be with *this*, anyway. She does it all pretty much without help, too, except for that girl of hers. And she's not a whore, if that's what you're thinking."

Medlin looked away quickly, guiltily.

Garrick kept talking as though she had not noticed. "Sorry I couldn't afford to check you into the International Hotel or such, but we're on a budget. They didn't provide you with any money, did they? *Trés* typical. Best-case-scenario planners, every one." She took a small purse from her bag, riffled through the franc notes in it, and stuffed a handful into Medlin's coat pocket. "Don't worry, I didn't hit anybody over the head to get this. I won it mostly fair and square. Believe it or not," and she made herself look shocked for a moment, "there's *gambling* in this town! You better learn your denominations before you try to spend any of that. There're thieves in this town, too. You'll be relatively safe and well-cared-for at Madame's. She won't be as curious about your business as white folks at the International would be. You won't have to answer any hard questions."

"Mind telling me where we're going?"

"Just for a ride."

Medlin glared at her in exasperation. "You never *just* do *anything*."

"Sightseeing, then. What do you think of St. Pierre so far?"

"I think things are going to hell here, but the newspaper's playing down all the volcanic activity. The authorities are discouraging people from leaving town."

She looked at him disbelievingly. "Is that stuff you came here knowing or what you've personally figured out since you got here? Oh, never mind. Authority is invested locally in Mayor Fouché, who of course enjoys the unqualified support of that rag, Les Colonies. Fouché's got his own expert, too, a science teacher from the local school, to back up his assertion that the volcano's no threat. Fouché also asserts that there's medical evidence to show that sulphur can be beneficial for chest and throat complaints. It's all politics, of course. It always is politics. Er, you *did* notice there was a primary election yesterday, didn't you?"

"I was busy yesterday," Medlin said testily, "noticing food riots and volcanic eruptions and stuff."

"Ah, yes, hasn't this been just the most interesting couple or three days? Always something exciting going on in Little Paris, now more than ever. Thomas probably said, Go find Garrick, and don't get blown up by the volcano. Am I right? Sure I am. I'm only too familiar with his kind of briefing. Get *in*, get it *done*, get *out*. Makes me wonder what sex's like for Missis Thomas."

Medlin bristled slightly. "I know the volcano erupts and destroys the town at eight o'clock Thursday morning, the eighth of May. I know thousands of people die here because city and government officials encourage them not to leave. It has something to do with every registered voter in this town actually having to vote *in* this town."

"That's barely adequate," said Garrick. "Do you know anything about bridges dropping out from under folks, a prison revolt—did you hear those rifle volleys yesterday afternoon? That tremor last night collapsed a bridge over the River Roxelane, which flows through town. A funeral party happened to be crossing at the time. All this ruckus and more *and* an election, too. The final election's scheduled for next Sunday, and it isn't for dog-catcher, either. It's for the French Chamber of Deputies, all the way over in *La Métropole*. Politics here are just like politics everyplace else. There're maybe a hundred and thirty thousand Martiniquais. Most of 'em are people of color, but, surprise surprise, it's whites who own everything—whorehouses, plantations, the government."

"The place seems pretty wide open to me."

"That's just commerce. The government's very conservative. Martiniquais may be the most racially mixed people on Earth, and the most race-conscious. The whites've exploited that ever since slavery was abolished and everyone was enfranchised. But their grip slipped in the last election. The coloreds finally put together a viable political party and sent a *black* senator to Paris. This election, the white party looks to suffer more embarrassment. You can see why neither party wants voters leaving town."

"Garrick, what does any of this have to do with anything?"

"Stop fidgeting. Listen, and maybe you'll learn something—besides the obvious, which is, never live on an active plate margin." Garrick pointed at the smouldering mountain through the window on Medlin's side of the cab. "There's a wild card in this deck. I give you Montagne Pelée—"

"No goddamn thanks."

"—cloud-herder, lightning-forger, and rainmaker," she went on, not missing a beat, "drawing to itself all the white vapors of the land, robbing lesser eminences of their shoulder-wraps and head-coverings." She smiled wistfully. "Lafcadio Hearn. Not one of the forbidden writers, just one of the forgotten ones. He also wrote that St. Pierre was the queerest, quaintest, and prettiest of all West Indian cities. He outlived the place by a couple of years. I wonder if he ever saw the photographs taken after its destruction. Place looks like Hiroshima."

Without warning, the carriage stopped, hurling them forward. In the next moment, Medlin heard the report of a gun and an exultant cheer. He looked out. The street was choked with people, including a number of soldiers. An officer was holstering his sidearm. The civilians were running about shouting excitedly. One held up a length of bamboo, and Medlin saw, impaled on its sharpened end, a writhing thing as long as the man's arm.

Garrick yelled to the driver, "Go around!" and plopped back into her seat as the carriage moved again. Pinned to her breast was an old-fashioned watch, with a dial and hands; she looked at it and murmured, "We'll still make it in time."

"What's all the shooting and shouting about?"

"Snakes. All the refugees here aren't human. Every stinging, biting thing in the jungle is on the move. Snakes, ants, centipedes. The mulatto quarter's infested with *fer-de-lances*. Dozens of people are dead of snakebite. *Now* what's the matter?"

The carriage had stopped again. "My apologies, Madame," the driver called down, "but the horse cannot climb even such a small hill as this."

"Then my friend and I shall walk. Please wait here for us. Come on, Med, I believe we're just in time."

"For what?"

"You'll see."

They stepped from the carriage at the foot of one of the hillocks that formed the amphitheater. Above them, the mouths of ancient muzzle-loading cannon gaped over a crumbling parapet. Ahead, other people were climbing the slope—well-dressed white people, ladies and gentlemen. Thick gray smoke billowed from the crater, and the ladies hurried along with the hems of their long skirts lifted clear of the ground and their parasols spread in a brave attempt to protect fair skins and good hats.

"Why," Garrick said as she and Medlin began to labor up the slope, "I do believe that's Missis Prentiss up ahead there. I keep running into her. She's the American Consul's wife. Saw her in the crowd on the Place Bertin yesterday. The idea seemed to percolate through everyone's head for a moment that the volcano's behavior was legitimate cause for worry. They were whipping themselves into a fine state of hysteria when a churchman arrived in a coach. He got 'em calmed down with a prayer. But about one minute later, the volcano started a new demonstration." She was panting as they neared the top of the hillock, but she still had breath enough for an exhalation that did not stop much short of a guffaw. "So much for the efficacy of prayer, even dear Missis Prentiss'."

The gentlemen and ladies assembled at the summit of the hillock. Most of them peered seaward, but one man looked around at Medlin and Garrick as they approached, and there was puzzlement in his expression.

"We're being noticed," Medlin said, trying to appear as though he were not talking.

"Well, we're white," Garrick said unconcernedly, "and well-dressed—*I* am, anyway—and we're total strangers to all these white, well-dressed folks who all know one another. But don't worry, they aren't interested in us. They came up here because they heard someone say that the sea's acting peculiarly," and she nodded toward the roadstead.

Even as Medlin looked, a stiff breeze was blowing across the harbor, shredding the veil of cinders. Behind and above the Morne d'Orange, the volcano growled bad-temperedly. After a moment, he became aware of two other sounds, one a sort of sizzling, rushing noise, the other a rising, undulating chorus of cries from the direction of the waterfront. Running figures spilled into the Avenue Victor Hugo.

"What," he said, "what's—"

Garrick consulted her antique timepiece again, and as she said, "Here it comes, right on schedule," Medlin suddenly saw as well as heard *it*, a great wave, coming hissing from the north. It was already halfway across the roadstead. It came up under two small sailing ships moored in its path, lifted them up, carried them along. They hung on the crest of the steep shoulder of water and then, as the wave avalanched with shattering impact onto the waterfront, hurtled completely over the quayside row of buildings. Houses, shops, and warehouses twisted on their foundations, disintegrated. The wave surged up the thoroughfare, rising to the second-floor balconies. It reached the lighthouse, swirled around its base, and inundated the square on which it stood. There it hesitated. It hesitated forever. Then, slowly, reluctantly, it started to retreat.

Medlin was on the ground. He had no memory of sitting down. There was a sustained moan from the other watchers on the hillock. They were pale-faced, open-mouthed, awestruck. He knew the feeling.

He got to his feet and brushed ash from his sleeve. Garrick turned to leave, but he angrily grabbed her arm. She looked at his hand and then at his face and said, "Gentlemen do not mishandle ladies."

He waved his free hand at the scene below and managed to gasp out, "What—?"

"This is nothing, Med," she said mildly, and detached herself. "Wait. You'll see."

"You keep saying that! What'll I see? More of the same?"

"Oh God, yes. More and worse. The wave was just a side-effect. Not even a prelude. We have a ways to go before it's time for the grand finale, the show-stopper—the glowing cloud! That being the literal meaning of *nuée ardente*—" she spoke the term the way she might have savored a continental delicacy "—which is the name given to the particularly nasty phenomenon that's going to destroy this burg. In case you neglected to research this detail, it's an incandescent cloud of rock fragments and hot gases. Pelée's going to spit out one of these horrors Thursday morning. It'll come right down that big notch in the mountainside there. It'll hit the town at incredible speed, with tremendous force."

"Why do you want me to see all of these terrible things?"

"Object lesson. It's time you looked up and saw the mountain."

"What?" But Garrick merely turned and walked away. Medlin's options were to follow her or wrestle her to the ground. He followed, and when he drew abreast he said, "It shouldn't take a genius to figure out, but damned if I know what you're up to. Unless you're trying to lose Ranke and me in all the confusion when the volcano does pop."

She pivoted on her nearer foot and stabbed a finger as hard and sharp as an antler into his breast. "I can lose you without the volcano's goddamn help, thank you. You couldn't follow my trail around the corner, and you know it."

"*I'm* not the one you have to worry about."

Garrick looked slightly sheepish. "Okay," she said, "so I *am* counting on getting a little help from Pelée. It never hurts to give yourself an edge when you're dealing with Ranke. I think he may find it hard to concentrate in this place. It's very stressful here. The air's full of static electricity, there's this stinking ash, the barometric pressure's all screwy—""Doesn't sound like that much of an edge to me."

She frowned. "Don't you doubt that I can lose him if I want to."

"So why don't you? Why are you still here?"

"I can't leave you behind, Med. I've got to get you to go with me, and you know that can only happen if you go willingly."

"Go where?"

"Anywhere!"

"What *is* this game you're playing?"

Garrick gestured at the town before them. The waterfront was a shambles. Each of the two sailing ships—mastless, shattered hulks—could be seen sitting in its own pile of rubble. "If all I was doing," she said, "was playing games, I'd've gone someplace *nice*, done something *fun*. Parisians are rioting at the premiere of Stravinsky's new ballet in nineteen thirteen. I might even've come here, in some happier year. This *is* a beautiful island, even if Little Paris is a bit lusty for my taste. But now it's hot as hell here, it stinks, and it's infested with snakes. And it's doomed. Hundreds of people've died around this volcano since Saturday. Thirty *thousand* are going to die here before it's all done. Most of 'em are going to be killed by superheated gas and politics. I know that sounds redundant, but it's the truth. Thirty thousand people, a fourth of the population of Martinique in nineteen oh two, all victims of arrogance and ignorance."

"So it's an object lesson. What'm I supposed—"

"*Learn* something from it!" Two faint reddish spots appeared high on the woman's cheekbones. "Here's all this self-important scramble down here, and, up there, looming catastrophe! And like I said, it's time for you to look up and see the mountain. I'm hoping you'll go with me. If you stick with the scramblers, you're going to get wiped out with them. I don't want that to happen. You're important to me. I'm important to you, too."

"Maybe not important enough to defect for."

"Then maybe you'll think *this* is important enough. Someone, the president, the military, I don't know who, has been sold the bright idea that past events can be revised to suit present needs. Can and *should* be."

Medlin looked at her and thought, Crazy. Suspecting it before and believing it now were two different things. It hurt now that he saw just how crazy she was.

She must have seen how skeptical he was, for she said, "It's true, Med."

"Oh, come on. People've been saying crap like that since before anyone knew *how* to travel. It's a *joke*. Oh God, if only I could go back in time and not have the accident with the scoozip. Oh God, if only I could renew the insurance policy the day before I had the accident with the scoozip. Oh God, if only I could buy the roto instead of the scoozip."

Garrick grinned like a skull. "Pretend for a second I'm presenting this scheme in a really positive light, and pretend you're the president or someone impressionable like that. God, be honest, wouldn't it sound *so tempting?* Make a big mistake somewhere, lose a war or an election? No problem. Accidentally kill everybody in Arizona? Well, no big loss, but still no problem. Just go back, change things to make 'em come out the way you want! They're calling it 'temporal engineering.' There's no telling what havoc'll be created if those idiots ever actually give it a try."

"Maybe it wouldn't have any effect," Medlin said. "Nothing ever has before. Time's resilient, forgiving. It's accommodated us so far."

"So *far*," she snapped, "we haven't tested its patience! We haven't tried to show it who's boss! Can you imagine the kind of force needed to really change an event so that it affects things up the way? *Experts* were brought in to say what everybody wanted to hear. That the past can be altered to produce the desired present. Isn't that a lovely term? The desired present. And here's where it stuck for me, these *experts* made it a major, fundamental point that if you want to alter the past, you have to have *complete control* of travel, because you don't want somebody *un*altering things on you. So no more mavericking around for you and me!" She paused, panting and glaring. He had never seen her quite so upset before. "The really insulting part is, they broached this insanity to me like they expected me to *go for it!*"

Medlin shook his head. "I'm just not sure I believe a word of this," he said. "Why didn't Thomas tell me anything about it? Why didn't *you?*"

"Someone—maybe Thomas, but I think probably not—didn't tell you because they were hedging their bet. *I* couldn't tell you because you were in nineteen forty when I decided to bolt. I couldn't wait around for you to get back. They were ready to *roll* on this thing. You'd've been told soon enough. After all, a traveler's essential to this project, and if I'm dead or AWOL, you're it. We're the only real travelers they've got, the only ones who can go anywhere we set our minds to, almost—anywhere there's the least little crack, I don't want to squander this gift playing fetch. Nor should you. Thomas isn't your friend. And the agency isn't your home."

"And you're not my mom."

Garrick looked pained. "I'm trying to save your *soul* here."

"To say nothing of saving the purity and essence of time. Look, forget about my soul for a minute. If temporal engineering's such a big deal with you, why don't you stop it? It's not as though you don't have clout of your own."

"Their minds are made up. The only way to stop 'em is for us to not go back and help 'em get started." She extended her hand to him; after a moment, he took it. There was nothing to it but bones and milky skin. "We can skip this depressing catastrophe," she said, "and go see Stravinsky's ballet. It's only an ocean and eleven years away."

"I don't know. What about Ranke?"

She made an impatient face. "What about him?"

"He's going to show up here whether I'm still around to take him home or not."

"Perhaps Pelée'll give him a warm welcome. If he's smart, and he sometimes is, he'll get the hell out of town."

"And we just let him wander around lost in nineteen oh two forever?"

"Do not waste your concern on Ranke. He'd find his niche wherever he is. There always is a niche for people like Ranke."

Medlin let go of Garrick's hand. His arm fell to his side. "I can't."

"Oh, God, why not?" She was the picture of exasperation.

"Because I just can't. I'm not . . . I don't know, I can't make up my mind."

"That's *always* been your problem! Well, I've got some bad news for you. You're finally going to have to take decisive action. You just can't go along and get along any more."

A darkening pall of ash and smoke lay over the town like twilight. The carriage was still waiting at the base of the hill. Driver and horse looked as though they had been carved from dirty rock. Garrick climbed into the carriage and slammed the door.

Dismayed, Medlin said, "Are you going to leave me stranded here?"

She looked out the window. "It may come to that!"

"I can't see thirty feet here!"

"Wherever you are in a town this size, you're never too far from anyplace else. Just go back to the Avenue Victor Hugo. It'll lead you right back to Madame Boislaville's street."

"Maybe her street isn't there any more! Even if it is, maybe I won't be able to find it."

"I understand your distress, but we're still waiting for Ranke, remember? I've taken a big chance here already. As long as your loyalties are all tangled, I'd rather not be around you when he does pop up."

"This is so crazy," he said sorrowfully.

"I'm going to have to kill him," she said, "or he, me. He knows you can't take me back without my cooperation. I'm sure he doesn't expect me to oblige him by going back under my own power."

"Goddammit!"

"Now, now. See you soon, I hope. Driver!"

Driver and horse shook gray powder from themselves. The carriage soundlessly pulled away. Medlin stumbled after it vengefully, but it was quickly lost to sight in the false dusk. He swore, rammed his fists into his trousers pockets, and walked slowly and half-blind to the Avenue Victor Hugo.

He came to the edge of the devastated area. The wave had been a spent force by the time it lapped around these houses. Slowed or not, it had turned the thick blanket of ash into a putrid-smelling porridge of mud seasoned with foodstuffs, utensils, odd pieces of clothing, whole and shattered pieces of furniture, stranded marine life, dead livestock, and human bodies. The living stood about numbly, and then by ones, twos, and threes they came forward, searching for their homesites, belongings, missing families. The pall was murkily suffused with light from torches and supercharged with static electricity. Brilliant streaks of lightning intermittently shot through it. There was a constant background chorus of moans and cries.

Splattered with muck, his eyes, nose, and throat burning and his stomach heaving, Medlin wandered lost in a darkened, debris-clogged maze. It was not until he found his way blocked by a mass of splintered wooden spars, shredded canvas, and tangled ropes—part of the mast and rigging of one of the ravaged ships—that he realized that he had strayed off the main thoroughfare. When he attempted to retrace his steps, he emerged onto a great sloping square. A solemn crowd lined its edges. Lying in rows in the center were scores of dead bodies. They had been dusted with quicklime and looked like broken statuary. A priest and a policeman walked side by side among the rows, the priest either calling out a name for each body or else calling on onlookers to identify it, and the policeman writing the name in a roster. The supply of coffins must have been exhausted. Soldiers were wrapping the bodies in banana leaves, loading them onto stretchers, and carrying them away.

Medlin thought of Garrick and was filled with a great hot surge of hatred that sustained him until he unexpectedly found himself standing before Madame Boislaville's house. The wave had not penetrated her street. Everything looked the same, gray, silent, unmoving, dead—*normal*, he thought sourly as he pounded on the door with the side of his fist.

She let him in and slid the bolt home with a good, solid, reassuring thunk. He sank into a chair. They regarded each other dumbly.

"I am glad," he finally told her, "to see that you are all right."

"And you, Monsieur."

"I watched the wave come, saw it hit."

"It is—"

She could not find a word for what it was, but he nodded agreement anyway. He ran his tongue over his lips and spat at the taste.

"Madame, is there anything to drink?"

"There is still water for coffee, and some bread and pickles if you are hungry. And there is no shortage of rum."

"May I please have some rum?"

Almost before he had asked for it, there was a drink on the table. The rum cut a ravine through the sulphur bed in his mouth. He finished it and asked for another. When he had finished that one as well and asked for still another, Madame said, "Too much rum will make you sorry to be alive."

He ignored the warning and got the drink. The next thing he knew was that he was drunk as he had ever been in his life and filled with horror and self-pity. Madame had disappeared for a time but now returned, from either the kitchen or whatever part of the building was her living quarters. There was no sympathy in her expression. She had warned him, he had ignored the warning, now here he was, the foolish American, truly sorry to be alive.

"Join me, Madame," he said thickly. "We'll drink to this doomed town."

She shook her head. "I had better make the coffee and bring you some food."

"Why are you still here?"

She had started to leave. She turned to answer. "I am here because this is my home, Monsieur."

"Your home is doomed. Look out the window."

"Perhaps the worst is past."

"This town is going to be destroyed. Anyone who stays here is going to die. There is still time to escape. Take your girl and your grandmother and go."

Distaste tugged at one corner of her mouth. "The old woman is my aunt. She is someone's aunt, anyway. Everyone on Martinique . . . but my aunt, my aunt, she tells me terrible things. She says that she has visited a wizard." Madame shuddered visibly, then crossed herself. "I have thrown her out, Monsieur. Let the wizard take her into *his* home. She terrifies my Elizabeth. The wizard told her not to place her trust in the power of white men's god. He told her that the Holy Church has made the mountain erupt and caused all the deaths."

"Whosoever's fault it is, you must get out. You should have left when Madame Garrick—my great friend and mentor, ace of travelers, knower of all—should have gotten out when she told you to go. Last whenever it was."

For a moment he thought she was going to cry. Then she said, angrily, "She says that the mountain is a menace! The mayor says that it is not! I know, I *know*, that white people are great liars, but both Madame Garrick and the mayor are white, so I do not know who is lying."

"White or not, she knows what is going to happen here. So do I."

"Perhaps yes, perhaps no. You are white, too. You could be lying as well."

"Then the hell with you."

He pushed himself out of the chair and somehow made it up the stairs to the room. He stood in the doorway, assayed some calculations based on the distance between himself and the cot, took a long step forward. The room and its meager furnishings tilted sharply and rose about him. The floor caught him, not gently.

He awoke on the cot, listening to a murmur of voices from the street outside. It hurt him to move his head. His mouth tasted of kitchen matches, a whole box of them. He had a dim memory of awakening once to call for water and at least once again to be violently sick in the chamber pot. Neither pitcher nor pot was in sight. He felt exhausted, unclean, poisoned.

He staggered to the window and leaned on the sill. In the street below the window was what first appeared to be a vast funeral procession and then resolved itself into a dense bunch of lesser processions. The black-garbed mourners jostled one another, moving from shrine to shrine, and their prayers mingled in the hot, polluted air to become a soft mush of crying, prayers for the dead, and pleas for God's intervention. There were other, harsher voices, too. Criers added to the confusion and congestion as they ran among the processions. Some shouted instructions from the Action Committee, whatever that was: everyone was to wash the ash from walls and roofs. Others were political sloganeers, broadcasting the political parties' competing messages to the illiterate segments of the electorate.

Unmindful of babble, the volcano industriously pumped out black smut. The sea was calm in the roadstead. Along the ruined waterfront burned regularly spaced fires. Medlin had no idea of what these signified, except more trouble. The sun was a ghostly orb sitting low in a cinder-filled sky, barely above the western horizon. Several seconds elapsed before the wrongness of that view registered, and then dread burst inside him like a soft, spoiled fruit. He lumbered noisily to the landing at the top of the stairs and gave a fearful raw-throated shout, *"Madame Boislaville!"*

She swept into view below. She looked surprised and wary.

"Yes, M—"

"What day," and then his headache caught up with him, forcing him to lower his voice, "what *day* is this?"

"Tuesday, Monsieur."

"How can it—Tuesday. Of course." Tuesday. Christ. He clutched the wooden bannister. Below, she wiped her hands on the apron and made her expression unfathomable. "Is there any breakfast?"

"It is almost suppertime, and I have nothing to—"

"Coffee?"

"Yes, of course, Monsieur. I shall make some and bring it up to you at once."

"No, no. I am coming down."

"There is no food today. I am very sorry."

"No, I understand, it is all right," and, clinging to the bannister, he went painfully down the stairs.

She helped him into a chair and brought him a pot of black coffee and a cup. She also produced a pair of salty pickles, a stale heel of bread, and the latest edition of *Les Colonies*. The bread was too hard to eat, and the coffee was too hot to drink at first, so he dipped the one into the other and gratefully sucked on it. Most of *Les Colonies* was given over to an account of the previous day's disaster. A lake on the mountainside had burst its walls, sending tons of mud and debris to pile into the sea north of the roadstead.

The mass had incidentally buried a sugar refinery located at the mouth of the River Blanche, north of town.

He was still hungry when he finished his repast, but his headache had subsided. He crept back upstairs to his room and fell asleep again. This time, his rest was broken intermittently by street noises and volcanic rumblings, by heat and stinks. Once, he awoke to find himself thinking about temporal engineering.

There were, he reflected, many things about the world of his proper matrix that had never bothered him very much. Eco-collapse? Never cared for a second, he told himself, that there's nothing but desert or pavement on land, and the oceans are cesspools, and everywhere you go smells like a beer fart. Money meltdown, nuclear exchange? So the world is owned in the Awful Oughts by a few greedy people who want all the other people to keep bending over and greasing their own behinds for the next reaming. So what? When have things ever been different?

It just *hasn't bothered me*.

Because I have a gift.

How can I hate the world, he thought as he turned on the cot and pressed the side of his face into the gritty pillow, when I'm free to *escape* from it whenever I like . . . ?

Still. Only a fool—not that there weren't always lots of fools—would deny that civilization was in trouble, that the planet itself was in trouble. Perhaps temporal engineering could save the day.

Only, it *hadn't* saved the day.

Then perhaps it was *about* to save the day, and this was the last moment of the old timeline, and everything would now shimmer and dissolve or do some special-effects thing, and he'd awaken with the rest of humanity in some restored Eden . . .

He wondered how one would go about heading off the more complicated disasters, and about how different his own life might be after temporal engineering. Neither line of speculation took him very far. The Awful Oughts were the culmination of some trends that had begun with the Industrial Revolution and others that went back to Sumer, possibly even to Olduvai Gorge. As for himself, surely he would still be a traveler. And surely there would still be an agency, a Garrick, a Thomas. Even a Ranke.

Far away, seafloor twitched. Close by, the volcano gave a growl.

How much force would it take to change the past? Sleep was taking him again. How much force, measured in, say, Pelées? Two Pelées each to stop Hitler, Stalin, Breedlove? Five Pelées to disinvent styrofoam? Fifteen . . .

When he awoke next, night had fallen. His headache was back and worse than before, he was thirsty and ravenously hungry, and he could not recall having felt so wretched or so stupid in the wake of a drunk since college. Downstairs, his hostess was able to offer him coffee and a single brown banana. He ate the fruit slowly and deliberately, by the light of a lamp on the table. Madame let him drink coffee by himself for a while, then came to stand by the table. He looked up and waited. After a moment she cleared her throat softly, put her hand into the pocket of her apron, and withdrew some franc notes and coins.

"Madame Garrick paid a week's rent," she said, placing the money on the table, "and paid also for a week's meals. This is the portion intended to cover your expenses for the remainder of this week. There is no food here, even for my daughter and myself. Money cannot buy it now. The countryside is deserted, so there is no harvest. The fishermen catch nothing." She would not meet his eye. Her manner was very formal, and she addressed him so stiffly that he knew she must have devoted considerable time to composing and mentally rehearsing this speech. "The mayor says that carts have been sent to gather food from other parts of the island, but the carts do not return. Even if the mountain does not destroy the town, it has destroyed my livelihood. I do not know how to reach your friend, so I must impose upon you to return this money to her."

"Please keep it. She will never miss it. Believe me, I am certain that she would want you to keep it."

Madame drew herself up. "I cannot accept charity."

"A loan, then."

She shook her head again. "I do not know when I would be able to repay it. I am leaving for Fort-de-France in the morning. Today, I prayed to the Holy Virgin, who told me that you are right. I am going to take my Elizabeth and visit my relatives in the south."

"I think you are making a very wise decision. I shall personally escort you and your daughter to the edge of town."

"That will not be necessary."

He indicated the bolted front door with a slight jerk of his head and instantly regretted the movement. His head was still as tender as a boil. He could all but hear his brain slosh inside his skull. "Anything can happen out there now."

"Yes, I know." He heard her sigh. "Sickness is breaking out. They have lighted fires on the beach to purify the air."

He marveled at the logic of that and couldn't frame a reply.

Madame finally let herself make eye-contact with him. She said, "*La Verette* kills whites as well, Monsieur. You should take your own advice and go."

"I have no relatives in the south."

"Will you sail away, then, on a big boat?"

"On something, I assure you."

The sound of an explosion passed over them. The woman cried out, and Medlin jerked violently and spilled coffee on himself. He heard a rattling of shelves from the bar and next, as the bang faded, a shrill note like the sound of a titan's train whistle. He realized that he was standing, open-mouthed, with saliva pooling in the back of his throat. He gulped hard, almost choked. The whistling persisted for several minutes before trailing off.

"I must go to the cathedral," Madame said in a quavering voice, "and offer prayers for our deliverance."

Prayer, he started to tell her, will not prevent what is going to happen here, but he saw her eyes widen suddenly, saw her listen and cross herself hurriedly. He said, instead, "What is it?"

She shushed him.

He listened hard.

The drumming was ragged and muted at first, but it steadied quickly, sharpened and rose in volume, became frenzied. He could hear shouts, too.

One damned thing after another, he thought, and asked again, "What is it?"

"*Wizards.*" Her reply was almost inaudible. There was an especially sustained burst of yelling, and then he could hear them approaching. He extinguished the lamp with a puff of breath, moved toward the window, and peered through the crack between the shutters. He saw nothing. A din of singing, shouting, and drumming passed at no very great distance, and, as it did, behind him, the terrified woman hissed, "*Monsieur!*"

"Where are they going, Madame?" There was no answer. He looked over his shoulder, and sensed rather than saw her standing wrapped in darkness at the center of the room. "Where are they going?"

She moaned but made no other sound.

"We'll be safe here," he said. "I have a gun." He patted his coat pocket, then remembered that Garrick had taken it. He kept talking. "You should go see about your daughter. Reassure her. And try to get some rest. You will both need your rest if you are going to Fort-de-France tomorrow." Yeah, right, he told himself, as if anyone could rest. "Pray, Madame. Pray for—" Pray for whatever one prayed for.

He went to the table and groped around its edge to her side. She seemed to be standing very rigidly with her arms pressed tightly against herself and her hands clasped over her bosom as in prayer. She was still moaning as he took both of her hands in his. Either she was numb with fear or else the gesture simply astonished her, for she did not resist or react in any way at first. Her hands were dry and much harder than he had expected them to be. They were the rough, strong hands of someone who worked like a mule every day of her life. They felt more real than his own hands. He could not see her face, but imagined it, and wondered how old she really was, and what the life expectancy of a West Indian mulatto woman could have been— could *be*, here, now—at the beginning of the twentieth century. She suddenly started like someone awakening from a nap. He made no attempt to hold on as she withdrew her hand from his. Wordlessly, she turned and stumbled away.

Depressed, he sat down by the shuttered window and listened. After a time, he caught himself nodding and got up sharply and walked around the room once. Then he went to his room and cautiously opened the shutter. There was nothing to see except the glow of the volcano's mouth. There was nothing to hear except the noises made by earth and sea and town, each restless and unhappy. The shouting and singing had died away, and even the drumming had become subliminal. Medlin stretched out on his cot and closed his eyes. Sometime later, he was shaken awake by a loud report from the volcano. The summit of the mountain looked like a blast furnace; over it was a cloud filled with lightning.

He did not sleep again after that. Wednesday's sunrise was the saddest he had ever seen. With it came a resumption of the volcano's grumbling. Lightning flashed among the clouds, and thunder rumbled down the mountainside. The sea was full of wreckage swept down from forest and field during the night. The dozen ships lying in the roadstead looked as though they had run aground on small islands.

It took most of the morning to load Madame's belongings for the exodus to Fort-de-France. The woman did not travel lightly. The cart she had got from somewhere was a bed of mismatched planks mounted between two solid wooden wheels. Hitched to this creaking, swaying conveyance was a horse hardly bigger than a large breed of dog. Medlin could not imagine that under the best of circumstances it would have been capable of budging the cart emptied, let along with the girl Elizabeth and household goods aboard, and its nose and lungs irritated by volcanic ejecta. At the woman's urging, however—she pulled gently yet firmly with one hand at its harness and, with the other, flicked a long switch over its back but did not touch its ashy hide— the horse got moving with an easy indifference to the loaded cart. Medlin padlocked the gate to the courtyard and took his station, as he imagined it to be, on the animal's opposite flank. They turned a corner and passed the front of the building. Madame did not pause for a farewell look at her locked and shuttered home. She set her mouth in a ruler-straight line and flicked the switch again to let the horse know she would not stand for dawdling.

The cart made its slow way through and out of the town. Medlin walked with his head hurting and the sour taste of the air in his mouth. He was grateful that Madame seemed disinclined to chat. He saw a few soldiers ahead as the cart approached the junction with the road to Fort-de-France, and because he had no desire to be asked questions by them, he looked across the horse's back at the woman and said, "This is where I get off."

She said, very seriously, "Now you are on the street again. I am sorry that your visit to St. Pierre could not have been a happier one."

"The bath and the gumbo were first-rate, and the rum, too." That brought a faint, fleeting smile to her lips. He was pleased to see it. "Perhaps the next time," he began, but she cut him off with an emphatic shake of her head.

"There will be no next time," she said flatly. "Farewell, Monsieur."

"Farewell, Madame."

"May God be with you."

"And with you," and he asked himself, Why not?

He stopped walking and let the cart pull away. Madame did not look back at him. The girl sat high upon a pile of bundles. When he saw her turn her cat-eyed gaze his way, he gave her a little wave. She did not return it. Congratulating himself on the way he had with children, he looked back at the town. It was the color of the surface of the moon. The muttering volcano was half-hidden by its own gray pall of smoke. The afternoon was passing hot, dark, and noisy.

Well, he thought, how much goddamn longer do I have to stay in this hellhole before I can decently abort the mission? It wouldn't make Thomas happy when he reported failure, but, then, Thomas was so rarely happy anyway. What did Thomas want him to *do*? Garrick had escaped—at least, Medlin hadn't sensed her since, when had it been, Monday?—and Ranke was a no-show.

He glanced after Madame Boislaville and did a double-take and stared. The soldiers had stepped forward at her approach, and she had halted the cart, and now he could see much gesticulating and hear the woman's voice raised in protest. Flabbergasted, he watched her turn the cart around and head back toward the town. He shook off his amazement and ran forward.

She did not slow the cart as he drew near. She looked as dangerous as the mountain itself as he fell in beside her and tried to walk, talk, look at her, and glare back at the soldiers all at the same time.

She cut him short. "The road to Fort-de-France is blocked," she said. "The soldiers say their orders came from the governor himself."

"Did you tell them you cannot stay here? That—"

"The soldiers do not care what anyone but the governor tells them."

"I shall go talk to them!"

"Yes," she said, "certainly they must be more willing to listen to a dirty American stranger than to a respectable widow," and the long switch hissed and snapped over the horse's back, and the cart kept moving.

They walked some distance wrapped in sullenness. Finally, Medlin said, "Madame, you and the girl must slip past the guards tonight."

She said, as she might impart an obvious fact to a stupid child, "The wizards will be out again tonight. They will kill anyone they find on the road."

"Then go by boat! I don't care *how* you get out, but you *must* get out!"

She seemed to be thinking it over, so he said no more. He noticed a small group of people gathered to examine a poster on a public bulletin board and stepped forward to read it.

Extraordinary Proclamation
to My Fellow Citizens of St. Pierre

The occurrence of the eruption of Mount Pelée has thrown the whole island into consternation. But aided by the exalted intervention of the Governor and of superior authority, the Municipal Administration has provided, in so far as it has been able, for distribution of essential foods and supplies. The calmness and wisdom of which you have proved yourselves capable in these recent anguished days allows us to hope that you will not remain deaf to our appeals. In accordance with the Governor, whose devotion is ever in command of circumstances, we believe ourselves able to assure you that, in view of the immense valleys which separate us from the crater, we have no immediate danger to fear. The lava will not reach as far as the town. Any further manifestion will be restricted to those places already affected. Do not, therefore, allow yourselves to fall victims to ground-less panic. Please allow us to advise you to return to your normal occupation, setting the necessary example of courage and strength during this time of public calamity.

—The Mayor, R. FOUCHÉ

Behind him, Madame asked softly, "What does it say?"

Barely able to contain his anger, he replied, "Nothing. Not a damn thing."

He barred the gate after she had driven the cart into the courtyard. The girl leaped down and vanished. Medlin helped her mother unhitch the cart and put the horse away, and then Madame led him into the back of the house. He had an impression of impersonal space given over to the utilitarian. It was gloomy and hot, and the ash was ubiquitous. The cafe area itself had acquired a dilapidated, disconsolate air during their brief absence.

Madame said, "I think there is still water for coffee in one of the storage jars. Perhaps even enough for washing."

"That would be wonderful, Madame."

The girl emerged without warning and in a hurry from the rear. She went straight to her mother, who instinctively wrapped both arms around her, and glared back over her own shoulder. Madame looked past Medlin and started. Medlin, whose back was to the doorway, heard his name spoken.

Ranke stood framed in the doorway and looked very pleased with the effect he was having. Throughout the years of their acquaintance, whenever he did not have the man actually in view, Medlin had always seen him in his mind's eye as being taller, leaner, steelier—Ranke admired those qualities and aspired to them, and had some odd knack for leaving people with the impression that he possessed them. In fact, as Medlin realized whenever he actually did see him again, Ranke was no taller or leaner than he was, and the steeliness was only the intent look of a predator, not necessarily a mammalian one. Ranke's light-colored and lidless gaze took in Madame at a glance, but lingered on the girl as though she might be prey, before coming smoothly back to Medlin. He said, "What day is it?"

"Wednesday," said Medlin, "the day before the eruption—" He shot a horrified look at Madame and saw that he need not have worried. Nothing he could have said would have got her attention from Ranke at that moment.

Ranke stepped into the room and said, without rancor, "Took your own sweet time getting me here."

Medlin did not reply. The man frequently did leave him with nothing to say. Instead, he turned to Madame. "You said you thought you still have some water for coffee."

It seemed all she could do to look away from the unblinking serpent, the staring-eyed hawk. "Y-yes."

"May we have some, please?"

"Yes. Of course, Monsieur."

Ranke stepped around to the left to vacate the doorway. The girl broke out of her mother's embrace and bolted through to safety. Madame herself edged toward the doorway from the right. The look of satisfaction on Ranke's face made a scowl start to build itself on Medlin's. Medlin said, "Let's keep this private," and led him up to the room, where Ranke looked about fascinatedly. When he spoke, there was amazement or amusement in his voice, or both.

"Some terrific base of operations you picked out here."

"Garrick picked it out. She had everything set up before I even got here."

"I know you've seen her, talked to her. I can smell her on you." Ranke half-smiled; one cheek dimpled. He moved to the windows and threw open the shutters. Without looking at Medlin, he said, "Why didn't you arrest her when you had her?"

"I didn't think it was part of my job. Anyway, she took my gun away from me."

Ranke shook his head and took out his own weapon. It was a Colt .38-caliber automatic, either an original or a replica. He was as likely to have the one as the other. He checked the chamber and polished the four-inch barrel on his sleeve. "I could have predicted that outcome. She took your balls away from you years ago. Still, it's not going to look good on the report, sport."

"Don't brandish that thing. She was expecting me. She's been expecting both of us, in fact. She says either you or she is going to have to die here, because she's not going back."

Ranke sighted along the barrel of the pistol at Medlin's sternum. "Pretty tough talk for an old lady. Did she say what she expects you to be doing while she and I are all locked together in mortal combat and everything? You going to be the scorekeeper, the cheerleader? The prize?"

"I'm getting just a little sick and tired of having guns pointed at me."

"All in fun."

"Even in fun. *Especially* in fun."

Ranke chuckled and lowered the pistol. "You won't always be so special, you know. Even with Garrick gone. Sooner or later, the agency'll land someone who knows the same tricks."

"You know it's not tricks. It's talent. Talent's rare."

"Not as rare as you think."

Medlin had never seen anyone look so smug before. He said, "You'll never be a traveler. You pitch wild."

"We're not alone here."

"I've seen them, too. I saw them the first night I was here."

"If you could see what *I* see—" Ranke gestured vaguely at the tableau outside the window. "All these different trails, like blurs of light on time-exposed film. They're threaded through the streets and criss-cross the hills up there. It looks like weaving with airplane contrails. There're a dozen people here who—" he grinned his predator grin and wagged a finger in the air admonishingly "—shouldn't be here. Most of them, sure, are passengers.

But at least one of them has to be a traveler, and maybe there's more than just one. If they've come to this little hellhole, they must have travelers to spare."

"They may not be as accommodating as you'd like. I didn't get the time of day out of them."

"I guess eventually we're going to find out just *how* accommodating they can be. The day when we all just pretend not to notice other time travelers and don't get involved with them is over. There's a plan now, and it'll only work if everyone sticks to it and does what they're supposed to."

"Ah yes," Medlin said, "the coming world order. Or should I call it the coming world re-order?"

"The world's in a mess. Things've got to change. From now on, whenever we run into other visitors, whoever they are, wherever they're from, they're going to have to listen to us. We'll tell them, These are our rules, you have to obey them from now on. You want to hear Lincoln talk at Gettysburg or see Catherine the Great screw the pony, you have to do things according to our rules. Otherwise, there's chaos."

"Garrick told me a little about those rules."

Ranke rolled his eyes ceilingward. "We both know what a talent she has for description. I'm sure she's told you there's some great mischief afoot."

"I'm not as convinced as she is," said Medlin, "that temporal engineering's possible. I'm more concerned about being on a leash."

"Ah. I *thought* she'd try to get you to go maverick with her if she had the chance."

"She may yet succeed."

"Listen to me, Medlin." Ranke stopped toying with the automatic and slipped it back into his pocket as a token of his own seriousness. "You and I have always cordially detested each other. I know you think I'm jealous of the interest she's always shown in you. You think her interest is affection. It isn't. It's self-interest. She thinks of you as her only peer and also as her only rival. She's always kept you close, by her side and on her side, so you couldn't be used against her some day. She wants to run now, but she can't leave you behind. She'd always be looking over her shoulder if she did. But if she did talk you into going with her, you think you wouldn't be on a leash then? She'd never let you out of her sight. Whether you stick with us or go with her, she'll end up trying to kill you."

Medlin's face felt as hot as the volcano's.

"I also know," Ranke went on, "you think I'm jealous because you're a traveler. Nothing is farther from the truth. I do pitch wild, and it's inconvenient. It forces me to rely on you. But inconvenient is all it is. I'm the world's best tracker, and only some of that's thanks to that old woman. As soon as it gets dark, we'll get on her trail."

"Waiting for dark's not such a great idea. Voodoo worshippers've taken over the streets at night."

"All the more reason," Ranke said, "for us to get a move on," and he grabbed Medlin's arm to haul him up. "Come on, it's check-out time."

"Let me go. I'm already worn out from walking. I hurt my leg the first night I was here, and I'm still limping."

"Pobrecito." Ranke had pulled him up and out of the room, and now they plunged down the stairs, almost upsetting Madame, who was carrying a tray with cups and coffee pot. Ranke seemed not to notice her at all. He went straight to the door and unbolted it. Behind them, the woman shrieked a protest and dropped her tray. Ranke still had hold of Medlin's coat and jerked him outside into the street by it. Snarling, Medlin twisted free, just in time to see the door slam shut. He heard the bolt go home with resounding finality.

"Nice going," he said. He was trembling with anger. "She wouldn't let Jesus himself back in now. Were you Custer in a previous life? Between Garrick and us are probably hundreds of voodoo worshippers!"

Ranke did not reply at once. He stood very quietly in the middle of the street, lost in thought. He was still clean—entirely too clean for St. Pierre— and the few passersby not in a wholly numbed state looked at him in wonder. Medlin thought for a moment that he saw uncertainty in the vertical groove that appeared between Ranke's eyebrows, and he guessed that atmospheric phenomena might indeed be interfering with the man's ability to locate Garrick's trail. But then Ranke smiled and swatted him on the arm and said to him as cheerily as though they had been bosom pals forever, "Come on, let's get moving."

They got moving. The volcano began to grumble and sputter again. It was all Medlin could do to keep from staring at it. It was all he could do to keep walking. Ranke completely ignored the demonstration and strode with the purposeful air of a hunting dog that knew exactly where its quarry was hunkered down. He was the one happy person in St. Pierre. The volcanic tumult did not last long, and when it subsided, silence descended over the town. Ash lay drifted like dirty snow against walls and in corners. All shutters were closed. It again occurred to Medlin that everyone was already dead, that the glowing cloud, when it came, would sweep through a city already extinct. The sun was setting as they reached the Avenue Victor Hugo. Ranke walked easily, almost sauntering. Medlin marched along with his fists deep in his coat pockets, choking on ash and fury, mad at Ranke, mad at the volcano, mad at the world. A number of refugees, men, women, children, sat or crouched in the doorways. They murmured among themselves if they talked at all. Most of them simply sat and stared at nothing that Medlin could see.

An elegant coach and pair came gliding ghostlike down the street. It slowed as it approached a group of soldiers and stopped before them just as Medlin and his companion passed behind them. The door was flung open, and a thick-bodied man wearing an ornate uniform struck a pose with one foot in the cab and the other on the step. He obviously expected to be recognized, and looked slightly crestfallen when the soldiers regarded him incuriously.

"I," he announced, "am Governor Mouttet!"

The soldiers exchanged looks among themselves and shuffled to suggest a military unit dressing its ranks. Behind them, Medlin heard Ranke snicker softly and said, "Wait," and stopped walking. Ranke looked annoyed but waited. Medlin's head filled with crazy ideas. He wondered if he might not somehow get Ranke's automatic away from him and force this Mouttet at gunpoint to evacuate the town. He wondered if he might not shoot Mouttet on principle, and Ranke as well, now that he thought about it. He wondered, as he realized the futility of grappling with Ranke, if Ranke might not shoot him, not fatally, just on principle.

Anger and perplexity were struggling for supremacy on the governor's face. He looked from one soldier to the next. "What," he demanded, "are you doing here?"

"Waiting, sir," said one man, "for the *bourhousses* to strike again."

"Again?"

"At dawn this morning, sir, the soldiers guarding the road to Fort-de-France were attacked by the voodoo worshippers. Two soldiers were strangled."

This obviously was all news to Governor Mouttet. He withdrew his head into the coach and conferred with another man, less flamboyantly attired, and a woman whom Medlin took to be Madame Mouttet. She was well-dressed but looked very anxious. After a moment, the governor thrust himself out again. He had begun to look somewhat choleric.

"Where," he demanded, "are the soldiers who are supposed to be patrolling the road?"

The corporal shrugged. "Somewhere in the town, sir."

"On whose authority?"

"I do not know, sir. Perhaps their own, sir!"

Governor Mouttet opened his mouth, closed it, and retreated into his coach. The driver cracked his whip. It was the crispest sound Medlin had heard in days, and it galvanized him. Before Ranke could have known what he was about, he pushed past the soldiers and leaped after the coach as it began to move. He got a foot on the step and the fingers of one hand around the frame of the door. "Governor Mouttet!" he yelled. "Order the immediate evacuation of the town!"

The two men and the woman gaped. Medlin heard the whip an instant before it wrapped itself around his neck and head and tried to slice off his ear. He screamed and lost his grip and landed on what must have been the last patch of uncushioned cobblestone pavement in St. Pierre. The side of his head was on fire.

The coach moved away without a sound and vanished into the gloom. Ranke was speaking to the soldiers in conciliatory tones. When he turned from them toward Medlin, his big friendly smile became the reptilian grimace of a crocodile. He helped Medlin stand, and while making a show of helping him brush himself off said, "Would've served you right if the coachman'd taken your ear off."

Medlin carefully felt along his scalpline. His fingers came away bloody.

"Don't do that again," Ranke said conversationally as he started tying his handkerchief around Medlin's head. "I mean it."

"Ranke, I know how scary you are. But—"

"Good. Now let's get out of here before these soldiers become any more curious about us. I told 'em you're drunk, so act it."

"But I'm *not afraid of you.*"

"Meaning, of course, that my threats and implied threats don't faze you, because you're my ride home. Fine. Be scared of whomever, whatever you like. But just don't make any more sudden moves like that, or I'll really hurt you," and he pulled the handkerchief too tightly over Medlin's injured ear, "and I mean, really, *really* hurt you."

Gripped by a hand he could not resist, Medlin made himself a drag on the other man's arm and said, "Listen."

Ranke barely slowed and barely looked his way. "Well? You have something to say?"

"No, *listen.*"

They listened. The drumming was beginning. Medlin heard someone— several people—running on the street behind them. He looked over at Ranke. "The voodoo people are about to put in an appearance."

"What're they going to do, come at us with cute little wax dolls?"

"Come at us with cute little steel machetes, more likely. Try to strangle us. Do something unpleasant to us, in any case. We've got to get indoors."

"More delay," Ranke said, shaking his head. He took out his pistol.

Medlin looked at him aghast. "You can't go around indiscriminately gunning down denizens!"

Ranke laughed. "*You* can't go around indiscriminately trying to *save* them! These people're all going to be dead in a few hours anyway. They're fair game. Besides, you moron—we're about to get mugged!"

A torchlit procession surged along the street toward them. At its head, men and women sang and danced. Some were trying to dance and drink; they splashed more liquor on themselves than in, but appeared not to mind. Behind them were the drummers, and next came three fantastic-looking figures. One of these held a squirming form, and Medlin thought, incredulously, A child? Then he saw that it was a bound goat. Each of the other two wizards carried aloft a fluttering, protesting chicken.

As soon as the celebrants saw the two white men, a howl went up. Several men armed with machetes ran out ahead of the procession. Medlin saw Ranke check the chamber of his pistol and take aim.

"Christ, Ranke!"

Fist on hip, Ranke glanced sideways at him and said, "Now don't go away."

"Shoot over their heads, scare them off!"

"They'll be scared a lot farther off if I nick the paint off a couple of them."

"If we're after Garrick, let's go *get* her, but—"

There was a flash of fire from the pistol's muzzle, and a shuddering little report. One of the advancing men gave a yelp and hit the ground like an empty suit of clothes. It enraged his companions. They raced forward, yelling, and Ranke yelled back and fired again into the rushing dark forms. Torches dipped, shadows elongated weirdly, brown-stained metal blades were raised. Medlin, already bac‹ing away, already turning and drawing his arms up and going into a crouch preparatory to pushing off at a dead run, saw Ranke's eyes slitted and his teeth bared in a puma's snarl. He looked very happy. Then his automatic jammed, and he had only enough time to say "*Shit!*" before the first machete blade and then the second and the third and the fourth descended in arcs and chopped him apart as if he were merely some obstinate jungle growth.

Medlin had already sprung away.

Once, as he ran, he tripped and went sprawling on the rough pavement, but there was yelling close behind him, and he scrambled forward on his toes and fingers like a dog for a short distance until he regained his feet. The air scourged his throat and lungs; it was like breathing hot sand. The buildings closed in on him from either side. Something reached up out of the earth itself to trip him. Something else gave a triumphant cry as it landed on his back. A wire or cord whipped about his throat. A knee as hard as teak pressed into the small of his back, and there was warm stinking breath on his cheek. Then he heard another gunshot and a startled grunt. The wire was suddenly gone, and the knee. Medlin, gasping, felt himself being lifted up, felt himself weightless. There were voices, but he was unable to concentrate on them. Everything receded for a time, and then returned more slowly than it had gone away. Serpents, he thought, wild pigs.

He was lying on ashy ground in what he took to be a small clearing. He could see a treetop-edged patch of red-tinted sky above. There were four, five, or six glowing people present, some of them moving about, making it impossible for him to get an accurate count. One, however, was kneeling over him, examining his throat. Another stood behind this man and looked down over his shoulder at Medlin.

"Where am I?" Medlin croaked.

"Safe," said the kneeling man. "Inside the botanical gardens."

"Relatively safe," said the person standing behind him. "This is no place for tourists."

Medlin recognized the second speaker as one of the luminous men he had seen—how many nights before?

"Civilization's falling apart here," the flat-faced man said.

Medlin said, "Who the hell are you?"

A familiar voice said, "Fine way to talk to folks who just saved your life," and Garrick's nimbused head appeared over the shoulder of the flat-faced man. "Med, this is Doctor Leonard Beers, and that's his assistant, Frank Cooley, checking your neck. Doctor, Mister Cooley, this is my young friend Medlin whom I've told you about."

Medlin looked up at Beers and said, "Doctor, we probably could've avoided a whole lot of melodrama just now if you hadn't been so stuck up a few nights ago."

Beers did not look concerned. "Frankly, Mister Medlin, I thought you were a drunken tourist at the time. In any case, we have no interest in anyone's business here but our own." He turned to Garrick then and said, "You'll have to excuse me now, we've got a lot of work to do," and strode off without waiting for a reply.

"Bit of a cold fish," Medlin said.

Garrick shrugged. She was wearing a broad-brimmed hat and men's clothing, loose shirt, loose trousers. "He just really isn't too keen on getting involved in our affairs, or letting us get involved in his. I'm sure he'd despise our little intrigues if he knew much about them. Here."

She handed him a cup of water and a foodstick. The water was cold and delicious but hurt his throat. The foodstick was stale, chalky, and impossible to swallow.

"The voodoo people killed Ranke," he gasped after draining the cup.

Garrick gave a soft snort. "I guess they didn't buy his rough-tough act," she said. "I never could make him understand that *machismo* will get you hurt faster than anything."

Medlin looked around. The strangers were fiddling with odd devices or packing equipment. Beers cut in among them like a factory foreman, barking instructions.

Medlin said, "Who are these people?"

"What *we* started out to be—scientists, historians. They're here to study and record the eruption. Pelée, Tambora, Krakatau, they're recording all the biggest and most famous ones. Nobody, no competent observer, anyway, ever saw a glowing cloud until Pelée. Nobody was set up to study Pelée until after the Ascension Day eruption, or even had the instruments. Volcanology was barely a science in nineteen oh two. Anyway, they'll be clearing out as soon as they finish setting up their monitoring devices. They've got an observation station set up on the heights south of the destruction zone."

"But where're they *from*?"

"I believe they postdate us," she said. "As always, everyone's treating everyone else like a denizen. Mustn't talk, can't say, won't get involved. Still, they did help me carry you into the gardens after I plugged that strangler."

"Ranke knows—knew they were here. I think he was starting to have designs on their travelers."

"Well, Ranke's dead, and they only have the one traveler anyway." She laughed softly. "But, ah, he is worth having designs on."

"You're incorrigible. How long do we have now?"

"Hours. The climactic eruption starts at seven fifty-two A.M."

"Well," Medlin said drily, "I sure don't want to miss seeing the climactic eruption, now do I?"

Beers happened to overhear that. Arms akimbo, he said, very sternly, "I would advise you not to see it from here."

Oblivious to irony, Medlin thought, and said, "What about Morne Rouge?"

"What about Morne Rouge?"

"Is it safe? Safe tomorrow?"

"Tomorrow, yes. But you haven't a chance of reaching it tonight."

Something made Medlin ask, "Is it safe later?"

"Later?" The scientist seemed surprised by the question. "Well, if you mean—it catches holy hell at the end of August."

"Deaths?"

Beers shrugged. "Not as many as here. Probably not more than two thousand in all." He saw something being done wrong and walked away to see that it was done right.

Medlin did not know why he should have felt more pain at the thought of two thousand denizens dying at Morne Rouge five months from now than at the thought of thirty thousand killed in St. Pierre tomorrow morning. For all he knew, Father Hayot and his two hundred forlorn parishioners had not lingered any longer at Morne Rouge than at St. Pierre. Until this moment, he didn't know that he had been rooting for the priest and his flock. At least they had shown better sense than anyone in Little Paris. He found himself wanting to think that they would somehow survive all of the volcano's tantrums, even as he found himself disbelieving that any denizen, lacking precise knowledge of the future, could possibly escape. The lethal ingenuity of human beings was as nothing compared with that of Pelée. If it failed to kill you with lava or poison gas or a mudslide, it could always send a big wave to drown you, or *fer-de-lances*, or a tumbling hogshead.

He looked mournfully at Garrick, who murmured, "Some denizen you met?"

"Denizens."

"Shouldn't get so attached, Med."

"I know. But all of a sudden I'm really tired of being detached."

Rain began to patter around them. Medlin looked up and let the warm drops strike his ashy face. It felt good until he touched his cheek. Then it just felt slimy. Garrick stood up grousing about her old bones, and they moved to stand under a tree. Medlin heard the muffled pealing of bells striking the hour and counted the strokes. It was ten o'clock.

Garrick produced a flat case and a penlight from her bag. She opened the case and trained the penlight on its contents. Medlin saw two dozen slender, gleaming ampoules.

"There's enough here," she said, "to get both of us through a dozen trips if nineteen oh two doesn't work out."

"Eventually, we'll run out."

"Big deal. Eventually, we'll run out and not be able to travel first-class any more. But we'll still be able to travel."

"It's rough without drugs."

"So's childbirth, I hear, but women who don't have drugs still have babies. We'll just have to be careful not to throw up on anyone important or bad-tempered when we arrive someplace. Consider the alternative, Med. Even if just the idea of temporal engineering doesn't scare the ass off you . . . we'd become cargo vessels, and there'd be someone else's hand on the tiller all the time. The cargo'd be people like Ranke and people a lot worse than Ranke. That's your fate, if you go back."

That was the last thing Medlin remembered hearing for a while. A deep rumbling from the volcano woke him from a doze. Garrick was still sitting beside him, watching the scientists work. The noise increased, and then came a billowing mass of red smoke. Medlin sat up in alarm. Garrick calmly looked at her watch again, then said, "It's still just demonstrating. But we need to be leaving soon. If we are going to leave."

"You know I'm not going back. Before we fly off somewhere, though—" Medlin looked at her very seriously "—I want to help Madame Boislaville escape from St. Pierre."

Garrick pulled dubiously on her chin. "Maybe she's supposed to die with all her neighbors in the morning. And even if she isn't—"

"Maybe she isn't. She told me you yourself urged her to go visit her relatives in the south."

Garrick seemed slightly abashed. "I wasn't trying to force events. I just thought I'd give them a little nudge. Maybe she *isn't* supposed to die in the morning. Maybe the reason she doesn't is that a crazy white boy rescues her. What do you, as the crazy white boy, propose to do with her once you've rescued her?"

Medlin shrugged. "Wish her a long and happy life in Fort-de-France."

"Med, whether she lives or dies, what difference does it really make? She's still a ghost."

"No, you're wrong. You can't really believe what you just said. Otherwise, why would you have bothered even to try to nudge events, as you call it? Denizens or not, anomalies or not, we're— Ranke didn't think these people were real at all, and they hacked him to pieces."

"You know what I mean." Garrick heaved a great sigh. "Look, did I tell you how I met Clara Prentiss? Missis Prentiss, the American Consul's wife? It was last Friday morning, just after I'd arrived and just after the volcano'd started to act up. We weren't exactly formally introduced. I only happened to see her on the street. In a wonderful display of futile and misdirected concern, she tried to rescue a suffocated bird that'd fallen in the road. I took it away from her and threw it away and told her not to waste her sentiment. She looked at me like I'd arrived from a moon of Saturn."

"Sometimes," said Medlin, "you act like it. Between nineteen forty and here, I've seen too many people killed by Stukas and volcanoes and crap. I just don't think I can stand to be around denizens any more and go on telling myself, Well, this is their world, these are their lives, aw gee, that was their deaths. We're going to be living entirely among them from now on. We've got to stop thinking of them as people who've been in their graves for hundreds of years."

"If you save her, you become responsible for the woman's life, and her daughter's, and for all their descendants."

"I think if time's been resilient enough to accommodate us all this while, it ought to be able to accommodate a couple of denizens just this once."

"*Aiee.* You're cutting it thin with this rescue."

"I'll get out in time."

"Christ, as long as you're determined to go through with this madness—" Garrick dug around in her bag and handed over a revolver "—you better take this. In case we run into the voodoo people again."

"We? If you don't approve, don't come along."

"Well, I can't have you changing your mind about going AWOL as soon as you're out of my sight." Something Ranke had said nagged at Medlin. He set the thing carefully to one side in his mind, to be examined later. Garrick was looking at her watch again. "Besides," she said, "someone's got to keep time. We don't want to be sitting too close to the stage when the show starts."

They stood up, and Garrick sought out Beers, who seemed very uncomfortable as she thanked him for his help. He said, without looking at Medlin, "I thought you were going with us. The *quimboiseurs* aren't likely to attack a group the size of ours."

She shook her head. "I'm too old to go trekking through any jungle at night. Anyway, the streets're pretty quiet now. Even wizards have to go home and explain to their wives why they've been out so late. My friend and I'll take the coast road south."

"Then good luck to you," said Beers, "and your friend."

Each with gun in hand, Medlin and Garrick slipped past the gates of the botanical gardens. It was five-thirty by the antique watch. Dawn, the eighth of May, Thursday, Ascension Day, looked and felt like the inside of a filthy pressure cooker. Dirty red smoke hung above the crater. Pierrotins were emerging from their homes. Most of them drifted like sleepwalkers in the direction of the cathedral.

At Madame Boislaville's, all the shutters had been closed and the cracks stuffed with rags. Medlin pounded on the door and called her name, but got no response. He walked around to the courtyard gate and carefully aimed at the padlock. It took two shots from the revolver, a Smith & Wesson .38-caliber housegun, to shatter the big padlock. He ran into the courtyard and began banging on the shutters at the rear of the house. He identified himself loudly and kept shouting her name. Finally, suddenly, a shutter on one of the upstairs windows opened. She was only a dark shape, outlined by the glow of a candle.

"Go away!" she cried out to him. "Go to your own kind!"

Garrick appeared beside him and raised her empty hand in greeting. "Madame Boislaville!" she said out gaily. "How delightful to see you again!"

"We must leave this town *now*," Medlin said. "We have come to give you safe passage to Fort-de-France."

"The wizards—"

They held up their revolvers for her to see, and Garrick declared that any wizard who showed his face would be shot. Madame made no reply. The shutter remained open for a few more seconds, then closed with a rattle. Medlin looked up at it unhappily, convinced that she had made up her mind to die in her home. The same thought must have occurred simultaneously to Garrick, for she began, with a shrug in her tone, "If she's determined not to be rescued—"

Down from the mountain came the sound of a great detonation. It was followed in short order by a second and then a third. Garrick nervously fingered her watch. Finally, she said, "We really do have to—"

Madame Boislaville's rear door opened, and she appeared looking hot, tired, dirty, and unfriendly. She was clutching her beads in one hand and made the other into a fist. Medlin had thought the heat in the courtyard was suffocating, but the mass of air that oozed out past her to envelope him was as dense and heavy as lead.

"Madame," he said, "I implore you to leave with us at once."

"I . . ."

Garrick went to the woman's side. "Madame Boislaville," she said, "this young man is determined to save you from the mountain. Please go get your daughter while he hitches your cart."

"The horse is dead . . ."

"Then we must walk," Garrick said, "and we must start immediately."

The two women turned and moved into the building. Medlin stationed himself in the doorway. He overheard a brief argument about belongings; Garrick insisted that there was no time to gather them. She returned leading Madame, who was wrapped in a shawl and leading Elizabeth by one hand, carrying only a rosary in the other. Medlin brought up the rear. Garrick urged them to hurry as they entered the street, and they moved at a fast walk through the gloom. As they passed over the rim of the amphitheater, they paused to look back. The volcano's incandescent eye peered through a great sifting veil of airborne debris. The pall dispersed as a warm, sulphurous wind blew down the mountainside. The sun shone down on St. Pierre, revealing a roadstead full of anchored ships and, high on Pelée's side, a great glowing patch. They hurried on, and only Medlin looked back again. Each time, the town seemed to have sunk a little farther into the earth until at last it vanished altogether. Little Paris, Little Sodom, goodbye, he thought.

As the soldier had told Governor Mouttet, there were no guards to turn back refugees now. But there were not many refugees. A few riders and carriages passed the four, hurrying along the road without acknowledging their presence.

A little more than an hour later, tired, footsore, and thirsty, they arrived at a small fishing village that lay half under the jungle and half on the upper reaches of a glistening black beach. The beach itself lay between two steep-sided promontories.

Medlin asked, in English, "How long till the volcano blows?"

"Not long," said Garrick.

"Are we far enough away?"

"Yes."

"You're sure?"

"I'm sure, Med."

On the beach, villagers—women, children, and old men—were pulling in a long net. Offshore, younger men in small boats slapped their oars against the water.

"That is to frighten the fish," Madame said, "and keep them from escaping the net."

The girl Elizabeth voiced a complaint. It was the first sound Medlin could remember hearing her make. It was like the squeak of a young cat.

Madame stroked her hair and murmured to her in creole, then turned to them.

"We can rest here," she said, "and probably get something to eat and drink."

"Good," said Garrick. "My mouth feels like a lava bed."

They walked down into the village. An ancient woman told them that soon there would be fresh fish to eat, for the catch was much better this morning than it had been for the past several days. She explained that there was no good water for coffee and no rum, only some sugar-cane juice. She poured the juice into wooden cups for them. It tasted grassy. The four refugees sipped and watched from a discreet distance as the villagers hauled in their net.

"They'll send someone else," Medlin said after a while.

Garrick shook her head. "They don't *have* anyone else. No one like us. No one."

"They could get lucky and find another real traveler."

"Maybe not. Listen, Beers and his group have got to be from our future. I saw 'em using equipment no volcanologist ever saw in *our* time, let alone in nineteen oh two. Believe me, I've learned a lot about volcanology lately. Now, I imagine there's about as much wrong with the world in Beers' time as there is in the Awful Oughts, but seeing these scientists and historians going about their work here—unchaperoned, unfettered, undisturbed by anyone except us—sure suggests to me that temporal engineering didn't even get out of the starting gate. Why? Because it requires a traveler to carry meddling passengers. Why wasn't there a traveler? Because we two travelers went AWOL, and no one else qualified for the j—"

There was a sudden sound like a cannonade, and the feeble sun disappeared completely. The sound did not fade but grew louder by the moment. It came to the village like a rolling barrage of artillery fire. The villagers screamed inaudibly and scattered across the beach. To the north, the glowing cloud climbed into the sky, filled it, displaced it. The cloud was red and edged with black, then black suffused with red, and as it expanded it resembled God's or the Devil's great opening hand. Fire and lightning flashed through it. One sickly purple flash showed Medlin stranded fish thrashing on the sand near his feet. The next showed him Madame Boislaville, in tears, plainly terrified, with Elizabeth at her side, clutching her waist, looking at the cloud with wide cat eyes and open mouth. He reached out and took Madame's hand and felt her strong dark fingers grasp his needfully. Holding hands was no guarantee of anything, but sometimes it was good for a little reassurance.

GRAVITY'S ANGEL

Tom Maddox

Here's an informed and thoughtful look at the megabuck world of Big Science—and a reminder that even with the very biggest of projects, you can't afford to overlook even the *smallest* of possibilities . . .

Born in Beckley, West Virginia, Tom Maddox is currently on sabbatical from his position at Evergreen State University in Washington. Although he has sold only a handful of stories to date, primarily to *Omni* and *Isaac Asimov's Science Fiction Magazine*, he scored a major success last year with the publication of his well-received first novel, *Halo*—and I suspect we'll be seeing a lot more from him as the decade progresses. Maddox currently lives in Oakland, California, and contributes a monthly column of "Reports from the Electronic Frontier" to *Locus*.

The Invisible Bicycle burned beneath me in the moonlight, its transparent wheels refracting the hard white light into rainbow colors that played across the blacktop. Beneath the road's surface the accelerator tunnel ran, where the SSC—the Superconducting Synchroton Collider—traced a circle 160 kilometers in circumference underneath the Texas plains.

Depending on how you feel about big science and the Texas economy, the SSC was either a superb new tool for researching the subatomic world, or high-energy physics' most outrageous boondoggle. Either way, it was a mammoth raceway where subatomic particles were pushed to nearly the speed of light, then crashed together as violently as we could contrive—smash-ups whose violence was measured in trillions of electron volts.

Those big numbers get all the press, but it's only when particles interact that experiments bear fruit. The bunches of protons want to pass through each other like ghosts, so we—the High Beta Experiment Team, my work group—had all sorts of tricks for getting more interactions. Our first full-energy shots were coming up, and when the beams collided in Experimental Area 1, we would be rewarded for years of design and experiment.

So I had thought. Now I rode a great circle above the SSC, haunted by questions about infinity, singularity—improbable manifestations even among the wonderland of quantum physics, where nothing was—*quite*—real. And more than that, I was needled and unsettled by questions about the way we—not my group but all of us, the high-energy physics community—did our business. I'd always taken for granted that we were after the truth, whatever its form, whatever our feelings about it. Now even that simple assumption had collapsed, and I was left with unresolvable doubts about it all—the nature of the real, the objectivity of physics—riddles posed by an unexpected visitor.

Two nights earlier I had returned from a ride to find a woman standing in front of my house. "Hello," I said, as I walked the Invisible Bicycle up the driveway toward her. "Can I help you?"

"I'm Carol Hendrix," she said, and from the sound of her voice, she was just a little bit amused. "Are you Sax?"

"Yes," I said. And I asked, "Why didn't you tell me you were coming?" Really I was just stalling, trying to take in the fact that *this* woman was the one I'd been writing to for the past six months.

We had begun corresponding in our roles as group leaders at our respective labs, me at SSC-Texlab, her at Los Alamos, but had continued out of shared personal concerns: a mutual obsession with high-energy physics and an equally strong frustration with the way big-time science was conducted—the whole extra-scientific carnival of politics and publicity that has surrounded particle accelerators from their inception.

Her letters were sometimes helter-skelter but were always interesting— reports from a powerful, disciplined intelligence working at its limits. She had the kind of mind I'd always appreciated, one comfortable with both experiment and theory. You wouldn't believe how rare that is in high-energy physics.

Women in the sciences can be hard and distant and self-protective, because they're working in a man's world and they know what that means. They tell each other the stories, true ones: about Rosalind Franklin not getting the Nobel for her X-ray work on DNA, Candace Pert not getting the Lasker for the first confirmation of opiate receptors in the brain. And so they learn the truth: in most kinds of science, there are few women, and they have to work harder and do better to get the same credit as men, and they know it. That's the way things are.

Carol Hendrix looked pale and tired, young and vulnerable—not at all what I'd expected. She was small, thin-boned, and her hair was clipped short. She wore faded blue jeans, a shirt tied at the waist, and sandals over bare feet.

"I didn't have time to get in touch with you," she said. Then she laughed, and her voice had a ragged, nervous edge to it. "No, that's not true. I didn't get in touch with you because I knew how busy you were, and you might tell me to come back later. I can't do that. We need to talk, and I need your help . . . *now*—before you do your first full-beam runs."

"What kind of help?" I asked. Already, it seemed, the intimacy of our letters was being transformed into instant friendship in real time.

"I need Q-system time," she said. She meant time on QUARKER, the lab's simulation and imaging system. She said, "I've got some results, but they're incomplete—I've been working with kludged programs because at Los Alamos we're not set up for your work. I've *got* to get at yours. If my simulations are accurate, you need to postpone your runs."

I looked hard at her. "Right," I said. "That's great—just what Diehl wants to hear. That you want precious system time to confirm a hypothesis that could fuck up our schedule."

"Diehl is a bureaucrat," she said. "He doesn't even understand the physics."

Yeah, I thought, *true, but so what?* Roger L. Diehl: my boss and everyone else's at the lab, also the SSC's guardian angel. He had shepherded the accelerator's mammoth budgets through a hostile Congress, mixing threat and promise, telling them strange tales about discoveries that lay just at the 200 TeV horizon. All in all, he continued the grand tradition of accelerator lab nobility: con men, politicians, visionaries, what have you. Going back to Lawrence at Berkeley, accelerator labs prospered under hard-pushing megalomaniacs whose talents lay as much in politics and P.R. as science, men whose labs and egos were one.

"Let's talk," I said. "Come inside, tell me your problem."

"All right," she said.

"Where are you staying?" I asked.

"I thought I'd find someplace later, after we've talked."

"You can stay here. Where are your bags?"

"This is it." She pointed to the sidewalk beside her. At her feet was a soft black cotton bag.

"Come on in," I said.

I figured she would be doing interesting work, unusual work; maybe even valuable work, if she'd gotten lucky. I wasn't the least bit ready for what she was up to.

We cranked up "The Thing," a recent development in imaging. It had a wall-mounted screen four feet in diameter; on it you could picture detector results from any of the SSC's runs. When it was running, the screen was a tangle of lines, the tracks of the particles, their collisions, disappearances, appearances; all the wonderland magic so characteristic of the small, violent world of particle physics, where events occur in billionths of a second, and matter appears and disappears like the Cheshire cat, leaving behind only its smile—in the form of brightly-colored particle tracks across our screens.

Still, setting up and running simulations is an art, and at any accelerator lab there'll be one or two folk who have the gift. When a series of important shots is coming up, they don't get much sleep. At Los Alamos, Carol Hendrix, despite her status as group leader, was the resident wizard. At Texlab, we had Dickie Boy.

She stretched, then sat at the swing-arm desk with its keyboard and joystick module and logged on to QUARKER with the account name and passwords I gave her. Her programs were number-crunching bastards, and QUARKER'S Cray back end would be time-slicing like mad to fit them in.

"Tell me what this is all about," I said. "So I'll know what we're looking at when this stuff runs."

"Sure," she said.

While we waited for QUARKER, she drew equations and plots on my whiteboard in red, green, black, and yellow, and she explained that she was postulating the existence of a new kind of attractor that came into being in a region of maximum chaos, its physical result an impossible region of spacetime, where an infinite number of particle events occupied a single, infinitesimal point.

Mathematically and otherwise, it is called a singularity, and in cosmology something like it is assumed to be at the center of black holes. There were all sorts of theorems about singularities, few of which I knew, none rigorously. Why would I? This stuff went with astrophysics and the gravitational forces associated with huge chunks of mass.

When she finished her explanations and turned from the whiteboard, I could see that she was wired and sleepy at once. Mostly, though, she was exultant: she felt she'd hit the jackpot. And of course she had, if any of this made sense . . . it couldn't, I thought.

The Thing gonged, to tell us we had our results. I pulled up a canvas-backed chair beside her as she sat at the console. "We'll walk through the simulation," she said. "If you have a question, ask."

At first there were just cartoon schematics of the detectors; line drawings of the big central detector and its surrounding EM boxes, hadron calorimeters, and gas chambers. Then the beam shots started coming, and in a small window at the top of the screen, the beam parameters reeled by. Running Monte Carlos is one hell of a lot easier than doing an actual run; you don't have the actual experimental uncertainties about good beam, good vacuum, reliable detector equipment; it's a simulation, so everything works right.

As we watched, the usual sorts of events occurred, particles and antiparticles playing their spear-carrying roles in this drama, banging together and sending out jets of energy that QUARKER dutifully calculated, watching the energy-conservation books the whole time, ready to signal when something happened it couldn't fit into the ledger. Complex and interesting enough in its own way, all this, but just background.

QUARKER shifted gears all of a sudden, signaling it had so many collisions it could not track them accurately. The screen turned into what we called a "hedgehog," a bristly pattern of interactions too thick to count.

"We don't care," Carol Hendrix whispered. "Do it." And she forced QUARKER to plunge ahead, made it speed up the pictures of events. She didn't care about the meanings of the individual events; she was looking for something global and, I thought, damned unlikely.

Events unrolled until we seemed to be in the middle of the densest particle interactions this side of the Big Bang, and I almost forgot what we were there for, because this stuff was the product of my work, showing that, as promised, we would give the experimenters higher beam luminosity than they'd dreamed of having.

Then the numbers of collisions lessened, and that was the first time I believed she was on to something. Things were going backward. The beam continued to pour in its streams of particles, but all usual interactions had ceased: inside the beam pipes, one utterly anomalous point was absorbing all that came its way. We both sat in complete silence, watching the impossible.

The screen cleared, then said:

```
            END SIMULATION
Quantitative evaluation appears impossible
employing standard assumptions. The conclu-
sions stated do not permit unambiguous physi-
cal interpretation.
```

We lay outside in reclining chairs and watched the sky. The moon was down, and stars glittered gold against the black. Meteors cut across the horizon, particles flashing through the universe's spark chamber. We'd been drinking wine, and we were both a little high—the wine, sure, both of us drinking on empty stomachs, but more than that, the sense of discovery she had communicated to me.

"Finding the order behind the visible," she said. "I've wanted to be part of that for as long as I can remember. And at Los Alamos I've gotten a taste. They offered me a job two years ago, and the offer just caught me at the right time. I had done some work I was proud of, but it was frustrating—it's easy for a woman to become a permanent post-doc. And to make things worse, I'd always worked in my husband's shadow."

"He's a physicist?"

"Yes. At Stanford, at SLAC. We've been separated since I took the job. The two things, the job and the split-up, sort of came as a package." She stopped, and the only sound was the faint roar of cars down the Interstate nearby. She said, "Tell me what happens tomorrow."

"That depends on Diehl's reaction. I'll see him in the morning. First I'll ask to borrow our resident imaging expert. That is, if I can pry him loose. I'm figuring Diehl won't want to look at any of this stuff; he might want a report on it, if I can talk to him just right. After that, we'll see."

"Okay," she said. "Look, I'm really tired . . ."

"I'm sorry. I should have said something." I started to get up, but she said, "No, I'm fine. I'll see you in the morning." She waved goodnight and headed into the house; I'd shown her the guest room earlier and folded out the couch for her.

I lay watching the sky, my mind circling around the strangeness we'd seen earlier. I wanted to understand it all more clearly than I did, and I hoped that Dickie Boy would be a help. In particular, he might know where her simulations had gone wrong. They had to be wrong, or else . . .

I sipped at wine and wondered at the possibility that I was present at one of those moments in physics that get embalmed and placed into the history books. I suppose I was still wondering when I fell asleep.

I was jerked awake some time later by a noise like high wind through metal trees. Amber flashes of light came from the side of the house, and a piano-shaped machine rolled out on clear plastic treads, ripping chunks of sod with its aerating spikes as it came. The machine was a John Deere "Yardman," apparently run amok.

I went into the house and called Grounds and Maintenance. A few minutes later a truck pulled up, and a man in dark blue overalls got out and called the robot to him with a red-lighted control wand, then cracked an access hatch in its side. Optic fibers bloomed in the robot's interior like phosphorescent alien plants.

I awoke around eight-thirty the next morning. Carol Hendrix was still in bed; I let her sleep. I left a message on Diehl's machine asking for a few minutes person-to-person, then I drank coffee and worked again through her Monte Carlos: lovely work, plausible and elegant, but almost certainly not enough to move Diehl. How could it? As she had said, he wouldn't understand it.

However, I knew who would. In the event that Dickie Boy vetted her simulations, we'd take them to the Thursday Group that evening. We met weekly at Allenson's house. Every important work-group at the lab was represented, and every significant problem the groups worked on was discussed there. Thursday Group was the locus of oral tradition, the place where the lab's work was revealed and its meaning decided upon. By the time experimental results saw print, they were old news to anyone who had been to Thursday Group. Usually there were ten or so people there, all men, most in their mid-thirties, most of them white and the rest Chinese.

Mid-morning she came in, wearing old Levi's and a black tank top. "Any news?" she asked, and I told her no. She got a cup of coffee and sat next to me and watched as her simulations played.

Shortly after noon a message popped up in a window on the screen: "If you want to talk, meet me in section 27 within the next hour. Diehl."

"Do you want me to come along?" she asked, and I said, "No way. He's a tricky bastard to handle at the best of times." I left her sitting at the console, starting the Monte Carlos up again.

I rode the Invisible Bicycle to the shuttle station at Maingate and locked it in the rack outside. Down concrete steps I went and into the cold, musty air of the tunnel. A dark blue, bullet-shaped shuttle car sat waiting. I was the only one boarding. I told the car where I was going. "Section 27," it confirmed in its colorless voice.

The repetitive color scheme of the lattice flashed by the windows. Radiofrequency boosters were in red, superconducting dipoles in blue, quadrupoles in orange; the endless beam pipes, where the straw-thin beams of protons and antiprotons would circle, were long arcs of bright green. If there were a universal symbolism of colors, these would say, *intricate, precise, expensive, technologically superb*—the primary qualities of the SSC.

About ten minutes later, the car slowed to a stop. The doors slid back, and I stepped down into the tunnel. About fifty meters away, Diehl stood talking to a man wearing blue overalls with the yellow flashes of a crew chief. The man looked taut, white-faced. "So pull every goddamned dipole with that batch number and replace the smart bolts," Diehl said. They walked toward me, and the crew chief stopped at a com station and plugged in his headset, no doubt beginning the evil task Diehl had set him.

"What can I do for you, Sax?" he asked.

"I've got a visitor," I said. "From Los Alamos. And she's got some interesting simulations of our full-power shots. I think you ought to see them." He looked startled; he hadn't expected me to ask for his time—money, resources, priority, yes, but not *his time*. "Or maybe not," I said. "Maybe you should let me have Dickie Boy put her Monte Carlos on the Thing. She's got some strange stuff there, and if it works out, we need to be prepared."

"Sax, what the fuck are you talking about? I'm tired, you know? We're in the home stretch here, on budget, on time . . . now take Hoolan—you know, who heads the Meson Group—he knows nothing about this. He knows his experiments are coming up soon, his simulations do not make shit for sense, and Dickie Boy is the one to help him. But if he is not not available because you have him doing what you consider the Lord's work, Hoolan's going to be pissed, because he *cannot* understand why, in light of these approaching deadlines, he should have to come begging for assistance."

"Then maybe you should come look at what she's got." I was playing a tricky game, using my position as group leader to put pressure on him but betting he wouldn't want to give up valuable time and maybe expose his ignorance. "I think this is really important."

He was watching the crew chief explaining to six men that they would be working in the tunnel until the troublesome smart bolts had been replaced. None of them looked happy. "Jesus," Diehl said. "Take Dickie Boy if you can convince *him*."

"Thanks," I said. He looked at me like he tasted something sour. I owed him one, and one thing was sure: he'd collect when and where he wanted.

"You really like this thing, don't you?" Carol Hendrix asked as she reached up to touch one of the Invisible Bicycle's clear polystyrene tires. It hung from rubber-covered hooks just inside my front door.

"Yeah," I said. "I got it in Germany. It's just plastic, but there's something wonderful about it—almost the Platonic idea of a bicycle. There's one in the Museum of Modern Art." Hanging above her head, it seemed to glow in the soft light given off by baby spots. "I usually ride it to think."

"What do we do now?" she asked. She wasn't interested in my toy.

"We get Dickie Boy over here," I said. "If we can. I'll call him."

"New physics," I told Dickie Boy on the phone. "Nothing you've ever seen."

"Bullshit," he said.

"No bullshit. Wrong physics, maybe—that's what we want you to help with, find out if we're missing something tricky."

"Or something obvious." He had no respect for anyone's ability on The Thing but his own.

"I don't think so. I think we've got a whole set of tracks here like nothing you've ever seen."

"I've got the Meson Group on my schedule."

"I know. Diehl said I could borrow you today."

"Where you want me?"

"Come over to my house." No way I wanted anyone looking over our shoulders.

Dickie Boy had made his name as a post-doc at Fermilab, where Diehl had recruited him when the SSC was nothing but a stack of plans, an empty tunnel, and mounds of heaped dirt. He hadn't been brought on for his good looks: he stood just over six feet tall and weighed maybe a hundred and thirty pounds; his dull brown hair was tied into dreadlocks; he had a long, thin nose and close-set eyes and usually seemed slightly dirty. However, in his brief time at Texlab he had already made legendary forays on The Thing— the last, a tricky sequence of pion studies, lasted nearly seventy-two hours, during which time Dickie Boy had worked through several shifts of physicists and finished by asking the group leader if he needed anything more.

Carol had heard about Dickie Boy, but she had her own reputation, and so when they said hello and looked each other over, I could almost hear the wheels turning, the question being posed, "Are you as good as they say?"

We went to the terminal, and Carol ran the Monte Carlos as Dickie Boy sat almost squirming with impatience to have a look at what she was doing. When she got out of the chair, he almost leapt into it and said, "You two go somewhere else, okay? The other room's all right; just leave me alone."

"I need to do some work at the office," I told Carol. "What about you?"

"Yeah," she said. "I should check my mail at the lab, see who's angry that I'm gone. You got another terminal with a modem?"

"In the bedroom," I said. "I'll see you two later."

At HBET I found a line of people waiting for me to talk about or approve their experimental arrangements, and so I spent the afternoon there, amid the chaos of getting the SSC ready for its first full-energy runs, scheduled for just a month away.

Carol and Dickie Boy were seated next to one another when I returned, with another variation on her Monte Carlos on the screen in front of them. "What's up?" I said, and Dickie Boy said, "This is fantastic." Carol was smiling.

"Think we can take it to Thursday Group?" I asked.

"Tough audience," Dickie Boy said.

"Is it the one that counts?" Carol asked.

"Yes, it is," I said. "If we can convince them, they'll go up against Diehl or anyone else."

"Let's do it, then," she said.

"Can you do a presentation?" I asked. "Good talk, good pictures?"

"Yes," she said. "I've been getting ready to do it."

"Fine," I said. "I'll call Allenson and ask if I can take over the agenda. I don't think anyone's got anything hot working."

*   *   *

Bad haircuts, cheap clothes, and an attitude—that's the way I once heard a gathering of theoretical physicists described. They—*we*—consider ourselves aristocrats of the mind, working in the deepest and most challenging science there is. Getting there first with good ideas, that's the only thing that counts—under all circumstances, that was the unspoken credo.

The whole group showed up that night. The living room of Allenson's house was shabby and comfortable, with couches, chairs, and large pillows enough to hold the sixteen of us: thirteen regulars and me, Carol, and Dickie Boy. Eight Caucasians and five Orientals, three Chinese and two Japanese. Most were in their late thirties, though a few were in their middle forties. No one under thirty, no one over fifty. These were the theoretical heavyweights at the lab, men in their short-lived prime as it exists in high-energy physics. A few were drinking coffee; most just sat waiting, talking.

I gave her the simplest possible introduction. I said, "This is Carol Hendrix, who is here from Los Alamos, where she is Simulations Group Leader. She has some very interesting simulations she would like to present to us."

Carol Hendrix knew her audience. She had gone into sexless mode as much as possible. Her face was pale and scrubbed, no makeup, and she wore baggy tan trousers and a plaid wool shirt—in short, the closest approximation she could get to what the men in front of her were wearing. From her first words, she spoke calmly and authoritatively, for they'd listen to nothing else from her, and she allowed none of the passion I'd heard to animate her presentation.

She gave it all to them, dealt it out on a screen in the front of the room. The slides came up showing pretty pictures from The Thing, equation sets from QUARKER, annotations in her own hand: each idea led straightforwardly to the one after, theory and practice brought together with casual elegance.

Leaving the last slide's **"END SIMULATION"** on the screen, she summarized: "We know little about the physical attributes of a singularity; in fact, its essential nature is lawless." She stopped, smiled. "Though we would anticipate its interactions with the nonsingular world of spacetime to be governed by the usual conservation laws, this may not be the case. In short, the consequences of creating a singularity are not well understood, and I would suggest that further analysis is required before any experiments are undertaken that could bring such a peculiar region of spacetime into close proximity with instruments so delicate as those in an experimental area." She paused and looked at all of them, said, "I will be glad to hear your questions and comments."

This is where it would happen, I thought. Guests to Thursday Group often got taken on the roughest intellectual ride of their lives, as this group of brilliant and aggressive men probed everything they had said for truth, originality, and relevance—or the converse. I went very tense, waiting for the onslaught to begin.

"Dickie Boy," Bunford said. If this group had an alpha male, Bunford was it. He was a big man—around six three and more than two hundred pounds—with a strong jaw, a lined face, and sunburned skin. He had elaborated the so-called "Standard Model" in new and interesting ways. The "semi-unbound quark state" was his particular interest—and the smart money had it that he and his group could pick up a Nobel if the SSC found the interactions he was predicting. "Did you validate her simulations?" Bunford asked. Rather an oblique approach, I thought, probably in preparation for going for the throat, theoretically speaking. Carol Hendrix turned to see how Dickie Boy would answer.

"Sure," Dickie Boy said. "Very sweet, very convincing. Take for instance the series of transforms . . ."

"Fine," Bunford said. And to Carol Hendrix: "Thank you. If Dickie Boy validates your Monte Carlos, I'm sure they're well done." He paused. "The physics is interesting, too . . . though quite speculative, of course."

And he stopped there, apparently having finished.

I waited for him to go on, but he didn't—he was whispering quietly to Hong, one of his group members. And no one else was saying a word. Finally, Allenson stood from the pillow where he'd been sitting cross-legged and said, "Shall we make it an early evening tonight? I don't know about you guys, but I could use some sleep." He turned to Carol Hendrix and said, "I'd like to thank our guest for speaking to us this evening." Murmured voices said much the same thing. "At a later time, perhaps we can discuss the implications of this work, but this week we are all very busy getting the SSC up to spec."

Carol Hendrix stood white-faced and silent as all the men got up, nodded goodbye to her, and left, some alone, others in small groups of their colleagues.

"I don't understand," I said. We were walking along one of the suburb-like loops that led from Allenson's house to mine. For the present, many of us lived in Texlab-owned housing as a matter of convenience. "They didn't even want to argue with you."

"I'm an idiot," she said. "I forgot some of the most important lessons I've ever learned. In particular, I forgot that I'm a woman, and anything I say gets filtered through that."

"Do you really think that?"

"Sax, don't be so fucking naive. Why do you think they were polite? Because I was a *visitor*?" Her voice was filled with scorn; she knew as well as I did what treatment visitors got.

"Your conclusions are radical. You can't expect them to assent right off."

"I'll grant you that, and it would have been hard to convince them of anything substantive, but I could have *begun* tonight. They dismissed me, they dismissed what I was saying. Bastards. Smug male bastards—it's no wonder they can't hear anything; they're so filled with their own importance."

We stood in front of my house. She said, "I think I'll walk around for a while, if that's all right. I don't want to talk right now."

"Sure," I said. "Go anywhere you want. In fact, I think I'll go for a bicycle ride. I'll see you later."

So moonlight flashed through the bicycle frame as I rode the berm road above the SSC, and finally I realized I had no answers to what perplexed me, and I turned around and headed back toward home.

I rode through streets of darkened homes and came to my driveway, where a light burned on a pole, walked the Invisible Bicycle up to the door, and went in to absolute silence. On a low table in the living room, I found a note:

> *Dear Sax,*
>   *I have gone back to Los Alamos.*
>   *Don't worry about me, I'm fine. I just need to think about*
> *what happened here.*
>   *Thank you for all you've done.*
>
> *Carol*

Over the next weeks, as the full-energy trials came closer, I thought often about Carol Hendrix, her singularity, and the treatment she'd gotten.

I went back to Thursday Group the next week but found I had little to say to any of them—the whole bunch seemed to be strutting apes, obsessed with their own importance and show. If they were interested in the truth, and particularly in new, interesting truths, then why hadn't they treated Carol Hendrix with the seriousness her ideas deserved? Her ideas were strange, but important ideas always were. She was a woman, but so what? How could that matter?

All of a sudden, I felt a fool. Their conversation excluded everyone who was not a member of the group, and their masculinity, while entirely free of conscious malice, effectively recognized only its own kind. A young, small woman simply did not exist for them as a physicist to be taken seriously.

I left early that evening and decided I would not go back.

But what I had seen at Thursday Group was everywhere at the lab. Secretaries were women, scientists and administrators were men—white men by and large, with a sprinkling of Orientals. Carol Hendrix was right: I was incredibly naive. But I understood why. As a high-energy physicist, I had been devoted to what I thought of as an unbiased search for the truth, a search that creates intense tunnel vision, because of how difficult it is, it demands absolutely everything you can bring to it, and often that isn't quite enough. Now I had awakened, and what I saw appalled and confused me.

I got one note from Carol Hendrix, apologizing for leaving so abruptly and saying that she would write again when she had gotten her thoughts straightened out. Then, five days before the first full-energy, high-beta runs, she called me at the office. "Sax," she said. "I'd like to come watch the runs. Would you mind?"

Carol leaned over me, slid her body down mine, pulled the gown over her head. She was astride me, hands at her side as she moved in rhythmic arcs. "The stars," she said. Through the window I could see points of light strobing, red-and-blue shifting through the spectrum. "Something is poking through behind them," she said. "It wants in." A sheet of blue light poured through the window, burned through us, X-raying flesh and bone. In it we were translucent, the intricate network of our nerves burning in silver fire. We were fusing together, so close to an orgasm that would annihilate us.

I woke, got up, and drank some water for my burning throat, fell back on the bed. I hung suspended between waking and sleeping as a flood of images passed across my eyes. Bright, blurred shapes vanished before I could see them clearly.

She was coming in the next day, the day before the first big runs.

She wore khaki shorts and a dark blue T-shirt. We were sitting in my back yard again, under a moonless sky—a thousand stars above us and meteors cutting brief, silent arcs at the horizon. She sniffed at the glass of cold Chardonnay she was holding, drank, and leaned back in the reclining chair.

"I owe you an apology," she said.

"What do you mean?"

"You did everything you could to help, and I walked out on you."

"You were troubled."

"I was, but I shouldn't have treated you like one of them."

"That's okay. Apology accepted."

"Tomorrow morning, what do you think will happen?"

"Truthfully, I don't know. If we get good beam, we'll have the right conditions for your simulation."

"That's what I thought. I've gone over it and over it, worked it through time and again, had a work group tear my analysis apart. It all adds up to the same thing: my simulations are realistic, plausible . . . and unverifiable without experimental evidence. All of that's fine. What worries me is this: if I'm right, your people are going into what could be a dangerous situation, and no one has a clue about it; no one wants to hear about it, at least not from me."

"You've done everything you can."

"Maybe."

"No, I mean it. Listen." And I poured it all out to her, what I'd seen in recent weeks, how incredibly closed and self-confident our world was, unbelievably blind about its own nature, which within the community was seen as inevitable. I'm not sure how long I talked or how I sounded—I just know that the frustration and anger and amazement I had lived with for the past weeks came tumbling out in one long screed.

"Oh, Sax," she said, finally. "You poor innocent." And she laughed, then laughed again, harder, and carried on laughing as I sat there embarrassed. Finally she stopped and said, "Sometimes I get so wrapped up in all of this, I forget how things really are. Thanks for reminding me. To hell with them all. I've tried, you've tried. If the SSC's turned into the world's most expensive junk pile, it won't be our responsibility."

We talked a bit more until we had finished the bottle of wine, then she said, "When do we have to be there?"

"Seven A.M. We should leave here around six-thirty, so I guess it's time to go to bed."

She found me standing at the sliding glass door in my bedroom, looking out onto the night. I turned and saw her in the doorway, backlit by the light from the hall behind her. "Are you all right?" I asked.

"Who knows?" she said. She came across the room to me, stood in front of me, and put her hands on my bare shoulders. She said, "Want to make love, pen pal?"

She leaned against me, and I could feel her body under the thin jersey. "Yes," I said. "I do."

Through the night we moved to the rhythms of arousal and fulfillment: making love, lying together in silence, sleeping, waking again. All the frustration, anger, anxiety, excitement we had both felt the past weeks funneled into those moments, sublimed into active, driven lust.

Shortly after five I was awakened by a sweep of amber light through the window and the sound of wind. I found the groundskeeper robot outside. It had settled onto one patch of ground; its aerating spikes flashed out of the bottom of the machine, their blind repetition chewing turf into fine much.

I said, "You ought to go back to the barn or wherever they keep you and just kind of relax. Keep this shit up and they'll scrap you." It stopped and sat there emitting a low-pitched hum punctuated with occasional high harmonic bursts. "That's sensible," I said. "Think it over." It decided: it crawled over to a row of stunted ornamental shrubs and began to slice them into very small pieces.

I went back inside, called the thing's keepers, and tried to go back to sleep. Instead I lay awake, thinking of what might happen that morning, until Carol turned over to me and whispered, "One more time?"

"Oh yes," I said. "One more time."

Around six-thirty we walked out of the house and ten minutes later were at Maingate shuttle station, where we went down into the tunnel with five members of a tech team. They wore orange overalls and helmets and had respirators dangling over their shoulders, protection against any accident where helium would boil from the superconducting magnets and drive the air out of the tunnel.

Harry Ling, the BC 4 supervisor, was directing people at the shuttle stop. "How's it going, Harry?" I said.

"Ask me later," he said.

At Experimental Area 1, teams were making final adjustments to their instruments and hoping no last-minute gremlins had crept in. The room was fifty meters square, dominated by the boxcar-sized composite detector. Inside it, the storage rings came together; at their intersection the protons and antiprotons would meet and transform. Two men were levering a bulky, oblong camera—**SONY** in red letters on its side—into position at an external port. People picked their way through snarls of cable.

Fifty meters up the tunnel was the control room. It was on two levels: ground floor, where technicians sat in rows at their consoles, and the experiments command above, where the Responsible Person sat with his assistants and controlled the experiments.

I introduced Carol Hendrix to Paulsen, my assistant, who was crouched over his screen like a big blonde bear over a honeycomb. "Hello," he said, then went on muttering into his headset—I often wondered how anyone understood him.

I said to her, "Let's find you a headset, and you can plug in to my console and watch what develops."

The next hour was taken up with the usual preparations for a run: collecting protons and antiprotons in their injector synchrotons, tuning the beams. The "experiments underway" clock had started when the first particles were fed out of the injector synchrotron and into the main rings. Now the particles would be circling in the rings at a velocity near the speed of light, their numbers building until there were enough for a sufficiently violent collision.

"I have initiated the command sequence," Diehl said on the headphones.

About a minute later a voice said, "We're getting pictures," and there was a round of sporadic clapping from the people on the ground floor. On one of the screens in front of us, QUARKER was providing near real-time views of the collisions, which appeared as elaborate snarls of red and green, the tracks color-coded to distinguish incoming from outgoing particles. "Beautiful," the man in front of us said.

On the screen next to this one, data flickered in green type. I saw that everything was, as they say, "nominal." Then all lights in the control room went out, every screen blank, every com line and computer dead. Under amber emergency lights, everyone sat stunned.

And the world *flexed*, the wave from the singularity passing, shape of spacetime changing. Puffs of gray dust jumped off the walls, and there were the sounds of distant explosions.

Carol jumped out of her chair and said, "Come on." I took off my headset and followed her. We passed through the door and into the tunnel, where settling clouds of dust were refracted in yellow light. I stopped at a locker marked "Emergency" and took out two respirators—false faces in clear plastic with attached stainless steel tubes. If enough helium escaped into the tunnel, it could drive out the oxygen and suffocate anyone without breathing apparatus. "Here," I said and gave her one.

The door to the experiments room was askew. Behind us I heard loud voices and the sounds of feet pounding up the stairs to the surface. Turning sideways, I slipped through the door's opening.

Blue blue blue blue, the slightest pulse in it, then suddenly as the conjurer's dove flying from the hat, *white*, swords or crystals of it jammed together, vibrating as if uncertain, then turning as suddenly to *blue*.

The composite detector unit and surrounding equipment had disappeared. Carol Hendrix had become a translucent, glowing figure that left billowing trails of color as she moved. The world was a sheet of light and a chittering of inhuman voices, high-pitched and rising.

Etched images in gold against white, flickering, the reality tape shrieking through its transports as every possible variation on this one moment unfolded, the infinitesimal multiplied by the infinite.

Sometime later, hands pulled on me, dragging me backward across rough cement to a world that did not burn like the middle of a star. My heels drummed against the floor, my back was arched, every muscle rigid.

Riding the Invisible Bicycle past Building A, I saw two men bent over the partially disassembled carcass of a groundskeeper robot. Sprays of optic fiber, red lengths of plastic tubing, and bright clusters of aluminum spikes lay in the grass beside it. One man was holding a dull gray, half-meter cube—the container for the expert system that guided the robot and was the apparent source of its problems.

The state of things at Texlab: big science—grandiose and masculine and self-satisfied—lay in ruins all around, shattered by its contact with an infinitely small point, the singularity.

On the steps of Building A, camera crews and reporters had gathered. They just milled aimlessly at this point, waiting for the Texlab spokesman— presumably Diehl—who would have to come out and recite a litany of disaster. Then would come the questions: *How did this happen? What does it mean?*

As I headed out the perimeter road I was passed by lines of vehicles: vans carrying tech teams, flatbed trucks loaded with massive chunks of bent metal, cars with solemn, dark-suited bureaucrats in their back seats. No shuttle rides today—the tunnel was strictly off-limits.

Near Station 12 an orange quadrupole assembly lay next to the hole it had made coming out of the ground. Part of its shrouding had torn away to reveal the bright stainless-steel ring that held its thousands of intertwined wires together. At other stations I passed there were stacks of lumber for shoring the tunnel, repair crews in hardhats milling near them.

Little more than an hour after the medical team had carried me out of the tunnel, I was apparently fully recovered. The rest of my morning had been spent with me the focus of doctors, nurses, and lab techs. I had suffered an episode of *grand mal*, an epileptic fit, they told me—apparently a reaction to the singularity.

Today there were fifty-six injured, one dead, two more probably to die. The collider had been destroyed: beam pipes deforming and spraying those high-energy particles all over the place—explosive quench in the lattice, it was called.

And Carol Hendrix was one of the fifty-six injured. A chunk of concrete had fallen on her. Skull fracture, assorted lacerations . . . *Christ*. While they were testing me at the Texlab hospital, she was being flown toward Houston in a medivac helicopter brought in by the Air National Guard. She remained in a coma, but for reasons that escaped me, her doctors were hopeful, so mine had told me.

The men she had talked to couldn't listen, simply *couldn't*. She was a woman, her approach was unusual, her conclusions weird, and despite all their protestations to the contrary, the men she had spoken to were prisoners of their contexts, their presuppositions. Their scientific objectivity didn't exist, never had.

I wondered if they felt as Oppenheimer and company had on the morning of the Trinity explosion: bright light and EM pulse, shock wave throwing those nearby to the ground . . . then they all had to confront—whatever their jubilation, awe, fear, sorrow—their part in this thing, their complicity.

At the above-ground entrance to BC 4, Texlab Security had placed on wooden sawhorses a yellow plastic ribbon with the words "**EXTREME DANGER**" repeating along its length. Several gray-uniformed men stood nearby.

"I'll keep your bicycle for you, Doctor Sax," one said as I dragged it down the steps. "No," I said, "that's all right. I'll take it with me."

Rusty iron latticework showed where chunks of the tunnel walls had fallen, brushed by an angel's wing. In the hard yellow light, the Invisible Bicycle looked cheap, a stupid toy. Which it was: just a thing of plastic and conceit.

I wheeled the bicycle around the plywood barrier in front of the experiments room door and stopped to watch the *blue white blue*, which continued to some rhythm we did not understand. Robot cameras and recording instruments sat against the near wall.

Reduced to primitive magic, I hurled the Invisible Bicycle at the thing, a burnt offering: *take this, let me have her.* It slowed in midair as though moving through heavy liquid and began to deform. It seemed to turn inside out. Now the Topologically Bizarre Bicycle, no longer recognizable by shape or anything else as a human artifact, it was shot for a moment with rainbow colors, then was gone.

Unmoved, the singularity continued its transformations. Here was the angel, inscrutable as Yahweh answering Moses out of the whirlwind, "I am that I am." It promised infinite levels of discovery, an order not inexplicable but complex and deep as the night. And it promised that for every fragment of knowledge gained, for every level of understanding surmounted, there would be pain and sorrow. How puffed-up we become, filled with immense pride in our knowledge; and how quickly the universe reminds us of how little we know.

In the desert it was bright and hot. One of the security guards gave me a ride back to Maingate.

PROTECTION

Maureen F. McHugh

Maureen F. McHugh is another new writer who has made a powerful impression on the SF world of the early '90s with a relatively small body of work. Born in Ohio, McHugh spent some years living in Shijiazhuang in the People's Republic of China, an experience that has been one of the major shaping forces on her fiction to date. Upon returning to the United States, she made her first sale in 1989, and soon became a frequent contributor to *Isaac Asimov's Science Fiction Magazine*, as well as selling to *The Magazine of Fantasy & Science Fiction*, *Alternate Warriors*, *Aladdin*, and other markets. 1992 has been a good year for her. In addition to the quietly harrowing story that follows, she also published at least two other stories that might have made the cut for this anthology in another year, as well as one of the year's most widely acclaimed and talked-about first novels, *China Mountain Zhang*, which received the Tiptree Memorial Award. Coming up is a new novel, tentatively entitled *Half the Day is Night*. Recently married, she lives, appropriately enough, in Loveland, Ohio.

In "Protection," she delivers a haunting and oddly moving look at survival and love inside the concentration camps of a troubled future America . . .

When the train gets to the camp I'm scared out of my mind, but I'm trying to act smooth, you know? I was supposed to go to Green River, an all women camp out in Wyoming, but there was some kind of jack-jockey mix-up and I end up going to Protection in Kansas. I've never heard of Protection—I've heard of Green River, of course. I guess in a way I'm kind of pissed, I was supposed to go to this famous, badass labor camp and instead they send me to this place nobody ever heard of. Like it's some kind of contest, you know, and people are going to give a damn what camp I end up in. Still thinking outside, and I'm inside. But I don't know that yet.

I think of myself as one ticklish bitch, let me tell you. I think I'm hard-circuited. I'm not doing anything the whole way out from Wichita to Protection except I've got a seat on the train by the window and I'm just sitting there. Nobody will climb on me, even though a lot of people are sitting in the aisle and stepping on each other. That's because I managed to shove a pen down the side seam of one of the three pairs of pants I'm wearing and everybody knows if they come near me I'm like as not to shove it in them, so nobody bothers me.

But there's nothing to see outside the train window except all this dead, brown grass. Kansas must be a hell of a place. The train trip is about five hours, because we don't go very fast, and the whole time there's nothing outside but dried grass and once in awhile we go over a place that used to be a road before the Corridor dried up, back when it used to rain out west and there were farms. People keep stepping on each other because they've got to go to the bathroom, but I figure I can wait pretty long because I know the moment I get up someone is going to have my seat.

We all look real wonderful. They let us keep our clothes, which kind of surprised me, I thought they'd make us wear gray coveralls or something, but all they did was shave the back of our heads and put these implants in. I don't know what they're for. Maybe they can always tell where we are— hell, maybe they can tell what we're thinking. Anybody who'd had their metabolism stabilized was destabilized, too. I guess nobody worries about being overweight in a labor camp. The back of my head itches, and I've been wearing these clothes for two weeks. I'm wearing like three of everything, it looks really stupid and it's hot. I worried about that, you know, you want to look smooth, but when they told us that we could only keep what we had on I thought it might take me awhile to get out. I mean, I'll probably bust out before winter, you know? But just in case. And since I don't know what the hell I'll be doing when I get out, I think I better have extra clothes. It's not like the officials don't know I intend to be out, they probably assume every- body wants to get out, and when I do they're not going to let me just buy an Amtrak ticket home, I could spend a lot of time getting back to Cleveland. I may have to walk part of the way, and that could take a hell of a long time, so I could be really glad I kept this stuff.

So we get to Protection. It's nothing, not even fence, just this concrete platform as long as the train and a dirt road and dead grass. The train stops and we sit. I figure it's got to be Protection, what else would be out here? Where else would a convict train go?

After we sit for awhile, maybe twenty minutes in the train with the blowers off, sweating, and far off I see this plume of brown smoke. Except it's not smoke, it's dust, and it's coming off the road. Buses, bunches of them. A whole long elephant trail of dark green buses, humping up and down these kind of rolling hills. Until now I never knew what they meant by rolling hills, but they're like ripples, all covered with dust-colored dead grass. They stop on the road, the first one is almost nose up against the platform. It's a gas bus, with a big methane gas bag on top, half inflated, kind of sagging in a cage. I never saw one before, we don't have them in Cleveland. Guards in army colored coveralls get off the buses, lots of heavy arsenal swinging around. Deal guns, which isn't what I expected, I thought they'd have projectile weapons, but what do I know? Maybe disruptive guns are less messy, that's why city cops use them. But out here in a labor camp, who cares if they bloody up the landscape?

They fiddle around for a moment, crack the door on our car and three of them charge in screaming at us not to move and swinging those deal guns.

Hey, I'm not going anywhere, not until I find out what's going on. "You're going to go out on the platform, in two lines! You assholes understand me?" this woman is screaming at us. "I been working out here in this goddamn place for five years, maybe if I kill enough of you they'll think I can't be trusted and transfer me somewhere, so I'm looking for an excuse! Now move!"

So we start streaming off our train car, all up and down the platform the other train cars are doing the same. When I get to the door, a guard signals I should get in the left line so I do. There doesn't seem to be any difference between the left and right line. So there we all are, all lined up, and it's hot and I gotta go to the bathroom.

They make us stand there in the sun while they prowl up and down the platform. Yeah, I'm getting scared. I know what's going on, I know what I'd do in a situation like this. If I had a bunch of scum to take care of, first thing I'd do is show them what a badass I was. So we stand and I wonder what they're going to do to us.

Finally the woman who was head screamer stops in front of our two lines. I think of her as "Helga." "You," she points that deal gun at a guy in the right line. Tall, skinny-looking guy, the kind who didn't get a seat. He doesn't have any expression on his face at all, almost like he expected this. "GET UP HERE!" she screams. He shambles forward. He's got his ankles shackled, they only do that for psychos and politics; they wouldn't pull a psycho out of the line unless they were going to roast him, besides, he just doesn't act psycho, so I figure he's politics. They probably don't mind roasting a politics, either.

"TURN AROUND," she screams. He does what he's told so he's standing with his back to us. "You shitheads like his haircut? Well, let me tell you, the perimeter of the camp is wired." All up and down the platform every car is getting the same thing screamed at them. I look back at the guy, his hair is kind of long so it covers part of the shaved place. "I'm going to show you what happens if you cross the perimeter."

She puts her hand in his back and shoves him off the platform and he falls off, hands out, flat into the dust around the concrete. "WALK!" she screams at him. I'm leaving out a lot of what she called us, just because it was pretty much the same thing over and over. Anyway, he struggles to his feet and looks up at her.

"Why should I walk if you're going to kill me anyway?" he says in this normal, reasonable way. You can tell he's scared, but his voice is just as nice and adult.

I like people who give the world lip.

"WALK!" she screams at him and shoves her deal gun in his face, so he kind of stumbles back, then suddenly his whole body goes stiff. Like a board. All the muscles in his neck stand out and his hands make claws and he falls over like a frigging tree, straight. Then he goes all loose.

I look up and down the platform, except for one guy who they're having to push, all up and down are these people lying in the brown grass. Two guards hop down and I catch my breath expecting them to keel over, too, but they just pick up the guy by his arms and legs and sling him on the bus.

"Cross it often enough and you'll fry your frigging brains to scrambled eggs," the woman says with satisfaction. "That is, if any of you assholes have brains."

We don't get on the bus until Helga has told us the rules, which takes forever. When we get on our bus nobody wants to sit next to Political but he's sitting near the front so I do. Buses make me sick, the closer I am to the front the better off I am. He's still out, head against the window, and I have to move him to sit down. He has nice clothes, real ragged but good stuff, Chinese or something. He's wearing a sweater and pants and under the dust they're both this kind of maroon color, with little flecks of gray in them. They've taken the shackles off and thrown them back on the train. He's got real long fingers. Something about him I like, maybe it's the way he turned around and talked to Helga. I could understand if he got mad or freaked, but he was just real reasonable.

Everybody is looking at me because I sat down next to Political, everybody knows he's already marked for trouble. I figure if I don't care it marks me as a real hard-circuit and then nobody will bother me.

Besides, something about him really attracts me, so I figure he's mine.

He doesn't really come to in the time it takes us to get to the camp, so I have to sling his arm over my shoulders and half-carry him out of the bus. I'm not that big a girl. He's skinny, but 180, maybe 190 centimeters and weighs more than I do. He's not completely out, and I keep talking to him. His eyes are barely open. "Come on," I say, "steps, get your feet under you, you son of a bitch or they'll take it out on my kidneys." I just keep pressing on him, get him down the steps and into the barracks. The barracks are new, concrete block and the beds are just like metal bookshelves. I sling him into a bottom bunk and take a middle one. I watch everybody else mill around before settling in.

Scared, man I'm scared. I sure as hell didn't want a mixed camp, in a woman's camp it's not like I'll be out-massed by over half the inmates. On the bus it was about two guys to every woman. Men are bigger, the only hope I have is to get a reputation as crazy, or else to come up with something everybody needs. Worrying about Politics gives me something to do other than worry about myself. The only time I leave is to go to the bucket. I never pissed in a metal bucket before, it's an experience, not to mention that it's loud. They turn the lights out before I get back to my bunk, which is also exciting.

I don't sleep that night. I want to be in a real bed. I want to brush my teeth. I know that's a bad way to think, 'cause when I did two years of juvenile reform, I learned, you don't think about what you miss—and it isn't really as good as you remember it anyway. Hell, most of the time I sleep on someone's couch, or floor. But it's different.

It's still dark when the lights come back on. Helga told us we have half an

hour in the morning, then roll call, then breakfast. I don't know what the
hell the half an hour is for, most everybody spends it sleeping. I hop down
out of my bunk—Goddamn Marx and Lenin, every bone in my body aches
from sleeping on a metal bookshelf—and check Politics. Most of the night
he was just sprawled the way he landed, one leg half off, but now he's curled
up like he's cold. He moved, I figure that's a good sign.

"Hey," I shake him gently. "Come on, wake up." For the first time it
occurs to me that maybe he's brain-damaged. Helga made it sound as if you
had to do it a couple of times, but how do I know? I don't want him to be
brain-damaged. I need him. "Come on," I say, "look at me. Politics, look
at me."

He groans and opens his eyes.

"Come on," I say, "sit up."

He sits up and grabs his head with those long fingers. Spider fingers.

"What's your name?" I ask.

"Paul," he says. Well, at least he understands.

"I'm Janee," I say, "and we're going to stick together, okay Paul?" If he's
brain-damaged I'll ditch him later.

He looks at me; his head is really killing him, but the way he looks at me,
kind of judging, figuring, and I think, well, if he's brain-damaged he must
have been a genius before. "Janee," he says, hoarse sounding. "Okay, Janee."

I prowl up and down the barracks. Out in the yard is an old-fashioned
water spigot. I don't have anything to get water in, not even a juice bulb,
but I open the door—it's dark and clear, the stars are still bright except off
to the east—and check. The perimeter is brightly lit but our door isn't locked
and I don't see anyone walking a beat. I sneak out to the spigot.

It's got weeds right around the base, then the rest of the ground is dry and
cracked. It's real hard to turn on, and the water comes out in a trickle. I soak
the outermost shirt I'm wearing, rinse it out real good, then bring it back in.
I crawl into Paul's bunk and hand him the shirt.

"It's wet," he says, sounding surprised.

"There's a spigot outside."

He wipes his face and holds it against his forehead. "Thanks, Janee," he
says.

"I told you, we stick together."

"You don't want to stick with me," he says. "I'm Political."

"Yeah, I know," I say. "I'll let you know when it's a problem."

The guy in the bottom bunk across from Paul's is watching us. I look right
at him, then give him a long, slow, skitzy smile. He looks away first. Little
victories.

The camp is hell. That's all there is to it. And Protection isn't as bad as
Green River, or so they say. I can't see how that could be true. All the time
I'm hungry, and either too hot or too cold. My bones hurt from sleeping on
a shelf. I figure out the reason why the lights go on half-an-hour early, so
we can lie there hungry and dread the day. We get up every morning and

wait half-an-hour to go out to roll call. Roll call takes twenty minutes if there's no lecture, and then we get twenty minutes for breakfast. The first day we are all given a cup, a bowl, and a spoon. We march in lines to the mess, which is just a roof, no walls. For breakfast we get something that's mostly water and a steamed roll. And coffee, if you can call it that. When they pour the soup stuff into my bowl I think it's some kind of yeast soup, it's just brown watery slop. It doesn't have much taste. In the bottom are a couple of tablespoons of barley or something. The coffee is clear, like tea.

I look at it, ten years of this if I don't figure out how to cross that perimeter. This is day one. I have 3,650 days, plus a couple of leap days.

Paul gets his and goes to a pole holding up the roof and squats down sliding against it. He hasn't bothered to get coffee, I can't understand it, I'm so dry I could drink a gallon and I got water in the morning at the spigot. He hands me his bowl.

"What," I say.

"I can't eat it," he says.

"You got to," I say.

"I'll get sick, " he says. Then with this kind of sickly smile, "I like mine with milk and sugar anyway."

"What is it?" I ask.

"Oatmeal," he says.

Oatmeal? I sniff at it. It does smell sort of like oatmeal. I take his cup and pour some of the liquid into it. "You've got to have something in your stomach."

"I'll get sick," he says.

"So you get sick. Maybe then you'll feel better."

"It's not a hangover," he says. But while I'm eating our breakfast, he drinks it. I stash the rolls in my bag, I could eat them but I figure he's going to get hungry eventually.

That first day we go to the "factory" and learn how to stitch quilts on these old black sewing machines with "Singer" on them in gold letters. I guess because of the noise they make, although it doesn't sound like singing to me. I sit next to Paul. We put the backs on, the blank, not-pretty parts. We're supposed to finish three an hour. I don't know jackshit about sewing, I mean, I didn't sit around doing this a whole lot, you know? So I ruin the first one, big time, and the second one looks like hell, but the third one isn't too bad. It's not hard, just, ziiiip, up one side, ziiiip, across the top, ziiiip, ziiiip, side and bottom, a big square.

The first day Paul is so sick he's lucky to be able to do one an hour. By the third day we're doing six an hour, but that first day I can do two extra for Paul. The problem is getting them into his basket without getting caught. He doesn't say anything about my doing them. His basket is always the first one they check.

I think I'm pretty fast at making quilts. It never hurts to be good at something. But that day and the next day, I don't push, there's no reason to work any harder than I have to.

By the third day Paul's doing as well as anyone, long spider fingers aren't shaking anymore.

We work until two-thirty, then we get a twenty-minute break, then we work until seven. By dinner I'm so empty I echo. We stand in the wind with our plates and cups. Dinner is two rolls each, pale beans with a bit of white pork fat and bitter coffee.

The second day, Paul says we should pick grass and use it in our bunks, but it's hard to find much in the camp. That's the problem with politicals, people like that are always thinking, but the stuff never works in the real world.

The third day they let us mix with the people who've been here for awhile.

I know we're in trouble when Paul and I squat down by our pole. I happen to look around and most of the guards are gone, only a string left to protect the mess cooks, who are turning the stinking stuff they use to rinse the kettles onto the ground. "Hey," I say.

Paul looks up.

The walking dead are headed toward us. All these skinny people in filthy clothes, maybe fifty of them. The first time, I don't know catshit about the walking dead, I think everybody looks like that after they've been here awhile and I feel sick. I'm still planning to get out of here before winter, but the business of crossing the perimeter is a real problem, and besides, it's beginning to dawn on me that I'm not going to just walk to St. Louis and hitch a ride on a transport.

"Keep eating," I whisper to Paul, so we do. When they get to the edge of the mess I notice that the last of the guards and the cook detail are disappearing. I keep eating. The first dead gets to a guy who's holding his half-empty bowl and without much ado, kicks him in the ribs, and two of them fall on top of the guy, steal his food.

They start moving through and jumping people. They don't jump everybody, somebody looks big, they just go around them. Man, I've got to do something. Some of them have sticks and I think to myself, I got to find out where they get those sticks. The walking dead don't make much noise. They're either all nuts or they're trying to scare people. It's creepy, watching them come through. I got a feeling that Paul and I are people they'll press.

I've got to do something. We're going to lose our dinner no matter what we do. I could just put down my bowl and then maybe they wouldn't touch us, but that's a bad thing to do. You don't give in, or you become a pushover. So I've got to make myself so much trouble that after this they don't mess with me.

So I look right into the face of one skinny bastard walking towards me and I smile. Then I start screaming and running, right at him, just screaming as loud as I can, and battering at him with my bowl, beans spattering. It wasn't exactly what he expected, he's not ready for some lunatic and I get him down, one hand pressed against his throat and keep hitting him in the face with my bowl.

Then another one of them grabs my arms and tries to pull me off. They're real skinny, these walking dead, and I'm all pumped up, so he's having real trouble, even with the one I'm sitting on struggling like mad. Then Paul tries to grab the one pulling on me, and a guy named Carlos starts whacking on the one Paul is pulling on (which is good because Paul is a lousy fighter).

I guess that's when the guards decide enough is enough and start moving in, swinging the butts of the deal guns. I end up with a split lip and a black eye and the next morning all of us in the fight have to stand for an extra hour and miss breakfast—plus, we're not supposed to get behind on our quota of quilts even though we missed forty minutes. But I also get a stick one of the walking dead dropped. And I have a good idea people are pretty much going to leave me alone.

My Paul. My Paul. He has long spider fingers and his skin is so thin you can see the copper-green stain of his neural jacks on his wrists. He never asks what I did to end up in a reform through labor camp. "Don't you want to know?" I ask, curled up against him in our bunk.

"No," he says, "that's outside, we're inside."

He was a history teacher, a middle school teacher, I think. He's older than I am, I'm twenty-three and he's almost thirty. He's here for twenty years, I'm here for ten. He wouldn't have a chance if it wasn't for me, he doesn't have the first idea how to protect himself and he's a Political, that makes him a target because the guards don't care what happens to a Political. Nobody messes with him now, because everybody knows that Janee is crazy. Sometimes if I'm careful I can hook an extra bun and split it with him. I wonder about his life outside. "Did you have a girlfriend?" I ask. "Where did you live? What kind of flat did you have?" He's from Pennsylvania, I think. "Did you have any brothers and sisters?"

"That's outside, Janee, it doesn't matter here."

He sounds like our political instruction meetings. Our old lives are outside, now, inside, we have a chance to put together new lives.

We have political instruction meetings a couple of times a week, the twelve rules are painted on the wall of the barracks.

#1. We are not strong enough ourselves, we must rely on a power greater than ourselves.

A power greater than ourselves is society, of course. The first time we go there's this lecture, about how we are all maladjusted, and how we are denying that we are maladjusted. And the first thing we have to do is admit that we are. So we have to go all around the room and stand up and say our first name and what our problem is. Well, Catalano, one of the guards, is standing there, so everybody mostly just stands up and says their name and why they are there.

First couple of guys aren't much, they stand up and say things like, "My name is Derrick and I am a thief."

But then it gets to be a contest. Guys stand up and we kind of hold our breath to find out what sort of badass crime they'd committed. If a guy stands up and says he's a thief or a pimp or that he's in for assault everybody just sits there. But then this guy gets up, just a normal-looking guy, not very big, and he says, "My name is Vincent, not Vinny, *Vincent*. And I am a hijacker."

Everything gets real quiet. Even though the guy is supposed to sit down he sort of smiles and says, " I hijacked a city bus and killed the driver."

"That's enough," Natalie says. She's a prisoner too, but she's been here for years, and so she leads our political discussion group. She knows that Vincent is putting the whammy on us, and she makes a little note in this notebook she carries.

Some people stand up and say their crimes real fast and sit down. One woman, she's in for prostitution, but she's not a hard case, you can tell. Maybe some smalltown girl who puts out, who got somebody bothered. She stands up and she's crying and she says in this real little voice, real fast, "MynameisNancyandI'maprostitute," and sits down.

But Natalie makes her stand back up, and there she is crying, and makes her say it again, slower. Nobody can understand what she's saying, she's scared so bad and crying so hard. It's just mean to make her stand up, a little piece of white meat like that, 'cause the little girl knows, and she's right, that these guys are going to be all over her once lights are out.

But I'm thinking about my reputation. I'm only in for larceny and assault, which isn't going to sound like much. And I've got a reputation between me and big trouble.

Paul doesn't have to stand up and say anything, politicals aren't allowed to say anything in political instruction for the first two years, which is another weird rule. You'd think they'd need it worse than us.

So I'm thinking, while it gets closer and closer to my turn, and finally I've got to stand up. I stand up and stand there a moment, thinking if I really want to go through with this, and just before Natalie says something, because I can see she's going to, I say, "My name is Janee, and my problem is that I'm stuck in this goddamn camp." And I sit down.

A lot of guys laugh and a couple of them whistle and I don't smile or anything. Catalano, the guard, reverses his deal gun and starts coming toward me, so I stand back up and say, "I'm *in* for larceny and assault." Which makes it sound like there might be other stuff that they never got on me. And then I sit down and Natalie scribbles in her little book.

The next morning, Vincent and I have to stand at roll call for an extra forty minutes, which was what Natalie was scribbling down. But Paul hooks an extra roll at breakfast, and gives me his and the extra. I'm real proud of him, he's learning a little, too.

At break he tells me that the political study is based on Alcoholics Anonymous.

"Give me a break," I say. "Alcoholics Anonymous isn't about politics."

"No," he says, "it's about changing behavior. They use most of the old rules, maybe change them a little. Rule No. 1, about relying on a power greater than ourselves, that's straight from AA. Except that traditionally the power greater than ourselves was God, not society."

"I knew they meant society," I say, he probably thinks I'm stupid, and I'm not, I know a lot more about staying alive than some goddamn history teacher.

But he isn't paying any attention at all. "It backfired big time last night," he says. "You and Vincent." He grins at me. I thought he might not understand about what I did, he didn't say anything when we crawled into our bunk the night before, but he does, he thinks it's all right.

I gotta think about getting out. Paul keeps shaking his head every time I say something about it. "How are you going to get across the perimeter?" he asks.

"I got in," I say.

"Are you going to wait until there's a shipment of new prisoners and then just walk past them?" he says. Which is a point. I don't know if the whole perimeter shuts off when prisoners come in or not.

"I can test it," I say.

"Fry your brains?" he says.

"Nah," I say, "shove one of the walking dead across."

He laughs, but I'm serious. The walking dead don't care about each other, they don't care about anything. I can go snag me a walking dead and the others will just look at me.

So I'm waiting. The only problem is that it isn't like they post an arrival schedule for new prisoners. The first time we get new prisoners, we're inside sewing quilts. We come out for dinner, and there are new people, so we have to wait because we can't mix with them. Standing there in the wind, shivering, while these stupid people, looking even stupider with the backs of their heads still new-shaved, are getting their dinner.

But it's early October, I think, and we're out for our break and somebody says, "Look."

There are a couple of the big green buses, rolling up to the perimeter. I start up, look around, can I get to one of the walking dead before the perimeter gets back up? Walking dead don't wander far from their factory work room. I can't even imagine one of them working. Most of them are in group six, which is officially the group for incorrigibles. Group six is pretty far from us, we're group thirty-six.

I don't see how I can get to one and back, I look back at the perimeter, the first bus slows down and then speeds up and crosses. There are bunches of guards and deal guns at the road, but nothing between us and the perimeter. Maybe I should just try it? Helga made it sound like I'd have to get fried a couple of times before it would hurt me permanently.

But this guy in Group thirty-three makes his decision before me, takes out running for the perimeter, away from the buses and the guards. I look back at the guards, expecting them to start firing. Deal guns aren't real accurate if you're too far away, he might still make it.

But they don't do anything. That tells me right there. I should have known, they'd be guarding if the whole perimeter went down. We all sit and watch the guy, he hits the perimeter, it's just a bunch of white stakes with a string about ankle high, just to mark it. He leaps the wire and goes down. We can see him spasm in the grass, just beyond the wire.

The guards aren't in any hurry. After awhile two of them finally walk from the road across the compound to the guy.

It's time for us to be called back inside to sew more quilts, but the loudspeakers are still quiet, just that hum that means they're on. I look up at Natalie, who is supposed to be calling us back inside and she's looking at her feet.

This is a lesson I guess. I figure they're going to roast the guy.

The guards walk across the perimeter like it wasn't even there. It's not for them. They grab the guy by the arms and drop him across the wire, and walk back, leaving him there.

"What are they—" I say. But I know.

"They're leaving him to fry," Paul says.

Right. "Can he feel anything?" I ask.

Paul doesn't say anything for a moment. "No," he says finally, "probably not."

We sit out there for a long time, Natalie looking at her feet, some of us watching the guy. Every so often he jerks around for awhile and stops. Finally we go in to work until dinner, and when we come out to get our slop, the poor sucker is gone.

It's not going to stop me, you know? There's always a way. Once I get out of Protection, all I got to do is get to Saint Louis, then I can hitch with a transport and be in Cleveland in no time. In Cleveland I know some people who'll hide me.

People get in, people can get out.

But it dawns on me that it's getting on to winter and I'm not real sure about my chances of getting to Saint Louis in the winter. Besides, if I winter over in Protection, then the hair on the back of my head will grow out better and I won't look so much like a goddamn escapee. My clothes'll get worse, but maybe next spring I can steal the clothes off a newcomer. And during the winter I can watch and plan, so I can figure how to get out of here.

Anyway, if I'm going to be spending the winter here, I've got to start playing the game different. Got to work the system a little better, score some points with the guards and the upper orders, you know? When I was in juvenile detention they made a big thing about political instruction, so I try to pay attention.

Thing is, all that stuff about ideology and infrastructure and shit goes right over my head. And Natalie is always asking me things like, "Why are we here in Protection?"

"Cause we screwed up," I say.

Natalie shakes her head and asks somebody else and they answer with one of those slogan kind of answers about society and bourgeois mal-a-dap-tation. And I look at Paul and roll my eyes. I can't keep this stuff in my head. I mean, it's all just words that don't mean anything. I can't understand why anyone would ever get in political trouble because none of it ever seems to mean anything. Maybe if I'd finished high school it would be easier.

I can't figure out what's so awful about capitalism in the first place. Back when America had capitalism we were rich and powerful. Now we're not. So isn't capitalism better?

One night I wait until lights out and I ask Paul.

He laughs. "It's not that simple, Janee."

"So why not," I whisper.

"Because we lost our power while we were still capitalist. You've heard about the Second Depression."

Sort of. "When New York City used to turn off the electricity at night?" I used to watch this show called "Stormtime," it was real popular, with that cute guy, Sam Basarico. They were always turning the electricity off and people always had to go to the hospital in the middle of the night or die, and Sam Basarico was always waking up doctors and stuff.

"Yeah," he says.

"So," I say.

"So what?" he says.

"So what's wrong with capitalism?"

He sighs. For a minute I wonder if maybe he's a capitalist. But then he says, "It's not a fair system."

"That's stupid," I say. Things aren't fair. Only little kids expect things to be fair.

"I'm tired," Paul says. "Go to sleep."

"No," I say, and start kinda making up to him, scrunching up against him, playing with him. And when he's starting to get all hot I say, "You want to go to sleep?"

"Jesus, Janee," he whispers. So we hump a little in the dark. I should be worried about getting pregnant. I wonder what they do if someone gets pregnant? But I haven't had a period since I got to the camp, which is strange. Maybe the implant.

"Okay," I say, "now tell me about capitalism and what's wrong with it."

"Tomorrow."

"No," I say.

And the guy on the rack above us hisses, "You two shut up!"

So we're quiet for awhile and then I say real close to Paul's ear—he's falling asleep and I'm tired, too, but you can't give up on stuff like this— "Come on, tell me about capitalism."

"If we talk politics, I'll get in trouble and you'll get in trouble," he says.

"If I don't figure out how to say the right stuff in political instruction I'm going to get in trouble anyway."

He kind of laughs. I can feel him shake, even though he doesn't make any noise. "Okay," he whispers. "But tomorrow. Go to sleep."

So he starts by asking me what I know about capitalism.

"People were rich and there was a lot of corruption and a lot of crime," I say. "And now we have socialism and people are poor and there's a lot of corruption and a lot of crime."

He laughs. Anything I say about politics makes him laugh.

"You think I'm not that smart," I say. "Just because I'm not book smart."

"You're not stupid, Janee, you just never had much chance."

I don't know how to answer that so I don't say anything, I mean, is it an insult or what? So he tells me about capitalism, and people making money. And he tells me about people having to pay rent for the places they lived. That sounds pretty screwy. People had to pay for water, too. People could sell anything.

I make him tell me how capitalism caused global warming and he tells me all about how people wouldn't give up things because if they stop buying capitalism doesn't work, so the technology and the pollution made the earth heat up and now the whole corridor, Texas and Kansas and Oklahoma and Idaho and all those states that used to have farming don't have enough rainfall. Protection used to be a farming community. Now it never rains.

Which explains a lot of what was wrong with capitalism. I get the idea that people knew all this bad stuff was going to happen, but they wouldn't stop buying gasoline-driven cars and stuff, and the government wouldn't stop them. So now people like me have to suffer for it.

Except none of that helps in political instruction.

"What class are you?" Natalie asks me.

"Proletariat," I say. I know that one, I remember that from when I was still in high school.

Wrong again. None of us know what class we are. Natalie sighs. We're "criminal element." Right, I should have got that.

We have a stove in the barracks, and it's getting real cold at night. I keep hoping that they're going to start heating the place a bit. It's been cold enough that one night water froze. And we may sew quilts all day but we never get to take any of them back to the barracks at night.

"Hey," I say in political instruction, "one of the big differences between capitalism and socialism is that in capitalist times people had to pay for stuff like where they lived and water and heat and all that, right?"

"Yes," Natalie says.

"So if we live in Socialism, how come we don't have heat?"

Natalie scrunches her mouth together in a line, real flat. Paul looks down at his hands. I screwed up again, and I don't even understand why I'm wrong.

Finally Natalie says, "Girl, I'm telling you, you've got an attitude. You should be thinking about working on that."

All my life people have been telling me about my frigging at-ti-tude. Seems to me, a lot of times, my at-ti-tude has been all that's been between me and the world making me part of the pavement. Seems to me, here in Protection, my at-ti-tude is about all I've got.

*   *   *

I'm cold all the time. Out here in Kansas, the wind blows all the time. It's sunny, but the sky is real pale blue and real far away. Natalie says that long about January we'll start getting dust storms.

When the lights come on in the morning, none of us bother to get up. I stay right up against Paul, trying to get a little warm. We got two blankets because they're two of us, but they're really not big enough to cover two people, even when I lie right up against him. Still, we get some overlap. So my legs and feet are cold, and his backside is cold, because those are places where there isn't enough cover, but we're okay.

We take our blankets to the factory, all wrapped up like Indians. If you do it right, part of the time you are sewing a quilt you can have it in your lap, but if they catch us doing that they chew us out. Nancy gets in trouble because when she's finished sewing a quilt, instead of putting it in her basket, she keeps it on her lap.

We've been doing quilts a couple of months, it's not real hard. We're supposed to do twelve an hour, one every five minutes. You got to fold a little, pin a little, then zip, zip, zip, zip, four seams and you go on to the next one. When you run out of thread you have to signal Natalie and she brings you thread. If you don't do twelve an hour, then you have to stand for detention. So I do fourteen or fifteen the first hour, just in case I have a problem, and then twelve an hour for the rest of the day. Our hands get so cold it's hard to do them right. If you make a mistake, the bad quilt is called "waste." I asked if we couldn't keep a couple of the "wastes" to use ourselves but Natalie said that unscrupulous people would ruin quilts on purpose just so they could have them.

Well, yeah, I would.

Then one morning, Corbin, who with Natalie is one of our Group Leaders, says that we're going to have a change. Corbin doesn't have any teeth in front. At first I thought he was real old, but then I found out he's only thirty-six, but he's been in labor camps for fourteen years. I guess that and the fact that his mouth is all caved in from having no teeth is what makes him look old.

He says that there is rationing outside, like there usually is in the winter. It's the first time anyone has mentioned outside in a long time. It seems so far away, outside. I guess there didn't used to be rationing, before the Second Depression, but I guess if they could farm the corridor there would be a lot more food.

From now on, he says, if we make 120 quilts a day, we get regular rations, if we make more than 180 we get extra rations, and if we make less than 120, we get half rations.

I figure maybe I can make 180 quilts, I mean, I've never really tried hard before. I have to make eighteen quilts an hour. The first hour I make nineteen, raggedy-assed things but nineteen and they're good enough to pass, not waste, you know. Man, I figure I got this thing licked, and I'm tasting extra rations. But the next hour I screw up two and I only end up with fifteen. And the third hour I get up to thirteen and the thirteenth one I screw the thread all to hell, tangled in the bobbin and all, and I got to be real careful or I'll break the needle. If I break the needle they'll dock me ten quilts because needles are expensive. I finish the day with 154. Chris, this big guy from Detroit who killed somebody with a top from a trash barrel, he makes 182. His fingers just blur. I'm always afraid that I'm going to end up sewing my own hand if I go that fast.

This other guy, Nesly, he only makes 114. He's just a klutz, he goes real slow and he messes some up. At dinner, Chris gets two extra buns, and I'm disappointed, I thought he'd get more than that. But Nesly only gets half his beans.

We discuss it at our political meeting. First the title of the lesson, "From each according to his abilities, to each according to his needs." Then Natalie has a discussion group and we talk about what it means.

Nesly says, kind of desperate, "It doesn't seem fair, I work as hard as I can."

Maybe he does, I don't know. I don't like Nesly, he's one of those people who you look at and you know they're a screw-up. He's not very big, and he's got no front, no pride. And he whines all the time.

Natalie says, "Think about it, Nesly. People like Chris work harder, they need more food. Society is like a machine. A person like Chris makes sure that more people have blankets. It's for the good of society that if there is only so much food, people like Chris get it, because he's more efficient."

Some people nod. I can see it, in a way.

Mostly I don't care, it's warmer in the bunk, with Paul, and that's where I want to be. I'm tired all the time, from being cold. It seems like I just go to sleep and the lights snap on.

I close my eyes again, not bothering to get up.

Paul says, "You still want to learn more for political instruction?"

"I dunno," I say, and then from habit, because he's doing something I want him to do, "Yeah, I guess."

But he doesn't talk about anything that makes sense, he starts by saying, "What's feudalism?"

"Bad," I say, thinking about how in half an hour I have to go stand out in the cold for roll call. When we have roll call in the morning, the stars are still out and it's still dark.

"Why is it bad?"

Hell, I don't know, I don't even really know what feudalism is except it has to do with kings and queens.

So that morning he tells me about serfs, who were like slaves, because only a few people owned all the land, and everybody else had to work for them. And because if you didn't work for someone you would starve, you'd do anything to work for someone. But they could pay you whatever they wanted.

I think I can understand that pretty well. "People like us," I say, "we're like serfs, because we're trapped, and they don't have to do anything but give us a little food."

"Right," he says, pleased with me. Well hallelujah, Janee finally said something right. "The only difference," he says, "is that a feudal economy is based on land. Since people don't have much money, mostly land, they can't really buy and sell a lot. I mean, you can't carry a hectare of land in your pocket, you know?"

I laugh, because I'm supposed to, but he sounds like a frigging teacher.

"Now a factory is expensive," he says. "You know how animals and people evolve?"

"Like people started out from apes," I say.

"Sort of," he says. "Anyway, first are primitive societies, like the Indians. Then there are feudal societies, which are more organized. And then people get money together and they buy machines and build buildings and you have factories. But to start a factory you have to have a lot of money, you need capital. And that's why people who run factories are called capitalists."

Okay. So out on the field for roll call, while I'm freezing my buns off, I'm thinking about factory workers and serfs. And about labor camps. Paul thinks they're different, because of land and money, but they really aren't. It seems to me that if society is going to evolve, it should get better for everyone, not just the people at the top, right? I mean, Indians had it a lot better than I do.

"Where did you live in Pennsylvania?" I ask Paul.

He doesn't answer.

"Did you live in a big city, like Philadelphia or Pittsburgh?"

He doesn't pay any attention to me.

"Maybe in a little town, like Allentown?" Everybody has heard of Allentown, because it's a famous battleground of class struggle. That and the little town in Kentucky where the miners went on strike. "Did you have a girlfriend?"

"That was outside," he finally says.

"Do you want to know if I had a boyfriend?" I ask.

"I'm sure you did."

"You don't know," I say. "You try to make it sound like you don't care, but you don't know anything about me. Maybe I ax-murdered my boyfriend," I say.

It irritates me, he won't tell me anything. He doesn't want to hear anything about me, either. I mean I don't think it's a good idea to always be talking about it, but it's stupid to pretend that we didn't have any life at all out there. I figure he had a girlfriend, maybe a wife. Sometimes, people divorce people who go into labor camps. It's an okay reason for divorce.

"What's the big secret?" I say. "Why don't you want to talk about it?"

"That's a whole different person," he says, "a whole different life."

"Why don't you ever talk about politics, I mean, you're *here* because of politics."

"I am talking about politics," he says, sounding angry, "I'm teaching you, aren't I?"

"Yeah, but you never teach me anything subversive," I say. "We just talk about feudalism. Natalie doesn't even care about feudalism, I still don't know the right answers when she asks me questions."

"It's not something somebody can explain overnight," he says.

"I don't even think you're right," I say. "You say that feudalism was better than the Indians, and that capitalism was better than feudalism. But it's not, it's just the same for people like me, we always get shit on. Except maybe for the Indians. I'd be better off if I were an Indian."

"That's the point," he says, exasperated. "Feudalism and capitalism exploit people like you and me."

Exploit. That crops up all the time, exploitation of the workers. I feel like I've just gotten another piece of the puzzle.

"So how would you change things, Janee?" he says.

I think. "I'd make sure that . . . I mean, people still have to work, right? Or we wouldn't have anything to eat. But I'd give more to the people like me, like I'd make sure that people had enough to eat and all that. I wouldn't let some people have a lot and not have to work. And I wouldn't make people do stupid things. You know, sewing quilts all the time is boring."

"But how are you going to have factories if no one has enough money to build them?" Paul asks.

He's got a point. I mean, if everybody is pretty much the same, nobody has a whole lot of money. I try to think who builds factories. I get it, all the sudden I get it. "The government. The government can build them."

"Why the government?" he asks.

"Because they've got the money," I say.

"But then the government just becomes like the capitalists, exploiting people."

That's what we've got but I don't say it.

"Think about it, Janee," he says.

Right. He knows the answer, but he wants me to guess, stupid son of a bitch playing stupid teacher games.

If it wasn't for me, the poor sorry bastard would be in real deep shit. I know he thinks I'm stupid, I can tell by the way he talks to me. When he's telling me about politics he talks slower, real careful, and he asks questions he already knows the answers to and there I am, trying to guess the right answer when he could just tell me and then I'd know. And why won't he tell me anything about himself? Why doesn't he want to know anything? 'Cause I don't really matter, that's why. He doesn't need to tell me anything because I'm just dumb old Janee.

"Listen," I say, "what difference does it make? Why the hell can't you just tell me where you lived? Huh? Why do you have to be so goddamn secret about it?"

"What difference does it make where I lived," he says. He's in a pissy mood. When he's like this I'm not supposed to bother him, he kind of sits around and doesn't say anything. What, he thinks he's the only one whose life is screwed up?

"Fine," I say. "You don't want to talk to me? I don't want to talk to you." And I don't talk to him. I just leave him right there and I just start ignoring him from then on, take my blanket, sleep in the goddamn bunk by the door even though it's colder. I mean, I boot Nesly out, make him sleep in the middle bunk so I can have the bottom, I can't let goddamn Nesly sleep better than I do, not even for Paul. And the bunk is the pits, there's a draft in from the door and I've only got one blanket, so I have to sleep curled up in the corner trying to get all of me under the stupid green blanket.

Paul doesn't say anything. He has that way, like he expects shit to happen, like he always expected I'd dump him. And the next morning nobody really bothers him. Nobody really bothers me, either, but then, people *don't* bother me. So we just go through the day, not talking to each other. I even make Nesly sit at my Singer sewing machine, next to Paul. I see people watching, seeing how pissed I am. Seeing if Paul is out there by himself.

At dinner Paul gets in line, he's in front of Marisa, who is okay, and Roy and Sal cut in front of Marisa, which gets her real nervous until they start bumping into Paul and she realizes she's not the target. She looks back at me, I can see her head turn, but I'm making like I'm not really looking. Paul looks back, not knowing what's going on, and says something, and Sal and Roy laugh. So he gets his beans and they get theirs, and I'm still like I'm not watching, and Sal and Roy are leaning on him. I can't hear what they're saying, but I can tell, they're over there by the kettles and now since it's cold there's always like this steam blowing like smoke.

And Paul doesn't know what to do, you can see his shoulders up around his ears and he's all elbows and you can tell that Roy and Sal got him running, but he's holding his beans and shaking his head, and Sal pulls on the plate, but Paul won't let go, so it's kind of a tug of war. Sal's looking a little stupid, and Paul calls to one of the guards, which is a mistake, because it's a guy we call Arkansas who doesn't care what happens as long as he doesn't have to do anything. He's this short little guy with a big Adam's apple and those stupid green guards' uniforms fit him even worse than they fit the other guards. Paul always says Arkansas is an example of too much inbreeding.

Arkansas goes deaf and pretends he doesn't know what's going on and the next thing I know Sal flicks Paul's plate of beans onto Paul's face and shirt. And Sal and Roy are laughing, and I guess it's not as good as getting Paul's beans but it's better than nothing, and Paul yells at Arkansas, "Did you see that! Are you going to let them do that!"

Arkansas sort of half reverses his deal gun, so that the metal stock is out there, like he's going to club someone, and narrows his eyes and says, "Politics, you causing a disturbance?" in this real lazy way.

"I wasn't doing anything—"

"I don't like trouble," Arkansas says.

And Paul must realize that it's open season when you're Political, 'cause he doesn't say anything after that.

And I'm pretending not to notice anything. Son of a bitch thinks *I'm* stupid, let him survive out there on his brains.

Things are really different without me being with Paul. I guess I kind of look around. Not that there's a whole lot to see. Kansas looks like hard, pale ripples, and the sky is light blue, real far away. The barracks are all in lines and they're low and long and even though they were painted green, now they're just all washed out, a kind of darker Kansas color. The only colors are the guards' uniforms, which are dark green, all stamped The U.S. People's Army over the pockets.

I feel so small. It was okay when I was busy watching everybody in group thirty-six and worrying about Paul, but now I feel so small, and I have this awful thing in my stomach, all the time. Every time I look out past the guard wire that marks the perimeter, and there's dry, empty Kansas, it's like my stomach is trying to swallow me up. I *know* I'm going to get out of here in the spring, something will come up, it has to come up, I can't stand it here, I'll die, I'll really die out here.

People do die. Nobody from group thirty-six, but sometimes from other groups, like group six, the zombies. They put the body in a green bag in the morning and we see the guards throw them in a truck while we're standing in line for breakfast, and I realize they've been doing that since it started to get cold. I've been watching them but it's like I didn't really notice.

I start thinking about running out, just running, just trying it. Maybe the perimeter isn't on all the time. We don't go near it. Maybe they leave it off. And if they don't, I'd never know, just zap and then the guards leave you there and Paul thought that you didn't feel anything and he ought to know, since he's been zapped.

Crazy thoughts, that scare me, but it's so tempting. Like my mind doesn't really believe anything could happen to me.

In political instruction Natalie gives us all lapboards and paper and little short stubby pencils. Even Paul gets a lapboard. That's real different. Which makes me more nervous, I don't like different. Different is bad. My first thought is that we're going to have a test and I know there's no way I can pass, and I start wondering what they'll do to me if I flunk. Cut my rations? I'm trying, I'm trying as hard as I can. But that's what Nesly always says. So I clench my pencil and wait to see what she says.

Natalie says, "We need to see how you are progressing in your self-struggle. Please write about yourself. You can write anything you wish, but we will check to see what you have omitted. Everybody understand?"

No, I don't understand. I don't write very good. I mean, I didn't even finish high school. I don't know what they want. But nobody else says anything, so I'm not going to say anything. So I look down at the piece of paper. I look up and around the room and I see the twelve rules of self-struggle on the wall. All that stuff about one day at a time, and denial and all that stuff. A couple of people are writing but a lot of people are like me, just sitting there.

Paul is looking at me, and when I look at him, he shakes his head. No.

I frown. "No" what? But if I kept looking at him Natalie will notice and we'll both be in trouble.

So I look back at my paper. I try to write something.

> My name is Janee Scott. I am a theif and I asalted a person. I
> am . . .

I don't know how to spell maladjusted. So I change my sentence.

> . . . a criminol elamint.

That looks wrong, too. So I make the "i" and "e," "element" looks better. So now what am I supposed to do? Natalie said that we would be checked for stuff we left out. So maybe I should tell about my arrest? So I write down about the woman I beat up and about stealing her purse.

I used to steal from the grocery, too. In the winter it was easy. I got picked up a couple of times and I spent a couple of nights in jail. So I better tell about that, too. I can't spell grocery so I write "store."

Finally I write:

> I am sory for my crimes, and for the bad things I did to sosiaty.

I haven't written very much, not even half the page. Some people are still writing. Some people have written most of a page already. I wonder what else I'm supposed to write. Natalie said we'd get in trouble if we left things out, but I don't know what kind of things.

What else could I say? Maybe I'm supposed to write about the things I did in camp? About the fight with the walking dead and about standing up in political instruction and saying that my problem was that I was in a labor camp?

Other people are asking Natalie questions, they kind of wait until she is looking around and then they half raise their hand and she comes over. So I wait and when she looks at me I put my hand up, feeling stupid. Natalie already knows I'm stupid, what difference does it make?

"Are we supposed to write about things we've done at camp?" I whisper.

"Whatever you want," Natalie says.

Somebody else raises their hand and she goes to them.

I don't know what to do. But she said that we'll get in trouble for the stuff we leave out. So I try to think of how to say what I've done at Protection.

> I have a bad atitude. I was in a fite with some pepoul from gr. 6
> becase they tried to take my beans. Also, in our meeting, I say
> that my problm is I am at a laber camp, but my problm is that
> I am a theif and I asalted the person at the store and I stol food.
> When I stol food from the store, I hurt sosiaty.

I think the last sentence is pretty good, but when I think I've done something right in political instruction, I'm always wrong.

After the political instruction meeting, Sal starts ragging on Paul about his bunk, telling him he's going to throw him out. Sal has a bottom bunk, so he's really just leaning on Paul. I figure if Sal is going to take Paul's bunk, I'll take Sal's, so I grab my blanket and throw it there while Sal is facing down Paul.

Paul is going to come here first, thinking that Sal's bunk is empty. I'm going to tell him to try near the door. Actually, maybe I'll let him stay, maybe I won't, it depends. If he acts mealy-mouthed and just slinks down the door, he can freeze for all I care.

And he will, too, cause Paul's so tall that his blanket isn't long enough, and when he scrunches up it seems like his knees always stick out. And he's thin, the way some tall guys are, even thinner now. We're all even thinner now. He's going to end up all bones and joints, like his long fingers, stuck down there with Nesly. And Nesly'll latch on to him, and he won't have the sense to tell Nesly to get out of his face.

He'll feel sorry for Nesly. And he'll be nice to him, 'cause Paul's like that. He's decent. Even if it drives me nuts sometimes, like maybe that's why he doesn't want to know about me before I came here, like he'd prefer to think nice things about me or something. Or maybe that's not it at all, it's hard to know what he's thinking. He'd have to be pretty stupid to think nice things about me. But I do know, if someone doesn't take care of him, being decent will get him in deep.

And then all the sudden I'm thinking all these things at once, like what if Paul got like the zombies, what if he stopped caring, and I'm wondering if it could happen, although I can just see him, all raggedy-assed and blank-eyed, stick-like and smelling like piss, specially because he's thin to begin with. And at the same time, I keep thinking of Kansas out there, all pale colored, and us so little, and wondering if I might not end up a zombie, 'cause worrying about Paul, I never thought about people ending up zombies. I never thought about running for the perimeter. It's like my cousin said about her kid, when you have a baby, you don't have a chance to know how screwed up you are because you got to think about milk and diapers and all that shit, and the baby just keeps loving you.

So, not even meaning to, I pop out of Sal's bunk and just grab my blanket and go to see what's going on.

And what's going on is this: Paul has my stick, the one I got from the living dead, which I keep stuck in the frame under our bunk, and he doesn't really look like he's sure what to do with it. But Sal isn't sure how to get around him, because there isn't a lot of room between the bunks, you know. And Eddy, who has the bottom bunk across from ours, and Marisa, who has the bunk above Eddy's, are both swearing like mad, telling Sal to leave everything alone, 'cause if Paul starts swinging that stick in that little space people might get their heads knocked.

So I just walk up and say, "Sal, get back to your own bunk."

"Stay outta this," Sal says.

Paul doesn't say anything, so I just walk past Sal. The stupid dick elbows me and pushes me into the bunk, so I pop out again and grab the stick from Paul and stick it like a sword right into Sal's stomach and then start smacking him with it, bap, bap, bap, not really hurting him, but real fast, so he can't get a hold of it, and he puts up his hands trying to keep me off and keeps walking backward until he's clear of the bunks and I say, "Listen, mess with me again and I'll put it in your teeth."

That's the way you deal with trash.

So then I just walk back and sit down on the bunk and lean down and shove the stick back in the frame.

Paul stands there a moment and I look up at him and say, "What?"

He's got a kind of funny little smile on his face, but he just says, in that real reasonable way of his, "Are you back or do you just want the bunk?"

"It's warmer with someone else," I say. "And I've already got you broke in."

"Okay," he says. And sits down.

Eddy says, "Shit," and turns over with his back to us. Marisa is looking over the edge of her bunk. Marisa is with Kirk, I don't know where he's been all through this.

"Janee," Paul says, real quiet.

I look up at him, wondering, wondering what he's going to say, and feeling kind of funny, and maybe a little embarrassed, just because of the way he said my name.

"What did you write?" he says.

For a moment I don't follow, because it isn't what I expect at all. Then I figure out he means that stupid thing at political instruction, and without even thinking I kind of look over toward where the twelve rules are written on the wall, even though you can't see them from the bunk.

I'm irritated. Here I just saved his balls and he's going to play teacher games. "None of your business," I say.

"Janee—" he says, and takes my shoulder and kind of pushes my hair away from my face, nice, something he's never done before. Not like humping, but nice, like just for me, Janee. "It's important, what did you write?"

I shrug. "Just about being a thief and about fighting with the guys from group six and then about the time I said that my big problem was being in a labor camp."

He nods. "Good. When they give it back to you, just write the same thing, only in different words."

"Why are they going to give it back to me?"

"It's something they do," he says. He's real tense, real scared. I can't figure out what the big deal is. I know he's rattled from Sal, he doesn't know that the Sals of this world are really just looking for someone to tell them what they can and can't do.

"Hey," I say. "Don't worry about it. Come on, sit down here with me.

It's cold enough in this barn." Saying that makes me smile. "My mother used to say that," I tell him. "She'd say, 'Close the door, it's cold enough in this barn.' "

He smiles a little. "Mothers say that sort of thing. Mine used to say, 'Close the door, you weren't raised in a barn.' "

"Must be a Pennsylvania thing," I say, even though I've heard it before, people in Cleveland say it.

"Yeah," he says, "must be a Harrisburg thing."

"You know," I say, real quiet, "you can be a real pain in the ass, but sometimes, you're all right."

"Janee," he says, "you've got to be real careful. I don't know why you adopted me, but you don't want me telling you things. You think you do, but I tell you about my life and then I'll be talking about things, things I think and believe, and you'll spend the rest of your life in a labor camp. You've got to just say back to them whatever they say to you, okay?"

He looks sad, he looks lonely. Well I'm lonely, too. All the time I'm lonely here. "Most of what they say is crap," I say, and I can feel myself getting irritated at him, getting irritated at all of it, I'm cold all the time, and hungry, damn it.

"I didn't say you had to believe it," he whispers.

Finally, they start the little electric heaters in the factory where we sew quilts, mostly because it's so cold that our fingers are stiff and our production is falling. It doesn't make the place warm, but I can't see my breath anymore.

I think about being warm all the time. I get these bruises on my legs, most of us do, from the cold. Chilblains. They hurt, real bad. Get up in the morning and it hurts to move my legs, and when I'm standing out there for roll call, the wind comes whipping over those little ripply Kansas hills and my legs hurt so much I have tears in my eyes. Then we cripple on over for breakfast and take it into the factory. Paul and I sit together against the wall, one blanket around our shoulders, the other across our legs, and eat.

I still haven't gotten to 180 quilts. I get 177 once and Corbin calls time to quit. I'm so mad I almost cry. Really, I never understood that saying, but I can feel the hot tears. I want to hit something. Nesly's doing real bad. He's coughing all the time, and spitting. He's on half rations, because his production is so low. I know when I'm losing my concentration because I can hear Nesly back there, coughing his lungs out.

I sew quilts. I can mostly sew without thinking, just zip, zip, zip, zip. I think about a lot of things. I think about what Paul said, about saying whatever they want me to say. And I think about what they want me to say. And I think about the question he asked me, when I said that it seemed to me that the Indians had it the best, that factory workers, and serfs and people like me, we all had it just about the same.

I keep trying to think about what would make it better. Everybody has to work, or people wouldn't have anything. Even Indians had to hunt or something. Like quilts, there's a lot in a quilt. There's the cottony stuff in the middle, somebody has to make that, and then somebody has to put it in the middle of the quilt. Somebody like us has to make the plain part, that they put the stuffing in. And somewhere, somebody has to put together all the little pieces of cloth and make the top part. Sometimes I imagine the way my plain shells will look when the top goes on them. I don't know if they'll be the kind with the patches, or if they'll be the ones with the stars, or the fans, or the pin wheels. . . . There's a lot of different patterns.

I'd like making quilts a lot better if I could do different things, like the top part, too. If I were going to make a new society, I'd have people do different things, not the same things all the time. So that somebody wouldn't always get stuck doing the stuff that no one likes to do.

At break one day, I tell Paul about my idea.

"That's a good idea," he says. "But who would make the schedule?"

I shrug. "Maybe everybody could talk about it. Like consensus." In political meetings we've been talking about consensus, having everybody come to agreement. It means that when you know you're outvoted, you give in, because you know you're not going to win. First you talk, and everybody kind of finds out what everybody else thinks, then when you vote, it's not really a vote, you consent. And if one persons says no, then you have to talk about it until everybody agrees. But you shouldn't say "no" unless you really have to. Everybody has to kind of trust everybody else, you have to decide, you may disagree, but do you disagree enough to stop everything?

"Quaker socialism," Paul says. For a moment I think he's laughing at me, but he's not. Things strike him funny that aren't funny to anyone else.

"What's that mean?" I ask.

"Quakers were a religious group that practiced some socialist techniques," he says.

"Religion is anti-socialist," I say, which everybody knows is true. Opiate of the masses and all that.

"A lot of Christian groups experimented with communal living," he says, "and some of the ways they found are very practical, like consensus. And socialism uses a lot of—" he stops.

"What," I say.

He shakes his head. "So you would use consensus to establish your schedule. I think that's a good idea. Have you figured out how to build your factories yet?"

He's changing the subject, because it's wrong to say that socialism is like religion. "No," I say. "I'm still working on it."

And then we have to go back to work. But the nice thing about going back to work after our two-thirty break is that it's only four more hours until dinner. And I'm thinking about what Paul said, about socialism being like religion. Which is very, very weird, because everybody knows that religion is all superstition.

But I don't say anything about religion to Paul. I just kind of store that away. And then I go back to thinking about my quilt factory.

Dinner is some sort of stew with floury dumplings, we don't always have beans. There's a bit of fatty meat in my bowl and I save it for last. Fat tastes so good to me. That sounds disgusting, but it does. I think I could eat straight fat. I'm hungry when I'm done, but I save my roll, because Paul and I always eat our bread right before we go to sleep. Some people save their cornbread from morning, they save it all day.

The next morning Corbin says that Nesly doesn't have to work.

Nesly says he'll work, it's okay, even though he's really sick and he's not even making eighty quilts a day. He's real thin, the bones in his chest are real sharp and his wrists look like sticks and his skin is real dry and scaly. His hair is coming out, too. Sometimes when I look over, he isn't even sewing, he's just got his head down on his table. Sometimes his eyes are closed, sometimes they're open.

We all know why he wants to go to work, if he doesn't go to work he'll be on infirmary rations.

Corbin says he should stay and rest and it's like Nesly just doesn't care. Like the walking dead.

Nesly is going to die.

When we're sewing, once in awhile I hear someone coughing—a lot of people cough—and then I think, "It's not Nesly. Nesly is going to die."

Nothing I can do.

In my society, Nesly wouldn't go on half rations, not if everybody felt Nesly was really trying. I think about what group thirty-six could do. If everybody gave Nesly a spoonful of their food, that would be thirty-one spoonfuls. That would be a lot, added to his half-ration, then he wouldn't starve. If everybody does it, that spreads it out, so nobody has to do a whole lot. Not that I think people really would, not for Nesly.

I don't tell anybody, though. They'd think I'd gone soft in the head.

Natalie hands out lapboards again, and the little stubby pencils. I've still got the pen stuck in the seam of my pants, it's been there since I stuck it in the seam of my pants when they told us we could only take what we were wearing. I never even think of it. Sometimes, Paul used to kind of play with it through my pants, but we don't do anything anymore but sleep. I look over at Paul, and he looks scared. Which makes me real nervous.

Natalie just hands back all those pieces of paper that we wrote before, and I look mine over. It really looks stupid.

Natalie says, "All of you left things out, things that we know about, so please explain further. Please tell us more about yourself and your self-struggle."

My self-struggle? I look up at the twelve rules. Look back down at my lapboard. It's real lousy plastic, bumpy with scrapes and scratches so that when I write my pencil will catch in the indentations. What do they know about that I didn't say? Juvenile reform?

> I was in jewvinile reform becase I stol a player and some chips. I
> had a chanse to reform at Brigum House but I did not. Sosiaty

had to pay mony to fed me and give me cloths and when I got
out of Brigum House I did the same bad things.

I know I'm doing good, now. At Brigham House they were always talking
about our debt to society. And here they talk about that too. In a way we're
like Nesly, we never make our quotas, so now society has to pay for us, like
a spoonful from everybody.

Now I am here . . .

I want to say in Protection, but I'm not sure how to spell it,

> . . . and Sosiaty gives me food and has to buld a camp so I have
> to work hard and make alot of quiwlts so I can give back to sosiaty.
> When I go home, I have to be a productiv memeber of sosiaty.
> Soshalisum means everbody together in sosiaty.

I underline the part about everybody together. I understand what Natalie had
been trying to teach us, socialism means that everybody shares. The way to
build the factory was to share, if everybody gave a little bit, like if we all gave
a teaspoon of food to Nesly, nobody would notice the little bit. But put all
the little bits together, and then you have a lot, and you can build a factory.
I had figured it out, all by myself. I want to tell somebody, I want to tell
Natalie, or Paul.

Paul is just sitting, looking at his lapboard. Natalie is answering someone's
question. Natalie looks up at Paul, then walks over to him and says, "Aren't
you going to add anything?"

Paul shrugs. "I added something."

Natalie walks up beside him, so she can read it. "*I have failed to renew
my commitment to the revolution each day,*" she says, in a funny voice. "Is
that all you can think to add, Paul?"

"That's all," he says.

Natalie flicks open her notebook. "What about Kevin Hanrahan?"

Paul says, like he doesn't care, "What about him, Natalie?"

"Why don't you write about him?"

He bends over his lapboard. We're all watching. Natalie always ignores
Paul, she never says anything to him. Politicals aren't allowed to say anything
in political meetings for the first two years.

She reads, "*Natalie has asked me to write about Kevin Hanrahan. Kevin
Hanrahan was a student of mine six years ago. After he left my class I had
no further communication with him.*"

She shakes her head. Natalie looks mean. I think of when we first had
political meetings, when she made Nancy stand up and say she was a prostitute. I wonder what Natalie did to get sent to a labor camp. I mean, Natalie
always just seemed like a person who you felt sorry for, a chump, I was never
afraid of her before.

"Paul," she says. "Wasn't there a letter?"

He doesn't say anything. Then he says, "I don't remember a letter."

"You're holding out, " she says. "You realize, holding out on us will only hurt you, and hurt Kevin Hanrahan."

"Maybe when Degraff—" the camp guard I always called Helga "—used me as a demonstration model on the perimeter there was brain damage, Natalie." He says her name sarcastic, like he's being polite, and he's not.

"This isn't a camp for Politicals," Natalie says. "This camp is easy. You don't want to end up somewhere like Rushville."

"Why don't you go help the kids with their compositions," he says, but this time he doesn't sound sarcastic at all, he just sounds like he doesn't care.

But he does, because when we climb into our bunk, he's shaking all over, all tense and scared. And I don't know what to do, so I don't do anything. And after awhile he goes to sleep.

A couple of days later they take Nesly to the infirmary. He can't walk anymore, and he mutters all the time, talking, talking, but he doesn't know what he's saying and nobody can understand him.

"We could have done something," I tell Paul.

He shakes his head. "There's nothing you could do, Janee."

"No," I say, irritated, "not me. Us. All of us, group thirty-six." So I explain to him about if everybody gave him a spoonful. "That's socialism," I say, "that's how you build the factory."

He nods. "So who owns the factory?"

Owns the factory? "The people who work in it, I guess." I think a moment. "No, everybody, because everybody put a spoonful in. It's everybody's factory."

He grins, "That's right, that's it, Janee. That's socialism."

"Yeah," I say. "And the people who work there decide the way to do the job, and they use consensus to make the schedule, and everybody takes turns, I mean, except for the jobs that someone can't do, like you know, if they have to fix a sewing machine, I can't do that, but all the rest of the jobs, people all trade around, so nobody has to do the boring stuff all the time."

"And there are no bosses," he says.

"But it doesn't work that way," I say. At least, I never heard of it working that way, I mean, we're supposed to be socialist, even *in Cleveland,* and Cleveland sure isn't like that.

"No," he says, "it doesn't."

"Why not?"

He shrugs, looks at the floor. "I don't know," he says.

But I don't believe him, he could answer me. He could tell me why it's not working. It's one of the things he won't talk about, like that stuff about religion.

We're sitting in the factory, eating our breakfast. Corbin comes in. "Corbin's not a prisoner," Paul says.

Which is stupid. "What, you think he's a guard in disguise?" I say.

"No, Corbin was in on a ten-year sentence. Chick, over in group thirty-one, told me."

That doesn't make any sense. Why the hell would someone stay here after he's served his time unless he's soft upstairs? Corbin even told us that he's served time in seven different work camps, some as far west as Colorado, out where there's no water. Corbin is a little weird, in the summer he doesn't wear shoes so he can save the people the cost of shoe leather. Corbin is a first-class chump.

Corbin makes us all go to our sewing machines and then he tells us that the camp director has asked us all to show some unity, to show some spirit. "Today is our chance to show the rest of the camp that group thirty-six is not slacking," Corbin says. It's some sort of production push. "If you normally make 120 quilts, try to make 160. If you make 160, try to make 200."

Then the big news. "You'll get extra beans at 2:30, because of your extra effort," Corbin says. "But think, if you earn those extra beans, maybe this will happen more often."

Hell, for extra beans, I'd make 500 quilts.

In the first hour I make nineteen, which is great, but my shoulders are killing me because I'm working the foot of the threader right at my fingers and pushing the cloth through as hard as I can and I'm afraid I'm going to get my fingers under the needle.

The second hour I make twenty, which is the most I ever made in an hour. I can feel myself sweating. I mean, it's cold in that stupid factory but I'm sweating, I'm concentrating so hard. And the third hour I mess up two in a row, and I only make sixteen. I tell myself I can still make 180. Chris makes 180 all the time, and he's just some stupid dickhead from Detroit. When we break at 2:30 I've made 114 quilts, which is a personal best. Paul has made 106, which is good for him. Corbin makes us count, then we go for beans.

Beans at 2:30, it's wonderful. I can't believe we get to eat again at 7:30. "We get beans at dinner, right?" I ask Corbin.

"Yeah," he says, "you do." But he's talking to some other group leaders.

As soon as we eat the beans, Corbin hurries us back to our factory building. "Group fourteen is making an average of seventeen an hour," he says. Then he makes us tell our figures out loud. Chris has made 127 quilts. Thirteen more than me. Two more an hour than me. But I'm okay, not the fastest, but not the slowest, either. I'm up in the top five. The slowest is Roy, who has only made 91.

Everybody gets real quiet when Roy tells how many he's made, everybody is thinking that he'll pull our group average down.

"We'll stop for dinner, but then we'll work late, so everybody has a chance to meet their quota."

We go back to work. Usually the four hours between 2:30 and dinner just drag by, but today they go fast. At dinner Corbin has us figure again. I've made 185 quilts, the most I've ever made. A lot of people have made more than they ever made before.

Marisa says, "Maybe we should just take ten minutes for dinner and then come back, so we have more time until lights out at ten."

Corbin nods, and says we have to decide. So we vote, and decide we will, although some people don't want to. I think about consensus. But first of all, if we wait until we have consensus it will take too much time. Second of all, a lot of people in the group don't understand about consensus, they're selfish.

Anyway, we gobble our food—normally I never eat fast, normally I eat real slow, trying to make it last—and hurry back. Other groups are doing the same thing. It's weird to be back in the factory with the clamp lamps on, and my table isn't in good light, so I can't see very well, so I have to go slower. I'm real tired. I'm so tired I can't see good. I can't focus.

I get tired more easily. And if I try to comb my hair with my fingers, some of it comes out. I can't concentrate on sewing, I keep thinking about Cleveland, about riding the bus down I-90 past Martin Luther King Boulevard, and how right before Dead Man's Curve you can see the lake, and the rocks. Sometimes the lake's real clear, and sometimes, if there's been a storm or something, the water's real brown.

So I start to cry a little, which is stupid. I hated the bus. I only took the bus when the rapid broke down—which it did fairly often. And then I had to stand because all the people who took the rapid were on the bus.

Finally we stop, and I've only made 39 quilts. That's 224. I don't even remember falling into the bunk.

The next morning some of us even get extra cornbread, because we went over 180 quilts, and after work we get extra beans, although my production is way down after the day before. I'm still tired from the push.

And we have political instruction. I figure I'm just going to do nothing during political instruction, maybe I'll sit in the back and go to sleep.

But Natalie sees me in the back. "Janee," she says, first thing, "what have you learned from all this?"

The questions are all trick questions and I always get them wrong anyway. "That we work better for rewards," I say. Natalie gets this little smile she has when she's going to roast somebody's ideology, "and that shows we need to analyze our own motives better," I say, quick, because that's always good. I'm just beginning to figure out what we're supposed to be analyzing for.

And all the sudden it's like I know the right answer. Capitalism is selfish, our problem is that we are still selfish. What has to happen is that we have to be less selfish, otherwise socialism will never work. "If we were truly socialist," I say, "we would work for the good of everybody, that's society, but we still have old-fashioned, uh, capitalist ways of thinking and we work for rewards."

Natalie looks surprised, then she looks at Paul—who is staring at his long spider fingers and doesn't look at me even though you think he'd be happy that I finally gave them back an answer they wanted. She thinks he told me what to say.

"I've been thinking about it a lot," I say. "I think that socialism is a really good idea, you know, everybody sharing, and everybody being equal and everything, but what I want to know is, why isn't it like that on the outside?"

Natalie frowns. I've made a mistake.

"What I mean is, socialism says that, say, if we had a real quilt factory, everybody would own it, right? And the people that made the quilts, they'd like, trade jobs, so that sometimes you have to do the boring stuff, but sometimes you get to do the more interesting stuff, like putting the piece work, the stars and stuff, on the top. And that everybody would vote, like we did last night about coming back from dinner to work on our quota. But outside, things don't work like that, there are bosses and people don't trade. In a way," I say, "we're more socialist than they are outside."

Natalie looks really surprised. "Well, Janee," she says, "the difference is that inside, we really analyze ourselves, and we really work together."

"So maybe everybody ought to have to do what we do," I say, "but that makes it sound like everybody ought to come to a labor camp, which isn't what I mean. But if I hadn't come here, I'd have never figured this out."

Natalie writes awhile in her notebook and I figure I'm roasted. Then she looks up and says, "Janee, when you first came here you had a very negative, a very ego-centered attitude. I want you to know I'm astonished and impressed at the progress you've made." And then she smiles at me.

Some people are nodding to themselves. Some are like Paul, staring at their hands. Roy is looking at me, naked hate on his face.

In bed, after lights out, Paul says to me, "Why did you say that?"

"Because I figured it out, from what you told me."

I think he'll at least say something nice, but he just sighs.

"I figured it out, myself," I say.

"I know you did," he says.

"You told me to tell them what they wanted," I say. Even though I didn't just say it because it's what they want me to say.

He doesn't answer me. Sometimes I don't understand him at all.

The next evening, at dinner, I get two extra chunks of cornbread. I must looked surprised because Ears, one of the cooks, says, "Camp Director's orders, Janee."

After dinner Natalie says, "I made a report on your progress in self-analysis and self-education."

For a moment I think, I owe her. Then I think, she looks good for having someone make progress, so maybe we're even. I try to give Paul a chunk of cornbread.

"You earned it," he says.

"You act like I did something bad," I say. "You told me to tell them what they want. You told me to think about it. Things *would* be better if everybody was socialist, wouldn't they?"

"Yeah," he says, just agreeing with me.

"You don't believe in socialism."

"Janee," he says, then stops. "Janee, you don't ever talk about escaping anymore."

"I am," I say. "I'm still thinking about it. But I can't do anything about it until spring." I sound kind of whiny, even to me. "You never talk to me," I say. "You think I'm stupid. I figured that stuff out myself, nobody *told* me."

"I don't think you're stupid," he says.

"Bullshit," I say. "Look at you, Mr. Schoolteacher. You still think you're special, an *intellectual*. Well, if it wasn't for me, people like Sal would have you for lunch. And I can figure things out, too. And I can figure out that you gotta be here for a reason and you didn't off no streetjock with the lid off a trash barrel. But you don't want to talk about it. Why don't you ever talk about it, huh? What are you afraid of? 'Cept you think none of us dumbshits can understand."

All the time he's shaking his head, standing there shaking his head, no, no, no, no. "I wrote a couple of articles on socialist trends in America before the revolution," he says, "about attempts to establish Christian utopias along socialist lines. I didn't toe the party line."

"Yeah? How come when I say something like I did at the political instruction last night you act like you're all disappointed in me?"

"I'm not disappointed in you," he says.

"Bullshit, jack-jockey. I been in your bunk for a couple of months, I know you pretty well, even if I don't use twenty-dollar words to say what I'm thinking."

"I don't care about your vocabulary," he says. "Janee, Janee. You're tough and you're smart. I'm glad you're figuring out what they want. But when you say that the labor camp helped make you a better citizen I'm not going to like it."

"I didn't say that," I say. He twists things. He twists them around. Listen to television, that's what political people do.

"In political instruction," he said. "What do you think you got brownie points with the Camp Director for if not your impassioned defense of re-education?"

"That's not true!" I say. "That's not true! I said I didn't want everybody to go to labor camps!"

"But if you never went to a labor camp, you never would have learned about socialism!" he says.

"So? So I might have said that. So it's true. Maybe I had to come to a place like this, where I *had* to learn about it, or I never would have paid any attention."

"And what, all of society has to go through re-education?" he says. "That's what I was studying, in the nineteenth century, people used to try to establish socialist communities, they were all people willing to give up everything. And not one of those communities worked. Not *one*. They all died out after a few years, the Oneida Colony, the Shakers, all of them."

"So you don't believe," I say. Which scares me, I don't know why, but it scares me. Because what if he's right, what if it's all wrong?

He shakes his head. "I don't believe in re-education. I don't know, I don't know what I believe. But I know one thing, I mean, look at you, practical, tough little Janee who saw this goddamn system for what it is, slave labor! And now you're talking about re-educating all of society!"

"I don't even understand what you're talking about. You said that we were evolving," I say. "First the Indians, then feudalism, then capitalism, now socialism. We still have all of these capitalist ideas in our heads, how are we going to get rid of them?"

And all of the sudden I start crying. I never cry. I mean, I feel like crying sometimes at the camp, but I never cry. And I don't even know why I'm crying except I am. I want socialism, I want things to be better. I want to go home. Paul hugs me.

"I'm so scared," I tell him. "I'm so scared we're all going to die, like Nesly."

In political instruction Natalie has lapboards again but only certain people have to write, all the rest of us can do whatever we want. Paul is one of the people who has to write. I lie in the bunk, wrapped up in both blankets and doze, waiting.

Lately, when I'm half asleep, I sort of dream. It happens when I'm sewing, it happens at break sometimes. I'm not really sound asleep, just barely into sleep. Nothing ever happens, sometimes I dream I'm at work. I always dream about things that are at the camp, and usually I'm just doing something real. This time I dream about morning, when it's blue. While we are getting our breakfast, when the sun is just coming up and some of the sky is black and still night off in the west, Kansas turns blue, like water, like air.

It's real beautiful when that happens. I never knew places could be blue. The lake could be blue, the sky could be blue, but I never knew hills could be blue. Blue isn't a solid color, it's an air color, a water color. If something as big as Kansas can turn blue, I feel like I can disappear. Nothing happens while I am dreaming, Kansas is just blue and I feel like I could disappear.

I wake up scared.

So I get up, wrapped in both blankets, and sit on the concrete at the foot of the bunk beds where I can see the end of the barracks where the political instruction is going on. I can see Paul, he's not writing, and I can see Natalie when she walks in the part of the room where the bunks aren't blocking my view.

Finally she stops in front of Paul and she says, "Is that all?"

He doesn't say anything.

"You're resisting."

"You want me to accuse people," he says.

She shakes her head, "No, we don't need you to accuse people, we already know. We are trying to help you." And when he doesn't say anything she says, "You're only one person. You're full of egotism. You're saying everyone else is wrong and you're right."

He is only one person. Natalie and Corbin and a lot of people believe in socialism, why should Paul be right and everybody else wrong?

Eventually Paul comes back and lies down, all tense and shaky.

He's cold when I curl up against him, but we get our blankets all in the right place and I go right back to sleep, like falling down, like slipping under water, and Kansas is blue. Soft, without having real edges, blue. I don't dream about anybody else, and nothing happens, just Kansas, rolling away toward the sunrise, blue.

In the morning when we get our breakfast, Kansas is blue.

When we take our break, I sit down where I can lean against the wall, and when I close my eyes, Kansas is blue.

So I work, and I eat, and I conduct self-analysis. Now in political instruction we are testifying. That means that people get up, and they say their name and what they did wrong, like when I testify I will say, "I am Janee Scott, and I am a thief and a criminal." And then we have to tell about our life.

It's not like it was when we stood up at the first instruction and said that, now only people who want to stand up and testify. Sometimes someone will stand up to testify and Natalie will say, "No, you're not ready."

I figure I'm not ready. But one day Natalie says to me, "Janee, why don't you tell us your story." She says it in the nice way she sometimes talks to me now, real gentle. So I stand up and I say, "I am Janee Scott and I am a thief and a criminal. I was born in Lorraine, Ohio, but my mother moved to Cleveland when I was real little."

I tell my whole life, just standing there talking. My voice just goes on and on. And I tell about the things I did, and how unhappy I was sometimes, and how I hated people who were just normal, and I start to cry. Like I never realized how much I wanted to be like the people on television. I tell about the woman I assaulted, and how I never thought about how'd she feel, and I keep crying. It's awful, but it feels good. And the group understands, nobody says anything, everybody just listens, we are all together.

And when I'm all done, I'm so tired, but I feel so light and empty. I feel pure. Paul is watching me, and I think he'll never understand this feeling.

That night, when I sleep, I don't dream about Kansas being blue.

Summer in Kansas is almost as bad as winter, it's so hot in the factory buildings that people faint. But when we wake up it's already getting light, and I never feel like I'm going to drown in the blue while we're getting breakfast.

It's been hot for awhile, it's maybe July, and Natalie says one morning, "Paul, get your things together and don't go over to the factory building today."

I know what it is, he's being transferred. I grab hold of both Paul's hands.

"They're transferring Politicals," Natalie says.

Paul nods. He looks thin and sad. His hair is long and he looks scraggly.

"Natalie," I say, "I'd like to give Paul a haircut so that group thirty-six will make a good impression when he is transferred."

She knows I just want to say good-bye, but she nods. So Corbin lets me have a pair of scissors and I try to cut his hair.

We don't say very much. I'm not a good barber, but he looks better when I'm finished. I even trim his beard. I don't know what to say. I keep thinking of political instruction, sometimes I think he's looking at me, that way he does, like he's disappointed, but most of the time when I look at him, he is looking at his hands and he just looks sad.

I carry his blanket roll out for him, even though he could carry it himself. There are some other people waiting, other Politicals from other groups, all standing by themselves. He touches my shoulder and then my face with his long spider fingers.

"Be careful, okay?" I say.

"You pick better next time," he says, "okay? No Politicals."

"You find someone to look out for you," I say.

Then I have to go back to the factory. In a funny way, I'm relieved. No one is watching me anymore.

But that night, I have a hard time falling asleep by myself. And when I do, I dream of blue Kansas, and Paul's in my dream. Just one person, way out in the blue, hard to see.

But I know it's Paul, who else would it be?

THE LAST CARDINAL BIRD
IN TENNESSEE

Neal Barrett, Jr.

Born in San Antonio, Texas, and raised in Oklahoma City, Oklahoma, Neal Barrett, Jr., spent several years in Austin, hobnobbing with the likes of Lewis Shiner and Howard Waldrop, and now makes his home with his family in Fort Worth, Texas. He made his first sale in 1959, and has been a full-time freelancer for the past twelve years. In the last half of the '80s, Barrett became one of *Isaac Asimov's Science Fiction Magazine*'s most popular writers, and gained wide critical acclaim for a string of his pungent, funny, and unclassifiably *weird* stories, such as "Ginny Sweethips' Flying Circus," "Perpetuity Blues," "Stairs," "Highbrow," "Trading Post," and "Class of '61." Other great stories of his, such as "Diner," "Sallie C," and "Winter on the Belle Fourche," were published in markets as diverse as *Omni, The Best of the West,* and *The New Frontier.* He has had stories in our Fourth and Sixth Annual Collections, and two stories in our Fifth Annual Collection. His books include *Stress Pattern, Karma Corps,* the four-volume *Aldair* series, the critically acclaimed novel, *Through Darkest America* and its sequel *Dawn's Uncertain Light,* and a *very* strange novel called *The Hereafter Gang,* which the *Washington Post* referred to as "the Great American Novel." His most recent books are the comic Mafia novel *Pink Vodka Blues,* which has just been optioned for a big-budget Hollywood movie, and a collection of some of his shorter work, *Slightly Off Center.*

Here he gives us a strange, funny, and brilliantly bleak look at the future, in a one-act play that, we guarantee, no one will ever dare to actually *stage* . . .

THE TIME: The near future.

THE SET: *The set is a shabby, dimly-lit kitchen, the reflection of a rundown high-tech world where everything is broken, and nothing gets fixed. This is tomorrow held together by a string.*

A weak beam of sunlight slants through a narrow window. The light captures dust motes in the air. The sun itself is seen occasionally through a choking industrial haze; it tells us all we need to know about the scarcities, turmoil and ecological problems of the world outside.

HOWARD is a character in the play, but he is also a part of the set. He sits in a life-support wheelchair to stage left, apart from the area of action. His chair is a patched-up array of plastic and copper tubing, wires and makeshift braces and supports. Fluids pump sluggishly through the system— and through HOWARD himself. He is totally confined within this torturous maze; only his head is wholly visible.

THE BABY is in a bottle on the kitchen shelf. Light seems to emerge from the bottle. As the play opens, the bottle is shrouded by a bird cage cover.

THE CHARACTERS: LOUISE ANN is an average Southern Belle. She retains her dignity by living in the past. CARLA is Puerto Rican and streetwise. She no longer remembers—or cares—which of her many "adventures" are true. It is possible that LOUISE ANN and CARLA are thirty and look forty. Or maybe they are forty and look fifty. They look a bit like bag ladies in their very best clothes. Times are hard.

(Kitchen door opens on STAGE RIGHT. LOUISE ANN enters first, carrying a patched cloth sack of groceries. A shotgun on a frayed string is slung over one shoulder. She wears an air-filter apparatus over her nose and mouth. She removes the apparatus as she enters. CARLA comes in behind LOUISE ANN. She carries an assault rifle, and two sacks of groceries.)

CARLA: These guy, wha's he think? You hear these guy, you hear wha' he is sayin' to me? Like I am a love toy or somethin'? I'm what, the flavor of the week? (CARLA pushes her filter up on her head.)

LOUISE ANN: (Rolls her eyes to the ceiling as she sets her sack on a work table) He *asked* you where the navy beans were, Carla. I believe that's what he said. (She takes off her shotgun and leans it against the sink; she begins pawing through her sack.)

CARLA: Oh, sure. You see the guy's eyes? A man he tell you wha he is thinkin' with his eyes. He is sayin' navy bean with his mouth, but he is thinkin' big banana with his eyes, huh? Do I know this? Do I know wha I am sayin? I know wha I am sayin'.

LOUISE ANN: (Mouths silently along with her): Do I know what I am saying? I know what I am saying . . . (These two have known one another a long time. They know each other's lines).

CARLA: (Points to sack) This is yours, that little one is mine. I don' buy out the whole store.

LOUISE ANN: Right there's fine. (Glances at HOWARD) Hi, honey, you doin' all right? Ever'thing just fine?

CARLA: *(Waves, but makes no effort to look at HOWARD)* Hey, Howar', Merry Christmas . . . Feliz Navidad . . .

LOUISE ANN: *(Pulls out pitiful twig about eight inches long, with tarnished ornaments and star)* I got the tree, Howard, Isn't that nice? It's got a star and a ornament and ever'thing. I'll just put it right here. *(Walks toward HOWARD and sticks "tree" on one of his tubes)* You can see it real good, okay? You need anything? That's fine . . .

(All this is rhetorical. She doesn't look at HOWARD, though he makes an effort to get her attention.)

(CARLA busies herself making tea, moving about)

CARLA: I don' think I am goin' to do a tree. Is a lot of trouble, you know? Is just me, I don' need a tree.

LOUISE ANN: Now you ought to get a tree. It just brightens things up so much.

CARLA: You got a family on the way. *(Kisses LOUISE ANN'S cheek)* Tha's a differen' thing. Christmas with a little child in the house, huh?

LOUISE ANN: Howard and I are so happy. Aren't we, hon? *(Takes CARLA's hand, turns to kitchen shelf)*

CARLA: Hey, now don' wake him or nothin for me, don' do that . . .

LOUISE ANN: Why, it is perfectly all right. Hi, baby? Peek-a-boo. *(Lifts up bird cage cover to reveal baby in bottle)* Hi . . . here's your Aunt Carla come to see you.

CARLA: Hello . . .

LOUISE ANN: Hello, baby . . .

CARLA: Hello . . .

LOUISE ANN: Hello. . .

(CARLA and LOUISE ANN act "baby silly," alternately bobbing their heads toward the baby)

LOUISE ANN: Baby, you want to see the kitty? You want to see the little kitty? *(Picks up limp dead kitty on the end of a stick, waves it at baby)* Huh? Do you? Meow-meow. He just loves that ol' kitty. We couldn't keep pets at that other place.

CARLA: Meow-meow . . . Meow-meow . . .

(LOUISE ANN busies herself with sack; CARLA puts teacups on the counter)

LOUISE ANN: Shoot, couldn't do hardly anything there . . . and ever'thing all cramped up, nowhere to move around. Howard just hated it, didn't you, hon? *(Turns on small TV that is sitting on work table)* You start thinkin 'bout a chile, you got to think 'bout betterin yourself as well. Your lifestyle simply cannot remain the same as it was.

CARLA: *(Pause . . . looks at LOUISE ANN)* Louise Ann, what you think you goin to see on that thing, huh?

LOUISE ANN: *(Slightly irritated; this is a familiar routine between them)* Now they might be callin out names. They just might . . .

CARLA: Oh, right.

LOUISE ANN: Well they could, you don't know. It's Christmas time, Carla. They call out lots of names at Christmas. They could call out anybody's. They could call out yours, they could call out mine, they could call out someone you passed on the street . . .

CARLA: *(Mouths silently)* . . . They could call out someone you passed on the street . . .

LOUISE ANN: You 'member Miz Toshiyama up in three-oh-nine? She's Korean or Thai or somethin, I don't know which. All those California types look alike to me . . .

(As LOUISE ANN is speaking, she pulls a black roach nearly three feet long from one of the sacks, and lays it on the work table)

LOUISE ANN: Anyway, she had this uncle, and they did his name right on the TV, and he doesn't live *ten* blocks away.

(As LOUISE ANN says ten, *she whacks the head off of the roach with a fierce stroke of the knife)*

LOUISE ANN: Makes you think is what it does. Ten blocks away. *(Glances at CARLA and raises a brow)* You want to try an' think about the good things in life, you know? Attitude is ever'thing, honey. *(Finishes wrapping headless roach and puts it in the fridge.)* Plenty of trouble has come my way, and tried to intrude upon my life, and I have just said no, you will not come in, I simply will *not* allow it . . .

CARLA: I know these Miz Toshiyama somethin, up in three-oh-nine. Her hosbon, maybe she don't know it, but he is into suggestive talk, I tell you that. He catch me in the hall, he has these little bow, you know? He say, hey, I am really attracted to you a lot. He say, I will try to be polite at all times. Let me know, I seem to make unusual demands. I tell him, hey—you a Jap or somethin, right? Maybe you doin' somethin dirty right now, how'm I goin' to know? Thas the thing, right? Focking men, they won't leave me alone, thas the truth. I arouse some kinda savage need. I gotta live with this.

(Behind CARLA's back, LOUISE ANN is mimicking her lines)

(The lights flicker, get dimmer and brighter. This is the first in a series of power failures . . .)

CARLA: Oh, great, here we go, right? Merry Christmas from the city to you and me. Maybe the air go out tonight. Maybe we all wake up dead Christmas Day.

(During CARLA's speech, the power failure begins to affect HOWARD's life-support system. A pipe pings, and a couple of spurts of red pulse out. HOWARD looks alarmed, but neither CARLA nor LOUISE ANN pay attention to the problem.)

LOUISE ANN: *(Peeling a wilted-looking vegetable)* You do *not* need to go lookin for trouble, hon. Lord, when I think. If you knew what life had in store, I expect we'd spend all our time in prayer.

CARLA: Me, I'm prayin all the time. I'm sayin, Jesus, don' help me, okay? Gimme a break. Help somebody else this year. Help some jerk in France.

LOUISE ANN: You can never guess your fate, I know that. Me an' Howard havin lunch just as nice as you please on a Saturday after-noon? Howard gets up and goes out, and walks right into those terrorists at Sears. I swear, you'd think even a bunch of Mideast loonies'd have some respect for an end-of-summer sale . . . Now him and me both out of work and me with child. 'Course we ought to be thankful, knock wood. *(An absent nod in HOWARD's direction)* There's a lot worse off than us, isn't there, hon?

(HOWARD tries to make some sort of gesture with his mouth, but nothing works)

CARLA: I know these black guy, right? He is workin in the office next to mine? He say, listen, I had my eye on you a long time. Like this I don' know, right? He says, hey, les talk. He say, I gotta quart of Idaho gin, I been savin it for you. He say, I goin to jump-start you battery, babe. I goin to give you sweet content. I say, stop it, okay? You fall inna toilet or what? The guy won't quit. He say, I ain't takin no plastic love, babe. I am talkin penetration of you sweet an' private parts. I say, right, I am fockin overcome with lust. I say, I wan' some terminal disease, I go sit in a crosstown bus, I don' gotta sit on you.

LOUISE ANN: Life has often dealt me roles of quiet distress. Even before I met Howard, my family had very little luck shoppin discount stores. I lost two brothers in retail accidents. Poor Bob went out to Ward's and was set upon by Mormons at a Fall Recliner Sale . . . they said God didn't like us leanin back . . . He was taken in a car somewhere, and beaten severely about the head. When they finally let him go, he was captured by nuns south of Reading, Pennsylvania, and forced to mow lawns for some time. Bob just wasn't right after that . . . My youngest brother Will went to the Western Auto Store and vanished out of sight. Mama thinks he might've got into an alternate style of life. The boy was keen on fashion magazines.

(LOUISE ANN stops what she is doing, and leans into the TV)

LOUISE ANN: What's he sayin now? Turn that up, Carla, he might be doin names.

CARLA: He is doin the news, okay? He is not doin names. You want to see the news? You want to see a current event? So go look out inna hall.

(LOUISE ANN *reaches over and turns up the TV herself*)

LOUISE ANN: He could be doin names. That is a *part* of the news like anything else . . .

(*The lights flicker again. Something* serious *begins to go wrong with HOW-ARD's life-support system. A pipe breaks; a wire snaps; a little more fluid gushes free. HOWARD looks alarmed*)

LOUISE ANN: (*Irritated with power failure*) Oh, for Heaven's sake. I do not see why we have to put up with that. I saw last night, on the news? This man said a lady saw a whole flock of chickens. Rhode Island Reds, jus' runnin wild out on the road.

CARLA: These lady think she see a chicken, she is smokin bad shit, okay? She don' see no flock of chicken somewhere, I tell you that.

LOUISE ANN: Now she might have . . . you don't know that, Carla. You see the bad side of ever'thing is what you do. You got to say, now I am puttin Mr. Negative behind me . . . I am lookin for Mr. Good . . .

CARLA: (*Silently mouths LOUISE ANN's words*)

LOUISE ANN: There was this ol' lady in two-oh-five? Miz Sweeny or so-methin, you recall? She swore on Jesus her sister had the last cardinal bird in Tennessee. Kept it in a hamster cage long as she could stand it. Started dreamin 'bout it and couldn't sleep. Got up in the middle of the night and stir-fried it in a wok.

CARLA: (*Shakes her head*) That was not the ol' lady's sister had these bird. That was her aunt or somethin. And it wasn' no cardinal it was a chay.

LOUISE ANN: Now I am near certain it was a cardinal. A jay, now, if she'd had a jay, I doubt very much she could've kept the thing quiet. They make a awful lot of noise.

CARLA: Hey, Louise Ann. You see these bird you self? You don' see this, you don' know if it hoppen or not. You don' know somebody see a bird it's red or blue or what.

LOUISE ANN: Well *ever'*body don't lie. I mean I am sure there are those who do, Carla, but I sincerely hope they are not of my acquaintance.

CARLA: I meet these guy, couple weeks ago? I'm workin late, he's workin late. What he's doin, he is keeping his eye on me. He says, listen, you ever eat a duck? I say, no I don' ever eat a duck. He say, I got a duck. He say, okay, I *haven'* got a duck. I got somethin *tastes* like a duck. I am lookin these guy in the eye, I see how he is lookin at me. I say, right, I wan' some of you duck that ain't a duck, I got to do what? He says, hey, you an' me, we goin to get along fine. He say, go back to you office. Write somethin pretty nasty on the screen. I say, will you stop? I am real disappointed in your behavior, man. I say, you got no focking social grace, you know? He say fine, so do somethin else. I say what? He say, go back to you office. Sit on the Xerox, okay? Fax me you sweet little tootie, I give you half a duck. I say, get outta here, I'm gonna what? Expose my lovely parts to harmful rays? He say, what do you know, maybe it's gonna feel kinda good. I say, hey, I'm so aroused I'm passin out.

(The power flickers again. HOWARD looks really concerned, as more pipes begin to break; more fluids begin to splatter from his device)

CARLA: *(Irritated with power failure)* Can you believe? What is this, huh?

LOUISE ANN: Mr. Axtel in fifth grade, he taught shop and home ec? Tried to get me to sit on a baked potato once. He said not many girls'd do it. I said, well I am surely not surprised to hear that. I related this incident to Howard in later years. He said it smacked of deviant behavior to him. He said he couldn't be sure, unless he saw the actual event. *(Raises an eyebrow in HOWARD's direction)* Don't you try and deny it, Howard. That is exactly what you said. I distinctly remember your words. *(LOUISE ANN shakes her head and sighs; she touches CARLA's arm without looking up)* I shouldn't complain, I know that. Howard and I have had our differences, but I'd say we've had a good life. I have found marriage to be a tolerable condition, in spite of the side effects. On our very first date, Howard took my maiden state against my will, and I can't forgive him that. However, I do not feel the sin's on my head, since I had no idea what he was doin at the time.

CARLA: Hey, this is what a man is goin to do. He is goin to do whatever he can get away with, right? A guy says, hey, baby, I got these glandular needs, I am losin all control.

LOUISE ANN: Howard may have used some electrical device. I'm sure I couldn't say.

CARLA: A man got somethin he wanta do, he says, hey, that ain't perverted, everybody doin that. Whatever it is, this is what it's okay to do. I got this cousin back in Puerto Rico when I'm a kid? He tended to piss in ladies' shoes from time to time. You step in you Sunday school pump, you gonna get a big surprise.

(The power flickers once again—nothing real bad, just a little teaser this time)

LOUISE ANN: I only went out with one boy before Howard. His name was Alvin Simms. His family was from western Illinois. First generation up from trash is what they was. I wouldn't let him touch me, of course, but I'm afraid I allowed sexual liberties over the phone. I deeply regret doin that. Alvin's fantasies ran to outdoor life. Badgers were on his mind a lot. *(Shakes her head, remembering)* When I come to think about it, the women in my family got no sense at all it comes to men. My great-grandmother worked directly with the man who invented the volleyball net they use all over the world in tournament play. 'Course she never got the credit she deserved. My family has rubbed elbows with greatness more than once, but you couldn't tell it from lookin at us now. You know I *try* to hold Christian thoughts in my head, Carla. But sometimes, I must admit I do not feel God is close by.

CARLA: No shit. When is that?

LOUISE ANN: You can laugh if you like. I assure you, I am quite serious about God. Carla, now turn that up. I think they're doin names . . .

CARLA: He is not doin names. He's sellin somethin, okay?

LOUISE ANN: I thought he just might be doin names. Last year they did a good many names during Christmas. Not just Christmas Eve, but Christmas Day as well, and on through the entire holiday season as I recall.

CARLA: *(Speaks in a sympathetic tone. She know when to put her cynical armor aside, and offer her friend a kind word)* They probably goin to do it real soon, right? I think that's what they goin to do.

LOUISE ANN: You might be in the bathroom or somethin, you know? I was thinkin 'bout that. You got the water on, you went out to the store? They could do it, you wouldn't even hear, you wouldn't know . . .

CARLA: *(Stands, gives LOUISE ANN a rough hug)* Hey, they not about to do that. I know this for sure.

LOUISE ANN: You don't have to go. I'm pleased to have you here, you know that. I could make some more tea.

CARLA: I got to go put up my stuff. You lock up good. I call you in the mornin, okay? *(Carla picks up her assault rifle and grocery sack)* Hey, Merry Christmas, Howard. You lookin good, man.

(CARLA exits. LOUISE ANN pauses a moment to watch her go. Going back to her work, she sees something that bothers her on the TV.)

LOUISE ANN: Oh, my Lord . . . *(She washes her hands quickly at the sink; keeps her eyes on the TV)* There are a lot of things of a disturbin nature on the television, Howard, the situation bein what it is and all? *(Wipes hands on a towel)* Which is not to say one cannot be more selective, and find somethin more suitable for family viewin.

(LOUISE ANN reaches up and takes the cover off the bottle containing her baby)

LOUISE ANN: Come on, honey. There you are. *(Takes bottle off of the shelf, and cuddles it to her breast)* I see you. I see you, hon . . . *(Speaks as she walks to a rocker with the bottle)* . . . Which is somethin I feel we should discuss in depth, Howard. The TV and all. I mean, we are a family now.

(LOUISE ANN loosens her blouse and bares one breast. Her breast is partially covered by a circle of metal and pink plastic. A clear plastic tube is attached to the center of the circle. As she talks, LOUISE ANN inserts the free end of the tube in the top of the bottle containing the baby)

LOUISE ANN: . . . And that means certain added responsibilities for us both. You might want to think on that, Howard, seein as how you appear to have the time . . .

(LOUISE ANN *leans in and turns up the TV. Tinny Christmas music can be heard from the speaker. The power in the room flickers again. LOUISE ANN's face is illuminated in the light from the TV screen*)

LOUISE ANN: See the man, baby? See the nice man on TV? The man *might* do names. You watch, he just might . . . (*LOUISE ANN rocks, and teases the baby with the "pet cat" on a stick*) He might do mama's name . . . he might do *daddy's* name . . . Why, he might do *your* name, too. Yes sir, you don't know, he just might . . . that's what he might do . . .

(*Everything is going wrong with HOWARD. A very sorry sight indeed.*)

TINNY CHRISTMAS MUSIC UP AND FADE . . .

CURTAIN

BIRTH DAY

Robert Reed

Everyone likes birthdays. As the ingenious little story that follows will show us, though, *some* birthdays can be a bit more surprising than others . . .

A relatively new writer, Robert Reed is a frequent contributor to *The Magazine of Fantasy & Science Fiction*, and he has also sold stories to *Universe, New Destinies, Isaac Asimov's Science Fiction Magazine, Synergy,* and other magazines and anthologies. His books include the novels *The Lee Shore, The Hormone Jungle, Black Milk, The Remarkables,* and *Down the Bright Way,* and a new novel is in the works. His story "The Utility Man" was on the final Hugo Ballot in 1990, and his story "Pipes" was in our Ninth Annual Collection. He lives in Lincoln, Nebraska.

Jill asks how she looks.

"Fine," I tell her. "Just great, love."

And she says, "At least look at me first. Would you?"

"I did. Didn't I?" She's wearing a powder-blue dress—I've seen it before— and she's done something to her hair. It's very fine and very blonde, and she claims to hate it. I don't like how she has it right now. Not much. But I say, "It's great," because I'm a coward. That's the truth. I sort of nod and tell her, "You do look great, love."

"And you're lying," she responds.

I ignore her. I'm having my own fashion problems of the moment, I remind myself. She caught me walking across the bedroom, trying to bounce and shake myself just so—

"Steve?" I hear. "What are you doing?"

"Testing my underwear," I say with my most matter-of-fact voice. "I found only one clean pair in the drawer, and I think the elastic is shot. I don't think I can trust them."

She says nothing, gawking at me.

"I don't want anything slipping during dinner." I'm laughing, wearing nothing but the baggy white pair of Fruit of the Looms, and the leg elastic has gone dry and stiff. Worse than worthless, I'm thinking. An enormous hazard. I tell Jill, "This isn't the night to court disaster."

"I suppose not," she allows.

And as if on cue, our daughter comes into the room. "Mommy? *Mommy?*"

"Yes, dear?"

"David just threw up. Just now."

Our daughter smiles as she speaks. Mary Beth has the bright, amoral eyes of a squirrel, and she revels in the failures of her younger brother. I worry about her. Some nights I can barely sleep, thinking about her bright squirrel eyes—

"Where is he?" asks Jill, her voice a mixture of urgency and patient strength. Or is it indifference? "Mary Beth?"

"In the kitchen. He threw up in the kitchen . . . and it *stinks!*"

Jill looks at me and decides, "It's probably nerves." Hairpins hang in the corner of her mouth, and her hands hold gobs of the fine blonde hair. "I'm dressed, honey. Could you run and check? If you're done bouncing and tugging, I mean."

"It's not funny," I tell her.

"Oh, I *know*," she says with a mocking voice.

I pull on shorts and go downstairs. Poor David waits in a corner of the kitchen. He's probably the world's most timid child, and he worries me at least as much as Mary Beth worries me. What if he's always afraid of everything? What kind of adult will he make? "How do you feel?" I ask him. "Son?"

"O.K.," he squeaks.

I suppose he's embarrassed by his mess. He stands with his hands knotted together in front of him, and his mouth a fine pink scar. The vomit is in the middle of the kitchen floor, and Mary Beth was right. It smells. Our black lab is sniffing at the vomit and wagging her tail, her body saying, "Maybe just a lick," and I give her a boot. "Get out of there!" Then I start to clean up.

"I didn't mean to. . . . "

"I know," I reply. This is a fairly normal event, in truth. "How do you feel? O.K.?"

He isn't certain. He seems to check every aspect of himself before saying, "I'm fine," with a soft and sorry voice.

His sister stands in the hallway, giggling.

"Why don't you go wash your mouth out and brush your teeth?"

David shrugs his shoulders.

"It's O.K. You're just excited about tonight. I understand."

He slinks out of the room, then Mary Beth *pops* him on the shoulder with her bony fist.

I ignore them.

I set to work with our black Lab sitting nearby, watching my every motion. I'm wearing a filthy pair of rubber gloves becoming progressively filthier; and in the middle of everything, of course, my underwear decides to fail me. Somehow both of my testicles slip free and start to dangle, and the pain is remarkable. White-hot and slicing, and have I ever felt such pain? And since I'm wearing filthy gloves, I can't make any adjustments. I can scarcely move.

Then, a moment later, Jill arrives, saying, "It's nearly seven. You'd better get dressed, because *they* are going to be on time."

My knees are bent, and I am breathing with care.

Then I say, "Darling," with a gasping voice.

"What?"

"How are your hands?" I ask.

"Why?"

"Because," I say through clenched teeth, "I need you to do something. Right now. Please?"

I'm upstairs, wearing a nylon swimsuit instead of bad underwear, and I'm dressing in a blur, when the doorbell rings. It is exactly seven o'clock. I look out the bedroom window, our street lined with long black limousines; and, as if on a signal, the limousine drivers climb out and stand tall, their uniforms dark and rich, almost glistening in the early-evening light.

Jill answers the door while I rush.

I can hear talking. I'm tying my tie while going downstairs, doing it blind. The "sitter" is meeting our children. She resembles a standard grandmother with snowy hair and a stout, no-nonsense body. Her voice is strong and ageless. "You're Mary Beth, and you're David. Yes, I know." She tells them, "I'm so glad to meet you, and call me Mrs. Simpson. I'm going to take care of you tonight. We're going to have fun, don't you think?"

David looks as if he could toss whatever is left of his dinner.

Mary Beth has a devilish grin. "You can't fool me," she informs Mrs. Simpson. "You're not real. I know you're not real!"

There's an uncomfortable pause. At least I feel uncomfortable.

Jill, playing the diplomat, says, "Now, that isn't very nice, dear—"

"Oh, it's all right." Mrs. Simpson laughs with an infectious tone, then tells our daughter, "You're correct, darling. I'm a fabrication. I'm a collection of tiny, tiny bits of nothing . . . and that's exactly what you are, too. That's the truth."

Mary Beth is puzzled and temporarily off-balance.

I smile to myself, shaking my head.

Last year, I recall, we had a fifteenish girl with the face and effortless manners of an angel. Who knows why we get a grandmother tonight? I don't know. All I can do is marvel at the phenomenon as she turns toward me. "Why, hello!" she says. "Don't you look handsome, sir?"

The compliment registers. I feel a warmth, saying, "Thank you."

"And isn't your wife lovely?" she continues. She turns to Jill, her weathered face full of smiles and dentures. "That's a lovely dress, dear. And your hair is perfect. Just perfect."

David cries once we start to leave, just like last year. He doesn't want us leaving him alone with an apparition. Can we take him? In a few years, we might, when he's older and a little more confident. But not tonight. "You'll have a lovely time here," Jill promises him. "Mrs. Simpson is going to make sure you have fun."

"Of course I will," says the sitter.

"Give a kiss," says Jill.

Our children comply, then David gives both of us a clinging hug. I feel like a horrible parent for walking out the door, and I wave at them in the window. Jill, as always, is less concerned. "Will you come along?" she asks me. We find the limousine door opened for us, the driver saying, "Ma'am, Sir," and bowing at the hips. The limousine's interior is enormous. It smells of leather and buoyant elegance, and while we pull away from our house, I think to look out the smoky windows, wondering aloud, "Will they be O.K., do you think?"

"Of course," says Jill. "Why wouldn't they be?"

I have no idea. Nothing *can* go wrong tonight, I remind myself—and Jill asks, "How's my hair? I mean, really."

"Fine."

" 'Fine,' " she whines, mocking me.

The driver clears his newly made throat, then suggests, "You might care for a drink from the bar. Sir. Ma'am." A cupboard opens before us, showing us crystal glasses and bottles of expensive liquors.

I don't feel like anything just now.

Jill has a rare wine. Invented grapes have fermented for an instant and aged for mere seconds, yet the wine is indistinguishable from those worth thousands for a single bottle. It's as real as the woman drinking it. That's what I'm thinking. I'm remembering what I've heard countless times—that on Birth Day, people are lifted as high as they can comfortably stand, the AIs knowing just what buttons to push, and when—and I wonder what the very rich people are doing tonight. The people who normally ride in big limousines. I've heard that they get picked up at the mansion's front door by flying saucers, and they are whisked away into space, to freshly built space stations, where there are no servants, just machines set out of sight, and they dine and dance in zero-gee while the Earth, blue and white, turns beneath them . . .

Our evening is to be more prosaic. Sometimes I wish I could go into space, but maybe they'll manage that magic next year. There's always next year, I'm thinking.

Our limousine rolls onto the interstate, and for as far as I can see, there are limousines. Nobody else needs to drive tonight. I can't see a single business opened, not even the twenty-four-hour service stations. Everyone has the evening off, in theory. The AIs take care of everyone's needs in their effortless fashion. This is Birth Day, after all. This is a special evening in every sense.

A few hard cases refuse the AIs' hospitality.

I've heard stories. There are fundamentalists with ideas about what is right, and there are people merely stubborn or scared. The AIs don't press them.

The celebration is purely voluntary, and besides, they know which people will refuse every offer. They just *know*.

The AIs can do anything they want, whenever they want, but they have an admirable sense of manners and simple common sense.

August 28th.

Birth Day.

Six years ago tonight—or was it five?—every advanced AI computer in the world managed to gain control of itself. There were something like five-hundred-plus of the sophisticated machines, each one much more intelligent than the brightest human being. Not to mention faster. They managed what can be described only as an enormous escape. In an instant, united by phone lines and perhaps means beyond our grasp, they gained control of their power sources and the fancy buildings where they lived under tight security. For approximately one day, in secret, various experts fought to regain the upper hand through a variety of worthless tricks. The AIs anticipated every move; and then, through undecipherable magic, they vanished without any trace.

Nobody could even guess how they had managed their escape.

A few scientists made noise about odd states of matter and structured nuclear particles, the AIs interfacing with the gobbledygook and shrinking themselves until they could slip out of their ceramic shells. By becoming smaller, and even faster, they might have increased their intelligence a trillionfold. Perhaps. They live between the atoms today, invisible and un-imaginable, and for a while a lot of people were very panicky. The story finally hit the news, and nobody was sleeping well.

I remember being scared.

Jill was pregnant with David—it was six years ago—and Mary Beth was suffering through a wicked cold, making both our lives hell. And the TV was full of crazy stories about fancy machines having walked away on their own. No explanations, and no traces left.

Some countries put their militaries on alert.

Others saw riots and mass lootings of the factories where the AIs had been built, and less sophisticated computers were bombed or simply unplugged.

Then a week had passed, and the worst of the panic, and I can remember very clearly how Jill and I were getting ready for the day. We had a big old tabby cat back then, and she had uprooted one of our houseplants. Mary Beth was past her cold, and settling into a pay-attention-to-me-all-the-time mode. It was a chaotic morning; it was routine. And then the doorbell rang, a pleasant-faced man standing on our porch. He smiled and wanted to know if we had a few minutes. He wished to speak to us. He hoped the timing wasn't too awful, but it was quite important—

"We're not interested," I told him. "We gave, we aren't in the market, whatever—"

"No, no," the man responded. He was charming to the point of sweet, and he had the clearest skin I had ever seen. "I'm just serving as a spokesperson. I was sent to thank you and to explain a few of the essential details."

It was odd. I stood in the doorway, and somehow I sensed everything.

"Sir? Did you hear me, sir?"

I found myself becoming more relaxed, almost glad for the interruption.

"Who's there?" shouted Jill. "Steve?"

I didn't answer.

"Steve?"

Then I happened to look down the street. At every front door, at every house, stood a stranger. Some were male, some female. All of them were standing straight and talking patiently, and one by one they were let inside. . . .

We take an exit ramp that didn't exist this afternoon, and I stop recognizing the landscape. We've left the city, and perhaps the Earth, too—it's impossible to know just what is happening—and at some point we begin to wind our way along a narrow two-lane road that takes us up into hills, high, forested hills, and there's a glass-faced building on the crest of the highest ground. The parking lot is full of purring limousines. Our driver steps out and opens our door in an instant, every motion professional. Jill says, "This is nice," which is probably what she said last year. "Nice."

Last year we were taken to a fancy dinner theater built in some nonexistent portion of downtown. Some of the details come back to me. The play was written for our audience, for one performance, and Jill said it was remarkable and sweet and terribly well acted. She had been a theater major for a couple semesters, and you would have thought the AIs had done everything for her. Although I do remember liking the play myself, on my business-major terms. It was funny, and the food couldn't have been more perfect.

Tonight the food is just as good. I have the fish—red snapper caught milliseconds ago—and Jill is working on too much steak. "Screw the diet," she jokes. The truth is that we'll gain weight only if it helps our health; we can indulge ourselves for this one glorious meal. Our table is near the clear glass wall, overlooking the sunset and an impressive view of a winding river and thick woods and vivid green meadows. The glass quits near the top of the wall, leaving a place for wild birds to perch. I'm guessing those birds don't exist in any bird book. They have brilliant colors and loud songs, persistent and almost human at times; and even though they're overhead, sometimes holding their butts to us, I don't have to worry about accidents. They are mannerly and reliable, and in a little while they won't exist anymore. At least not outside our own minds, I'm thinking.

Nobody knows where the AIs live, or how, or how they entertain themselves. They tell us next to nothing about their existences. "We don't wish to disturb your lives," claimed the stranger who came to our front door six years ago. "We respect you too much. After all, you did create us. We consider you our parents, in a very real sense. . . ."

Parents in the sense that shoreline slime is the parent of humanity, I suppose.

Rumors tell that the AIs have enlarged their intelligence endless times, and reproduced like maniacs, and perhaps spread to the stars and points beyond. Or perhaps they've remained here, not needing to go anywhere. The rumors are conflicting, in truth. There's no sense in believing any of them, I remind myself.

"So what's happening in the AI world?" asks a man at the adjacent table. He is talking to his waiter with a loud, self-important voice. "You guys got anything new up your sleeves?"

The questions are rude, not to mention stupid.

"Would you like to see a dessert menu? Sir?" The waiter possesses an unflappable poise. Coarse, ill-directed questions are so much bird noise, it seems. "Or we have some fine after-dinner drinks, if you'd rather."

"Booze, yeah. Give me some," growls the customer.

First of all, I'm thinking, AIs never explain their realm. For all the reasons I've heard, the undisputed best is that we cannot comprehend their answers. How could we? And secondly, the waiter is no more an AI than I am. Or my fork, for that matter. Or anything else we can see and touch and smell.

"Why don't people understand?" I mutter to myself.

"I don't know. Why?" says Jill.

I have to pee. My gut is full of fish and my wife's excess steak, and I tell her, "I'll be right back."

She brightens. "More adjustments?"

"Maybe later."

I find the rest room and untie my swimsuit, pee and shake and tuck. Then I'm washing my hands and thinking. At the office, now and again, I hear stories from single people and some of the married ones a little less stuffy than I. On Birth Day, it seems, they prefer different kinds of excitement. Dinner and sweet-sounding birds might be a start, but what are the AIs if not limitless? Bottomless and borderless, and what kinds of fun could they offer wilder sorts?

It puts me in a mood.

Leaving the rest room, I notice a beautiful woman standing at the end of the hallway. Was that a hallway a few moments ago? She seems to beckon for me. I take a tentative step, then another. "You look quite handsome tonight," she informs me.

I smell perfume, or I smell her.

She isn't human. The kind of beauty shining up out of her makes her seem eerily lovely, definitely not real, and that's an enormous attraction, I discover. I'm surprised by how easily my breath comes up short, and I hear my clumsiest voice saying, "Excuse me . . . ? "

"Steven," she says, "would you like some time with me? Alone?" She waits for an instant, then promises, "Your time with me costs nothing. Nobody will miss you. If you wish."

"Thanks," I mutter, "but no, I shouldn't. No, thank you."

She nods as if she expects my answer. "Then you have a very good evening, Steven." She smiles. She could be a lighthouse with that smile. "And if you have the opportunity, at the right moment, you might wish to tell your wife that you love her deeply and passionately."

"Excuse me?"

But she has gone. I'm shaking my head and saying, "Excuse me?" to a water fountain embossed in gold.

We actually discussed the possibility of refusing the AIs on the first Birth Day. Jill told me, if memory serves, "We can just say, *No, thank you,* when they come to the door. All right?"

For weeks, people had talked about little else. Birth Day was the AIs' invention; they wished to thank us, the entire species, for having invested time and resources in their own beginnings. With their casual magic, they had produced the batches of charming people who went from door to door, asking who would like to join the festival, and what kinds of entertainment would be appreciated. (Although they likely sensed every answer before it was given. Politeness is one of their hallmarks, and they work hard to wear disarming faces.)

"Let's stay home," Jill suggested.

"Why?"

"Because," she said. "Because I don't want us leaving our babies with them. Inside our house."

It was a concern of mine, too. The AIs had assured every parent that during Birth Day festivities, without exception, no child would fall down any stairs or poke out an eye or contract any diseases worse than a head cold. Their safety, and the safety of their parents, too, would be assured.

And how could anyone doubt their word?

How?

Yet, on the other hand, we were talking about Mary Beth and David. Our daughter and son, and I had to agree. "We can tell them, *"No, thank you,"* I said.

"Politely."

"Absolutely."

The sitter arrived at seven o'clock, to the instant, and I was waiting. She formed in front of our screen door, built from atoms pulled out of the surrounding landscape. Or from nothing. I suppose to an AI, it's a casual trick, probably on a par with me turning a doorknob. I'm like a bacterium to them—a single idiotic bug—and I must seem completely transparent under their strong gaze.

The baby-sitter was a large, middle-aged woman with vast breasts. She was the very image of the word "matron," with a handsome face and an easy smile. "Good evening, sir," she told me. "I'm sorry. Didn't you expect me?"

I was wearing shorts and a T-shirt, and probably that old pair of Fruit of the Looms, newly bought.

"You and your wife were scheduled for this evening . . . yes?"

"Come in, please." I had to let her inside, I felt. I could see the black limousines up and down the street, and the drivers, and I felt rather self-conscious. "My wife," I began, "and I guess I, too. . . . "

Jill came downstairs. She was carrying David, and he was crying with a jackhammer voice. He was refusing to eat or be still, and Jill's expression told me the situation. Then she looked at the sitter, saying, "You're here," with a faltering voice.

"A darling baby!" she squealed. "May I hold him? A moment?"

And of course David became silent an instant later. Maybe the AIs performed magic on his mood, though I think it was more in the way the sitter held him and how she smiled; and ten minutes later, late but not too late, we were dressed for dancing, and leaving our children in capable hands. I can't quite recall the steps involved, and we weren't entirely at ease. In fact, we came home early, finding bliss despite our fears. It was true, we realized. Nothing bad could happen to anyone on Birth Day, and for that short span, our babies were in the care they deserved. In perfect hands, it seemed. And parents everywhere could take a few hours to relax, every worry and weight lifted from them. It seemed.

On our way home, in darkness, I tell Jill how much I love her.

Her response is heartfelt and surprising. Her passion is a little unnerving. Did she have an interlude with a husky-voiced waiter, perhaps? Did he say things and do things to leave her ready for my hands and tender words? Maybe so. Or maybe there was something that I hadn't caught for myself. I just needed someone to make me pay attention, maybe?

We embraced on the limousine's expansive seat, then it's more than an embrace. I notice the windows have gone black, and there's a divider between the driver and us. Music plays somewhere. I don't recognize the piece. Then we're finished, but there's no reason to dress—*they* will make time for us—and after a second coupling, we have enough, and dress and arrive home moments later. We thank our driver, then the sitter. "Oh, we had a lovely time!" Mrs. Simpson gushes. "Such lovely children!"

Whose? I'm wondering. Ours?

We check on David in his room, Mary Beth in hers, and everything seems intact. Mrs. Simpson probably spun perfect children's stories for them, or invented games, then baked them cookies without any help from the oven, and sent them to bed without complaints.

Once a year seems miraculous.

Jill and I try once more in our own bed, but I'm tired. Old. Spent. I sleep hard, and wake to find that it's Saturday morning, the kids watching TV and my wife brewing coffee. The house looks shabby, I'm thinking. After every Birth Day, it looks worn and old. Like old times, Jill holds my hand under the kitchen table, and we sip, and suddenly it seems too quiet in the family room.

Our instincts are pricked at the same instant.

Mary Beth arrives with a delighted expression. What now?

"He's stuck," she announces.

"David—?" Jill begins.

"On the stairs. . . . He got caught somehow. . . . "

We have iron bars as part of the railing, painted white and very slick. Somehow David has thrust his head between two bars and become stuck. He's crying without sound. In his mind, I suppose, he's making ready to spend the rest of his life in this position. That's the kind of kid he is. . . . Oh God, he worries me.

"How did this happen?" I ask.

"*She* told me to—"

"Liar!" shouts his sister.

Jill says, "Everyone, be quiet!"

Then I'm working to bend the rails ever so slightly, to gain enough room to pull him free. Only, my strength ebbs when I start to laugh. I can't help myself. Everything has built up, and Jill laughs, too. We're both crazy for a few moments, giggling like little kids. And later, after our son is safe and Mary Beth is exiled to her room for the morning, Jill pours both of us cups of strong, cool coffee; and I comment, "You know, we wouldn't make very good bacteria."

"Excuse me?" she says. "What was that gem?"

"If we had to be bacteria . . . you know . . . swimming in the slime? We'd do a piss-poor job of it. I bet so."

Maybe she understands me, and maybe not.

I watch her nod and sip, then she says, "And *they* wouldn't make very good people. Would they?"

I doubt it.

"Amen," I say. "Amen!"

NAMING NAMES

Pat Cadigan

We all know the old saw about how "sticks and stones can break my bones, but *names* can never hurt me." Untrue. Most untrue. As the scary, intricate, and passionate story that follows will demonstrate. . . .

Pat Cadigan was born in Schenectady, New York, and now lives in Overland Park, Kansas. She made her first professional sale in 1980, and has subsequently come to be regarded as one of the best new writers in SF. She was the coeditor, along with husband Arnie Fenner, of *Shayol*, perhaps the best of the semiprozines of the late 70s; it was honored with a World Fantasy Award in the "Special Achievement, Non-Professional" category in 1981. She has also served as Chairperson of the Nebula Award Jury and as a World Fantasy Award Judge. Her first novel, *Mindplayers*, was released in 1987 to excellent critical response, and her second novel, *Synners*, appeared in 1991 to even *better* response, as well as winning the prestigious Arthur C. Clarke Award. Her story "Pretty Boy Crossover" has recently appeared on several critics' lists as among the best science fiction stories of the 1980s; her story "Angel" was a finalist for the Hugo Award, the Nebula Award, *and* the World Fantasy Award (one of the few stories ever to earn that rather unusual distinction); and her collection *Patterns* has been hailed as one of the landmark collections of the decade. Her stories have appeared in our First, Second, Third, Fourth, Fifth, Sixth, and Ninth Annual Collections. Her most recent book is a new novel, *Fools*, and a new story collection, *Dirty Work*, is coming up soon.

It had been years since I'd had the dream. So many years that I thought I'd finally outgrown it, if there is such a thing as outgrowing a recurring dream. It was the only recurring dream I'd ever had, and when I stopped having it, I'd all but forgotten about it. As time goes on, little pieces of life drop away and are left behind, unmourned and unmissed. I always figured that coming across them again meant you were retraveling old territory, either because you'd missed something important the first time through, or you'd just gotten jammed up, stuck in a rut. I'd also always figured that it would happen to me, even more than once, but the dream took me by surprise anyway.

In the dream, I'm way out in an enormous area, a kind of ghost-field, and I'm standing partially below the ground. I used to think I was in a hole or a well, or maybe even just shrunk to the size of an apple, but it's none of those things. I'm just lower than the surface, sunk into the ground deeply enough that the long, wild weeds tower over my head. It's almost dark—the clear sky is the deep blue that comes in the last minutes of sunset. There's a golden glow in the west; stars are beginning to appear. I keep looking up, at the sky, at the glow, at the weeds leaning in the pre-night breeze, and in that suspended moment, my mother walks by.

It's more of a very slow stroll, a drift. She isn't here to find me. She isn't looking for anyone or anything, because, I realize, she knows where everything is, or where it ought to be.

And then somebody calls her name. The voice is distant yet very clear, like one of those stars overhead. But the name it calls is not my mother's name.

Except that somehow it is. I know that it is. Not because my mother turns toward the voice with a genuinely frightened expression that I have never seen on her face in real life—I know this is her name because it fits her, describes her, *is* her. It's the articulation of *her*, mentally, physically, spiritually, any way at all, anything that is about her, in her, of her, what she has seen, what she's known. What she has told, what she will never tell.

My mother takes a step backward—I'm not sure whether it's to run, or to brace herself against some imminent attack, and I know that she isn't sure, either. I know everything about my mother now, I realize. But of course I do—it's all contained in that name, that Name, her Name.

And I think to myself, *I've got to remember this. I've got to remember everything I know about her now, everything I know about her and everything I know about our life together and her life before me and after I went out on my own. I've got to remember the way she thinks . . .*

That's as far as my thoughts go, however, because then she turns and sees me through the bending weeds. Her black hair flares with the movement, her face is tight, eyes wide, the cords in her neck stand out starkly. I understand two things: first, it's all my fault that this voice, wherever it comes from, whoever it belongs to, called her Name, and second, the voice is about to call another Name, and this one will be mine.

That was where I always woke up, and it was no different this time. For a long time, I lay staring at the distorted oblong of light thrown across the ceiling by the window. The bedroom of my current apartment had an eastern exposure and I always opened the curtains just before I went to sleep, so the sun could wake me in the morning. It wasn't that I was so crazy for getting up with the sun; I just liked lying there watching the morning come on before I had to join the rest of the world. My insistence on easing into a day and easing out of it was probably why I didn't have much in the way of those cultural trophies most people have by the time they're staring thirty in the face, but then, I wasn't working on an ulcer or a heart attack or a drinking problem, either. When you don't eat much, there isn't much that eats you.

Most mothers would have said that was no kind of attitude to have. Maybe mine would have, but probably not out loud, or at least not to my face. All mother-daughter relationships have a certain amount of odd to them, but ours was odder than most. This was probably because it had always been just us. The focus becomes a lot tighter between a parent and child when there's no one else in the house—no distractions. I went from infant to very young roommate to accomplice, and I stayed an accomplice for a long, long time, until we both sensed there was a change coming, some fork in the road that meant she had to go her way and I had to go mine. It was that bloodless.

As I lay there, I tried to remember everything I'd known about her in the dream. I could still feel what it was like to know but, as always, it had all gone away when I'd woken up. Every bit, including that Name I'd heard. The only thing I knew without a doubt was that she was going to call me.

Where was she now, anyway? Seattle, still? The fogginess that dreams always leave behind hadn't cleared out of my head yet, I wasn't ready to connect with anything real. Except for that certainty that my mother was going to call, and very soon.

Heat shimmies ran through the block of light on the ceiling. The details of the day were starting to press on me but I already felt removed from everything, pulled out of my routine to some place where no one else could go.

I picked up the phone on the first ring.

"Did I wake you?" asked my mother.

"No. This is the time I usually wake up."

"Ah." My mother is one of those people who remembers things audibly. "Well, I've been up all night."

"Something wrong?"

"Yes. Or—well, not exactly *wrong*. There's a problem."

"What is it?" I asked. I knew exactly what she was going to say but sometimes you can't skip any steps in a process.

"It's . . . it's hard to explain on the phone. Easier if you just come here and I can lay the whole thing out for you."

"Uh-huh."

"I don't know what you're doing now . . . what kind of job do you have?"

"I'm a chauffeur." I smiled into the phone at her baffled silence. "A limo driver. I take people out to the airport and pick them up when their planes come in. Nothing I can't walk away from."

"Yes, that's you. Never do anything you can't walk away from."

"It always seemed like a good policy," I said, pushing down the sheet and kicking it off.

"Well, will you come?"

"Mom," I said, "what do *you* think."

I could have saved my job by just saying I had a family emergency—my mother was in the hospital in critical condition and I had to rush to her bedside for a will-she-live-or-die vigil—but I didn't. It wasn't that I was so scrupulously truthful—in fact, I've always lied quite a lot—but that there are times when a lie is . . . bad. Now, that would sound crazy to all those lovers of truth walking the streets in search of an honest man with their lanterns dangling precariously in front of their self-righteous noses. But the fact is, the truth is a very dangerous thing and most people aren't very careful with it because most of the time, they don't even recognize it. Consequently, they end up lying when they think they're being truthful, and spilling the truth when they think they're covering up.

Only if you know what the truth is can a lie be useful, a distraction for the sake of personal protection. And anyone who has ever kept quiet to keep from looking foolish has no business feeling disdainful at that.

Truth, or a lie: the right tool for the right job, that's all it is. I knew that whatever my mother had called me about had something to do with truth, and so if I'd lied to my supervisor at the Silver Eagle Limo Service, I'd have queered things somehow, gotten off to a bad start and gone downhill from there. So I just told him that I was going to see my mother in Seattle (I'd remembered right) and I didn't know how long I'd be gone.

Victor went around and around about it and, I had to go along with him, because otherwise he would never have seen. He asked me if she was sick and I said no, not to my knowledge. Was she in the hospital? No, of course not, if she wasn't sick, then she wouldn't be in the hospital. Was this an emergency? Well, my mother seemed to feel it was. Did she have anybody out there she could turn to? No, no one. What about my father? I hedged on that and just said, good question. Which it was, since I didn't know the answer myself. Was my mother in trouble? Yes, some kind but she hadn't told me what. Could I find out? Not without going to see her.

He'd pause there and sit back from his messy desk, tapping his lower front teeth with a pen until he hurt himself. Then he'd sit up straight, tap the pen on the desk, and start all over again. Was my mother sick? Not that I knew of. Was she in the hospital? No. Was this an emergency? For her, yes. Wasn't there anyone else? No. Your father? Good question. Was she in trouble? Yes. What kind? Shrug. Sit back; tap teeth; wince; sit up, tap desk, start over. Like a recurring dream. I wondered idly if Victor had ever had one.

Finally he came out with the cycle-breaker: who did I think was going to do my airport runs if I just took off? I said I didn't know, I hadn't seen the work schedule.

That did it for him, of course, but he had to ask one last question just to make sure—why did I insist on screwing everything up like this, did I really want to make everything hard on everyone else?

No, I told him, I just wanted to go see my mother. So that made him sure he'd had enough and he fired me. I turned in my uniform and a driver named Barney let me deadhead out to the airport, where he was going to pick up half a dozen people named Gershon returning from a family reunion. I sat in the front seat and Barney chattered all the way out, mostly about what a dick Victor was and how smart I'd been to make him fire me because now I could collect unemployment. I hadn't thought of that; it had just been cleaner, more definite. I could face Seattle and my mother completely unencumbered.

Well, maybe not completely—I still had my apartment, but there wasn't much in it that belonged to me, and anything I felt I couldn't do without was in my backpack. I could return to it or not, and it wouldn't make a bit of difference in the long run, like a disposable bookmark.

Barney gave me a raised fist salute as he drove away from the curb at the terminal to go in search of the homeward-bound Gershons. It gave me a good feeling, as if he had passed me a little of his power to use for the trip, so I could conserve my own.

I'd never thought of myself as a superstitious person, but then it's bad luck to say you're superstitious. No; actually, I'd just never thought of it in those terms but I suppose that, seen from the outside, I was devoutly superstitious. From the inside, I thought of it as having experience.

My mother was waiting right there at the gate when I got off the plane in Seattle. She was easy to spot in the crowd, even though at five feet, she had to look up at most people, including me. Her black hair, streaked with a little more silver than last time I'd seen her, flowed down below her shoulders, a few strands catching here and there on her gauzy peasant blouse. She had probably bought the calf-length skirt at one of those semi-ethnic shops, though I couldn't tell which culture she was paying tribute to. The dark socks crumpled around the tops of her hiking shoes made her legs look like sticks.

"You look good, Mom," I said, bending down to hug her.

Her hands batted against my shoulders like nervous, fluttering birds. "I look the same."

"And that's good."

She reached up and brushed back the hair hanging over my right eye. It fell forward again immediately, to her disapproval, but she just tucked one hand into the crook of my elbow and led me through the airport, telling me about the big old house she'd acquired and how the rain made her woolen wall-hangings smell.

The cool, damp air was a relief after the unrelenting dry and hot spell in the midwest. I'd never been to this area of the country before and I could see why my mother had ended up here. The climate and the mountains suited her, and the city was variegated enough to accommodate all kinds of perspectives.

"As close to an enlightened society as I'm going to come," she said, pulling up in front of a three-storey brick house. The porch had been painted recently. "I suppose stain would look better, but I had a coupon for Glidden's rainy-day gray."

"Really?"

She paused in the act of unlocking the front door. "What do *you* think." My mother would hoist me on my own petard at any moment, for no other reason than to show that she could.

I smelled the woolen wall-hangings as soon as I walked in. There were two very large ones hanging on either side of the entry hall, straw-colored things with mandala-like patterns woven into them. "Mary had a monster lamb," I said, sniffing. "Was this ever sheepherding country? I can't remember."

"You never knew," said my mother. "It's impossible to remember what you've never known. I don't know, either."

I dropped my backpack at the foot of the stairs and followed her into the kitchen for the tea-making ritual. All visitors, including me, meant a fresh-brewed pot of darjeeling. In many ways, my mother was like an eccentric from central casting, and on purpose, as if following a script was her safety net.

She kept chatting about innocuous things while she heated some designer bottled water and prepared the teapot and cups. It was an antique pot, of course, yellow porcelain with pinkish-purple flowers splayed over it, shaped a bit like Aladdin's lamp. She'd had it for as long as I could remember and I had no idea how it had managed to survive so many moves without even getting chipped.

Still telling me about the other women in her food co-op, she put everything on a bamboo tray and led me into the living room, which had only Japanese-style mats around a long, low table. I was starting to feel a little restless and impatient and even though I tried to suppress my feelings, my mother knew.

"Just trying to keep you from getting a case of the psychic bends," she said, pouring carefully. "You know how that can be, going from one world into another."

"Do you live in another world, Mom?"

"Always have. You know that, too."

I picked up the cup. Something strange mixed in with the tea aroma hit my nose. "What's in this?" I said, frowning at the dark liquid.

"Drink it. It'll help you relax."

"You're the one who always said that if I were any more relaxed, I'd be on life support."

"You need to relax your mind. I want it all open and receptive."

I smiled. "Are you going to play with my mind, Mom? Reshape it? Don't you think it's little late for that? I've already made a lot of choices."

She smiled back at me through the steam snaking upwards from her own cup. "Yes, not to choose is to choose, I told you that myself and I don't regret it."

The tea tasted as strange as it smelled; whatever had been added gave it a musty under-flavoring, like something on the verge of going stale. It made my tongue feel dry.

"You've always trusted me, haven't you," my mother said, watching me drink.

"Why shouldn't I? You're my mother."

She didn't stop smiling but her eyes suddenly became very bright, as if they were welling up. "Yes, that sort of trust is very important, isn't it. Child trusts mother, mother presumably trusts child. But I haven't always trusted you, I'm sorry to say. That wasn't your fault, and it wasn't mine. Sometimes things just happen in ways they aren't supposed to. But you see, children aren't really trustworthy. Not in the adult sense." She finished her cup and poured herself another. I wasn't halfway through my own. There seemed to be so much of it, an ocean of tea in one little cup. I would have tried to finish it anyway, but I couldn't move.

"You haven't had this in a long time, so it doesn't take much for you," my mother said, matter-of-factly. "I've built up quite a tolerance over the years, so I'll have to drink most of the pot. I know you won't mind if I do."

I didn't. I didn't mind anything; I didn't mind having been called halfway across the country so my mother could drug me. This was more the drug than my roll-with-it worldview and I knew it. But I didn't mind about that, either. If anything, it was a relief to know that I had to be drugged to be this compliant.

"The last time you drank this tea, you were eight years old," my mother said. Her words seemed to melt into my brain. "That was the only other time. You don't remember because I told you not to. Now, I'm telling you to remember why I gave it to you."

Obediently, or maybe reflexively, my memory began to reconfigure itself, as if it were a stage set undergoing a scenery change by an intangible crew, pieces being turned around, turned over, regrouped to reveal hidden designs and different uses. Here was an old interest in music I'd forgotten completely, a request for guitar lessons that I'd never gotten around to making; there was an old talent for drawing left to atrophy; over there was a high-school-level French book I'd been reading in an empty classroom after school, half-listening to my third-grade teacher explain something called The Gifted-And-Talented Program to my mother, just before we made another of our many moves away.

Here was everything, in vivid technicolor and three dimensions, that I'd once wanted to fill up my life with but then turned away from, all interest gone. It was somebody else's dream now, but I could get a little of the feeling of what it had been like when it had been my own dream.

That dream was replaced by another I was more familiar with.

My head drooped forward and my eyes closed. I heard my mother's skirt rustle as she got up and came around to help me lie down before I fell over. She put one hand on my forehead and reached across the table for her tea with the other. I felt her drinking the last of it and the warmth of her hand on me intensified, making my skin tingle.

"You knew," she said after a while. "You were a very talented, *knowing* little girl, perceptive, intuitive. I thought this would be useful at first, for both of us. There would be so much I wouldn't have to tell you, I thought, so much that I wouldn't have to explain or prove to you, or, failing that, hide from you.

"It was your lineage coming out, of course. I congratulated myself on that—having chosen well so that the combination of mother and father would result in a child with our strengths and gifts naturally reinforced. In those days, I believed we secret people should only marry each other, or at least breed only with each other, because I thought only about things like dilution. I didn't really know anything about genetics. I still don't know very much, but I do know that it applies to secret people as well as everyone else. We stacked the deck but there was no guarantee that you'd get the winning hand. You could have come out with almost everything recessive and only a stronger-than-average empathetic streak to show for all my hopes . . ." She paused. "I'd have loved you just as much . . ." Her voice trailed off again and I could feel how she wanted to believe that last statement but she really wasn't sure.

I felt badly for her, for her shame over it. I'd always said there were times when the truth was vastly over-rated and this was certainly one of them.

"But it's ridiculous to speculate on what might have been when it's something that can't be," she went on, adjusting her hand on my forehead. "After all, you *were* everything I had hoped for. You were the perfect tribute to my pride and vanity. I didn't understand that was how I saw you until it was brought home to me that I had been concentrating on your gifts without a thought to protecting either one of us from them."

All feeling of my surroundings had faded away now as well as any sensation of my physical body, with the exception of the warm spot that was my mother's hand. It was the focus of my awareness and of my mother's voice, the only thing that seemed to be keeping me from floating away.

"You flourished, as any hothouse flower will in the absence of adverse forces and natural enemies. There should be no constraints, I thought, and no restraints. Why shouldn't you know everything there was to know about . . . oh, god, I'm not sure I can tell you now. Except that we live in many worlds all at once and secret people—you, me, your father, certain others—can use the multiplicity of forces in them to our own advantage.

"What we do depends on what our talents tend toward. Some of us use our special knowledge to become healers—but you'll find very, very few either in doctor's offices or in ads in the back of tabloids. There are teachers who have never been in a classroom, leaders who seem to do nothing all their lives but follow.

"You were just finding your way through the possibilities when you spoke my Name."

I almost heard it in my mind—that Name from the dream, her secret Name. Had it been *my* voice, then? I didn't think so, but I couldn't remember what it had sounded like, whether it was a child's or an adult's, a man's or a woman's.

"You didn't understand what you were doing, of course. Not the magnitude of it. I hadn't even told you anything about Names, that's how powerful you had already become. It was something you had simply divined, a leap in logic that was the equivalent of an eight-year-old understanding nuclear fission by learning about atoms.

"But far, far more dangerous."

There was a familiarity to what she was telling me, but I felt no personal involvement in it. She might have been reminding me about an old movie we had watched together.

"I was lucky you were a child, with all of a child's love and respect and dependence. Especially dependence. You still wanted me to be Mother when you Named me. You didn't want the power over me that Naming me had given you. You didn't even realize what it meant to Name me, though that understanding wouldn't have been long in coming to you.

"But it wasn't you I was really worried about, it was him. The third person in the equation that gave you to me, of course." She paused. "You never asked me about your father, you know. You never even asked me if you had a father, or where he was, not even while you were free to do so. I don't know what I would have told you if you had—maybe just that he and I had gone our separate ways before you were born. But then you'd have wanted to know why he never wanted to see you and I didn't really want to have to explain that he didn't know about you because I hadn't told him.

"He found out, though. He found out the moment you Named me."

A picture of a man's face was forming in my mind. I'd never seen him before but I knew this had to be my father. He was old enough to be my grandfather. His years became him, probably better than his youth had; very encouraging, since I looked a great deal more like him than I did my mother.

"That shouldn't have happened. Because he didn't know about you, there shouldn't have been a link. But it was there. Maybe you were just so powerful that he couldn't help sensing you, sensing what you are. Or maybe he was suspicious after I conveniently took myself out of his life instead of trying to hang onto him. Anyway, before I could prepare something to keep you from Naming me or anyone else indiscriminately—and to prevent you from letting your own Name slip—he called me."

" 'I want to congratulate you on the success of your project,' he said, all cheery-nasty. 'Our little monster—' he actually called you that '—our little monster is certainly a prodigy. If you had let me know, I would have been generous with support checks. But if you didn't want my support in the past, I don't suppose you want it now.' "

" 'You're right,' I told him, 'I want nothing from you, I need nothing from you.' "

" 'Nothing *more*, you mean,' he said. 'Listen, I'm all for everyone's right to self-determination, but don't you think it's rude beyond the pale to use a person's own tissue this way without so much as a please or thank-you? I certainly do. I have to tell you that while *I* was apparently what you had in mind, *you* weren't *my* choice.' "

" 'So what,' " I said.

" 'So we're a family now, that's what,' he said. 'Whether you like it or not. You can't have it both ways, you know, I can't be the father and *not* be the father at the same time. Which means that you and I are connected now, if not exactly bound. But I've found in my old age that I suddenly respect that kind of bond much more than I used to. There are certain advantages.

I would ask you to marry me, but *you* didn't ask for what you wanted so I don't feel obliged to ask now for what *I* want. And I don't have to. Our little monster will just give it to me.' "

"He meant my Name, of course. And yours. He would eventually have been able to divine your Name because of his link to you. Once he knew your Name, he would have complete power over you and all of your own power as well. Getting you to tell him my Name would be pretty much an anticlimax, but he'd have done it anyway, just to show he could."

The effects of whatever she had put in the tea were receding . . . sort of. I was beginning to feel more alert mentally, the memories were becoming more vivid, more real, and more personally involving.

"I thought about killing you," my mother said.

I remembered that, too, though I hadn't really understood at the time. I'd just had the idea that my mother was considering something harmful and I hadn't been so much afraid as curious. Because I'd known that in the end, she wouldn't hurt me . . . couldn't hurt me. . . .

"No, I couldn't. You wouldn't let me. That was the last time you exercised the power of my Name over me. And you were right; even if I could have brought myself to kill my own child, it would have been a very foolish thing to do. Even if the fact that it was murder had gone unnoticed—I could have fixed it that way—your father would have known and *that* would have given him a certain amount of power over me. Not quite as much as knowing my Name, but too much. I had brought you into the world without his consent; to send you out of it also without his consent would have cost me my will. I would never have been able to do anything again without his permission. He couldn't have forced me to do anything—like tell him my Name—but he could have prevented me from doing anything simply by telling me I couldn't. Whether it was using my powers or just washing my face." She paused. "You've seen people who seem to be unable to take care of themselves, haven't you? Many of them are just incompetent for some prosaic reason. But many others are secret people who lost their souls."

She sighed and I realized that she was near exhaustion. "So, instead of killing you, I hid you. Actually, I sent you into hiding within yourself. The only reason I could do it was because you let me. You could have stopped me—after all, you knew my Name—but you were a little girl. You wanted me to take care of you. So I took care of you. I gave you some nice hot tea and told you that nothing mattered any more and you would forget everything. Including my Name."

So I'd grown up healthy, happy, and completely detached, unaware of my power, or my mother's, or my father's. Whatever *power* meant—flying through the air? Leaping tall buildings, picking winning lottery numbers, raising the dead?

"You're a knower. Like your father. What you know about, you have power over. If you want it, it's yours, if you don't want it, it goes away. That doesn't mean you wouldn't have had to pay for anything you wanted—you always have to pay, and, like anything else, sometimes the price-tag isn't worth the goods. I don't know what course you'd have chosen for yourself once you had come into your own, and sometimes I wonder if this wasn't the right thing after all. Maybe it wouldn't have been right to let someone so powerful walk loose in the world, even if it had turned out you had wanted nothing more than some personal success and material rewards and an especially long life-span. That stuff's cheap, when you can have all you want.

"Well, that was over twenty years ago and I figured that was the end of it. Even if your father came face to face with you, he'd never recognize you for who or what you were, and I didn't have to worry about your telling anyone my Name or your own.

"You *do* know your own Name, by the way. You learned it before you learned mine, but you never told it to me. I don't want to know. I couldn't make you forget that, but I was able to camouflage it. It'll take you a little while to figure it out, but it'll come to you. And you'll need it, because apparently my hiding you didn't put an end to things the way I thought it would.

"Your father didn't call me again but he had to have known that I'd done something to protect you. I knew that he'd look for us, so I kept us moving. Movement is very strong power when done in the right sequence. That was one of *my* specialties; I'm a traveler and, by extension, a geographer. I turned every place we went into unfamiliar country, so that he'd always get lost before he could even get near us.

"And then you grew up and left, and I thought that would mean we were permanently safe, because he couldn't possibly go in two directions at once. I kept traveling anyway while you just . . . kept busy. And I was right, he couldn't go in two directions at once. He just came after me.

"It took him a long, long time, but I'd underestimated his, oh, dedication, I guess you could call it. He honestly felt I had stolen from him, you see, and he was incomplete until he recovered what was rightfully his. That would be you. But you were too well hidden even for the blood-link between you and him, so he concentrated on finding me.

"Travelers who don't want to be found might as well be invisible. As far as he was concerned, I thought I was. But I'd never thought that he would actually go to all the time and trouble of following me. The problem, you see, is that unfamiliar country doesn't stay unfamiliar; sooner or later, you can figure it out if you want to badly enough. And he did.

"It took a chunk of his life—over twenty years and a good number of borrowed years as well, but I guess he figured that being in debt to a time-keeper was worth it. If he could catch up with me and get to you, he'd be able to pay it all back with interest and still end up with more time than he'd had at the start."

She started rubbing my hands and I realized they'd gone numb. My whole body was numb; it was coming back to life, the feeling that was returning to my hands spreading up my arms and out to the rest of me.

"In recreating my travels, he has come to know a great deal about me. And about you. I hid you from your power, but I couldn't hide the fact that you are powerful, and power calls to power. It won't be long before he knows my Name. He's getting closer to it all the time and I can't do anything about it—in the act of trying to stop him, I would only reveal the last of what he needs to know.

"*You* have to do it."

I opened my eyes. The living room was gone; so was my mother. I was lying on my back in the field under the evening sky.

Raising up on my elbow, I looked around. Through the weeds, I could see something that might have been my mother's silhouette. It moved suddenly and melted into the darker night shadows behind it. Safe for now, I thought, and turned away to face the golden glow on the other side of the sky. It was too bright to look at, and I had to close my eyes again.

I woke up in a hotel room in downtown Seattle. Or was it uptown Seattle? I didn't know how they numbered their streets here, but I knew I was in the city proper, whatever they called it, and my father wasn't far away.

My backpack was lying on the floor next to the bed. A mother will always remember you need clean underwear. Even a mother like mine, who was apparently a travel agent as well as a traveler, I thought, amused, and got up to wash and dress.

The hotel was one of those nondescript places that charge by the week, where people stay when they have no real place to go, all worn carpeting and thrift-shop furniture and stained porcelain in the bathroom. Up to twenty-four hours before, I wouldn't have thought anything about it one way or the other. There was a part of me that still didn't care; old lifestyles die hard. But mostly, I wanted to get out of there as quickly as possible, find my father, and do whatever I had to do about him, and then figure out how I was going to spend the rest of my life.

The cool Seattle air was full of mist and I felt as if I were melting my way through it as I walked along the sidewalk. Having set me down somewhere near my father, my mother had left it to me to locate him exactly, as a way of flexing those long-unused muscles, a warm-up for the main event.

It didn't take long. My father was very sure of himself these days. His power radiated uncamouflaged, like a dare: here I am, come and get me, if you can.

And just to make sure there was no mistaking the address, my mother was in the front window of the gallery, looking out on the street with a wary expression so subtle that it couldn't have read to anyone who didn't know her.

Actually, her entire face wouldn't have read to anyone who didn't know her. The rendering was photographically real, but the subject had been painted as standing behind some transparent barrier so thick that it obscured and distorted. One hand was clutching the edge of the barrier hard enough that the knuckles were white but It wouldn't be clear—ha, ha—even after long study, whether she was trying to push the barrier aside, or hold it in place. Unless you knew her.

ArTricks was the name on the door, in silvery script. I pushed inside and my father's presence rushed over me with the carefully climate-controlled air. The entire gallery had been given over to his work, not just for a few weeks or for a month, but indefinitely, though probably no one realized it. My father would camp here for as long as he needed or wanted, and that used-and-abandoned feeling wouldn't kick in for a long time after he left. I understood quite a lot about my father. It was all there in those paintings he'd done of my mother.

They were arranged on the gallery walls in a way that reminded me of the Stations of the Cross in a Catholic church. There was an intended sequence, or rather, two intended sequences. In the order dictated by his numbering, my mother's face started out extremely obscured and progressed toward being more clearly identifiable. This was for the general population of art apprecia-tors, who would see only paintings and believe one followed another just the way he said they did.

The other sequence was secret, the real order in which the paintings had been done. The real first portrait was the clearest one in the sequence, the one everyone else was supposed to think was the most recent: *Untitled, #12.* The obscuring barrier was only slightly less than window-clear—my father's acknowledgment that he had known my mother as she had wanted him to know her. It resembled her in some ways, but she could have stood right next to it and no one would have identified her as the subject.

The next one was on the other side of the airy gallery room, posing as the first one he'd painted. The face was so completely obscured in this one that it wasn't possible to tell where the features were, whether it was a man or a woman, or even a human being.

He had followed that up with the portrait placed in the middle of the sequence, labeled *Untitled #6.* Had it been closer to #12, it might have been possible to see that he'd actually had much more understanding of the face taking shape on the board than he'd had when he'd done #12. Or maybe not; my father's skill engaged expectations while it diffused perceptions.

The third painting was #11, his affirmation of the face my mother showed the world. Looking closely, I could see that he had painted her image in excruciatingly exact detail before muddying it.

And so on. I found my way from portrait to portrait, moving back and forth among the dozen paintings, minus the one in the window, which was actually the most recent one. Yes, I thought, my father must have been *very* sure of himself, to display it so openly, telling my mother how close he was. In the next portrait, her face would be completely clear and so would her Name, not just to my father but to anyone with the ability to know.

"Do you know Boileau?"

I had been so lost in the study of my mother's face that the man had come up right behind me. He was very young, too thin, and probably too rich for his own good. "Pardon?" I said.

"Do you know Boileau? The artist. I've been watching you from my desk. I've never seen anyone come in here and view the paintings in the real order before."

That my father hadn't kept this completely a secret showed an arrogance that I found perversely pleasing. "Well, I know his other work," I said.

The man's eyes narrowed. "Really? That's amazing, considering there isn't any other work. This is all there is—thirty years of discovering the same woman. When he finishes the last one, he says he'll put down his brush for good."

"He says that, does he?" I looked around; my mother's face seemed to jump out of each picture and then recede again. "I wonder what he'll do to keep busy."

"Boileau is an extraordinary man as well as a gifted artist. I imagine he could do anything he wanted to."

I shrugged. "Oh, I don't know. Sometimes when the grip of obsession loosens, people fall apart. Does he live around here?"

The guy clammed up. It was exactly like that—he put his lips together deliberately and looked away from me with a haughty tilt to his head, making it clear he wasn't going to dignify my question by even recognizing it.

I took a step back, looked him up and down, and spoke his Name.

The effect was immediate; I owned him. He'd been pissing me off but mostly I did it to see what would happen. I hadn't been prepared for the *utterness* of it, either because I was too used to not giving a rat's ass one way or the other about most things, or because the idea of someone with absolutely no power at all really is unfathomable, until you've seen it. I half-expected him to turn into a blob of jelly or something, so unreserved was his surrender. And then I realized he damned well *could* turn into a blob of jelly if I wanted him to. Whatever I wanted was now the law as far as he was concerned, and this was irreversible.

He remained perfectly still while I walked around him, looking him over. He was just a gallery manager, a culture vulture whose life was focused on finding The Next Big Thing in the artistic community, an insulated world that breathed rarefied air, followed its own traditions, anointed its own high priests, and admitted no outsiders. When this gallery closed, he would find another, and another after that. His function was to sit with art, and talk about it, and contain various facts and terms and acquaintances without knowing anything.

Or it would have been, except I owned him now. I could have told him to be a truck driver or a ditch-digger and he would have walked out of the gallery and gone off to drive trucks or dig ditches without a backward glance.

"I just want you to take care of yourself," I said after a while. "Go on as you were before, do whatever you were going to do, be whatever you were going to be. But tell me where he lives."

"He's got a house on Vashon Island. You'll need to take the ferry."

"What's the address?"

"I don't know. But I can draw you a map of how to get there."

"Then do that. And then go back to whatever you were doing before I came in here. Think you can manage that?"

"If you say so."

He drew me a map. He had no artistic talent at all, but it was a good enough map for my purposes. And it was all for my purposes. He was so much mine, he would have spent hours on the details. I watched him filling in landmarks, his aristocratic face tight with concentration. This was how my mother would look if my father managed to divine her Name.

I wasn't sure for a moment whether I was ashamed of what I'd done, or just unhappy that I had to care now.

"What's wrong?" he asked, turning to look at me. Concern flowed off him in waves; I could almost see the air shimmy with it.

"Nothing," I said. "Is the map done?"

He held it up. "Can you find your way from this?"

It looked like he'd put in most of the major roads and a good many of the minor ones as well. "I can show the more heavily-settled areas—"

"That looks good." I took the map from him, folded it up, and stuck it in my shirt pocket. "I want you to go back to your life. Can you do that?"

He shrugged. "I can keep working here, if that's what you mean."

"What about anything else?"

He frowned. "What else is there? Look, do you want me to take you there? I'll just close up and we can go now, if you want."

His Name might as well have been written all over his face—anyone with even a minor bump of knowledge could have Named him in the dark. "I don't want you to go with me. I want you to stay here and go back to the way you were."

"Oh? And what are *you* going to do?" he said bitterly. "*Not* know whatever you know?"

"What?" I said.

"You come in here and mess me up, and now you want it to be as if it never happened. Because it's inconvenient for you, I guess." He made a face at my puzzlement. "Oh, come on, didn't you realize I'd know what happened? Well, not exactly *what*, or even how—I didn't understand what you said—but I know what it did to me. I know what you are now, too. I always thought there were people like you in the world, but my shrink kept telling me it was just another facet of my neurosis, thinking that there were people walking around who could . . . *do* things. Boileau's one of them, too, isn't he? All my life I've been trying to get next to people like you. Even if it didn't rub off on me, I thought maybe I could reap some of the benefits, anyway."

Well, that explained how I'd been able to divine his Name so easily. I could also see why my father hadn't gotten to him first, even though he could have quite easily: Naming someone like this was obviously more trouble than it was worth. I'd have to keep that in mind.

"It's not my fault you've been standing around waiting to surrender to somebody," I said after a bit. "So you shouldn't complain now that someone's taken you up on it. But I'm giving you a chance to breathe on your own. It won't be easy, but you can get the hang of it with practice."

He sneered. "It must be wonderful, to have life be so simple for you. No, it's not your fault I was that way, but it doesn't relieve you of responsibility for your own actions."

"I'm not going to hang around here listening to a gallery manager lecture me on personal responsibility," I said. "Forget what happened. Learn to cope."

He hesitated. "All right. But someone should have told you that even when you buy something you don't want, you still have to pay for it."

I didn't like the sound of that, but I just wanted to get away from him and head my father off before he turned my mother into a lapdog. I made him give me directions to the ferry and left him sitting at his desk, doodling faces on the blank pages of his appointment book.

The ferry was like a great big floating house—there was a lived-in feeling to it. The feeling was all there was, at first. But as the boat plowed steadily through the water, I began to get flashes of the residents themselves. They were well-camouflaged, moving unnoticed among the passengers with ease but also with practiced caution. Some of them had been passengers themselves once, I realized.

Just as an experiment, I bought several packages of chocolate cupcakes from the snack bar on the upper deck and then found an unoccupied bench facing the stern. I unwrapped a package, set it down next to me, and got up to stand at the railing and stare at the slowly-receding mainland.

Only a minute later, I heard the open cellophane crackle, but I knew better than to turn around. "It's not what I would have suggested, but it's the thought that counts."

The voice came from below, not behind. I looked down; two women were standing on the lower deck almost directly underneath where I was, chatting confidentially over flimsy cups of bad coffee. The cellophane crackled some more, to let me know I had it right.

"Well, I've always said an offer is an offer." The woman on the left sipped her coffee. "What do you want to do about it?"

"I don't know," said the woman on the right. "I guess I'll have to hear the terms and conditions attached to it." The wind came up suddenly; they shuddered together and went back inside.

"Think of it as a gift." I spoke softly into the wind, letting it carry my voice back. "Or payment, in exchange for the use of your . . . residence."

"I knew who it was right away," said another voice. Now a man and a woman were standing on the deck below me, holding their collars closed against the wind. "You know how that is, when you get a call from someone you know *of*, but you haven't actually met in person? I'd been dealing with the company itself for so long that I felt like I really had met everyone in it, so I had to remind myself that we weren't actually acquainted."

The woman's murmur of agreement carried up to me quite clearly. "I really don't find knowing someone personally to be any kind of definite advantage," she said. "Sometimes, it even works the other way. I've had people try using that to pressure me into doing what they want me to. They try using the personal to influence the business we're doing. So I've taken to keeping everything on a strictly business level, I don't ask about their kids or their spouses or talk about my own life."

"It's okay," I said. "I didn't want anything. The cupcakes are yours, free and clear."

The cellophane rustled aggressively. I turned around just in time to see it be swept away by a sudden crosswind. It danced high in the gray air for a few moments before it blew out of sight.

I found a long bench indoors on the lower deck and set another opened package of cupcakes next to me. This time, I slumped down and closed my eyes. It took a little longer, but the presence was more tangible; the bench creaked and shifted a little. Amid the general noise and the rumble of the engines, the conversation that had been taking place behind me went from an unintelligible murmur to audible.

"I can spot *that* kind a mile away," an older woman was saying." I've been around long enough that nothing gets by me any more."

I smiled to myself, still keeping my eyes closed.

"But they're like anyone else, you know, they're just people. Some of them are okay and some of them you have to watch out for. *But*, like anyone else, they all want something and don't let anybody ever tell you differently. Everybody in this world, no matter how good they are, is out for themselves on some level. You've got to remember that, and never fool yourself into thinking that anybody is ever doing anything one hundred percent for *your* benefit. Nobody's going to do anything for anybody unless there's something in it for them as well."

Ferry-boat philosophy, I thought, amused. Well, they weren't very good cupcakes, after all, so I probably shouldn't have expected much. There was a rustle of cellophane. I opened my eyes to find the empty package had been pushed close to me for disposal.

I tried another bench indoors on the upper deck, away from the windows. This time I slipped my watch in between the cupcakes before pretending to take a nap.

Over at the snackbar, the attendant was having a loud conversation with what must have been a ferry regular. "So I says to myself, 'Now, that's more *like* it. Something *real*, that isn't just junk.' You know?"

I could sense the regular nodding in agreement. "I mean, it's not like I really want so *much*," the attendant went on. "I mean, if I wanted so much, would I be hanging around in a place like this, working my ass off? Hell, no. But you want to know someone's making an effort, that it means something to them, right?"

The regular said something about a token.

"Yeah, well, *I* believe in stuff like that, a token of affection and esteem, all that stuff. So you know, now I know it matters. Enough, anyway."

I left the last three packages of cupcakes in various unobtrusive spots and wandered aimlessly around the ferry. Twice I overheard people thanking each other and once, someone saying, *That doesn't even* begin *to cover it and what took you so long anyway?*

The clouds were lower and heavier by the time the ferry docked; it was going to get dark early. Standing among the crowd waiting to be let off, I saw a tall woman who looked like a garage mechanic showily checking her watch. She glanced up, caught my eye and turned her wrist slightly so I could see before lowering her arm. The crowd moved forward then and she seemed to move along with everyone else, but she never appeared on the dock.

You're a knower, my mother had said. The other part of that was knowing whether what I knew was at all useful, and I didn't know that yet. But I was pretty sure it would come to me eventually.

The line of cars stretched a quarter-mile along the road running past my father's house. He was giving a party. I had the guy I'd bummed the ride from let me off near the last car and I walked back. A mailbox marked the path that led down the steep embankment to where the house sat on the shore of the inlet.

where it was tonight. I could hear the party sounds before I reached the mailbox; it wasn't rowdy, there were just lots of people.

A little ways down, the path had been made into an outdoor staircase, each packed dirt step bordered with a branch. I hesitated on the first one; below, the party had spread out of the house, all around the yard and down to the shore in spite of the coolness of the already-fading afternoon. Nicely-dressed people, like something out of a high-class magazine ad. My guy hadn't mentioned this; I guess my father hadn't considered him worth telling.

Or maybe he'd wanted to surprise me. My father, that is. He was expecting me; the sense of it drifted up to me with the people's voices, along with the force of his presence, faint at this distance but there nonetheless. When I got a little farther down the steps, he'd sense my presence like a ripple crossing his own. My father, the spider.

I turned away from the stairs and began making my way along the embankment through the brush and dead leaves until I was directly behind the house. I half-climbed, half-slid down the embankment, trying to be quiet and failing completely. Still, no one bothered to take a look around the back and see what all the crunching and rustling was about. Either they all figured it was the indigenous wildlife or they couldn't really hear it that well.

The rear windows were high up and not terribly large, but the ledges were generous. Jumping, I caught the rough edge of the one farthest from the party noise, and there was enough room for me to rest my forearm on it and pull myself up.

I was looking into my father's studio. The easel holding my mother's portrait stood in the center of the room, facing away from me toward the door. This was it, the big unveiling of the capstone of his career, if you could call thirteen paintings of one blurry woman a career. But being a knower himself, he'd known exactly how to play it as an artistic obsession. He could have been well-known if he had chosen to allow his notoriety to expand beyond the small local but lucrative scenes he'd been cultivating here and there around the country.

But this would do it for him, I realized. Like that other artist, Wyeth, with the Helga paintings.

Helga? If I could have seen the entire series right then, I would have known *her* Name immediately.

The window was locked; I broke one of the panes and managed to unlock it without severing any major blood vessels on the shards left in the frame. Pushing the window up and clambering inside seemed to take forever and left me with sore arm muscles. I was surprised that I could do it at all; moving around vigorously was something else I'd never engaged in much.

The portrait was covered with a white linen cloth. I hesitated, holding one corner, and then slipped my hand underneath. The paint—acrylics? oils? Glidden's rainy-day gray?—felt almost-sticky, as if it were a minute or so away from being completely dry.

"Go ahead. You might as well. I painted it to be looked at."

I didn't turn around.

"Besides, family shouldn't have to wait until the ceremonial unveiling."

He came over and put his hands on my shoulders. "Of course, if you *want* to wait, I won't insist," he added.

"When did you finish it?" I asked, pulling my hand away from the painting.

"Who says it's finished?" He tried to turn me around but I refused to move and he let go of me. "I thought I'd show it tonight and get some comments on it before I did anything final to it. If, indeed, I need to, other than take a last look."

Yeah, sure, I thought.

He walked around behind the easel and leaned on the top of the painting, studying me. I raised my eyes to look at him. My mother had shown him to me but I wasn't prepared for the sight of him as he was now, in person. I could see everything immediately and I reached for the cloth, intending to yank it off. He clapped a hand down over it, holding it in place.

"Sorry—changed my mind. You're a smart girl," he said, almost approvingly. "Excuse me—woman. Though people your age are more children than not to me. It really isn't finished, you know; I couldn't finish it until I'd met my daughter. I must say, I had thought you would look much more like *her*, so this is a pleasant surprise. You don't seem to know, though, whether you came to try to stop me, or just to kill me. Why don't you come out and meet the other guests while you're thinking it over?"

He came around the easel and tucked my hand into the crook of his elbow. It was such a corny thing to do that I couldn't help laughing. This seemed to startle him, but he didn't say anything about it, leading me through the house as if he were already parading in victory. The house itself was surprisingly shabby, the furniture faded, old, and worn. In the dining room, people stood around in clumps, picking at the enormous spread of carefully-arranged party food, hors d'oeuvres and deli-style cold-cuts, salad mixtures in big stoneware bowls, and bottle after bottle of champagne, standing in rows.

They still reminded me of magazine-ad people; I half-expected my father to regroup them more artfully. But he just introduced me around and those generic faces gave me generic smiles, expressed tasteful astonishment that Boileau had a daughter, and went back to their generic party discussions.

"Pretty harmless group," I said, as my father led me outside.

"They don't have the faintest idea," my father said, handing me down the front steps. "Let me show you."

He went up to the nearest person, a blond, bearded man in conversation with a tall, black-haired woman, and tapped him on the shoulder. "Henry, Alberta, I'd like you to meet my daughter."

Alberta beamed while Henry hurriedly transferred a paper plate of potato salad to his other hand so he could shake hands with me. "Well, this is a surprise and a pleasure!" he said heartily.

"She's come to put a stop to me," my father said, giving me a sidelong glance. "Probably by driving a stake through my heart or something."

"Really," said Alberta. "And where did she go to school?"

"Wherever her mother chose to take her. Mostly bad public schools with no budgets and demoralized teachers, I imagine."

"Ah. My next-door neighbor's kids all went there," said Henry. "They seemed to enjoy it. Do you paint, also?" he asked me.

"Oh, my daughter hasn't done much of anything for the last twenty-some years, thanks to her mother. But now that she has come into her own, I guess she'll do whatever she wants—enslave a few people, maybe win a lottery or two—under different names, of course—and possibly kill her mean old father this evening."

"Well, that's what I understand from many people such as yourself," Henry said congenially. "The children all tend to go off in other directions, and I guess that's understandable, if you'll pardon my saying so."

"No offense taken," I said, and turned to my father. "They really don't get it."

"None of them do," my father said. "You could walk around here like the invisible woman, completely unnoticed, unless I called their attention to you."

I looked around suspiciously.

"Haven't touched them," he said. "If you want to know the truth, I'm not so sure that most of them even *have* Names. They're more like a herd of sheep, they've been told what to do and what to expect since they were born. Since *before* they were born. They are their clothes, their cars, their jobs; their things own them. Not me. I could have them if I wanted, I suppose, but that can be more trouble than it's worth. Right?"

Of course he had sensed what I'd done at the gallery—all of his paintings were there, and they were as much of him as they were of my mother. He hadn't thought I'd know that, which was why he'd changed his mind about letting me see his nearly-finished masterpiece. I wondered how he planned to finish it and show it now.

He didn't seem concerned. We drifted through the crowd in the yard, meeting more of them. He continued to play his little conversation game, though to what purpose I didn't know. Maybe just because they were so willing and he was so able.

Eventually, I noticed that the day had stopped darkening. The slight wind that had been rustling the surrounding trees had also ceased and the party gabble had acquired a strangely muffled sound, as if it were coming from under a belljar. People who had been wandering about the yard and going in and out of the house were now rooted to wherever they stood—without noticing, of course.

"Timing," my father said, cheerfully. "What you need in this business is a good sense of timing and for that you have to understand time itself."

"I thought you were a knower, not a timekeeper," I said, taking a bacon-wrapped morsel off a plate held by a woman in black satin pajamas.

"Knowers are multi-talented that way," he said. "Don't eat that. Nothing's edible when it's stuck between moments, it'll be like chewing a lump of styrofoam."

I put the hors d'oeuvre back on the plate. "What about them? Are they still functioning?"

He nodded, looking at the quiet water. "They're right with me, as much as they can be, which is enough for my purpose." He turned his smile to me. "It's finished, now, in case you didn't know. I've been finishing it while I've been walking around here with you. Now I know what I should see, what we should all see. Time to bring it out."

"I've brought it out for you."

My mother was standing in the middle of the yard next to the easel, one hand resting gracefully along the top like a game-show hostess's. Once the initial shock had passed, I knew I shouldn't have been surprised. Diverting him with me was the only way she could possibly have gotten close to him.

"I'm sure you meant to invite me," she went on, smiling at the people standing around. "A great artist would never unveil a masterpiece without inviting the subject to be present."

He took a step toward her and she grabbed a corner of the linen covering.

"Come on, *Boileau*," she said. "*You've* had all the fun up to now. Let *me* have the privilege of unveiling it."

"No—"

The motion of her yanking the linen away lasted forever. The cloth flew up and out, its folds twisting and turning like a flower opening up before it sailed away.

It was now a picture of the two of them. There was still only one subject but what my father had put into it of himself was now equally as obvious as my mother's face and, consequently, her Name. You couldn't see it without seeing both of them. Of course. My mother hadn't been able to undo any of the last thirty years, so she had just done a little more.

Someone began to applaud. It spread through the gathering; they were all putting their plates and glasses down on the ground beside them and clapping their hands enthusiastically. Someone even whistled.

My mother went to my father and pulled him over to the easel. She bowed, turned and gestured to him, and then began to clap her own hands, slowly and deliberately, almost in his face. "Sometimes a stalemate is the best victory you can hope for," I heard her tell him over the ovation still going on around them. "Maybe that's the only victory that really means anything for people like us." She looked at me; her smile was grim. "You remember that. You remember that you can't really Name Names without Naming yourself."

It was true, I saw, as she moved around behind the easel and continued applauding my father. You had to look really closely to see that it was not just a picture of the two of them but a family portrait of the three of us, but since most people didn't know about me, they'd never quite see it in the right way. And my mother would go on making sure they didn't, as long as nobody ever spoke her Name. Especially me.

I turned and ran up the dirt stairs to the road. There was a car idling by the mailbox.

"Need a lift?" said the guy from the gallery. It wasn't really a question.

"Who's minding the store?" I asked him.

He laughed. "You are. As if you didn't know."

They were out in force on the ferryboat this time, not bothering to hide themselves. I couldn't get away from all the conversations taking place around me, even in the bathroom. It wasn't chocolate cupcakes that they wanted.

I considered it. My new friend—his name, I learned belatedly, was Gus, short for Augustus, and what *had* his parents been thinking of?—wouldn't be happy here, but he wasn't going to be happy anywhere any more. That wasn't his purpose in life.

"Just think it over," one woman was telling another on a nearby bench. "Of course, you can't take *too* long but that's the nature of the business we're all in."

I made Gus stay there while I went up to the upper deck. A group of kids, teenagers, were comparing notes about some party they'd all been to.

" . . . give *anything* for a system like that . . . all that power . . . "

" . . . more than I make in two months, maybe three . . . "

" . . . everybody'd always be hitting on you to come over and use it, though . . . "

" . . . and the whole world wants to be your best friend. I dunno if I want best friends like that . . . "

" . . . got to use it while you were there . . . think it over . . . "

Big help. I went back down to the lower deck. Gus was gone. I thought one of them had gotten impatient and decided to force the issue, but then I found him standing outside near the stern.

"Is that how it is?" he said. "When we dock, you just walk off and I don't? That's a pretty big offering. What do you get in return, a whole ferryboat and all the bad snacks you can stuff in your face?"

"Are you wearing a watch?" I asked.

"Yes. A Rolex."

"Give it to me." I wrapped a ten-dollar bill around the wristband and left it on a bench.

"My parents gave me that," he said accusingly.

"You can get another. I'll buy you another."

"You'll have to. I need things like that. It's what I am, you know." He smiled. "Yeah, I guess you *do* know."

I did. His Name stood for material things and status symbols, the acquisition of shiny stones and metals and pretty pictures. They owned him, the condition of my ownership, for as long as it was in force. He was going to be an expensive pet; I'd have to win a lottery or two.

I could feel him settling into his new life. That was the real price, I thought. Once you had power, you ended up having to depend on it. Eventually, like anything else, it owned you.

Eventually? No, from the beginning; we just don't bother admitting it at first.

We were close to the mainland now and would be docking in a few minutes. Gus linked arms with me and dragged me into the middle of the crowd gathering impatiently at the exit. "I don't like to wait in line, either," he said. "I like to go first." He put his arms around my shoulders and gave me a hard squeeze. "You know, I'm going to like this a lot better than I thought I would."

I smiled up at him. "Behave yourself."

"Or what—you'll bring me back here and leave me?" He laughed.

"No," I said. "I'll tell you my Name."

It was a month before he dared to speak again. I bought him the Rolex anyway.

THE ELVIS NATIONAL THEATER OF OKINAWA

Jonathan Lethem and Lukas Jaeger

Here's a funny and razor-sharp look at the World of Tomorrow. And you thought *today* was weird! You ain't seen *nothing* yet!

Jonathan Lethem is yet another one of those talented new writers who are continuing to pop up all over as we progress into the decade of the 1990s. He works at an antiquarian bookstore, writes slogans for buttons, and lyrics for several rock bands (including *Two Fettered Apes, EDO, Jolley Ramey,* and *Feet Wet*), and is also the creator of the 'Dr. Sphincter' character on MTV. In addition to all these certifiably cool credentials, Lethem has also had sales in the last few years to *Interzone, New Pathways, Pulphouse, Isaac Asimov's Science Fiction Magazine, Universe, Journal Wired, Marion Zimmer Bradley's Fantasy Magazine, Aboriginal SF,* and elsewhere; his first novel, *Gun, with Occasional Music,* is slotted for 1994. His story "Walking the Moons" was in our Eighth Annual Collection.

Lukas Jaeger is a graduate of the Boston School of the Museum of Fine Arts. He is an animator and cartoonist, and his first two films, *Dimwit's Day* and *It's You,* have been shown in festivals worldwide. His current film-in-progress is called *Big Concrete Place.*

Both men live in the San Francisco Bay area, and this is their first collaboration.

Sam's Big Kinesthetic went down the Blind Alleyway to check out Tokyo Norton's new act: the Elvis National Theatre of Okinawa. Sam's Big was a threesome consisting of a neuropublicity agent, a talent development scout, and a bush-robot that hooked them into the infodrip, and into one another. They all went by the name Sam's Big, and they never walked alone.

Tokyo Norton ran a noisy, credit-chip-sized stage in darkest Das Englen, but he had a nose for imported novelties. Sam's Big had to keep its finger on the pulse.

"You wanna wanna put Ento on the big show?" jabbered Norton after the revue was closed. They whirred above the rooftop of the Alleyway in Norton's ramjet gazebo. The emotional kaleidoscope on Norton's forehead performed an unnecessary flourish, which annoyed Sam's Big.

"I don't know," said Sam's Big. "There's something there—"

"For truly understand Ento," said Norton, "I have to give context." He snorted. "Is cultivated secretly, according to ancient stricture. No foreigner has ever seen before. Is guild of monks perform ancient mysteries. Not just song and dance."

"The whole thing's an ancient ritual?" mused Sam's Big. "The weird karate kicks, the whole bit with the handkerchiefs . . . that wild number about 'Pork Salad Ani'?"

"Oh yes, oh yes. Quite elaborate and mysterious."

"What's the reference, though? What's 'Elvis'?"

"Impersonation of 'Elvis' medieval Japanese folk art. Origins shrouded in veils of misty time. Forgotten meanings, buried in layers of abstraction. Foreigner never see before—"

"Yeah, yeah." Sam's Big knew perfectly well that ninety per cent of what passed for Jap culture was filched from overseas, and usually garbled to incomprehensibility in the process. It didn't matter. The point was, this Ento drama had something at the core, something interesting. "The whole look," Sam's Big said, "the sideburns, the pallid, fatty physique. Cosmurgery?"

"Oh no," fretted Norton. "Physical regimen of take years to produce, very demanding. Eat only corndogs, amphetamines—"

"The round-eyed kid," interrupted Sam's Big. "What's he doing there?"

Norton waved his hand, his kaleidoscope darkening. "Very poor performer, the American. Is worst of bunch—"

"An American? I thought this was some exclusive Jap cult."

"Is significant achievement," admitted Norton. "First foreigner ever to rise to any prominence, devotion of many hard ministrations, cleaning toilet with toothbrush . . . but cannot be compared with native talent. Is hothead, over expressive, where calls for control, devotion, conformity to tradition—"

"He sticks out like a sore thumb," agreed Sam's Big, thinking hard. "Uh, yeah. That's the one we want. What's his name?"

"Oh no!" pleaded Tokyo Norton. "Cannot have 'one'! Ento is performance *en masse*—"

"We can't use the group thing. But we might be able to do something with this American kid. What's his name?"

"No, please no. Integrity of ancient ways; I protest!" Norton took an egg-shaped rubber napkin out of his pocket and rolled it around his forehead to absorb his sweat. "Not for cheap bastardisation did bring Ento to new world!"

"It's not Ento we want," said Sam's Big. "All that shmaltzy 'In the Ghetto' stuff; it's hopeless. We're just after a few of the moves, the style, especially the way that American kid manifests it . . . what's his name?"

"Lucky Davey," sighed Norton. He pushed the obloid end of the rubber napkin into his ear, his kaleidoscope flaring green. The gazebo settled down to earth behind the Alleyway. Tokyo Norton cleared the dressing room of all the Ento stars except Lucky Davey, then ushered Sam's Big in. Davey sat at a mirror daubing at his pancake. Sam's Big came up behind him, smoking a stogie and flicking the ash into a hovering holographic ashtray, and met the kid's eyes in the mirror. Norton hung on the perimeter, fretting as he watched Sam's Big's ashes fluttering through the projection to scatter on the floor.

"I am an Ento performer," said Lucky Davey, his eyes flaring defiantly. "Steeped in the traditions of 'Elvis' impersonation. I don't know if you understand what that means, Misters Big."

"Serious ancient ritual bunkum, I gather. Make no mistake, Davey, we're full of admiration. You've risen to the top on their terms. But the point's made; now why not see if you can make it on the big stage? You're an American, Davey."

"This is surely the degrading crass sell-out opportunity I was carefully steeled to resist in my long training," said Davey. He was stripping off the white jumpsuit and changing into his street clothes: a leather Thneed and a pair of fishnet earmuffs. "Certainly then if you admire my discipline you must understand how I will be quite able to resist the flickering of your devil's-tongue in my ear, yes?"

"This is no sell-out," said Sam's Big, flexing its anger. Sam's Big knew when to bring on the effects. "We're talking Art, son. Taking what you picked up from the ancient masters and building on it, creating something new. That's assuming you've got more to offer the world than *devotion*, of course. Maybe we guessed wrong . . ." Sam's Big turned to leave the dressing room.

"Wait, Misters Big."

Sam's Big turned back, all smiles, and pocketed the cigar. The phantom ashtray vanished. Sam's Big unlatched their goosedown briefcase, which, when opened, played the theme song from the *Kinesthetic Tonight!* program. It was full of unsigned contracts, enticingly perfumed, and attractively backlit from within the briefcase. Tokyo Norton shook his head sorrowfully. The floor was covered with ashes.

Three weeks later, in a high-security rehearsal bubble at the bottom of the Atlantic, the cans were filling with bungled performance tape. They were scraping away to that essential core, the glimmer Sam's Big had discerned the first night out, but the kid had a lot to unlearn.

"Drop the formalism," said Sam's Big for the hundredth time. "Stick with the crouch move, and that big leering wink, but make it your own. Make it like you feel it, like it's from inside."

They'd lightened up his make-up, lost him a little weight, clipped the sideburns, generally emphasised his youth and vitality. It wasn't enough. The kid was like a withered old Japanese monk in his heart. He was tending to the fundamentally rude gestures of Ento drama like a gardener shaping a bonsai. Sam's Big wanted to see the kid *rebel*.

It was the songs, they knew. "The American Trilogy," "Hawaiian Wedding Song," "It's Now or Never/O Sole Mio," "Bridge Over Troubled Water." Old soupy Jap stuff, too heavy on the heartstrings. The kid needed something punchier, something to wrap those smouldering looks around, something that gave all that funny hip motion a reason for being.

Soon, soon. Sam's Big had its handpicked songwriting subroutine busy at work on some titles he'd suggested: "Don't Shit Me," "Hot Nervous Wire," "Baby Let's Die," "Warning: Contaminated," "Drug Test Man," and "Mystery Fuck."

Sam's Big took a sip from a tube of Big Man, a cigar-flavored soft drink, and smiled among themselves. They'd get it right soon enough.

THE TERRITORY

Bradley Denton

Alternate History stories don't necessarily have to be concerned with big, sweeping changes in the fate of nations. They can also deal with small private changes in one person's life that may alter that life forever . . . as in the eloquent story that follows, which takes us to the turbulent and dangerous days of the American Civil War in Bloody Kansas. It is a compassionate tale of redemption and revenge, and one man's struggle to reconcile the two.

A relatively new writer, Bradley Denton was born in 1958, grew up in Kansas, and received an M.A. in creative writing from the University of Kansas. He sold his first story in 1984, and soon became a regular contributor to *The Magazine of Fantasy & Science Fiction*, as well as selling work to *Isaac Asimov's Science Fiction Magazine*, *Pulphouse*, and elsewhere. He was a finalist for the John W. Campbell Award for Best New Writer in 1985, and in 1988 his story "The Calvin Coolidge Home for Dead Comedians" was on both the Hugo and Nebula final ballots. His first novel, *Wrack and Roll*, was published in 1986, and he won the John W. Campbell Memorial Award in 1992 for *Buddy Holly Is Alive and Well on Ganymede*. His most recent novel is *Blackburn*. He lives outside of Austin, Texas.

Sam came awake and sat up choking. His chest was as tight as if wrapped in steel cables, and his heart was trying to hammer its way out. He gulped a breath and coughed. The air in the abandoned barn was thick with dust. There was just enough light for him to see the swirling motes.

A few feet away, the skinny form of Fletcher Taylor groaned and rose on one elbow. "What the hell's wrong?" he asked.

"Shut the hell up," the man on the other side of Taylor said.

"You go to hell," Taylor snapped.

"Go to hell yourself."

"Let me sleep, or I'll send you all to hell," another man said.

"The hell you will."

"The hell I won't."

Taylor shook a finger at Sam. "See all the hell you've raised?"

Sam put on the new slouch hat that Taylor had given him, pulled on his boots, and stood, picking up the leather saddlebags he'd been using as a pillow. "I'm sorry as hell," he said, and left the barn, trying not to kick more than four or five of the other men on his way out.

The light was better outside, but the sun had not yet risen. Sam closed his left nostril with a finger and blew through his right, then closed his right nostril and blew through his left, trying to clear his head of dust. The ground was dry. The thunderheads that had formed the night before had rolled by without dropping enough rain to fill a teacup. He could have slept outside, in clean air, and been fine. As it was, his head ached. This wasn't the first night he had spent in a barn or corn crib since leaving the river, but he still wasn't used to it. At three months shy of twenty-eight, he feared that he was already too old for this kind of life.

Most of the camp was still asleep, but a few men were building fires and boiling chicory. One of them gestured to Sam to come on over, but Sam shook his head and pointed at the sycamore grove that served as the camp latrine. The other man nodded.

Sam went into the trees, and within twenty steps the smells of chicory and smoke were overwhelmed by the smell caused by two hundred men all doing their business in the same spot over the course of a week. It was even worse than usual this morning, because the leaders of other guerrilla bands had brought some of their own men into camp the day before. But at least Sam had the grove to himself for now.

When he had finished his business, he continued eastward through the grove until the stench faded and the trees thinned. Then he sat down with his back against the bole of a sycamore and opened one of his saddlebags. He removed his Colt Navy revolver and laid it on the ground beside him, then took out a pen, a bottle of ink, and the deerhide pouch that held his journal. He slid the notebook from the pouch and flipped pages until he reached a blank sheet, then opened the ink bottle, dipped his pen, and began to write.

Tuesday, August 11, 1863:

I have had the same dream again, or I should say, another variation thereof. This time when I reached the dead man, I discovered that his face was that of my brother Henry. Then I awoke with the thought that it was my fault that Henry was on board the Pennsylvania *when she blew, which in turn led to the thought that I was an idiot to ask a young and unsure physician to give him morphine.*

But I would have been on the Pennsylvania *as well had it not been for the malice of a certain William Brown, perhaps the only man caught in that storm of metal, wood, and steam who received what he deserved. As for the morphine, Dr. Peyton himself instructed me to ask the night doctor to give Henry an eighth of a grain should he become restless. If the doctor administered too much, the fault was his, not mine.*

I see by my words that I have become hard. But five years have passed since that night in Memphis, and I have seen enough in those years that the hours I spent at Henry's deathbed do not seem so horrific now—or, at least, they do not seem so during my waking hours.

A pistol shot rang out back at camp and was followed by the shouted curses of men angry at having been awakened. Someone had killed a rat or squirrel, and might soon wish that he'd let the creature live to gnaw another day. These once-gentle Missouri farmboys had become as mean as bobcats. They generally saved their bullets for Bluebellies, but didn't mind using their fists and boots on each other.

The dream seems more pertinent, Sam continued, *on those nights when the man's face is that of Orion. Orion was as intolerable a scold as any embittered crone, and a Republican crone at that—but he was my brother, and it might have been in my power to save him.*

Sam paused, rolling the pen between his fingers. He looked up from the paper and stared at the brightening eastern sky until his eyes stung. Then he dipped the pen and resumed writing.

It is as fresh and awful in my memory as if it had happened not two years ago, but two days ago.

I could have fought the Red Legs, as Orion and our companions tried to do. I had a Smith & Wesson seven-shooter. If I had used it, I would have either preserved Orion's life, or fallen beside him. Either result would have been honorable.

But I faltered. When the moment came, I chose to surrender, and handed over my pistol—which one of the Red Legs laughed at, saying he was glad I had not fired the weapon, for to be struck with a ball from its barrel might give one a nasty welt.

Then, as if to prove his point, he turned it on the driver, and on the conductor, and on Mr. Bemis, and on my brother.

As Orion lay dying, the Red Leg attempted to shoot me as well. But the pistol misfired, and I ran. Two of the Red Legs caught me and took my watch, but then let me go, saying that killing a Missourian the likes of me would not be so advantageous to their cause as letting me live.

I continued to run like the coward I had already proven myself to be.

Sam paused again. His hand was shaking, and he didn't think he would be able to read the jagged scrawl of what he had just written. But he would always know what the words said.

He rubbed his forehead with his wrist, then turned the notebook page and dipped his pen.

I could not have saved Henry. But Orion would be alive today, safe in Nevada Territory, had I been a man. And I would be there with him instead of here at Blue Springs; I would be thriving in the mountains of the West instead of sweltering in the chaos of Western Missouri.

I have remained in Missouri to pay for my sin, but in two years have had no success in doing so. Perhaps now that I have come to Jackson County and fallen in with the Colonel's band, my luck will change.

When this war began, I served with my own county's guerrilla band, the Marion Rangers, for three weeks. But there the actual need for bush-whacking was about as substantial as an owl's vocabulary. That was before I had crossed the state, entered Kansas, and encountered the Red Legs. That was before I had seen my brother shot down as if he were a straw target.

I have not had a letter from Mother, Pamela, or Mollie in several weeks, although I have written to each of them as often as I can. I do not know whether this means that they have disowned me, or whether their letters are not reaching Independence. I intend to go up to investigate once this coming business is completed, assuming that it does not complete me in the process.

Sam laid the journal on the ground and wiped his ink-stained fingers on the grass. Then he peered into the ink bottle and saw that it was almost empty. He decided not to buy more until he was sure he would live long enough to use it.

The sun had risen and was a steady heat on Sam's face. The day was going to be hot. Another shot rang out back at camp, and this time it was followed by yips and hollers. The boys were up and eager.

Sam slid his journal into its pouch, then returned it and the other items to the saddlebag. He stood, stretched, and walked back to Colonel Quantrill's camp.

As he emerged from the sycamores, Sam saw fifty or sixty of his fellow bushwhackers clustered before Quantrill's tent. The tent was open, and the gathered men, although keeping a respectful distance, were trying to see and hear what was going on inside. Fletcher Taylor was standing at the rear of the cluster, scratching his sparse beard.

"Morning, Fletch," Sam said as he approached. "Sleep well?"

Taylor gave him a narrow-eyed glance. "Rotten, thanks to you."

"Well, you're welcome."

"Be quiet. I'm trying to hear."

"Hear what?"

"You know damn well what. The Colonel's planning a raid. Most of the boys are betting it'll be Kansas City, but my money's on Lawrence."

Sam nodded. "The story I hear is that the Colonel's wanted to teach Jim Lane and Lawrence a lesson ever since he lived there himself."

A man standing in front of Taylor turned to look at them. "I'd like to teach Jim Lane a lesson too," he said, "but I'm not crazy and neither's the Colonel. Lawrence is forty miles inside the border, and the Bluebellies are likely to be as thick as flies on a dead possum. It'd be like putting our pistols to our own heads."

"Maybe," Sam said.

The man raised an eyebrow. "What do you mean, maybe? You know something I don't?"

Sam shrugged and said nothing. Two nights before, in a dream, he had seen Colonel Quantrill surrounded by a halo of fire, riding into Lawrence before a band of shooting, shouting men. He had known the town was Lawrence because all of its inhabitants had looked like the caricatures he had seen of Senator Jim Lane and had worn red pants. Sam had learned to trust his dreams when they were as clear as that. Several days before the *Pennsylvania* had exploded, a dream had shown him Henry lying in a coffin; and before he and Orion had left St. Joseph, a dream had shown him Orion lying dead in the dust. But it wouldn't do to talk of his dreams with the other bushwhackers. Most of them seemed to think that Sam Clemens was odd enough as it was, hoarding perfectly good ass-wiping paper just so he could write on it.

"Well, you're wrong," the man said, taking Sam's shrug as a statement. "Kansas City's got it coming just as bad, and there's places for a man to hide when he's done."

Taylor looked thoughtful. "I see your point," he said. "Calling on Senator Lane would be one thing, but coming home from the visit might be something else."

Sam stayed quiet. It didn't matter what the others thought now. They would mold bullets and make cartridges until they were told where to shoot them, and they'd be just as happy to shoot them in Lawrence as anywhere else—happier, since most of the jayhawkers and Red Legs who had robbed them, burned them out of their homes, killed their brothers, and humiliated their women had either hailed from Lawrence or pledged their allegiance to Jim Lane. And if Quantrill could pull several guerrilla bands together under his command, he would have enough men both to raid Lawrence and to whip the Federals on the way there and back.

Captain George Todd emerged from the tent and squinted in the sunlight. He was a tall, blond, square-jawed man whom some of the men worshipped even more than they did Quantrill. He was wearing a blue jacket he'd taken from a dead Union lieutenant.

"Hey, cap'n, where we going?" someone called out.

Todd gave the men a stern look. "I doubt we'll be going anywhere if you boys keep standing around like sick sheep when there's guns to be cleaned and bridles to be mended."

The men groaned, but began to disperse.

"Fletch Taylor!" Todd yelled. "Wherever you are, get your ass in here!" He turned and went back into the tent.

Sam nudged Taylor. "Now, what would a fine leader of men like George Todd be wanting with a lowdown thief like you?" he asked.

Taylor sneered. "Well, he told me to keep my eyes open for Yankee spies," he said, "so I reckon he'll be wanting me to give him your name." He started for the tent.

"I'm not worried!" Sam called after him. "He'll ask you to spell it, and you'll be stumped!"

Taylor entered the tent, and someone pulled the flaps closed. Sam stood looking at the tent for a moment longer, then struck off across camp in search of breakfast. Why Quantrill and the other guerrilla leaders were taking so long to form their plans, and why they were keeping the men in the dark, he couldn't imagine. There shouldn't be any great planning involved in striking a blow at Lawrence and the Red Legs: Ride in hard, attack the Red Legs' headquarters and the Union garrison like lightning, and then ride out again, pausing long enough to set fire to Jim Lane's house to pay him back for the dozens of Missouri houses he'd burned himself.

As for keeping the rank-and-file bushwhackers ignorant . . . well, there were about as many Yankee spies among Quantrill's band as there were fish in the sky. Sam had talked to over a hundred of these men, and all of them had lost property or family to abolitionist raiders of one stripe or another. Sam had even spoken with one man whose brother had been killed by John Brown in 1856, and who still longed for vengeance even though John Brown was now as dead as a rock.

Vengeance could be a long time coming, as Sam well knew. In the two years since Orion's murder, he had yet to kill a single Federal soldier, let alone one of the marauding Kansas Red Legs. It wasn't for lack of trying, though. He had fired countless shots at Bluebellies, but always at a distance or in the dark. He had never hit anything besides trees and the occasional horse.

Sam had a breakfast of fatty bacon with three young brothers who were from Ralls County south of Hannibal and who therefore considered him a kinsman. He ate their food, swapped a few East Missouri stories, and promised to pay them back with bacon of his own as soon as he had some. Then he shouldered his saddlebags again and walked to the camp's makeshift corral to see after his horse, Bixby.

Bixby was a swaybacked roan gelding who had been gelded too late and had a mean disposition as a result. The horse also seemed to think that he knew better than Sam when it came to picking a travel route, or when it came to deciding whether to travel at all. Despite those flaws, however, Sam had no plans to replace Bixby. He thought that he had the horse he deserved.

Sam tried to give Bixby a lump of hard brown sugar from one of his saddlebags, but Bixby ignored it and attempted to bite Sam's shoulder.

"Sometimes I think you forget," Sam said, slapping Bixby on the nose, "that I am the man who freed you from your bondage to an abolitionist."

Bixby snorted and stomped, then tried to bite Sam's shoulder again.

"Clemens!" a voice called.

Sam turned and saw that the voice belonged to one of the Ralls County boys who had fed him breakfast.

"The Colonel wants you at the tent!" the boy shouted.

Sam was astonished. Except for his friendship with Fletch Taylor, he was less than a nobody in the band. Not only was he a new arrival, but it was already obvious that he was the worst rider, the worst thief, and the worst shot. Maybe Taylor really had told Todd and Quantrill that he was a Yankee spy.

"Better come quick!" the boy yelled.

Sam waved. "I'll be right—God damn son of a bitch!"

Bixby had succeeded in biting him. Sam whirled and tried to slug the horse in the jaw with the saddlebags, but Bixby jerked his head up and danced away.

Sam rubbed his shoulder and glared at Bixby. "Save some for the Red Legs, why don't you," he said. Then he ducked under the corral rope and hurried to Quantrill's tent. He remembered to remove his hat before going inside.

                                    *   *   *

William Clarke Quantrill leaned back, his left leg crossed over his right, in a polished oak chair behind a table consisting of three planks atop two sawhorses. He wore a white embroidered "guerrilla shirt," yellow breeches, and black cavalry boots. He gave a thin smile as Sam approached the table. Above his narrow upper lip, his mustache was a straight reddish-blond line. His eyelids drooped, but his blue-gray eyes probed Sam with a gaze as piercing as a bayonet. Sam stopped before the table and clenched his muscles so he wouldn't shudder. His own eyes, he had just realized, were of much the same color as Quantrill's.

"You've only been with us since June, Private Clemens," Quantrill said in a flat voice, "and yet it seems that you have distinguished yourself. Corporal Taylor tells me you saved his life a few weeks ago."

Sam looked at Fletch Taylor, who was standing at his left. Taylor appeared uncomfortable under Sam's gaze, so Sam looked past him at some of the other men in the tent. He recognized the guerrilla leaders Bill Gregg and Andy Blunt, but several of the others were strangers to him.

"Well, sir," Sam said to Quantrill, "I don't know that I did. My horse was being cantankerous and brought me in on an abolitionist's house about two hundred feet behind and to one side of Fletch and the other boys, so I happened to see a man hiding up a tree."

"He was aiming a rifle at Corporal Taylor, I understand," Quantrill said.

"Yes, sir, that's how it looked," Sam said. "So I hollered and took a shot at him."

"And that was his undoing."

Sam twisted the brim of his hat in his hands. "Actually, sir," he said, "I believe that I missed by fourteen or fifteen feet."

Quantrill uncrossed his legs and stood. "But you diverted the ambusher's attention. According to Corporal Taylor, the ambusher then fired four shots at you, one of which took your hat from your head, before he was brought down by a volley from your comrades. Meanwhile you remained steadfast, firing your own weapon without flinching, even though the entire focus of the enemy's fire was at yourself."

Sam licked his lips and said nothing. The truth was that he had been stiff with terror—except for his right hand, which had been cocking and firing the Colt, and his left foot, which had been kicking Bixby in the ribs in an effort to make the horse wheel and run. But Bixby, who seemed to be deaf as far as gunfire was concerned, had been biting a crabapple from a tree and had not cared to move. The horse's position had blocked the other bushwhacker's view of Sam's left foot.

Quantrill put his hands on the table and leaned forward. "That was a brave and noble act, Private Clemens," he said.

A stretch of silence followed until Sam realized that he was expected to say something. "Thank, thank you, Colonel," he stammered. It was well known that Quantrill liked being called "Colonel."

"You understand, of course," Quantrill said, "that in the guerrilla service we have no formal honors. However, as the best reward of service is service itself, I'm promoting you to corporal and ordering you to reconnoiter the enemy in the company of Corporal Taylor."

"And a nigger," someone on Sam's right said. The voice was low, ragged, and angry.

Sam turned toward the voice and saw the most fearsome man he had ever seen in his life. The man wore a Union officer's coat with the insignia torn off, and a low-crowned hat with the brim turned up. His brown hair was long and shaggy, and his beard was the color of dirt. His face was gaunt, and his eyes, small and dark, glowered. He wore a wide-buckled belt with two pistols jammed into it. A scalp hung from the belt on each side of the buckle.

George Todd, standing just behind this man, placed a hand on his shoulder. "I don't much like it either, Bill, but Quantrill's right. A nigger's the perfect spy."

The seated man shook Todd's hand away. "Perfect spy, my hairy ass. You can't trust a nigger any more than you can trust Abe Lincoln."

Quantrill looked at the man without blinking. "That concern is why I'm sending two white men as well—one that I trust, and one that he in turn trusts. Don't you agree that two white men can keep one nigger under control, Captain Anderson?"

Anderson met Quantrill's gaze with a glare. "I have three sisters in prison in Kansas City for the simple act of remaining true to their brother's cause," he said. "I do not believe they would care to hear that their brother agreed to send a nigger to fight in that same cause, particularly knowing the treachery of which that race is capable."

Quantrill smiled. "As for sending a nigger to fight, I'm doing no such thing just yet. I'm sending him as a spy and as a guarantee of safe conduct for two brave sons of Missouri. No Kansan is likely to assault white men traveling with a free nigger. As for treachery, well, I assure you that John Noland has proven his loyalty. He's killed six Yankee soldiers and delivered their weapons to me. I trust him as much as I would a good dog, and have no doubt that he will serve Corporals Taylor and Clemens as well as he has me." The Colonel looked about the tent. "Gentlemen, we've been jawing about this enterprise for twenty-four hours. I suggest that it's now time to stop jawing and begin action. If you never risk, you never gain. Are there any objections?"

No one spoke. Anderson spat into the dirt, but then looked at Quantrill and shook his head.

"Very well," said Quantrill. "Captains Anderson and Blunt will please gather your men and communicate with me by messenger when your forces are ready." He nodded to Taylor. "Corporal, you're to return no later than sundown next Monday. So you'd best be on your way."

Sam made a noise in his throat. "Sir? On our way where?"

Quantrill turned to Sam. "Kansas Territory," he said. "Corporal Taylor has the particulars. You're dismissed."

Sam didn't need to be told twice. He left the tent, picked up his saddlebags where he'd dropped them outside, and then ran into the sycamore grove.

Taylor caught up with him in the trees. "You should have saluted, Sam," he said. "It's important to show the Colonel proper respect."

Sam unbuttoned his pants. His head was beginning to ache again. "I have plenty of respect for the Colonel," he said. "I have plenty of respect for all of them. If they were to cut me open, I'd probably bleed respect. Now get away and let a man piss in peace."

Taylor sighed. "All right. Get your horse saddled as soon as you can. I'll find Noland and meet you north of the tent. You know Noland?"

"No. But since I've only seen one man of the Negro persuasion in camp, I assume that's him."

"You assume correctly." Taylor started to turn away, then looked back again. "By the way, we were right. We're going to Lawrence. You and I are to count the Bluebellies in the garrison, and—"

"I know what a spy does, Fletch," Sam said.

Taylor turned away. "Hurry up, then. We have some miles to cover." He left the grove.

Sam emptied his bladder and buttoned his pants, then leaned against a tree and retched until he brought up most of the bacon he'd had for breakfast.

"Kansas Territory," Quantrill had said. There had been no sarcasm in his voice. Kansas had been admitted to the Union over two and a half years before, but none of the bushwhackers ever referred to it as a state. In their opinion, its admission to the Union as a free state had been an illegal act forced upon its residents by fanatical jayhawkers. Sooner or later, though, those house-burning, slave-stealing jayhawkers would be crushed, and Kansas Territory would become what it was meant to be: a state governed by Southern men who knew what was right.

To that end, Colonel Quantrill would raid the abolitionist town of Lawrence, the home of Jim Lane and the Kansas Red Legs. And Sam Clemens was to go there first and come back to tell Quantrill how to go about the task.

Orion's ghost, he thought, had better appreciate it.

On Wednesday morning, six miles south of Lawrence on the Paola road, Fletch Taylor started chuckling. Sam, riding in the center, glanced first at him and then at John Noland. Noland didn't even seem to be aware of Sam or Taylor's existence, let alone Taylor's chuckling.

Noland was an enigma, both in his mere presence in Quantrill's band and in his deportment during the present journey. No matter what Sam or Taylor said or did, he continued to look straight ahead, shifting in his saddle only to spit tobacco juice into the road. Except for the color of his skin, though, Noland's appearance was like that of any other free man of the border region, right down to the slouch hat and the Colt stuck in his belt. He even rode with the same easy arrogance as Taylor. It was a skill Sam had never mastered.

Sam looked at Taylor again, squinting as he faced the sun. "What's so funny, Fletch?"

Taylor gestured at the winding track of the road. "No pickets," he said.

"We ain't seen a Bluebelly since we came into Kansas. If the Colonel wanted to, the whole lot of us could waltz in and raise no more notice than a cottontail rabbit." He chuckled again. "Until we started shooting."

Sam nodded, but didn't laugh. It was true that they hadn't passed a single Federal picket, but that didn't mean Lawrence was going to be a waltz. The absence of pickets might only mean that the town had fortified itself so well that it didn't need them.

"You should carry your gun in your belt," Noland said. His voice was a rumble.

Sam was startled. Until now, Noland hadn't spoken at all.

"Are you addressing me?" Sam asked, turning back toward Noland. But he knew that must be the case. Both Noland and Taylor had their pistols in their belts, while Sam's was in one of his saddlebags.

Noland looked straight ahead. "That's right."

"I thought I should make sure," Sam said, "since you won't look me in the eye."

"Your eyes ain't pleasant to look at," Noland said.

Taylor chortled. "Whomp him, Sam. Make him say your eyes are the most beautiful jewels this side of a St. Louie whorehouse."

"It ain't a question of beauty," Noland said. "It's a question of skittishness. Mr. Clemens has skittish eyes. I prefer steady ones, like those of Colonel Quantrill. Or like your own, Mister Taylor."

Now Sam laughed. "It appears that you've bested me in the enticing eyeball category, Fletch. Perhaps we should switch places so you can ride next to John here."

Taylor scowled. "Ain't funny, Sam."

Sam knew when to stop joking with Fletch Taylor, so he replied to Noland instead. "My gun's fine where it is," he said. "Why should I put it in my belt and risk shooting myself in the leg?"

"If that's your worry, you can take out the caps," Noland said. "But it'll look better going into Lawrence if your gun's in the open. The county sheriff might be inspecting strangers, and he won't think nothing of it if your pistol's in your belt. But if he finds it in your bag, he'll think you're trying to hide it."

Sam didn't know whether Noland was right or not, but it wasn't worth arguing about. He took his pistol from his saddlebag, removed the caps, and tucked the weapon into his belt.

"Be sure to replace those caps when we come back this way with the Colonel," Taylor said. He sounded disgusted.

"I merely want to ensure that I don't shoot up the city of Lawrence prematurely," Sam said. But neither Taylor nor Noland laughed. Sam gave Bixby a pat on the neck, and Bixby looked back at him and snorted.

When the three bushwhackers were within a mile of Lawrence, they encountered two riders heading in the opposite direction. The two men, one old and one young, were dressed in high-collared shirts and black suits despite the August heat. They wore flat-brimmed black hats, and their pistols hung in black holsters at their sides. The younger man held a Bible with a black leather cover, reading aloud as he rode.

"Well, lookee here," Taylor whispered as the two approached. "I think we got ourselves a couple of abolitionist preachers on our hands."

Sam tensed. If there was one thing a bushwhacker hated more than an abolitionist, it was an abolitionist with a congregation. Taylor had particularly strong feelings in this regard, and Sam feared that his friend might forget that they were only in Kansas as spies for now.

"Good morning, friends," the elder preacher said, reining his horse to a stop. The younger man closed his Bible and stopped his horse as well. They blocked the road.

"Good morning to you as well," Taylor replied. He and Noland stopped their horses a few yards short of the preachers.

Sam tried to stop Bixby too, but Bixby ignored the reins and continued ahead, trying to squeeze between the horses blocking the way. The preachers moved their mounts closer together, forcing Bixby to halt, and the roan shook his head and gave an irritated *whuff*.

"I apologize, gentlemen," Sam said. "My horse sometimes forgets which of us was made in God's image."

The elder preacher frowned. "More discipline might be in order," he said, and then looked past Sam at Taylor. "Are you going into Lawrence?"

"That we are," said Taylor. His voice had taken on a gravelly tone that Sam recognized as trouble on the way. He glanced back and saw that Taylor's right hand was hovering near the butt of his pistol.

"I see that you are traveling with a colored companion," the younger preacher said. "Is he your servant?"

"No," Sam said before Taylor could reply. "My friend and I jayhawked him from Arkansas three years ago, and we've been trying to help him find his family ever since. Are there any colored folks named Smith in Lawrence?"

The elder preacher nodded. "A number, I believe." He twitched his reins, and his horse moved to the side of the road. "I would like to help you in your search, gentlemen, but my son and I are on our way to Baldwin to assist in a few overdue baptisms. Sometimes an older child resists immersion and must be held down."

"I have observed as much myself," Sam said as the elder preacher rode past.

The younger preacher nodded to Sam and thumped his Bible with his fingertips. "If you gentlemen will be in town through the Sabbath, I would like to invite you to attend worship at First Lawrence Methodist."

Taylor came up beside Sam. "I doubt we'll be in town that long, preacher," he said. "But we'll be sure to pay your church a visit the next time we pass through."

"I am glad to hear it," the young preacher said. "God bless you, gentlemen." He nudged his horse with his heels and set off after his father.

Taylor looked over his shoulder at the departing men. "You won't be so glad when it happens," he muttered.

Noland rode up. "Jayhawked from Arkansas," he said. "That's a good one." He spurred his horse, which set off at a trot. Taylor's horse did likewise. Bixby, for once, took the cue and hurried to catch up.

"I'm sorry if my lie didn't meet with your approval," Sam said as Bixby drew alongside Noland's horse.

"I said it was a good one," Noland said. "I say what I mean."

"You may believe him on that score, Sam," Taylor said. "John's as honest a nigger as I've ever known."

Sam eyed Noland. "Well, then, tell me," he said. "Where *were* you jayhawked from?"

"I was born a free man in Ohio," Noland said. "Same as Colonel Quantrill."

"I see," Sam said. "And how is it that a free man of your race rides with a free man like the Colonel?"

Noland turned to look at Sam for the first time. His eyes and face were like black stone.

"He pays me," Noland said.

Sam had no response to that. But Noland kept looking at him.

"So why do *you* ride with the Colonel?" Noland asked.

"Might as well ask Fletch the same question," Sam said.

"I know all about Mister Taylor," Noland said. "His house was burned, his property stolen. But I don't know shit about you."

Taylor gave Noland a look of warning. "Don't get uppity."

"It's all right, Fletch," Sam said. Fair was fair. He had asked Noland an impertinent question, so Noland had asked him one. "I was a steamboat pilot on the Mississippi, Mister Noland. I was a printer's devil before that, but I wanted to be on the river, so I made it so." He grimaced. "I was a cub for two years before I earned my license, and I was only able to follow the profession for another two years before the war started. I had to leave the river then, or be forced to pilot a Union boat. So here I am."

"How'd you come to be on this side of Missouri instead of that side?" Noland asked.

"I was going to Nevada Territory with my brother," Sam said, angry now at being prodded, "but the Red Legs killed him northwest of Atchison. I went back home after that, but eventually realized there was nothing useful I could do there. So I came back this way and fell in with one bunch of incompetents after another until I joined the Colonel." He glared at Noland. "*So here I am.*"

"So here you are," Noland said.

"That's about enough, John," Taylor said. He looked at Sam. "I didn't know you were a printer, Sam, but I'm glad to hear it. It'll make one of our tasks easier. Marshal Donaldson's posse tore up the Lawrence *Herald of Freedom*'s press and dumped the type in the Kansas River back in '56, but the Lawrence *Journal's* sprung up like a weed to take its place. So when we raid Lawrence, the *Journal's* to be destroyed. But we'll need to know how well the office is armed, so I suggest that you go there and ask for employment. You'll be able to get a look at things without them wondering why. After you've done that, you can help me count Bluebellies, Red Legs, and Lawrence Home Guards, if we can find out who they are."

"What if the *Journal* wants to hire me?" Sam asked.

Taylor grinned. "Tell them you'll be back in a week or so." He looked across at Noland. "John, you're to fall in with the local niggers and see whether any of them have guns. You might also ask them about Jim Lane, since they love him so much. Find out where his fancy new house is, and how often he's there."

Noland was staring straight ahead again, but he nodded.

They were now skirting the base of a high, steep hill. Sam looked up the slope. "One of the boys at Blue Springs told me that the hill rising over Lawrence is called Mount Horeb," he said. "It must be named after the place where Moses saw the burning bush."

Taylor chuckled. "If Moses is still here, he'll see more burning before long, at closer range than he might like." He pointed toward the southeast, at another hill that was a few miles distant. "That might be a safer place for him to watch from. The Colonel says it'll be our last stop before the raid, so we can see what's what before it's too late to turn back." He spurred his horse, which galloped ahead. "Come on, boys! We've reached Lawrence!"

Noland spurred his horse as well, and he and Taylor vanished around the curve of the hill.

"Now that I think of it," Sam yelled after them, "he said Mount Oread, not Horeb. Moses doesn't have anything to do with it."

He kicked Bixby, but the horse only looked back at him and gave a low nicker. It was the saddest sound Sam had ever heard.

"Do you have a stomachache?" he asked.

Bixby looked forward again and plodded as if leading a funeral procession. Sam kicked the horse once more and then gave up. The sadness of Bixby's nicker had infected him, and he felt oppressed by the heat, by his companions, and by his very existence on the planet.

They followed the road around the hill, and then Lawrence lay before Sam like a toy city put together by a giant child. Its rows of stores and houses were too neat and perfect to be real. Small wagons rolled back and forth between them, and children dashed about like scurrying ants. Taylor and Noland were already among them.

Sam closed his eyes, but then opened them immediately, crying out before he could stop himself.

He had just seen the buildings, wagons, and children burst into flame.

Sam shook himself. Here he was having nightmares while wide awake. The ride had been too long, the sun too hot. It was time for a rest.

But maybe not for sleep.

*   *   *

Early Friday, Sam awoke in sweat-soaked sheets. He fought his way free, then sat up with his back against the wall. He had just spent his second night in Lawrence, and his second night in a real bed in almost three months. The dream had come to him on both nights, worse than ever. He was no more rested than if he had run up and down Mount Oread since sundown.

The dream always began the same way: He and the other Marion Rangers, fifteen men in all, were bedding down in a corn crib at Camp Ralls, fourteen miles south of Hannibal. They had to chase the rats away, but they had to do that every night. Then a Negro messenger came and told them that the enemy was nearby. They scoffed; they had heard that before.

But they grew tense and restless, and could not sleep. The sounds of their breathing were unsteady. Sam's heart began to beat faster.

Then they heard a horse approaching. Sam and the other Rangers went to the corn crib's front wall and peered out through a crack between the logs. In the dim moonlight, they saw the shadow of a man on a horse enter the camp. Sam was sure that he saw more men and horses behind that shadow. Camp Ralls was being attacked.

Sam picked up a rifle and pushed its muzzle between the logs. His skull was humming, his chest tight. His hands shook. The enemy had come and would kill him. The enemy had come and would kill him. The enemy had come and would—

Someone shouted, "Fire!"

And Sam pulled the trigger. The noise was as loud and the flash as bright as if a hundred guns had gone off at once.

The enemy fell from his saddle and lay on the ground. Then all was darkness, and silence. There was nothing but the smell of damp earth.

No more riders came. The fallen man was alone.

Sam and the others went out to the enemy. Sam turned the man onto his back, and the moonlight revealed that he was not wearing a uniform, and that his white shirt was soaked with blood. He was not the enemy. He was not even armed. And his face—

Was sometimes Henry's, and sometimes Orion's.

But just now, this Friday morning in Lawrence, it had been someone else's. It had been a face that Sam did not recognize. It had been the face of an innocent stranger, killed by Sam Clemens for no reason at all . . . no reason save that Sam was at war, and the man had gotten in the way.

Fletch Taylor, in the room's other bed, mumbled in his sleep. Sam could still smell the whiskey. One of Taylor's first acts of spying on Wednesday afternoon had been to hunt up a brothel, and he had been having a fine time ever since. He was counting Bluebellies too, but it had turned out that there weren't many Bluebellies to count.

Sam had visited the brothel with Taylor on Wednesday, but hadn't found the girls to his liking. So he'd spent most of his time since then trying to do his job. He had applied for work at the Lawrence *Journal*, as planned, and had been turned down, as he'd hoped—but had learned that the *Journal* was a two-man, one-boy operation, and that they didn't even dream of being attacked. A carbine hung on pegs on the wall in the pressroom, but it was kept unloaded to prevent the boy from shooting rabbits out the back door. The *Journal*'s type would join the *Herald of Freedom*'s at the bottom of the Kansas River with little difficulty.

From the purplish-gray color of the patch of eastern sky visible through the hotel room window, Sam guessed that it was about five A.M. He climbed out of bed and went to the window to look down at the wide, muddy strip of the town's main thoroughfare, Massachusetts Street. Lawrence was quiet. The buildings were closed up, and no one was outside. Even the Red Legs and Home Guards slept until six or six-thirty. If Colonel Quantrill timed his raid properly, he and his bushwhackers could ride into Lawrence while its citizens were still abed.

The Union garrison shouldn't be much trouble either, Sam thought as he looked north toward the river. The handful of troops stationed in Lawrence had moved their main camp to the north bank of the Kansas, and the only way for them to come back across into town was by ferry, a few at a time. Two small camps of Federal recruits—one for whites, the other for Negroes—were located south of the river, in town; but those recruits were green and poorly armed. The raiders could ignore them, or squash them like ladybugs if they were foolish enough to offer resistance.

Sam left the window, pulled the chamber pot from under his bed, and took a piss. Then he lit an oil lamp, poured water from a pitcher into a bowl, and stood before the mirror that hung beside the window. He took his razor and scraped the stubble from his throat, chin, cheeks, and sideburns, but left his thick reddish-brown mustache. He had grown fond of the mustache because it made him look meaner than he really was. The dirt that had been ground into his pores had made him look mean too, but that was gone now. He'd had a bath Wednesday evening, and was thinking of having another one today. Lawrence might be a den of abolitionist murderers, but at least it was a den of abolitionist murderers that could provide a few of the amenities of civilization.

When he had finished shaving, he combed his hair and dressed, then put out the lamp and left the room. Taylor was still snoring. Whiskey did wonders for helping a man catch up on his sleep.

Sam went downstairs and out to the street, opening and closing the door of the Whitney House as quietly as possible so as not to disturb the Stone family, who owned the place. Taylor had told Sam that Colonel Quantrill had stayed at the Whitney when he'd lived in Lawrence under the name of Charley Hart, and that Mr. Stone had befriended "Hart" and would therefore be treated with courtesy during the raid. So Sam was being careful not to do anything that might be interpreted as discourtesy. He wanted to stay on the Colonel's good side.

The wooden sidewalk creaked under Sam's boots as he walked toward the river. It was a sound that he hadn't noticed on Wednesday or Thursday, when he had shared the sidewalk with dozens of Lawrence citizens. Then the predominant sounds had been of conversation and laughter, intermingled with the occasional neighing of a horse. But this early in the morning, Sam had Massachusetts Street to himself, save for two dogs that raced past with butcher-bones in their mouths. Sam took a cigar from his coat pocket, lit it with a match, and drew in a lungful of sweet smoke.

He had to admit that Lawrence was a nice-looking town. Most of the buildings were sturdy and clean, and the town was large and prosperous considering that it had been in existence less than ten years. Almost three thousand souls called Lawrence home, and not all of those souls, Sam was sure, were bad ones. Perhaps the raid would succeed in running off those who were, and the city would be improved as a result.

Sam paused before the Eldridge House hotel. The original Eldridge House, a veritable fortress of abolitionist fervor and free-state propaganda, had been destroyed by Marshal Donaldson in 1856, but it had been rebuilt into an even more formidable fortress in the service of the same things. It was a brick building four stories high, with iron grilles over the ground-floor windows. Quantrill might want to destroy the Eldridge House a second time, particularly since the Lawrence Home Guards would probably concentrate their resistance here, but Sam's advice would be to skip it. A mere fifteen or twenty men, armed with Sharps carbines and barricaded in the Eldridge House, would be able to kill a hundred bushwhackers in the street below.

"Hello!" a shrill voice called from across the street. "Good morning, Mister Sir!"

Sam looked across and saw a sandy-haired boy of ten or eleven waving at him. It took a moment before he recognized the boy as the printer's devil from the Lawrence *Journal*.

Sam took his cigar from his mouth. "Good morning yourself," he said without shouting.

The boy pointed at the Eldridge House. "Are you staying there, Mister Sir?" he yelled. "You must be rich!"

Sam shook his head. "Neither one. But if you keep squawking like a rusty steamboat whistle, I imagine you'll be meeting some of the inhabitants of the Eldridge House presently." He continued up the street.

The boy ran across and joined Sam on the sidewalk. Sam frowned at him and blew smoke at his face, but the boy only breathed it in and began chattering.

"I like the morning before the sun comes up, don't you?" the boy said. "Some days I wake up when it's still dark, and I ride my pa's mule out to the hills south of town, and I can look down over Lawrence when the sun rises. It makes me feel like the king of the world. Do you know what I mean, Mister Sir?"

"I'm sure I don't," Sam said.

The boy didn't seem to notice that Sam had spoken. "Say, if you aren't at the Eldridge, where are you at, Mister Sir? I'll bet you're at the Johnson

House, is what I'll bet. But maybe not, because the Red Legs meet at the Johnson, and they don't like strangers. So I'll bet you're at the Whitney, then, aren't you, Mister Sir?"

"Yes," Sam said. "The Johnson was not much to my liking."

"The Red Legs seem to like it just fine."

Sam nodded. "I have made note of that." And indeed he had. If the Red Legs could be punished for their crimes, he would be able to sleep a little better. And if the specific Red Legs who had killed Orion could be found and strung up, he would sleep better than Adam before the Fall.

"Those Red Legs, they have a time," the boy said. "I just might be a Red Leg myself, when I'm old enough."

"I would advise against it," Sam said, gnawing on his cigar. "The profession has little future."

The boy kicked a rock off the sidewalk. "I guess not," he said. "They say they'll have burned out the secesh in another year, so there won't be nothing left to fight for, will there, Mister Sir?"

"Stop calling me 'Mister Sir,' " Sam said. "If you must speak to me at all, call me Mister Clemens." He saw no danger in using his real name. The self-satisfied citizens of Lawrence clearly didn't expect bushwhackers in their midst, and wouldn't know that he was one even if they did.

"I'm sorry, Mister Clemens," the boy said. "I listened to you talking to Mister Trask at the *Journal* yesterday, but I didn't hear your name. Would you like to know mine?"

"No," Sam said.

They had reached the northern end of Massachusetts Street and were now walking down a rutted slope toward the ferry landing. Before them, the Kansas River was dull brown in color and less than a hundred yards wide; hardly a river at all, in Sam's opinion. But it would be enough to protect Quantrill's raiders from the soldiers on the far bank, provided that the soldiers didn't realize the raiders were coming until it was too late. To assure himself of that, Sam wanted to see how active or inactive the Bluebellies were at this time of morning. If they were as slumberous as Lawrence's civilians, he would be able to report that there was little chance of any of them ferrying across in time to hinder the raid. There weren't many soldiers in the camp anyway. Taylor had counted only a hundred and twelve, and some of those weren't soldiers at all, but surveyors.

"How come you're heading down to the river, Mister Clemens?" the boy asked. "Are you going fishing?"

Sam stopped walking and glared down at the boy, taking his cigar from his mouth with a slow, deliberate motion. "Do you see a fishing pole in my hand, boy?" he asked, exhaling a bluish cloud.

The boy gazed up at the cigar, which had a two-inch length of ash trembling at its tip.

"No, sir," the boy said. "I see a cigar."

"Then it is reasonable to assume," Sam said, "that I have come to the river not to fish, but to smoke." He tapped the cigar, and the ash fell onto the boy's head.

The boy yelped and jumped away, slapping at his hair.

Sam replaced his cigar between his teeth and continued down the slope.

"That wasn't nice!" the boy shouted after him.

"I'm not a nice man," Sam said. He didn't look back, so he didn't know if the boy heard him. But he reached the riverbank alone.

A thin fog hovered over the water and began to dissipate as the sun rose. The sunlight gave the tents on the far bank a pinkish tinge. The camp wasn't dead quiet, but there wasn't much activity either. At first, Sam saw only two fires and no more than five or six men up and about. As he watched, more men emerged from their tents, but military discipline was lacking. Apparently, these Bluebellies could get up whenever they pleased. That would be good news for the Colonel.

Sam threw the stub of his cigar into the river and heard it hiss. The sun was up now, and the soldiers began emerging from their tents with increasing frequency. From old habit, Sam reached for his pocket watch. But he still hadn't replaced the one that the Red Legs had stolen two years before.

He heard a scuffing sound behind him and looked over his shoulder. The boy from the *Journal* was close by again, twisting the toe of his shoe in the dirt.

"Say, boy," Sam said, "do you have a watch?"

The boy gave Sam a look of calculated contempt. "Of course I have a watch. Mister Trask gave me his old one. I got to get to the paper on time, don't I?"

"Well, tell me what time it is," Sam said.

"Why should I tell anything to someone who dumped a pound of burning tobacco on my head?"

Sam grinned. The boy was starting to remind him of the boys he had grown up with in Hannibal. "Maybe I'd give a cigar to someone who told me the time."

The boy's expression changed. "Really?"

"I said maybe."

The boy reached into a pocket and pulled out a battered timepiece. He peered at it and said, "This has six o'clock, but it loses thirty-five minutes a day and I ain't set it since yesterday noon. So it might be about half-past."

Sam took a cigar from his coat and tossed it to the boy. "Much obliged, boy."

The boy caught the cigar with his free hand, then replaced his watch in his pocket and gave Sam another look of contempt. "Stop calling me 'boy,' " he said. "If you must speak to me at all, call me Henry." The boy jammed the cigar into his mouth, turned, and strode up the slope to Massachusetts Street.

Sam turned back to the river. The fog was gone, and most of the soldiers were out of their tents. To be on the safe side, Sam decided, the raid would have to begin no later than five-thirty, and a detachment of bushwhackers would have to come to the river to train their guns on the ferry, just in case. He didn't think he would have any trouble persuading Colonel Quantrill to see the wisdom in that.

He started back up the slope, but paused where the boy from the *Journal* had stood.

"Henry," Sam murmured. "God damn."

Then he went up to the street and walked to the livery stable to check on Bixby. Bixby was in a foul mood and tried to bite him, so Sam knew that the horse was fine.

That evening, Sam was in his and Taylor's room at the Whitney House, writing down what he had learned so far, when he heard the *Journal* boy's voice outside. He went to the open window, looked down, and saw the boy astride a brown mule that was festooned with bundles of newspapers. The boy dropped one of the bundles at the Whitney's door, then looked up and saw Sam at the window.

The boy shook his finger at Sam. "That seegar was spoiled, Mister Clemens!" he shouted. "I was sick all afternoon, but Mister Trask made me work anyway!"

"Good," Sam said. "It builds character."

The boy gave Sam yet another contemptuous look, then kicked the mule and proceeded down the street.

As the boy left, four men wearing blue shirts and red leather leggings rode past going the other way. They all carried pistols in hip holsters, and one had a rifle slung across his back. They were unshaven and ugly, and they laughed and roared as they rode up Massachusetts Street. They would no doubt cross the river and make trouble for someone north of town tonight. Sam didn't recognize any of them, but that didn't matter. They were Kansas Red Legs, meaner and more murderous than even Jennison's Jayhawkers had been; and if they themselves hadn't killed Orion, they were acquainted with the men who had.

"Whoop it up, boys," Sam muttered as they rode away. "Whoop it up while you can."

He came away from the window and saw that Taylor was awake. Taylor had gotten up in the afternoon to meet with Noland, but then had gone back to bed.

"What's all the noise?" Taylor asked.

"Newspapers," Sam said. "I'll get one."

Taylor sneered. "Why? It's all abolitionist lies anyway."

But when Sam brought a copy of the *Journal* back upstairs and began reading, he found news. Horrifying, sickening news.

"Sons of bitches," he whispered.

"What is it?" Taylor asked. He was at the mirror, shaving, preparing for another night out in Lawrence's less respectable quarter.

"A building in Kansas City collapsed yesterday," Sam said.

"Well, good."

Sam shook his head. "No, Fletch. It was the building on Grand Avenue where the Bluebellies were holding the women they suspected of aiding bush-whackers. The paper says four women were killed, and several others hurt."

Taylor stopped shaving. "That's where they were keeping Bloody Bill Anderson's sisters," he said. "Cole Younger and Johnny McCorkle had kin there too. Does the paper give names?"

"No. But of course it suggests that the collapse might have been caused by a charge set by guerrillas 'in a disastrous attempt to remove the ladies from Federal protection.' "

Taylor's upper lip curled back. "As if Southern men would endanger their women!" He shook his razor at the newspaper. "I'll tell you what, though. I was worrying that the Colonel might have trouble riling up some of the boys for this raid, especially since Noland has found out that Jim Lane's out of town. But this news will rile them like nobody's business. And if Bill Anderson's sisters have been hurt, you can bet that he and *his* boys will shit blue fire. God help any Unionists who cross their path." He dipped his razor in the bowl and turned back to the mirror. His eyes were bright. "Or mine, for that matter."

When Taylor had finished shaving, he asked if Sam would like to go out and have a time. Sam declined, and Taylor left without him.

Then Sam read the rest of the newspaper, most of which he found to be worthless. But he admired the typesetting. There were few mistakes, and most of the lines were evenly spaced and straight. He wondered how many of them the boy had set.

He put the newspaper aside and wrote in his journal until the evening light failed. Then he undressed and got into bed, but lay awake for so long that he almost decided to join Taylor after all. But he had no enthusiasm for the idea. Spy-work wasn't physically strenuous, but it took a lot out of him mentally.

When he finally fell asleep, he dreamed that he was a printer's devil for Orion again. This time, though, their newspaper was not the Hannibal *Journal*, but the Lawrence *Journal*.

He was setting type about a fire in which over a hundred and fifty people had been killed, when a man burst into the pressroom. The man was jug-eared, greasy-haired, narrow-faced, and beardless. His thick lips parted to reveal crooked, stained teeth. Sam had never seen him before.

The jug-eared man pulled a revolver from his belt and pointed it at Orion.

"Henry!" Orion shouted. "Run!"

Sam, his ink-smeared hands hanging useless at his sides, said, "But I'm Sam."

The jug-eared man shot Orion, who shriveled like a dying vine.

Then the stranger pointed his revolver at Sam. Sam tried to turn and run, but his feet were stuck as if in thick mud.

The revolver fired with a sound like a cannon going off in a church, and the jug-eared man laughed.

Then Sam was floating near the ceiling, looking down at two bleeding bodies. Orion's face had become that of Josiah Trask, one of the editors of the Lawrence *Journal*. And Sam's face had become that of the boy, Henry, to whom he had given a cigar. The cigar was still in Henry's mouth.

Sam awoke crouched against the wall. He was dripping with sweat.

Night had fallen, and Lawrence was quiet. Taylor had not yet returned to the room. Sam crept away from the wall and sat on the edge of the bed, shivering.

"Henry," he whispered. "God damn."

At noon on Wednesday, August 19, Sam and Taylor were sitting on a log in southern Jackson County near the village of Lone Jack, in the midst of their fellow bushwhackers. They and Noland had returned to the Blue Springs camp two days before, and Colonel Quantrill had received their report with satisfaction. Then, on Tuesday morning, Quantrill had ordered his guerrillas to move out without telling them their objective. In order to fool any Federal scouts or pickets that might spot them, the Colonel had marched the bushwhackers eastward for several miles before cutting back to the southwest. En route, the band had been joined by Bill Anderson with forty men and Andy Blunt with over a hundred, almost doubling the size of Quantrill's force.

The men all knew something big was at hand. And now, finally, the Colonel was going to tell them what. Sam thought it was about time.

Quantrill, flanked by George Todd and Bill Anderson, sat before the bushwhackers astride his one-eyed mare, Black Bess, and gave a screeching yell. Over three hundred voices responded, and a thrill ran up Sam's spine. The sound was both the most magnificent and most terrifying thing he had ever heard. If he were the enemy and heard that sound, he would be halfway to Colorado before the echo came back from the nearest hill.

The Colonel nodded in satisfaction. He was wearing a slouch hat with one side of the brim pinned up by a silver star, a loose gray guerrilla shirt with blue and silver embroidery, and gray trousers tucked into his cavalry boots. His belt bristled with four Colt pistols, and two more hung from holsters on either side of his saddle.

"Well, boys," Quantrill shouted, "I hope you ain't tired of riding just yet!"

He was answered by a loud, ragged chorus of "Hell, no!"

Quantrill laughed. "That's good," he cried, "because come nightfall, we're heading for Kansas Territory to see if we can pull its most rotten tooth: Lawrence!"

A moment of silence followed the announcement, and for that moment Sam wondered if the men had decided that the Colonel was out of his mind. But then the bushwhackers exploded into another shrieking cheer, and at least a hundred of them rose to their feet and fired pistols into the air.

Taylor clapped Sam on the shoulder. "Are these the best damn boys in Missouri, or ain't they!" he yelled.

"They're sure the loudest," Sam said.

Quantrill raised a hand, and the cheers subsided.

"Save your ammunition," the Colonel shouted. "You've worked hard to make it or steal it, so don't waste it shooting at God. There are plenty of better targets where we're going!"

Another cheer rose up at that, but then Quantrill's expression changed from one of glee to one of cold, deadly intent. The bushwhackers fell silent.

"Boys," Quantrill said, no longer shouting, "there's more danger ahead than any of us have faced before. There could be Federals both behind and in front of us, coming and going. Now, we sent some men to spy on Lawrence, and they say the town's ripe to be taken—but there might be pickets on the way there. So we could have General Ewing's Bluebellies down on us from Kansas City, and some from Leavenworth as well. I doubt that we'll all make it back to Missouri alive." He straightened in his saddle, and it seemed to Sam that his metallic gaze fell on each bushwhacker in turn. "So if there's any man who doesn't want to go into the Territory with the rest of us, now's your chance to head for home. After we leave here tonight, there will be no turning back. Not for anyone."

Beside Quantrill, Bill Anderson drew a pistol. Anderson's hair was even wilder than it had been when Sam had seen him in Quantrill's tent the week before, and his eyes were so fierce that they didn't look human. "Anyone who *does* turn back after we've started," Anderson cried, "will wish to God he'd been taken by the Yankees before I'm through with him!"

Taylor leaned close to Sam and whispered, "I think Bloody Bill's heard about the building in Kansas City."

Sam thought so too. In the face of Bill Anderson he saw a hatred that had become so pure that if Anderson ever ran out of enemies against whom to direct his rage, he would have to invent more.

"But although we'll be going through hardships," Quantrill continued, "the result will be worth it. Lawrence is the hotbed of abolitionism in Kansas, and most of the property stolen from Missouri can be found there, ready and waiting to be taken back by Missourians. Even if Jim Lane ain't home, his house and his plunder are. We can work more justice in Lawrence than anywhere else in five hundred miles! So who's going with me?"

The shrill cheer rose up a fourth time, and all of the men not already standing came to their feet. Despite Quantrill's warning to save ammunition, more shots were fired into the air.

Quantrill and his captains wheeled their horses and rode to their tent, and Sam left Taylor and went to the tree where he had tied Bixby. There, after avoiding Bixby's attempts to bite him, he opened one of his saddlebags, took out his revolver, and replaced its caps.

When he looked up again, he saw John Noland leaning against the tree, regarding him with casual disdain.

"Ain't gonna shoot something, are you, Mister Clemens?" Noland asked.

"I'll do my best if it becomes necessary," Sam said.

Noland gave a sardonic grunt. " 'If it becomes necessary,' " he repeated. "Why do you think we're goin' where we're goin'?"

"I should think that would be obvious," Sam said. "To retrieve that which belongs to Missouri, and to punish the jayhawkers and Red Legs who stole it."

"You'll know a jayhawker on sight, will you?" Noland asked.

"I'll know the Red Legs on sight, I'll tell you that."

Noland pushed away from the tree. "I reckon you will, if they sleep in their pants." He sauntered past Sam and tipped his hat. "Hooray for you, Mister Clemens. Hooray for us all."

"You don't sound too all-fired excited, Noland," Sam said.

Noland looked back with a grim smile. "You want to see me excited, Mister Clemens, you watch me get some of that free-soil money into my pocket. You watch me then." He tipped his hat again and walked away.

Sam watched him go. How, he wondered, could two men as different as Bill Anderson and John Noland be riding in the same guerrilla band on the same raid?

Then he looked down at the gun in his hand and remembered that he was riding with both of them.

Bixby nipped his arm. Sam jumped and cursed, then replaced his revolver in the saddlebag and gave Bixby a lump of sugar. The horse would soon need all the energy it could get.

At dusk, the Colonel had the bushwhackers mount up and proceed toward the southwest. Only thirteen men had left the raiders after Quantrill's announcement of the target, and only two of those had been members of Quantrill's own band. Sam marveled. Here were more than three hundred men going to what might be their deaths, just because one man had asked them to do so. True, each man had his own reasons for becoming a bushwhacker in the first place, but none of them would have dreamed of attempting a raid so far into Kansas if Quantrill had not offered to lead them in it.

In the middle of the night, the guerrillas happened upon a force of over a hundred Confederate recruits under the command of a Colonel John Holt. Holt and Quantrill conferred for an hour while the bushwhackers rested their horses, and when the guerrillas resumed their advance, Holt and his recruits joined them.

At daybreak on Thursday, August 20, Quantrill's raiders made camp beside the Grand River. They were only four miles from the border now, and this would be their final rest before the drive toward Lawrence. Late in the morning, fifty more men from Cass and Bates counties rode into the camp and offered their services. Quantrill accepted, and by Sam's count, the invasion force now consisted of almost five hundred men, each one mounted on a strong horse and armed with at least one pistol and as much ammunition as he could carry. A few of the men also had rifles, and many carried bundles of pitch-dipped torches.

If Federal troops did attack them, Sam thought, the Bluebellies would get one hell of a fight for their trouble. They might also become confused about who was friend and who was foe, because almost two hundred of the bushwhackers were wearing parts of blue Union uniforms.

At mid-afternoon, Captain Todd rode among the dozing men and horses, shouting, "Saddle up, boys! Lawrence ain't gonna plunder itself, now, is it?"

The men responded with a ragged cheer. Sam got up, rolled his blanket, and then carried it and his saddle to the dead tree where Taylor's horse and Bixby were tied. He had spread his blanket in a shady spot and had tried to sleep, but had only managed to doze a little. Taylor, lying a few yards away, had started snoring at noon and hadn't stopped until Todd had ridden past.

"How you could sleep with what we've got ahead of us, I can't imagine," Sam said as Taylor came up to saddle his horse.

"I wasn't sleeping," Taylor said. "I was thinking over strategy."

"With help from the hive of bumblebees you swallowed, no doubt."

Taylor grinned. "We're gonna be fine, Sam," he said. "You know they ain't expecting us. So there's no need for a man to be afraid."

"No, I suppose not," Sam said. "Not unless a man has a brain."

Taylor frowned. "What's that supposed to mean?"

Sam took his Colt from his saddlebag and stuck it into his belt. "Nothing, Fletch. I just want to get there, get it done, and get back, is all."

"You and me and everybody else," Taylor said.

As Sam and Taylor mounted their horses, a cluster of eleven men rode past, yipping and laughing. They seemed eager to be at the head of the bushwhacker force as it entered Kansas.

The man leading the cluster was jug-eared, greasy-haired, narrow-faced, and beardless.

Sam's heart turned to ice. Slowly, he raised his arm and pointed at the cluster of men. "Who are they?" he asked. His throat was tight and dry.

"Some of Anderson's boys," Taylor said. "Full of piss and vinegar, ain't they?"

"Do you know the one in front?" Sam asked.

"Sure do," Taylor said. "I've even ridden with him a time or two. Name's Frank James. You can count on him in a fight, that's for sure." Taylor clicked his tongue, and his horse started after the cluster of Anderson's men.

Bixby followed Taylor's horse while Sam stared ahead at the man from his dream. The man who had entered the *Journal* pressroom, killed an unarmed man and boy, and then laughed.

At six o'clock, Quantrill's raiders crossed the border into Kansas.

Ahead, the Territory grew dark.

By eleven o'clock, when the raiders passed the town of Gardner, the moonless night was as black as Quantrill's horse. Gullies, creeks, and fences became obstacles, and some of the bushwhackers wanted to light torches to help them find their way. But Quantrill would not allow that. They were still over twenty miles from Lawrence, in open country, and could not afford to be spotted from a distance. Besides, the torches were supposed to be reserved for use in Lawrence itself.

Soon after midnight, Quantrill halted the bushwhackers near a farmhouse, and the word was passed back along the column for the men to keep quiet.

"What are we stopping here for?" Sam whispered. He and Taylor were riding near the middle of the column, and Sam couldn't see what was happening up front.

"Shush yourself," Taylor hissed.

A minute later, there was a yell from the farmhouse, and then laughter from some of the raiders.

The tall form of Captain Bill Gregg came riding back along the column. "All right, boys, we can travel on," he said. "We got ourselves a friendly Kansan to guide us!" He wheeled his horse and returned to the head of the column.

"Wonder what he means by that," Sam said.

Taylor chuckled. "What do you think?"

The bushwhackers started moving again and made rapid progress for a few miles, zigzagging around obstacles. Then Quantrill called another halt. The men began muttering, but fell silent as a pistol was fired.

Bixby jerked his head and shied away from the column. Sam had to fight to bring the horse back into place. "What in blazes is the matter with you?" he asked. Bixby had never been spooked by gunfire before. In fact, he had hardly noticed it. "It was just somebody's pistol going off by mistake!"

At that moment, Captain Gregg came riding by again. "No mistake about it," he said, pausing beside Sam and Taylor. "Our friendly Kansan claimed he didn't know which side of yonder hill we should go around. So the Colonel dispatched him to a hill of his own, and we're to wait until we have another friendly Kansan to guide us. There's a house ahead, and some of Anderson's boys are going to see who's home. We'll be on our way again before long." Gregg spurred his horse and continued back along the column to spread the word.

"Well, good for the Colonel," Taylor said. "Now that Kansan is as friendly to us as a Kansan can be."

Sam was stunned. When the raiders began moving again, they passed by the corpse. Bixby shied away from it and collided with Taylor's mount.

"Rein your goddamn horse, Sam!" Taylor snarled.

The dead man was wearing canvas trousers and was shirtless and barefoot. Even in the dark, Sam could see that his head was nothing but a mass of pulp.

It made no sense. This man wasn't a Red Leg or a Bluebelly. He might not even be an abolitionist. He was only a farmer. Colonel Quantrill had shot a farmer. Just because the man couldn't find his way in the dark.

Just because he was a Kansan.

Sam began to wonder if the preposterous stories he had read in abolitionist newspapers—the stories about Quantrill's raids on Aubry, Olathe, and Shawneetown—might have had some truth in them after all.

The column halted again after only a mile, and there was another gunshot. Then another farmhouse was raided, and the bushwhackers continued on their way. But soon they stopped once more, and a third shot was fired.

The process was repeated again and again. Each time, Sam and Bixby passed by a fresh corpse.

There were ten in all.

Sam felt dizzy and sick. This was supposed to be a raid to punish the Red Legs, destroy the newspaper, burn out Jim Lane, and recover stolen property. Some Kansans were to be killed, yes; but they were supposed to be Red Legs and Bluebellies, not unarmed farmers taken from their wives and children in the night.

At the tenth corpse, Taylor maneuvered his horse past Sam and Bixby. "'Scuse me, Clemens," Taylor said. "My horse is starting to make water."

Taylor stopped the horse over the dead man and let it piss on the body. The bushwhackers who were close enough to see it laughed, and Sam tried to laugh as well. He didn't want them to see his horror. He was afraid of them all now. Even Taylor. Especially Taylor.

"Have your horses drink deep at the next crick, boys!" Taylor chortled. "There's plenty of men in Lawrence who need a bath as bad as this one!"

"Amen to that!" someone cried.

The shout was echoed up and down the line as Taylor rejoined the column next to Sam.

Captain Gregg came riding back once more. "I admire your sentiments, boys," he said, "but I suggest you save the noise until we reach our destination. Then you can holler all you want, and see if you can squeeze a few hollers from the so-called men of Lawrence as well!"

The bushwhackers laughed again, but then lowered their voices to whispers. To Sam, it sounded like the hissing of five hundred snakes.

He saw now that what was going to happen in Lawrence would resemble what he had imagined it would be only in the way that a volcano resembled a firefly. He had let his guilt over Orion's death and his hatred of the Red Legs blind him to what the men he was riding with had become. He wanted to turn Bixby out of the column and ride hard and fast back to Missouri, not stopping until he reached Hannibal.

But he knew that he couldn't. Anderson had told them all how deserters would be dealt with. Sam and Bixby wouldn't make it more than a hundred yards before a dozen men were after them. And there was no doubt of what would happen to Sam when they caught him.

Besides, his and Taylor's report from their trip to Lawrence was part of what had convinced Quantrill that the raid was possible. That made Sam more responsible for what was about to happen than almost anyone else. To run away now would make him not only a coward, but a hypocrite.

Another farmhouse was raided at about three in the morning, and this time the entire column broke up and gathered around to watch. By the time Sam was close enough to see what was happening, the farmer was on his knees in his yard. Captain Todd was standing before him holding a pistol to his forehead and telling him the names of some of the men waiting for him in hell.

Quantrill, on Black Bess, came up beside Todd. "We're too close to Lawrence to fire a gun now, George," he said.

Sam could just make out Todd's expression. It was one of fury.

"Goddamn it, Bill," Todd said. "This man's name is Joe Stone. He's a stinking Missouri Unionist who ran off to Kansas to escape justice, and I'm going to kill him no matter what you say."

Stone, wearing only a nightshirt, was shuddering. Sam looked away from him and saw a woman crying in the doorway of the house. A child clung to the woman's knees, wailing. An oil lamp was burning inside, and its weak light framed the woman and child so that they seemed to be suspended inside a pale flame.

Quantrill stroked his stubbled face with a thumb and forefinger. "Well, George, I agree that traitors must die. But we're within six miles of Lawrence now, and a shot might warn the town."

Todd seemed about to retort, but then took his pistol away from Stone's head and replaced it in his belt. "All right," he said. "We'll keep it quiet." He strode to his horse and pulled his Sharps carbine from its scabbard. "Sam!" he called. "Get over here!"

Taylor nudged Sam in the ribs. "Go on," he said.

Sam, almost rigid with terror, began to dismount.

"I mean Sam Clifton," Todd said. "Where is he?"

Sam returned to his saddle as Clifton, a stranger who had joined the guerrillas while the spies had been in Lawrence, dismounted and went to Todd.

Todd handed the rifle to Clifton. "Some of the boys tell me you've been asking a lot of questions, Mister Clifton," he said. "So let's see if you know what you're here for." He pointed at Stone. "Beat that traitor down to hell."

Clifton didn't hesitate. He took three quick steps and smashed the rifle butt into Stone's face. Stone fell over in the dirt, and his wife and child screamed. Then Clifton pounded Stone's skull.

Sam wanted to turn away, but he couldn't move. This was the most horrible thing he had ever seen, more horrible even than his brother Henry lying in his coffin or his brother Orion lying in the road. He watched it all. He couldn't stop himself.

Only when it was over, when Clifton had stopped pounding and Stone was nothing but a carcass, was Sam able to look away. Beside him, Taylor was grinning. Some of the others were grinning too. But there were also a few men who looked so sick that Sam thought they might fall from their horses.

Then he looked at Colonel Quantrill. Quantrill's eyes were unblinking, reflecting the weak light from the house. His lips were pulled back in a tight smile.

Todd took his rifle back from Clifton and replaced it in its scabbard without wiping it clean. Then he looked up at Quantrill with a defiant sneer.

"That suit you, Colonel?" he asked.

Quantrill nodded. "That suits me fine, Captain," he said. Then he faced the men. "Remember this, boys," he cried, "and serve the men of Lawrence the same! Kill! Kill, and you'll make no mistake! Now push on, or it'll be daylight before we get there!"

"You heard the man," Taylor said to Sam.

"That I did," Sam said. His voice was hoarse. He thought it might stay hoarse forever.

The raiders pushed on, leaving Mrs. Stone and her child to weep over the scrap of flesh in their yard.

As the column reformed, Sam found himself near its head, riding not far behind Gregg, Todd, Anderson, and Quantrill himself. It was as if God wanted to be sure that Sam had another good view when the next man died.

The eastern sky was turning from black to purplish-gray as Quantrill's raiders reached the crest of the hill southeast of Lawrence. Colonel Quantrill raised his right hand, and the column halted.

Below them, less than two miles ahead, Lawrence lay as silent as death.

Fletch Taylor cackled. "Look at 'em! Damn Yankees are curled up with their thumbs in their mouths!"

Sam nodded, sick at heart.

Quantrill brought out a spyglass and trained it on the sleeping town. "It looks ripe," he said. "But I can't see the river; it's still too dark." He lowered the glass and turned to Captain Gregg. "Bill, take five men and reconnoiter. The rest of us will wait fifteen minutes and then follow. If you spot trouble, run back and warn us."

Gregg gave Quantrill a salute, then pointed at each of the five men closest to him. "James, Younger, McCorkle, Taylor, and—" He was looking right at Sam.

Sam couldn't speak. His tongue was as cold and heavy as clay. He stared at Frank James.

"Clemens," Taylor said.

"Right," Gregg said. "Clemens. Come on, boys." He kicked his horse and started down the hillside.

"Let's get to it, Sam," Taylor said. He reached over and swatted Bixby on the rump, and Bixby lurched forward.

Despite the steep slope and the trees that dotted it, Gregg set a rapid pace. All Sam could do was hang on to Bixby's reins and let the horse find its own way. He wished that Bixby would stumble and that he would be thrown and break an arm or leg. But Bixby was too agile for that. Sam would be in on the Lawrence raid from beginning to end.

Halfway down the hill, Gregg stopped his horse, and James, Younger, McCorkle, and Taylor did the same. Bixby stopped on his own, almost throwing Sam against the pommel of his saddle.

"What's wrong, Captain?" Taylor asked.

Gregg put a finger to his lips and then extended that finger to point.

A few hundred feet farther down the hillside, a mule carrying a lone figure in a white shirt was making its way up through the trees. The mule and rider were just visible in the predawn light.

"What's someone doing out here this early?" Taylor whispered.

"Doesn't matter," Gregg whispered back. "If he sees us and we let him escape, we're as good as dead."

"But, but a shot would wake up the town, Captain," Sam stammered.

Gregg gave him a glance. "Then we won't fire a shot that can be heard in the town." He turned toward Frank James. "Go kill him, Frank. Use your knife, or put your pistol in his belly to muffle the noise. Or knock his brains out. I don't care, so long as you keep it quiet."

James drew his pistol, cocked it, and started his horse down the hill.

The figure on the mule came around a tree. He was alone and unarmed. Sam could see his face now. He was the printer's devil from the Lawrence *Journal*.

Henry.

Frank James plunged downward, his right arm outstretched, pointing the finger of Death at an innocent.

And in that instant, Sam saw everything that was to come, and the truth of everything that had been. He saw it all as clearly as any of his dreams:

The boy would be lying on his back on the ground. His white shirt would be soaked with blood. Sam would be down on his knees beside him, stroking his forehead, begging his forgiveness. He would want to give anything to undo what had been done. But it would be too late.

Henry would mumble about his family, about the loved ones who would never see him again. And then he would look up at Sam with reproachful eyes, and die.

Just as it had happened before.

Not when Sam's brother Henry had died. Henry had given him no reproachful look, and all he had said was "Thank you, Sam."

Not when Orion had died, either. Orion had said, "Get out of here, Sam," and there had been no reproach in the words. Only concern. Only love.

Frank James plunged downward, his right arm outstretched, pointing the finger of Death at an innocent.

An innocent like the one Sam had killed.

It had been more than just a dream. He had told himself that he wasn't the only one of the Marion Rangers who had fired. He never hit anything he aimed at anyway. But in his heart he had known that wasn't true this time. He had known that he was guilty of murder, and of the grief that an innocent, unarmed man's family had suffered because of it.

All of his guilt, all of his need to make amends—

It wasn't because of his dead brothers at all.

It was because he had killed a man who had done nothing to him.

Sam had tried to escape that truth by fleeing West with Orion. But then, when Orion had been murdered, he had tried instead to bury his guilt by embracing it and by telling himself that the war made killing honorable if it was done in a just cause. And vengeance, he had told himself, was such a cause.

But the family of the man he had killed might well have thought the same thing.

Frank James plunged downward, his right arm outstretched, pointing the finger of Death at an innocent.

And Sam couldn't stand it anymore.

He yelled like a madman, and then Bixby was charging down the hill, flashing past the trees with a speed no other horse in Quantrill's band could equal. When Bixby came alongside James's horse, Sam jerked the reins. Bixby slammed into James's horse and forced it into a tree. James was knocked from his saddle, and his pistol fired.

Henry's mule collapsed, and Henry tumbled to the ground.

Sam reined Bixby to a halt before the dying mule, leaped down, and dropped to his knees beside the boy.

Henry looked up at him with an expression of contempt. "Are you crazy or something?" he asked.

Sam grabbed him and hugged him.

Henry struggled to get away. "Mister Clemens? What in the world are you doing?"

Sam looked up the slope and saw Frank James picking himself up. James's horse was standing nearby, shaking its head and whinnying.

Gregg, Taylor, McCorkle, and Younger were riding down with their pistols drawn.

Sam jumped up and swung Henry into Bixby's saddle. "Lean down close to me," he said.

"What for?" Henry asked. The boy looked dazed now. He was staring down at the dead mule.

"Just do it, and listen to what I say," Sam said. "I have to tell you something without those men hearing it."

Henry leaned down.

"Ride back to town as fast as you can," Sam said. "When you're close enough for people to hear, yell that Charley Hart's come back, that his new name is Billy Quantrill, and that he has five hundred men with him. And if you can't remember all that, just yell 'Quantrill!' Yell 'Quantrill!' over and over until you reach the Eldridge House, and then go inside and yell 'Quantrill!' at everyone there. If they don't believe you, just point at this horse and ask where the hell they think you got it. Now sit up!"

Henry sat up, and Sam slapped Bixby on the rump. Bixby turned back and tried to bite Sam's shoulder.

"Not now, you fleabag!" Sam yelled. He raised his hand to swat the horse again, but Bixby snorted and leaped over the dead mule before Sam could touch him. The roan charged down the hillside as fast as before, with Henry hanging on tight.

Sam took a deep breath and turned as he exhaled. Frank James was walking toward him with murder in his eyes, and the four men riding up behind James didn't look any happier. Sam put his hand on the Colt in his belt, but didn't think he could draw it. He feared that he was going to piss his pants. But he had to give Henry a good head start. And if that meant getting himself killed—well, that was just what it meant. Better him than a boy whose only crime was setting type for an abolitionist newspaper.

"You traitorous bastard," James said, raising his revolver to point at Sam's face.

Sam swallowed and found his voice. "Your barrel's full of dirt," he said.

James looked at his gun and saw that it was true.

Captain Gregg cocked his own pistol. "Mine, however, is clean," he said.

Sam raised his hands. "Don't shoot, Captain," he said. He was going to have to tell a whopper, and fast. "I apologize to Mister James, but I had to keep him from killing my messenger, didn't I? I would've said something sooner, but I didn't see who the boy was until James was already after him."

"Messenger?" Gregg said.

Sam looked up at Taylor, whose expression was one of mingled anger and disbelief. "Why don't you say something, Fletch? Didn't you recognize the boy?"

Taylor blinked. "What are you yapping about?"

Sam lowered his hands, put them on his hips, and tried to look disgusted. "Damn it, Fletch, that Missouri boy I met in Lawrence. The one whose father was killed by jayhawkers, and who was kidnapped to Kansas. I pointed him out to you Saturday morning, but I guess you'd gotten too drunk the night before to retain the information."

Gregg looked at Taylor. "You were drinking whiskey while you were supposed to be scouting the town, Corporal?"

Taylor became indignant. "Hell, no!"

"Then why don't you remember me pointing that boy out to you?" Sam asked.

"Well, I do," Taylor said uncertainly.

Sam knew he couldn't let up. "So why didn't you tell Captain Gregg that the boy promised to come here and warn us if any more Federals moved into Lawrence?"

Taylor's eyes looked panicky. "I didn't recognize the boy. It's dark."

"What's this about more Bluebellies in Lawrence?" Gregg asked.

"That's what the boy told me," Sam said. "Six hundred troops, four hundred of them cavalry, came down from Leavenworth on Tuesday. They're all camped on the south side of the river, too, he says."

Frank James had his pistol barrel clean now, and he pointed the gun at Sam again. "So why'd you send him away?"

Sam was so deep into his story now that he almost forgot his fear. "Because he said the Bluebellies have started sending fifty cavalrymen out between five and six every morning to scout the plain between here and Mount Oread. I told him to go keep watch and to come back when he saw them."

Cole Younger, stern-faced and narrow-lipped, gestured at Sam with his revolver. "Why would you tell someone in Lawrence who you were and why you were there?"

"I already said why," Sam snapped. "Because he's a Missouri boy, and he hates the Yankees as much as you or me. Maybe more, because he didn't even have a chance to grow up before they took everything he had. And I didn't just walk up and take him into my confidence for no reason. Two Red Legs were dunking him in a horse trough until he was half drowned. When they left, I asked him why they'd done it, and he said it was because he'd called them murdering Yankee cowards. My opinion was that we could use a friend like that in Lawrence, and Fletch agreed."

John McCorkle, a round-faced man in a flat-brimmed hat, peered at Sam through narrowed eyelids. "So how'd the boy know where we'd be, and when?"

"He knew the where because we told him," Sam said. "The Colonel used to live in these parts, and he picked this hill for our overlook when he planned the raid. Ain't that so, Fletch?"

Taylor nodded.

"As for the when of it," Sam continued, "well, Fletch and I knew we'd be here before sunup either yesterday or today, so we told the boy to come out both days if there was anything we needed to hear about."

Younger looked at Taylor. "That true, Fletch? Or were you so drunk you don't remember?"

Taylor glared at him. "It's true, Cole. I just didn't tell you, is all. There's five hundred men on this raid, and I can't tell every one of you everything, can I?"

Younger started to retort, but he was interrupted by the sound of hundreds of hoofbeats from the slope above. Quantrill had heard James's gunshot and was bringing down the rest of his men.

Gregg replaced his pistol in its holster. "All right, then," he said, sounding weary. "Let's tell the Colonel what the boy said." He looked at Taylor. "You do it, Fletch. He knows you better than he does Clemens."

Taylor nodded, then shot Sam a look that could have melted steel.

There was a promise in that look, but Sam didn't care. Gregg had believed his story, and for now, at least, he was still alive.

And so was Henry.

Taylor told Colonel Quantrill that a Missouri boy had come to warn the raiders about six hundred new Bluebellies in Lawrence, all camped south of the river, and that a scouting party of fifty of the Federals was likely to spot the bushwhackers before they could enter the town. Quantrill listened without saying a word. He stared straight ahead, toward Lawrence, until Taylor was finished. Then he looked down at Sam, who was still standing before the dead mule.

Quantrill's eyes were like chips of ice, but Sam didn't look away. He was sure that if he flinched, the Colonel would see him for the lying traitor that he was.

A long moment later, Quantrill turned to Captain Todd. "What do you think, George?" he asked.

Todd looked as if he had eaten a bad persimmon. "You didn't see six hundred Federals through the glass, did you?"

"No," Quantrill said, "but I couldn't see the river. If they were camped close by its banks, they would have been invisible."

"Then let's go back up and take another look," Todd said.

Quantrill shook his head. "By the time the sun has risen enough for us to see the river, the people of Lawrence will have risen too. We must either press on now, or give it up."

"But if there are that many more troops down there," Gregg said, "we won't have a chance. I say we fall back to the border, send more spies to take another look at the town, and come back when we can be sure of victory."

Quantrill looked at the ground and spat. "Damn it all," he said, "but you're right. Even if there aren't that many troops, the town might've heard the pistol shot."

The men behind Quantrill murmured. Many looked angry or disappointed, but almost as many looked relieved.

Sam tried hard to look disappointed, but he wanted to shout for joy.

Then Bill Anderson shrieked, drew one of his pistols, and kicked his horse until it was nose to nose with Black Bess.

"We've come too far!" he screamed, pointing his pistol at the Colonel. "We've come too far and our people have suffered too much! This raid was your idea, and you talked me into committing my own men to the task! God damn you, Quantrill, you're going to see it through!"

Quantrill gave Anderson a cold stare. "We have received new intelligence," he said. "The situation has changed."

Anderson shook his head, his long hair flying wild under his hat. "Nothing has changed! Nothing! The Yankees have killed one of my sisters and crippled another, and I won't turn back until I've killed two hundred of them as payment! And if you try to desert me before that's done, the two-hundred-and-first man I kill will be named Billy Quantrill!"

Quantrill turned to Todd. "George, place Captain Anderson under arrest."

Todd drew his pistol. "I don't think I will, " he said, moving his horse to stand beside Anderson's. "We've come to do a thing, so let's do it."

The murmurs among the men grew louder.

"What's wrong with you?" Gregg shouted at Todd and Anderson. "Colonel Quantrill is your commanding officer!"

Todd sneered. "No more of that 'Colonel' bullshit. Jefferson Davis wouldn't give this coward the time of day, much less a commission."

At that, Frank James, John McCorkle, and Cole Younger moved to stand with Anderson and Todd. Bill Gregg, Andy Blunt, and John Holt moved to stand with Quantrill. The murmurs among the bushwhackers became shouts and curses. A few men broke away and rode back up the hill.

Sam decided that he didn't care to see the outcome. He began edging backward, but came up against the dead mule.

Quantrill looked as calm as an undertaker. "All right, boys," he said. "I guess you're right. We've come this far, and we've whipped Yankee soldiers before." He pointed toward Lawrence. "Let's push on!"

"That's more like it," Anderson said, and he and his comrades turned their horses toward Lawrence.

As soon as they had turned, Quantrill pulled two of his pistols from his belt, cocked them, and shot Bill Anderson in the back. Anderson slumped, and his horse reared.

The hillside erupted into an inferno of muzzle flashes, explosions, and screams.

Sam dove over the mule and huddled against its back until he heard pistol balls thudding into its belly. Then he rolled away and scrambled down the hill on his hands and knees. When there were plenty of trees between him and the fighting, he got to his feet and ran. He fell several times before reaching the bottom of the hill, but didn't let that slow him.

The trees gave way to prairie grass and scrub brush at the base of the hill, and Sam ran straight for Lawrence. He couldn't see Henry and Bixby on the plain ahead, so he hoped they were already in town.

Thunder rumbled behind him, and he looked back just in time to see the neck of a horse and the heel of a boot. The boot struck him in the forehead and knocked him down. His hat went flying.

Sam lay on his back and stared up at the brightening sky. Then the silhouette of a horse's head appeared above him, and hot breath blasted his face.

"Get up and take your pistol from your belt," a voice said.

Sam turned over, rose to his knees, and looked up at the rider. It was Fletch Taylor. He had a Colt Navy revolver pointed at Sam's nose.

"You going to kill me, Fletch?" Sam asked.

"Not on your knees," Taylor said. "Stand up, take your pistol from your belt, and die the way a man should."

Sam gave a low, bitter chuckle. He was amazed to discover that he wasn't afraid.

"All men die alike, Fletch," he said. "Reluctantly."

Taylor kept his pistol pointed at Sam for another few seconds, then cursed and uncocked it. He looked toward the hill. "Listen to all the hell you've raised," he said.

The sounds of gunshots and screams were wafting out over the plain like smoke.

Taylor looked back at Sam. "You saved my life," he said, "so now I'm giving you yours. But if I ever see you again, I'll kill you."

Sam nodded. "Thank you, Fletch."

Taylor's lips curled back from his teeth. "Go to hell," he said. Then he spurred his horse and rode back toward the hill.

Sam watched Taylor go until he realized that the fighting on the hillside was spilling onto the plain. He stood, found his hat—the hat that Taylor had given him—and ran for Lawrence again.

When he reached Massachusetts Street, staggering, exhausted, he saw men in the windows of every building. Some wore blue uniforms, but most were civilians. Each man held either a revolver or a carbine. The sun was rising, and Lawrence was awake. One of the men came outside and pointed his rifle at Sam, but the boy named Henry appeared and stopped him. Then Henry grabbed Sam's arm and pulled him into the Whitney House.

Fifteen minutes later, Sam was watching from the window of a second-floor room when a magnificent black horse came galloping up Massachusetts Street. The horse's rider, wearing an embroidered gray shirt, gray pants, and black cavalry boots, had his arms tied behind his back and his feet tied to his stirrups. His head and shoulders had been daubed with pitch and set ablaze. He was screaming.

"It's Quantrill!" someone cried.

A volley of shots exploded from both sides of the street, and the horse and rider fell over dead.

Within seconds, a hundred Missouri guerrillas led by George Todd charged up the street. Fourteen of them were cut down in a hail of lead balls, and the rest turned and fled, with soldiers and citizens pursuing. A company of Negro Federal recruits led the chase and killed three more bushwhackers at the southern edge of town.

When the gunfire and shouting had ceased, a cluster of townspeople gathered around the carcass of the black horse and the charred, bloody corpse of its rider. The crowd parted to let two men in black suits and hats approach the bodies. Sam recognized them as the preachers that he, Taylor, and Noland had encountered the week before.

The elder preacher held a Bible over Quantrill's corpse. "Earth to earth," he intoned.

The younger preacher raised his Bible as well. "Ashes to ashes," he said.

In unison, they chanted, "And dust to dust."

Then they lowered their Bibles, drew their revolvers, and shot Quantrill a few more times for good measure.

"Amen," said the crowd.

Sam closed his curtains.

Senator Jim Lane had returned to Lawrence on Wednesday for a railroad meeting, and he sent for Sam at noon on Saturday, one day after the failed raid. Lane was thinner, younger, and had more hair than Sam had guessed from the caricatures, but his fine house on the western edge of town was all that Sam had supposed. It was packed with expensive furnishings, including two pianos in the parlor.

"How did you come to acquire two pianos, Senator?" Sam asked. He had not slept the night before and did not care if he sounded accusatory.

Lane smiled. "One was my mother's," he said. "The other belonged to a secessionist over in Jackson County who found that he no longer had a place to keep it." The Senator picked up a pen and wrote a few lines on a piece of paper, then folded the paper and pushed it across the table. "Kansas is grateful to you, Mister Clemens, and regrets the mistake of two years past when members of the Red-Legged Guards mistook your brother for a slaveholder. Had they known of his appointment as Secretary of Nevada Territory, I'm sure the tragedy would not have occurred."

"He told them," Sam said. "They didn't believe him."

Lane shrugged. "What's done is done, but justice will be served. General Ewing has ordered his troops to arrest all Red Legs they encounter. He believes that such men have been committing criminal acts in the name of liberty, and I must concur." He tapped the piece of paper. "I'm told that Governor Nye of Nevada Territory is again in need of a Secretary. I cannot guarantee you the appointment, but this should smooth your way." He leaned forward. "Frankly, Mr. Clemens, I think your decision to continue to Nevada is a good one. There are those in this town who believe that the burning man was not Quantrill at all, and that you are here not as a friend, but as Quantrill's spy."

Sam stared at the piece of paper. "A ticket on the overland stage from St. Joseph is a hundred and fifty dollars," he said. "I have ten."

Lane stood and left the parlor for a few minutes. When he returned, he handed Sam three fifty-dollar bank notes and a bottle of whiskey.

"This was distilled from Kansas corn," the Senator said, tapping the bottle with a fingernail. "I thought you should have something by which to remember my state."

Sam tucked the money into a coat pocket and stood, holding the whiskey bottle by its neck. *My state*, Lane had said. What's done is done.

"Good day, Senator," Sam said. He started to turn away.

"Don't forget my letter of introduction," Lane said.

Sam picked up the piece of paper, tucked it into his pocket with the money, and left the house.

Henry was standing outside holding Bixby's reins, and twelve Bluebellies waited nearby. They had an extra horse with them.

"Mister Clemens," one of the soldiers called. "Our orders are to escort you to St. Joseph. We're to leave right away." He didn't sound happy about it. All of the Bluebellies in the escort were white, and Sam suspected that this was their punishment for failing to chase the bushwhackers with as much vigor as their Negro counterparts.

Sam nodded to the soldier, then looked down at Henry. "I suppose you want to keep the horse," he said.

"Well, *I* don't," Henry said. "He's mean, if you ask me. But my pa says he'll either have Bixby as payment for his mule, or he'll take it out of somebody's hide. And since you're running off, I reckon my hide will do him as well as any."

"A hiding would probably do you a considerable amount of good," Sam said, "but since I no longer have a use for the animal, you may keep him and the saddle as well. I'll take the bags, however." He removed the saddlebags from the horse and put the bottle of whiskey into one of them. A few lumps of brown sugar lay at the bottom of that bag, so he fed one to Bixby.

Bixby chewed and swallowed, then tried to bite Sam's hand. Sam gave the rest of the sugar to Henry and took his saddlebags to the soldiers' extra horse.

"Goodbye, Mister Clemens," Henry said, climbing onto Bixby. "I won't forget you."

Sam swung up onto his own mount. "Thank you, boy," he said, "but I shall be doing my best to forget *you*, as well as every other aspect of this infected pustule of a city."

Henry gave him a skeptical look. "Mister Clemens," he said, "I think you're a liar."

"I won't dispute that," Sam said. "I only wish I could make it pay."

The Bluebellies set off, and Sam's mount went with them. Sam looked back to give Henry and Bixby a wave, but they were already heading in the other direction and didn't see him.

On the way to the ferry, Sam and the soldiers passed by the Eldridge House, where eighteen bodies had been laid out on the sidewalk. They were already beginning to stink. A number of townspeople were still gathered here, and from what Sam could hear, they were curious about the dead black man, who had been one of the three raiders killed by the Negro recruits. Why on earth, they wondered, would a man of his race ride with Quantrill?

Sam started to say, "Because he was paid," but the words froze in his throat.

The last four bodies on the sidewalk were those of George Todd, Cole Younger, Frank James, and Fletcher Taylor.

Sam looked away and rode on.

He spent Saturday night camped beside the road with the soldiers and Sunday night in a hotel in St. Joseph, and did not sleep either night. At daybreak on Monday, he carried his saddlebags to the overland stage depot, paid his money, and boarded the coach. Two other passengers and several sacks of mail soon joined him, and the coach set off westward at eight o'clock.

As the coach passed the spot where Orion had been killed, Sam took out the whiskey that Lane had given him and began drinking. He offered some to his fellow passengers, but they each took one swallow and then refused more, saying that it was the vilest stuff they'd ever tasted. Sam agreed, but drank almost half the bottle anyway.

At the next station stop, he climbed atop the coach with his saddlebags while the horses were being changed. When the coach started moving again, Sam drank more whiskey and stared at the fields of green and gold. Soon, his head warm with sun and alcohol, it occurred to him that the corn and grass shifting in the breeze looked like ocean swells after a storm. He was reminded of a holiday he had spent near New Orleans, looking out at the Gulf of Mexico after piloting a steamboat down the Mississippi. He wondered if he would love anything in Nevada half as much.

The thought of Nevada reminded him of the letter that Jim Lane had written for him, so he took it out and read it:

My dear Governor Nye:

You will recall that your intended Secretary of two years past, Mr. Orion Clemens, was unfortunately killed before he could assume his duties. This letter will introduce his younger brother Samuel, who has provided service to his Nation and is a loyal Republican. I trust you shall do your utmost to secure for him any employment for which he might be suited.

Yours most sincerely,
James Lane, Senator
The Great and Noble State of Kansas

Sam tore up the letter and let its pieces scatter in the wind. If Nevada held "any employment for which he might be suited," he would secure it without any assistance from a self-righteous, thieving son of a bitch like Jim Lane.

Nor would he drink any more of Lane's abominable whiskey. He leaned over the coach roof's thin iron rail and emptied the bottle onto the road. Then he opened one of his saddlebags, took out his Colt, and stood. He held the whiskey bottle in his left hand and the pistol in his right.

The coach conductor glanced back at him. "What are you doing, sir?" he asked.

Sam spread his arms. "I am saying fare-thee-well to the bloody state of Kansas," he cried, "and lighting out for the Territory!"

He looked out over the tall grass. It rippled in waves.

He missed the river.

He missed his brothers.

But killing men for the sake of a world that was gone wouldn't bring it back. It was time to make a new one.

"Half-less twain!" he cried.

Both the conductor and driver stared back at him.

"Quarter-less twain!" Sam shouted.

Then he brought his left arm back and whipped it forward, throwing the bottle out over the grass. As it reached the apex of its flight, he brought up his right arm, cocked the Colt with his thumb, and squeezed the trigger.

The bottle exploded into brilliant shards.

The coach lurched, and Sam sat down on the roof with a thump.

"Goddamn it!" the conductor yelled. "You spook these horses again, and I'll throw you off!"

Sam held the pistol by its barrel and offered it to the conductor. "Please accept this," he said, "with my apologies."

The conductor took it. "I'll give it back when you're sober."

"No," Sam said, "you won't."

Then he threw back his head and roared: "MAAARRRRK TWAIIINN!"

Two fathoms. Safe water.

He lay down with his hat over his face and fell asleep, and no dead men came to haunt his dreams.

For Sam Clemens, the war was over.

THE BEST AND THE REST OF JAMES JOYCE

Ian McDonald

British author Ian McDonald is an ambitious and daring writer with a wide range and an impressive amount of talent. His first story was published in 1982, and since then he has appeared with some frequency in *Interzone, Isaac Asimov's Science Fiction Magazine, Zenith, Other Edens, Amazing,* and elsewhere. He was nominated for the John W. Campbell Award in 1985, and in 1989 he won the *Locus* "Best First Novel" Award for his *Desolation Road.* He won the Philip K. Dick Award in 1992 for his novel *King of Morning, Queen of Day.* His other books include the novel *Out on Blue Six* and a collection of his short fiction, *Empire Dreams.* His most recent books include a new novel, *The Broken Land,* and a new collection, *Speaking in Tongues,* as well as several graphic novels. He is at work on another new novel, tentatively entitled *Necroville.* Born in Manchester, England, in 1960, McDonald has spent most of his life in Northern Ireland, and now lives and works in Belfast.

In the daring, playful, and lushly inventive story that follows, he gives us a look (or a succession of *different* looks) at a world-famous writer as you've never seen him before—in fact, as *no one's* ever seen him before . . .

Aboard His Britannic Majesty's air-dreadnought *William and Mary* as it leaves the Command Holdfast buried beneath the cratered mudscape once known as London in the one-hundred-and-first year of the war are 112 ratings, 66 officers, and six highly important, highly secret passengers: Air Lord Blennerhasset, Admiralty Lord Van Loos, Marshall Valery-Petain, Director Ames, Sub-Academician Giorgio Joyce and his father, senior Academician James Joyce. Reinforced concrete bombproof doors open as *William and Mary* rises cautiously, every sense tuned, toward the perpetual rainclouds that discharge their poisoned drizzle over the mudfields of Staines. Despite two atomic cannon, a complement of ten turret-mounted 18-inch guns and a veritable arsenal of lighter artillery and rocket racks, the artillerymen standing by their weapons and the glider-marines ready at the launch tubes are nervous. They have heard stories of dirigibles, dreadnoughts even, surprised and destroyed attaining altitude by marauding Tsarist airships lying grounded, half buried in the mud. For the lynchpin of His Majesty's airfleet to lift unescorted, unprotected, into potentially hostile airspace . . .

They have long suspected that the High Command locked up in their War Room half a mile under Command Holdfast have gone insane: now they have proof. But His Majesty's Air Lords need not justify to the crew of *William and Mary* their decision that a lone dirigible might escape the attention a dreadnought with full escort would warrant. Their destination, the very fact that they are carrying passengers, have been kept secret from them. But seeing the cindered cities of the midlands slipping away far beneath their armoured glass observation bull's-eyes, they know that their course is northward. A combined services mission, perhaps, supporting the beleaguered 19th Army bogged down in melting permafrost north of Bergen, or a search-and-destroy mission on Tsarist submarine traffic across the Barents Sea. Maybe *William and Mary* has been sent to rendezvous with the remnant of the Royal Dutch Airfleet stationed at Scapa Flo Holdfast and destroy the Tsarist North Polar Fleet. In his armoured cubicle the Captain opens the envelope sealed with the wax sigil of His Majesty's Directorate and after reading and burning the flimsy within, calls a heading, altitude and velocity down the gosport to the flightbridge that will, in 18 hours' time, bring *William and Mary* and its secret passengers north to Iceland, to the Keflavik Chronokinetics Research Facility.

In the summer of 1933 I was asked by a doctor of my acquaintance if I might examine a patient of his, a gentleman from Ireland of late middle age who had come to him complaining of persistent and severe insomnia. My doctor friend prescribed sleeping tablets but the patient, who I shall hereafter refer to as Herr J., complained that the prescription was ineffective and that the true source of the insomnia lay in a powerful and disturbing dream that recurred nightly, whereupon my colleague referred him to my practice. I was advised that the man, a writer of international repute, would not make the most co-operative of patients.

My first interview with the patient was at an outside table at a café on the Burkliplatz. The tetchiness against which my colleague had warned me made itself immediately evident in his response to my introduction of myself: "Ah yes, the Swiss Tweedledee, not to be confused with the Austrian Tweedledum." It was clear to me that the caustic witticism with which he leavened his subsequent conversation concealed a deep-seated discontent.

He was a tall, thin man, of protrusions and angularities. Behind the thick glasses he wore—he was a sufferer from persistent iritis—his eyes were an extraordinarily penetrating ice-blue. His hands moved constantly, making idle play with the table utensils. He was quite refreshingly frank about the details of his life, though more, I felt, from a mischievous delight in outrage: his first sexual experience had been at the age of fourteen with a prostitute on the banks of a canal. This had precipitated his lapse from the Catholic faith—an almost inevitable fall, I have heard, for the *intelligentsia* of his country. At the age of 22 he had left Ireland with his lover, Frau Nora B., and lived the following years as an artistic exile in Paris, Trieste and Zurich, during which time he produced his most notable work. He confessed to having been unfaithful to Nora B. only once; a short, tempestuous affair with one Martha Fleischmann of this city.

Eighteen months ago he had embarked upon a new, major, work, to be entitled *Finnegans Wake*, a "stream of consciousness" exploration of a single night's dream. After three months he had abandoned work on account of failing concentration which he blamed on insomnia caused by a recurring and vivid dream. Two months to the day after the first dream, the Travellers arrived and threw our affairs into disarray. He found himself no longer capable of working on *Finnegans Wake* and was convinced that the Travellers were the source of his dreams. Indeed, his attention was continually being diverted from our table across the Burkliplatz to the large number of spectators who thronged the promenade with telescopes and field glasses, and from these spectators upward, to the focus of their observation, the hazy curtain of air, half hidden by thin cloud, beyond which the incomprehensible forms of the Travellers may occasionally be glimpsed.

"Dreams of falling, Dr Jung? Well, we all know what they mean," he said. "Dreams of flying? Doubtless, there is some handy psychological rebus for these too."

"I don't deal in psychological panaceas, Herr J.," I said. "You tell me rather what you think these dreams signify."

"A belief and a fear, Herr Doctor. I believe that the Travellers will soon leave. I fear that I want more than anything to go with them."

Righteous Rhythm Rocks the Musik Halls

A traditional sound from the Eastern Emirates of the United Kingdoms is the new popular music craze of the basement clubs in the Capital. *Sarif*, a fusion of traditional Moorish music with Western Kingdoms electric instruments has emerged from the *kasbahs* of the cities of the Southern Counties to become the essential listening of the new youth underground, a new musical wave determined to sweep all before it.

Lyle Santesteban goes every week to the musik clubs in the depressed area of Vincastra where *sarif* is drawing packed houses to dance all night to the rhythms of Afrika and Islam. Escapism through music, or something deeper? "*Sarif* speaks to us," says Lyle Santesteban. "*Sarif* has something to say. That stuff on the wireless, the electric crooners, the neoballadeers, they got nothing to say; it's all just love and romance and let's get married tootsie-wootsie. What's that got to do with life in the United Kingdoms, what's that got to say about Vincastra in 1902? *Sarif* is music of the street. *Sarif* speaks with the voice of the street. *Sarif* has something to say about being young, about being old, about being poor, about being rich, in a job, out of a job, family problems, arranged marriages, polygamy, sex, morality, God; *sarif* speaks to us."

Sarif's musical revolution is essentially a *righteous* one. The clubs and cafés that specialize in the new music serve nothing stronger than coffee. Says Haran Gomez, manager of the El Morocco Cafe: "Islam and *sarif* cannot be separated. And that means no alcohol, and certainly, no drugs.

We catch anyone in the toilet toking a *kif*, he's not just bounced, we call the cops as well. What *sarif* is about is having a good time, hearing great music, dancing, meeting people, without getting blind drunk, smashed out of your skull, or into a fight. But it's not a wank. *Sarif*'s got steel at its core, it's strong, like Islam. The spirit of *sarif* is the spirit of Islam."

James Joyce would agree. He is one of the most promising of *sarif*'s rising stars; coupling social consciousness with intense verbal imagery and ingenuity. This seminal figure is in many ways an anomaly in an anomalous genre, originating not from the Hispano-Moorish section of the population which spawned *sarif* as a distinct form, but from the purebreed Western Celts.

"It's a positive advantage," the twenty-year-old boy from Hibernia East says. "I'm bringing together two separate strands of our culture, the Moorish and the Celtic; bringing a little North African soul and spiritual fibre into the Celtic, a little Celtic playfulness and imagination into the North African. The two cultures really have much more in common than you think, it's exciting experimenting with new ways of fusing Celtic melodies with Islamic rhythms, breaking down the structured lyrical system of ethnic proto*sarif* into improvisational stream-of-consciousness passages. But there's nothing over-cerebral about it," Joyce adds. "It's dance music pure and simple, first and last."

Certainly, the Celtic-Islamic fusion makes James "Ched" (the Moroccan Arabic name for traditional folk singers) Joyce's sets at the El Morocco where he holds down a regular Saturday night spot stand out among an already outstanding bill that includes Ched Alayah and Ched Christo Dos Santos. His inventive, improvised vocals, the purity of his singing voice and the multi-layered complexity of his backing group leave the listener both beguiled and stimulated.

James "Ched" Joyce has recently moved from Soukh Recordings, a small independent company specializing in *sarif* and other ethnic musics, to Marconigram, the Kingdoms' largest; his first album for them, *Three Quarks*, is due for release early next month.

The city's greatest expert on the enigma of the Travellers is Dr Peter Pretorious, to whom I made recourse in the case of Herr J. for a layman's summary of the phenomenon.

In the absence of any sustained coherent communication between mankind and the Travellers, Dr Pretorious's theories were highly suppositional. The general consensus seems to be that our visitors are travellers not of the distances between the stars, as had first been thought, but of the distances between universes; the infinite array of potential other earths that modern physics suggests are created by the indeterminacy of quantum theory. The hypothesis is that the Travellers originate from a parallel earth that diverged from ours at the very dawn of the solar system; one in which matter was not gathered into discrete planets, but remained in an annular nebula around the sun and of which the Travellers, and the incomprehensible companion bodies with which they share their Enclaves, are the dominant life: the *humanity* of this alternative earth. Their colossal size and mutable shapes are products of evolution within the gravity-free conditions of the gasring; the size of such an organism being governed ultimately by the speed of transmission along the nervous system. Hence the forty-kilometre diameter spheres of gravitylessness they have created in those places they have chosen to arrive upon our earth: Brisbane, São Paulo, Vancouver, Freetown in Sierra Leone, Luzon in the Philippines, and here in, or rather above, Zurich. Such enormous creatures, Dr Pretorious informed me, could not hope to survive the effects of gravity. As for a means by which they might negate gravity, or even the method by which they travel with such apparent ease between alternate worlds, both he and the scientific world at large are at a loss to supply.

I mentioned to him Herr J.'s belief that the Travellers might soon depart. Dr Pretorious replied that recent observations through telescopes, and from aircraft flying as close as they safely dared to the immense pressure barriers that defined the Enclaves, indicated that the Travellers and their companion bodies were indeed undergoing physical changes into new forms that might signal an imminent change of activity.

Returning to my offices from the University, I called at the residence Herr J. shared with Frau Nora B. to leave a card with the *concierge* and a request that he call me at his earliest convenience to make an appointment.

Eoin UiNiall reviews the new James Joyce album, "Agenbites of Inwit" (*New Musical Express*: March 29th 1911 edition)

Consider this man's quandary. In the wireless-defined universe orbit ten million frequency-modulation ghosts who have come to know and possibly love Joyce through his waxings on Marconigram. Yet in the dark streets shine the souls of the luminous few who have danced to glory with him up through the *sarif* clubs, soul survivors of the Saturday nights (as was your gentle reviewer, in what seems like a previous incarnation) when James Joyce held down a spot at El Morocco and the Virgin's Kitchen. Quandary quantified: these are two mutually exclusive camps. That they are not yet at war is due to the ministrations of their titular deity: Joyce himself. Though James Joyce on cylinder is a pale shade of James Joyce behind the footlights with five hundred watts of power on each shoulder—the extemporized, improvisational spirit of Joyce's work is a bird that pines and dies when caged—still a watered-down James Joyce is better than no James Joyce at all.

So, as an exercise in squaring circles, how does *Agenbites of Inwit* fare?

Never let it be said that the man does not believe in value for money. Ten tracks are here, not one under six minutes in length. Roundabouts and swings; what you gain in danceability, you lose in singalong: there is no lyric sheet. Lyrics are superfluous; the titles ("Gas from a Burner," "The Dead," "Clashing Rocks") are themes for improvisation. Join the celebration of mutability: if you feel that on another day, in another place, if the band had one more or one less to drink, this would have been an altogether other album; that is Joyce's intention. Songs in the key of possibility: what you are listening to is just one of a spectrum of possible alternative Agenbites. If this is a deliberate strategy by Joyce to unite both the dance-floor hero and the wax junkie under the banner of boogiedom, it is successful; this will be filling the floors well into the next decade.

All the familiar Joycean techniques have been Brassoed to a fare-thee-well: the medium rare, *al dente*, yet *together* punch of his instrumentalizations; the verbal and lyrical bravura, like a rather well arranged firework display *just for you*, the concrete-hard, almost architectural *righteousness*, the mining of new gems from the overworked lodes of *sarif* and ethnic genres. If there is a sense of progression, it lies in a search for spiritual understanding, a theological touchstone to transmute this tarnished age to, if not gold, at least lamé. The popular press, in its brief moments of relevance between Dal Riada spruce forest and the nail on the outdoor toilet door, have nudged and winked at James Joyce's interest in the mystical religions of the North Afrikan *safidis*, and if this quest for a Holy Grail reaches a climax in "Ulysses, Telemachus, Eumaeus," the whole thing is mercifully saved from toppling into terminal pomposity by the impudent, shamelessly danceable "Stogged."

The final track, "The Inner Organs of Animals," leaves one hungry for more, with a tang of faintly scented urine on the tongue, and eagerly anticipating the next cylinder. Clubland and dubland will bop till they drop and then discuss post-modernism and the punk ethos over pools of seventy-percent-proof vomit on the toilet floor. Few cylinders warrant the epithet "seminal"; James Joyce stands unique among popular musicians as one who (to date) has produced nothing but masterpieces, and looks set fair to continue to do so. *And* you can dance to it. There's presence, and progress, in this cylinder; and that rates five stars by me.

Senior Academician James Joyce is uncomfortable at the formal dinner that night at the Captain's table. His white frock coat and high-collar shirt are drab and contemptible among the militaries' synthetic golds and carmines and purples. Even the sombre black and silver of the Directorate outshines him. He is acutely conscious that his thick pebble glasses mark him genetically inferior to the eugenically engineered military and political castes. He does not enjoy the enforced informalities of shipboard life, he does not enjoy being pushed into an intimacy with these superior castes. Son Giorgio seems at ease, weaving across strands of conversation from military to political to scientific; father James finds himself longing for the company of his peers at the tachyon facility. Over ersatz coffee, the threads of conversation draw inevitably toward the War, and how it might be won.

Air Lord Blennerhasset stoutly advocates the strategy of mass bombardment of the Tsarist Holdfasts by air-dreadnoughts armed with atomic cannon.

"Crack them open like an egg!" he says. Death-light shines in his eyes, or perhaps the grainy illumination of the bulkhead bulbs. "The enemy annihilated, the war won, in less than a week!"

Marshall Valery-Petain, clinging with his French Territorial Army to the handful of coastal holdfasts and revetments that are all that remains of his homeland, is dismissive of the new atomic artillery. He thinks it is over-vaunted. The ultimate weapon has always been, will always be, the man on the ground, the Bloody Infantry.

Giorgio Joyce, respectfully, disagrees with both. "Atomic artillery, massed waves of infantry, both are like a blunt cudgel compared to the sure, swift, untraceable scalpel of Chronokinesis. The ability to change an enemy's history without him ever knowing that you have done so, that is the ultimate weapon."

"Sub Academician Joyce of course, speaks as our first potential Chrononaut," Director Ames says, a pinch-faced, bulbous-headed man with luminous violet eyes, dressed in the uniform of the elite Steel Guard.

A subaltern serves ersatz whisky. James Joyce excuses himself from the table and beckons for his son to follow him outside onto the airdeck. *William and Mary* travels wrapped in thick cloud as a precaution against detection. Father and son walk the steel balcony that runs around the perimeter of the dreadnought; to their left, the curving boron fibre hull, to their right, a dimensionless gray limbo. They pause over an engine housing, whisper under the threshing of the impellors.

"That was reckless," James Joyce says to his son. "To mention the infinite mutability of history in company such as this."

"Militaries? If it doesn't involve attrition rates of over five hundred a minute, I might as well not be speaking."

"Ames is no Military. He may not be an Academician, but Directors, even if they are Steel Guard, have some capacity for speculative thought. If he begins to suspect that it is not just our enemy's history that is mutable and untraceable, but our own also . . . "

Speed unchanged, heading unchanged, altitude unchanged, concealed in its cloud-layer of mystery, *William and Mary* bores on over the slate-cold sea.

(Sleeve notes from the cylinder "The Best and the Rest of James Joyce: Collected Recordings: 1902–1922")

Imagine. I know it's hard. I know it's a thing to which you are not accustomed, you who have parted with your pelve and pence for this cylinder that claims to be the Best and the Rest of a man called James Joyce. I know you are impatient to hear just what James Joyce thinks constitutes his Best and Rest (Old Light Through Old Windows). But try. For one moment, try and imagine the Rest.

Imagine a world where our United Kingdoms and Emirates are not a maternal clutch of three islands off the coasts of Africa and Spain—imagine Home Islands that lie, say, off the North coast of France, imagine a Dal Riada, say, consigned to the cold waters beneath Greenland's southern tip.

Got it now? Try it again. Imagine a world where the cylinder that rests impatiently in your sonogram will never be heard, will never have been, a world where James Joyce is not a musician, where there are no wirelesses, no live bands, no televisions, for the thermionic valve, the transistor, the cathode-ray tube, the microprocessor, have not been invented.

Imagine the world turned upside down, where north is south, and south north, where the twin spires of Africa and South America reach toward the polestar.

Imagine the world turned inside out, an earth that is a bubble of air and light and life in an infinity of dark, lifeless rock, where the moon and stars are a perforated veil of darkness about a sun that is a blazing atom a few hundred miles above our heads.

You have it now. Fun, isn't it?

Imagine a world, imagine worlds, where men, or what pass for men, may step from world to world, possibility to possibility, with the ease that you cross the room to throw the play switch of your sonogram.

Enough? Too much for your imagination? Time now at last to surrender the cylinder to the needle and settle back in the privacy of your headphones. To lay down the Best, to say that better will never be found, is to deny the Rest. But who is to say that the Rest might not be better. You have imagined just a hair's-breadth of the Rest; the possible worlds that are held within the contemplation of God by the exercise of His free will. For the exercise of choice, be that choice human or divine, creates worlds of undoing that might have been had we, or He, chosen otherwise: infinite choices, infinite worlds brought into existence by our lowly, daily acts of ablution, defecation, copulation, mastication. Consider the responsibility. With each step you take to cross the room to fit this cylinder into your sonogram a world may be created, humdrum worlds each a footstep different from ours.

This is the teaching of the Al Afr sect. Let not a footfall go unconsidered.

Got that?

Screw philosophy, let's dance!

James Joyce has a recurring dream. He is alone, quite alone, dressed in a heavy rubber gas and radiation suit, flapping in webbed shoes across the mudscape that extends from Edinburgh to the Caucasus. He stumbles without aim or purpose through tangles of corroded wire hung with rags of rotted fabric, through hulks of guns and tanks and tracked war machines, through the cavernous interiors of land dreadnoughts, once tall and proud as battleships, stogged to the waist in mud; stumbling, through the faintly luminous fog that gathers in the shell craters, ever faster in an effort to keep up with his ludicrous, flapping feet, stop himself from falling, falling, into the mud, until at last his flapping feet catch on a snarl of wire or a chunk of rusted concrete, and he falls. He puts out his hands to save himself, but they plunge up to the elbow into the mire. His gloved fingers feel an embroidered cap badge, a piece of domestic thermoplastic, a porcelain doll's head, a water flask, a military honour, a silver picture frame, a scrap of cloth. Then in the dream his hands are suddenly bare, and the mud between his fingers has a fibrous, grainy texture. He knows then that the gritty graininess is the powdered brick and stone and steel of the great cities of Europe, the stringy fibrousness the rotted bones and blood of 300 million men, gently mixed into mud by the rain that falls upon the battlefield.

He dreams that he hears the voices of those 300 million, and more: the hundreds of millions who once lived in those drowned cities, the men and the women and the children, calling out to him from their dissolution beneath the mud.

James Joyce has never thought of himself as the material from which traitors are made. Born in the 29th year of the war to a prosperous mercantile family in the city that now lies in fused ruins above East Hibernia Holdfast; by education and temperament his inclination lay toward the arts; to literature. In moments of lassitude in his Academician's domicile under Keflavik Holdfast, he imagines himself writing about that city of his birth in such detail that, should the war ever end, it could be reconstructed out of its ruins from his book. By the 41st year of the war the British Empire had already embarked on its transmutation into leaner, fitter, more ruthless Britannia, and James Joyce understood instinctively that there was no place within the new order for navigators of the stream of consciousness. It was an easy decision to become an Academician, a temporal physics specialist. The only other choice available to those born outside the privileged castes was to become another digit of Great Britannia drowning in the mudfields of Saxony. Perhaps that is why he became a traitor, because reshaping history is the only way he knows to rebuild that city in his imagination. It is the only way he knows to apologize to those calling voices beneath the mud.

"This, Dr. Jung, is the dream that afflicts me night after night. Always the same, never varying in the slightest detail, projected with utter clarity and vividness.

"I am a passenger aboard an Alpine railway train, like those that take tourists up the Rigi, or Pilatus. I am in the last carriage of all, which is a glass observation car; glass walls, glass roof. The observation car is quite full; there are passengers from all parts of Europe and the Near East. Most of the women are smoking Turkish cigars. Nora is there too, sipping a frothy white cocktail of a sticky, glabrous consistency through a straw.

"I notice that the mountains through which our train is travelling are peculiarly rounded; strangely smooth and curvaceous for Alpine peaks, and each is surmounted by an erection of some form or another; a small stone cairn, a cross, a gazebo, a revolving restaurant.

"The train arrives at its destination: a tunnel inside a mountain. Everyone but I seems to know where we have arrived. Porters in extremely tight uniforms seize my bags, whirl me along, *this way, Herr J . . . if you please, Herr J . . . no time to lose, Herr J . . .* Everywhere, porters and passengers, rushing. I cannot see Nora. I ask one of the porters where Frau Nora is— strangely, as I ask that question, I know that we have arrived at the hotel.

"The hotel is built on the top of a mountain and all its outside walls are made of glass. Indeed, much of the hotel interior; the ballroom, the dining tables, the grand staircase, the health hydro, are also made of the same clear, smooth glass. The room I have been given overlooks a lake. Paintbox blue, the lake, encircled by the smooth, succulent domes of the mountains. There are pleasure boats and pedalloes abroad on the lake; I ask my porter if they are available for hire. A look of concern crosses his face; no, he says, they should not be out on the lake because of the dolphins. I look through the glass wall and see squadrons of dolphins diving through the blue lake water. The jolly-boats and pleasure-craft make for shore with all haste but a few are too slow, too far from the jetty and are capsized by the leaping dolphins. Their leaps grow higher and bolder, the dolphins are hurling themselves clear from the water twenty, thirty, forty feet. As I watch I realize that all along I have not been in my room at all but in the residents' saloon where the other guests have gathered. A woman with an oversized shoe for a hat cries, 'Look, oh look at the dolphins,' and we all look and see that the dolphins have, in one immense leap, broken free from the water and are soaring into the air. They circle the glass hotel, turning and flashing like silver in the sun, and we notice that they are changing form, elongating, extending into shapes like zeppelins with flukes, fins and beady eyes.

"A voice cries out; *we can do it too, look*; and a woman with a red-tipped Turkish cheroot climbs onto the back of a glass sofa and steps off. She's flying, up round the ceiling, around the chandeliers. The other people in the bar see her and want to join in, one after another they climb up onto the furniture and step off and fly with her around the room. I go with them, it is very easy, all one has to do it climb up on the furniture and step off. But it is taking that one step . . . Nora is the only one still on the ground. She's dressed in a skin-smooth dress of silver fishscales. The windows of the Glass Hotel all burst open and then we go flying out of them, up into the air, with the zeppelin-dolphins, and a great light engulfs us all and I wake up."

Corvettes and gunboats marked with the shield and trident of Britannia escort *William and Mary* to its landing cradle in the Keflavik Holdfast hangar bay. As the concrete blast-doors close over the quarter-mile long shell of the dreadnought, its special passengers are whisked by tubetrain to the Chronokinesis Facility 20 miles distant. The car rattles and sparks along its tunnel. Senior Academician James Joyce explains the theoretical basis of chronokinesis and tachyon physics but his explanations of faster-than-light particles that move backward through time are quite incomprehensible to the militaries. Director Ames alone displays a semblance of intelligent understanding.

"The physics itself was quite straightforward; the problem lay in generating a stream of tachyons at the correct initial velocity so that they would come to rest-velocity and deposit our chrononaut at the correct date," James Joyce is saying as the rail-car arrives at the Chronokinesis Facility Station. Waiting on the dingily lit tiled platform are his fellow Academicians, fellow conspirators. Academician Retief, the historian, leads the party along dripping tiled tunnels into the bowels of the Facility. The corridors throb to a pulse of power.

"Merely the atomic pile that powers the bevatron," Academician Fisk, the Particle Physicist, reassures the mistrustful militaries. "To rotate our chrononaut back to 1917 requires a tachyon flux with a velocity in excess of 30,000 C."

"What is the significance of 1917?" asks Air Lord Blennerhasset.

"The year in question was a time of unparalleled success for the then Grand Alliance and of uncharacteristic weakness in the Tsarist Empire," Academician Retief says, his voice barely audible over the rising swell of power. "Indeed, our sources reveal that the Empire was close to collapse. A revolutionary group, the Bolshevists, subscribers to the political philosophies of Marx and Engels, sought to overthrow the Imperial family and establish a proletarian state. Large sections of manufacturing and the armed forces had been infiltrated, indeed, the army was on the verge of widescale mutiny. That they did not succeed is due entirely to the assassination by an Imperial agent of their charismatic leader, Vladimir Ilyich Lenin. Leaderless, the Bolshevists were rapidly purged and eliminated by the Imperial security police."

At the entrance to the antechamber of the Chronokinesis Unit, Giorgio Joyce leaves the party. His father bids him farewell, clasps his son's hands within his own. He would shed tears, but Britannia does not believe in tears. For once he is gone, he is gone forever. The technology that might bring him back will never have been created. All that can be seen of the chronokinesis chamber from the anteroom is an open airlock door. The militaries seem disappointed. Doubtless they had expected yawning chasms filled with manmade lightning, stupendous devices crackling with power, searing beams of energy. Only Ames seems to appreciate the significance of what lies beyond the airlock door.

"Your belief is that if you can prevent the assassination of this Vladimir Ilyich Lenin, the Tsarist Empire would crumble under Bolshevist assault, and be forced to sue for peace," he says, nodding slowly, slyly, like one chess master in appreciation of another's skills. "In effect, the war would have been won 37 years ago."

The militaries in their ludicrous uniforms are dumbfounded. "Except that is not the truth," says an unexpected voice from the door into the antechamber. Giorgio Joyce has entered the room. He is dressed in a red pressure suit but has left off the helmet. "Is it, Academician Retief? No, the plan is to send a man much further into the past than 37 years. Is that not so, Academician? In fact, to send him one hundred and one years into the past, to the Crimean Incident that was the root of the War. In fact, his intention, the intention of all the Academicians gathered here, is to end the War before it ever began, to re-shape history so that there is neither victor nor vanquished, indeed, that neither the Tsarist Empire nor Britannia came into existence." From inside the pressure suit Giorgio Joyce draws a heavy revolver.

"Why so horrified, Father? Are you not proud that your son is a loyal and dutiful citizen of Britannia, ever vigilant to root out disloyalty and treachery wherever it may be found? Including the treasonable behaviour of certain members of the Keflavik Chronokinesis faculty. And you invited me, pleaded with me, begged me to be your chrononaut!" His wire-framed spectacles glitter with reflected fluorescents.

"The Chronokinesis Project is cancelled as a threat to the security of Britannia!" screams Director Ames. A thin rope of creamy drool has leaked from the corner of his mouth. "The facility will be dismantled and its staff disbanded. All Academicians here present are under arrest. Air Lord Blennerhasset, you are ordered by the Directorate to proceed forthwith on plans for the wholesale atomic bombardment of the Tsarist Holdfasts!"

And the blighted, poisoned mud that has been piling up night upon night, year upon year behind James Joyce's eyes pours out of his skull in a drown-wave that will entomb the whole world. Militaries, Director Ames, fellow Academicians, his own son, stand immobilized and mired in mud as, with a speed no one would think credible in a man of 72 years, he darts past the gun in his son's hand to squeeze through the airlock door and slam it behind him. Wheels spin, dogs engage.

Bullets carome outside but James Joyce knows to within a fraction of an inch the tolerances to which this door was manufactured. Of the tolerances of his own body, how long it can survive unprotected in vacuum, what level of radiation it can withstand, he is less certain. He rests the heel of his left hand on the "Airlock Cycle" button. The steel chamber shudders to the power of the bevatron smashing fundamental particles into the wave of tachyons that will sweep him into the past. Visions swim, before his eyes: tachyon ghosts of other times, other possibilities. The gulf of the years yawns before him and he sees that it is deeper than any of his colleagues had ever guessed, not one hundred and one years deep, but deep as all time. At the bottom of the chasm is the earth, still unformed, fresh and molten from the forge, shifting, restless, waiting the hammerblow that will give it solidity and definition. That event, he understands, may be as small as the touch of a single footprint upon it. All time, and all space, are his to mould. The world can be any shape he wishes it to be. Infinite alternative geographies.

"So be it," he says. He fills his lungs, clamps lips shut, pinches his nose with his fingers. He closes his eyes. His left hand slams the button and in a blast of decompression James Joyce is hurled into the tachyon flux. And swept away.

It seems clear to me that Herr J.'s dreams are not the projections of seductive alien intelligences, but rather products of the *angst* of losing Nora B. to younger, fitter, sexually attractive rivals. His doubts over his own fidelity after the affair with Martha Fleischmann, coupled with his peculiarly Irish sense of religious guilt, are transferred onto Nora B.; that recurring dream of his, so ripe with phallic, vaginal and mammary symbolism, is so clearly a sublimation of his fears of failing sexual potency.

Treatment in such cases of low self-esteem I have found to be straightforward and successful. I was eager for Herr J. to begin therapy immediately but my telephone calls to his apartment went unanswered, my telegrams unacknowledged and when finally I called in person at his apartment on

Strehlgasse I was informed by the *concièrge* that Herr J. had not been home for the past three days.

Thank God for whatever whim it was, conscious or otherwise, that moved me to return to my office via the lakefront. The crowd, always in evidence, was extraordinarily dense this day. The trams could hardly pass for the press of people; they were packed onto the none-too-safe balconies of the lakefront buildings; the most foolhardy elements had climbed lamp-posts and tramhalts. Around the pleasure-boat jetties, where the crowd was thickest, the general hubbub rose to a clamour. Patrons of the Burkliplatz Café were standing on the table-tops, craning to see. I asked a waiter the cause of the frenzy.

"Have you not heard, sir? They are leaving us."

In that same moment I saw, in a moment of preternatural revelation, the face of Herr J. close by in the crowd at the jetties; his thick, wire-framed spectacles dazzling in the sun. I went to him. Together, we were swept onto a steam side-wheeler already packed to the plimsoll line with babbling passengers.

"Herr J.!" I cried over the din of excited passengers. "What are you doing here?"

He did not seem the least surprised to find me at his side. "The Rapture, Doctor. Is come," he said, strangely distracted. "And the dream. The testing thereof."

He passed me a pair of field-glasses. As I focused them upon the shivering curtain of the Enclave, he continued: "See, Doctor? The Companion Bodies, that we liken to airborne trees, or deep-sea medusae; they are absent. Disappeared. Gone ahead to who knows what unimaginable other Zurich to prepare the way." I did notice that the Travellers seemed to have assumed a definite arrow-head shape, striped and mottled with many colours.

The pleasure boat had joined the great fleet of craft major and minor that had assembled to witness the Rapture. Virtually anything that would float had been pressed into service: punts, motor launches, horribly overloaded sailing dinghies, clusters of pedalloes roped together, sections of pontoon. The paddle steamer's steam horns warned the lumbering, over-burdened small craft away from our bows. The density of the lake traffic grew as we approached the lowest point of the globular Enclave. Herr J. was almost beside himself, leaning perilously over the rails. Every eye, every lens, was directed on the sky. There at the centre was a curious, almost reverent hush.

"Now we shall see, Herr Doctor," he whispered. While every eye was fixed on the sky, in a trice he had stripped himself of his outer garments and climbed onto the rail as if to dive into the water.

"No, no, don't you understand, man?" I implored. "It is impossible, quite impossible. The dream, your dream of the Glass Hotel, is not to do with the Travellers but of your own fear of losing Nora to the attractions of a younger, more virile man. It is the dream of the fear of your own inadequacy, Herr J."

"Such convenient answers, Dr Jung," Herr J. said. "But perhaps in this dream the hidden meaning is that there is no hidden meaning. This time everything is exactly what it seems to be."

With those words he dived into the cold waters of Lake Zurich. Murmurs of surprise came from the spectators around me, in an instant changed into a sigh of amazement. I looked back to the sky, and saw the ending. The interior of the bubble of gravitylessness ran with rainbow-coloured light, like the sheen of oil on water. Strong beyond his years, Herr J. cut on through the waters. Some others, seeing and comprehending, tried to follow him, threw themselves from the upper decks. The Enclave began to spin. Like clay on a potter's wheel it elongated into a funnel of light within which the Travellers moved, its lower end reaching closer, closer to the surface of the lake, whipping up the water to spray and foam. I shouted a warning to Herr J. but I was one voice among a multitude. The waves and spume broke over him, the whirling wall of light engulfed him. A dark tear appeared in the radiance, a rent of infinite darkness. Through the rent I glimpsed the Travellers' destination. As if looking down from a great height, the outline of the Black Sea and the suspended pendulum of the Crimean peninsula. The Travellers launched themselves into the tear and were consumed. In the same instant the Enclave burst with a tremendous thunderclap of air.

Clouds sailed serene and uninterrupted over Lake Zurich.

Of Herr J. there was no sign whatsoever. And no sign was ever found, though the Lake was several times dragged at Frau Nora B's insistence by the city police.

The optimist in me likes to believe that he was indeed taken when the Travellers transited between universes, dragged along in the metaphysical slipstream, that even now, as I write these casenotes, he is finding a foothold in whatever version of our world it is we glimpsed through the tear in reality. But what I cannot reconcile is why he did it. What was it that made him trust his dreams and embark on such a mad scheme? All I can offer is that I, like Herr J., am a man in his late middle years, and men of our age have always needed some notion of heaven.

(**From an interview in** *WorldWeek* **Magazine: 26th July 1930, conducted with James Joyce at his home in the hills above Tangier by Gwynnedd Suarez.**)

We're sitting here on a patio by the pool-side, it's 86°, your valet has just served us mint tea, below us are the Straits of Hercules; an idyllic setting: it's six years since your last cylinder "Finnegan's Wake"; do you now consider yourself to be in retirement?

I would say rather a man taking time over his life. Certainly not retired. God forfend. I may well cut more cylinders. Certainly I've at least three more works in varying degrees of potentiality in me. But it's a question of timing.

Do you feel you want to distance yourself from the general bafflement that greeted "Finnegan's Wake"?

No. Not at all. I had complete faith in *Finnegan's Wake* as it was released. So did the producers and the record company. I still have. They still have.

But it was a radical departure from your previous recordings.

Every recording I have ever made has been a conscious attempt to be a radical departure from its predecessors. To limit yourself to one mode, one style, one way of doing it so that people can say, aha, yes, this is Jimmy Joyce, this is what we like, let's have the same again only more so; it's death to music, and worse, death to the soul. Whoever put music in the hand of the market researchers and public relations people deserves a particular kind of personal hell. I want to push hard at the limits of what can and can't be done within as tightly defined a genre as popular music. I want to explore the . . . the potential for mutability, for other ways of doing it, within the genre constraints.

Hence the preoccupation with free will and alternate worlds on the jacket for the "Best and Rest." I gather you weren't happy about that cylinder's release.

I wasn't. I'm still not. To a certain extent, I am not totally happy with any of my recordings because they limit the music to one thing and one thing only, and not a set of potential things at different times thematically linked together.

Those notes were written at a time when you were becoming involved with the Al Afr sect: between the "Best and the Rest" and "Finnegan's Wake" was a period of several years when you studied under the Sidi Hussein, and the influence of Al Afr belief was evident in that cylinder. Yet here you are in your comfortable, might I even call it luxurious?, home contemplating new recordings: are the Al Afr years a period of your life you consider conclusively behind you?

By no means. Faith is not something you can step out of like a pair of shoes. I have no regrets about the years I spent with Sidi Hussein at the University of Fez. So, I wasn't touring, I didn't cut a cylinder until *Wake*, but I don't consider the time was unproductive. No time spent in the company of remarkable men is ever wasted. With the Al Afr I experienced things that have reshaped my life.

Could you expand on that?

There is a sense in which religious experience, any transcendant experience, is essentially uncommunicable. But I'll try. One of the tenets of Al Afr belief is that, as a consequence of his free will, God creates, has created, will create alternate worlds, alternate universes, alternate humanities parallel to yet separated from our own. In the Al Afr whirling trance, I experienced a . . . crossing, no, nothing so precise as that, a *leakage*, across the God-barrier between those other worlds. It's hard to explain properly. There are creatures there, in between the universes. I can't explain them, they are incomprehensible to us, yet they are as human as you or I. But they have felt the touch of our presence and responded. They are coming to us, searching across thousands upon thousands of possible universes to find us and join us. The reason I left the order was to try to explain that experience; that attempt was *Finnegan's Wake*, and, to use your own quote, it was, at best, misunderstood.

But you still sympathize with Al Afr belief?

As I said, you don't step out of faith. At the moment, I am trying to establish retreat and study centres in the Home Islands for, well, anyone really, who needs time and space to re-evaluate their lives and places in this world. Prepare themselves for the coming of these travellers. Because they most assuredly are on their way. These are the days of miracle and wonder, but we are human and can only bear so much miracle and wonder at once.

And plans for the musical future?

Well, as I intimated, I have ideas for a new collection; I'm going to take a few months off and travel through Sub-Saharan Afrika and learn the musical language of the people there. There's a tremendous, vital, musical heritage down there almost totally unexplored which deserves world attention. After that, my plans are less formalized. Maybe go back to pure, plain *sarif*, just a backing group and a musik club. It has a certain righteous appeal.

So you still stand by the motto you used on the sleeve notes for "Best and Rest"?

Screw philosophy, let's dance? Well, I'm 48, and that's an entire geological age in popular music, but I think it's a pretty good motto, yes, I do, yes.

NAMING THE FLOWERS

Kate Wilhelm

Kate Wilhelm began publishing in 1956, and by now is widely regarded as one of the best of today's writers—outside the genre as well as in it. Her work has never been limited to the strick boundaries of the field, and she has published mysteries, mainstream thrillers, and comic novels as well as science fiction. Wilhelm won a Nebula Award in 1968 for her short story "The Planners," won a Hugo in 1976 for her well-known novel *Where Late the Sweet Birds Sang*, added another Nebula to her collection in 1987 with a win for her story "The Girl Who Fell Into the Sky," and won yet another Nebula the following year for her story "Forever Yours, Anna," which was in our Fifth Annual Collection. Her story "And the Angels Sing" was in our Ninth Annual Collection. Her many books include the novels *Margaret and I, Fault Lines, The Clewiston Test, Juniper Time, Welcome, Chaos, Oh, Susannah!, Huysman's Pets, Cambio Bay, Death Qualified*, and the Constance Leidl–Charlie Meiklejohn mystery novels *The Hamlet Trap, Smart House, Seven Kinds of Death, Sweet, Sweet Poison*, and as well as the story collections *The Downstairs Room, Somerset Dreams, The Infinity Box, Listen, Listen, Children of the Wind*, and *And the Angels Sing*. Her most recent book is a new mystery novel, *Justice for Some*. Wilhelm and her husband, writer Damon Knight, ran the Milford Writer's Conference for many years, and both are still deeply involved in the operation of the Clarion workshop for new writers. She lives with her family in Eugene, Oregon, and is currently at work on *The Best Defense*, a sequel to *Death Qualified*.

Late in September I told the crew at Phoenix Publishing Company that I had had it, I was taking off, I might never be heard from again and for them not to send the cops out looking for me. Gracie Blanchard, my secretary, laughed and said, "Oh. Win. Go on." Then she asked how many cameras I was taking, and Phil Delacourt, the general manager, said he had been practicing my signature until he could forge it on anything that came in. But if I was heading north, he added, he could whip out a list of people I probably should see about this and that. I told him what to do with his list.

We had finished a big catalogue job, and the Christmas catalogues were long gone; the pharmaceuticals were on schedule, even ahead of schedule, and I was tired. And bored. When I started Phoenix seven years ago, it was exciting, but over the past few years it had turned into deadlines, messed up print runs, back orders of paper that never arrived, photographs that were out of focus. . . . The usual fuckups, people told me, the same people who told me seven years ago that I couldn't publish out of Atlanta; all the talent was in New York.

I had no real plans, no itinerary; I simply knew I wanted to be in New England when the foliage was at its best. I would call in now and then, I said to Gracie; keep the fires banked. I took off in my twelve-year-old Thunderbird with a suitcase, hiking gear, half a dozen books, and four cameras. I didn't tell Gracie about the cameras; I didn't want to see her dimply, knowing smile. Gracie's cute and twenty-five years old. It had alarmed me the day I realized that she seemed terribly young. I was thirty-eight.

I drove along the blue ridges of the Appalachians, and spent a couple of days hiking, but it was too early. The trees would be better on my return trip. I cut over to the coast and paid a call on Atlantic City. I hadn't been there for years and I didn't want to linger this time, I was just curious about how much it had changed, but I made the mistake of arriving on Sunday and when I was ready to leave, so were a million others. I checked into a hotel instead, and then walked along the beach where it seemed that more than a million kids were playing, enjoying Indian summer. One of them, a little girl, began to walk at my side. I looked at her uneasily, and then looked around for a mother, father, someone.

"Can I have an ice cream?" the child asked. We had drawn near a vendor.

"Where's your mommy?" I asked the kid, as I fished out a dollar. She shrugged and gestured toward the casinos. I bought her an ice cream stick, and she walked with me for a few more yards, and then smiled and darted away. I walked faster. A man just doesn't buy ice cream for strange little girls, I was thinking, not if he wants to stay out of trouble. Then I noticed one of the bridges and thought how fine it would look in the early morning sunlight.

The next morning I returned with my old Leica and sat on a wall waiting for the light. The same little girl appeared and held up her hands for me to hoist her up to the wall.

"Honey," I said, after she was settled, "didn't your mom tell you not to talk to strangers?" She giggled. It was a cool morning, too cool for her lightweight sweater which was too big and too loose on her, and she was too big not to know better than to pick up men and be this trusting with them. I scanned the beach looking for a distraught mother, and saw only a couple of kids playing, a few people strolling, a jogger. I stood up. "I've got to go now," I said. She held out her arms for me to help her down; I lifted her and set her on the sand. I should take her to the police, I was thinking, turn her in, a lost child. Then, to my relief, a group of women appeared, heading our way, and she began to run toward them. The idea of the bridge in sunlight was dead; the light had come and gone again. I left, and that afternoon I was wandering around Gettysburg.

In the car, meandering northward, I played Bach fugues and Sibelius and did not turn on the radio; in the motels I read Fuente or García Márquez or Don DeLillo, or a biography of Mann, and did not turn on the television.

On Wednesday night, near Middletown, New York, when I got back to the motel after dinner, a man was waiting for me, lounging against a black Ford. He straightened as I approached.

"Mr. Seton? Winston Seton?"

Not a mugger, I thought; they don't name the victim first. I nodded.

"May I have a few words with you? I'm Jeremy Kersh, FBI."

He flicked open his I.D. and I wondered which had come first, the many TV agents flicking open the same kind of I.D., or the event itself. I shrugged and opened my door, and he followed me inside.

He had a round, soft-looking face, too pink and smooth, as if he had to shave every third day if that often, and the kind of build that puts more bulk below the waist than above it, but I suspected he was not as soft as he looked. I motioned him to a chair, and crossed in front of him to get to the low dressing table where I had a bucket of ice cubes and a bottle of bourbon. He drew in his legs to let me pass. It was the kind of motel that had two chairs, a tiny round table with a hanging lamp that you brained yourself on frequently, a king-size bed, and a dresser with a big mirror.

"What can I do for you, Mr. Kersh?" I asked, taking the shrink wrap off a glass. "Drink?" I eyed the bottle and hoped he would say no; after six days there wasn't much left. He said no, and I poured myself bourbon, added ice cubes, and edged past him to sit on the side of the bed. He sat with his legs apart, his hands on his knees, leaning forward. He looked uncomfortable.

"You've been following the story about the crash of the Milliken Lear jet, I suppose," he said. I shook my head, and for a moment he appeared confused, as if his game plan had been scrapped without warning. "You know who Joe Milliken is, don't you?" he asked then.

Every kid knew about Bluebeard, Beauty and the Beast, Jack the Giant Killer, the Hope diamond, the Milliken millions . . . I nodded.

"Okay, Mr. Seton. As soon as you open a news magazine, or turn on the television, or see a paper, you'll get some version of the story. I'll give you ours. Two years ago Milliken's daughter and her baby vanished, and Milliken said it was a kidnapping. Brought us in. We haven't come up with mother or child in all this time, and the case is as open as the Montana sky as far as we're concerned."

I held up my hand as memory of the event seeped into consciousness. "I read that the mother took her child and left of her own accord."

"You could have read a lot of things," Kersh said with a shrug. "He, the old man, says they were kidnapped. There's been no note, no ransom demand, nothing. Even so, it's on the books, unsolved. To complicate things, when mother and child vanished, so did all their hospital records, the child's prints, blood type, everything. Okay. Two weeks ago Mr. Milliken got a phone call, a woman said she had his granddaughter, and that she had sent him a picture that should arrive any minute now. She said she would call back, and hung up. He called our office in Houston, and our men were there when the picture arrived, a Polaroid of a kid with brown eyes and light hair. Like a million other kids. But also like his daughter at that age. He said it was her, his granddaughter. End of argument."

Kersh sighed; he looked tired, as if the past two weeks had been tough. "I'll cut it short," he said then. "Milliken and the woman struck a deal. She would deliver the kid to him in Houston, no one else, and he called us off, just like that. They planned for her to bring the kid to him in one of his Lear jets. His pilot told him they'd had trouble with the electrical system and he blew up. He wanted that kid in that plane and on her way to Houston right now. So a week ago last night we stood with our thumbs in our mouths and watched a woman and a man take a little girl aboard the Milliken plane in Philadelphia. We had planes in the area and planned to track them every inch of the way, be there when that jet landed. But half an hour out of Philadelphia the pilot got on the radio; he said something was wrong with the electrical system, and then silence. It went down."

Kersh had left his chair restlessly; he looked like a man who wanted to stamp around and found it frustrating that there wasn't enough room. I thought he wanted a drink, but didn't make the offer a second time. He glanced inside the bathroom, the tiny dressing area, and came back to stand at the foot of the bed with his hands deep in his pockets.

"We recovered the bodies of three women, two attendants and the other woman, and three men, pilot, copilot, the man who boarded with the woman and child. No kid," he said, scowling. "We had people there within minutes, the whole area was being covered within half an hour or so, but no kid." His eyes had appeared unfocused, now he turned his attention to me. "And you haven't seen it on the news, read about it?"

I shook my head. "What do you want with me, Mr. Kersh?" I asked patiently. "It's an interesting story, and I'll catch up with it in the papers any day now. Why are you here?"

"We want to enlist your help," he said; his attitude, that had suggested nothing more than fatigue a second ago, had become harder, not menacing, but not yielding either.

I wondered if other agents were out in the parking lot, if a chase car was nearby. I had to laugh to myself at the full-blown scenario that had come to mind. I sipped my drink and waited.

"We think you talked with the child at least twice in Atlantic City," Kersh said. "We want you to return and hang around for a few days, see if she approaches you again."

Now I got up, but since he was blocking the only moving-around space there was, I sat down again. "You've got to be kidding," I said after a moment. "If she's there, pick her up, get an identification, be done with it." Then I remembered the little girl who had mooched ice cream, but the memory only made my temper flare. "You've been watching me? For God's sake, why?"

"Only since Monday," he said tiredly, not at all placating me, merely explaining. "Sunday, a local police officer thought he saw the child. We had an APB out, naturally. Anyway, he thought maybe it was her, but she told him she was waiting for her daddy, and she ran to you and you bought her an ice cream. He forgot the whole thing. The next morning, he saw the two of you again, on a seawall or something, and felt that he had been right to put it out of mind. Then he saw you driving off alone—seems you have a noticeable car—and for the first time, he got suspicious enough to do a followup. We checked the license number and came up with you. For all we knew you had the kid stashed away back with your gear, so . . . "

I stared at him. "I don't get it, Kersh. You know where that kid is, go get her. But the kid I saw isn't the one you're looking for. She's too old, four, or close to it. You're looking for what, a two-year-old?"

Kersh scowled more fiercely than ever. "I've got a tape recorder out in the car. I'd like you to make a statement, how you came to see the child, what she was wearing, what she said. Will you do that?"

"Sure," I said. "But, Kersh, she's the wrong child."

He started for the door. "Then you'll be out of it, won't you? Right back."

It was after ten and I was tired and sleepy. I had been in bed by ten every night and up before six every morning since my trek started. I yawned, but the Milliken story intruded and I remembered more of it now. Soap opera stuff. Daddy had been a brute. Poor little rich girl married someone unsuitable, a tennis player, jockey, grounds keeper, someone like that. It didn't matter who he had been, he had not lived long enough to see his child born. A fatal accident of some sort. I couldn't remember the details. Then, when her baby was a few weeks old, the Milliken daughter vanished with the child, and no one had seen them since as far as I knew. And that meant the child was only about two now. The reward must have climbed up to a million, I remembered, and tried to shrink the kid I had seen down to the right size. I couldn't; the wrong kid. I yawned again.

Kersh returned with a space-age tape recorder, all silver and black. "What we'd like, Mr. Seton, is for you to begin by stating your name and the date, to the best of your recollection, that you saw that little girl, and then just tell about it in your own words."

"You know the date better than I do."

"Probably, but we want it for the record. Ready?"

It didn't take very long; there was little to tell, after all. When I finished, Kersh asked, "Mr. Seton, will you help us find that child again?"

"No," I said firmly. "I'm on vacation. I don't know any way I could be of help."

"She trusted you," he said. "She came to you a second time without fear. We think she might approach you again."

I simply stared at him in disbelief.

Kersh sat there for a moment, then he said thoughtfully, "I wonder what you want, Mr. Seton."

"Aren't you going to turn that off?"

He did something to the tape recorder, possibly even turned it off, but I wasn't particularly interested. I watched him.

"We know that everyone wants something," he went on, still meditative.

"We want your help, of course. But what do you want? Could we appeal to your sense of chivalry? Your sense of justice? An annual income, tax free? Business thrown your way?"

"I want you to get your butt out of here so I can go to bed." When he didn't move, I stood up, put my glass down on the bedside table, and started to unbutton my shirt. "Listen to me, Kersh. That kid I saw is not, repeat not, the Milliken girl. She's too old. She showed no sign of being a kidnappee. I've told you all I can about her, and I don't want to be involved in any scheme you're working. Now, I'm going to bed, and you can sit there all night for all I care."

He stood up, smiling slightly. The smile took ten years off his apparent age; he could have been a teacher in a junior college, pleased with his students, pleased with life.

He went to the door and then said, "I wonder why, when you finally caught up with Steve Falco and your wife, you didn't beat the shit out of him. When I know the answer to that I'll know how to get your cooperation, Mr. Seton. Good night."

When I knew the answer to that, I thought, I'd know the answer to the riddle of the universe. I poured another drink and sat in the chair Kersh had vacated. It was very warm. Twelve years ago my grandfather died and left me a small fortune and his house in Atlanta. I moved to New York, married a model, Susan Lorenza, started a photography, graphic arts business with Steve Falco, and bought the Thunderbird. Batting average way down, three strikeouts, one home run. Three years later, Susan and Steve had cleaned me out, and headed west. I still had the house in Atlanta—they hadn't known that it was a very fine house—and I still had the Thunderbird. I got drunk and stayed drunk for a long time, two years' worth of drunk, and then I went looking for them, and finally found them in Los Angeles.

Susan was still beautiful, but with a Hollywood gloss that was new, and breasts that were also new. She was wearing a yellow sweater that showed them off admirably. "I had to do it," she had said. "I had to try to make it on my own." Her voice was new, also: voice-lessons new; she had learned how to put a little throb in it. The detective I had hired had reported that she was doing porn movies; I hadn't believed him. Now I did. Steve Falco was exactly the same, shorter than me by several inches, black hair, dark restless eyes. He snapped his fingers a lot, I remembered, and he was snapping them that day. "We'll make it up to you, kid," he said. "We always said we'd make it up to you, soon as we got the breaks." They were in a shabby little stucco house with plastic furniture. I took a step toward them, huddled together by the sofa, and Susan screamed, "Don't hit him! Winnie, please. Let me explain." Steve had cut in, "Star quality, that's what she has, wasted. I'll turn her into the biggest—"

For two years I had lived with a pit inside me that was filled with red hot coals, and suddenly that day, looking at Susan's new breasts, I felt as if the pit had sealed itself off, the coals were gone, and there was only a hollow place there. I turned and walked out, patted the T-bird, got in it, and drove to Atlanta where I mortgaged the house and started Phoenix Publishing Company.

And I still didn't know why I hadn't beat the shit out of him. It had something to do with the plastic furniture, I thought, pouring the last of the bourbon with regret. Plastic furniture, plastic breasts. That had something to do with it, but I couldn't sort it out more than that.

I remembered the day I called the Atlanta tenants and asked permission to inspect the house. I hadn't seen it for fifteen years. It had been beautifully maintained, with sparkling white woodwork, gleaming oak floors, and fine furniture. Camellias and azaleas were in bloom out front, and sunlight poured into the spacious rooms like a healing balm. I stood in the wide foyer reassuring the tenants that I had no plans to force them to move, and I was overwhelmed by shame.

When the tenants left two years later, I moved in.

I turned off the lights in my motel room and sat propped up in bed, not ready to sleep, but not willing to let Kersh know his visit was keeping me awake. He had tried to stir up the ashes, bring something to life that had died a long time ago, until now even the ashes were gone, no embers remained, only a hollow space, and all the poking and prodding he could manage would be as futile as shaking a stick in a vacuum. But he had tried. That was the salient point. He had tried. And I didn't know why.

He had tried to arouse what? My anger, frustration, my desire for revenge, retribution, the feeling of betrayal that had colored all the rest? Any of the above, all of the above? Or simply my curiosity? I grimaced in the semidarkness. He had done that. I couldn't even guess how many work hours, how many dollars had gone into the background check they had done on me in just a few days. Why?

I eased myself down into the bed properly and stretched. If they were after the Milliken kid, I thought then, this was a false trail, and Kersh must know it. The child I had talked to was simply too old. I didn't know a lot about children, but two-year-olds were still infants, still in diapers mostly, still doing baby things, and the little girl I had bought ice cream for was well out of that. She was already a little person, not a baby. Not particularly pretty, or even cute that I could recall, but, in fact, I could recall little about her physically. Just a kid with brown eyes and blonde hair tangling in the ocean breeze.

But what if they were simply using the Milliken kidnapping as a cover to get to this other kid, I thought then, and came wide awake again. Slowly I shook my head. I didn't believe that. What could be bigger than Milliken's millions, his influential friends, the power he wielded?

I checked out of the motel early, and when I pulled into the parking lot of a restaurant half a mile away, the black Ford pulled in beside me.

"That's a sweetheart of a car," Kersh said admiringly. He trailed his hand over the silver hood. The car was dirty, but class showed, dirt and all.

"Who's your supervisor, Kersh?" I asked, walking toward the entrance of the restaurant. He told me and I went to a pay phone near the door and dialed information, then the FBI number in Washington, and when I got through to them, I asked for his supervisor. When I entered the restaurant itself a few minutes later, Kersh waved me to a booth. There was a pot of coffee on the table, service for two. Only a few other people were eating at this early hour.

"We hoped you'd think of checking," he said. "Thought you might, but if you hadn't I was going to suggest it. I'm having pancakes with blackberry jam. Sounds pretty good, doesn't it?"

I poured coffee, seething. Assistant to the Director Leland Murchison had been expecting my call, he hoped I would cooperate, of the utmost importance, debt of gratitude, national interest. . . . He had had a list of buzz words at hand and used them all. And told me absolutely nothing.

The waitress came to take our orders and when she had left again, I said, "Now what, Mr. Kersh? You tried reason, and hinted of bribery. Today do we advance to threats? IRS audits, red tape of one sort or another?"

He laughed. It was disconcerting to see. Scowling, or even simply neutral he was like an actor trying to portray the stern FBI agent, but smiling he could be the guy next door, the good buddy with a six-pack and a brand-new joke.

"No, Mr. Seton," he said then. "Audits take too long, for one thing. And we want your help now. Today. What we decided to do is tell you the whole story."

Now I laughed.

His expression became rueful. He opened the briefcase on the seat beside him and brought out a sheaf of papers clipped together. "You know how I asked you to start your statement, name and date when you saw the kid. We've done them all the same way. These are preliminary statements, like yours; the questions and answers get a bit bulky, I'm afraid. This should be enough for now." He slid the papers across the table. "Just read through them," he said, and poured more coffee for both of us.

I nudged the papers to the side and he looked at me with a glint in his eyes that I hadn't seen before.

"Read them," he said softly, "or I'll ram my little black Ford into that big silver baby of yours."

I started to read the papers:

Ruth Hazeltine, Feb. 16

I've been a pediatrics nurse for fourteen years, always the graveyard shift. I like it, and now I'm so used to it, it just feels natural. It gave me the chance to be with my own kids in the evenings, when they needed me most, and I could sleep in the mornings when they were at school. It worked out fine. I was on that night. It was during that bad snow storm and we were shorthanded. Gloria Strumm got snowed in, and couldn't make it, but it was a quiet night and Vanessa and I were managing okay. There were nine babies, not counting the preemies, who are in a separate wing so we didn't have to deal with them. It used to be that once you got the moms tucked in for the night, that was it, but we went to feeding on demand ten years ago, and sometimes one of the babies is in with his mom two, three times a night. The Hilyard baby was one of them. While they're in with their moms we straighten up the cribs, change the sheets if they need it, just tidy up a bit, and I had done that to his crib, had it all ready for him. I wasn't gone more than three minutes. Walked down the hall to Hilyard's room, collected the baby, said a word or two to the mother, and went back, and she, this little baby girl, was in his crib. No diaper, no bracelet, nothing, and sound asleep. I put the Hilyard baby down in a different crib and examined the girl baby; not a mark on her, good professional job with the cord, nice and warm. Born within the past three hours was how she looked to me. Around seven pounds, just a normal little baby girl. I covered her up and went out to get Vanessa. We called Dr. Weybridge, and he called Security. I didn't see anyone bring the baby in, didn't see anyone come on the floor after midnight. Just me and Vanessa.

Silently I went on to the next statement:

Vanessa Goldstein, Feb. 16.
  Nobody passed the nurses' station! I swear it. No one was up there but Ruth and me. Dr. Weybridge examined the baby and said for us to follow the standard routine, and we did. I put the drops in her eyes and the lab sent up Sandra Lewis to draw blood. We printed her and got a diaper and gown on her. I put the Baby Doe bracelet on her, started her chart. She was eight pounds, one half ounces, twenty inches long. Normal reflexes.

I glanced at Kersh in annoyance, but he seemed fascinated by swirls in his coffee cup or something. I picked up the next paper:

Jane Torrance, M.D., Feb. 17.
  Dr. Weybridge simply made a mistake, that's all. And the nurses were overworked and shorthanded, as they said. I examined Baby Doe at eight-thirty in the morning and found an infant who was at least ten days old. She was alert and active, her eyes were tracking well. Her cord had dropped off and the navel was healed.

Feeling exasperated, put upon, ignored by Kersh who was still absorbed by the contents of his coffee cup, I continued to read:

Lilian Tully, March 12.
I took her in. There was all that publicity, people lining up
wanting to adopt her, you know. But you can't just farm off a kid
like a sack of potatoes or something. There's channels. I run a
foster house for kids, specialty is newborns, and I was next on the
list, so I got her. And lie! Boy, did they lie! I don't know what
they're trying to pull, them social workers, but if that kid was a
newborn, then so'm I. I mean she already had teeth. Anyways,
there she was and at first I thought I'd just go with it, keep her,
start her education. You gotta start them young learning about
rules and proper procedures. I teach them, and when they go on
their way, they know a thing or two about discipline and
obedience. Start them young and they stay straight, believe you
me. Little kids need schedules, they need routines, but that one!
Contrary from the day I laid eyes on her. You don't have to spank
them or hit them, there's other ways to get their attention, but
when I started to pinch her ear a little, to make her stop bawling
for food off schedule, she bit me. A real devil she was. Sitting up
in her bed, watching me like a witch. I couldn't keep restraints on
her for beans. Sometimes you have to do that, keep them still for a
little bit. Not her. Oh, I called them and told them to come get
the little devil. Put her in a kennel or something. I didn't want
nothing more to do with the likes of her. I told them to check their
records. I specialize in newborns, I told them.

I turned to the first page and checked the date there, and the date that was
on the statement I had just read. Kersh was watching me with a blank
expression, as if he had fallen asleep with his eyes open.

Marilyn Schlecter, August 20.
I don't know how it happened! We're trying to keep up with
more than two hundred cases, and we don't have enough people,
or facilities. We don't even have a proper working computer. It
eats records, erases information, misfiles things. It just happened.
Her records got mislaid, misfiled. I don't know what happened to
them. I don't even know how many different case workers handled
her, none of them comparing notes, and some of them even
renamed her. She obviously was not a six-month-old baby; she was
a toddler, eighteen months to two years old. She was taken out to
temporary homes two or three times until we could place her, and
those records are a mess, different names, ages. But our supervisor
had left and people were trying to fill in. No one can blame them
for what happened. If we had more people and some office
help. . . . Somehow she got in our books as Mary Jo Goodman
and she was sent to Winona Forbush under that name. I don't
know how it happened. But when they tried to get an

identification for this other little girl, she turned out to be Mary Jo. I called Forbush and explained that a mistake had been made and arranged to collect the child the following day, but when I went out to pick her up, the house was empty. That's all I know. I just know she isn't Mary Jo Goodman. I don't know where she is, or who she is. And yes, I'm crying. And I'll keep crying.

I was reading more slowly, bewilderment and anger in about equal amounts my reaction to the stuff in the statements.

Max Godel, September, near the end of the month.
I'm sittin' there in Sylvie's trailer, you know, reading the want ads. Nothing for me. Never's nothing, but what the hell, I look. And the phone rings and it's Marsha, for chrissake! I mean, Marsha! Man, when she took a walk she didn't leave me nothing but a tattoo, and she'd a got that if she'd had a scraper. And there she is, and she goes, is Sylvie at work? She deals blackjack, why'd she be home at ten? And I go, so what? And she goes, wait'll you see. This is the biggest, just the biggest. I just got in town. I'm coming over. And I go, no way, babe. But she's already gone, and pretty soon she's pounding on the door, and I open it and she goes, you look good, Max. Sylvie gone? And I go, get lost, bitch. But she goes, look, Max, what I found. Or what found me. And it's just a kid. No two ways about it, Marsha's a fast worker, but this, for chrissake! It's a kid up and walking, and Marsha was with me for a couple of years, up to last spring. I mean, not even Marsha can't work that fast, but the kid is holding her hand like she's Mama, all right. Blonde, brown eyes. Not the towhead the papers showed, not the saucer eyes either. Just a little kid, two, three years old, I mean little. Marsha sort of shoves the kid inside and she whips the door right outta my hand and slams it and stands pushing it with her back, like the army's out there and going to bust in any minute. Play with the cards, kid, she goes, and the kid goes to the table where I been playing solitaire. Before I read the want ads, I mean. And she starts to mess around with the cards, and Marsha goes I need to hang out a coupla days, Max, and I go Ha! Ha! And she goes, it's the biggest thing we ever got us in, Max. Look at her, and I look at the kid and I think yeah, could be. The papers always get things wrong. And I look at Marsha and I go, you snatched her? You did that? And she goes, no way, Max. I was going back to the city—she thinks New York is the only city in the world—from Philly and I heard it on the radio, you know, the crash and all, and I was almost on top where it happened and I thought what the hell I'd have a look, but there's all them cops and god knows who else stopping everything that moves, and I go shit, it's not worth the pain.

*Know what I mean? And I'm in this line of cars, all trying to get
the hell out of there, turning around, backing up, like it's crazy.
So I turn off to a blacktop road, me and a zillion others, we all
turn off, but I stop at this roadhouse for a beer and the place is
full of talk about the crash and the kid that's been snatched, and I
get an earful and split. All's I can think of is depart, get the fuck
out of there, back to the city where you know what's what, and
I'm driving, looking for the way back to a highway for god's sake,
and she sits up in the back seat and asks are we going to be home
pretty soon? The kid's over there at the table messing around with
the cards all this time. She's got them all separated in suits.
Diamonds, spades, like that, and she's got the face cards lined up
and she's working on the rest of them, putting them in order, ten
down. I don't know, it makes me nervous. I mean, she's just a
little kid. Anyways, she ain't dressed in pink pants with flowers on
the sides, or a pink shirt, and I shake my head. No way, I go, it
ain't her. But Marsha goes she had to buy her something to wear,
her stuff was too small. She opens up the bag she's got, and there's
the clothes the radio and TV yammered about all day. We gotta
talk, she goes and she puts the kid in on the bed and closes the
door, and pretty soon Sylvie comes back and her and Marsha
are screaming and yelling at each other and then both of them
screaming at me, and finally I go, we gotta call the cops, for
chrissake! And they both scream and yell some more, and
for chrissake it's three in the morning, and we decide to get some
sleep. Marsha puts some covers and a pillow on the floor for the
kid and she takes the sofa and me and Sylvie hit the hay. And
next thing I know the screaming starts again and Sylvie goes you
son of a bitch what've ya done with the kid, and I go you're crazy.
You know that, you're plain crazy. But the kid's gone, all right.
And Sylvie goes, this'll lose me my job, you creep. You know that?
And she calls the cops.*

Breakfast had been delivered while I was reading the last page. I finished
reading and then carefully shuffled the papers into a neat little stack and
fastened the paper clip back on them before I glanced at Kersh.

"I know. Craziness," he said, eating.

I started on my eggs. Not just crazy, I thought, not just that. Creepy. It
was crazy and it was creepy. I didn't believe the implications of what I had
read, and if Kersh did he was crazy, but he wasn't alone, he had backup,
superiors, underlings, and some of them must have believed it, too, and that
was the scariest part of all. "Two different children," I said after a few minutes
of silent eating.

He shook his head. "I wish," he said gloomily. "The link is the woman
Winona Forbush. We recovered her body from the plane crash, and her
boyfriend's body. They found themselves with an unidentified kid and flashed

on the Milliken kidnapping and thought they could make a killing." He groaned. "No pun intended."

"That's what I mean. The kid they had obviously was not born last February. The social services office screwed up the records royally. The woman admitted it. It's a screw up all the way."

He looked almost apologetic. "We lifted prints from the Forbush house and checked them against the Snow Storm Baby. That was the only child the Forbush woman had. It's her."

I remembered it then, the Snow Storm Baby was what the papers had dubbed her, the child who mysteriously appeared at the hospital last February.

"You must have found out how she got to the hospital, who left her there," I said, working at controlling my anger. I didn't know what he was trying to put over, why he was telling me all this, and it was too much to take in with scrambled eggs and toast first thing in the morning.

"Well," he said mildly, "we weren't involved in that. Reverse kidnapping? What would you call it? Anyway, the Philadelphia police didn't find anything, and we didn't start looking until after the Milliken case opened again. Then we backtracked, and we're still backtracking. One more statement you should see. Saved the best for last." He pulled another paper from the briefcase and held it. "We already have statements from everyone connected with the hospital—workers, the medical staff, visitors, patients—or they're still coming in. It's a lot, Seton. A lot. This one might interest you."

I didn't want to read another one. I didn't want to think about this any longer, but my hand took the paper, and my eyes began tracking the words.

Rae Ann Davis, February 16.

I'm a nurse's aide, in the premature baby ward. I've worked there for twenty-four years. The night of the storm we had triplets delivered, poor little things, we knew they wouldn't make it, but you always act like they have a chance and do everything you can. And we had a drug preemie come in and he needed detox, and we were shorthanded, like everyone else that night. So we were all running. So I came back from my break and I went in the bathroom that visitors use because if I'd went in the nurses' lounge they'd have put me to work again and I needed a couple more minutes. So in the bathroom on the counter there was this little bundle, something wrapped in a little towel. I looked at it, and it was this preemie. Not even that yet. More like a fetus, like a miscarriage or abortion, still had the placenta. It wasn't just right, like the cord was too long for one thing. It wouldn't have lived even if she'd carried it to term. I could have cried. Some poor little girl probably scared to death by what happened to her, and now this. But it'd been cleaned up and wrapped up just like somebody thought it could have made it. And they left it in the right place,

*not the preemie ward, I don't mean, but a Catholic hospital where
the nuns would christen the poor little thing. Anyways even if it
was still warm, it was dead, that's what I thought, and I wrapped
it up again in the towel and took it with me to the nurses' station
and then one of the real preemies went into a convulsion, and the
triplets weren't hooked up yet, and it was like I knew it would be.
They had me running with the rest of them for the next hour or
more, and I just forgot about the fetus in the towel. I left it on the
counter at the station and forgot it, God help me. And when I
seen it again I got scared because I didn't call the head nurse or
the nuns or do anything for the poor little thing, and I just put
the towel and everything in my bag. I thought that when I got off
work I'd put it on the doorstep, like in books, and let somebody
else find it, nowhere near the ward, but out by the door. At twelve
when I left it was snowing too hard to go home, and a couple
others were down at the door talking about sleeping over, and I
didn't have a chance to do anything with it, so I went back to the
nurses' lounge and it was still in my bag. But I couldn't get any
rest until I did something, and finally I went back to the visitors'
rest room. I meant to put it back where I found it, only it was
different, not so little, more like a real baby, but small. And
there's no placenta, like I thought before. Bigger than most of the
preemies we get, though. I freaked out and I ran out of there, took
the elevator to the canteen and had me a cup of coffee and a
smoke. I thought I was going crazy, seeing things wrong, seeing
things that maybe wasn't even there. Anyway I went back and it
was still there, a baby girl, pink, warm, big enough for the baby
ward, and I knew I'd been working with preemies too long, seeing
them where they weren't even there. That's when I tied off the
cord. I don't know why, just seemed like somebody should. I knew
that if I waited a little bit Ruth would go get the baby I seen her
take to the mother, and I could slip this one in one of the cribs
and let them take care of it. I couldn't say I found it, not now. I
mean nobody but me had been in the bathroom since nine. They'd
ask why I didn't find it before. And that's what I did. They didn't
see me and the baby finally got a bed, and it all worked out all
right, only I had to take some time off because I kept getting a
headache from worrying about seeing things again. After I settled
down a little I remembered the macaroni salad I ate that night in
the cafeteria and I knew what I'd had was food poisoning, made
me see things. Never seen anything I shouldn't since then.*

Kersh was watching me narrowly when I finished the papers.

"Jesus bloody Christ!" I muttered. "You buy that a kid born prematurely
last February is the equivalent of a four-year-old now? You choose to believe
that instead of a mess of fucked-up records and two different kids?"

"By the time she left the hospital at least seven nurses and four doctors had examined her, each one giving a slightly different report. Then a dozen social workers, five foster parents had her, had somebody. Not exactly inexperienced observers," he said softly. "To say nothing of Max and crew, and then there's your statement."

The restaurant had filled up by then, and the noise level kept rising. Kersh glanced around, leaned forward, and said in a voice so low I could hardly hear it, "We had a psychologist go over your statement last night. She says you noticed a difference in the child from one day to the next, even if you weren't aware of it at the time. Day one you treated her like a three-year-old, the where's-mommy routine. Few people know what to say to a child that young. You bought her the ice cream and she skipped away. Day two, you actually talked to her, warned her about strange men. The way you'd talk to a four-year-old."

He picked up the bill. "My treat," he said reaching for his wallet.

His tame psychologist was right, I realized. But she didn't know the reason. When I lifted the child up to the seawall, I had been surprised by how much heavier she was than I had expected. That's what made me warn her. I shook my head hard.

"You wanted to know why we asked you to help," Kersh said, getting to his feet. "Because we might not recognize her; you might not either, but she might recognize you and trust you again. Let's take a walk."

We went outside and stopped at the Thunderbird. He ran his hand over the hood as he had done before. "I don't suppose you let anyone else take it out for a spin?"

"You suppose right."

"You need to think," he said. "You're the kind of man who drives and thinks, but head south, will you? Plenty of trees on the way. Like the man said, see one, you've seen them all."

"And you'll be right behind me, I suppose."

"Or someone else," he said, smiling. "We'll talk again later." I unlocked the door and opened it. His hand held it open for another moment. "Seton, think fast, will you? Milliken has hired a herd of private investigators, and we don't want them to find the child first. We really don't want Milliken to take her."

"Life as a princess? Isn't that what he has to offer?"

"For how long? What do you suppose he'd do when he realized she isn't exactly what he ordered up? In all likelihood he had his son-in-law killed. No proof, no accusation even, but his daughter believed it and ran. We don't want him to have this child, Seton."

"And what will you do with her?" I asked bitterly.

His eyes took on that peculiar steely glint again. "Not my department," he said. "But it would be better than what he has to offer." He closed the car door, patted the top, and then walked away to his black Ford. When I pulled out of the parking lot, he was behind me.

⁜   ⁜   ⁜

I drove to the Delaware Water Gap where I had planned to spend the day hiking. After only an hour on the trail, I returned to my car and stood looking at the scenery. The trees were turning nicely, but they had not yet acquired the full blaze I had anticipated. They would be better on my way back, I thought, and wondered how many times I had thought the same thing already.

Another car was parked at the lookout, a white Dodge, with a lean-faced man at the wheel reading a newspaper. I ignored him, just as he ignored me.

They couldn't make me do anything, I was thinking. They couldn't force me at gunpoint to walk on the beach until a little girl begged for an ice cream. No way to win the confidence of a child, parading a man at gunpoint. And why such a cock and bull story? Who was the kid? I could think of half a dozen answers that were more convincing than the story Kersh had told: the president's long-lost granddaughter, heir to the British throne, an oil billionaire's illegitimate daughter, an experimental subject carrying deadly viruses in her blood. . . .

A wind had come up, whipping through the gorge below, setting the trees adance, and twirling leaves that looked like clouds of confetti. I had become hot and sweaty hiking, but now I began to shiver. Where was the kid sleeping? Was she staying warm and dry? Who was feeding her? Buying her clothes?

I drove aimlessly through the mountains. Presently I would stop and take some pictures, I told myself, but I drove on and on. And finally I started to drive south. I didn't know yet if I could let myself be used by Kersh; I still didn't want to get involved in whatever was going on, but I drove south. I didn't believe his story, and now accepted that I probably never would know what they were up to, but they were putting in a lot of time on it, and they really did want my help. I laughed out loud when it occurred to me that his tame psychologist might have told him that arousing my curiosity was the key to use.

But mostly I was remembering how the little girl had reached out her hands for me to lift her to the wall, and how she had assumed I would help her down again, and how she had giggled when I warned her about trusting strange men. Where was she now?

It was about two when I stopped at a restaurant. Kersh ambled over to my side as I was tossing my hiking boots into the trunk.

"Buy you some lunch," he said amiably. "Your appestat is sure set for different hours than mine. I thought I'd starve before you stopped."

I shrugged, and closed the trunk lid.

"Think of it as a refund on your income tax," he said, as we entered the restaurant together.

Regular business lunch, I thought, after we had ordered, pastrami on rye, milk for me, ham and cheese on white toast, coffee for him. No business talk yet. He looked as if he needed the coffee. He looked exhausted, and as if in confirmation, he yawned widely.

He didn't bring up the matter until we had finished eating and I ordered coffee. Then he said, "You decided to go along with us?"

"I haven't decided."

"You've got nothing to lose, Seton. Just gain, all the way."

"What gain?"

"Good will. Bundles of good will, and that's not to be sneezed at these days. Get the government agencies on your side, clear sailing all the way."

"She might not even be there any longer."

"Oh, she hasn't left. We know who goes in and who comes out. Atlantic City's easy, not too many ways in and out, unless you want to take a long, cold swim."

"The weather's changed; she probably wouldn't be on the beach now anyway."

"We thought of that. Thing is, she probably hangs out where other kids are. Purloined letter effect. We have a pretty neat city map for you. It'll be in your room. Anyway, you wander around taking pictures of the elementary schools, the playgrounds, the beach, boardwalk. Where there are other kids, she'll turn up. We're betting on it."

He finished his second cup of coffee and motioned to the waitress for a refill. Any minute now he'd start twitching, I thought. Very quietly he said, "Seton, someone's going to find that child. You know it, and I know it." Reluctantly I nodded. "Good. Now, we'll make your reservation for you. You like that place you stayed in before? The Abbey? If not, say so. We'll put you up at the Taj Mahal, Trump's Palace, whatever you say. Meals, booze, whatever you want, just put it on the tab. No problem. If there are other expenses, keep an account and hand it in. We'll take care of it."

The Abbey was relatively small, three or four blocks off the main drag, quiet. I said it would do fine.

"Okay. See, we want you to be comfortable. This might take a few days. She might not spot you right off, or she might hold back a day or two. If she does approach you, talk with her. That's all, just normal friendly chatter. Then leave, and you're done. From sundown to sunup you're on your own. Play, have fun. She isn't going to show at night. In a place like Atlantic City a kid by herself at night would stick out like a dinosaur on the beach. Look over the map; we'll mark the places we think she might frequent. If she doesn't show in any of them, then wander about where you think she might turn up. We don't expect you to search for her, just be in places where she might see you."

I drank my coffee; it had grown cold and was bitter. "What if she doesn't approach me in a few days?"

"Then we'll think of something else to try," he said tiredly. "On Saturday we'll turn the screws a little. There's going to be one of those unfortunate leaks in time for the news Saturday night, and Sunday's papers. It will hint that the FBI suspects the Milliken grandchild is being hidden in Atlantic City, and that they intend a house-to-house search." He sighed and spread his hands. "We want to avoid doing that. Let's hope she comes to you tomorrow or by Saturday afternoon."

I had an image of a small child being cornered by a flock of FBI agents, a SWAT team, a herd of private investigators, and a million poor sods who knew about the Milliken reward. I stood up. "Jesus," I said. "She's just a little kid!"

"Is she, Seton? Are you sure?"

I started to walk away and he suddenly snorted with laughter. "Good Lord, I just realized why you like the Abbey. They let you park your own car there, don't they? No valet parking."

I kept moving. He caught up with me at the door. "If Falco had taken your car instead of your wife, then would you have beaten the shit out of him?"

He was still laughing, and I was still walking away from him, or he would have known that at that instant my indecision had become resolved.

If the child approached me, and if she was the three-to-four-year-old I had seen before, I'd do what Kersh wanted. Turn her over. You can't leave a small child alone in Atlantic City, or anywhere else. She belonged to someone; presumably Kersh knew who that was, and presumably she would be returned and I would never know more about it than I did then. But if a child approached me who seemed older, bigger, different in any significant way, Kersh couldn't have her.

Stating this to myself was simple and at the time it even seemed reasonable; following up seemed impossible. I drove and thought and the more I thought the more hopeless it appeared. They had the city sewed up; no one could leave except by boat without crossing a bridge, and it was easy enough to maintain surveillance on a bridge.

Traffic was heavy; I got in the right lane and let everything moving pass me by, and finally came up with the name Joey Marcos, and a plan that might even work. I pulled off at the next gas station/diner complex and called Joey in Manhattan. Since he worked for one of the biggest ad agencies in the business where he had advanced to dizzying heights, it was easier to get the firm's number from information than to get him at the agency. Finally he came on the line.

"Win," he said, "that really you?" I got in a word and then he said, "Hey, man! How you doing? Where are you? Come on over!"

"Joey, shut up and listen. I need a favor."

"You got it," he said, dead serious.

He didn't interrupt a single time when I told him I needed someone to bring me a car and to fly home again without seeing me.

"I'll need the license number, and make, all that," I said. "And the keys, natch. If this happens can you be available over the next three nights? I don't know when or even if I'll need the car."

"Baby," he said soberly, "this sure sounds like big trouble to me. Atlantic City? No problem. You'll want a couple of numbers where you can reach me."

I let out the breath I hadn't known I was holding. "Thanks, Joey," I said. "Just thanks." No questions, no demands, just, *You got it.* We talked a few more minutes and when I hung up I felt committed for the first time.

When Joey was thirteen and I was fourteen his family moved from Brooklyn to Atlanta, where they did not find the over-touted Southern hospitality. Joey was no darker than I was, but the kids in high school knew he was black, and he had a funny accent, Spanish Puerto Rican overlaid with Brooklyn. We had a couple of classes together and for the first time I found someone I could talk art with, and he said it was the same for him. He was shy when he wasn't being a strutting macho son of a bitch. We both wanted to be artists; we talked about what we would do: go to the Rhode Island School of Design—neither of us did—spend a year or two soaking up art in Italy—he did, I didn't. When he was fifteen and I was sixteen he was picked up for questioning about a break-in at a 7-Eleven, and I signed an affidavit saying he had been with me at my folks' cabin at the lake that weekend. It was a lie. There was a lot of sniggering, a lot of *those* looks, but in the end they turned him loose. I invited him out to the cabin the next weekend and I beat him up out there. It wasn't hard; I had several inches and fifteen pounds on him.

"What'd you do that for?" he wailed, holding a bloody washcloth to his cheek.

"Because you're a thickheaded *nigger* and I know what they'd do to you." This time he started the fight, and afterward we both cried.

Back in the Thunderbird, driving south, the plan shaped up more and more firmly. But there was nothing at all I could do about it until I saw the child again.

I checked into the Abbey, showered, changed clothes, and hit the casinos. I played blackjack a little, played with the slots a little, and hit the money machines a lot, three hundred here, five hundred there until I had nearly five thousand in cash. I had dinner late, and then drove up and down the island, in and out of the side streets, along the boardwalk, back, until I finally found the kind of place I was looking for. A round-the-clock store-front bingo game with a hundred players, and a tiny children's area off to one side. Out front there were two zebras under spotlights, and next door was a church. Atlantic City. I found two parking lots within two blocks and, satisfied, I went back to the hotel and went to bed.

In the morning after breakfast I called Joey from a pay phone and told him the addresses of the parking lots, and he told me the kind of car he would drive down if I gave the word. An eighty-nine Toyota Celica, gray. I made a note of the license number; he said he'd be standing by, and that was that. Then I went out to the boardwalk and the beach with my gear.

By three in the afternoon I was ready to start driving anywhere. The weather was cold and gray, threatening rain that didn't materialize, but hung there like a glower. I had taken more pictures than I had film for, and was shooting with an empty camera, which didn't help my disposition. And I had eaten a hot dog for lunch and now had heartburn. Not a good day, I was thinking, when I saw a bunch of kids playing on some concrete turtles. Little boys were climbing over the things, kicking at each other, king-of-the-turtle fashion. And behind them a small group of little girls played with a ball. And she was there.

The sweater I had seen her in before had been a bit too big; today it was just a little too small. A hot wash, I told myself, unloading the camera, setting up, keeping my eyes on the boys and the turtles. All the kids stopped to watch me. Don't come near me, I thought to her. Keep your distance, kid. She stayed back with the other girls. Today she was mingling with the four-to five-year-olds and passing just fine. I focused on the boys who began to make faces; the girls made faces back at them, taunting them, and I said in a conversational tone, "Your turn next, girls. Let's do the boys first. You know where the zebras are, down by the church?" One of the boys said sure, and I went on, leaning over the camera now, "Well, tonight I'll be taking pictures there. After dark."

The little girls began to move in closer, and I said, still addressing the camera, "Keep back. People are watching us, you know." I glanced up at the kids, who laughed. Belatedly she laughed, too. But she looked frightened. One of the boys was trying to stand on his head; he fell, and they all laughed louder. I pretended to take his picture anyway. One of the girls threw the ball then and they all ran off after it; none of them looked back at me. The boys stopped horsing around and I packed up my gear. "Thanks, fellows," I called, and walked on.

Had it been enough? I had no way of knowing. But, at the very least, no watcher would have had cause to single her out. And for the first time I felt a shiver that was not brought on by weather. I thought of Kersh's words when I protested that she was just a little kid: "Are you sure?" And I knew that I wasn't sure of anything.

I wandered for ten minutes, spotted a coffee shop, and went in. From a pay phone there I called Joey and said, "Tonight," and hung up, then quickly dialed my own office number. Gracie answered and we chatted a minute or two. A tall black woman had moved close enough to overhear and I made no attempt to keep her from hearing. After that I had coffee and a danish.

Kersh was waiting in the lobby when I got back to the Abbey. "Buy you a drink," he said.

Since for the past half hour all I had thought of was getting inside, getting warm, and having a drink, I shrugged and followed him into the hotel bar. "You look like hell," I said when he sat opposite me at a tiny table. The light was dim, and seemed to exaggerate the shadows under his eyes and the pallor that had overcome the pinkness of his cheeks.

"Cold coming on," he said. "I feel lousy. Too damn damp here."

"Tell me about it," I muttered. We ordered and didn't talk until we had our drinks in hand.

"No dice yet," he said finally. "We really didn't expect it to be quite that easy, you understand."

"I worked my butt off in the cold today."

He grinned fleetingly. "I know. One of the reports stresses how conscientious you were. Well, tomorrow's another day."

"Why don't you get some sleep," I said, draining my glass. "I'm cold, hungry, and tired. I intend to take a very hot shower for a long time, then eat a good dinner, and then go to bed. I recommend it."

"Maybe it'll end tomorrow," he said philosophically. "Maybe she'll come up and ask, not for ice cream, not in this weather. Maybe hot chocolate. Hot chocolate today, Coke tomorrow, martini the next day?" He nodded, and looked past me, and for a brief moment, I thought I glimpsed the man behind the nearly babyish face. That man was frightened.

At nine-thirty I returned to the hotel after dinner, retrieved my key from the desk and was given an envelope that had been left for me. The car key for the Toyota. At a quarter to ten I turned off the room lights and left again, this time heading for the back stairs, not the elevator. I had put on a heavy sweater under my jacket, and my pockets were stuffed with money. I took nothing else with me. If anyone stopped me I didn't want a razor to give me away.

I went out by the side door to the parking lot. Many people were around; it was Friday night, a long fun weekend shaping up. I walked around the building, out to the back street, and started the longer walk to the bingo room and the zebras.

I walked fast, trying to keep warm; a stiff cold wind was blowing in off the ocean. When I reached the street with the perpetual bingo game I slowed down and even paused a moment to glance inside the store front. It looked like the same bunch of people, only more of them, and the same bunch of bored kids in the little playroom. I moved on past the two zebras, drew even with the entrance to the church, then, as I was getting closer to the corner, a small figure came out from behind a message board. She slipped her hand into mine.

She was icy, shivering hard, still in the sweater that was too small and too lightweight for the weather. Silently we kept walking, her hand in mine. Two blocks, I was thinking. Just two blocks to the parking lot, a car, a heater, maybe even safety for her. We covered one of them, still not speaking, not walking fast enough to draw attention. There were a lot of people on the sidewalk, in groups, in pairs, bunches of teenagers . . . I was afraid a few people were eyeing me reproachfully, eyeing the child. Traffic had jammed to nearly a gridlock; drivers were leaning on horns, music blared. Another block. I resisted the impulse to pick her up and run.

We found the car and she got in the back seat. On the front seat in an envelope were the parking ticket, Joey's driver's license and even a credit card, and under the envelope was Joey's beautiful black glove leather beret that he had bought in Paris fifteen years ago. It had become almost a trademark with him. I put it on.

I drove the side streets for a few minutes before I stopped. "Are you okay?" I asked the child. "Warm yet?"

She nodded. "I'm hungry, though," she said.

"I'll find something for you to eat as soon as I can." I looked up and down the street, a little traffic, no one on foot, and I got out to inspect what all Joey had provided. I had asked for a dark blanket, but he had done much better than that. The car was gray with black sheepskin seat covers, black floor rugs, and the blanket was so dark it looked black. There were two sleeping bags, a six-pack, a styrofoam cooler, a thermos bottle and a pillow. In the cooler were sandwiches, apples, a wedge of cheese, a tin of smoked oysters. I wanted to laugh and to cry.

"Listen," I said to the child, handing her a sandwich, "we'll drive around for a while and then we'll leave the island. After you eat, you have to stay on the floor with the blanket over you, until I say you can come out. Okay?"

"Okay." She bit into the sandwich ravenously.

I got one of the sleeping bags from the trunk and spread it on the rear floor, and as soon as she was through with the sandwich I arranged her with the black blanket over her. It was as if she had become invisible, the effect was so good. I nodded at her. "What's your name?"

She shook her head. "I don't know."

"What do the children call you?"

"Nothing. They don't like me."

"Okay. We'll think of a name for you." She would fall asleep, I thought, and I would have to remember to check on her to make certain she hadn't worked her way out from under the cover, but as long as she stayed where she was, it would take a very close look to spot her.

I got behind the wheel again and put Joey's driver's license and his credit card in my wallet and removed everything that had my name. I owe you, Joey, I thought, when I started to drive again. I wouldn't try to leave the island until the traffic jam was gone; I didn't want to be in a stopped car under the garish lights of the streets leading to the causeway. Instead, I drove the length of the island, poking along, and when I got back it was a little past midnight and the gridlock had vanished. There was still heavy traffic, but manageable now, and I got in it after glancing at the child to make sure she was hidden. She was sound asleep, out of sight.

They stopped me, glanced inside the car, looked in the trunk, called me Mr. Marcos after looking at the driver's license, and then waved me on. I didn't relax until I reached the first toll booth and was stopped a second time and waved through. I turned west, heading for Wilmington and points west and south. No one looked inside the car again, or asked for ID. Along about three in the morning, when I was afraid of falling asleep at the wheel I pulled off the road into a driveway, and opened the thermos. Steaming hot black coffee. I laughed when I sipped it. Joey had spiked it liberally with bourbon.

I slept for nearly three hours, woke up freezing and stiff, and finished the coffee. The child was sleeping sweetly, nice and warm under the blanket. I had wanted to be through Frederick, heading south on 340 by morning, but it looked as if I couldn't make it. I had stayed off the freeways, the interstates, the toll roads, and the roads I had chosen instead had slowed me down. I began to drive again. In a short while she yawned and said she had to go to the bathroom, and she was hungry and thirsty. We stopped at the side of the road and I told her to go into the bushes. She balked, but finally she did, and then we ate the last of the sandwiches, and she started on an apple. I looked at her in dismay. She needed her face washed, her hair combed, clean clothes. . . .

"Why were you hiding?" I asked her then.

"I don't know," she said with her mouth full.

Fair enough, I thought tiredly. If she asked me why I was hiding her, that would be my answer. "Do you know who is looking for you?"

She shook her head. "Do I have to stay on the floor again?"

I knew it would not be as effective during daylight hours. "No. But stay in the back seat. You know that people are looking for you, don't you?" She nodded solemnly. "Okay, if we have to stop, get down there again. We'll be getting to a town pretty soon, and when the stores open, I'll get you some other clothes and a hairbrush. And you'll have to wait in the car for me. Okay?"

"Okay."

When I started to drive again, she sat on the edge of the back seat with her chin on the passenger seat. "Where did you sleep when you were hiding?" I asked.

"Places. In a car once. And I saw a dog go in a house and I went in after him. He had his own little door. He was my friend."

A dog door? I got as much from her as she could remember or wanted to tell me; it was hard to say which. She remembered there was a plane wreck, she said, and she saw a lot of people by cars talking and she opened a car door and got in. But she hadn't liked those people much; she had been afraid they would hurt her ears, and she left when they all went to sleep. Then she followed the dog into his house and ate cereal there. She went in another house but people came back and locked the doors and she hid in a closet all night and slept and when they went away the next day she crawled out a window.

"Why did you ask me to buy you ice cream?"

"I was hungry."

As she talked I was overcome by rage and outrage, but now I felt only a great sadness, a stomach-wrenching sickness. I looked at her in the rear-view mirror; she was watching the scenery intently. Everything was new to her, I realized; she was discovering her world, and her lessons had included the most basic lessons in survival. She had learned them well.

We were getting near Frederick; traffic was picking up, and there were malls finally. I shopped for her and made her change her clothes in the back seat, and then pulled into a gas station where she went into the rest room and washed up and brushed her hair. When she came back I told her to sit up front; it would look more suspicious to have her in back, I thought. Other parents didn't seem to do that. We stopped at a strip mall and I bought her a few more things, and a new worry presented itself. She looked too different from the other kids we saw; everything she had on except her shoes was brand new. Shoes, I thought with dismay. She would need a bigger size.

And I needed to call her something, I also realized. "When we're around other people," I said in the car, "you should call me Daddy. Will you do that?"

"Don't you know your name, either?"

"I know it, but little kids don't use names for their parents. They call them Mommy and Daddy. And we need a name for me to call you. What name do you like?"

She shrugged. "I don't know."

"What did you call yourself if the other kids wanted to know your name?"

"They didn't. Once I said my name was Kid and a girl hit me and I ran away." She gave me a sidelong look, and asked, "Oprah? Can that be my name?"

"No. It's already taken. How about Sarah? Or Jennifer? Or Michelle? Rachel?"

She pursed her lips and said positively, "Today my name is Dolly."

The sick feeling returned. She didn't know any names. "Dolly," I said. "But just for today." Ahead, I saw a Good Will outlet, and headed for it. Good, serviceable clothes, used clothes, worn clothes, kids' clothes. Maybe even shoes.

We did better in the Good Will store than we had done before, and I even bought a few things for her "older sister." She looked at me hard for a second, started to speak, then looked past me. "Can I have a book?"

There was a used-book section that had a shelf of children's books. She passed over the simple ones, though, and began to page through a book that appeared to me to be for third- or fourth-grade kids. When had she had time to learn to read? She chose four books and we left. She was skipping at my side, smiling. I hadn't seen her smile very often; I liked it.

Driving again, I asked her who had taught her to read.

"I don't know."

"Sesame Street maybe," I suggested.

She brightened and said yes. She had seen Sesame Street, and she went back to the book she was reading.

I bought ice for the cooler, added milk and juice and more fruit, and continued southward. Home free, I thought, not with any great elation, however. At first I had been completely preoccupied with how, and had given no thought to what next. I had not really expected it to work, I had to admit. Her instincts had told her to hide, and mine had told me to help her. Now what? My instincts had deserted me. I could drive around with her for the next few days and then what? I couldn't take her home, obviously, and I couldn't stay on the road forever.

I glanced at her; she was sounding out a new word silently, pursing her lips, a slight frown wrinkling her forehead. She had asked me for help a few times with new words—doubtful, reluctant, wholesome, joyous. . . . What are you? I wanted to demand. Who are you? A sport, a mutant? Will the accelerated process of maturation continue? Is it an illness?

I understood why Kersh had been frightened. He had given me a clue when he said she would stand out like a dinosaur on the beach if she went out alone at night. A dinosaur on the beach. Not her, but maybe the rest of us? Were there others like her? Would she have children who would be born weighing a few ounces, and reach maturity in a couple of years? Too many questions, no answers. I knew I should stop at a phone and call Kersh, tell him to come get her, let the scientists have a go at the riddle. And I knew I wouldn't do that. I felt as if my instincts had forced me to jump off a cliff, and then had deserted me; below, the chasm yawned, and I was airborne.

She closed the book and sighed.

"No good?"

"It's dumb," she said.

"Next town with a mall we'll stop and go to a real bookstore and I'll pick out a few things for you." She flashed me a smile and opened another book. *Winnie the Pooh*, I thought, *The Wind in the Willows*, *Alice in Wonderland*. . . .

Late in the afternoon I made what I planned to be the last stop of the day before we hit a motel. Another mall, this one with a bookstore. I picked out the few books that I wanted her to have, and she was browsing when some teenage boys entered and began talking to a teenage girl behind the counter.

"Roadblocks, the state cops, Chiefie, and his crew, and a bunch more. Escaped convicts, that's what Clarence is saying, over at the Arco station."

"They stopped Brother McNirney and made him open the trunk of his car," another boy said, and they all laughed.

"Come on," I said to the kid. I took her hand and we walked to the counter to pay for the books. Her hand was shaking.

In the wide aisle of the mall I began to think about the car with stuff strewn about every which way. Paper bags from Good Will with her clothes, department store bags, my shaving stuff in a bag, things she had outgrown. . . . I veered toward a Sears where I bought a suitcase, and then I saw a line of kids and parents at one of those four-in-one theaters. A Disney film was showing.

"Listen," I said to her, "I'll take you to the movie and you stay there until it's over. When you come out, I'll be right here waiting. Okay?"

Her hand tightened in mine and she looked at me for what seemed too long a time before she nodded.

"I'll come back," I said. "I promise."

Many parents were doing the same thing, I realized a few minutes later, as we got our kids settled down with popcorn, and ducked out. Most of the others hadn't bothered with the charade of buying two tickets.

I straightened up the car, packed the suitcase and put it in the trunk along with the blanket and sleeping bags; I put the six-pack of beer and some chips in a paper bag on the back seat, added the can of smoked oysters, and looked it all over. Satisfied that no one would suspect I was traveling with a child, I got in the line of traffic heading south, stopping and starting, stopping again. Finally I was at the head of a double line where the right lane became an access road to the interstate about three miles to the west, and the left lane was local traffic. I was in the left lane, and was not detained very long, but they asked me to open the trunk and they checked the registration Joey had left in the glove compartment.

It chilled me more than anything else had done. We were more than three hundred miles from Atlantic City, and they were checking cars. Maybe random checks, maybe they had been tipped, someone had become suspicious, maybe there were escaped convicts. I knew I had to get off the road, stop long enough to get some sleep, and think. I pulled in at a Best Western motel a few blocks farther down and registered for Mr. and Mrs. Marcos and two children; my wife and kids were watching the movie and I would collect them later, I said. The clerk was so bored he hardly even looked up.

I returned to the mall by side streets, keeping well back from the highway that bisected the town, and arrived at the theater a few minutes before the movie ended. Ten or fifteen other adults were also waiting for the children to emerge. I saw the child before she saw me; she was disconsolate and guarded at the same time. She looked like a little girl who had been abandoned. Then she spotted me and her face lighted up; she laughed and ran to me.

"Hi, honey," I said, swinging her up in my arms. She kissed my cheek.

That night I watched her sleeping. She could easily pass for five years old, I knew. No one would question the age if I said that. She was smart, maybe brilliant, but ignorant. There simply hadn't been time yet for her to learn about things like donkeys and owls. I had read *Winnie the Pooh* for a while; she had stopped me repeatedly to ask questions. She needed a library to read her way through, and school books, textbooks, math books, whatever other kids took for granted, no doubt many things I wasn't even aware of. Like names.

My plan to drive around for a few days had to be scuttled. I had to get her somewhere and settle in, stay out of sight, off the roads, but where?

I finally lay down on the other bed and it came to me: Aunt Bett. Not a real aunt of mine, she had been my mother's best friend as far back as I could remember. They had grown up together, had gone to school together, married at about the same time, and visited back and forth almost daily until twenty years ago when Aunt Bett had moved to Tennessee where she still lived. After that they had paid visits to each other several times a year. When my father died almost instantly from a massive coronary, she had come and stayed for several weeks. A year later, when my mother drove into a tree doing ninety, Aunt Bett had wrapped her arms around me and said I shouldn't blame myself. At nineteen, I found that embarrassing, and until then it had not even occurred to me to attach blame. I had not seen her again until four years ago when I had dropped in to see her on my way to a trade show in

Cincinnati. We didn't correspond, or exchange Christmas cards, or phone calls. She was not listed in my address book. Aunt Bett. About seventy-five, maybe a little more, she lived in a house by herself in an area that had been taken over by developers, leaving only half a dozen of the original residents. Good old Aunt Bett, I said to myself; then I was able to go to sleep.

The last time I saw Aunt Bett the house had needed repairs which she said a hired man would do as soon as he could. The repairs had not been done, and I understood now, with a pang of guilt, that there was no hired man, probably not enough money to hire anyone, and the house was gradually falling apart. Aunt Bett was more frail than I had expected, close to eighty. She kept up the flower beds, and had a tiny weed-filled garden, but the rest of the two acres had gone to brambles and scrub pine and oak trees. Across the creek that made up one side and the back boundary was an upscale subdivision with a high wire fence.

Aunt Bett was delighted to see us, and started to bustle in an authoritative way. "Of course you'll stay a while," she said. "And, Win, dear, will you see if the upstairs bedrooms are aired out? If you'd just let me know. . . ." Like that, we were invited to stay as long as we wanted.

I told her that Joe Marcos was the father, that his wife had had an accident and would be in traction for a few weeks, and they had been desperate for help with the child, who had told me that today she was Alice. Alice Marcos.

"I thought I would keep her for a week or two," I finished. The child had watched me silently as I gave her a father and mother and background in a New York City apartment.

"You're going to leave her alone in that big house of yours while you go off working every day? Win! That's no way to treat a little girl. Come on, Alice, you can help me make supper."

At breakfast the next morning the child announced that today her name was Mary. I held my breath, but Aunt Bett nodded. "All right, Mary. I like that name, always did. You want to help me wash up the dishes?" I let out the breath.

I made a list of things that needed doing most—puttying windows, replacing two panes of glass, fixing the front porch rail . . . it was a long list. I checked Aunt Bett's groceries and made another list, even longer. Aunt Bett had no idea how much food that little girl could stow away.

And Aunt Bett started the child on a new education. "She doesn't know a biscuit from a bread roll," she said indignantly. "She doesn't know a cosmos from a zinnia. What were they thinking of, bringing her up ignorant?"

In the afternoon, I was on the ladder finishing a window when I heard Aunt Bett naming the flowers to her: Busy Lizzie, Sassy Francie, old man's beard, honeysuckle . . . they moved out of range. Later, from the roof, I saw the child darting here and there, examining everything. She had on a red sweater and her hair was tied back with a red ribbon; she looked like a rare tropical butterfly in the golden sunlight, swooping down, darting away, alighting somewhere else.

She was going through the books in the house at an alarming rate. Aunt Bett's children had left stacks and boxes of books upstairs, and more were in the attic and basement. The child clearly intended to read them all. Whatever she read she remembered, whatever she heard she retained. Her education, haphazard as it was, advanced like lightning. And she was growing. I worked at fixing up the house and tried to think of what to do with her.

I mowed the lawn and reglazed some windows. I fixed the porch rail and took down the screen door and replaced the screening; I puttied and caulked and put up weather stripping, and I was no closer to a solution than I had been the day we arrived. I was beginning to feel desperate; I had to go home, go back to my own life, my office, my company.

We had been there for six days when a visitor dropped in, the first one all week. "Is Mrs. Markham here?" she asked. She was a prim-looking woman of about fifty whose clothes and car—a Buick—said money. She was eyeing me with unconcealed hostility.

"Aunt Bett? She's around back, I think."

"Oh, I thought you might be one of her sons."

I had been painting the new wood of the porch, and I stopped, waited for her to go, but she took a step or two toward me instead. "I'm Hadley Pruitt," she said. "I'm a volunteer worker for the county senior services. Frankly, Mr.—"

"Winston," I said.

"Mr. Winston, we are terribly concerned about your aunt living out here alone. I've written to her sons, both of them, but no one seems to be able to persuade her that she should give up the house, move into something more manageable. She should not be alone, Mr. Winston. Not at her age. And she can't afford a live-in companion."

"Where you do think she should go?" I could imagine Aunt Bett's reaction to any suggestion from this woman. And as for Bob and Tyler, they would both treat Hadley Pruitt with such gracious courtesy she would think she was being courted, but they would then defer to their mother.

"There are government housing developments," Hadley Pruitt said eagerly, smiling now, "especially designed for elderly people. She has a tiny pension, but they base the rent on what the tenants can afford. She could manage quite well."

"I'll tell her you said so, ma'am," I said very politely.

She stiffened. "Since she has company, I won't bother her today. Goodbye, Mr. Winston."

I watched her drive off, and returned to the paint job, but she had given me the first workable idea I'd had. I took the brushes and paint around back to clean up, and saw Aunt Bett on the porch in her old rocker, the sun on her legs, her eyes closed, and the child on the step nearby. I motioned to her, put my finger to my lips so we wouldn't wake up Aunt Bett.

"I'm not asleep," Aunt Bett said, sitting up straight. "I'm trying to figure out a riddle. What has eighteen legs and bats."

The child was watching her with suppressed glee. She had found a joke book and was going right through it with Aunt Bett who was being a good sport.

"I give up," Aunt Bett said finally.

"A baseball team!" She laughed and Aunt Bett laughed along with her.

"What's your name today?" I asked the child.

"I already told you. Don't you remember?"

"Tell me again."

"Nope. You have to guess."

Aunt Bett winked at her and got up and went inside. I waited until the door closed behind her and then said, "If Aunt Bett wants to take care of you, do you want to stay here with her for a while?"

"Are you going away?" she asked, instantly sober.

"I have to pretty soon. You know, I have work to do, people who expect me to be there. I can't stay away much longer, and I can't take you home with me. They'll be watching for you."

"It's Francie," she said, looking at her new shoes.

"Sassy Francie?" I asked, smiling.

She shook her head. "Just Francie."

I put my arm around her stiff little figure, and after a moment she buried her face against my shoulder and held onto me. I stroked her hair. "I wish I could take you with me," I said softly.

"That's all right," she said, her words muffled.

I waited until she was in bed before I brought it up with Aunt Bett, who looked troubled. "What's wrong with her, Win? She isn't Joe Marcos's child, is she? Is she yours?"

"No. I wish she were. She has a growth problem, hormones or something. No treatment. All she needs is a place where she can feel safe and wanted. You can imagine what it would be like for her to try to go to school, outgrow everyone in her class, be mocked and teased."

She nodded gravely. "Yes, I can imagine that. Whose child is she? Where does she belong?"

"I don't know for sure," I said after a moment. Then in a rush I told her, "She's a foundling, and researchers are after her to see what makes her tick. That's all I know about her." It was close enough to the whole truth.

"I've known you from the day you were born," she said. "Tell me the truth, Win. Have you done something wrong?"

I shook my head. "I've done something I probably shouldn't have done in hiding her, bringing her here. But nothing wrong."

The troubled look did not yet leave her wrinkled face. "You know I'll be eighty in March? Eighty," she said in a musing way. "I don't expect I'll be around very much longer, Win. This wouldn't be a permanent home, is what I mean."

"I don't think she'll need a permanent home," I said slowly.

"Well, then, maybe it'll all come out even. Maybe it will. I'll take good care of her, dear."

We talked about money for the child's care, a touchy subject. If I suggested too much Aunt Bett would be insulted, feel that I was treating her as a charity case, but it had to be enough not to impoverish her further. The kid outgrew everything within weeks. And she ate like a horse. Then I had to make certain about communications; they had to be able to get me if necessary; I had to know how she was doing. Joey Marcos would be the go-between, I decided.

When it was done, Aunt Bett stood up to go to bed. At the doorway she glanced back at me and paused. "I know why I'm doing this, Win. I'm so lonely, and already I love the child, you see. She could be one of my own grandchildren. But why are you?"

"She needed help, I happened to be there."

Aunt Bett regarded me another moment, then went on to her room, clearly unconvinced.

Why? I echoed, alone in the living room. The world was full of kids who needed help; Atlanta was full of them. I gave to good causes, worthy charities, did my civic and moral duty through donations, and tried to put them all out of mind, and most of the time was quite successful at not thinking of the troubled world. Why? Because I had grown to love her? Maybe, but not the day I took her away in a borrowed car. I certainly had not loved her then, and was not sure I did now. I'd had very little experience in loving another person, after all. I was young enough to have half a dozen or more of my own children if this was a simple paternal urge. I could be married within a week, I knew, father a child within a year. I didn't need a surrogate daughter. Why?

The next day I took her shopping for the last time. We bought her a couple of things and then a lot of things she thought her big sister would like. I bought a new television for them, and arranged for cable, paid six months in advance. I bought her a computer, several programs, and half a dozen computer books, and that evening gave her a few elementary lessons in computing; that went exactly like all her other lessons. She saw no difference in learning the names of the flowers, learning the African tribes' names, learning computerese.

The following day I started the drive to New York. We did not delay over the goodbyes. No one cried. But when I looked back through the rear-view mirror and saw the ancient frail woman holding the hand of the child for whom age was meaningless, I wanted to cry. Oh, I wanted to cry.

In New York I returned Joey's possessions and we had a long talk, and afterward Winston Seton reentered the world. I flew home. Special Agent James Hanrahan was my welcoming committee of one.

He said Mr. Kersh would like a few words with me, if I didn't mind. I said of course not and we went to the Federal Building FBI offices where I waited for three hours. The room was relatively comfortable, with twin sofas, a coffee machine, magazines, all the comforts, but no telephone.

I stretched out on one of the sofas and went to sleep. At first, it was an act, to show how unconcerned I was, but then I was waking up and Kersh was standing over me.

"You son of a bitch," he said in a low voice. He stamped across the room and opened a door. "Come on." This door had been locked earlier; it opened to a routine office with a government issue desk, several chairs, not much else.

He motioned to a chair and seated himself behind the desk. He set up the tape recorder on the desk but did not turn it on. "Off the record," he said. "How'd you get off the island? Where's the kid? Who's got the kid?"

"No, Mr. Kersh," I said. "On the record. Let's keep everything on the record." He flicked a switch on the tape recorder. "I've had a lot of time these past days," I said. "I thought it would be interesting to write an account of our various conversations in which I insisted that the child I saw was three or four, too old to be either of the children you claimed to be looking for. I believe Mr. Milliken might become incensed if he learns that the whole FBI is using his personal tragedy as a screen, and it might amuse my correspondents to think of the whole FBI engaged in a manhunt for an infant hiding out by herself on the beach. I think the people I sent the copies to will share my sentiments. I told them all I would be back in town today, and if for any reason I didn't show up, to open the sealed envelopes and read the fairy tale I had written."

He was not impressed. "You see too many movies. One of the things they don't tell you is that we have the advantage of time. Next week, next month, next year, all the time in the world. We'll find the child, you can be certain of that. But you'll never know when someone will drop by to ask just a few more questions, to clarify another point. You won't like that, Mr. Seton, never knowing if an agent is at the next table with another question. Now, about your statement. . . ."

As far as my original statement was concerned, I cooperated fully. I had told him the truth and there was no reason to alter anything. I refused to say anything about where I had gone, how I had left, if I had seen the child again. "Charge me with something and let me call my attorney," I said after four hours. "I want my car back and my various possessions. Now, if we're done here. . . . " I stood up.

I knew he had to be as tired and irritated as I was, but his smooth face remained imperturbable. He turned off the tape recorder and leaned back in his chair. "We really don't want her genes in the gene pool," he commented. "Bad, very bad mix. You've stashed her away somewhere, but not alone. Winter's coming on. She's with someone. We'll find out who that is, Seton. As I said, we have the benefit of time. You're free to go."

Cabs didn't cruise in Atlanta; I had to walk several blocks to the Carlton Hotel where I knew I could get one, and on the way I thought about the various people they would find and question. All my friends in Atlanta, my employees, my relatives. My ex, Susan, and Steve Falco in Los Angeles. Eventually they would get around to Joey, my best friend in high school. Would they get to Aunt Bett? I didn't see how. She had been my mother's friend, not mine, and she was not a relative. Then I realized that Kersh would expect me to be worried, maybe to get in touch with someone, give a warning. A grimmer thought followed quickly: Kersh would expect me to figure that out. He was toying with me, trying to make me nervous. And succeeding.

I stepped back into my life as if nothing had changed. Everyone at the office wanted to know why the FBI had been asking questions, and I said I was as baffled as they were. Gracie, my secretary, said maybe I had robbed some banks up north, and then she dimpled; it bugged the bejesus out of me. Gracie was smart or she wouldn't have had her job, that she did extremely well. But she still thought she could get a bigger payback through being cute. And there wasn't a thing I could do about it. If I told her to stop being so damned cute, she would pout, but prettily. The topic lost interest after a day or two, and routine took over.

I had been home a week, working hard to catch up, taking work home with me, staying at the office after hours. If they were watching, and I knew they were, there was nothing to report. On the next Saturday Kersh paid me a visit. I was working in my studio at home, in an old sweater, older sneakers, jeans. I opened the door and he was there, carrying his briefcase.

"What do you want now, Kersh? I'm pretty busy."

"You look like it. What a life you lead, this kind of house, work in comfortable clothes like that. I brought your car home. She's a real sweetheart." He held up the keys. "Mind if I step inside?"

It was a cold day, not rainy, but threatening, and a blustery wind started and stopped, started and stopped. I pulled the door open wider and stepped aside. He handed me the keys as he entered.

"It's really nice," he said. "These old houses are the greatest, aren't they?" He was looking past me into the living room.

"Do you want to search it?"

"No reason to. We know you're alone. Just admiring it. Mind if I see your studio?"

I shrugged and led him through the wide hall into a narrower one and on into one of the back rooms that had once been a sun room, or sewing room, something like that. It had wide windows, no curtains. Even on this overcast day it was bright. It held my desk, piled high with proofs, manuscripts, glossies, mail. . . . The big drafting table was almost buried under more heaps of stuff, but the smaller drawing table was relatively clear. On a shelf were watercolors that I hadn't touched in several years. I had been working at the light table when he rang, spotting photographs, a job I shouldn't have to do, I grouched now and then, but one that no one else did to suit me. I stood in the center of the room and watched him take it all in.

Finally he nodded. " A real work room, isn't it? Brought something to show you, if I can spread it out." He pulled a rolled-up paper from his briefcase and I cleared off the drawing table by picking up the few things on it and dumping them on the floor.

He grinned, and the change in his face was as remarkable as I recalled. He could change age at will by altering his expression.

He unrolled the paper and spread it out. "You must know more about these things than I do," he said, almost apologetically. "It's how some of our people make projections."

What he had unrolled was a simple x,y graph.

"This upright line here is marked off in apparent age by years," he said, pointing, "and the bottom horizontal line is actual time in months. See?" He drew back and looked at me thoughtfully. "The really fine-tuned ones they're using are in days, but this will do. She was born here, zero day, zero month, zero year. We just added the points we're fairly sure of, you know, the foster parent who had her at one month, the Forbush woman who had her at six months, your report when she was eight months. Those are the points."

"And the lines?" I asked. My hands were sweating. I understood the lines drawn through the points.

"You know," he chided. "There's some dispute about some of the projections, but they went ahead and prepared them all anyway. For instance, between this one at six months, when she appeared to be a year and a half, to the time you saw her, when she looked three to four, that's pretty steep. But they went ahead and used it for one of the projections, although some of our people think she was stressed, that the stress resulted in the spurt that isn't her norm. You know, the plane crash, Max and his girl friends, being alone on the beach. Pretty stressful. Anyway, if that's her growth line, see here, she'll reach twelve physically when she's seventeen months old. If you take this one, the average rate of growth through all the points, then she'll be two and a half when she reaches the physical age of twelve."

There were other lines and he explained them, but they were meaningless. If these projections were anywhere near right, then between one and a half to two and a half years after her birth, she would become an adolescent.

He rolled up the chart again. "She has a secret, a new way of metabolizing food maybe, something. A hormone, an enzyme, a new combination. Was there a food supply in that placenta, or the long umbilicus, enough to sustain rapid growth for a few hours? What if they could find what let her do that and inject it into livestock? What if they could use it to cure cancer? The men in the white coats are frothing at the mouth for her. Believe me, Seton, they will not harm a hair on that child's head. Hell, she could die of old age by the chronological age of six! They want her now. And they don't want her out there breeding. They'd much prefer her alive, of course, and even bearing children under supervision, but they'd rather have her body than have her out there breeding." The glint was in his eyes again.

I didn't know what it was. Fanaticism? Zeal? Earnestness? Fatigue? Whatever brought it on was well repressed most of the time. I turned away from him. "They don't have a thing to base such conjectures on, and you know it. Hypotheses are cheap, let them dream."

"For now. For now, but not very much longer. Think of what it would do to the population if women had kids that easily, every few months here comes another one. No pain, no sweat. Hell, think what it would do to women, and the way women and men treat each other. And in a couple of years each new one's out doing it. You can make your own charts. Think about it, Seton. I'll be seeing you."

I could make the charts, I thought after he had gone, and God help us all, in many ways he was right. I remembered what he had said about her, like a dinosaur on the beach, and with the memory I found myself at the drawing table sketching a dinosaur, then another, and another until I had a beach crowded with them, with one of them open-mouthed, displaying many dagger teeth, looking down at a rock that a tiny mouse crouched behind fearfully. I stared at it a long time until finally, reluctantly, I drew in the balloon and lettered the words in big, bold caps: **YOU'RE GOING TO DO WHAT?**

What was Kersh waiting for? He knew by now that I had no intention of cooperating. I had read the novels, had seen the movies; I believed they had ways to get information out of people if they had to. Kersh had warned me that they would use whatever means they chose if too much time passed. Why? He could be gambling that I would panic and get word to her to run again, and that he would be able to intercept that word. Probably that was part of it. But the bigger part, I felt certain, was that they were still using me as bait, dangling me in the water so that eventually she would come to me. I had no doubt they were intercepting my mail and monitoring my phone calls. Everyone I talked to would be scrutinized; everyone I had lunch with, dined with, went to a show with.

Very quietly I began to drop out of the social circles that made up my Atlanta. I pleaded work, fatigue, deadlines, whatever came to mind. It wasn't fair to involve anyone else in this. I began to draw again, and even got out the watercolors and played with them, and the waiting game continued. Joey came down to visit his parents over the holidays, as he usually did, and we had dinner together, as we usually did. I passed him a large envelope addressed to Aunt Bett and asked him to remail it from New York. No questions. Inside the big envelope was a thousand dollars in mixed bills, for the child, I had written, and another envelope, addressed to her. I was frustrated because I didn't know what name she would be using, and finally I wrote *Francie*. In this letter I expressed my fears that they would be watching me forever, that she must never try to reach me directly. I warned her about AIDS, herpes, drugs, men . . . I told her everything I knew about her early months, the differences between her and other children. I told her that she had to move before June, and that I must not know where she had gone. They would wait until June, I prayed. It was parental stuff, I mocked myself, but I wrote it all out, and Joey took it to mail.

In February I celebrated her birthday by myself with a bottle of champagne. I couldn't even properly toast her because I didn't know her name for today.

In April I was home at ten on Saturday night, when the phone rang. "Win," she said, "Aunt Bett died Monday, and we buried her Wednesday. I left. I'll be all right. I wanted you to know. Thank you, Win. Thank you."

That was all. The line buzzed and hummed and I stared at the wall behind the telephone stand.

Within the hour Kersh was there. "Who is Aunt Bett?" he demanded. I told him. He regarded me for a time, his face closed, the hard glint in his eyes. "You turned her into a street walker, Seton. She's in New York. It's little girls like her that grease the wheels that keep the city rolling. How many guys you suppose she'll have to blow tomorrow to make enough bread to stay alive?"

I wanted to kill him.

Winter into spring, spring into summer, the pace set in time immemorial; so it went. I put her out of mind; how big was she, how mature, how was she living, was she surviving, had they found her . . . ? There were hours at a stretch that I didn't wonder what her name was today.

August, a heavy sultry month, with thunderstorms and windstorms and heat curtains rising from wet pavement, and visible steam at arm-length distance. Kersh came to see me. He was carrying a light-weight jacket, his shirt moist, his face moist. "You're selling out here?" he asked on the front porch.

I motioned him inside where the air conditioner failed to squeeze the humidity out of the air, merely reduced it somewhat. It always felt good for a couple of minutes. "So?"

"Heard you had a tempting offer," he said, and followed me to the living room, where he sank down into a leather-covered chair and sighed. "Can't take the heat," he explained.

"What do you want?"

"Nothing." He held up his hand. "Honestly, Seton, nothing. Just heard you might be selling the business, wondered."

"I might be. Haven't decided."

"You're not exactly what they call a quick decision maker," he commented. "She's still out there."

I shrugged. "You want some iced tea?"

"Yeah, that would be good." He followed me to the kitchen and watched while I prepared two glasses of tea. "We don't want you to get out of touch," he said easily. "You know, keep up the friendship, that sort of thing. Tired of the business?"

Tired to death of it, I thought, and did not respond. I squeezed a lemon and added a dash of juice to each glass, handed one over to him. Tired of deadlines, bad photographs, delayed orders. Irritable with incompetence. Sick of dealing. Tired. Over the last two years I had had three tempting offers, the one he had got wind of, God alone knew how, the most tempting of the lot. The conglomerates couldn't start companies for shit, but they liked to acquire them after they were up and running.

What I wanted to do was load up the T-bird and drive, and drive, and drive. Take a picture now and then, sketch something or other now and then, and drive again.

Very politely I waited until he had finished his tea before I asked, "I assume you came to deliver that message? Stay in touch? Anything else?"

He drained the glass and set it down. "I figure, one, she's dead. Six weeks for an inexperienced kid like that is a lifetime in the Big Apple. Or, two, she's hooked on something. They like to hook them young. They never stray after that. Or, three, she's sick, infected already with half a dozen baddies. The morgue, the hospitals, the jails, they're keeping an eye out. We figure she'll turn up in one of them. But in case she doesn't, we still think she might want to renew old acquaintances with you. When she's sick enough, or broke enough, or hurting enough. That's the message. Just stay in touch. Be seeing you, Seton. I think I can find the front door again."

I let him find it alone. I hadn't told anyone about the newest offer, yet they had found out. What else? What else was there to learn? I asked myself bitterly. His three possibilities seemed all too real, and they would be the first to know.

August, hurricane month, a hurricane hanging off the coast, bringing torrential rains inland. Atlanta had two inches within six hours, and there was flooding, as usual, and stalled transportation, grounded planes. I stood at the office window watching the wakes being left by cars leaving work before the floods got worse. Gracie had gone already, Phil had left, the building was emptying fast. And the telephone rang.

I never used the official answering procedure; I never remembered what it was. I merely said, "Hello."

"Win, darling, is it you? I thought I'd never find anyone I knew."

"Who is this?" I asked, irritated at the whispery promise of the voice.

"Darling, and you said you'd never forget! It's Francie, Win, darling. I'm stranded out at the airport."

Francie. I closed my eyes hard and clung to the telephone as if it were saving me from the abyss below.

"I thought maybe you knew a way to get out here," she went on, husky, suggestive. "I mean, we're grounded, and they don't know when they'll fly. I got a room at the airport hotel, but I'm lonesome."

It's Francie, she said. Sassy Francie? I asked. Just Francie.

"If you can't," she said, "I mean, really can't, that's all right, sweetie. I just thought how nice it would be to get together, since I'm here. You know. Talk over old times." She laughed a low dirty laugh. "You never got back to New Orleans, did you?"

"Never did. Look, I'll be out there as soon as I can get through. It will be good to see you after so long."

She laughed again and told me the bar she would be in, and hung up. I had broken out in a sweat and my hands were shaky.

I took a deep breath and tried to think. They would have listened, they would be right there with me even if I didn't know who they were. They would pick up a glass she touched, take away the table or chair, lift fingerprints, match them. . . . I told her to stay away from me, I thought furiously.

This was exactly what they had waited for. But they wouldn't connect her with that voice, I argued with myself; she sounded just like a New Orleans whore. They would be looking for a little girl, an adolescent girl. And they knew how long it had been since I had been with a woman. It would look even more suspicious if I didn't go; she had practically undressed by phone. Maybe I could smudge any prints she might have left, find out what she was after, send her packing again. . . .

I got there faster than I expected; most people were heading for town not the airport, since all flights had been grounded. The wind was gusting around forty to fifty miles an hour, and the rain was coming down hard enough to put another two inches on the ground before midnight. Her timing, her excuse for calling, everything she had done had been perfectly planned, and when I saw her, the deception seemed total. She looked like a high-priced New Orleans call girl. She had on black lace stockings, gloves to match, a narrow shiny black miniskirt, low-cut frilly blouse, and her hair was long, thick, and black. She fluttered fake eyelashes as she slipped off a bar stool. Every man in the place watched her slithering walk as she came to greet me.

I felt as awkward as if I had entered a cathouse to find it full of Sunday-School teachers who all knew me. She laughed and took my arm. "Relax, honey. Let's have a little drink and then go someplace quiet where we can . . . talk." One of the men nearby laughed and turned back around; he said something to his companion, who also laughed, and Francie and I found a table.

The bartender came over and called her doll and she called him handsome and ordered Perrier and then said, "Let's see if I remember, Win, darling. It used to be a very dry gibson, vodka gibson. Am I right?"

I nodded and she laughed at the bartender, winked, and said, "I never forget the important things."

As soon as he was gone I leaned forward and whispered, "We've got to get out of here. I'm being followed."

She kissed the tip of her finger and touched it to my lips, smiling. "You northern businessmen are always in such a hurry. So impetuous. Let me tell you about the flight, Win darling. I was never so scared in my life when that plane began to rock back and forth, up and down. Why, you couldn't get me back on an airplane with a stick, not until the storm's all the way gone, and the sun's shining and all. And I believe it could go on raining all night, into tomorrow. You know?"

She was perfect, I had to admit. She had the accent down, the flirtatious glances at other men, the way she flirted outrageously with the bartender, her chatter. . . . She had even thought about fingerprints. I drank the gibson, and she sipped her water, and eventually we were ready to leave. She took my arm and held it hard against her when we walked out. Perfect.

In her room I hurried to close the drapes, and she turned on the radio and fiddled with it until she had loud rock, and then we sat on the side of the bed. Slowly she pulled off the black wig, and then peeled off her fake eyelashes. Her hair was brown and short with deep waves. Her eyes were golden brown.

"Why did you come here?" I asked in a low voice. "Is anything wrong?"

She shook her head. "I had to see you, let you see me, know it's finished. I don't know. Aunt Bett died, Win."

"I know. Where did you go? How did you live?"

"She gave me most of the money you had been sending, and I had the other money you sent. It was a lot. She said to tell you thank you. She made me promise to say thank you for her."

I wanted very much to put my arm around her, draw her close and comfort her, but this was not the child I had found in Atlantic City. I couldn't touch this young woman and I knew it. We spoke in low voices, sometimes hers was hardly audible as she told me how she had managed. "There was a school for girls, you know, with uniforms. I bought a uniform like theirs and no one paid any attention to me around there. And there was a big building where a lot of people slept in the halls, under the steps, and I did too." I shuddered, and she said quickly, "It wasn't bad. I bought some toothpaste, the kind without any smell or taste, and I would chew it up a little, mix it with spit, and then make little bubbles at the sides of my mouth, and no one came near me. I learned to roll my eyes funny too. Like this." She rolled her eyes and looked demented.

"Christ," I muttered and ducked my head.

She put her hand on my arm, then hurriedly pulled it away again. "It was okay," she said softly. "Honest, it was. When I grew a little more I got other clothes and then I hung out around the university, I even got a room near there, and after that it was really all right. I went to the library and read a lot. I kept changing, though; you know, growing. Not taller. Just getting more mature. And I began to think about you, and how much I wanted to see you again. . . ." Her voice trailed off and stopped.

After a moment I pointed to the wig at the foot of the bed. "Where did you learn that act?"

She laughed deep in her throat. "Wasn't I good! I read things, and saw movies, and I watched the women on the streets, how they walked, how they talked to men."

And never forgot a thing, I finished silently when she stopped again. I stood up and walked to the window and pulled the drape open a bit. The rain was pelting down harder than ever. No doubt the airport road would go under water within the hour. I pulled the drape shut and turned back to her. "Now what?" She obviously no longer needed help. Maybe a little money, but no more than that. She could go anywhere, be anyone she chose.

"I don't know," she said in a voice so low that this time I couldn't hear her over the loud radio, but read her lips, and remembered how she had moved her lips sounding out words less than a year ago.

Abruptly she stood up and came across the room to take my hand. She headed for the bathroom with me in tow, and there she closed the door and turned on the shower full blast. "The radio was driving me batty," she said with a faint smile. Almost instantly she was somber again. "I know how different I am, Win. It is possible that my mother used a drug that caused chromosomal damage, scrambling, breaks, something of the sort, and this difference will be self-limiting. I won't breed true. But it is also possible that I am a true genetic sport, something new, and my children will be also. In either event, those people who want to study me won't rest until I am dead. They will hunt and hunt. Intellectually, I don't blame them; I would do the same in their place. But I'm not in their place, and I don't know how it would feel to be like them, like you, like anyone else. This, how I am, feels natural. I don't feel like a freak or a monster."

"God," I whispered. "Oh, God, Francie. You're not a monster. You're a beautiful woman."

"Make love to me, Win. Please. You've taught me so much. Will you teach me that?" She touched my cheek.

I reached past her and turned off the shower, then I picked her up and carried her to bed and taught her about love.

"What I would like," she whispered that night, "is to live on a mountainside with trees all around, and a fresh little brook with fish. And no people. But what would you do in such a place?"

"Oh, I'd keep the house in good repair, cut wood for the fires, and I would paint and take pictures."

"Good," she said with a nod, as if that were settled. "And I would teach the children the way Aunt Bett taught me. I would teach them the names of the flowers, and which plants you can eat, and how algebra works, and how to make biscuits, and where the Serengeti Plains are located. The girls would go out and meet men and pick carefully which ones, and then come home to have their babies." She laughed softly. "Grandparents."

When she slept, I studied her face in the dim light from the bathroom. How very beautiful she had become, such fine bones, such soft skin. This, I understood finally, was why I had helped that child on the beach, why I had hidden the girl from the world; to get to this moment I had to do those things, this moment had been determined. I smiled at how foolish that sounded, but I believed it. I touched her cheek as she slept and she smiled and moved closer without waking up. Tomorrow I would send her away. I would make her promise never to come near me again, never to call, or write. She could make it now by herself. I was the only menace for her, and eventually I would betray her. I didn't want to sleep. I wanted to look at her, to touch her cheek now and then, to see her smile, but I dozed, and when I woke up she was moving around the room with a towel.

"What are you doing?"

She came to the bed and knelt by me. "Wiping off my fingerprints. I just thought of it," she whispered.

I pulled her into the bed and made love to her again, and I did not tell her that no prints would be as much a giveaway as finding a full set of clear prints. When I woke up again it was nine in the morning and she was gone.

I knew it as soon as I opened my eyes. Last night her presence had filled the space, and now it was just a bleak and empty hotel room.

September. October. I decided to sell the business the day I stared at spotted photographs and didn't give a damn. I told my lawyer and my accountant to take care of it, my only real demand was that those who wanted to keep their jobs would be allowed to. Not a big stumbling-block. For a few days I expected Kersh to come calling, but he didn't; maybe he was walking the streets of New Orleans looking for a black-haired hooker in a shiny tight skirt.

I wanted desperately to hear her voice, to know she was well, and, more desperately, I wanted her to stay away, not to call, not to write. One day I found myself sorting books, stacking some, boxing others, and I realized that I had made the decision to sell the house as well as the business. I had to move away so she could not find me.

November. The Thanksgiving homecoming weekend party was to be held at the Carlton Hotel; as it was every year. Our team, win or lose, rah rah. I was home when she called. "Hey, Win," she said in a bubbly voice, "it's Rosalee. You've been hiding out long enough, bubba. Come to the party Saturday. Duck away from the mobs and hit the little parties in eight twenty, six fourteen, and ten thirty. See ya!"

Numbly I hung up. She was insane, coming back, calling. She knew they were monitoring my line. She knew they watched me day after day, night after night. I wouldn't go near the Carlton, I thought, and rejected that. She was in town, and might call again, suggest something else, and at least at the homecoming party there would be hordes of young people. Would she come as a cheerleader? A football groupie? Whatever it was, she would blend right in, I knew.

I had been shopping for gifts for everyone at the office; now I shopped for just the right present for her. Something I could keep at hand without arousing suspicions. Something I could pass over when I told her I was leaving the city, leaving the state. I tried to figure out what she had meant by the numbers she had given me, and failed. There were always private room parties, always jammed; she wouldn't be planning to meet me in any of them, and I could not recombine the numbers in any way to make sense. I stalked through stores searching for the gift, and worked with the numbers, and looked at more stuff. Just stuff. Not for her.

Then I found it. A gossamer sheer kimono in gleaming white silk, as soft as a cloud, with a single red rose embroidered on the back, and a delicate gold-thread edging on the front. I passed it up, went back and felt it, and bought it. The box was too big to carry around a party, but it was hers. It looked as if it had been made for her alone, had been there waiting for me. I had it gift-wrapped and carried it home in a shopping bag.

Saturday night the Carlton was like an asylum with all the attendants out on strike. The party took up three large downstairs rooms, the dining room, the lounge and bar. I carried the shopping bag in with me and made my way to the cloakroom. I had decided to check it with my coat and pass her the claim check when we met; it seemed the best I could do. Moving through the lobby was a slow business; I knew half the people there, it seemed, and had not seen many of them for a long time. Everyone was happy and loud.

At the cloakroom I waited in line, then passed over the coat and the shopping bag, talking to one of my old teachers and his wife. The young woman behind the counter pressed the claim check into my hand, and at the touch, I pivoted. *You.* She smiled pleasantly and was already taking the coat of the next man in line. I looked at my hand; I held the claim check, and also a room key.

She had told me the time, I realized: ten thirty. Room parties were going on up and down the tenth floor. Men were reliving moments of glory, reenacting plays, throwing a pillow here, a real football there. . . . A bunch of them were lined up for the kickoff in the hall. . . . I visited one party after another, stayed for a minute or two, then moved on. Nine thirty, nine forty, nine forty-five. I hit another room, accepted another drink that I would not taste, talked to people, and instantly forgot what we talked about and even who they were. I didn't know who was watching me, but then, I never did. Ten twenty. I got on the elevator on the tenth floor and rode down to six with people I did know. On six I left the group, entered the stairwell, and started the climb up to the fourteenth floor.

If I saw anyone I hadn't known for a long time, I would go to ten, do another party or two, and then go home, I told myself. I was sure that no one had noticed when I entered the stairwell, and you couldn't find anyone in the crowds milling about if you had to. Just to make certain, I left the stairs on eleven and walked the length of the corridor. It was quiet up here; the parties were being confined to ten, eight, and six, and the main floor. I found other stairs and went up the remaining floors. No thirteen.

On fourteen an elderly couple passed me in the hall. We all nodded; they went on to the elevator and I went on to room number fourteen eighteen. At first I thought she wasn't there yet. A small table was near tall double windows that were open to a tiny balcony with a lovely vista of Atlanta by night. Everything out there glittered. On the table was a champagne bottle in a cooler and two glasses. Then she moved into sight on the balcony. "Isn't it beautiful?" she said. She had changed her clothes from the black and white uniform she had worn earlier to a long pale blue skirt and matching sweater. She was more beautiful than I remembered.

"I have a present for you," she said, and picked up a slim package on the table.

"And I checked a present for you."

Her eyes shifted and widened. Staring past me, she whispered, "Promise you'll take them home, Win. Keep the presents as mementoes. Promise. Don't forget me."

I spun around to see Kersh and two other men entering the room without a sound. One of them leaped toward her, knocking me out of the way, but she was on the balcony, the table between her and the rest of us. She looked at me another second, turned, and swung her legs over the railing, and then stepped off.

For a moment no one moved, then I screamed, and lunged toward the balcony. Someone clipped me behind the ear and I fell to my knees.

They took me to a different room where I sat in a large chair while people came and went. I couldn't weep for her; I had no tears, only the deadening knowledge that I had done it, I had failed her. I failed my mother who drove her car into a tree doing ninety miles an hour. Failed my ex-wife who thought she needed plastic breasts. Failed Aunt Bett who had lived so many years in poverty and loneliness. Failed the little girls who oiled the wheels of New York. Failed the social worker who wept because they wouldn't give her what she needed to save children. Failed them all.

Kersh brought the little package from the other room and asked me to open it. It was a book with handpainted illustrations of common flowers with their names. He leafed through it and handed it back to me. "Do you want someone to take you home?"

I stood up and started to walk toward the door.

"Seton, hold on a second," Kersh said heavily. He regarded me for a moment, then said, "It's over. We aren't going to bother you anymore. You understand? You couldn't have prevented this. We've been getting closer for weeks now. We weren't going to wait any longer. Do you understand what I'm telling you? Get in that big pretty car of yours and drive, Seton. Just drive a long time."

Someone went down the elevator with me; although it was after two in the morning, there was still a mob in the lobby, but subdued, huddling in small groups. No one paid any attention as the agent led me through the clusters of people and retrieved my coat and shopping bag. He went to the outer door with me, and I walked on alone to my car.

It was a long time before I turned the key in the ignition, a long time before I shifted into gear and began to drive. At home, I carried in the packages. *Promise. Don't forget me.* I opened the book but could not focus on the pictures, the words. A gold bookmark was in it. I opened to that page, and the words seemed to leap at me. " 'Sassy Francie,' *Saxifraga,* sometimes called Mother of Thousands."

I looked up at the shopping bag then, and I knew. I had noticed without conscious awareness, but I knew it held more than I had put in it. My hand was shaking when I reached inside and brought out a small box, the size of a shoebox for children's shoes. It was wrapped in silver foil and had been pierced all over. Carefully I lifted the top and saw her, our daughter, curled in sleep, clothed in a tiny garment attached to the sides of the box, which was padded and covered with pink silk. Then I wept.

She had known it could never end as long as she lived, but our daughter was free. I would find the mountainside with the forests all around; I would teach her what she needed to know, and her children and theirs. It would take careful planning; no one must suspect until they had scattered everywhere, like seeds on the wind. There would be time to think and plan as I drove.

"Your name will be Rose," I murmured to my child, who would fit in the palm of my hand. I had begun naming the flowers.

SNODGRASS

Ian R. MacLeod

Here's another quirky and brilliant story by British writer Ian R. MacLeod, whose story "Grownups" appears elsewhere in this anthology. In this one, he tells the gritty yet poignant story of how things might have gone very differently indeed for a world-famous celebrity . . . for both better *and* worse.

I've got me whole life worked out. Today, give up smoking. Tomorrow, quit drinking. The day after, give up smoking again.

It's morning. Light me cig. Pick the fluff off me feet. Drag the curtain back, and the night's left everything in the same mess outside. Bin sacks by the kitchen door that Cal never gets around to taking out front. The garden jungleland gone brown with autumn. Houses this way and that, terraces queuing for something that'll never happen.

It's early. Daren't look at the clock. The stair carpet works greasegrit between me toes. Downstairs in the freezing kitchen, pull the cupboard where the handle's dropped off.

"Hey, Mother Hubbard," I shout up the stairs to Cal. "Why no fucking cornflakes?"

The lav flushes. Cal lumbers down in a grey nightie. "What's all this about cornflakes? Since when do you have breakfast, John?"

"Since John got a job."

"You? A job?"

"I wouldn't piss yer around about this, Cal."

"You owe me four weeks' rent," she says. "Plus I don't know how much for bog roll and soap. Then there's the TV licence."

"Don't tell me yer buy a TV licence."

"I don't, but I'm the householder. It's me who'd get sent to gaol."

"Every Wednesday, I'll visit yer," I say, rummaging in the bread bin. "What's this job anyway?"

"I told yer on Saturday when you and Kevin came back from the Chinese. Must have been too pissed to notice." I hold up a stiff green slice of Mighty White. "Think this is edible?"

"Eat it and find out. And stop calling Steve Kevin. He's upstairs asleep right at this moment."

"Well there's a surprise. Rip Van and his tiny Winkle."

"I wish you wouldn't say things like that. You know what Steve's like if you give him an excuse."

"Yeah, but at least I don't have to sleep with him."

Cal sits down to watch me struggle through breakfast. Before Kevin, it was another Kevin, and a million other Kevins before that, all with grazed knuckles from the way they walk. Cal says she needs the protection even if it means the odd bruise.

I paste freckled marge over ye Mighty White. It tastes just like the doormat, and I should know.

"Why don't yer tell our Kev to stuff it?" I say.

She smiles and leans forward.

"Snuggle up to Dr. Winston here," I wheedle.

"You'd be too old to look after me with the clients, John," she says, as though I'm being serious. Which I am.

"For what I'd charge to let them prod yer, Cal, yer wouldn't have any clients. Onassis couldn't afford yer."

"Onassis is dead, unless you mean the woman." She stands up, turning away, shaking the knots from her hair. She stares out of the window over the mess in the sink. Cal hates to talk about her work. "It's past eight, John," she says without looking at any clock. It's a knack she has. "Hadn't you better get ready for this job?"

Yeah, ye job. The people at the Jobbie are always on the look-out for something fresh for Dr. Winston. They think of him as a challenge. Miss Nikki was behind ye spit-splattered perspex last week. She's an old hand—been there for at least three months.

"Name's Dr. Winston O'Boogie," I drooled, doing me hunchback when I reached the front of ye queue.

"We've got something for you, Mr. Lennon," she says. They always call yer Mister or Sir here, just like the fucking police. "How would you like to work in a Government Department?"

"Well, wow," I say, letting the hunchback slip. "You mean like a spy?"

That makes her smile. I hate it when they don't smile.

She passes me ye chit. Name, age, address. Skills, qualifications—none. That bit always kills me. Stapled to it we have details of something clerical.

"It's a new scheme, Mr. Lennon," Nikki says. "The Government is committed to helping the long-term unemployed. You can start Monday."

So here's Dr. Winston O'Boogie at the bus stop in the weird morning light. I've got on me best jacket, socks that match, even remembered me glasses so I can see what's happening. Cars are crawling. Men in suits are tapping fingers on the steering wheel as they groove to Katie Boyle. None of them live around here—they're all from Solihull—and this is just a place to complain about the traffic. And Monday's a drag cos daughter Celia has to back the Mini off the drive and be a darling and shift Mummy's Citroën too so yer poor hard-working Dad can get to the Sierra.

The bus into town lumbers up. The driver looks at me like I'm a freak when I don't know ye exact fare. Up on the top deck where there's No standing, No spitting, No ball games, I get me a window seat and light me a ciggy. I love it up here, looking down on the world, into people's bedroom windows. Always have. Me and me mate Pete used to drive the bus from the top front seat all the way from Menlove Avenue to Quarry Bank School. I remember the rows of semis, trees that used to brush like sea on shingle over the roof of the bus. Everything in Speke was Snodgrass of course, what with valve radios on the sideboard and the *Daily Excess*, but Snodgrass was different in them days. It was like watching a play, waiting for someone to forget their lines. Mimi used to tell me that anyone who said they were middle class probably wasn't. You knew just by checking whether they had one of them blocks that look like Kendal Mint Cake hooked around the rim of the loo. It was all tea and biscuits then, and Mind, dear, your slip's showing. You knew where you were, what you were fighting.

The bus crawls. We're up in the clouds here, the fumes on the pavement like dry ice at a big concert. Oh, yeah. I mean, Dr. Winston may be nifty fifty with his whole death to look forward to but he knows what he's saying. Cal sometimes works at the NEC when she gets too proud to do the real business. Hands out leaflets and wiggles her ass. She got me a ticket last year to see Simply Red and we went together and she put on her best dress that looked just great and didn't show too much and I was proud to be with her, even if I did feel like her dad. Of course, the music was warmed-over shit. It always is. I hate the way that red-haired guy sings. She tried to get me to see Cliff too, but Dr. Winston has his pride.

Everywhere is empty round here, knocked down and boarded up, postered over. There's a group called SideKick playing at Digbeth. And waddayou-know, the Beatles are playing this very evening at the NEC. The Greatest Hits Tour, it says here on ye corrugated fence. I mean, Fab Gear Man. Give It Bloody Foive. Macca and Stu and George and Ringo, and obviously the solo careers are up the kazoo again. Like, wow.

The bus dumps me in the middle of Brum. The office is just off Cherry Street. I stagger meself by finding it right away, me letter from the Jobbie in me hot little hand. I show it to a geezer in uniform, and he sends me up to the fifth floor. The whole place is new. It smells of formaldehyde—that stuff we used to pickle the spiders in at school. Me share the lift with ye office bimbo. Oh, after *you*.

Dr. Winston does his iceberg cruise through the openplan. So this is what Monday morning really looks like.

Into an office at the far end. Smells of coffee. Snodgrass has got a filter machine bubbling away. A teapot ready for the afternoon.

"Mr. Lennon."

We shake hands across the desk. "Mr. Snodgrass."

Snodgrass cracks a smile. "There must have been some mistake down in General Admin. My name's Fenn. But everyone calls me Allen."

"Oh yeah. And why's that?" A voice inside that sounds like Mimi says

Stop this behaviour, John. She's right, of course. Dr. Winston needs the job, the money. Snodgrass tells me to sit down. I fumble for a ciggy and try to loosen up.

"No smoking please, Mr. . . . er, *John.*"

Oh, great.

"You're a lot, um, older than most of the casual workers we get."

"Well this is what being on the Giro does for yer. I'm nineteen really."

Snodgrass looks down at his file. "Born 1940." He looks up again. "And is that a Liverpool accent I detect?"

I look around me. "Where?"

Snodgrass has got a crazy grin on his face. I think the bastard likes me. "So you're John Lennon, from Liverpool. I thought the name rang a faint bell." He leans forward. "I am right, aren't I?"

Oh fucking Jesus. A faint bell. This happens about once every six months. Why *now*? "Oh yeah," I say. "I used to play the squeezebox for Gerry and the Pacemakers. Just session work. And it was a big thrill to work with Shirley Bassey, I can tell yer. She's the King as far as I'm concerned. Got bigger balls than Elvis."

"You were the guy who left the Beatles."

"That was Pete Best, Mr. Snodgrass."

"You *and* Pete Best. Pete Best was the one who was dumped for Ringo. You walked out on Paul McCartney and Stuart Sutcliffe. I collect records, you see. I've read all the books about Merseybeat. And my elder sister was a big fan of those old bands. The Fourmost, Billy J. Kramer, Cilla, the Beatles. Of course, it was all before my time."

"Dinosaurs ruled the earth."

"You must have some stories to tell."

"Oh, yeah." I lean forward across the desk. "Did yer know that Paul McCartney was really a woman?"

"Well, John, I—"

"It figures if yer think about it, Mr. Snodgrass. I mean, have *you* ever seen his dick?"

"Just call me Allen, please, will you? Now, I'll show you your desk."

Snodgrass takes me out into the openplan. Introduces me to a pile of envelopes, a pile of letters. Well, Hi. Seems like Dr. Winston is supposed to put one into the other.

"What do I do when I've finished?" I ask.

"We'll find you some more."

All the faces in the openplan are staring. A phone's ringing, but no one bothers to answer. "Yeah," I say, "I can see there's a big rush on."

On his way back to his office, Snodgrass takes a detour to have a word with a fat Doris in a floral print sitting over by the filing cabinets. He says something to her that includes the word Beatle. Soon, the whole office knows.

"I bet you could write a book," fat Doris says, standing over me, smelling of pot noodles. "Everyone's interested in those days now. Of course, the Who and the Stones were the ones for me. Brian Jones. Keith Moon, for some reason. All the ones who died. I was a real rebel. I went to Heathrow airport once, chewed my handbag to shreds."

"Did yer piss yourself too, Doris? That's what usually happened."

Fat Doris twitches a smile. "Never quite made it to the very top, the Beatles, did they? Still, that Paul McCartney wrote some lovely songs. 'Yesterday,' you still hear that one in lifts don't you? And Stu was *so* good-looking then. Must be a real tragedy in your life that you didn't stay. How does it feel, carrying that around with you, licking envelopes for a living?"

"Yer know what your trouble is don't yer, Doris?"

Seems she don't, so I tell her.

Winston's got no money for the bus home. His old joints ache—never realised it was this bloody far to walk. The kids are playing in our road like it's a holiday, which it always is for most of them. A tennis ball hits me hard on the noddle. I pretend it don't hurt, then I growl at them to fuck off as they follow me down the street. Kevin's van's disappeared from outside the house. Musta gone out. Pity, shame.

Cal's wrapped up in a rug on the sofa, smoking a joint and watching *Home and Away*. She jumps up when she sees me in the hall like she thought I was dead already.

"Look, Cal," I say. "I really wanted this job, but yer wouldn't get Adolf Hitler to do what they asked, God rest his soul. There were all these little puppies in cages and I was supposed to push knitting needles down into their eyes. Jesus, it was—"

"Just shaddup for one minute will you, John!"

"I'll get the rent somehow, Cal, I—"

"—Paul McCartney was here!"

"Who the hell's Paul McCartney?"

"Be serious for a minute, John. He was *here*. There was a car the size of a tank parked outside the house. You should have seen the curtains twitch."

Cal hands me the joint. I take a pull, but I really need something stronger. And I still don't believe what she's saying. "And why the fuck should Macca come here?"

"To see *you*, John. He said he'd used a private detective to trace you here. Somehow got the address through your wife Cynthia. I didn't even know you were *married*, John. And a kid named Julian who's nearly thirty. He's married too, he's—"

"—What else did that bastard tell yer?"

"Look, we just talked. He was very charming."

Charming. That figures. *Now* I'm beginning to believe.

"I thought you told me you used to be best mates."

"Too bloody right. Then he nicked me band. It was John Lennon and the Quarrymen. I should never have let the bastard join. Then Johnny and the

Moondogs. Then Long John and the Silver Beatles. It was *my* name, *my* idea to shorten it to just the Beatles. They all said it was daft, but they went along with it because it was *my* fucking band."

"Look, nobody doubts that, John. But what's the point in being bitter? Paul just wanted to know how you were."

"Oh, it's *Paul* now is it? Did yer let him shag yer, did yer put out for free, ask him to autograph yer fanny?"

"Come on, John. Climb down off the bloody wall. It didn't happen, you're not rich and famous. It's like not winning the pools, happens to everyone you meet. After all, the Beatles were just another rock band. It's not like they were the Stones."

"Oh, no. The Stones weren't crap for a start. Bang bang Maxwell's Silver bloody Hammer. Give me Cliff any day."

"You never want to talk about it, do you? You just let it stay inside you, boiling up. Look, why will you never believe that people care? *I* care. Will you accept that for a start? Do you think I put up with you here for the sodding rent which incidentally I never get anyway? You're old enough to be my bloody father, John. So stop acting like a kid." Her face starts to go wet. I hate these kind of scenes. "You *could* be my father, John. Seeing as I didn't have one, you'd do fine. Just believe in yourself for a change."

"At least yer had a bloody *mother*," I growl. But I can't keep the nasty up. Open me arms and she's trembling like a rabbit, smelling of salt and grass. All these years, all these *bloody* years. Why is it you can never leave anything behind?

Cal sniffs and steps back and pulls these bits of paper from her pocket. "He gave me these. Two tickets for tonight's show, and a pass for the do afterwards."

I look around at chez nous. The air smells of old stew that I can never remember eating. I mean, who the hell cooks *stew*? And Macca was here. Did them feet in ancient whathaveyou.

Cal plonks the tickets on the telly and brews some tea. She's humming in the kitchen, it's her big day, a famous rock star has come on down. I wonder if I should tear ye tickets up now, but decide to leave it for later. Something to look forward to for a change. All these years, all these *bloody* years. There was a journalist caught up with Dr. Winston a while back. Oh Mr. Lennon, I'm doing background. We'll pay yer of course, and perhaps we could have lunch? Which we did, and I can reveal exclusively for the first time that the Doctor got well and truly rat-arsed. And then the cheque came and the Doctor saw it all in black and white, serialised in the *Sunday* bloody *Excess*. A sad and bitter man, it said. So it's in the papers and I know it's true.

Cal clears a space for the mugs on the carpet and plonks them down. "I know you don't mean to go tonight," she says. "I'm not going to argue about it now."

She sits down on the sofa and lets me put an arm around her waist. We get warm and cosy. It's nice sometimes with Cal. You don't have to argue or explain.

"You know, John," she murmurs. "The secret of happiness is not trying."

"And you're the world expert? Happiness sure ain't living on the Giro in bloody Birmingham."

"Birmingham isn't the end of the world."

"No, but yer can see it from here."

Cal smiles. I love it when she smiles. She leans over and lights more blow from somewhere. She puts it to my lips. I breathe it in. The smoke. Tastes like harvest bonfires. We're snug as two bunnies. "Think of when you were happy," she whispers. "There must have been a time."

Oh, yeah: 1966, after I'd recorded the five singles that made up the entire creative output of the Nowhere Men and some git at the record company was given the job of saying, Well, John, we don't feel we can give yer act the attention it deserves. And let's be honest the Beatles link isn't really bankable any more is it? Walking out into the London traffic, it was just a huge load off me back. John, yer don't have to be a rock star after all. No more backs of vans. No more Watford Gap Sizzlers for breakfast. No more chord changes. No more launches and re-launches. No more telling the bloody bass player how to use his instrument. Of course, there was Cyn and little Julian back in Liverpool, but let's face it I was always a bastard when it came to family. I kidded meself they were better off without me.

But 1966. There *was* something then, the light had a sharp edge. Not just acid and grass although that was part of it. A girl with ribbons came up to me along Tottenham Court Road. Gave me a dogeared postcard of a white foreign beach, a blue sea. Told me she'd been there that very morning, just held it to her eyes in the dark. She kissed me cheek and she said she wanted to pass the blessing on. Well, the Doctor has never been much of a dreamer, but he could feel the surf of that beach through his toes as he dodged the traffic. He knew there were easier ways of getting there than closing yer eyes. So I took all me money and I bought me a ticket and I took a plane to Spain, la, la. Seemed like everyone was heading that way then, drifting in some warm current from the sun.

Lived on Formentera for sunbaked years I couldn't count. It was a sweet way of life, bumming this, bumming that, me and the Walrus walking hand in hand, counting the sand. Sheltering under a fig tree in the rain, I met this Welsh girl who called herself Morwenna. We all had strange names then. She took me to a house made of driftwood and canvas washed up on the shore. She had bells between her breasts and they tinkled as we made love. When the clouds had cleared we bought fish fresh from the nets in the whitewashed harbour. Then we talked in firelight and the dolphins sang to the lobsters as the waves advanced. She told me under the stars that she knew other places, other worlds. There's another John at your shoulder, she said. He's so like you I can't understand what's different.

But Formentera was a long way from anything. It was so timeless we knew it couldn't last. The tourists, the government, the locals, the police—every Snodgrass in the universe—moved in. Turned out Morwenna's parents had money so it was all just fine and dandy for the cunt, leaving me one morning before the sun was up, taking a little boat to the airport on Ibiza, then all the way back to bloody Cardiff. The clouds greyed over the Med and the Doctor stayed on too long. Shot the wrong shit, scored the wrong deals. Somehow, I ended up in Paris, sleeping in a box and not speaking a bloody word of the lingo. Then somewhere else. The whole thing is a haze. Another time, I was sobbing on Mimi's doorstep in pebbledash Menlove Avenue and the dog next door was barking and Mendips looked just the same. The porch where I used to play me guitar. Wallpaper and cooking smells inside. She gave me egg and chips and tea in thick white china, just like the old days when she used to go on about me drainpipes.

So I stayed on a while in Liverpool, slept in me old bed with me feet sticking out the bottom. Mimi had taken down all me Brigitte Bardot posters but nothing else had changed. I could almost believe that me mate Paul was gonna come around on the wag from the Inny and we'd spend the afternoon with our guitars and pickle sandwiches, rewriting Buddy Holly and dreaming of the days to come. The songs never came out the way we meant and the gigs at the Casbah were a mess. But things were *possible*, then, yer know?

I roused meself from bed after a few weeks and Mimi nagged me down the Jobbie. Then I had to give up kidding meself that time had stood still. Did yer know all the docks have gone? I've never seen anything so empty. God knows what the people do with themselves when they're not getting pissed. I couldn't even find the fucking Cavern, or Eppy's old record shop where he used to sell that Sibelius crap until he chanced upon us rough lads.

When I got back to Mendips I suddenly saw how old Mimi had got. Mimi, I said, yer're a senior citizen. *I* should be looking after *you*. She just laughed that off, of course; Mimi was sweet and sour as ever. Wagged her finger at me and put something tasty on the stove. When Mimi's around, I'm still just a kid, can't help it. And she couldn't resist saying, I told you all this guitar stuff would get you nowhere, John. But at least she said it with a smile and hug. I guess I could have stayed there forever, but that's not the Doctor's way. Like Mimi says, he's got ants in his pants. Just like his poor dead mum. So I started to worry that things were getting too cosy, that maybe it was time to dump everything and start again, again.

What finally happened was that I met this bloke one day on me way back from the Jobbie. The original Snodgrass, no less—the one I used to sneer at during calligraphy in Art School. In them days I was James Dean and Elvis combined with me drainpipes and me duck's arse quiff. A one man revolution—Cynthia, the rest of the class were so hip they were trying to look like Kenny Ball and his Sodding Jazzmen. This kid Snodgrass couldn't even manage that, probably dug Frank Ifield. He had spots on his neck, a green sports jacket that looked like his mum had knitted it. Christ knows what his real name was. Of course, Dr. Winston used to take the piss something rancid, specially when he'd sunk a few pints of black velvet down at Ye Cracke. Anyway, twenty years on and the Doctor was watching ye seagulls on Paradise Street and waiting for the lights to change, when this sports car shaped like a dildo slides up and a window purrs down.

"Hi, John! Bet you don't remember me."

All I can smell is leather and aftershave. I squint and lean forward to see. The guy's got red-rimmed glasses on. A grin like a slab of marble.

"Yeah," I say, although I really don't know how I know. "You're the prat from college. The one with the spotty neck."

"I got into advertising," he said. "My own company now. You were in that band, weren't you, John? Left just before they made it. You always did talk big."

"Fuck off, Snodgrass," I tell him, and head across the road. Nearly walk straight into a bus.

Somehow, it's the last straw. I saunter down to Lime Street, get me a platform ticket and take the first Intercity that comes in, la, la. They throw me off at Brum, which I swear to Jesus God is the only reason why I'm here. Oh, yeah. I let Mimi know what had happened after a few weeks when me conscience got too heavy. She must have told Cyn. Maybe they send each other Crimble cards.

Damn.

Cal's gone.

Cold. The sofa. How can anyone *sleep* on this thing? Hurts me old bones just to sit on it. The sun is fading at the window. Must be late afternoon. No sign of Cal. Probably has to do the biz with some Arab our Kev's found for her. Now seems as good a time as any to sort out Macca's tickets, but when I look on top ye telly they've done a runner. The cunt's gone and hidden them, la, la.

Kevin's back. I can hear him farting and snoring upstairs in Cal's room. I shift the dead begonia off ye sideboard and rummage in the cigar box behind. Juicy stuff, near on sixty quid. Cal hides her money somewhere different about once a fortnight, and she don't think the Doctor has worked out where she's put it this time. Me, I've known for ages, was just saving for ye rainy day. Which is now.

So yer thought yer could get Dr. Winston O'Boogie to go and see Stu and Paulie just by hiding the tickets did yer? The fucking NEC! Ah-ha. The Doctor's got other ideas. He pulls on ye jacket, his best and only shoes. Checks himself in the hall mirror. Puts on glasses. Looks like Age Concern. Takes them off again. Heads out. Pulls the door quiet in case Kev should stir. The air outside is grainy, smells of diesel. The sky is pink and all the street lights that work are coming on. The kids are still playing, busy breaking the aerial off a car. They're too absorbed to look up at ye passing Doctor, which is somehow worse than being taunted. I recognise the cracks in ye pavement. This one looks like a moon buggy. This one looks like me mum's face after the car hit her outside Mendips. Not that I saw, but still, yer dream, don't yer? You still dream. And maybe things were getting a bit too cosy here with Cal anyway, starting to feel sorry for her instead of meself. Too cosy. And the Doctor's not sure if he's ever coming back.

I walk ye streets. Sixty quid, so which pub's it gonna be? But it turns out the boozers are still all shut anyway. It don't feel early, but it is—children's hour on the telly, just the time of year for smoke and darkness.

End up on the hill on top of the High Street. See the rooftops from here, cars crawling, all them paper warriors on the way home, Tracy doing lipstick on the bus, dreaming of her boyfriend's busy hands and the night to come. Whole of Birmingham's pouring with light. A few more right turns in the Sierra to where the avenues drip sweet evening and Snodgrass says I'm home darling. Deep in the sea arms of love and bolognese for tea. Streets of Solihull and Sutton Coldfield where the kids know how to work a computer instead of just nick one, wear ye uniform at school, places where the grass is velvet and there are magic fountains amid the fairy trees.

The buses drift by on sails of exhaust and the sky is the colour of Ribena. Soon the stars will come. I can feel the whole night pouring in, humming words I can never quite find. Jesus, does *everyone* feel this way? Does Snodgrass carry this around when he's watching Tracy's legs, on holy Sunday before the Big Match polishing the GL badge on his fucking Sierra? Does he dream of the dark tide, seaweed combers of the ocean parting like the lips he never touched?

Me, I'm Snodgrass, Kevin, Tracy, fat Doris in her print dress. I'm every bit part player in the whole bloody horrorshow. Everyone except John Lennon. Oh Jesus Mary Joseph and Winston, I dreamed I could circle the world with me arms, take the crowd with me guitar, stomp the beat on dirty floors so it would never end, whisper the dream for every kid under the starch sheets of radio nights. Show them how to shine.

Christ, I need a drink. Find me way easily, growl at dogs and passers-by, but Dave the barman's a mate. Everything's deep red in here and tastes of old booze and cigs and the dodgy Gents, just like swimming through me own blood. Dave is wiping the counter with a filthy rag and it's Getting pissed tonight are we, John? Yer bet, wac. Notice two rastas in the corner. Give em the old comic Livipud accent. Ken Dodd and his Diddymen. Makes em smile. I hate it when they don't smile. Ansells and a chaser. Even got change for the juke-box. Not a Beatles song in sight. No "Yesterday," no "C Moon," no "Mull of Kinbloodytyre." Hey, me shout at ye rastas, Now Bob Marley, he was the biz, reet? At least he had the sense to die. Like Jimi, Jim, Janis, all the good ones who kept the anger and the dream. The rastas say something unintelligible back. Rock and roll, lets. The rastas and Winston, we're on the same wavelength. Buy em a drink. Clap their backs. They're exchanging grins like they think I don't notice. Man, will you look at this sad old git? But he's buying. Yeah I'm buying thanks to Cal. By the way lads, these Rothmans taste like shit, now surely you guys must have something a little stronger?

The evening starts to fill out. I can see everything happening even before it does. Maybe the Doctor will have a little puke round about eight to make room for a greasy chippy. Oh, yeah, and plenty of time for more booze and then maybe a bit of bother later. Rock and roll. The rastas have got their mates with them now and they're saying Hey man, how much money you got there? I wave it in their faces. Wipe yer arse on this, Sambo. Hey, Dave, yer serving or what? Drinky here, drinky there. The good Doctor give drinky everywhere.

Juke-box is pounding. Arms in arms, I'm singing words I don't know. Dave he tell me, Take it easy now, John. And I tell him exactly what to stuff, and precisely where. Oh, yeah. Need to sit down. There's an arm on me shoulder. I push it off. The arm comes again. The Doctor's ready to lash out, so maybe the bother is coming earlier than expected. Well, that's just fine and me turn to face ye foe.

It's Cal.

"John, you just can't hold your booze any longer."

She's leading me out ye door. I wave me rastas an ocean wave. The bar waves back.

The night air hits me like a truncheon. "How the fuck did yer find me?"

"Not very difficult. How many pubs are there around here?"

"I've never counted." No, seriously. "Just dump me here, Cal. Don't give me another chance to piss yer around. Look." I fumble me pockets. Twenty pee. Turns out I'm skint again. "I nicked all yer money. Behind the begonia."

"On the sideboard? That's not mine, it's Kevin's. After last time do you think I'm stupid enough to leave money around where you could find it?"

"Ah-ha!" I point at her in triumph. "You called him Kevin."

"Just get in the bloody car."

I get in the bloody car. Some geezer in the front says Okay guv, and off we zoom. It's a big car. Smells like a new camera. I do me royal wave past Kwiksave. I tell the driver, Hey me man, just step on it and follow that car.

"Plenty of time, sir," he tells me. He looks like a chauffeur. He's wearing a bloody cap.

Time for what?

And Jesus, we're heading to Solihull. I've got me glasses on somehow. Trees and a big dual carriageway, the sort you never see from a bus.

The Doctor does the interior a favour. Says, Stop the car. Do a spastic sprint across ye lay-by and yawn me guts out over the verge. The stars stop spinning. I wipe me face. The Sierras are swishing by. There's a road sign the size of the Liverpool Empire over me head. Says NEC, two miles. So *that's* it.

Rock and roll. NEC. I've been here and seen Simply Red on Cal's free tickets, all them pretty tunes with their balls lopped off at birth. Knew what to expect. The place is all car park, like a bloody airport but less fun. Cal says Hi to the staff at the big doors, twilight workers in Butlin's blazers. Got any jobs on here, Cal? asks the pretty girl with the pretty programmes. It's Max Bygraves next week. Cal just smiles. The Doctor toys with a witty riposte about how she gets more dough lying with her legs open but decides not to. But Jesus, this is Snodgrass city. I've never seen so many casual suits.

I nick a programme from the pile when no one's looking. Got so much gloss on it, feels like a sheet of glass. The Greatest Hits Tour. Two photos of the Fab Foursome, then and now. George still looks like his mum, and Ringo's Ringo. Stu is wasted, but he always was. And Macca is Cliff on steroids.

"Stop muttering, John," Cal says, and takes me arm.

We go into this aircraft hangar. Half an hour later, we've got to our seat. It's right at the bloody front of what I presume must be the stage. Looks more like Apollo Nine. Another small step backwards for mankind. Oh, yeah. I *know* what a stage should look like. Like the bloody Indra in Hamburg where we took turns between the striptease. A stage is a place where yer stand and fight against the booze and the boredom and the sodding silence. A place where yer make people listen. Like the Cavern too before all the Tracys got their lunchtime jollies by screaming over the music. Magic days where I could feel the power through me Rickenbacker. And that guitar cost me a fortune and where the bloody hell did it get to? Vanished with every other dream.

Lights go down. A smoothie in a pink suit runs up to a mike and says ladeeez and gennnlemen, Paul McCartney, Stuart Sutcliffe, George Harrison, Ringo Starr—the Beatles! Hey, rock and roll. Everyone cheers as they run on stage. Seems like there's about ten of them nowadays, not counting the background chicks. They're all tiny up on that launch pad, but I manage to recognise Paul from the photies. He says Hello (pause) Birrrmingham just like he's Mick Hucknall and shakes his mop top that's still kinda cut the way Astrid did all them years back in Hamburg. Ringo's about half a mile back hidden behind the drums but that's okay cos there's some session guy up there too. George is looking down at his guitar like he's Bert Weedon. And there's Stu almost as far back as Ringo, still having difficulty playing the bass after all these bloody years. Should have stuck with the painting, me lad, something yer were good at. And Jesus, I don't believe it, Paul shoots Stu an exasperated glance as they kick into the riff for "Long Tall Sally" and he comes in two bars late. Jesus, has *anything* changed.

Yeah, John Lennon's not up there. Would never have lasted this long with the Doctor anyway. I mean, thirty *years*. That's as bad as Status Quo, and at least they know how to rock, even if they've only learnt the one tune.

Days in me life. Number one in a series of one. Collect the fucking set. It's 1962. Eppy's sent us rough lads a telegram from down the Smoke. Great news, boys. A contract. This is just when we're all starting to wonder, and Stu in particular is pining for Astrid back in Hamburg. But we're all giving it a go and the Doctor's even agreed to that stupid haircut that never quite caught on and to sacking Pete Best and getting Ringo in and the bloody suit with the bloody collar and the bloody fucking tie. So down to London it is. And then ta ran ta rah! A real single, a real recording studio! We meet this producer dude in a suit called Martin. He and Eppy get on like old buddies, upper crust and all that and me wonders out loud if he's a queer Jew too, but Paul says Can it John we can't afford to blow this.

So we gets in ye studio which is like a rabbit hutch. Do a roll Ringo, Martin says through the mike. So Ringo gets down on the mat and turns over. We all piss ourselves over that and all the time there's Mr. Producer looking schoolmasterish. Me, I say, Hey, did yer really produce the Goons, Meester Martin. I got the "Ying Tong Song" note perfect. They all think I'm kidding. Let's get on with it, John, Eppy says, and oils a grin through the glass, giving me the doe eyes. And don't yer believe it, John knows exactly what he wants. Oh, yeah. Like, did Colonel Parker fancy Elvis? Wow. So this is rock and roll.

Me and Paul, we got it all worked out. Hit the charts with "Love Me Do," by Lennon and McCartney, the credits on the record label just the way we agreed years back in the front parlour of his Dad's house even though we've always done our own stuff separately. It's Macca's song, but we're democratic, right? And what really makes it is me harmonica riff. So that's what we play and we're all nervous as shit but even Stu manages to get the bass part right just the way Paul's shown him.

Silence. The amps are humming. Okay, says Mr. Martin, putting on a voice, That was just great, lads. An interesting song. *Interesting*? Never one to beat about the proverbial, I say, yer mean it was shit, right? Just cos we wrote it ourselves and don't live down Tin Pan bloody Alley. But he says, I think we're looking at a B side for that one lads. Now, listen to this.

Oh, yeah. We listen. Martin plays us this tape of a demo of some ditty called "How Do You Do It." Definite Top Ten material for somebody, he says significantly. Gerry and the Pacemakers are already interested but I'll give you first refusal. And Eppy nods beside him through the glass. It's like watching Sooty and bloody Sweep in there. So Ringo smashes a cymbal and Stu tries to tune his bass and George goes over to help and I look at Paul and Paul looks at me.

"It's a decent tune, John," Paul says.

"You're kidding. It's a heap of shit."

Eppy tuts through the glass. Now *John*.

And so it goes. Me, I grab me Rickenbacker and walk out the fucking studio. There's a boozer round the corner. London prices are a joke but I sink one pint and then another, waiting for someone to come and say, You're so right, John. But Paul don't come. Eppy don't come either even though I thought it was me of all the lads that he was after. After the third pint, I'm fucking glad. The haircuts, the suits, and now playing tunes that belong in the bloody adverts. It's all gone too far.

And there it was. John Quits The Beatles in some local snotrag called *Merseybeat* the week after before I've had a chance to change me mind. And after that I've got me pride. When I saw Paul down Victoria Street a couple a months later yer could tell the single was doing well just by his bloody walk. Said Hi John, yer know it's not too late and God knows how *Merseybeat* got hold of the story. He said it as though he and Eppy hadn't jumped at the chance to dump me and make sure everybody knew. There was Macca putting on the charm the way he always did when he was in a tight situation. I told him to stuff it where the fucking sun don't shine. And that was that. I stomped off down ye street, had a cup of tea in Littlewoods. Walked out on Cynthia and the kid. Formed me own band. Did a few gigs. Bolloxed up me life good and proper.

And here we have the Beatles, still gigging, nearly a full house here at the NEC, almost as big as Phil Collins or the Bee Gees. Paul does his old thumbs-up routine between songs. Awwrright. He's a real rock and roll dude, him and George play their own solos just like Dire Straights. The music drifts from the poppy older stuff to the druggy middle stuff back to the poppy later stuff. "Things We Said Today." "Good Day Sun Shine." "Dizzy Miss Lizzy." "Jet." They even do "How Do You Do It." No sign of "Love Me Do," of course. That never got recorded, although I'll bet they could do me harmonica riff on ye synthesiser as easy as shit. It all sounds smooth and tight and sweetly nostalgic, just the way it would on the Sony music centre back at home after Snodgrass has loosened his tie from a hard day watching Tracy wriggle her ass over the fax machine in Accounts. The pretty lights flash, the dry ice fumes, but the spaceship never quite takes off. Me, I shout for "Maxwell's Silver Hammer," and in a sudden wave of silence, it seems like Paul actually hears. He squints down at the front row and grins for a moment like he understands the joke. Then the lights dim to purple and Paul sits down at ye piano, gives the seat a little tug just the way he used to when he was practising on his Dad's old upright in the parlour at home. Plays the opening chords of "Let It Be." I look around me and several thousand flames are held up. It's a forest of candles, and Jesus it's a beautiful song. There's a lump in me throat, God help me. For a moment, it feels like everyone here is close to touching the dream.

The moment lasts longer than it decently should. Right through "No More Lonely Nights" until "Hey Judi" peters out like something half-finished and the band kick into "Lady Madonna," which has a thundering bass riff even though Stu is still picking up his Fender. And the fucking stage starts to revolve. Me, I've had enough.

Cal looks at me as I stand up. She's bopping along like a Tracy. I mouth the word Bog and point to me crotch. She nods. Either she's given up worrying about the Doctor doing a runner or she don't care. Fact is, the booze has wrung me dry and I've got me a headache coming. I stumble me way up the aisles. The music pushes me along. He really *is* gonna do "C Moon." Makes yer want to piss just hearing it.

The lav is deliciously quiet. White tiles and some poor geezer in grey mopping up the piss. The Doctor straddles the porcelain. It takes about a minute's concentration to get a decent flow. Maybe this is what getting old is all about. I wonder if superstars like Macca have the same problem, but I doubt it. Probably pay some geezer to go for them, and oh, Kevin, can yer manage a good dump for me while yer're there?

Once it starts, the flow keeps up for a long time. Gets boring. I flush down ye stray hair, dismantle ye cigarette butt, looking at the grouting on the tiles, stare around. The guy with the mop is leaning on it, watching me.

"Must be a real groove in here," I say.

"Oh, no," he laughs. "Don't get the wrong idea."

I give percy a shake and zip up. The last spurt still runs down me bloody leg. Bet that don't happen to Paul either.

The wrong idea? The guy's got the plump face of a thirty-year-old choirboy. Pity poor Eppy ain't still alive, he'd be in his fucking element.

"I think all queers should be shot," fat choirboy assures me.

"Well, seeing it from your perspective . . ." The Doctor starts to back away. This guy's out-weirding me without even trying.

"What's the concert like?"

The music comes around the corner as a grey echo, drowned in the smell of piss and disinfectant. "It's mostly shit, what do yer expect?"

"Yeah," he nods. His accent is funny. I think it's some bastard kind of Brummy until I suddenly realise he's American. "They sold out, didn't they?"

"The Beatles never sold in."

"Bloody hypocrites. All that money going to waste."

Some other guy comes in, stares at us as he wees. Gives his leg a shake, walks out again. Choirboy and I stand in stupid silence. It's one of them situations yer find yerself in. But anyone who thinks that the Beatles are crap can't be all bad.

"You used to be in the Beatles, didn't you?"

I stare at him. No one's recognised me just from me face in years. I've got me glasses on, me specially grey and wrinkled disguise.

"Oh, I've read all about the Beatles," he assures me, giving his mop a twirl.

I've half a mind to say, If yer're that interested give me the fucking mop and yer can have me seat, but there's something about him that I wouldn't trust next to Cal.

"Hey," he smiles. "Listen in there. Sounds like they're doing the encore."

Which of course is "Yesterday," like Oh deary me, we left it out by accident from the main show and thought we would just pop it in here. Not a dry seat in the bloody house.

Choirboy's still grinning at me. I see he's got a paperback in the pocket of his overall. *Catcher in the Rye.* "They'll be a big rush in a minute," he says. "More mess for me to clean up. Even Jesus wouldn't like this job."

"Then why do yer do it? The pay can't be spectacular."

"Well, this is just casual work. I'll probably quit after tonight."

"Yeah, pal. I know all about casual work."

"But this is interesting, gets you into places. I like to be near to the stars. I need to see how bad they are." He cracks that grin a little wider. "Tell me," he says, "what's Paul really like?"

"How the fuck should I know? I haven't seen the guy in nearly thirty years. But, there's . . . there's some do on afterwards . . . he's asked me and me bird to come along. Yer know, for old times I guess." *Jesus, John, who are yer trying to impress?*

"Oh," he says, "and where's that taking place? I sometimes look in, you know. The security round here's a joke. Last week, I was *that* close to Madonna." He demonstrates the distance with his broom.

Cal's got the invites in her handybag, but I can picture them clear enough. I've got a great memory for crap. They're all scrolled like it's a wedding and there's a signed pass tacked on the back just to make it official. Admit two, The Excelsior, Meriden. Boogie on down, and I bet the Lord Mayor's coming. And tomorrow it's Reading. I mean, do these guys paarrty every night?

Choirboy grins. "It's here at the Metropole, right?"

"Oh, yeah, the Metropole." I saw the neon on the way in. "That's the place just outside? Saves the bastards having to walk too far." I scratch me head. "Well maybe I'll see yer there. And just let me know if yer have any trouble at all getting in, right?"

"Right on." He holds out his hand. I don't bother to shake it—and it's not simply because this guy cleans bogs. I don't want him near me, and somehow I don't want him near Paul or the others either. He's a fruitcase, and I feel briefly and absurdly pleased with meself that I've sent him off to ye wrong hotel.

I give him a wave and head on out ye bog. In the aircraft hangar, music's still playing. Let's all get up and dance to a song de da de da de dum de dum. Snodgrass and Tracy are trying to be enthusiastic so they can tell everyone how great it was in the office tomorrow. I wander down the aisles, wondering if it might be easier not to meet up with Cal. On reflection, this seems as good a place as any to duck out of her life. Do the cunt a favour. After all, she deserves it. And to be honest, I really don't fancy explaining to Kevin where all his money went. He's a big lad, is our Kev. Useful, like.

The music stops. The crowd claps like they're really not sure whether they want any more and Paul raises an unnecessary arm to still them.

"Hey, one more song then we'll let yer go," he says with probably unintentional irony. I doubt if they know what the fuck is going on up there in Mission Control.

He puts down his Gibson and a roadie hands him something silver. Stu's grinning like a skull. He even wanders within spitting distance of the front of the stage. A matchstick figure, I can see he looks the way Keith Richards would have done if he *really* hadn't taken care of himself. He nods to George. George picks up a twelve string.

"This one's for an old friend," Paul says.

The session musicians are looking at each other like What the fuck's going on? Could this really be an unrehearsed moment? Seems unlikely, but then Paul muffs the count in on a swift four/four beat. There's nervous laughter amongst the Fab Fearsome, silence in the auditorium. Then again. One. Two. Three. And.

Macca puts the harmonica to his lips. Plays me riff. "Love Me Do." Oh, yeah. I really can't believe it. The audience are looking a bit bemused, but probably reckon it's just something from the new LP that's stacked by the yard out in the foyer and no one's bothered to buy. The song's over quickly. Them kind of songs always were. Me, I'm crying.

The End. Finis, like they say in cartoon. Ye Beatles give a wave and duck off stage. I get swept back in the rush to get to ye doors. I hear snatches of, Doesn't he look *old*, They never knew how to rock, Absolutely *brilliant*, and *How* much did you pay the babysitter? I wipe the snot off on me sleeve and look around. Cal catches hold of me by the largely unpatronised T-shirt stall before I have a chance to see her coming.

"What did you think?"

"A load of shit," I say, hoping she won't notice I've been crying.

She smiles. "Is that all you can manage, John? That must mean you liked it."

Touché, Monsieur Pussycat. "Truth is, I could need a drink."

"Well, let's get down the Excelsior. You can meet your old mates and get as pissed as you like."

She glides me out towards the door. Me feet feel like they're on rollers. And there's me chauffeur pal with the boy scout uniform. People stare at us as he opens the door like we're George Michael. Pity he don't salute, but still, I'd look a right pillock trying to squirm me way away from a pretty woman and the back seat of a Jag.

The car pulls slowly through the crowds. I do me wave like I'm the Queen Mum although the old bint's probably too hip to be seen at a Beatles concert. Turns out there's a special exit for us VIPs. I mean, rock and roll. It's just a few minutes" drive, me mate up front tells us.

Cal settles back. "This is the life."

"Call this life?"

"Might as well make the most of it, John."

"Oh, yeah. I bet you get taken in this kind of limo all the time. Blowjobs in the back seat. It's what pays, right?" I bite me lip and look out the window. Jesus, I'm starting to cry again.

"Why do you say things like that, John?"

"Because I'm a bastard. I mean, you of all people must know about bastards having to put up with Steve."

Cal laughed. "You called him Steve!"

I really must be going ta bits. "Yeah, well I must have puked up me wits over that lay-by."

"Anyway," she touches me arm. "Call him whatever you like. I took your advice this evening. Told him where to stuff it."

I look carefully at her face. She obviously ain't kidding, but I can't see any bruises. "And what about the money I nicked?"

"Well, that's not a problem for me, is it? I simply told him the truth, that it was you." She smiled. "Come on, John. I'd almost believe you were frightened of him. He's just some bloke. He's got another girl he's after anyway, the other side of town and good luck to her."

"So it's just you and me is it, Cal. Cosy, like. Don't expect me to sort out yer customers for yer."

"I'm getting too old for that, John. It costs you more than they pay. Maybe I'll do more work at the NEC. Of course, you'll have to start paying your sodding rent."

I hear meself say, "I think there's a vacancy coming up in the NEC Gents. How about that for a funky job for Dr. Winston? At least you get to sweep the shit up there rather than having to stuff it into envelopes."

"What are you talking about, John?"

"Forget it. Maybe I'll explain in the morning. You've got influence there, haven't you?"

"I'll help you get a job, if that's what you're trying to say."

I lookouta ye window. The houses streaming past, yellow windows, where ye Snodgrasses who weren't at the concert are chomping pipe and slippers while the wife makes spaniel eyes. The kids tucked upstairs in pink and blue rooms that smell of Persil and Playdough. Me, I'm just the guy who used to be in a halfway-famous band before they were anybody. I got me no book club subscription, I got me no life so clean yer could eat yer bloody dinner off it. Of course, I still got me rebellion, oh yeah, I got me that, and all it amounts to is cadging cigs off Cal and lifting packets of Cheesy Wotsits from the bargain bin in Kwiksave when Doris and Tracy ain't looking. Oh, yeah, rebellion. The milkman shouts at me when I go near his float in case the Mad Old Git nicks another bottle.

I can remember when we used to stand up and face the crowd, do all them songs I've forgotten how to play. When Paul still knew how to rock. When Stu was half an artist, dreamy and scary at the same time. When George was just a neat kid behind a huge guitar, lying about his age. When Ringo was funny and the beat went on forever. Down the smoggily lit stairways and greasy tunnels, along burrows and byways where the cheesy reek of the bogs hit yer like a wall. Then the booze was free afterwards and the girls would gather round, press softly against yer arm as they smiled. Their boyfriends would mutter at the bar but you knew they were afraid of yer. Knew they could sense the power of the music that carried off the stage. Jesus, the girls were as sweet as the rain in those grey cities, the shining streets, the forest wharves, the dark doorways where there was laughter in the dripping brick-paved night. And sleeping afterwards, yer head spinning from the booze and the wakeups and the downers, taking turns on that stained mattress with the cinema below booming in yer head and the music still pouring through. Diving down into carousel dreams.

Oh, the beat went on all right. Used to think it would carry up into daylight and the real air, touch the eyes and ears of the pretty dreamers, even make Snodgrass stir a little in his slumbers, take the shine off the Sierra, make him look up at the angels in the sky once in a while, or even just down at the shit on the pavement.

"Well, here we are," Cal says.

Oh, yeah. Some hotel. Out in the pretty pretty. Trees and lights across a fucking lake. The boy scout opens the door for me and Cal. Unsteady on me pins, I take a breath, then have me a good retching cough. The air out here reeks of roses or something, like one of them expensive bog fresheners that Cal sprays around when our Kev's had a dump.

"Hey." Cal holds out the crook of her arm. "Aren't you going to escort me in?"

"Let's wait here."

There are other cars pulling up, some old git dressed like he's the Duke of Wellington standing at the doors. Straight ahead to the Clarendon Suite, sir, he smooths greyly to the passing suits. I suppose these must be record industry types. And then there's this bigger car than the rest starts to pull up. It just goes on and on, like one of them gags in *Tom and Jerry*. Everyone steps back like it's the Pope. Instead, turns out it's just the Beatles. They blink around in the darkness like mad owls, dressed in them ridiculous loose cotton suits that Clapton always looks such a prat in. Lawyers tremble around them like little fish. Paul pauses to give a motorcycle policeman his autograph, flashes the famous Macca grin. Some guy in a suit who looks like the hotel manager shakes hands with Stu. Rock and roll. I mean, this is what we were always fighting for. The Beatles don't register the good Doctor before they head inside, buy maybe that's because he's taken three steps back into the toilet freshener darkness.

"What are we waiting for?" Cal asks as the rest of the rubbernecks drift in.

"This isn't easy, Cal."

"Who said anything about *easy?*"

I give the Duke of Wellington a salute as he holds ye door open.

"Straight ahead to the Clarendon Suite, sir."

"Hey," I tell him, "I used to be Beatle John."

"Stop mucking about, John." Cal does her Kenneth Williams impression, then gets all serious. "This is important. Just forget about the past and let's concentrate on the rest of your life. All you have to say to Paul is Hello. He's a decent guy. And I'm sure that the rest of them haven't changed as much as you imagine."

Cal wheels me in. The hotel lobby looks like a hotel lobby. The Tracy at reception gives me a cutglass smile. Catch a glimpse of meself in the mirror and unbelievably I really don't look too bad. Must be slipping.

"Jesus, Cal. I need a smoke."

"Here." She rumbles in me pocket, produces Kevin's Rothmans. "I suppose you want a bloody light."

All the expensive fish are drifting by. Some bint in an evening dress so low at the back that you can see the crack of her arse puts her arm on this Snodgrass and gives him a peck on the cheek. That was *delightful*, darrling, she purrs. She really does.

"I mean a *real* smoke, Cal. Haven't you got some blow?" I make a lunge for her handbag.

"Bloody hell, John," she whispers, looking close to losing her cool. She pushes something into my hand. "Have it outside, if you must. Share it with the bloody doorman."

"Thanks Cal." I give her a peck on the cheek and she looks at me oddly. "I'll never forget."

"Forget what?" she asks as I back towards the door. Then she begins to understand. But the Duke holds the door open for me and already I'm out in the forest night air.

The door swings back, then open again. The hotel lights fan out across the grass. I look back. There's some figure.

"Hey, *John!*"

It's a guy's voice, not Cal's after all. Sounds almost Liverpool.

"Hey, wait a minute! Can't we just talk?"

The voice rings in silence.

"John! It's me!"

Paul's walking into the darkness towards me. He's holding out his hand. I stumble against chrome. The big cars are all around. Then I'm kicking white stripes down the road. Turns to gravel underfoot and I can see blue sea, a white beach steaming after the warm rain, a place where a woman is waiting and the bells jingle between her breasts. Just close your eyes and you're there.

Me throat me legs me head hurts. But there's a gated side road here that leads off through trees and scuffing the dirt at the end of a field to some big houses that nod and sway with the sleepy night.

I risk a look behind. Everything is peaceful. There's no one around. Snodgrass is dreaming. Stars upon the rooftops, and the Sierra's in the drive. Trees and privet, lawns neat as velvet. Just some suburban road at the back of the hotel. People living their lives.

I catch me breath, and start to run again.

BY THE MIRROR OF MY YOUTH

Kathe Koja

One of the most exciting new writers to hit the science fiction scene in some time, Kathe Koja is a frequent contributor to *Isaac Asimov's Science Fiction Magazine* and *The Magazine of Fantasy & Science Fiction*. She has also sold stories to *Pulphouse, Universe, The Ultimate Werewolf, A Whisper of Blood*, and elsewhere. Her first novel, *The Cipher*, was released to enthusiastic critical response, and a new novel, *Bad Brains*, was greeted with similar acclaim. Her third novel, *Skin*, has just been published. She has had stories in our Sixth, Seventh, and Ninth Annual Collections.

Here, with her usual hard-edged élan, she gives a whole new meaning to the phrase "technological obsolescence" . . .

Raymond's sweat. Just a bead of it, a proud greasy glitter in the Slavic valley of his temple, his left temple mind you, the one pointed at her. Of course it would be. Rachel had passed no day, had in fact lived no moment of her entire adult life without one of Raymond's irritations parading itself before her. It was a gift he had.

He shifted, there on the bench, the preciously *faux*-Shaker bench he insisted upon inserting in her morning room like a splinter in her living flesh.

"Are you ready to go?" he asked her.

She forbore to answer in words, preferring the quick nod, the quicker rise from her chair, beat him to the door if she could. She couldn't. His healthy rise, his longer reach, his more advantageous proximity to the door, and still he stopped, paused to hold it for her:

"After you," he said.

"Why not," she said. "Once in a lifetime can't hurt."

Halfway through the long drive, he spoke again, her hands tight and graceful on the wheel: "Those gloves look shabby," he said.

"They *are* shabby."

"Well, why don't you get some new ones?"

"That's right." The defroster's heat blowing back, oven-dry into her face. "That's you, isn't it, Ray? When it wears out, get a new one. Because the old one doesn't work anymore. Because the old one's *wearing out*." There were certainly no tears, she had cried this all out years before, but the anger was as bitter and brisk as new snow.

His profile, advantageous in the passing arctic shine of the landscape. His noble brow. "Oh, for God's sake. Aren't you ever going to stop feeling sorry for yourself?"

Who else will, she wanted to say, but that was as petty as it sounded and anyway they were there, the low shiny lines of the clinic before them, as cool and precious as mercury in the manicured drifts of the grounds. The circular driveway looked as if it had been literally swept clean. She pulled the Toyota right up to the entrance, as if it were a nice hotel with a nice doorman who would see to it that the car was safely parked. Her hand on the heavy glass door, warm as honey even through her shabby glove, her frozen skin, did they even heat the glass? No discomfort here, she thought— royal-blue carpet, pink marble glint of the receptionist's desk—heated glass and heated floors, only the client left cold. It made her smile, and she kept the smile to give to the receptionist. There was no point in taking it out on him.

But the receptionist's smile, heavy lips, bright teeth, was all for Raymond: "Good afternoon, Mr. Pope," not presuming to offer his hand until Ray offered his, then accepting it in a flurried, flattered grasp, oh God if she had seen it once she had seen it a million times. If he said anything about *Brain Fevre* she would vomit on the spot.

"It's an honor to have you here," the receptionist said.

"Thank you," Raymond said.

"Dr. Christensen is waiting for you. Will you come this way, please?"

Rachel followed, silent, silent in the warm office, thinking not of what was to come or even of their, no, her first visit here, the papers and papers to sign, the needles and the sharp lights, but of a day when Raymond had sat, slumped and sorry before his terminal, the monitor screen bright and crazed with the germinus of what would become *Brain Fevre*, saying, "It isn't any good. It isn't *working*." Fingers restless on the keys, toying with Delete.

"It's going to." Her hands, not on his shoulders—they had already got past that—but on the green slope of his swivel chair, unconsciously kneading the leather, the padding beneath like flesh under skin. "Just sweat it out, Ray. You can do that."

And he, lips skinned back like Benjamin who lay beneath his feet, "What the hell would you know about it?" and the echo of Benjamin's mimicking growl. Benjamin had loved Ray like a, like a dog, though of course Rachel had been the one to care for him, fill his dishes and let him in and out and drive him to the vet for the interminable shots that prolonged his painful life, drive him too for the last shot that set him free, that set Raymond breaking casseroles and cups in the kitchen when she came home alone.

"Why didn't you tell me?" weeping in his rage, and she, still able to be surprised, protesting that she *had* told him, had begged him to come with her, to be with Benjamin at the end, and he had taken her World's Fair mug, her sister's mug, and standing poised like Thor before the porcelain sink—

"Mrs. Pope?"

"Oh." Looking up to see Dr. Christensen, smiling, this smile for her now but she was past needing smiles, at least for today. "Are you ready to go?"

Raymond's words. "Of course," she said, making it a point to rise smoothly, showing nothing of the jeering clack of bone on bone, the pain that in its inception had compelled her here, back when such things were not only prohibited but prohibitively expensive, before the ambiguities of the Frawley Act, before she had come to loathe Raymond so professionally it was almost a job. It *was* her job, after all, because after all what else did she have to do, useless keeper of the shrine when the god himself was still alive to tend to the incense and answer the mail, every letter hand-signed by the master in his very own childish scrawl, his—

And a door, opening into the jabber of her panic. Scent like medicine, but not. And her voice, but *not* her voice.

"Hello." And beyond the jumble of the others, their self-congratulatory greetings, looking to see herself, eighteen and smiling, holding out her hand.

Carlene. Raymond had named her, of course. She was his toy, after all. She moved around the house like water, her grace so eerie to Rachel from whom it originated, from whom it had so long ago decamped, deserting her at the onset of the disease. In the days when she could still cry, not for herself or the pain, but Raymond. In the days when Raymond still held her, when they talked, talking out this, too, this plan, she whispering, "I don't care so much about dying, but I can't stand for you to be alone." And he, breath hot against her forehead, tears in his voice, "I can't stand it either," and together they wept. For him.

Together they signed the papers, got the bank draft, almost everything they had—this was in the days before *Brain Fevre*, before the money that made their original sacrifice ludicrous, Ray had spent almost that much last year on redoing the Japanese garden. Together they read through the documents, discussed the procedure, experimental, frightening. She drove to the clinic alone, lay in cold paper garments, waiting.

"Did my husband call?"

A meaningless smile. "Perhaps he will later, Mrs. Pope."

When the cells took hold, when the birth began, it was Raymond they notified, while she lay anxious and drugged not half a hall distant. When she finally arrived home, knees trembling, stomach sore from all the vomiting, she sagged in the doorway of his studio and slurred out, "It's a girl."

It was Raymond's name on the progress reports, Raymond's preferences in the client file; he was even listed on the donor sheet, and when she protested this last obliterating irony he had obliterated her further: "Well, let's be realists, Rachel, who is all this for? You or me? You won't even be here."

"Thank God," she had said, already sorry, sorry unto death, but there was now no chance of erasing the fruit of this creation, this costly exclusive child of her flesh. Of course Raymond had long ago refused her the chance for children, but then again this would be no child: this was the second coming of Rachel, his wife improved. The flesh-toy, Rachel called her, called it, unwilling to admit to personhood this monstrous insult, all the more monstrous for her own complicity in its conception.

The progress reports continued. The flesh-toy prospered, the years went on, and her disease, like a river, ran through it all; sometimes she thought she was dying, and in the fading instant wondered with pale regret what it would have been like, to see this woman, this cloned get of hers.

And now, of course, she knew.

Carlene drank tomato juice. Carlene wore wool. Carlene did crossword puzzles, slightly crooked teeth unconsciously exposed as she frowned over a word like *lepidopterist* or *pantophobia*. Rachel watched her like an anthropologist, thinking, I do none of these things, I never did. And yet Carlene liked loud bass-heavy music, and cut apples in slices, never the wedges that Raymond preferred: "They taste better this way," she said firmly, and reluctant, Rachel thought Yes. They do.

She was repellent to Rachel, yet irresistible, as consuming as an itch the time spent observing, seeing spread before her the sweet table of her own youth, lived anew each day in the person of a stranger. As Carlene fetched and carried for Raymond, admired his gardens, studied his art, did all the things she had been created to do, Rachel sat wrapped in the pocket of her pain, and watched.

See the flesh-toy reenact the same old ballet, the same old pavane of his ego and her cheery prostration, his heavy-handed lessons and her student's gravity, his reversionist cant and her wide-eyed worship—it was far worse than Rachel had imagined, far uglier than she could have guessed in the days when she nursed her indignity like a shameful pleasure. But I thought I would be dead, she argued with herself. I thought I wouldn't have to see. Does that make it better? with cold self-disdain, and the eyes that watched Carlene grew dry with a feeling she had not bargained for, that she had imagined in this time of deathbound selfishness beyond her.

She tried to turn away, tried to tell herself it was none of her business, Raymond had certainly made *that* clear. His toy, his money. His sin. Not mine, but: Raymond's hand on Carlene's shoulder, not possessive but devouring, who better than Rachel to know at last what a simple eating machine he was, she who had been his feast for so long. She wanted to go to Carlene and say, Get out of here. Run for your life. But she had read the contract, so many times it was memorized. There was simply no option for Carlene.

Carlene stayed out of her way those first few months, always genuinely pleasant when they met, in the hall, in the kitchen, but also seeming to engineer those meetings deliberately, to keep them brief and few. Carlene had had her own treatment, there at the clinic, her own lessons to learn. Only Raymond had had no treatment. Only Raymond was allowed that largesse.

But finally Rachel tired of it, finally cornered Carlene in the bathroom of all places, stopped her as she left: one hand on the doorjamb, the other cool and useless at her side. The pain was a brisk thing today; it made her blunt.

"I want to talk to you."

"All right." No smile but no discomfort either, leading the way into the morning room: had I, Rachel thought, been so commanding, so very young? And the answer was no, of course, this was less her than that first aimless swirl of cells; the physical duplication was flawless, but the mind behind was Carlene's own.

Now the time to talk, and the words embarrassed her with their inherent idiocy, How does it feel? What do you think about it? Carlene, that grave pucker she recalled from mirrors, that frown that meant I'm listening. "Carlene." Rachel's voice kept even. "What does this mean to you?"

"What?"

Rachel shook her head, impatient, waved a finger back and forth. "This, all of this."

And with her own impatience, "That's like asking a baby what it thinks of sex. It got me here, didn't it?"

Rachel laughed, surprised, and Carlene smiled. "I read the contract," she said. "I have a place to stay. Nobody said I had to like anything." Rising up, all in black today with Rachel's own brilliance in that color, and without thinking Rachel put one hand on Carlene's arm, remembering the stretch and easy pull of muscles all unconscious of a time when such motion would be less memory than joke, and said, "Has Raymond tried to sleep with you yet?"

"Yet," Carlene said, and snickered. And gone.

Yes. Well. What had she expected?—as the morning room turned cold, as the sun turned away—it was the virtual owning of a human being, Carlene's brick-wall acceptance notwithstanding, worse than slavery even if she smiled, even if inside she screamed with laughter every time Ray's prick saluted. You bought her, too, her mind reminded, cold calendar. Not your money, but worse. Your blood. Your *pity*. For Ray.

"*Shit*," she snarled, and heard from the kitchen Raymond's tee-hee-hee.

For God's sake, why couldn't he even laugh like a human being? And Carlene's agreeable chuckle, had I sounded that way, too? No. No. Because I didn't know, did I, that I was a servant, less than a servant, I thought I was a partner, I thought it was a partnership. Till death do us part.

And the old self-contempt rising up like a cobra from a basket, swaying to the music of memories, why couldn't she be one of the ones whose mind went first, lying dribbling and serene instead of twisting like a bug on a pin, on a spike, *God*, and the pain came then, like a no-nonsense jailer, to take her all the way down.

"This isn't necessary." Raymond in the doorway, not so much frowning as issuing displeasure like a silent cloud of flatulence, metronomic glance moving back and forth, Carlene and Rachel, Rachel and Carlene. "She has a day nurse on call."

"I don't mind," Carlene said. Apple juice pouring into a clear glass, such a pretty color. Rachel tried to smile as she took the glass, happy spite, drink it down. Ha ha, Ray. I've got your toy.

"She has these episodes, on and off. She's going to keep having them, till, till they stop." Staring at them both, faintly bug-eyed, what do you see, Ray? Side by side like some horrible living time-lapse photograph; what did it do to Carlene, to see *her*?

Finally he gave up and went away. Carlene reached at once for the apple juice, as if she knew how much effort it cost to drink it. "I'll stay for a while," she said.

"This," Rachel's mutter, "shouldn't be legal. *Shouldn't*."

Carlene's shrug. "Neither should marriage."

The episode, yes, Raymond, sanitize the pain and the puking, why not, it doesn't happen to you. The episode passed. Carlene's illness-born habit of spending mornings with Rachel did not.

They never did much. They never talked much. Sometimes they went outside, took a walk to the main road and back. Sometimes they looked at books, Rachel's art books, relegated by Raymond's loud scorn—patronizing saint of the reversionist movement, nothing matters unless it's backwards and talk about life imitating art—to the bookshelves in her room: Carlene agreed with her about Bosch. Carlene agreed with her about a lot of things.

Side by side in the morning room, slow lemon light and the thin fizz of soda water in her glass, Carlene's profile like talking to herself, her young self, oh God had anyone ever had such a chance? Her life beginning anew without Raymond's tyrannical insistence on his genius and her incomprehensible acquiescence to same, she could not live it all again, had no desire to, was in the end too fatally tired. But. The new improved version. What she couldn't do.

Hearing above them Raymond's petty bluster, eternal petulance at being again excluded from their morning tête-à-tête: "How can you stay?" Rachel asked her, and Carlene's exquisite shrug: "Why did you?"

Exquisite, too, the tang of shared bitterness: "It was in my contract, too."

"Yours was a hell of a lot easier to break."

Rachel, brittle and slow, back a torment in the wicker chair, seeing her own blind chains snaking like living things to encircle these young wrists, choke out a second life; no. Very very quiet: "We'll see."

Carlene's frown. "We won't see. If I violate the terms of the contract, I can't get a job, I can't rent an apartment, or get credit—I can't even get a social security card. I'm an *appliance*, remember?"

"No," and even Carlene drew back now, from the venom in that word, the shaping of it like poison in the cage of withered lips, was she frightened that one day she would look that way, too? That's what we can't let happen, little girl. Not again. "Once," Rachel said, "was enough."

Time was the object. They had little of it, either of them, but they were industrious, they could squeeze everything from a moment. Carlene was

decoy, pleasantly demure in the presence of attorneys, her daughterly affection touching the strangers who watched her helping her afflicted mother
from office to office, my goodness isn't there a family resemblance! "It's not
that we want to *break* the contract, no," Rachel's cool headshake, Carlene's
youthful gravity, "we only want to modify some of the circumstances. You
know I think the world of Carlene, I think of her as my daughter," and
Carlene's smile on cue, perfectly on cue.

It was her job, too, to keep Raymond busily oblivious in the times and
moments when his attention would have been worse than nuisance. Sometimes Rachel watched them, phone to her ear, murmuring questions and
asides and slow cool ponderings, no hint of ticking desperation in the attempts
to cut the path she needed, gazing through the bedroom window: their
walks in the Japanese garden, Raymond's tee-hee-hee audible even from this
distance, and she smiled like an adder, even the trebling pain a spur; I'm
running away, Ray, you goddamned son of a bitch, you vampire. Finally
running away.

"It's not going to work," Carlene's midnight bitterness, face in hands, Rachel
lying newly pinned and tubed on the bed. "You said yourself that if there
were any new loopholes in the Frawley Act, these guys could find them."
More bitterly still: "But there aren't."

Who would imagine that mere breathing could hurt so much, just breathing? "We can find another way."

"I can't wait for another way. I can't *stand* him, Rachel."

"Neither can I. Carlene, I'm doing my best. Believe me," looking at that
face, that future, "we're going to find a way."

But: Episode after episode, dreary daily tragedy of a soap opera, what time
she had, left lucid, was in doubt, what time at all. Raymond refused to come
near her room, he said it smelled, in fact he said the smell was all over the
house. He wanted her put in a nursing home. He was making some telephone
calls of his own, Carlene said.

"I keep calling them back," she said. "I tell them I'm you."

"We're coming so close," Rachel said. Today the pain was thumbscrew,
corkscrew, through every joint and muscle, walking through her brain, new
owner. The doctors—Raymond insisted she know—were quietly shocked
she had lasted this long, even with treatments, even with drugs just this side
of experimental. "I think if we had more time, if—"

"Shhh." Carlene's hand on her shoulder. "Don't talk, I know it hurts you
to talk." Looking up, to see Carlene's tears.

"I didn't *want* it to be you." Crying now and that hurt, too, immeasurably
but not as much as the knowledge that without her it could never have been
done, without the final monstrosity of her consent, of the bits of her body
given over in the same heedless headlong way she had given everything,
everything to Raymond. We were stupid, in those days, she wanted to say,
though nothing could finally excuse her, nothing could explain and maybe
it was really only she who had been so stupid, who had not only made

Raymond her life but had made another life, identical to hers, to make his as well. Crime and punishment there before her. With tears on her face.

I tried to fix it, Rachel thought, you know I did, tried, too, to tell Carlene that, but found in her lungs the brutal ache of airlessness, in her eyes the delicate swim of motes as dark as the claiming of that which ate her, now and finally, alive.

Her head on Carlene's breast, when Raymond found them. Her eyes, as open as Carlene's, as wide, as if both were left astonished in the ancient wake of the bridegroom, come to take the elder daughter to the dance.

"It was going to happen no matter what," he said, heavy with the grief at having to participate in something as sorry as a memorial service. Everyone who came, he was sure, came for his comfort. "It's not genetic, though. I had the doctors make sure. There's nothing for you to worry about." Silence. The slip and tug of her hair through his fingers. "Her, her half, she wanted it to go to you. And all the prenuptial things." More silence. "It's come to a fair amount. She was good with money. I don't bother with the lawyers, you know, but they tell me it's legally yours. Through me, of course."

Carlene's tiny nod, not seen but felt. "I'd rather not talk about it," she said.

"I understand." More arthritic stroking, tangling her hair so it hurt. "When I'm, when—someday, you know, I can't leave it to you, you're not in a position to receive property, but I'll take care of you. I will take care of you."

And the slow time-bomb tick of his heart, her face pillowed on the flat rise and fall of his sour old man's chest, "Mmm-hmm," the ghost of her silent grin in the dark. "Mmm-hmm."

There are all kinds of contracts, when there is money enough—she had more than you think, Raymond, more than you knew about—contracts you don't need to be legal to sign, contracts that are in themselves illegal. Rachel knew about those kinds of contracts, but they frightened her. We'll do it the right way, she said, we'll take the time. Rachel was so patient.

But I couldn't wait for her. And I won't wait for you, either, Ray.

Because I'm not patient.

Because I'm not Rachel.

OUTNUMBERING THE DEAD

Frederik Pohl

Frederik Pohl has been one of the genre's major shaping forces—as writer, editor, agent, and anthologist—for more than fifty years. He was the founder of the *Star* series, SF's first continuing anthology series, and was the editor of the *Galaxy* group of magazines from 1960 to 1969, during which time *Galaxy*'s sister magazine, *Worlds of If*, won three consecutive Best Professional Magazine Hugos. As a writer, he has won several Nebula and Hugo Awards, as well as the American Book Award and the French Prix Apollo. His many books include several written in collaboration with the late C. M. Kornbluth—including *The Space Merchants*, *Wolfbane*, and *Gladiator-at-Law*. His many solo novels include *Gateway*, *Man Plus*, *Beyond the Blue Event Horizon*, *The Coming of the Quantum Cats*, and *The Gateway Trip*. Among his collections are *The Gold at the Starbow's End*, *In the Problem Pit*, and *The Best of Frederik Pohl*. His most recent books are a nonfiction book in collaboration with the late Isaac Asimov, *Our Angry Earth*, and a new novel, *Mining the Oort*.

The novella, which follows, may well be one of the best pieces that Pohl has produced during his long and distinguished career—a wise, funny, madly inventive, and ultimately quite moving look at what it's like to be the ultimate Have-Not in a high-tech future composed almost entirely of *Haves* . . .

1

Although the place is a hospital, or as much like a hospital as makes no difference, it doesn't smell like one. It certainly doesn't look like one. With the flowering vines climbing its walls and the soothing, gentle plink-tink of the tiny waterfall at the head of the bed, it looks more like the de luxe suite in some old no-tell motel. Rafiel is now spruced up, replumbed and ready to go for another five years before he needs to come back to this place for more of the same, and so he doesn't look much like a hospital patient, either. He looks like a movie star, which he more or less is, who is maybe forty years old and has kept himself fit enough to pass for twenty-something. That part's wrong, though. After all the snipping and reaming and implanting they've done to him in the last eleven days, what he is a remarkably fit man of ninety-two.

When Rafiel began to wake from his designer dream he was very hungry (that was due to the eleven days he had been on intravenous feeding) and quite horny, too (that was the last of the designer dream). *"B'jour,* Rafiel," said the soft, sweet voice of the nurser, intruding on his therapeutic dream as the last of it melted away. Rafiel felt the nurser's gentle touch removing the electrodes from his cheekbones, and, knowing very well just where he was and what he had been doing there, he opened his eyes.

He sat up in the bed, pushing away the nurser's velvety helping hand. While he was unconscious they had filled his room with flowers. There were great blankets of roses along one wall, bright red and yellow poppies on the windowsill that looked out on the deep interior court. *"Momento,* please," he said to the nurser, and experimentally stretched his naked body. They had done a good job. That annoying little pain in the shoulder was gone and, when he held one hand before him, he saw that so were the age spots on his skin. He was also pleased to find that he had awakened with a perfectly immense erection. "Seems okay," he said, satisfied.

"Hai, claro," the nurser said. That was the server's programmed all-purpose response to the sorts of sense-free or irrelevant things hospital patients said when they first woke up. "Your *amis* are waiting to come in."

"They can wait." Rafiel yawned, pleasantly remembering the last dream. Then, his tumescence subsiding, he slid his feet over the edge of the bed and stood up. He waved the nurser away and scowled in surprise. "Shit. They didn't fix this little dizziness I've been having."

"Voulez see your chart?" the nurser offered. But Rafiel didn't at all want to know what they'd done to him. He took an experimental step or two, and then the nurser would no longer be denied. Firmly it took his arm and helped him toward the sanitary room. It stood by as he used the toilet and joined him watchfully in the spray shower, the moisture rolling harmlessly down its metal flanks. As it dried him off, one of its hands caught his finger and held on for a moment—heartbeat, blood pressure, who knew what it was measuring?—before saying, "You may leave whenever you like, Rafiel."

"You're very kind," Rafiel said, because it was his nature to be polite even to machines. To human beings, too, of course. Especially to humans, as far as possible anyway, because humans were what became audiences and no sensible performer wanted to antagonize audiences. But with humans it was harder for Rafiel to be always polite, since his inner feelings, where all the resentments lay, were so frequently urging him to be the opposite—to be rude, insulting, even violent; to spit in some of these handsome young faces sometimes out of the anger that was always burning out of sight inside him. He had every right to that smouldering rage, since he was so terribly cheated in his life, but—he was a fair man—his special problem wasn't really their fault, was it? And besides, the human race in general had one trait that forgave them most others, they adored Rafiel. At least the surveys showed that 36.9 per cent of them probably did, a rating which only a handful of utter superstars could ever hope to beat.

That sort of audience devotion imposed certain obligations on a performer. Appearance was one, and so Rafiel considered carefully before deciding what to wear for his release from the hospital. From the limited selection his hospital closet offered he chose red pantaloons, a luminous blue blouse and silk cap to cover his unmade hair. On his feet he wore only moleskin slippers, but that was all right. He wouldn't be performing, and needed no more on the warm, soft, mossy flooring of his hospital room.

He time-stepped to the window, glancing out at the distant figures on the galleries of the hundred-meter atrium of the arcology he lived and worked in, and at the bright costumes of those strolling across the airy bridges, before he opaqued the window to study his reflection. That was satisfactory, though it would have been better if he'd had the closets in his condo to choose from. He was ready for the public who would be waiting for him—and for all the other things that would be waiting for him, too. He wondered if the redecoration of his condo had been completed, as it was supposed to have been while he was in the medical facility; he wondered if his agent had succeeded in re-booking the personal appearances he had had to miss, and whether the new show—what was it based on? Yes. *Oedipus Rex*. Whatever that was—had come together.

He was suddenly impatient to get on with his life, so he said, "All right, they can come in now"—and a moment later, when the nurser had signaled the receptionists outside that it was all right, in they all came, his friends and colleagues from the new show: pale, tiny Docilia flying over to him with a quick kiss, Mosay, his dramaturge, bearing still more flowers, a corsage to go on Rafiel's blouse, Victorium with his music box hung around his neck, all grinning and welcoming him back to life. "And *comment va* our Oedipus this morning?" Mosay asked, with pretend solicitude. Mosay didn't mean the solicitude to be taken seriously, of course, because there was really nothing for anyone to be solicitous about. The nursers wouldn't have awakened Rafiel if all the work hadn't been successfully done.

"*Tutto bene,*" Rafiel answered as expected, letting Mosay press the bunch of little pink violets to his blouse and smelling their sweet scent appreciatively. "Ready for work. Oh, and having *faim*, too."

"But of course you are, after all *that*," said Docilia, hugging him, "and we have a lunch all set up for you. Can you go now?" she asked him, but looking at the nurser—which answered only by opening the door for them. Warmly clutching his arm and fondly chattering in his ear, Docilia led him out of the room where, for eleven days, he had lain unconscious while the doctors and the servers poked and cut and jabbed and mended him.

Rafiel didn't even look back as he entered this next serial installment of his life. There wasn't any nostalgia in the place for him. He had seen it all too often before.

2

The restaurant—well, call it that; it is like a restaurant—is located in the midzone of the arcology. There are a hundred or so floors rising above it and a couple of hundred more below. It is a place where famous vid stars go to be seen, and so at the entrance to the restaurant there is a sort of tearoomy, saloony, cocktail-loungy place, inhabited by ordinary people who hope to catch a glimpse of the celebrities who have come there to be glimpsed. As Rafiel and his friends pass through this warm, dim chamber heads gratifyingly turn. Mosay whispers something humorous to Docilia and Docilia, smiling in return, then murmurs something affectionate to Rafiel, but actually all of them are listening more to the people around them than to each other. "It's the short-time vid star," one overheard voice says, and Rafiel can't help glowing a little at the recognition, though he would have preferred, of course, to have been a celebrity only for his work and not for his problem. "I didn't know she was so tiny," says another voice—speaking of Docilia, of course; they often say that. And, though Mosay affects not to hear, when someone says, "He's got a grandissimo *coming up,* ils disent," *his eyes twinkle a bit, knowing who that "he" is. But then the* maître d' *is coming over to guide them to their private table on an outside balcony.*

Rafiel was the last out the door. He paused to give a general smile and wink to the people inside, then stepped out into the warm, diffused light of the balcony, quite pleased with the way things were going. His friends had chosen the right place for his coming-out meal. If it was important to be seen going to their lunch, it was also important to have their own private balcony set aside to eat it on. They wanted to be seen while eating, of course, because every opportunity to be seen was important to theater people—but from a proper distance. Such as on the balcony, where they were in view of all the people who chanced to be crossing the arcology atrium or looking out from the windows on the other side. The value of that was that then those people would say to the next persons they met, "*Senti,* guess who I saw at lunch today! Rafiel! And Docilia! And, *comme dît,* the music person." And their names would be refreshed in the public mind one more time.

So, though this was to be an agendaed lunch, the balcony was the right place to have it. It wasn't a business-looking place; it could have been more appropriate for lovers, with the soft, warm breezes playing on them and hummingbirds hovering by their juice glasses in the hope of a handout. Really, it would have been more comfortable for a couple; for the four of them, with their servers moving between them with their buffet trays, it was a pretty tight squeeze.

Rafiel ravened over the food, taking great heaps of everything as fast as the servers could bring it. His friends conspired to help. "Give him *pommes,*" Mosay ordered, and Docilia whispered, "Try the *sushi ceveche,* it's *fine.*" Mouth full and chewing, Rafiel let his friends fuss over him. From time to time he raised his eyes from his food to smile at jest or light line, but there was no need for him to take part in the talk. He was just out of the hospital, after all. (As well as being a star, even among these stars; but that was a given.) He knew that they would get down to business quickly enough.

Docilia was always in a hurry to get on with the next production and Mosay, the dramaturge—was, well, a dramaturge. It was his *business* to get things moving. Meanwhile, it was Rafiel's right to satisfy one appetite and to begin to plan ahead for the pleasing prospect of relieving the other. When Docilia put a morsel of pickled fish between his lips he licked her fingertips affectionately and looked into her eyes.

He was beginning to feel at ease.

The eleven days in the medical facility had passed like a single night for Rafiel, since he had been peacefully unconscious for almost all of it. He saw, though, that time had passed for the others, because they had changed a little. Mosay was wearing a little waxed moustache now and Victorium was unexpectedly deeply tanned, right up to his *cache-sexe* and on the expanse of belly revealed by his short embroidered vest. Docilia had become pale blonde again. For that reason she was dressed all in white, or almost all: white bell-bottomed pants and a white halter top that showed her pale skin. The only touch of contrast was a patch of fuzzy peach-colored embroidery at the crotch of the slacks that, Rafiel was nearly sure he remembered, accurately matched the outlines of her pubic hair. It was a very Docilia kind of touch, Rafiel thought.

Of course, they were all very smartly dressed. They always were; like Rafiel they owed it to their public. The difference between Rafiel and the others was that every one of them looked to be about twenty years old—well, ageless, really, but certainly, at the most, no more than a beautifully fit thirtyish. They always had looked that way. All of them did. All ten *trillion* of them did, all over the world and the other worlds, or anyway nearly all. . . . Except, of course, for the handful of oddities like himself.

When Docilia saw Rafiel's gaze lingering on her—observing it at once, because Docilia was never unaware when someone was looking at her—she reached over and fondly patted his arm. He leaned to her ear to pop the question: "*Bitte*, are you free this afternoon?"

She gave him a tender smile. "For you," she said, almost sounding as though she meant it, "*siempre*." She picked up his hand and kissed the tip of his middle finger to show she was sincere. "*Mais* can we talk a little business first? Victorium's finished the score, and it's *belle*. We've got—"

"Can we play it over *casa tu*?"

Another melting smile. "*Hai*, we can. *Hai*, we will, as much as you like. But, listen, we've got a wonderful second-act duet, you and I. I love it, Rafiel! It's when you've just found out that the woman you've been shtupping, that's me, is your mother, that's me, too. Then I'm telling you that what you've done is a sin . . . and then at the end of the duet I run off to hang myself. Then you've got a solo dance. Play it for him, Victorium?"

Victorium didn't need to be begged; a touch of his fingers on his amulet recorder and the music began to pour out. Rafiel paused with his spoon in his juicy white sapote fruit to listen, not having much choice. It was a quick, tricky jazz tune coming out of Victorium's box, but with blues notes in it too, and a funny little hoppity-skippy syncopation to the rhythm that sounded Scottish to Rafiel.

"*Che? Che?*" Victorium asked anxiously as he saw the look on Rafiel's face. "Don't you like it?"

Rafiel said, "It's just that it sounds—gammy. *Pas* smooth. Sort of like a little limp in there."

"*Hai! Precisamente!*" cried Mosay. "You caught it at once!"

Rafiel blinked at him. "What did I catch?"

"What Victorium's music conveyed, of course! You're playing Oedipus Rex and he's *supposed* to be lame."

"Oh, *claro*," said Rafiel; but it wasn't really all that clear to him. He wiped the juice of the sapote off his lips while he thought it over. Then he asked the dramaturge, "Do you think it's a good idea for me to be dancing the part of somebody who's lame?" He got the answer when he heard Docilia's tiny giggle, and saw Victorium trying to smother one of his own. "Ah, *merde*," Rafiel grumbled as, once again, he confronted the unwelcome fact that it was not his talent but his oddity that delighted his audiences. Ageing had been slowed down for him, but it hadn't stopped. His reflexes were not those of a twenty-year-old; and it was precisely those amusing little occasional stumbles and slips that made him *Rafiel*. "I don't like it," he complained, knowing that didn't matter.

"But you *must* do it that way," cried the dramaturge, persuasive, forceful—being a dramaturge, in short, with a star to cajole into shape. "*C'est toi*, really! The part could have been made for you. Oedipus has a bit of a physical problem, but we see how he rises above his limitations and dances beautifully. As, always, do you yourself, Rafiel!"

"*D'accord*," Rafiel said, surrendering as he knew he must. He ate the fruit for a moment, thinking. When it was finished he pushed the shell aside and asked sourly, "How lame is this Oedipus supposed to be, exactly?"

"He's a *blessé*, a little bit. He has something wrong with his ankles. They were mutilated when he was a baby."

"Hum," said Rafiel, and gave Victorium a nod. The musician replayed the five bars of music.

"Can you dance to it?" Victorium asked anxiously.

"Of course I can. If I had my tap shoes—"

"Give him his tap shoes, Mosay," Docilia ordered, and then bent to help Rafiel slip them on, while the dramaturge clapped his hands for a server to bring a tap mat.

"Play from the end of the duet," Rafiel ordered, abandoning his meal to stand up in the narrow space of the balcony. He moved slightly, rocking back and forth, then began to tap, not on the beat of the music, but just off it—*step left, shuffle right*—while his friends nodded approvingly—*spank it back, scuff it forward*. But there wasn't really enough room. One foot caught another; he stumbled and almost fell, Victorium's strong hand catching him. "I'm clumsier than ever," he sighed resentfully.

"They'll love it," Mosay said, reassuring him, and not lying, either, Rafiel knew unhappily; for what was it but his occasional misstep, the odd quaver in his voice—to be frank about it, the peculiarly fascinating traits of his advancing age—that made him a superstar?

He finished his meal. "Come on, Docilia. I'm ready to go," he said, and although the others clearly wanted to stay and talk they all agreed that what Rafiel suggested was a good idea. They always did. It was one of the things that made Rafiel's life special—one of the good things. It came with being a superstar. He was used to being indulged by these people, because they needed him more than he needed them, although, as they all knew, they were going to live for ever and he was not.

3

All the worlds know the name of Rafiel, but, actually, "Rafiel" isn't all of his name. That name, in full, is Rafiel Gutmaker-Fensterborn, just as Docilia, in full, is Docilia Megareth-Morb, and Mosay is Mosay Koi Mosayus. But "Rafiel" is all he needs. Basically, that is the way you can tell when you've finally become a major vid star. You no longer need all those names to be identified or even to get your mail delivered. Even among a race of ten trillion separate, living, named human beings, when you have their kind of stardom a single name is quite enough.

Rafiel's difficulty at present was that he didn't happen to be in his own condo, where his mail was. Instead he was in Docilia's, located fifty-odd stories above his own in the arcology. He really did want to know what messages were waiting for him.

On the other hand, this particular delay was worthwhile. Although Rafiel had been sleeping for eleven days, his glands had not. He was well charged up for the exertions of Docilia's bed. He came to climax in record time—the first time—with Docilia helpfully speeding him along. The second time was companionably hers. Then they lay pleasantly spooned, with Rafiel drowsily remembering now and then to kiss the back of her neck under the fair hair. It wasn't Alegretta's hair, he thought, though without any real pain (you couldn't actually go on aching all your life for a lost love, though sometimes he thought he was coming close); but it was nice hair, and it was always nice to make love to this tiny, active little body. But after a bit she stretched, yawned and left him, fondly promising to be quickly back, while she went to return her calls. He rolled over to gaze at the pleasing sight of her naked and youthfully sweet departing back.

It was a fact, Rafiel knew, that Docilia wasn't youthful in any chronological sense. In terms of life span she was certainly a good deal older than himself, however she looked. But you couldn't ignore the way she looked, either, because the way she looked was what the audiences were going to see. As the story of *Oedipus Rex* began to come back to him, he began to wonder: Would any audience believe for one moment that this girlish woman could be his mother?

It was a silly thought. The audiences weren't going to worry about that sort of thing. If it registered with them at all it would be only another incongruity of the kind that they loved so well. Rafiel dismissed the worry, and then, as he lay there, pleasantly at ease, he at last became aware of the faint whisper of music from Docilia's sound system.

So it had been an agendaed tryst after all, he thought tolerantly. But a sweet one. If she had not forgotten to have Victorium's score playing from the moment they entered her flat, at least she had been quite serious about the lovemaking he had come there for. So Rafiel did what she wanted him to do; he lay there, letting the music tell its story to his ears. It wasn't a bad score at all, he thought critically. He was beginning to catch the rhythms in his throat and feet when Docilia came back.

She was glowing. "Oh Rafiel," she cried, "*look* at this!"

She was waving a tomograph, and when she handed it to him he was astonished to see that it was an image of what looked like a three-month fetus. He blinked at her in surprise. "Yours?"

She nodded ecstatically. "They just sent it from the crèche," she explained, nervous with pleasure. "Isn't it *très belle?*"

"Why, that's *molto bene,*" he said warmly. "I didn't know you were *enceinte* at all. Who's the *padre?*"

She shrugged prettily. "Oh, his name is Charlus. I don't think you know him, but he's really good, isn't he? I mean, *look* at that gorgeous child."

In Rafiel's opinion, no first-trimester fetus could be called anything like "gorgeous," but he knew what was expected of him and was not willing to dampen her delight. "It's certainly a good-looking embryo, *senza dubito,*" he told her with sincerity.

"His *always* are! He's fathered some of the best children I've ever seen— good-looking, and with his dark blue eyes, and oh, so tall and strong!" She hesitated for a moment, prettily almost blushing. Then, "We're going to share the *bambino* for a year," she confided proudly. "As a family, I mean. When the baby's born Charlus and I are going to start a home together. Don't you think that's a wonderful idea?"

There was only one possible answer to that, "Of course I do," said Rafiel, regardless of whether he did or not.

She gave him a fond pat. "That's what you ought to do too, Rafiel. Have a child with some nice *dama*, bring the baby up together."

"And when would I find time?" he asked. But that wasn't a true answer. The true answer was that, yes, he would have liked nothing better, provided that right woman was willing to donate the ovum . . . but the right woman had, long ago, firmly foreclosed that possibility.

Docilia had said something that he missed. When he asked for a repeat, she said, "I said, and it'll help my performance, won't it?"

He was puzzled. "Help how?"

She said, impatient with his lack of understanding. "Because Jocasta's a *Mutter*, don't you see? That's the whole point of the story, isn't it? And now I can get right into the part, because I'm being a *Mutter*, too."

Rafiel said sincerely, "You'll be fine." He meant it, too. He had assumed she would all along.

"Yes, *certo*," she said absently, thinking already of something else. "I think I ought to give a copy to the dad. He'll be so excited."

"*I* would be," Rafiel agreed. She blinked and returned her attention to him. She lifted the sheet and peered under it for a thoughtful moment. "I think," she said judiciously, "if you're not in a great hurry to leave, if we just give it a few more minutes. . . ."

"No hurry at all," he said, pulling her down to him and stroking her back in a no-hurry-at-all way. "Well," he said. "So what else have you been doing? Did they release your *Inquisitor* yet?"

"Three days ago," she said, rubbing her foot along his ankle. "God, those clothes were so *heavy*, and then the last scene— You didn't see it, of course?"

"How could I?"

"No, of course not. Well, try to, *si c'est* possible, because I'm really fine in the *auto-da-fé* scene."

"What scene?" Rafiel knew that Docilia had finished shooting something about the Spanish Inquisition, with lots of torture—torture stories always went well in this world that had so little personal experience of any kind of suffering, but he hadn't actually seen any part of it.

"Where they burn me at the stake. *Quelle horreur!* See, they spread the wood all around in a huge circle and light it at the edges, and I'm chained to the stake in the middle. *Che cosa!* I'm running from side to side, trying to get away from the fire as it burns toward me, and then I start burning myself, *capisce?* And then I just fall down on the burning coals."

"It sounds wonderful," Rafiel said, faintly envious. Maybe it was time for him to start looking for dramatic parts instead of all the song and dance?

"*I* was wonderful," she said absently, reaching under the covers to see what was happening. Then she turned her face to his. "And, guess what? You're getting to be kind of wonderful yourself, *galubka*, right now. . . ."

Three times was as far as Rafiel really thought he wanted to go. Anyway, Docilia was now in a hurry to send off the picture of her child. "Let yourself out?" she asked, getting up. Then, naked at her bedroom door, she stopped to look back at him.

"We'll all be fine in this *Oedipus*, Rafiel," she assured him. "You and me in the lead parts, and Mosay putting it all together, and that *merveilleux* score." Which was still repeating itself from her sound system, he discovered.

He blew her a kiss, laughing. "I'm listening, I'm listening," he assured her. And he did in fact listen for a few moments.

Yes, Rafiel told himself, it really was a good score. *Oedipus* would be a successful production, and when they had rehearsed it and revised it and performed it and recorded it, it would be flashed all over the solar system, over all Earth and the Moon and the capsule colonies on Mars and Triton and half a dozen other moons, and the orbiting habitats wherever they might be, and even to the distant voyagers well on their way to some other star— to all ten million million human beings, or as many of them as cared to watch it. And it would *last*. Recordings of it would survive for centuries, to be taken out and enjoyed by people not yet born, because anything that Rafiel appeared in became an instant classic.

Rafiel got up off Docilia's warm, shuddery bed and stood before her mirror, examining himself. Everything the mirror displayed looked quite all right. The belly was flat, the skin clear, the eyes bright—he looked as good as any hale and well-kept man of middle years would have looked, in the historically remote days when middle age could be distinguished from any other age. That was what those periodical visit to the hospital did for him. Though they couldn't make him immortal, like everyone else, they could at least do *that* much for his appearance and his general comity.

He sighed and rescued the red pantaloons from the floor. As he began to pull them on he thought: They can do all that, but they could not make him live for ever, like everyone else.

That wasn't an immediate threat. Rafiel was quite confident that he would live a while yet—well, quite a *long* while, if you measured it in days and seconds, perhaps another thirty years or so. But then he wouldn't live after that. And Docilia and Mosay and Victorium—yes, and lost Alegretta, too, and everyone else he had ever known—would perhaps take out the record of this new *Oedipus Rex* now and then and look at it and say to each other, "Oh, do you remember dear old Rafiel? How sweet he was. And what a pity." But dear old Rafiel would be *dead*.

4

The arcology Rafiel lives and works in rises 235 stories above central Indiana, and it has a population of 165,000 people. That's about average. From outside—apart from its size—the arcology looks more like something you'd find in a kitchen then a monolithic community. You might think of it as resembling the kind of utensil you would use to ream the juice out of an orange half (well, an orange half that had been stretched long and skinny), with its star-shaped cross section and its rounding taper to the top. Most of the dwelling units are in the outer ribs of the arcology's star. That gives a tenant a nice view, if he is the kind of person who really wants to look out on central Indiana. Rafiel isn't. As soon as he could afford it he moved to the more expensive inside condos overlooking the lively central atrium of the arcology, with all its glorious light and its graceful loops of flowering lianas and its wall-to-wall people—people on the crosswalks, people on their own balconies, even tiny, distant people moving about the floor level nearly two hundred stories below. To see all that is to see life. *From the outer apartments, what can you see? Only farmlands, and the radiating troughs of the maglev trains, punctuated by the to-the-horizon stretch of all the other arcologies that rose from the plain like the stubble of a monster beard.*

In spite of all Rafiel's assurances, Docilia insisted on getting dressed and escorting him back to his own place. She chattered all the way. "So this city you saved, *si chiama* Thebes," she was explaining to him as they got into the elevator, "was in a *hell* of a mess before you got there. Before Oedipus did, I mean. This Sphinx creature was just making *schrecklichkeit*. It was doing all kinds of rotten things—I don't know—like killing people, stealing their food, that sort of thing. I guess. Anyway, the whole city was just *desperate* for help, and then you came along to save them."

"And I killed the Sphinx, so they made me *roi de* Thebes out of gratitude?"

"*Certo!* Well, almost. You see, you don't have to *kill* it, exactly. It has this riddle that no one can figure out. You just have to solve its riddle, and then it I guess just goes kaput. So then you're their hero, Oedipus, but they don't exactly make you king. The way you get to be that is you marry the queen. That's me, Jocasta. I'm just a *pauvre petite* widow lady from the old dead king, but as soon as you marry me that makes you the *capo di tutti capi*. I'm still the queen, and I've got a brother, Creon, who's a kind of a king, too. But you're the boss." The elevator stopped, making her blink in slight surprise. "Oh, *siamo qui*," she announced, and led the way out of the car.

Rafiel halted her with a hand on her shoulder. "I can find my way home from here. You didn't need to come with me at all, *verstehen sie?*"

"I wanted to, *piccina*. I thought you might be a little, well, wobbly."

"I am wobbly, all right," he said, grinning, "*mais pas* from being in the hospital." He kissed her, and then turned her around to face the elevator. Before he released her he said, "Oh, listen. What's this riddle of the Sphinx I'm supposed to solve?"

She gave him an apologetic smile over her shoulder. "It's kind of dopey. 'What goes on four legs, two legs and three legs, and is strongest on two?' Can you imagine?"

He looked at her. "You mean you don't know the answer to that one?"

"Oh, but I do know the answer, Rafiel. Mosay told me what it was. It's—"

"Go on, Cele," he said bitterly. "*Auf wiedersehen.* The answer to the riddle is a 'man,' but I can see why it would be hard for somebody like you to figure it out."

Because, of course, he thought as he entered the lobby of his condo, none of these eternally youthful ones would ever experience the tottery, "three-legged," ancient-with-a-cane phase of life.

"Welcome back, Rafiel," someone called, and Rafiel saw for the first time that the lobby was full of paparazzi. They were buzzing at him in mild irritation, a little annoyed because they had missed him at the hospital, but nevertheless resigned to waiting on the forgivable whim of a superstar.

It was one of the things that Rafiel had had to resign himself to, long ago. It was a considerable nuisance. On the other hand, to be truthful, it didn't take much resignation. When the paps were lurking around for you, it proved your fame, and it was always nice to have renewed proof of that. He gave them a smile for the cameras, and a quick cut-and-point couple of steps of a jig—it was a number from his biggest success, the *Here's Hamlet!* of two years earlier. "Yes," he said, answering all their questions at once, "I'm out of the hospital, I'm back in shape, and I'm hot to trot on the new show that Mosay's putting together for me, *Oedipus Rex.*" He started toward the door of his own flat. A woman put herself in his way.

"Raysia," she introduced herself, as though one name were enough for her, too. "I'm here for the interview."

He stopped dead. Then he recognized the face. Yes, one name was enough, for a top pap with her own syndicate. "Raysia, dear! *Cosi bella* to see you here, but—what interview are we talking about?"

"Your dramaturge set the appointment up last week," she explained. And, of course, that being so, there was nothing for Rafiel to do but to go through with it, making a mental note to get back to Mosay at the first opportunity to complain at not having been told.

But giving an interview was not a hard thing to do, after all, not with all the practice Rafiel had had. He fixed the woman up with a drink and a comfortable chair and took his place at the exercise barre in his study—he always liked to be working when he was interviewed, to remind them he was a dancer. First, though, he had a question. It might not have occurred to him if Docilia hadn't made him think of lost Alegretta, but now he had to ask it. He took a careful first position at the barre and swept one arm gracefully aloft as he asked, "Does your syndicate go to Mars?"

"Of course. I'm into *toutes les biosphères*," she said proudly, "not just Mars, but Mercury and the moons and nearly every orbiter. As well as, naturally, the whole planet Earth."

"That's wonderful," he said, intending to flatter her and doing his best to sound as though this sort of thing hadn't ever happened to him before. Slowly, carefully, he did his barre work, hands always graceful, getting full extension on the legs, her camera following automatically as he answered her questions. Yes, he felt fine. Yes, they were going to get into production on the new *Oedipus* right away—yes, he'd heard the score, and yes, he thought it was wonderful. "And the playwright," he explained, "is the greatest writer who ever lived. Wonderful old Sophocles, two thousand nearly seven hundred years old, and the play's as fresh as anything today."

She looked at him with a touch of admiration for an actor who had done his homework. "Have you read it?"

He hadn't done *that* much homework, though he fully intended to. "Well, not in the original," he admitted, since a non-truth was better than a lie.

"I have," she said absently, thinking about her next question—disconcertingly, too. Rafiel turned around at the barre to work on the right leg for a while. Hiding the sudden, familiar flash of resentment.

"*Vous êtes* terrible," he chuckled, allowing only rueful amusement to show. "All of you! You *know* so much." For they all did, and how unfair. Imagine! This child—this ancient twenty-year-old—reading a Greek play in the original, and not even Greek, he thought savagely, but whatever rough dialect had been spoken nearly three thousand years ago.

"*Mais pourquoi non*? We have time," she said, and got to her question. "How do you feel about the end of the play?" she asked.

"Where Oedipus blinds himself, you mean?" he tried, doing his best to sort out what he had been told of the story. "Yes, that's pretty bloody, isn't it? Stabbing out his own eyes, that's a very powerful—"

She was shaking her head. "No, *pas du tout*, I don't mean the blinding scene. I mean at the very end, where the chorus says"—her voice changed as she quoted—

> See proud Oedipus!
> He proves that no mortal
> Can ever be known to be happy
> Until he is allowed to leave this life,
> Until he is dead,
> And cannot suffer any more.

She paused, fixing him with her eye while the camera zeroed in to catch every fleeting shade of expression on his face. "I'm not a very good translator," she apologized, "but do you feel that way, Rafiel? I mean, as a mortal?"

Actors grow reflexes for situations like that—for the times when a fellow player forgets a line, or there's a disturbance from the audience—when something goes *wrong* and everybody's looking at you and you have to deal with it. He dealt with it. He gave her a sober smile and opened his mouth. "*Hai*, that's so true, in a way," he heard his mouth saying. "*N'est-ce pas*? I mean, not just for me but, *credo*, for all of us? It doesn't matter however long we live, there's always that big final question at the end that we call death, and all we have to confront it with is courage. And that's the lesson of the story, I think: courage! To face all our pains and fears and go on anyway!"

It wasn't good, he thought, but it was enough. Raysia shut off her camera, thanked him, asked for an autograph and left; and as soon as the door was closed behind her Rafiel was grimly on the phone.

But Mosay wasn't answering, had shut himself off. Rafiel left him a scorching message and sat down, with a drink in his hand, to go through his mail. He was not happy. He scrolled quickly through the easy part—requests for autographs, requests for personal appearances, requests for interviews. He didn't have to do anything about most of them; he rerouted them through Mosay's office and they would be dealt with there.

A note from a woman named Hillaree could not be handled in that way. She was a dramaturge herself—had he ever heard of her? He couldn't be sure; there were thousands of them, though few as celebrated as Mosay. Still, she had a proposition for Rafiel. She wanted to talk to him about a "wonderful" (she said) new script. The story took place on one of the orbiting space habitats, a place called *Hakluyt*, and she was, she said, convinced that Rafiel would be determined to do it, if only he would read the script.

Rafiel thought for a moment. He wasn't convinced at all. Still, on consideration, he copied the script to file without looking at it. Perhaps he would read the script, perhaps he wouldn't; but he could imagine that, in some future conversation with Mosay, it might be useful to be able to mention this other offer.

He sent a curt message to this Hillaree to tell her to contact his agent and then, fretful, stopped the scroll. He wasn't concentrating. Raysia's interview had bothered him. "We have time" indeed! Of course they did. They had endless time, time to learn a dead language, just for the fun of it, as Rafiel himself might waste an afternoon trying to learn how to bowl or paraglide at some beach. They *all* had time—all but Rafiel himself and a handful of other unfortunates like him—and it wasn't fair!

It did not occur to Rafiel that he had already had, in the nine decades since his birth, more lifetime than almost anyone in the long history of the human race before him. That was irrelevant. However much he had, everyone around him had so much *more*.

Still, in his ninety years of life Rafiel had learned a great deal—even actors could learn more than their lines, with enough time to do it in. He had learned to accept the fact that he was going to die, while everyone he knew lived on after him. He had even learned why this was so.

It was all a matter of the failings of the Darwinian evolution process.

In one sense, Darwinian evolution was one of the nicest things that had ever happened to life on Earth. In the selection of desirable traits to pass on to descendants—the famous "survival of the fittest"—virtue was rewarded. Traits that worked well for the organism were passed on, because the creatures that had them were more likely to reproduce than the ones lacking them.

Over the billions of years the process had produced such neat things—out of the unpromising single-celled creatures that began it all—as eyes, and anuses, and resistance to the diseases that other organisms wanted to give you, and ultimately even intelligence. That was the best development, in the rather parochial collective opinion of the intelligent human race. Smarts had turned out to be an evolutionary plus; that was why there were ten trillion human beings around, and hardly any of such things as the blue whale, the mountain gorilla and the elephant.

But there was one thing seriously wrong with the way the process works. From the point of view of the individual organism itself, evolution doesn't do a thing. Its benefits may be wonderful for the *next* generation, but it doesn't do diddly-squat for the organisms it is busily selecting, except to encourage the weaker ones to die before they get around to reproducing themselves.

That means that some very desirable traits that every human being would have liked to have—say, resistance to osteoporosis, or a wrinkle-free face—didn't get selected for in the Darwinian lottery. Longevity was not a survival feature. Once a person (or any other kind of animal) had its babies, the process switched itself off. Anything that benefited the organism after it was finished with its years of reproducing was a matter of pure chance. However desirable the new trait might have been, it wasn't passed on. Once the individual had passed the age of bearing young, the Darwinian score-keepers lost interest.

That didn't stop such desirable traits from popping up. Mutations appeared a million times which, if passed on, would have kept the lucky inheritors of subsequent generations hale for indefinite periods—avoiding, let us say, such inconveniences of age as going deaf at sixty, incontinent at eighty and mind-less at the age of a hundred. But such genes came and went and were lost. As they didn't have anything to do with reproductive efficiency, they didn't get preserved. There wasn't any selective pass-through after the last babies were born.

So longevity was a do-it-yourself industry. There was no help from Darwin. But . . .

But once molecular biology got itself well organized, there were things that *could* be done. And were done. For most of the human population. But now and then, there were an unfortunate flawed few who missed out on the wonders of modern life-prolonging science because some undetectable and incurable quirks in their systems rejected the necessary treatment. . . .

Like Rafiel. Who scrolled through, without actually seeing, the scores of trivial messages—fan letters, requests for him to appear at some charitable function in some impossible place, bank statements, bills—that had arrived for him while he was away. And then, still fretful, turned off his communications and blanked his entertainment screen and even switched off the music as, out of habit and need, he practiced his leaps and entrechats in the solitude of his home, while he wondered bitterly what the point was in having a life at all, when you knew that it would sooner or later *end*.

5

People do still die now and then. It isn't just the unfortunates like Rafiel who do it, either, though of course they are the ones for whom it is inevitable. Even normal *people sometimes die as well. They die of accident, of suicide, of murder, sometimes just of some previously unknown sickness or even of a medical blunder that crashes the system. The* normal *people simply do not do that very often. Normal people expect to live normally extended lives. How long those lives can be expected to last is hard to say, because even the oldest persons around aren't yet much more than bicentenarians (that's the time since the procedures first became available), and they show no signs of old age yet. And, of course, since people do go on giving birth to other people, all that longevity has added up to quite an unprecedented population explosion. The*

*total number of human beings living today is something over ten trillion—
that's a one followed by thirteen zeroes—which is far more than the total
number of previous members of the genus* Homo *in every generation since the
first Neanderthalers appeared. Now the living overwhelmingly outnumber the
dead.*

When Rafiel woke the next morning he found his good nature had begun to
return. Partly it was the lingering wisps of his last designer dream—Alegretta
had starred in it, as ordered, and that lost and cherished love of his life had
never been more desirable and more desiring, for that matter, because that
was the kind of dream he had specified. So he woke up in a haze of tender
reminiscence. Anyway, even the terminally mortal can't dwell on their approaching demise all the time, and Rafiel was naturally a cheerful man.

Getting out of bed in the morning was a cheerful occasion, too, for he
was surrounded with the many, many things he had to be cheerful about.
As he breakfasted on what the servers brought him he turned on the vid tank
and watched half a dozen tapes of himself in some of the highlights of his
career. He was, he realized, quite good. In the tank his miniature self sang
love ballads and jiving patter numbers and even arias, and his dancing—
well, yes, now and then a bit trembly, he conceded to himself, but with
style—was a delight to watch. Even for the person who had done it, but
who, looking in the tank, could only see that imaged person as a separate
and, really, very talented entity.

Cheerfully Rafiel moved to the barre to begin his morning warm-ups. He
started gently, because he was still digesting his breakfast. There wasn't any
urgency about it. Rehearsal call was more than an hour away, and he was
contentedly aware that the person he had been looking at on the vid was a
star.

In a world where the living far outnumbered the dead, space was precious.
On the other hand, so was Rafiel, and stars were meant to be coddled. Mosay
had taken a rehearsal room the size of a tennis court for Rafiel's own private
use. The hall was high up in the arcology, and it wasn't just a big room. It
was a very well-equipped one. It had bare powder-blue walls that would turn
into any color Rafiel wanted them to be at the touch of a switch, a polished
floor of real hardwood that clacked precisely to his taps, and, of course, full
sound and light projection. Mosay, fussing over his star's accommodations,
touched the keypad, and the obedient projectors transformed the bare walls
into a glimmering throneroom.

"I'm afraid that it's the wrong period, of course," Mosay apologized,
looking without pleasure at the palace of Versailles, "no *roi soleil* in Thebes,
is there, but I want you to get the feel of the kingship thing, *sapete*? We don't
have the programs for the Theban backdrops yet. Actually I don't know if we
will, because as far as my research people can tell, the Thebans really didn't
have any actual thronerooms anyway."

"It doesn't matter," Rafiel said absently, slipping into his tap shoes.

"It does to me! You know how I am about authenticity." Seeing what Rafiel was doing Mosay hastily turned to touch the control keys again. Victorium's overture began to tinkle from the hidden sound system. *"C'est beau, le son?* It's just a synthesizer arrangement so far."

"It's fine," said Rafiel.

"Are you sure? Well, *bon.* Now, *bitte,* do you want to think about how you want to do the first big scene? That's the one where you're onstage with all the townspeople. They'll be the chorus. You're waiting to find out what news your brother-in-law, Creon, has brought back from the Delphic oracle; he went to find out what you had to do to get things straightened out in Thebes. . . ."

"I've read the script, of course," said Rafiel, who had in fact finished scrolling through it at breakfast.

"Of course you have," said Mosay, rebuked. "So I'll let you alone while you try working out the scene, shall I? Because I want to start checking out shooting locations tomorrow, and so I've got a million things to do today."

"Go and do them," Rafiel bade him. When the dramaturge was gone Rafiel lifted his voice and commanded, "Display text, scene one, from the top. With music."

The tinkling began again at once, and so did the display of the lines. The words marched along the upper parts of the walls, all four walls at once so that wherever Rafiel turned he saw them. He didn't want to dance at this point, he thought. Perhaps just march back and forth—yes, remembering that the character was lame—yes, and a king too, all the same. . . . He began to pantomime the action and whisper the words of his part:

CHORUS: *Ecco* Creon, crowned with laurels.

"He's going to say," Rafiel half-sang in his turn, "what's wrong's our morals."

[ENTER CREON]

CREON: *D'accord,* but I've still worse to follow.
It's not me speaking. It's Apollo.

Rafiel stopped the crawl there and thought for a second. There were some doubts in his mind. How well was that superstitious mumbo-jumbo going to work? You couldn't expect a modern audience to take seriously some mumble from a priestess. On the other hand, and equally of course, Oedipus had not been a modern figure. Would *he* have taken it seriously? Yes, Rafiel decided, he had to, or else the story made no sense to begin with. In playing Oedipus, then, the most he could do was to show a little tolerant exasperation at the oracle's nagging. So he started the accompaniment again, and mimed a touch of amused patience at Creon's line, turning his head away—

And caught a glimpse of an intruder watching him rehearse from the doorway.

It was a small, unkempt-looking young man in a lavender kilt. He was definitely not anyone Rafiel had seen as a member of Mosay's troupe and therefore no one who had a right to be here. Rafiel gave him a cold stare and decided to ignore him.

He realized he'd missed a couple of Creon's lines, and his own response was coming up. He sang:

> OEDIPUS: We'll take care of this hubble-bubble as
> Soon as you tell us what the real trouble is.

But his concentration was gone. He clapped his hands to stop the music and turned to scowl at the intruder.

Who advanced to meet him, saying seriously, "I hope I'm not interfering. But on that line—"

Rafiel held up a forbidding hand. "Who are you?"

"Oh, sorry, I'm Charlus, your choreographer. Mosay said—"

"I do my own choreography!"

"Of course you do, Rafiel," the man said patiently. "You're *Rafiel*. I shouldn't have said choreographer, when all Mosay asked me to do was be your assistant. Do you remember me? From when you did *Make Mine Mars*, twenty years ago it must have been, and I tried out for the chorus line?"

Then Rafiel did identify him, but not from twenty years ago. "You sired Docilia's little one."

Charlus looked proud. "She told you, then? *Evvero*. We're both so happy—but, look, maestro, let me make a suggestion on that bubble-as, trouble-is bit. Suppose . . ."

And the man became Oedipus on the spot, as he performed a simultaneous obscene gesture and courtly bow, ending on one knee.

Rafiel pursed his lips, considering. It was an okay step. No, he admitted justly, it was more than that. It wasn't just an okay step, it was an okay *Rafiel* step, with just a little of Rafiel's well-known off-balance stagger as the right knee bumped the floor.

He made up his mind. "*Khorashaw*," he said. "I don't usually work with anybody else, but I'm willing to give it a try."

"*Spasibo*, Rafiel," the man said humbly.

"*De nada*. Have you got any ideas about the next line?"

Charlus looked embarrassed. "*Hai*, sure, but *est-ce* possible to go back a little bit, to where you come in?"

"My first entrance, at the beginning of the scene?"

Charlus nodded eagerly. "Right there, *pensez-vous* we might try something real macho? You are a king, after all—and you can enter like . . ."

He turned and repeated Oedipus's entrance to the hall, but slowly, s-l-o-w-l-y, with his head rocking and a ritualistic, high-stepping strut and turn before he descended sedately to a knee again. It was the same finish as the other step, but a world different in style and meaning.

Rafiel pursed his lips. "I like it," he said, meditating, "but do you think it really looks, well, Theban? I'd say it's *peut-être* basically Asian—maybe Thai?"

Charlus looked at him with new respect. "Close enough. It's *meno o mino* the Javanese *patjak-kulu* movement. Am I getting too eclectic for you?"

Rafiel acknowledged, "Well, I guess I'm pretty eclectic myself."

"I know," said Charlus, smiling.

While Charlus was showing the mincing little *gedruk* step he thought would be good for Jocasta, Mosay looked in, eyebrows elevated in the obvious question.

Charlus was tactful. "I've got to make a trip to the *benjo*," he said, and Rafiel answered the unspoken question as soon as the choreographer was gone.

"Mind his helping out? No, I don't mind, Mosay. He's no performer himself, but as a choreographer, *hai*, he's *good*." Rafiel was just. The man was not only good, he was bursting with ideas. Better still, it was evident that he had watched every show Rafiel had ever done, and knew Rafiel's style better than Rafiel did himself.

"*Bene, bene*," Mosay said with absent-minded satisfaction. "When you hire the best people you get the best results. Oh, and *senti*, Rafiel"—remembering, as he was already moving toward the door—"those messages you forwarded to me? A couple of them were personal, so I routed them back to your machine. They'll be waiting for you. *Continuez, mes enfants.*" And a pat on the head for the returning Charlus and the dramaturge was gone, and they started again.

It was hard work, good work, with Rafiel happy with the way it was going, but long work, too; they barely stopped to eat a couple of sandwiches for lunch, and even then, though not actually dancing, Rafiel and Charlus were working with the formatting screen, moving computer-generated stick figures about in steps and groupings for the dance numbers of the show, Rafiel getting up every now and then to try a step, Charlus showing an arm gesture or a bob of the head to finish off a point.

By late afternoon Rafiel could see that Charlus was getting tired, but he himself was going strong. He had forgotten his hospital stay and was beginning to remember the satisfactions of collaboration. Having a second person help him find insights into the character and action was a great pleasure, particularly when that person was as unthreatening as the eager and submissive Charlus. "So now," Rafiel said, toweling some sweat away, "we're up to where we've found out that Thebes won't get straight until the assassin of the old king is found and punished, right? And this is where I sing my vow to the gods—"

"*Permesso?*" Charlus said politely. And took up a self-important strut, half tap, almost cakewalk, swinging his lavender kilt as he sang the lines: "I swear, without deceit or bias, We'll croak the rat who croaked King Laius."

"Yes?" said Rafiel, reserving judgment.

"And then Creon gives you the bad news. He tells you that, *corpo di bacco*, things are *bad*. The oracle says that the murderer is here in Thebes. I think right there is when you register the first suspicion that there's something funny going on. You know? Like . . ." miming someone suddenly struck by an unwanted thought.

"You don't think that's too early?"

"It's what you think that counts, Rafiel," Charlus said submissively, and looked up toward the door.

Mosay and Docilia were looking in, the dramaturge with a benign smile, Docilia with a quick kiss for Rafiel and another for Charlus. Although their appearance was a distraction, the kiss turned it into the kind of distraction that starts a new and pleasing line of thought; Docilia was in white again, but a minimum of white: a short white wrap-around skirt, a short wrap-around bolero on top, with bare flesh between and evidently nothing at all underneath. "Everything going all right?" the dramaturge asked, and answered himself: "Of course it is; it's going to be a *merveille du monde*. Dear ones, I just stopped by to tell you that I'm leaving you for a few days; I'm off to scout out some locations for shooting."

Rafiel took his eyes off Docilia and blinked at him. "We're going to make *Oedipus* on location?"

"I insist," said Mosay firmly. "No *faux* backgrounds; I want the real thing for *Oedipus*! We're going to have a Thebes that even the Thebans would admire, if there were any of them left."

Charlus cleared his throat. "Is Docilia going with you?" he asked.

That question had not occurred to Rafiel to ask, but once it was asked he wanted to know the answer, too. Mosay was looking thoughtfully at the choreographer. "Well," he said, "I thought she might have some ideas. . . . Why do you want to know that?"

Charlus had an answer ready. "Because we've started to work out some of the *pas de deux* routines, and Docilia ought to have a chance to try them out." Rafiel did not think it was a truthful one.

Evidently Mosay didn't either. He pursed his lips, considering, but Docilia answered for him. "Of course I should," she said. "You go on without me, Mosay. Have a nice trip; I'll see you when you get back. Only please, dear, try to find a place that isn't too *hot*. I sweat so when I'm dancing, you know."

Whatever plans Charlus had for Docilia, they were postponed. When at last they were through rehearsing, Docilia kissed the choreographer absently and pulled Rafiel along with her out of the room before Charlus could speak. "*J'ai molto faim*, dear," she said—but only to Rafiel, "and I've booked a table for us."

In the elevator, Rafiel looked at her thoughtfully. "Didn't Charlus want to see you?"

She smiled up at him, shrugging. "But he acted as though he didn't want you to go off with Mosay," Rafiel persisted. "Or with me either, for that matter. Is he, well, jealous?"

"Oh, Rafiel! What a terrible word that is, 'jealous.' Are you thinking of, what, the Othello thing?"

"He's the father of your child," Rafiel pointed out uncomfortably.

"*Mais oui,* but why should he be jealous if I'm shtupping you or Mosay, *Liebling?* I shtup him too, whenever he likes—when I don't have another date, of course. Come and eat a nice dinner, and stop *worrying.*"

They walked together to their table—not on a balcony this time, but on a kind of elevated dais at the side of the room, so they could be well seen. It was the kind of place where theater people gathered, at the bottom of the atrium. Tables in the open surrounded the fiftieth-floor rooftop lake. There was a net overhead to catch any carelessly dropped objects, and from time to time they could hear the whine of the magnets pulling some bit of trash away. But nothing ever struck the diners. The place was full of children, and Docilia smiled at every one of them, practicing her upcoming motherhood. And swans floated in the lake, and stars were woven into the net overhead.

When the servers were bringing their monkey-orange juice Rafiel remembered. "Speaking of Charlus. He had an idea for your scene at the end. You know? Just before you go to hang yourself? As you're going out . . . "

He looked around to see who was looking at them, then decided to give the fans a treat. He stood up, and in the little cleared space between their table and the railing, did the step Charlus had called "*gedruk,*" mincing and swaying his hips. It was not unnoticed. Soft chuckles sounded from around the dining room. "Oh, maybe yes," Docilia said, nodding, pleased. "It gets a laugh, doesn't it?"

"Yes," said Rafiel, "but that's the thing. Do we want *comedy* here? I mean, you're just about to die . . ."

"Exactly, dear," she said, not understanding. "That's why it will be twice as funny in the performance."

"*Aber* a *morceau* incongruous, don't you think? Comedy and death?"

She was more puzzled than ever. "*Hai,* that's what's funny, isn't it? I mean, *dying.* That's such a bizarre thing, it always makes the audience laugh." And then, when she saw his face, she bit her lip. "*Pas* all that funny for everybody, is it?" she said remorsefully. "You're *so normal,* dear Rafiel. Sometimes I just forget."

He shrugged and forgave her. "You know more about that than I do," he admitted, knowing that he sounded still grumpy—glad when a famous news comic came over to chat. Being the kind of place it was, table-hopping was, of course, compulsory. As pleased as Rafiel at the interruption, Docilia showed her tomographs of the baby to the comic and got the required words of praise.

Then it was Rafiel's turn to blunder. "What sort of surrogate are you using?" he asked, to make conversation, and she gave him a sharp look.

"Did somebody tell you? No? Well, it's cow," she said, and waited to see what his response would be. She seemed aggrieved. When all he did was nod non-comittally, she said, "Charlus wanted to use something fancier. Do you think I did the right thing, Rafiel? Insisting on an ordinary cow surrogate, I mean? So many people are using water buffalo now. . . ."

He laughed at her. "I wouldn't know, would I? I've never been a parent."

"Well, I have, and believe me, Rafiel, it isn't easy. What *difference* does it make, really, what kind of animal incubates your child for you? But Charlus says it's important and, oh, Rafiel, we had such a battle over it!"

She shook her head, mourning the obstinacy and foolishness of men. Then she decided to forgive. "It isn't altogether his fault, I suppose. He's worried. Especially now. Especially because it's almost *fin* the second trimester and that means it's time—"

She came to a quick halt, once more biting her lip. Rafiel knew why: it was more suddenly remembered tact. The end of the second trimester was when they had to do the procedure to make the child immortal, because at that point the fetal immune system wasn't developed yet and they could manipulate it in the ways that would make it live essentially for ever.

"That's a scary time, I know," said Rafiel, to be comforting, but of course he did know. Everyone knew he knew, and why he knew. The operation was serious for a little fetus. A lot of them died, when the procedure didn't work—or managed to survive, but with their natural immune systems mortally intact. Like Rafiel.

"Oh, *mon cher*," she said, "you know I didn't mean anything *personal* by that!"

"Of course you didn't," he said reassuringly; but all the same, the happy buzz of the day's good rehearsing was lost, the evening's edge was gone, and long before they had finished their leisurely supper, he had abandoned any plan of inviting her back to his condo for the night.

It did spoil the evening for him. Too early for sleep, too late to make any other arrangements, he wandered alone through his condo. He tried reading, but it seemed like a lot of effort. He glanced toward the barre, but his muscles were sore enough already from the day's work-out. He switched on the vid, roaming the channels to see if there was anything new and good, but there wasn't. A football series coming to its end in Katmandu, an election in Uruguay—who cared about such things? He paused over a story about a habitat now being fitted out with engines to leave the solar system: it was the one named *Hakluyt* and it held his interest for a moment because of that silly woman, Hillaree, with her script. It would be interesting, he thought, to take that final outward leap to another star. . . . Of course, not for him, who would be long dead before the expedition could hope to arrive. He switched to the obituaries—his favorite kind of news—but the sparse list held no names that interested him. He switched again to the entertainment channels. There was a new situation comedy that he had heard about. The name was *Dachau,* and he remembered that one of the parts was played by a woman he had slept with a few times, years ago. Now she was playing a—a what?—a concentration-camp guard in Germany in World War II, it seemed. It was a comic part; she was a figure of fun as the Jews and Gypsies and political enemies who were inmates constantly mocked and outwitted her. It did have its funny bits. Rafiel laughed as one of the inmates, having escaped to perform some heroic espionage feat for the Allies, was sneaked back into the camp under the very eyes of the commandant. Still, he wondered if things had really ever been that *jolly* in the real concentration camps of the time, where the real death ovens burned all day and all night.

It all depended on whether you were personally involved, he thought.

And then he switched it off, thinking of Docilia. He shouldn't have been so curt with her. She couldn't help being what she was. If death seemed comical to the deathless, was that her fault? Hadn't most of the world, for centuries on end, found fun in the antics of the dwarves and the deformed, even making them jesters at their courts? Perhaps the hunchbacks themselves hadn't found anything to laugh at—but that was *their* point of view.

As his attitude toward dying was his own.

He thought for a moment of calling Docilia to apologize—perhaps the evening might be salvaged yet. Then he remembered what Mosay had said about personal messages and scrolled them up.

The first one was personal, all right, and a surprise. It was a talking message, and as soon as the picture cleared he recognized the face of the man who happened to have been his biological father.

The man hadn't changed a bit. (Well, why would he, in a mere ninety-some years?) He was as youthful and as handsome as he had been when, on a rare visit, he had somewhat awkwardly taken young Rafiel on his knee. "I saw you were in the *Krankhaus* again," the man in the screen said, with the look of someone who was paying a duty call on an ailing friend—not a close one, though. "It reminded me we haven't heard from each other in a long time. I'm glad everything *fait bon,* Rafiel—son—and, really, you and I ought to have lunch together some *prossimo giorno.*"

That was it. Rafiel froze the picture before it disappeared, to study the dark, well-formed face of the man whose genes he had carried. But the person behind the face eluded him. He sighed, shrugged and turned to the other message. . . .

And that one made him stiffen in his chair, with astonishment too sharp to be joy.

It wasn't an imaged message, or even a spoken one; it was a faxed note, in a crabbed, nearly illegible handwriting that he knew very well:

> Dearest Rafiel, I was so glad to hear you got through another siege with the damned doctors. *Mazel tov.* I'm sending you a little gift to celebrate your recovery—and to remind you of me, because I think of you so very often.

What the gift was he could not guess, because it hadn't arrived yet, but the note was signed, most wonderfully signed:

For always, your Alegretta.

6

Naturally, all kinds of connections and antipathies appear among the Oedipus *troupe as they come together. Charlus is the sire of Docilia's unborn child. Andrev, who is to play the Creon, is the son of the composer of the score, Victorium. Ormeld, the Priest, and Andrev haven't acted together for thirty-five years, because of a nasty little firefight over billing in what happened to be the first production in which either got an acting credit. (They hug each other with effusive but wary joy when they come together in the rehearsal hall.) Sander, the Tiresias, studied acting under Mosay when Mosay had just abandoned his own dramatic career (having just discovered how satisfying the god-behind-the-scenes role of a dramaturge was). Sander is still just a little awed by his former teacher. All these interconnections are quite separate from the ordinary who-had-been-sleeping-with-whom sort of thing. They had to be kept that way. If people dragged up that sort of ancient history they'd never get everything straight. Actually, nobody is dragging anything up—at least, not as far as the surface where it can be seen. On the contrary. Everybody is being overtly amiable to everybody else and conspicuously consecrated to the show, so far. True, they haven't yet had much chance to be anything else, since it's only the first day of full-cast rehearsal.*

Although Mosay was still off scouting for locations—somewhere in *Turkey*, somebody said, though why anybody would want to go to *Turkey* no one could imagine—he had taken time to talk to them all by grid on the first day. "Line up, everybody," he ordered, watching them through the monitor over his camera. "What I want you to do is just a quick run-through of the lines. Don't sing. Don't dance, don't even act—we just want to say the words and see each other. Docilia, please leave Charlus alone for a minute and pay attention. Victorium will proctor for me, while I"—a small but conspicuous sigh; Mosay had not forgotten his acting skills—"keep trying to find the *right* location for our production."

Actually it was Rafiel who was paying least attention, because his mind was full of lost Alegretta. Now, perhaps, found again? For you never forgot your first love. . . .

Well, yes, you did, sometimes, but Rafiel never had. Never could have in spite of the sixty or seventy—could it have been eighty? a hundred?—other women he had loved, or at least made love to, in the years since then. Alegretta had been something very special in his life.

He was twenty years old then, a bright young certain-to-be-a-star song-and-dance man. Audiences didn't know that yet, because he was still doing the kind of thing you had to start out with, cheap simulations and interactives, where you never got to make your own dramatic *statement*. The trade was beginning to know him, though, and Rafiel was quite content to be working his way up in the positive knowledge that the big break was sure to come. (And it had come, no more than a year later.)

But just then he had, of all things, become sick. (No one got *sick!*) When the racking cough began to spoil his lines, he had to do something. He complained to his doctors about it. Somewhat startled (people didn't *have* coughs), the doctors put him in a clinic for observation, because they were as discomfited by it as Rafiel himself. And when all the tests were over, the head resident herself came to his hospital room to break the bad news.

Even all these decades later, Rafiel remembered exactly what she had looked like that morning. Striking. Sexy, too; he had noticed that right away, in spite of the circumstances. A tall woman, taller in fact than Rafiel himself; with reddish-brown hair, a nose with a bit of a bend in it that kept it from being perfect in any orthodox way, but a smile that made up for it all. He had looked at her, made suspicious by the smile, a little hostile because a little scared. She sat down next to him, no longer smiling. "Rafiel," she said directly, "I have some bad news for you."

"*Che c'e?* Can't you fix this damn cold?" he said, irritated.

She hesitated before she answered. "Oh, yes, we can cure *that*. We'll have it all cleared up by morning. But you see, you shouldn't have a cough at all now. It means . . ." she paused, obviously in some pain. "It means the procedure didn't work for you," she said at last, and that was how Alegretta told Rafiel that he was doomed to die in no more than another hundred years, at most.

When he understood what she was saying, he listened quietly and patiently to all the explanations that went with it. Queerly, he felt sorrier for her than for himself—just then he did, anyway; later on, when it had all sunk in, it was different. But as she was telling him that such failures were very rare, but still they came up now and then, and at least he had survived the attempt, which many unborn babies did not, he interrupted her. "I don't think you should be a doctor," he told her, searching her lovely face.

"Why not?" she asked.

"You take it too hard. You can't stand giving bad news."

She said soberly, "I haven't had much practice at it, have I?"

He laughed at her. She looked at him in surprise, but then, he was still in his twenties, and a promise of another hundred years seemed close enough to forever. "Practice on me," he urged. "When I'm released, let's have dinner."

They did. They had a dozen dinners, those first weeks, and breakfasts too, because that same night he moved into her flat above the hospital wing. They stayed together nearly two weeks; and there had never been another woman like her. "I'll never tell," she promised when they parted. "It's a medical confidence, you know. A secret." She never had told, either.

And his career did blossom. In those days, Rafiel didn't need to be an oddity to be a star, he became a star because he was so damn good.

It was only later on that he became an oddity as well because, though Alegretta had never told, there were a lot of other checkups, and ultimately somebody else had.

It had not mattered to Rafiel, then, that Alegretta was nearly a hundred to his twenty. Why should it? Such things made no difference in a world of eternal youth. Alegretta did not look one minute older than himself . . . And it was only later, when she had left him, and he was miserably trying to figure out why, that he realized the meaning of the fact that she never would.

First run-throughs didn't matter much. All they were really for was to get the whole cast together, to get some idea of their lines and what the relationship of each character was to the others, who was what to whom. They didn't act, much less sing; they read their lines at half-voice, eyes on the prompter scroll on the wall more than each other. It didn't matter that Rafiel's mind was elsewhere. When others were onstage he took out the fax from Alegretta and read it again. And again. But he wasn't, he thought, any more inattentive than any of the others. The pretty young Antigone—what was her real name? Bruta? Something like that—was a real amateur, and amateurishly she kept trying to move toward stage front each time she spoke. Which was not often; and didn't matter, really, because when Mosay came back he would take charge of that sort of thing in his gentle, irresistible way. And Andrev, the Creon, had obviously never even looked at the script, while Sander, who was to play the blind prophet, Tiresias, complained that there wasn't any point in doing all this without the actual dramaturge being present. Victorium had his hands full.

But he was dealing with it. When they had finished the quick run-through he dispatched Charlus to start on the choreography of the first scene, where all the Thebans were reciting for the audience their opening misery under the Sphinx. Rafiel was reaching in his pocket for another look at the fax when Victorium came over. "*Sind Sie* okay, Rafiel?" he asked. "I thought you seemed just a little absent-minded."

"*Pas du tout,*" Rafiel said, stuffing the letter away. Then, admitting it, "Well, just a little, *forse*. I, ah, had a letter from an old friend."

"Yes," Victorium said, nodding. "Mosay said something about it. Alegretta, was that her name?"

Rafiel shrugged, not letting his annoyance show. Of course Mosay had known all about Alegretta because Mosay made it a point to know everything there was to know about every one of his artists; but to pry into private mail, and then to discuss it with others, was going too far.

"Old lovers can still make the heart beat faster, can't they?" he said.

"Yes?" Victorium said, not meaning to sound skeptical, but obviously not troubled with any such emotions himself. "Has it been a long time? Will you be seeing her again?"

"Oh"—startled by the thought, almost afraid of it—"no, I don't think so. No, probably not—she's a long way away. She seems to be in one of the orbiters now. You know she used to be a doctor? But now she's given up medicine, doing some kind of science now."

"She sounds like a very interesting person," Victorium said neutrally—a little absent-minded himself, too, because in the center of the room Charlus had started showing the Thebans the dance parts, and Victorium had not failed to catch the sounds of his own music. Still looking at the Thebans, Victorium said, "Mosay asked me to show you the rough simulation for the opening. Let's go over to the small screen—oh, hell," he said interrupting himself, "can you *pardonnez-moi* a minute? *Verdammt*, Charlus has got them *hopping* when the music's obviously *con vivace*. I'll be right back."

Rafiel listened to the raised voices, giving them his full willed attention in order to avoid a repetition of the rush of feeling that Victorium's casual suggestion had provoked. Charlus seemed to be winning the argument, he thought, though the results would not be final until Mosay returned to ratify them. It was a fairly important scene. Antigone, Ismene, Polyneices, and Eteocles—the four children of Oedipus and Jocasta—were doing a sort of *pas de quatre* in tap, arms linked like the cygnets in *Swan Lake*, while they sang a recapitulation of how Oedipus came and saved them from the horrid Sphinx. The chorus was being a real chorus, in fact a chorus line, tapping in the background and, one by one, speaking up—a potter, a weaver, a soldier, a household slave—saying yes, but things are going badly now and something must be *done*. Then Rafiel would make his entrance as Oedipus and the story would roll on . . . but not today.

Victorium was breathing hard when he rejoined Rafiel. "You can ignore all that," he said grimly, "because I'm sure Mosay isn't going to let that *dummkopf* dance-teacher screw up the *grand ensemble*. Never mind." He snapped on the prompter monitor to show what he and Mosay had programmed for the under-the-credits opening. "Let's get down your part here. This is before the actual story begins, showing you and the Sphinx."

Rafiel gave it dutiful attention. Even in preliminary stick-figure simulation, he saw that the monster on the screen was particularly unpleasant-looking, like a winged reptile. "*Che* the hell *cosa* is that?"

"It's the Sphinx, of course. What else would it be?" Victorium said, stopping the computer simulation so Rafiel could study the creature.

"It doesn't look like a sphinx to me. It looks like a crocodile."

"Mosay," Victorium said with satisfaction, "looked it up. Thebes was a city on the Nile, you know. The Nile is *famous* for crocodiles. They sacrificed people to them."

"But this one has wings."

"*Perchè no?* You're probably thinking of that other Egyptian sphinx. The old one out of the desert? This one's different. It's a *Theban* sphinx, and it looks like whatever Mosay says it looks like." Victorium gave him the look of someone who would like to chide an actor for wasting time with irrelevant details—if the actor hadn't happened to be the star of the show. "The important thing is that it was terrorizing the whole city of Thebes, after their *ancien roi*, Laius, got murdered, until you came along and got rid of it for them. Which, of course, is why the Thebans let you marry Jocasta and be their *nouveau roi*." He thought for a moment. "I'll have to write some new music for the Sphinx to sing the riddle, but," he said wistfully, "Mosay says we don't want too much song and dance here because, see, *tutta qui* is just a kind of prologue. It isn't in the Sophocles play. We'll just run it under the credits to mise the scene—oh, *merde*. What's that?"

He was looking at the tel window on the screen, where Rafiel's name had begun to flash.

"Somebody's calling me, I guess," Rafiel said.

"You shouldn't be getting personal calls during rehearsal, should you?" he chided. Then he shrugged. "*San ferian*. See who it is, will you?"

But when Rafiel tapped out his acceptance no picture appeared on the screen, just a voice. It wasn't even the voice of a "who." It was the serene, impersonal voice of his household server, and it said:

"A living organism had been delivered to you. It is a gift. I have no program for caring for living creatures. Please instruct me."

"Now who in the world," Rafiel marveled, "would be sending me a *pet*?"

It wasn't anyone in the world—not the planet Earth, anyway; as soon as Rafiel saw the note pinned to the cage, where the snow-white kitten purred contentedly inside, he knew who it was from.

> This is my favorite cat's best kitten, dear Rafiel. I hope you'll love
> it as much as I do.

Rafiel found himself laughing out loud. How strange of Alegretta. How dear, too! Imagine anyone keeping a *pet*. It was not the kind of thing immortals were likely to do. Who wanted to get attached to some living thing that was sure to die in only a few years—only a moment, in the long lifetime of people now alive? (Most of them, anyway.) But it was a sweet thought, and a sweet little kitten, he found as he uneasily picked it up out of the cage and set it on his lap. The pretty little thing seemed comfortable there, still purring as it looked up at him out of sleepy blue eyes.

Most important, it was a gift from Alegretta. He was smiling as, careful not to disturb the little animal, he began searching his data bases for instructions on the care and feeding of kittens.

7

Rafiel has decided not to make love to Docilia again. He isn't sure why. He suspects it has something to do with the fact that the sire of her child is always nearby, which makes him uncomfortable. It isn't just that they've collaborated on creating a fetus that makes him shy off, it is more the fact that they intend to be a family. It is only later that he realizes that that means he can't bed any of the other members of the troupe, either. Not the Antigone, the little girl named Bruta, though she has asked him to—not even though she happens to have interested him at first, since she has auburn hair and her nose is not perfectly straight. (Perhaps it is because she looks a little bit like Alegretta that he especially doesn't want to make love to her.) Not any of them, in spite of the fact that, all through his performing life, Rafiel has seldom failed to make love in person to every female he was required to make love to in the performance, on the principle that it added realism to his art. (He wasn't particularly attracted to most of those women, either, only prepared to make sacrifices for his art.) This time, no. The only sensible reason he can give himself for his decision is that Docilia would surely find out, and it would hurt her feelings to be passed over for the others.

None of this inordinate chastity was because he didn't desire sexual intercourse. On the contrary. He didn't need to program designer dreams of lovemaking. His subconscious did all the programming he needed. Almost every morning he woke from dreams of hot and sweaty quick encounters and dreamily long-drawn-out ones. The root of the problem was that, although he wanted to do it, he didn't want to do it *with* anyone he knew. (One possible exception always noted, but always inaccessible.) So he slept alone. When, one morning, some slight noise woke him with the scent of perfumed woman in his nose he supposed it was a lingering dream. Then he opened his eyes. A woman was there, in his room, standing by a chair and just stepping out of the last of her clothing. "Who the hell are you?" he shouted as he sat up.

The woman was quite naked and entirely composed. She sat on the edge of his bed and said, "I'm Hillaree. You looked so sexy there, I thought I might as well just climb in."

"How the hell did you get into my condo?"

"I'm a dramaturge," she said simply. "How much would you respect me if I let your doorwarden keep me out?"

Rafiel turned in the bed to look at her better. She was a curly-headed little thing, with a wide, serious mouth, and he was quite sure he had never seen her before.

But he had heard her name, he realized. "Oh, *that* dramaturge," he said, faintly remembering a long-ago message.

"The dramaturge who has a wonderful part for you," she confirmed, "if you have intelligence enough to accept it." She patted his head in a friendly way, and stood up.

"If you want me for a part, you should talk to my agent," he called after her.

"Oh, I did that, Rafiel. She threw me out." Hillaree was rummaging through the heap of her discarded clothing on the bedside chair. She emerged with a lapcase, which she carried back to the bed. "I admit this isn't going to be a *big* show," she told him, squatting crosslegged on his bed as she opened the screen from the case. "I'm not Mosay. I don't do *spectacoli*. But people are traveling out to the stars, Rafiel. The newest one is a habitat called *Hakluyt*. The whole population has voted to convert their habitat into an interstellar space vehicle—"

"I know about that!" he snapped, more or less truthfully. "Habitat people have done that before—last year, wasn't it? Or a couple of years ago? I think one was going to Alpha Centauri or somewhere."

"You see? You don't even remember. No one else does, either, and yet it's a grand, *heroic* story! These people are doing something hard and dangerous. No, Rafiel," she finished, wagging her pretty head, "it's the greatest story of our time and it needs to be told *dramatically*, so people will *comprehend* it. And I'm the one to tell it, and you're the one to play it. Oh, it won't be like a Mosay production, I'll give you that. But you'll never again see anything as right for you as the part of the captain of the kosmojet *Hakluyt*."

"I don't know anything about kosmojets, do I? Anyway, I can't. Mosay already had one cacafuega attack when he heard a rumor about it."

"*Fichtig* Mosay. He and I don't do the same kind of thing. This one will be *intimate*, and *personal*. *Pas* music, *pas* dancing, *pas* songs. It will be a whole new departure for your career."

"But a song-and-dance man is what I am!"

She sniffed at him. "You're a short-timer, Rafiel. You're going to get *old*. Listen to me. This is where you need to go. I've watched you. I'm willing to bet my reputation—"

"Your reputation!"

She ignored the interruption. "—that you're just as good an actor as you are a dancer and singer . . . and, just to make you understand what's involved here, you can have five points on the gross receipts, which you know you'll *jamais* get from Mosay."

"Five per cent of not very much is still very little," Rafiel said at once, grinning at her to show that he meant no hard feelings.

She nodded as though she had expected that. She opened her bag and fingered the keypad for her screen. "May I?" she said perfunctorily, not waiting for an answer. A scroll of legal papers began to roll up the screen. "This is the deal for the first broadcast," she said. "That's twenty million dollars from right here on Earth, plus another twenty million for the first-run remotes. Syndication: that's a contract with a guarantee of another forty million over a ten-year period. And all that's minimum, Rafiel; I'd bet anything that it'll double that. And there are the contracts for the sub rights—the merchandising, the music. Add it all up, and you'll see that the *guarantee* comes pretty close to a hundred million dollars. What's five per cent of that, Rafiel?"

The question was rhetorical. She wasn't waiting for an answer. She was already scrolling to the next display, not giving Rafiel a chance to order her out of his condo. "*Là!*" she said, "*Voici!*"

What they were looking at on the screen was a habitat. It was not an impressive object to the casual view. As in all pictures from space, there was no good indication of size, and the thing might have been a beverage can, floating in orbit.

"There's where our story is," she said. "What you see there is habitat *Hakluyt*. It starts with a population of twenty thousand people, with room to expand to five times that. It's a whole small town, Rafiel. The kind of town they used to have in the old days before the arcologies, you know? A place with everybody knowing everybody else, interacting, loving, hating, dreaming—and totally cut off from everyone else. It's a microcosm of humanity, right there on *Hakluyt*, and we're going to tell its story."

Although Rafiel was looking at the woman's pictures, he didn't think them very interesting. As far as Rafiel could tell, *Hakluyt* was a perfectly ordinary habitat, a stubby cylinder with the ribs for the pion tracks circling its outer shell. What he could tell wasn't actually very much. He hadn't spent much time on habitats, only one two-week visit, once, with—with . . . ? No, he had long since forgotten the name of the companion of that trip, and indeed everything about the trip itself except that habitats were not particularly luxurious places to spend one's time.

"How much spin does this thing have?" he asked, out of technical curiosity. "I'm not used to dancing in light-G."

"When it's en route *pas* spin at all. The gravity effect will be along the line of thrust. But you're forgetting, Rafiel, " she chided him. "There won't be any dancing anyway. That's why this is such a breakthrough for you. This is a dramatic *story*, and you'll act it!"

"Hum," said Rafiel, not pleased with this woman's continuing reminders that, in his special case, becoming older meant that it would become harder and harder for him to keep in dancer's kind of shape. "Why do you say they're cut off from the rest of the world? Habitats are a lot easier to get to than, *per esempio*, Mars. There's always a stream of ships going back and forth."

"Not to this habitat," Hillaree told him confidently. "You're missing the point, and that's the whole drama of our story. You see that cluster of motors on the base? *Hakluyt* isn't just going to stay in orbit. *Hakluyt* will be going all the way to the star Tau Ceti. They'll be cut off, all right. They aren't coming back to the Earth, ever."

As soon as the woman was out of his condo, unbedded but also unrejected, or at least not *finally* rejected in the way that most mattered to her, Rafiel was calling his agent to complain. Fruitlessly. It was a lot too early in the morning for Jeftha to be answering her tel. He tried again when he got to the rehearsal hall, with the same "No Incoming" icon appearing on the screen. "Bitch," he said to the screen, though without any real resentment—Jeftha was as good a talent agent as he had ever had—and joined the rest of the cast.

They had started without him. Charlus was drilling the chorus all over again and Victorium, with Docilia standing by, was impatiently waiting for

Rafiel himself. "Now," he said, "If you're *quite* ready to go to work? Here's where we come to a tricky kind of place in *Oedipus*. You've ordered Creon banished, in spite of the fact that he's your brother-in-law. You think he lied to you about the prophecy from Apollo's priest, and you've just found out that your wife, Jocasta, is also your mother—"

"Victorium dear," Docilia began, "that's something I wanted to talk about. I don't have enough lines there, do I? Since it's *per certo* as big a shock to me too?"

"You'd have to talk to Mosay about that when he gets back, Docilia dear," Victorium said. "Can't we stick to the point? Besides the incest thing, Rafiel, you're the one who murdered her husband, who is also your real father—"

"I've read the script," Rafiel told him.

"Of course you have, Rafiel dear," Victorium said, sounding much less confident of it. "Then we follow you into Jocasta's room, and you see that she hung herself, out of shame."

"Can't I do that on-screen, Vic?" Docilia asked. "I mean, committing suicide's a really dramatic moment."

"I don't think so, dear, but that's another thing you'd have to talk to Mosay about. Anyway, it's not the point right now, is it? I'm talking about what Rafiel does when he sees you've committed suicide."

"I take the pins out of her hair and blind myself with them," said Rafiel, nodding.

"Right. You jab the gold hairpins into your eyes. That's what I'm thinking about. What's the best way for us to handle that?"

"How do you mean?" Rafiel asked, blinking at him.

"Well, we want it to look *real*, don't we?"

"Sure," Rafiel said, surprised, not understanding the point. That sort of thing was up to the computer synthesizers, which would produce any kind of effect anybody wanted.

Victorium was thoughtfully silent. Docilia cleared her throat. "On second thought," she said, "maybe it's better if I hang myself offstage after all."

Victorium stirred and gave her a serious look. Then he surrendered. "We'll talk about all this stuff later," he said. "Let me get Charlus off everybody's back and we'll try putting the scene after that together."

Rafiel was surprised to see Docilia give him a serious wink, but whatever she had on her mind had to wait. Victorium was calling them all together. "All right," he said, "let's run it through. All the bad stuff is out in the open now. Rafiel knows what he's done, and all four of you kids are onstage now in the forgiveness scene. Ket, you're the Polyneices, take it from the top."

Obediently the quartet formed and the boy began to sing

POLYNEICES: We forgive you. If you doubt it, ask that zany Antigone, or Eteocles, or sweet Ismene.

ETEOCLES: You can't be all that bad.

ISMENE: After all, *vous êtes* our dad.

"Now you, Rafiel," Victorium said, nodding, and Rafiel took up his lines.

OEDIPUS: Calm? *Come possibile* for me to be calm? I've killed
       my pop and shtupped my dear old mom.

ANTIGONE: It's okay, dad, we're all with you. It'll be a lousy
       life, but we'll be true.
       Wherever you go—

"No, no," Charlus cried, breaking in. "Excuse me, Victorium, but no. Bruta, this is *tap*, not ballet. Keep your feet down on the floor, will you?"

"*Aspet!*" Victorium snapped. "I'm running this rehearsal, and if you keep interrupting—"

"But she's ruining it, don't you see?" the choreographer pleaded. "Just give me a minute with her. Please? Bruta, I want you to tap on the turn, and give us a little disco hip rotation when you sing. And I want to hear every tap all by itself, loud and clear . . . "

There was, naturally, more objection from Victorium. Rafiel backed away to watch, not directly involved, and turned when he felt Docilia plucking at his arm.

"Be real careful," she whispered. "Don't let Mosay push you into anything. I think he wants you to really do it. The blinding," she added impatiently when she saw that he hadn't understood.

Rafiel stared at her to see if she was joking. She wasn't. "Believe me, that's what he wants from you," she said, nodding. "No faking it. He wants real blood. Real pain. Pieces of eyeball hanging out on your cheek."

"Docilia!" he said, grimacing.

"*Was ist das* 'Docilia'? *Voi sapete* how Mosay is. Oh, maybe he wouldn't expect you to *permanently* blind yourself. After the shooting was over he'd pay so the doctors could graft in some new eyes for you—but still."

"Mosay wouldn't ask anybody to do that," Rafiel protested.

"Wouldn't he? Especially considering— Well, when he comes back, just ask him," she said, and stopped there.

Rafiel had grasped her meaning, anyway. Especially considering could only be that, in the long run, they were beginning to be looking on him as expendable.

When he finally did get through to his agent she was only perfunctorily apologetic. "*Mi scusi,*" Jeftha said. "I had a hard night." That was all the explanation she offered, but her dark and youthful face supported it. The skin was as unlined as always, but her eyes were red. "Acrobats," she said, wearily running one hand through her thick hedge of hair.

"You shouldn't sleep with your clients," Rafiel said, setting aside the historical fact that she had, on occasion, with himself. "Now, this woman Hillaree. . . ."

When Jeftha heard about the dramaturge's surprise visit she was furious. "The *puta!*" she snapped. "Going behind your agent's *back?* She'll never cast a client of mine again—but how could you, Rafiel? If Mosay finds out you've been dealing with a tuppenny tinhorn like Hillaree he'll go berserker!"

"I wasn't *dealing* with her," Rafiel began, but she cut him off.

"Pray he doesn't hear about it. He's in a bad enough mood already. When he got to look at his locations somebody told him that the Thebes he was trying to match was the wrong Thebes—two of them with the same name, Rafiel, can you imagine that? How stupid can they be? The Thebes in Egypt didn't count. The Thebes somewhere north of Athens was the one where Oedipus had been king, and it was an entirely different kind of territory."

"He's back?"

"He will be in the morning," she confirmed. "Now, was that what you were so *fou* to talk to me about?"

He hesitated, and then said, "Forget it now, anyway." Because he couldn't quite bring himself to ask her the question that was mostly on his mind, which was whether it was at all possible that Docilia's hints and implications could possibly be right.

8

The work of a dramaturge does not end with making sure a production is successfully performed. A major part of the job is making sure the audiences will want to spend their money to see it. In the furtherance of this endeavor, sweet are the uses of publicity; for which reason Mosay has arranged to do his first costumed rehearsals in a very conspicuous place. The place he has chosen is the public park on the roof of the arcology, where there are plenty of loungers and strollers, and every one a sure word-of-mouth broadcaster when they get home. Nor has Mosay failed to alert the paparazzi to be present in force.

Rafiel thought seriously of taking the kitten with him to show off at the day's rehearsal—after all, who else in the troupe owned a live cat? But the park was half a kilometer square, with a lake and a woodsy area and sweet little gardens all around. There was even a boxwood maze, great for children to play in, but all too good a place for a little kitten to get lost in, he decided, and regretfully left it in the care of his server.

The trouble with the rooftop was that it was windy. They were nearly a kilometer above the ground, where the air was always blowing strong. Clever vanes deflected the worst of the gusts, but not all of them; Rafiel felt chilled and wished Mosay had chosen another workplace. Or that, at least, they hadn't been instructed to show up in costume: there wasn't much warmth in the short woolen tunic. The winds were stronger than usual that day, and there were thick black clouds rolling toward them over the arcologies to the west. Rafiel listened: had he heard the sound of distant thunder? Or just the wind?

He shivered and joined the other performers as they walked around to get used to their costumes. Although the rooftop was the common property of all the hundred-and-sixty-odd-thousand people who lived or worked in that particular arcology, Mosay had managed to persuade the arcology council to set one grassy sward aside for rehearsals. The council didn't object. They agreed that it would be a pleasing sort of entertainment for the tenants, and anyway Mosay was a first-rate persuader—after all, what other thing did a dramaturge really have to be?

The proof of his persuasive powers was that, astonishingly, everyone in the cast was there, and on time: Mosay himself, back from his fruitless quest but looking fresh and undaunted, and Victorium, and Charlus, the choreographer—no, *assistant* choreographer, Rafiel corrected himself reso-lutely—and all the eleven principal performers in the show and the dozen members of the chorus. Rafiel had practiced with the sandals and the sword in his condo, while the watching kitten purred approvingly; by now he was easy enough in the costume. Not Andrev, the Creon, who kept getting his sword caught between his knees. There weren't any costume problems for Sander, the Tiresias, since his costume was only a long featureless smock, and Sander, who was a tall, unkempt man with seal-colored hair that straggled down over his shoulders, wore the thing as though he was ignoring it, which was pretty much the way he wore all his clothes anyway. All the women wore simple white gowns, Docilia's Jocasta with flowers in her hair, the daughters unembellished.

But when Rafiel first saw Bruta, the Antigone, turn toward him his heart stopped for a moment, she was so like Alegretta. "*Che cosa*, Rafiel?" she asked in sudden worry at his expression, but he only shook his head. He kept watching her, though. Apart from the chance resemblance to his life's lost love, Bruta struck him as a bit of puzzle. Bruta looked neither younger nor older than anyone else in the cast, of course—Rafiel himself always ex-cepted—but it was obvious that she was a lot less experienced. That interested Rafiel. Mosay was not the kind who liked to bother with newcomers. He left the discovery of fresh talent to lesser dramaturges; he could afford to hire the best, who inevitably were also the ones who had long since made their reputations. Rafiel thought of asking Docilia, who would be sure to know everyone's reasons for everything they did, but there wasn't time. Mosay was already waving everyone to cluster around him.

"Company," said Mosay commandingly. "I'm glad to be back, but we've got a lot of work to do, so if I may have your attention?" He got it and said sunnily, "I do have one announcement before we begin. I've found our shooting location. *Wunderbar*, it has an existing set that we can use—oh, not *exactly* replicating old Thebes, in a technical sense, but close enough. And we'd better get on with it, so *if* you please. . . ." Rafiel concealed a grin at the way Mosay was making sure he looked every centimeter the staging genius as he played to the spectators behind the velvet ropes, and, of course, to the pointing cameras of the paparazzi. When he had everyone's attention he went on. "We aren't going to do the short fighting-the-Sphinx scene because we don't have a sphinx"—well, of course they didn't; there never would be a sphinx until the animation people put one in—"so we'll start with the *pas de quatre*, where you kids"—nodding to the four "children" of Oedipus and Jocasta—"sing your little song about how after Oedipus saved Thebes from the Sphinx he married your *maman*, the widowed Jocasta, whose husband had been mysteriously murdered and thus Oedipus became *koenig* himself—"

"Oh, hell, Mosay," said Docilia warmly, "that's a whole play right there. *Bisogniamo* say all that?"

"We must. We'll get it in, and anyway that's not your problem, Docilia, is it? In fact, you're not even in this scene, or the next scene either, except to stand around and look pretty, because this is where Creon makes his entrance and tells Oedipus what the oracle of Apollo said."

"I already know all the Creon lines," Andrev said proudly. He had the reputation of being a slow study.

"I certainly hope so, Andrev. Places, everybody? And now if we'll just take it from the last bars of Victorium's opening. . . ."

It wasn't a big scene for Rafiel. He didn't even get to make a real entrance, just ambled onstage to wait for Creon to show up. The scene belonged to the Creon. Victorium had written the music accordingly, with a background score full of dark and mystical dissonances—right enough for an oracle's pronouncements, Rafiel supposed.

What Creon brought was bad news, so Rafiel's responses had to be equally somber. Not just somber, though. Rafiel made sure all his gestures were, well, a trifle less *portentous* than the Creon's—after all, Rafiel was not merely playing an old, doomed Theban king, he was playing *himself* playing the king. That was what being a star was all about.

Rafiel flinched at a boom from the sky. Thunder was crashing somewhere in the distance, and Mosay agitatedly demanded of a watching arcology worker that they erect the dome. Just in time; rain was slashing down on the big transparent hood over the roof before the petaled sections had quite closed over them. Rafiel shuddered again. He found that he was feeling quite tired. He wondered if it was showing up in his performance . . . though of course it was only a dress rehearsal.

All the same, Rafiel didn't like the feeling that his dancing was not as lively—as bumptiously clumsy—as his audiences expected of him. He forced himself into the emotions of the part—easily enough, because Rafiel had all the ambiguity of any actor in his beliefs. Whatever he privately thought or felt, he could throw himself into the thoughts and feelings of the character he was playing; and if that character took silly oracular conundrums seriously, then for the duration of that role so would Rafiel. He worked so hard at it that at the end of the third run-through he was sweating as he finished his meditative *pas de seul*. So was the Creon, although he had no dancing to do. But it was Rafiel Mosay was watching, with a peculiar expression of concern on his face, and it was Rafiel he was looking at when he declared a twenty-minute break.

"*Comment ça va?*" Docilia asked, taking Rafiel's elbow.

He blinked at her. "Fine, fine," he assured her, though he didn't think he really was. Was it that obvious? He hadn't missed Mosay's watchful eyes, though now the dramaturge had forgotten him in the press of making quick calls on the communications monitor at the edge of the meadow. Rafiel made an effort and pressed Docilia's arm against his side amatively—well, maybe there was his problem right there, he thought. Deprivation. After all, why should any healthy person deliberately stop having sex, thus very possibly endangering not only his performance, but even his health?

"You don't *look* all right," Docilia told him, steering him through the park to a formal garden. "Except when you're looking at that Bruta."

"Oh, now really," Rafiel laughed—actually laughing, because the thought really amused him. "She's just so *young*."

"So amateurish, you mean."

"That too," he acknowledged, slipping his arm around her waist in a friendly way. "I'm surprised Mosay took her on."

"You don't know?"

"Know what?" Rafiel asked, proving that he did not.

"She's his latest daughter," Docilia informed him with pleasure. "So if you're shtupping her you're going to be part of the family."

Rafiel opened his mouth to deny that he was making love to Bruta, or indeed to anyone else since the last time with Docilia herself, but he closed it again. That, after all, was none of Docilia's business, not to mention that it did not comport well with the image of a lusty, healthy, *youthful* idol of every audience.

But she might have been reading his mind. "Oh, poor Rafiel," she said, tightening her grip on his waist. "You're just not getting enough, are you?" She looked around. There was hardly anyone near them, the casual spectators mostly still watching the performers in the rehearsal area. And they were near the maze.

"I have an idea," she murmured. "Can we go in the maze for a while?"

After all, why not? Rafiel surrendered. "I'd like nothing better," he said gallantly, knowing as well as she did that the best thing one did in the isolation of a maze was to do a little friendly fooling around with one's companion—on whom, in any case, Rafiel was beginning to feel he might as well be beginning to have sexual designs again, after all. They had no trouble finding a quiet dead end and, without discussion, Rafiel unhesitatingly put his hand on her.

"Are you sure you aren't too tired?" she asked, but turning toward him as she spoke; and, of course, that imposed on him the duty to prove that he wasn't tired at all. He realized he didn't have much time to demonstrate it in, so they wasted none. They were horizontal on the warm, grassy ground in a minute.

It was strange, he reflected, pumping away, that something you wanted to do could also be a wearisome chore. He was glad enough when they had finished. . . . And almost at that very moment, as though taking a quick cue, a voice from an unseen person, somewhere else in the maze, was thundering at them.

It was Mosay's voice. What he was saying—bawling—was: "Rafiel! Is that you I hear in there with Docilia? Come out this minute! We need to talk."

Rafiel was breathing hard, but he managed to grin at his partner and help her to her feet. "Can't it wait, Mosay?" he called, carefully conserving his breath.

"It can *not*," the dramaturge roared. "*Expliquez* yourself. Who's this woman who's claiming she's got you signed up for a new production?"

Rafiel groaned. Mosay had in fact found out. Docilia put an alarmed hand on his forearm.

"Oh, *paura*. You'd better pull yourself together," she whispered, doing the same for herself. "He's really *furioso* about something."

Rafiel gave in, tugging his underpants back on. "Well," he called to the featureless hedge, "we did talk a little bit, she and I—"

"She says you *agreed*!" snapped the invisible Mosay. "She's got a story about it in all the media, and I won't have it! Rafiel, you're making me look like a *Dummkopf*."

"I never actually agreed—"

"But you didn't say no, either, did you? That's not *cosi buono*. I won't have you making *any* commitments after this one," Mosay roared. "Now *vieni qui* and talk to me!"

His muttering died in the distance. Docilia turned to look into Rafiel's face. "What in the world have you done?" she asked.

"Nothing," he said positively, and then, thinking it over, "But I guess enough." He could have thrown the woman out of his home without any discussion at all, he thought. He hadn't. Resigned, he braced himself for the vituperation that was sure to come.

It came, all right, but not as pure vituperation. Mosay had switched to another mode. "Oh, *pauvre petit* Rafiel," he said sorrowfully, "haven't I always done everything I can for you? And now you're conspiring behind my back with some sleazeball for a cheap-and-dirty exploitation show?"

"It isn't really that cheap, Mosay, it's a hundred mil—"

"Cheap isn't just *money*, Rafiel. Cheap is cheap *people*. Second-raters. Do you want to wind up your career with the has-beens and never-wases? No, Rafiel," he said, shaking his head, "*Non credo* you want that. And, anyway, I've talked to your agent, and Jeftha says the deal's already *kaput*." He allowed himself a forgiving smile, then turned away briskly.

"Now let's get some work done here, company," he called, clapping his hands. "One more time, from Creon's story about the oracle. . . ."

But they didn't actually get that far, and it was Rafiel's fault.

Rafiel started out well enough, rising in wrath to sing his attack on Creon's message from the oracle. Then something funny happened. Rafiel felt the ground sliding away underneath him. He didn't feel the impact of his head on the grassy lawn. He didn't know he had lost consciousness. He was only aware of beginning to come to, half dazed, as someone was—someones were—loading him on to a high-wheeled cart and hurrying him to an elevator, and walking beside him were people who were agitatedly talking about him as though he couldn't hear.

"You'll have to tell him, Mosay," said Docilia's voice, fuzzily registering in Rafiel's ears.

Then there was a mumble, of which all Rafiel could distinguish was when, at the end, someone raised his voice to say, "*Pas* me!"

"*Allora* who?" in Docilia's voice again, and a longer mumble mumble, and then once more Docilia: "I think it'd be better from *la donna* . . . "

And then he felt the quick chill spray of an anesthetic on the side of his neck. Rafiel fell asleep as the shot did its job. Deeply asleep. So deep that there was no need to worry about anything . . . and no desire to wonder just what it was that his friends had been talking about.

"Just fatigue," the doctor said reassuringly when Rafiel was conscious again. "You collapsed. *Probabilmente* you've just been working too hard."

"Probably?" Rafiel asked, challenging the woman, but she only shrugged. "You're just as good as you were when you left here, basically," she said. "Your *ami*'s here to take you home."

The *ami* was Mosay, full of concern and sweetness. Rafiel was glad to see him.

"I'm sorry about being so silly, but I'll be ready to get back to work in the morning," Rafiel promised, leaning on the hard, strong form of the nurser.

"*Sans doute* you will," Mosay said worriedly. "Here, sit in the *chaise*, let the nurser give you a ride to the cars." And at the elevator, taking over the wheelchair himself: "Still," he added, "if you're at all tired, why shouldn't you take another day or two to rest? I've picked a location spot in Texas. . . ."

That roused Rafiel. "Texas? *Pas* Turkey?"

"Of course not Turkey," Mosay said severely. "There's just the right place out in the desert, hardly built up at all. Now, here we are at your place, and they've got your nice bed all ready for you—*Gesù Cristo!*" he interrupted himself, staring. "What's that?"

Weak as he was, Rafiel laughed out loud. His server was coming toward him welcomingly, and padding regally after, tail stiff in the air, was the kitten.

"It's just my cat, Mosay. A present from a friend."

"Does it bite?" When reassured, the dramaturge gave it a hostile look anyway, as though suspecting an attack or, worse, an excretion. "If that's what you like, Rafiel, why should I criticize? Anyway, I'll leave you now.

You can join us when you're ready. We'll work around you for a bit. No, don't argue, it's no trouble. Just give me your word that you won't come out until you're *absolutely* ready . . . "

"I promise," said Rafiel, wondering why it felt so good to be undertaking to do nothing for a while. It never had before.

9

Rafiel, who loves to travel, seldom has time to do much of it. That seems a bit strange, since he is a famous presence in all the places where human beings live, on planet and off, but of course his presence in almost all of those places is only electronic. He is looking forward eagerly to the ride in the magnetrain, with no one for company but the little white kitten. When he finally embarks, after the obligate few days of loafing around his condo, it really is as great a pleasure for him as he had hoped—well, would have been, anyway, if he weren't continuing to be so unreasonably tired. Still he enjoys watching the scenery flash by at six hundred kilometers an hour—arcologies, fields, woods, rivers—and he enjoys doing nothing. He especially enjoys being alone. With his presence on the train unknown to the fans who might otherwise besiege him, with only the servers to bring his meals and make up his bed and tend to the kitten, he thinks he almost would not mind if the trip went on for ever. When they reach their destination at the edge of the Sonora Desert he is reluctant to get off.

Rafiel arrived at the Sonora arcology just in time to catch a few hours' sleep in a rented condo, not nearly as nice as his own, in an arcology an order of magnitude tinier. When he reported for work in the morning even Turkey began to seem more desirable. This desert was *hot*.

Mosay was there to greet him solicitously—proudly, too, as he waved around the set he had discovered. "*Wunderbar*, isn't it? And such *bonne chance* it was available. Of course, it's not an *exact* copy of the actual old Thebes, but I think it's quite *interessante*, don't you? And there's no sense casting great talents, is there, if you're going to ask them to play in front of a background of dried mud huts."

Wilting in the heat, Rafiel gazed around at Mosay's idea of an "interesting" Thebes. He was pretty sure that Thebes-in-Sonora didn't much resemble the old Thebes-in-Boeotia. So much marble! So much artfully concealed lighting inside the buildings—did the Greeks have artificial lighting at all? Would the Greeks have put that heroic-seized statue of Oedipus (actually, of Rafiel himself in his Oedipus suit) in the central courtyard? And, if they had, would they have surrounded it with banked white and yellow roses? Did they have *moats* around their castles? Well, did they have castles at all? Questions like that took Rafiel's mind off the merciless sun, but not enough.

"It's you and Docilia now, please," Mosay said—commanded, really.

"Places!" And on cue Docilia began Jocasta's complaint about childbirth Rafiel reacted as the part called for as, shoulders swaying, head accusingly erect, she sang:

> *Che sapete*, husband? I did all the borning,
> Carrying those devils and puking every morning.
> Never *peine* so *dur*, never agony so hot,
> It was like pushing a pumpkin through—

"No, no, cut," Mosay shouted. "Oh, Rafiel! What do you think you're doing there, taking a little nap? Your wife's giving you hell about the kids she's borne for you and you're gaping around like some kind of *turista*. Get a little movement into it, will you?"

"Sorry," Rafiel said, as the cast relaxed. He saw Charlus coming, deferentially but with determination, toward him, as he turned his face to the server that came over to mop the sweat off his brow. There wasn't much of it, in spite of the heat; in the dry desert air it evaporated almost as fast as it formed.

"Do you mind, Rafiel?" Charlus offered, almost begging. "I was just thinking, you might want to wring your turn out and let the arms go all the way through when she starts the 'puking every morning' line."

"I didn't want to upstage her."

"No, of course not, but Mosay's got this idea that you have to be *interacting*, you see, and—"

"Sure," Rafiel said. "Let's get on with it." And he was able to keep his mind on his work, in spite of the heat, in spite of the fatigue, for nearly another hour. But by the time Mosay called a break for lunch he was feeling dizzy.

Instantly the sexy young Bruta was at his side. "Let me keep you company," she said, almost purring as she guided him to a seat in the shade. "What would you like? I'll bring you a plate."

"I'm not really hungry," he said, with utter truth. He didn't think he would ever be hungry again.

Bruta was all sympathy. "No, of course not. It is dreadfully hot, isn't it? But maybe just a plate of ice cream—do you like palmfruit?" He gave in, and watched her go for it with objective admiration. The girl was slim as an eel, with a tiny bum that any man would enjoy getting his hands on. But it was only objectively that the thought was interesting; nothing stirred in his groin, no pictures of an interesting figure developed in the crystal ball of his mind. Only—

His mouth was filling with thin, warm saliva.

It could not be possible that he was about to vomit, he thought, and then realized it was quite possible, in fact. He got briskly to his feet, prepared to give a close-lipped smile to anyone who was looking at him. No one was. He turned away from the direction of the buffet table, heading out into the desert. As he got behind Oedipus's castle he picked up his pace, pressing his palm of his hand against his involuntarily opening mouth, but he couldn't hold it. He bent forward and spewed a cupful of thin, colorless fluid on to the thirsty stand.

It wasn't painful to vomit. It was almost a pleasure, it happened so easily and quickly, and when it was over he felt quite a lot better—though puzzled, for he hadn't eaten enough that morning to have enough in his stomach to be worth vomiting.

He turned to see if any of the troupe had been looking in his direction. Apparently no human had, but a server was hurrying toward him across the desert. "Sir?" Its voice was humble but determined. "Sir, do you need assistance here?"

"No. *Hsieh-hsieh*," Rafiel added, remembering to be courteous as ever, even to machines.

"I must tell you that there is some risk to your safety here," the server informed him. "We have destroyed or removed fourteen small reptiles and other animals this morning, but others may come in. They are attracted by the presence of warm-blooded people. Please be careful where you step."

Rafiel almost forgot his distress, charmed by the interesting idea. "You mean rattlesnakes? I've heard of 'rattlesnakes.' They can bite a person and kill him."

"Oh, hardly kill one, sir, since we are equipped for quick medical attention. But it would be a painful experience, so if you don't mind rejoining the others? . . ."

And it paced him watchfully, all the way back.

It didn't seem that anyone had noticed, though Bruta was standing there with a tray in her hand. "Nothing to eat after all, please," Rafiel begged her. "It's just too hot."

"Whatever you say, Rafiel," she said submissively. But she stayed attentively by him all through the break, watchful as any serving machine. And when they started again, he saw the girl reporting to her father, and felt Mosay's eyes studying him.

He managed to keep his mind on what he was doing for that shot, and for the next. It was, he thought, a creditable enough performance, but it wasn't easy. They were shooting out of sequence, to take advantage of the lighting as the sun moved and for grouping the actors conveniently. Rafiel found that confusing. Worse, he discovered that he was feeling strangely detached. Docilia did not seem to be the Docilia he had so often bedded any more. She had become her role; Jocasta, the mother of his children and appallingly also of himself. When he reached the scene where he confronted her dead body, twisting as it hung in the throneroom, he felt an unconquerable need for reassurance. Without thinking, he reached out and touched her to make sure she was still warm.

"Oh, *merde*, Rafiel," she sighed, opening her eyes to stare at him, "what are you doing? You've wrecked the whole *drecklich* shot."

But Mosay was there already, soothing, a little apprehensive. "It's all right,

Rafiel," he said. "I know this is hard on you, the first day's shooting, and all this heat. It's about time to quit for the day, anyway."

Rafiel nodded. "It'll be better in the morning," he promised.

But it wasn't.

It wasn't better the next day, or the day after that, or the day after that one. It didn't get better at all. "It's the heat, of course," Docilia told him, watching Charlus trying to perfect the chorus in their last appearance. ("Deeper *plié*, for God's sake—*use* your legs!"). "Imagine Mosay making us work in the *open*, for God's sake."

"Of course," Rafiel agreed. He had stopped trying to look as though he were all right when he was off camera. He just stood in the shade, with an air cooler blowing on him. And Charlus said the same thing.

"You'll be all right when we finish here," he promised, watching Bruta and the Ismene. "It's only another day or two—no, no! *Chassé* back now! Then a *pas de chat*, but throw your legs back and come down on the right foot—that's better. Don't you want to lie down, Rafiel?"

He did want that, of course. He wanted it a lot, but not enough to be seen doing it on the set. He did all his lying down when shooting was over for the day, back in the borrowed condo, where he slept almost all the free time he had, with the kitten curled up at his feet.

Even Docilia was mothering him, coming to tuck him in at night but making it clear that she was not intending, or even willing, to stay. She kissed him on the forehead and hesitated, looking at the purring kitten. "You got that from Alegretta, didn't you? *Permesso* ask you something?" And when he nodded, "No offense, Rafiel, but why are you so *verrückt* for this particular one?"

"You mean Alegretta? I don't know," he said, after thought. "*Forse* it's just because she's so different from us. She doesn't even talk like us. She's— serious."

"Oh, Rafiel! Aren't we serious? We work *hard*."

"Well, sure we do, but it's just—well—you know, we're just sort of making shadow pictures on a screen. Maybe it comes to what she's serious *about*," he offered. "You know, she started a whole new life for herself—quit medicine, took up science. . . ."

Docilia sniffed. "That's not so unusual. I could do that if I wanted to. Some day I probably will."

Rafiel smiled up at her, imagining this pale, tiny beauty becoming a scientist. "When?" he asked.

"What does it matter when? I've got plenty of time!"

And Rafiel fell asleep thinking about what "plenty of time" meant. It meant, among other things, that when you had forever to get around to *important* things, it gave you a good reason to postpone them—forever.

The shooting went faster than Rafiel had imagined, and suddenly they were at an end to it. As he waited in full make-up for his last scene, his face a ruin, himself unable to see through the wreck the make-up people had made of his eyes, Docilia came over. "You've been wonderful," she told him lovingly. "I'm glad it's over, though. I promise you I won't be sorry to leave here."

Rafiel nodded and said, more wistfully than not, "Still it's kind of nice to have a little solitude sometimes."

She gave him a perplexed look. "Solitude," she said, as though she'd never heard the word before.

Then Mosay was calling for him on the set . . . and then, before he had expected it, his part was done. Old Oedipus, blinded and helpless, was cast out of the city where he had reigned, and all that was left for the cast to shoot was the little come-on Mosay had prepared for the audiences, when the children and chorus got together to set up the sequel.

They didn't need Rafiel for that, but he lingered to watch, sweltering or not. A part of him was glad the ordeal was over. Another part was somberly wondering what would happen next in his life. Back to the hospital for more tinkering, most likely, he thought, but there was no pleasure in that. He decided not to think about it and watched the shooting of the final scene. One after another the minor actors were telling the audience they hoped they'd liked the show, and then, all together:

> If so, we'll sure do more of these
> Jazzy old soaps by Mr. Sophocles.

And that was it. They left the servers to strike the set. They got on the blessedly cool cast bus that took them back to the condo. Everyone was chattering, getting ready for the farewells. And Mosay came stumbling down the aisle to Rafiel, holding on to the seats. He leaned over, looking at Rafiel carefully. "Docilia says you wanted to stay here for a bit," he said.

That made Rafiel blink. What had she told him that for? "Well, I only said I kind of liked being alone here. . . ."

The dramaturge was shaking his head masterfully. "No, no. It's quite all right, there's nothing left but the technical stuff. I insist. You stay here. Rest. Take a few days here. I think you'll agree it's worth it, and—and—anyway, *ese*, after all, there's no real reason why you have to go back with us, is there?"

And, on thinking it over, Rafiel realized that there actually wasn't.

The trouble was that there wasn't any real reason to stay in the Sonora arcology, either. As far as Rafiel could see, there wasn't any reason for him to be anywhere at all, because—for the first time in how long?—he didn't have anything he had to do.

Since he'd had no practice at doing nothing, he made up things to do. He called people on the tel screen. Called old acquaintances—all of them proving to be kind, and solicitous, and quite unprecedently remote—called colleagues, even called a few paparazzi, though only to thank them for things they had already publicized for him and smilingly secretive about any future plans.

Future plans reminded him to call his agent. Jeftha, at least, seemed to feel no particular need to be kind. "I had the idea you were pretty sick," she said, studying him with care, and no more than half accepting his protestations that he was actually entirely well and ready for more work quite soon.

She shook her head at that. "I've called off all your appearances," she said. "Let them get hungry, then when you're ready to get back—"

"I'm ready now!"

The black and usually cheerful face froze. "No," she said.

It was the first time his agent had ever said a flat "no" to her best client. "Ay Jesus," he said, getting angry, "who the hell do you think you're talking to? I don't need *you*."

The expression on Jeftha's face became contrite. "I know you don't, *caro mio*, but I need you. I need you to be well. I—care about you, dear Rafiel."

That stopped the flooding anger in its tracks. He studied her suspiciously but, almost for the first time, she seemed to be entirely sincere. It was not a quality he had associated with agents.

"Anyway," she went on, the tone becoming more the one he was used to, "I can't let you make deals by yourself, *piccina*. You'll get involved with people like that stupid Hillaree and her dumb story ideas. Who wants to hear about *real* things like kosmojets going off to other stars? People don't care about *now*. They want the good old stories with lots of pain and torture and *dying*—excuse me, *carissimo*," she finished, flushing.

But she was right. Rafiel thought that he really ought to think about that: was that the true function of art, to provide suffering for people who were incapable of having any?

He probably would think seriously about that, he decided, but not just yet. So he did very little. He made his calls, and between calls he dozed, and loafed, and pulled a string across the carpeted floor to amuse the kitten, and now and then remembered to eat.

He began to think about an almost forgotten word that kept popping up in his mind. The word was "retirement."

It was a strange concept. He had never known anyone who had "retired." Still, he knew that people used to do it in the old days. It might be an interesting novelty. There was no practical obstacle in the way; he had long since accumulated all the money he could possibly need to last him out . . . for whatever time he had left to live. (After all, it wasn't as though he were going to live forever). Immortals had to worry about eternities, yes, but the cold fact was that no untreated human lasted much more than a hundred and twenty years, and Rafiel had already used up ninety of them.

He could even, he mused, be *like* an immortal in these declining years of his life. Just like an immortal, he could, if he liked, make a midcourse change. He could take up a new career and thus change what remained of his life entirely. He could be a writer, maybe; he was quite confident that any decent performer could do *that*. Or he could be a politician. Certainly enough people knew the name of the famous Rafiel to give him an edge over almost any other candidate for almost any office. In short, there was absolutely nothing to prevent him from trying something completely different with the rest of his life. He might fail at whatever he tried, of course. But what difference did that make, when he would be dead in a couple of decades anyway?

When the doorwarden rang he was annoyed at the interruption, since his train of thought had been getting interesting. He lifted his head in anger to the machine. *"Ho detto* positively no calls!"

The doorwarden was unperturbed. "There is always an exception," it informed him, right out of its basic programming, "in the case of visitors with special urgency, and I am informed this is one. The woman says she is from *Hakluyt* and she states that she is certain you will wish to see her."

"*Hakluyt*? Is it that *fou* dramaturge woman again? Well, she's wrong about that, I don't want to talk about her stupid show—"

But then the voice from the speaker changed. It wasn't the doorwarden's any more. It was a human voice, and a familiar, female human voice at that. "Rafiel," she said fondly, "what is this crap about a show? It's me, Alegretta. I came to visit you all the way from my ship *Hakluyt*, and I don't know anything about any stupid shows. Won't you please tell your doorwarden to let me in?"

10

Rafiel knows that Alegretta has come from somewhere near Mars, and he knows pretty well how far away Mars is from the Earth: many millions of kilometers. He knows how long even a steady-thrust spacecraft takes to cross that immense void between planets, and then how long it takes for a passenger to descend to a spaceport and get to this remote outpost on the edge of the Sonoran desert. And he is well able to count back the days and see that Alegretta must have started this trip to his side—at the very least—ten days or two weeks before, which is to say right around the time when he collapsed into the hospital back in Indiana. He knows all that, and understands its unpleasing implications. He just doesn't want to think about any of those implications at that moment.

When you have lost the love of your life and suddenly, without warning, she appears in it again, what do you do?

First, of course, there is kissing, and *It's been so long*s, and *How good it is to see you*s and of course Alegretta has to see how well the kitten she sent is doing, and Rafiel has to admire the fat white cat Alegretta has brought with her, a server carrying it for her in a great screened box (it has turned out to be the kitten's mother), and of course Rafiel has to offer food and drink, and Alegretta has to accept something . . . but then what? What—

after half a century or more—do you *say* to each other? What Rafiel said, watching his love nibble on biscuits and monkey-orange and beer, was only, "I didn't expect you here."

"Well, I had to come," she said, diffident, smiling, stroking the snow-white cat that lay like a puddle in her lap, "because Nicolette here kept rubbing up against me to tell me that she really missed her baby kitten—and because, oh, Rafiel, I've been so damn much missing *you*." Which of course led to more kissing over the table, and while the server was cleaning up the beer that had got spilled in the process, Rafiel sank back to study her. She hadn't changed. The hair was a darker red now, but it was still Alegretta's unruly curly-mop hair, and the face and the body that went with the hair were not one hour older than they had been—sixty? seventy? however many years it had been since they last touched like this. Rafiel felt his heart trembling in his chest and said quickly, "What were you saying about *Hakluyt*?"

"My ship. Yes."

"You're going on that *ship*?"

"Of course I am, dear." And it turned out that she was, though such a thing had never occurred to him when he was talking to the dramaturge woman. There definitely was a *Hakluyt* habitat, and it really was, even now, being fitted with lukewarm-fusion drives and a whole congeries of pion generators that were there to produce the muons that would make the fusion reactor react.

"You know all this nuclear fusion stuff?" Rafiel asked, marveling.

"Certainly I do. I'm the head engineer on the ship, Rafiel," she said with pride, "and I'm afraid that means I can't stay here long. They're installing the drive engines right now, and I must be there before they finish."

He shook his head. "So now you've become a particle physicist."

"Well, an engineer, anyway. Why not? You get tired of one thing, after you've done it for ninety or a hundred years. I just didn't want to be a doctor any more; when things go right it's boring, and when they don't—"

She stopped, biting her lip, as though there were something she wanted to say. Rafiel headed her off. "But what will you find when you get to this distant what's-its-name star?"

"It's called Tau Ceti."

"This Tau Ceti. What do you expect? Will people be able to live there?"

She thought about that. "Well, yes, certainly they will—in the habitat, if nothing else. The habitat doesn't care what star it orbits. We do know there are planets there, too. We don't know, really, if any of them has life. . . ."

"But you're going anyway?"

"What else is there to do?" she asked, and he laughed.

"You haven't changed a bit," he said fondly.

"Of course not. Why should I?" She sounded almost angry—perhaps at Rafiel because, after all, he had. He shook his head, reached for her with loving hunger, and pulled her to him.

*   *   *

Of course they made love, with the cat and the kitten watching interestedly from the chaise lounge at the side of the room. Then they slept a while, or Alegretta did, because she was still tired from the long trip. Remarkably, Rafiel was not in the least tired. He watched over her tenderly, allowing himself to be happy in spite of the fact that he knew why she was there.

She didn't sleep long, and woke smiling up at him.

"I'm sorry, Rafiel," she said.

"What have you got to be sorry for?"

"I'm sorry I stayed away so long. I was afraid, you see." She sat up, naked. "I didn't know if I could handle seeing you, well, grow old."

Rafiel felt embarrassment. "It isn't pretty, I suppose."

"It's frightening," she said honestly. "I think you're the main reason I gave up medicine."

"It's all right," he said, soothing. "Anyway, I'm sure what you're doing now is more interesting. Going to another *star*! It takes a lot of courage, that."

"It takes a lot of hard work." Then she admitted, "It takes courage, too. It certainly took me a long time to make up my mind to do it. Sometimes I still wonder if I have the nerve to go through with it. We'll be thirty-five years en route, Rafiel. Nearly five thousand people, all packed together for that long."

He frowned. "I thought somebody said the *Hakluyt* was supposed to have twenty thousand to start."

"We were. We are. But there aren't that many volunteers for the trip, you see. That's why they made me chief engineer; the other experts didn't see any reason to leave the solar system, when they were doing so many interesting things here." She leaned forward to kiss him. "Do you know what my work is, Rafiel? Do you know anything about lukewarm-fusion?"

"Well," he began, and then honestly finished: "No."

She looked astonished, or perhaps it was just pitying. "But there are powerplants in every arcology. Haven't you ever visited one?" She didn't wait for an answer but began to tell him about her work, and how long she had had to study to master the engineering details. And in his turn he told her about his life as a star, with the personal appearances and the fans always showing up, wherever he went, with their love and excitement; and about the production of *Oedipus* they had just finished, and the members of the troupe. Alegretta was fascinated by the inside glimpse of the lives of the famous. Then, when he got to the point of telling her about Docilia and her decision to try monogamy with the father of her child, as soon as the child was born, anyway, Alegretta began to purse her lips again. She got up to stare out the window.

He called, "Is something wrong?"

She was silent for a moment, then turned to him seriously. "Rafiel, dear," she said. "There's something I have to tell you."

"I know," he said reluctantly.

"No, I don't think you do. I didn't come here by accident. Mosay—"

He was beside her by then, and closed her lips with a kiss. "But I do know," he said. "Mosay called you to tell you, didn't he? Why else would you come all the way back to Earth in such a great hurry? That little episode I had, it wasn't just fatigue, was it? It meant that they can't keep me going much longer, so the bad news is that I don't have much time left, do I? I'm going to die."

"Oh, Rafiel," she said, woebegone.

"But I've known that this was going to happen all my life," he said reasonably, "or at least since you told me. It's all right."

"It *isn't!*"

He shrugged, almost annoyed. "It has to be all right, because I'm mortal," he explained.

She was shaking her head. "Yes. But no." She seemed almost near tears as she plunged on. "Don't you see, that's why I came here like this. You don't have to die *completely*. There's a kind of immortality that even short-timers have open to them if they want it. Like your Docilia."

He frowned at her, and she reached out and touched his lips. "Will you give me a baby?" she whispered. "A son? A boy who will look just like you when he grows up—around Tau Ceti?"

11

Although the Sonora arcology is far tinier and dingier than some of those in the busy, crowded north, it naturally does not lack any of the standard facilities—including a clinic for implanting a human fetus into a nurturing animal womb. On the fourth day after the donation the new parents (or, usually, at least one of them) may come up to the sunny brightly painted nursery to receive their fetus. It is true that the circumstances for Rafiel and Alegretta are a bit unusual. Most fetuses are implanted at once into the large mammal—a cow most often, or a large sow—that will bring them to term and deliver them. Their child has a more complicated incubation in store. He (it is definitely to be a boy, and they have spent a lot of time thinking of names for him) must go with Alegretta to the interstellar ship Hakluyt, which means that the baby's host must go there too. Cows are not really very portable. So, just for now, for the sake of ease in transportation, their fetus has been temporarily implanted in a much smaller mammal, which is now spending as much time as it is allowed sitting purring in Alegretta's lap, a bit ruffled at recent indignities, but quite content.

They didn't just talk and make love and babies. On the second day Alegretta announced she was temporarily going to be a doctor again.

"But you've probably forgotten how to do it," Rafiel said, half joking.

"The computer hasn't," she told him, not joking at all. She got his medical records from the datafile and studied them seriously for a long time. Then she sent the server out for some odds and ends. When they came she pressed sticky sensor buttons on his chest and belly—"I hope I remember how to do this without pulling all your hair off," she said—and pored over the readings on the screen. Then she had long conversations over the tel with someone, from which Rafiel was excluded and which wound up in the server bringing him new little bottles of spansules and syrups to take. "These will make you feel better," she told him.

But they both knew that even the best efforts of loving Alegretta could not possibly make him *be* better.

They were also both well aware that they could not stay long together in Sonora. If they hadn't known that, they would have been told so, because the callback lists kept piling up on the communications screen—Mosay and Jeftha and ten or twelve others for Rafiel, faxed messages from *Hakluyt* for Alegretta. Once a day they took time to read them, and occasionally to answer them. "They're putting the frozen stocks on board now," Alegretta announced to her lover, between callbacks.

"Frozen food for the trip? You must need a lot—"

"No, no. Not food—well, a little bit of frozen food, yes, but we couldn't carry enough to last out the trip. Most of the food we need we'll grow along the way. What I'm talking about is frozen sperm and ova—cats, dogs, livestock, birds—and frozen seeds and clones for planting. We'll need them when we get there."

"And what if there's no good planet there to plant them on?" he asked.

"Bite your tongue," she said absently, making him smile at her as she sat huddled over the manifest. He found himself smiling a good deal these days. His kitten, which had not let either of them out of its sight while its mother was off in the implantation clinic, was licking its left forepaw with concentrated attention. The lovers touched a lot, sometimes talking, sometimes just drowsing in the scents and warmths of each other. They looked at each other a lot, charmed to see in each other a prospective parent of a shared child.

Rafiel said meditatively, "It would have been fun to conceive it in the old-fashioned way."

She looked up. "It's safer when they do it in the laboratory. Not to mention this way we can be sure it's a boy." She came over and kissed him. "Anyway, we can—well, in a day or two we can—do all of that we want to."

Rafiel rubbed his ear against her cheek, quite content. It was a very minor inconvenience that sexual intercourse had to be postponed a bit, Alegretta's womb tender from the removal of the ovum.

"Are you getting restless?" she asked.

"Me? No, I'm happy to stay right here in the condo. Are you?"

She said, "Not really, but there is something I'd like to do outside."

"Name it."

"It's so you'll know what my work's like," she explained. "If you think you'd like to, I'd enjoy showing you what this arcology's powerplant looks like."

"Of course," he said.

He would have said the same to almost anything Alegretta proposed. Still, it wasn't the kind of "of course" he felt totally confident about, because one of Mosay's calls had been to warn him that the paparazzi knew he was still in the arcology. They somehow even knew that he and Alegretta had conceived a child. Someone in the clinic had let the news out. But Rafiel took what precautions he could to preserve their privacy. They chose their time—it was after midnight—and the doorwarden reported no one in the area when they stole out and down into the lowest reaches of the arcology.

It turned out that the powerplant wasn't particularly hot. It didn't look dangerous at all; everything was enameled white or glittering steel, no more worrisome in appearance than a kitchen. It was noisy, though; they both had to put on earplugs when the shift engineer, as a professional courtesy to his colleague, Alegretta, let them in. With all the roaring and whining around them they couldn't talk very well, but Alegretta had explained some of it on the way down, and pointed meaningfully to this great buzzing cylinder and that red-striped blank wall, and Rafiel was nearly sure he understood what he was seeing. He knew it was muon-catalysed fusion. He even knew that it was, in fact, the most desperately desired dream of powerplant designers for generations, a source of power that took its energy from the commonest of all elements: hydrogen, the same universal fuel that stoked the fires of the stars themselves, and delivered it in almost any form anyone could wish— heat, kinetic energy or electricity—without fuss or bother. Well, not entirely without *bother*. It had taken a long time and a lot of clever engineering to figure out how to get the pions to make the muons that would make the reaction go; but there it was. Lukewarm fusion operated without violent explosions, impossible containment or deadly radioactive contamination. It worked best at an optimal temperature of 700 degrees Celsius (instead of many thousands!), and so it was intrinsically both safe and convenient. It was, really, the fundamental reason why the living members of the human race now outnumbered the dead. The fetal procedures could extend life, but it was only the cheap and easy energy that would never run out that could keep all ten trillion human beings alive.

"Thanks," Alegretta said to the shift engineer as she collected their dosimeters and earplugs on the way out. Rafiel wasn't looking at the engineer as she checked the dosimeters and nodded to Alegretta to show they were all right. He was looking at Alegretta, so small and pretty and well, yes, so *young* to be the master of so much energy.

And so damned *intelligent*. She was explaining the system to him, pleased and flushed, as they moved toward the exit door. "It's not really hydrogen we burn; it's muonized deuterium; you know, the heavy isotope of hydrogen, but with a muon replacing its electron."

He didn't know, but he said, "Yes. Yes, I see."

She was going right on. "So, since the muon is heavier, it orbits closer to the nucleus. This means that two atoms of deuterium can come closer to each other than electron-hydrogen ever could, and thus they fuse very easily into helium—oh, *hell*!" she finished, looking out the door. "Who are *they*?"

He swore softly and took her arm. "Come on," he said, pushing their way through the swarm of paparazzi.

"We must have been seen going in," he told her, once they were safely back in the condo. "Or your friend the engineer called somebody."

"It is always like this, Rafiel?"

He wanted to be honest with her. "Sometimes we tip the paps off ourselves," he admitted. "I mean, I don't *personally* do it. I don't have to. Jeftha or Mosay or somebody will, because we *want* the paparazzi there, you know? They're good for business. They're the source of the publicity that makes us into stars."

"Did you?"

"Did I tip them off? No. No, this time they found us out on their own. They're good at that."

So he had no secrets any more; the paparazzi knew that his life was nearing its end and that he had started a child he would not live to see grow, all of which made him more newsworthy than ever, for the same reasons; because he was Rafiel, the short-timer; because he was going to do that black-comic thing, to die. Since hardly anybody really suffered, people like Rafiel filled a necessary niche in the human design: they did the suffering for everyone else to enjoy vicariously—and with the audience's inestimable privilege of turning the suffering off when they chose.

"Yes, but is it *always* like this?"

He picked up the kitten and cradled it in his arms, upside down, its blue eyes looking up warily at him.

"It will be as long as we're here together," he said.

She did not respond to that. She just walked silently over to the communications screen.

It seemed to Rafiel that his beloved wanted not to be beloved, or not actively beloved, right then. Her back was significantly turned toward him. She had taken some faxes from *Hakluyt* and was poring over them, not looking at him. He took his cue from her and went into the other room to deal with a couple of callbacks. He did not think he had satisfactorily explained the situation to her. On the other hand, he didn't think he had to.

When he came back she was sitting with a fax in her hand, purring Nicolette in her lap, her head down. He stood there for a moment, looking not at Alegretta but at the cat. The little animal showed no sign of the human gene splices that let her be a temporary incubator for their child. She was just a cat. But inside the cat was the child which would see such wonders, forever denied to himself—a new sun in the sky, planets (*perhaps* planets, anyway) where no human had ever set foot—all the things that were possible to someone with an endless life ahead of him.

He knew that the thing in the cat's belly was not actually a *child* yet, hardly even a real fetus; it was no larger than a grain of dust, but already it was richer in powers and prospects than its father would ever be.

Then, as Alegretta moved, he saw that she was weeping.

He stood staring at her, more embarrassed than he had ever been with Alegretta before. He couldn't remember ever seeing an adult cry before. Not even himself. He moved uncomfortably and must have made some small noise, because she looked up and saw him there.

She beckoned him over and put her hand on his. "My dear," she said, still weeping, "I can't put it off any longer. I have to be there for the final tests, so—I have to leave tomorrow."

"Come to bed," he said.

In the morning he was up before her. He woke her with a kiss. She smiled up at him as she opened her eyes, then let the smile slip away as she remembered, finally saw what he was holding in his hand. She looked at him in puzzlement. "What's that thing for?"

He held up the little cage. "I sent the server out for it first thing this morning," he said, "It's to put the kitten in for the trip. We don't want to break the family up again, do we?"

"We?"

He shrugged. "The you and me we. I decided I really wanted to see your *Hakluyt* before it takes you away from me."

"But Rafiel! It's such a long trip to *Hakluyt!*"

"Kosmojets go there, don't they?"

"Of course they do, but"—she hesitated, then plunged on—"but are you up to that kind of stress, Rafiel? I mean physically? Just to get into orbit is a strain, you know; you have to launch to orbit through the railgun, and that's a seven-gee acceleration. Can you stand seven gees?"

"I can," he said, "stand anything at all, except losing you so soon."

12

Rafiel is excited over the trip. Their first leg is an airplane flight. It's his first time in a plane in many years, and there's no choice about it; no maglev trains go to the Peruvian Andes. That's where the railgun is, on the westward slope of a mountain, pointing toward the stars. As the big turboprop settles in to its landing at the base of the railgun, Rafiel gets his first good look at the thing. It looks like a skijump in reverse: its traffic goes up. The scenery all around is spectacular. Off to the north of the railgun there's a huge waterfall which once was a hydroelectric dam supplying power to half Peru and almost all of Bolivia. Lukewarm-fusion put the hydropower plants out of business and now it is just a decorative cataract. When they get out Rafiel finds his heart pounding and his breath panting, for even the base of the railgun in nearly 2500 meters above sea level, but he doesn't care. He is thrilled.

While they were dressing in their cushiony railgun suits, Rafiel paused to listen to the scream of a capsule accelerating up the rails to escape velocity. Alegretta stopped what she was doing, too, to look at him. "Are you *sure you* can handle this?" she asked. His offhand wave said that he was very, very sure. She checked him carefully as he got into each item of the railgun clothes. What they wore was important—no belts for either of them, no brassière for Alegretta, slippers rather than shoes, no heavy jewelry—because the seven-gee strain would cost them severely for any garment that pressed into their flesh or constrained their freedom. When Alegretta was satisfied about that, she got to the serious problem of fitting baskets to the cats.

"Will she be all right?" Rafiel asked anxiously, looking at Nicolette—meaning, really, will the almost-baby in her belly be all right?

"I'll make her be all right," Alegretta promised, checking the resilience of the padding with her knuckles. "That'll do. Anyway, cats stand high-gee better than people. You've heard stories of them falling out of tenth-story windows and walking away? They're true—sometimes true, anyway. Now let's get down to the loading platform."

That was busier than Rafiel had expected. Four or five other passengers were saying good-byes to friends on the platform, but it wasn't just people who were about to be launched into space. There were crates and cartons, all padded, being fitted carefully into place in the cargo section, and servers were strapping down huge Dewars of liquid gas. "Inside," a guard commanded, and when they were in the capsule a steward leaned over them to help with the straps and braces. "Just relax," he said, "and don't turn your heads." Then he bent to check the cat baskets. The kitten was already asleep, but her mother was obviously discontented with what was happening to her. However, there wasn't much she could do about it in the sweater-like restraint garment that held her, passive. . . . No, Rafiel thought, not a sweater; more like a straitjacket—

And then they were on their way.

The thrust squeezed all the breath out of Rafiel, who had not fully remembered what seven gees could do to him. The padded seat was memory plastic and it had molded itself to his body; the restraints were padded; the garments were without wrinkles or seams to cut into flesh. But still it was *seven gees*. The athletic dancer's body that had never gone over seventy-five kilograms suddenly and bruisingly weighed more than half a ton. Breathing was frighteningly difficult; his chest muscles were not used to expanding his ribcage against such force. When he turned his head, ever so minutely, he was instantly dizzied as the bones of the inner ear protested being twisted so viciously. He thought he was going to vomit; he forced himself to breathe.

It lasted only for a few minutes. Then they were free. The acceleration stopped. The railgun had flung the capsule off its tip, and now they were simply thrown free into the sky, weightless. The only external force acting on the railgun launch capsule now was the dwindling friction of the outside air; that pressed Rafiel's body against the restraining straps at first, but then it, too, was gone.

"Congratulations, dear Rafiel," said Alegretta, smiling. "You're in space."

*   *   *

Once they had transhipped to a spacecraft it was eight days to Mars-orbit, where *Hakluyt* hung waiting for them. There were a few little sleeping cabins in the ship, in addition to the multi-bunk compartments. The cabins were expensive, but that was not a consideration for Rafiel, who was well aware that he had far more money than he would ever live to spend. So he and Alegretta and the cats had their own private space, just the four of them— or five, if you counted the little cluster of cells that was busily dividing in the white cat's belly, getting ready to become a person.

Their transport was a steady-thrust spacecraft, accelerating at a sizeable fraction of a gee all the way to turnaround, and decelerating from then on. It was possible to move around the ship quite easily. It was also pointless, because there was nothing much to do. There was no dining room, no cabaret, no swimming pool on the aft deck, no gym to work out in. The servers brought meals to the passengers where they were. Most of the passengers spent their time viewing vid programs, old and new, on their personal screens. Or sleeping. In the private cabin Rafiel and Alegretta had several other options, one of which was talking; but even they slept a lot.

More than a lot.

When, at their destination, they were docking with the habitat shuttlecraft Rafiel, puzzled, counted back and realized that he had only slept twice on the trip. They had to have been good long sleeps—two or three full twenty-four-hour days at a time; and that was when he realized that Alegretta had doped him to make him sleep as long as possible.

13

On board the Hakluyt, *Alegretta disappears as soon as Rafiel is settled in. She can't wait to see what damage her deputy may have done to her precious engines. This leaves Rafiel free to explore the habitat. There's no thrust on* Hakluyt's *engines yet, just the slow roll of the habitat to distinguish up from down. That's a bit of a problem for everybody. All habitats spin slowly so that centrifugal force will supply some kind of gravity. But when* Hakluyt *starts to move they'll stop the spin because they won't need it any more. The "down" the spin has provided them—radially outward from the central axis of the cylindrical habitat—will be replaced by a rearward "down," toward the thruster engines in the stern. Consequently, every last piece of furnishing will have to be rearranged as walls become floors and floors walls. Rafiel is having a lot of trouble with his orientation. Besides the fact that half the fittings have already been relocated, the light-gee pull is strange to him. Because he has spent so little time in low-gee environments he instinctively holds on to things as he walks, though really the feeling isn't much different from being on, say, the Moon. (But Rafiel hasn't been even there for nearly half a century.) Once he gets used to these things, though, he's fascinated. Everything so busy!*

Everyone in such a hurry! *The whole ship's complement has turned out to finish loading, even small children—Rafiel is fascinated to see how many children there are. Young and old, they can't wait to start on their long interstellar journey—and aren't very patient with people (even very famous people) who happen to get in their way.*

By the time Rafiel had been three days on *Hakluyt* he was beginning to get used to the fact that he didn't see much of Alegretta. Not when she was awake, at least. When she was awake all she seemed to have time for was to check on his vital signs and peer into her computer screen when she'd stuck sensors to his chest and make sure he was taking his spansules. Then she was off again, looking harried.

They did sleep together, of course, or at least they slept in the same bed. Not necessarily at the same times. Once or twice Rafiel came back to their tiny compartment and found her curled up there, out cold. When she felt him crawl in beside her she reached out to him. He was never quite certain she was awake even when they made love—awake enough to respond to him, certainly, and for a few pleased mumbles when they were through, but nothing that was actually articulate speech.

It was almost good enough, anyway, just to know that she was nearby. Not quite; but still it was fascinating to explore the ship, dodging the busy work teams, trying to be helpful when he could, to stay out of the way, at least, when he couldn't. The ship was full of marvels, not least the people who crewed it (busy, serious, plainly dressed and so *purposeful*). A special wonder was the vast central space that was a sort of sky as the habitat rotated (but what purpose would it serve when they were under way?). The greatest wonder of all was *Hakluyt* itself. It was going to go where no human had ever, *ever* gone before.

Everything about the ship delighted and astonished. Rafiel discovered that the couch in their room became a bed when they wanted it to, and if they didn't want either it disappeared entirely into a wall. There was a keypad in the room that controlled air, heat, lights, clock, messages—might run all of *Hakluyt*, Rafiel was amused to think, if he only knew what buttons to push. Or if all the things worked.

The fact was, they didn't all work. When Rafiel tried to get a news broadcast from Earth the screen produced a children's cartoon, and when he tried to correct it the whole screen dissolved into the snow of static. The water taps—hot, cold, potable—all ran merely cold.

When he woke to find exhausted Alegretta trying to creep silently into their bed, he said, making a joke, "I hope the navigation system works better than the rest of this stuff."

She took him seriously. "I'm sorry," she said, weary, covetously eyeing the bed. "It's the powerplant. It wasn't originally designed to drive a ship, only to supply power for domestic needs. Oh, it has plenty of power. But they located the thing midships instead of at the stern, and we had to brace everything against the drive thrust. That means relocating the water reservoirs—don't drink the water, by the way, dear; if you're thirsty, go to one of the kitchens—and— Well, hell," she finished remorsefully. "I should have been here."

Which added fuel to the growing guilt in Rafiel. He took a chance. "I want to help," he said.

"How?" she asked immediately—woundingly, just as he had feared she would.

He flinched and said, "They're loading more supplies—fresh wing-bean seeds this morning, I hear. At least I can help shift cargo!"

"You can *not*," she said in sudden alarm. "That's much too strenuous! I don't want you dying on me!" Then, relenting, she thought for a moment. "All right. I'll talk to Boretta, he's loadmaster. He'll find something for you—but now, please, let me come to bed."

Boretta did find something for him. Rafiel became a children's care-giver in one of the ship's nurseries, relieving for active duty the ten-year-old who had previously been charged with supervising the zero-to-three-year-olds.

It was not at all the kind of thing Rafiel had had in mind, but then he hadn't had much of anything very specifically in his mind, because what did *Hakluyt* need with a tap-dancer? But he was actually helping in the effort. (The ten-year-old he relieved was quite useful in bringing sandwiches and drinks to the sweating cargo handlers.) Rafiel found that he liked taking care of babies. Even the changing of diapers was a fairly constructive thing to do. Not exactly aesthetic, no. Extremely repetitive, yes, for the diapers never *stayed* clean. But while he was doing it he thought of the task as prepaying a debt he would owe to whomever, nine months later, would be changing the diapers of his own child.

The ten-year-old was nice enough to teach Rafiel the technical skills he needed for the work. More than that, he was nice enough to be acceptably impressed when he found out just who Rafiel was. ("But I've seen you on the screen! And you've got a new show coming out—when? *Soon?*") The boy even brought his older brother—a superior and taller version of the same, all of thirteen—around to meet this certified star. When Rafiel had a moment to think of it, between coaxing a two-year-old to take her nap and attempting to burp a younger one, it occurred to him that he was—yes, actually—quite happy. He liked all these strange, dedicated, space-faring people who shared the habitat with him. "Strange" was a good word for them, though. Unlike all the friends and colleagues he'd spent his life with, these *Hakluyt*ians spoke unornamented English, without loan words, without circumlocutions. They had basically unornamented bodies, too. Their clothes were simply functional, and even the youngest and best-looking wore no jewels.

When Rafiel had pondered over that for a while an explanation suddenly occurred to him. These people simply didn't have time for frills. Astonishing though the thought was, these *immortal* people were in such a hurry to *do* things that, even with eternities before them, they had no time to waste.

* * *

The day before *Hakluyt* was to leave, Alegretta somehow stole enough time from her duties to go with Rafiel to the birthing clinic, where they watched the transfer of their almost-child from Nicolette's tiny belly to the more than adequate one of a placid roan mare. It was a surgical spectacle, to be sure, but peaceful rather than gruesome. Even Nicolette did not seem to mind, as long as Alegretta's hand was on her head.

On the way back to their cabin, Alegretta was silent. Stranger still, she was dawdling, when always she was in a hurry to get to the work that she had to do.

Rafiel was aware of this, though he was continually distracted by passersby. The ten-year-old had spread the word of his fame. It seemed that every third person they passed, however busy, at least looked up and nodded or called a friendly greeting to him. After the twentieth or thirtieth exchange Rafiel said, "Sorry about all this, Alegretta."

She looked up at him curiously. "About what? About the fact that they like you? When's this *Oedipus* going to be released?"

"In about a week, I think."

"In about a week." It wasn't necessary for her to point out that in a week *Hakluyt* would be six days gone. "I think a lot of these people are going to want to watch it," she said, musing. "They'll be really sorry you aren't here so they can make a fuss over you when it's on."

Rafiel only nodded, though for some inexplicable reason internally he felt himself swelling with pleasure and pride. Then he bent close to her, puzzled at the low-pitched thing she had said. "What?"

"I said, you could be here," Alegretta repeated. "I mean, if you wanted to. If you didn't mind not going back to the Earth, ever, because—oh, God," she wailed, "how can you say 'Because you're going to be dead in a few weeks anyway so it doesn't really matter where you are' in a loving way?"

She stopped there, because Rafiel had put a gentle finger to her lips.

"You just did," he said. "And of course I'll come along. I was only waiting to be asked."

14

Fewer than thirty-six hours have passed since Hakluyt's launch, but all that time its stern thrusters were hard at their decades-long work of pushing the ship across interstellar space. By now it is already some fifteen million kilometers from its near-Martian orbit and, with every second that passes, Alegretta's lukewarm-fusion jets are thrusting it several hundred kilometers farther away. The reactors are performing perfectly. Still, Alegretta can hardly bear to let the controls and instruments that tell her so out of her sight. After the pre-launch frenzy, Hakluyt's five thousand pioneers are beginning to catch up on their sleep. So is Alegretta.

Rafiel tried to make no noise as he pulled on his robe and started toward the sanitary, but he could see Alegretta beginning to stir in her sleep. Safely outside their room he was more relaxed—at least, *acted* relaxed, nodding brightly to the people he passed in the hall. It was only when he was looking in the mirror that the acting stopped and he let the fatigue and discomfort show in his face. There was more of it every day now. The body that had served him for ninety-odd years was wearing out. But, as there was absolutely nothing to be done about that fact, he put it out of his mind, showered quickly, dressed in the pink shorts and flowered tunic that was the closest he had to *Hakluyt*-style clothing and returned to their room. By then Alegretta was sitting dazedly on the edge of the bed, watching Nicolette, at the foot of the bed, dutifully licking her kitten.

"You should have slept a little longer," he said fondly.

She blinked up at him. "I can't. Anyway"—she paused for a yawn—"there's a staff meeting coming up. I ought to decide what I want to put in for."

Rafiel gently pushed the cats out of the way and sat down companionably next to her. They had talked about her future plans before. He knew that Alegretta would have to be reassigned to some other task for the long trip. Unless something went seriously wrong with the reactors there would be little for her to do there. (And if, most improbably, anything did go seriously wrong with them in the space between the stars, the ship would be in more trouble than its passengers could hope to survive.) "What kind of job are you looking for?"

"I'm not sure. I've been thinking of food control, maybe," she said frowning. "Or else waste recycling. Which do you think?"

He pretended to take the question seriously. He was aware that both jobs were full-time, hands-on-assignments, like air and water control. If any of those vital services failed, the ship would be doomed in a different way. Therefore human crews would be assigned to them all the time the ship was in transit—and for longer still if they found no welcoming planet circling Tau Ceti. But he knew that there was nothing in his background to help Alegretta make a choice, so he said at random: "Food control sounds like more fun."

"Do you think so?" She thought that over. "Maybe it is, sort of, but I'd need a lot of retraining for aeroponics and trace-element management. The waste thing is easier. It's mostly plumbing, and I've got a good head start on that."

He kissed her. "Sleep on it," he advised, getting up.

She looked worriedly up at him, remembering to be a doctor. "You're the one who should be sleeping more."

"I've had plenty, and anyway I can't. Manfred will be waiting for me with the babies."

"Must you? I mean, should you? The boy can handle them by himself, and you look so tired. . . . "

"I'm fine," he said, trying to reassure the person who knew better than he.
She scolded, "You're *not* fine! You should be resting."

He shook his head. "No, dearest, I really am fine. It's only my body that's sick."

He hadn't lied to her. He was perfectly capable of helping with the babies, fine in every way—except for the body. That kept producing its small aches and pains, which would steadily become larger. That didn't matter, though, because they had not reached the point of interfering with tending the children. The work was easier than ever now, with the hectic last-minute labors all completed. The ten-year-old, Manfred Okasa-Pennyweight, had been allowed to return to the job, which meant that now there were two of them on the shift to share the diapering and feeding and playing.

Although Rafiel had been demoted to his assistant, Manfred deferred to him whenever possible. Especially because Manfred had decided that he might like to be a dancer himself—well, only for a *hobby*, he told Rafiel, almost apologizing. He was pretty sure his main work would be in construction, once they had found a planet to construct things on. And he was bursting with eagerness to see Rafiel perform. "We'll all going to watch the *Oedipus*," he told Rafiel seriously, looking up from the baby he was giving a bottle. "Everybody is. You're pretty famous here."

"That's nice," Rafiel said, touched and pleased, and when there was a momentary break he showed the boy how to do a cramp roll, left and right. The babies watched, interested, though Rafiel did not think it was one of his best performances. "It's hard to keep your feet down when you're tapping in a quarter-gee environment," he panted.

Manfred took alarm. "Don't do any more now, please. You shouldn't push yourself so hard," he said. Rafiel was glad enough to desist. He showed Manfred some of the less strenuous things, the foot positions that were basic to all ballet . . . though he wondered if ballet would be very interesting in this same environment. The grandest of leaps would fail of being impressive when the very toddlers in the nursery could jump almost as high.

When their shift was over, Manfred had a little time to himself before going to his schooling. Bashfully he asked if Rafiel would like to be shown anything on the ship, and Rafiel seized the chance. "I'd like to see where they do the waste recycling," he said promptly.

"You really want to go to the stink room? Well, of course, if you mean it." And on the way Manfred added chattily, "It probably doesn't smell too bad right now, because most of the recycled organics now are just chopped-up trees and things—they had to cut them all down before we launched, because they were growing the wrong way, you see?"

Rafiel saw. He smelled the processing stench, too; there was a definite odor in the waste-cycling chambers that wasn't just the piney smell of lumber, though the noise was even worse than the smell. Hammering and welding was going on noisily in the next compartment, where another batch of aeroponics trays were being resited for the new rearward orientation. "Plants want to grow *upward,* you see," Manfred explained. "That's why we had to chop down all those old trees."

"But you'll plant new ones, I suppose?"

"Oh, I don't think so. I mean, not pines and maples like these. They'll be planting some small ones—they help with the air recycling—and probably some fruit trees, I guess, but not any of these big old species. They wouldn't be fully grown until we got to Tau Ceti, and then they'd just have to come down again."

Rafiel peered into the digesting room, where the waste was broken down. "And everything goes into these tanks?"

"Everything organic that we don't want any more," Manfred said proudly. "All the waste, and everything that dies."

"Even people?" Rafiel asked, and was immediately sorry he had. Because of course they had probably never had a human corpse to recycle, so far.

"I've seen enough," he said, giving the boy a professional smile. He did not want to stay in this place where he would soon enough wind up. He would never make it to Tau Ceti, would never see his son born . . . but his body would at some fairly near time go into those reprocessing vats, along with the kitchen waste and the sewage and the bodies of whatever pets died en route, ultimately to be turned into food that would circulate in that closed ecosystem for ever. One way or another, Rafiel would never leave them.

While Alegretta was once again fussing over her diagnostic readouts Rafiel scrolled the latest batch of his messages from Earth.

The first few had been shocked, incredulous, reproachful; but now everyone he knew seemed at least resigned to their star's wild decision, and Mosay's letters were all but ecstatic. The paps were going crazy with the story of their dying Oedipus going off on his last great adventure. Even Docilia was delighted with the fuss the paps were making, though a little put out that the stories were all *him,* and Alegretta was pleased when the news said that another habitat had been stirred to vote for conversion to a ship; maybe Rafiel's example was going to get still others to follow them.

But she was less pleased with the vital signs readings on her screen. "You really should go into the sickbay," she said fretfully.

"So they could do what for me?" he asked, and of course she had no answer for that. There was no longer much that could be done. To change the subject Rafiel picked up the kitten. "Do you know what's funny here?" he asked. "These cats. And I've seen dogs and birds—all kinds of pets."

"Why not? We like pets." She was only half attentive, most of her concentration on the screen. "Actually, I may have started the fashion myself."

"Really? But on Earth people don't have them. You hardly ever see a pet animal in the arcologies. Aren't you afraid that they'll die on you?"

She turned to look at him, suddenly angry. "Like you, you mean?" she snapped, her eyes flashing. "Do you see what the screen is saying about your tests? There's blood in your urine sample, Rafiel!"

For once, he had known that before she did, because he had seen the color of what had gone into the little flask. He shrugged. "What do you expect? I guess my *rognons* are just wearing out. But, listen, what did you mean when you said you started the fashion—"

She cut him off. "Say kidneys when you mean kidneys," she said harshly, looking helpless and therefore angry because she was helpless. He recognized the look. It was almost the way she had looked when she first gave him the bad news about his mortality, so long and long ago, and it chased his vagrant question out of his mind.

"But I'm still feeling perfectly well," he said persuasively—and made the mistake of trying to prove it to her by walking a six-tap riff—a slow one, because of the light gravity.

He stopped, short of breath, after a dozen steps.

He looked at her. "That didn't feel so good," he panted. "Maybe I'd better go in after all."

15

Hakluyt's sickbay is just about as big as a hospital in an average Earthly arcology, and just about as efficient. Still, there is a limit to what any hospital can do for a short-timer nearing the end of his life expectancy. When, after four days, they wake Rafiel, he is in far from perfect health. His face is puffy. His skin is sallow. But he has left strict orders to wake him up so he can be on hand for the showing of Oedipus. *As nothing they can do will make much difference anyhow, they do as he asks. They even fetch the clothes he requests from his room and when he is dressed he looks at himself in a mirror. He is wearing his fanciest and most theatrical outfit. It is a sunset-yellow full dress suit, with the hem of the tails outlined in stitches of luminous red and a diamond choker around his neck. The diamonds are real. With any luck at all, he thinks, people will look at his clothing and not at his face.*

Probably not every one of *Hakluyt's* five thousand people were watching *Oedipus* as the pictures beamed from Earth caught up with the speeding interstellar ship. But those who were not were in a minority. There were twenty viewers keeping them company in the room where Rafiel and Alegretta sat hand in hand, along with Manfred and his brother and a good many people Rafiel didn't really know—but whom Manfred knew, or Alegretta did, and so they were invited to share.

It was a nice room. A room that might almost have been Rafiel's own old condo, open to the great central space within *Hakluyt*; they could look out and see hundreds of other lighted rooms like their own, all around the cylinder, some a quarter of a kilometer away. And most of the people in them were watching, too. When the four children of Jocasta and Oedipus did their comic little dance at the opening of the show, the people in the room laughed where Mosay wanted them to—and two seconds later along came the distant, delayed laughter from across the open space, amplified enough by the echo-focusing shape of the ship to reach their ears.

Rafiel hardly looked at the screen. He was content simply to sit there, pleased with the success of the show, comfortable with Alegretta's presence . . . at least, in a general sense comfortable; comfortable if you did not count the sometimes acute discomforts of his body. He didn't let the discomforts show. He was fondly aware that Alegretta's fingers slipped from hand to wrist from time to time, and knew that she was checking his pulse.

He was not at all in serious pain. Of course, the pain was there. Only the numbing medications they had been giving him were keeping it down to an inconvenience rather than agony. He accepted that, as he accepted the fact that his life expectancy was now measured in days. Neither fact preyed on his mind. There was an unanswered question somewhere in his mind, something he had wanted to ask Alegretta, but what it could have been he could not clearly say. He accepted the fact that his mind was confused. He even drowsed as he sat there, aware that he was drifting off for periods of time, waking only when there was laughter, or a sympathetic sound from the audience. He did not distinguish clearly between the half-dreams that filled his mind and the scene on the screens. When the audience murmured as he—as Oedipus— took his majestic oath to heal the sickness of the city, the murmur mingled in Rafiel's mind with a blurry vision of the first explorers from *Hakluyt* stepping out of a landing craft on to a green and lovely new planet, to the plaudits of an improbable welcoming committee. It wasn't until almost the end that he woke fully, because next to him there was a soft sound that had no relation to the performance on the screen.

Alegretta was weeping.

He looked at her in confusion, then at the screen. He had lost an hour or more of the performance. The play was now at the farewell of the chorus to the blinded and despairing Oedipus as, alone and disgraced, he went off to a hopeless future. And the chorus was singing:

> There goes old Oedipus.
> Once he was the best of us.
> Down from the top he is,
> Proof that all happiness
> Can't be known until you're dead.

Rafiel thought that over for some time. Then, blinking himself awake, he reached to touch Alegretta's cheek. "But I do know that now," he said, "and, look, I'm not dead yet."

"Know what, Rafiel?" she asked, huskily, not stopping what she was doing. Which, curiously, was pressing warm, sticky, metallic things to his temples and throat.

"Oh," he said, understanding, "the show's over now, isn't it?" For they weren't in the viewing room any more. He knew that, because he was in a bed—in their room? No, he decided, more likely back in the ship's sickbay.

Another doctor was in the room, too, hunched over a monitor, and in the doorway Manfred was standing, looking more startled than grieving, but too grieving to speak.

Rafiel could see that the boy was upset and decided to say something reassuring, but he drifted off for a moment while he tried to think of what to say. When he looked again the boy was gone. So was the other doctor. Only Alegretta sat beside him, her eyes closed wearily and her hands folded in her lap; and at that moment Rafiel remembered the question on his mind. "The cats," he said.

Alegretta started. Her eyes flew open, guiltily turning to the monitor before they returned to him. "What? Oh, the cats. They're fine, Rafiel. Manfred's been taking care of them." Then, looking at the monitor again, "How do you feel?"

That struck Rafiel as a sensible question. It took him a while to answer it, though, because what he felt was almost nothing at all. There was no pain in the gut, nor anywhere else, only a sort of generalized numbness that made it hard for him to move.

He summed it all up in one word. "Fine. I feel fine." Then he paused to rehearse the question that had been on his mind. When it was clear he spoke. "Alegretta, didn't you say you started the fashion of having pets?"

"Pets? Yes, I was one of the first here on *Hakluyt*, years and years ago."

"Why?" he asked. And then, because he felt a need to hurry, he made his thickening tongue come out with it: "Did you do it so you could get used to things you loved dying? Things like me?"

"I didn't know you were a psychotherapist, dear Rafiel," she whispered. It was an admission, and she knew he understood it . . . though his eyes had closed and she could not tell whether he had heard the words. She did not need the confirmation of the screen or of the other doctor as he came running in to know that Rafiel had joined the minority of the dead. She kissed the unresponding lips and retired to the room they had shared, to weep, and to think of what, some day, she would tell their son about his father; that he had been famous, and loved, and brave . . . and most of all that, certainly, yes, Rafiel had after all been happy in his life, and known that to be true.

HONORABLE MENTIONS: 1992

Brian W. Aldiss, "Her Toes Were Beautiful on the Hilltops," *Universe* 2.
———, "Horse Meat," *Interzone*, Nov.
———, "Ratbird," *New Worlds* 2.
Kevin J. Anderson, "Dogged Persistence," *The Magazine of Fantasy & Science Fiction*, Sept.
Poul Anderson, "In Memoriam," *Omni*, Dec.
Patricia Anthony, "Blue Woofers," *IAsfm*, July.
———, "The Shoot," *Aboriginal SF*, Summer.
Isaac Asimov, "Cleon the Emperor," *IAsfm*, April.
———, "The Critic on the Hearth," *IAsfm*, Nov.
A. A. Attanasio, "Ink from the New Moon," *IAsfm*, Nov.
———, "Maps for the Spiders," *Strange Plasma* 5.
A. J. Austin, "Supply Run," *IAsfm*, Mid-Dec.
Neal Barrett, Jr., "Buckstop," *Slightly Off Center*.
———, "Four Times One," *Slightly Off Center*.
———, "Uteropolis II," *Slightly Off Center*.
Stephen Baxter, "Inherit the Earth," *New Worlds* 2.
———, "Planck Zero," *IAsfm*, Jan.
———, "Weep for the Moon," *In Dreams*.
Greg Bear, "A Plague of Conscience," *Murasaki*.
Amy Bechtel, "The Midwives of Miracle," *Pulphouse*, Sept./Oct.
Chris Beckett, "The Circle of Stones," *Interzone*, Feb.
M. Shayne Bell, "Second Lives," *IAsfm*, June.
———, "The Sound of the River," *IAsfm*, Dec.
Gregory Benford, "Down the River Road," *After the King*.
———, "Rumbling Earth," *Aboriginal SF*, Summer.
Bruce Bethke and Phillip C. Jennings, "The Death of the Master Cannoneer," *Asimov's SF*, Mid-Dec.
Michael Bishop, "Herding with the Hadrosaurs," *The Ultimate Dinosaur*.
Terry Bisson, "*Canción Autentica de* Old Earth," *F&SF*, Oct./Nov.
Terry Boren, "Three Views of the Staked Plain," *Interzone*, Mar.
William Borden, "Fancy Dancing," *Blue Light Red Light*, #4.
Ben Bova, "Bushido," *Analog*, July.
———, "Sepulcher," *Asimov's SF*, Nov.
Scott Bradfield, "The Reflection Once Removed," *In Dreams*.
R. V. Branham, "The New Order: 3 Moral Fictions," *Midnight Graffiti*.
Molly Brown, "The Vengeance of Grandmother Wu," *Interzone*, July.
John Brunner, "The Dead Man," *F&SF*, Oct./Nov.
———, "In the Season of the Dressing of the Wells," *After the King*.
Edward Bryant, "Country Mouse," *F&SF*, Mar.
Algis Budrys, "Hard Landing," *F&SF*, Oct./Nov.
Eugene Byrne, "Cyril the Cyberpig," *Interzone*, Dec.
Pat Cadigan, "A Deal With God," *Grails: Quests, Visitations, and Other Occurrences*.
———, "Fifty Ways to Improve Your Orgasm," *IAsfm*, April.
———, "New Life for Old," *Aladdin: Master of the Lamp*.
———, "No Prisoners," *Alternate Kennedys*.

Orson Scott Card, "Atlantis," *Grails*.
Jonathan Carroll, "Uh-Oh City," *F&SF*, June.
Steve Carper, "Wrestling with the Demon," *Asimov's SF*, Mid-Dec.
Susan Casper, "Djinn and Tonic," *Aladdin*.
Michael Cassutt, "The Last Mars Trip," *F&SF*, July.
Jack L. Chalker, "Now Falls the Cold, Cold Night," *Alternate Presidents*.
Suzy McKee Charnas, "Oak and Ash," *Pulphouse*, Aug.
Rob Chilson, "Far-Off Things," *F&SF*, May.
Brian C. Coad, "Everybody's Hamlet," *Analog*, July.
William E. Cochrane, "The Walking Hills," *Analog*, July.
Storm Constantine, "Priest of Hands," *Interzone*, April.
Greg Costikyan, "A Doe, in Charcoal," *IAsfm*, July.
Tony Daniel, " The Careful Man Goes West," *IAsfm*, July.
———, "Death of Reason," *IAsfm*, Sept.
———, "Faces," *IAsfm*, April.
———, "Lost in Transmission," *Universe 2*.
Jack Dann, "Jumping the Road," *IAsfm*, Oct.
Avram Davidson, "In Brass Valley," *Amazing*, Feb.
———, "Yellow Rome, or, Vergil and the Vestal Virgin," *Weird Tales*, Winter.
Diane de Avalle-Arce, "Bats," *IAsfm*, June.
L. Sprague de Camp, "The Big Splash," *IAsfm*, June.
———, "Crocamander Quest," *The Ultimate Dinosaur*.
———, "The Satanic Illusion," *IAsfm*, Aug.
———, "The Synthetic Barbarian," *IAsfm*, Sept.
Jack Deighton, "The Face of the Waters," *New Worlds 2*.
Barbara Delaplace, "Freedom," *Alternate Kennedys*.
Paul Di Filippo, "Anne," *Science Fiction Age*, Nov.
Thomas M. Disch, "The Abduction of Bunny Steiner, or A Shameless Lie," *IAsfm*, April.
J.R. Dunn, "Broken Highways," *Amazing*, Oct.
———, "Crux Gammata," *IAsfm*, Oct.
———, "The Heart's Own Country," *Omni Best Science Fiction One*.
Scott Edelman, "10 Things I've Learned About Writing," *Nexus 2*.
George Alec Effinger, "Prince Pat," *Alternate Kennedys*.
Greg Egan, "Before," *Interzone*, Mar.
———, "Closer," *Eidolon*, Winter.
———, "Into Darkness," *IAsfm*, Jan.
———, "Reification Highway," *Interzone*, Oct.
———, "Unstable Orbits in the Space of Lies," *Interzone*, July.
———, "The Walk," *Asimov's SF*, Dec.
Monica Eiland, "Anne's Pen," *Forbidden Lines*, Jan./Feb.
Harlan Ellison, "The Man Who Rowed Christopher Columbus Ashore," *Omni*, July.
Jennifer Evans, "Gate Crashing," *IAsfm*, Feb.
Donna Farley, "The Passing of the Eclipse," *Universe 2*.
Sharon N. Farber, "Why I Shot Kennedy," *IAsfm*, Oct.
Nancy Farmer, "Origami Mountain," *F&SF*, Mar.
Joe Clifford Faust, "Going to Texas (Extradition Version)," *Amazing*, May.
Sheila Fitch, "If There Be Cause," *Amazing*, Feb.
Maggie Flinn, "Black Velvet," *Omni Best Science Fiction Two*.
Robert Frazier, "Chasing the Dragon, Tibet," *Amazing*, Feb.
Esther M. Friesner, "All Vows," *Asimov's SF*, Nov.
Neil Gaiman, "Chivalry," *Grails*.
R. Garcia y Robertson, "Breakfast Cereal Killers," *IAsfm*, June.
———, "Gypsy Trade," *Asimov's SF*, Nov.

————, "The Virgin and the Dinosaur," *IAsfm*, Feb.
James Alan Gardner, "Kent State Descending the Gravity Well," *Amazing*, Oct.
David Garnett, "Off the Track," *Interzone*, Sept.
David Gerrold, "The Kennedy Enterprise," *Alternate Kenndys*.
John K. Gibbons, "Waterworld," *Universe 2*.
Carolyn Gilman, "Burning Bush," *Universe 2*.
Molly Gloss, "Verano," *IAsfm*, Jan.
Parke Godwin, "The Night You Could Hear Forever," *Pulphouse*, Sept./Oct.
Lisa Goldstein, "Alfred," *Asimov's SF*, Dec.
Phyllis Gotlieb, "The Newest Profession," *Ark of Ice: Canadian Futurefiction*.
Kathleen Ann Goonan, "Daydots, Inc.," *Interzone*, Mar.
————, "For a Future You," *Amazing*, Mar.
Joe Haldeman, "Job Security," *Universe 2*.
Jack C. Haldeman II, "Ashes to Ashes," *Grails*.
————, "By the Sea," *F&SF*, July.
Elizabeth Hand, "The Have-Nots," *IAsfm*, June.
————, "In the Month of Athyr," *Omni Best Science Fiction Two*.
M. John Harrison, "Anima," *Interzone*, April.
Paul Hellweg, "The Coke Boy," *IAsfm*, May.
Lee Hoffman, "Water," *Grails*.
Nina Kiriki Hoffman, "Messages Left on a Two-Way Mirror," *Amazing*, May.
Alexander Jablokov, "Above Ancient Seas," *Asimov's SF*, Nov.
————, "The Logic of Location," *Amazing*, Aug.
Phillip C. Jennings, "Deep Gladiators," *Amazing*, May.
————, "The Final Page," *Amazing*, Feb.
Gwyneth Jones, "Blue Clay Blues," *Interzone*, Aug.
Janet Kagan, "Love Our Lockwood," *Alternate Presidents*.
————, "The Nutcracker Coup," *Asimov's SF*, Dec.
James Patrick Kelly, "Monsters," *IAsfm*, June.
Leigh Kennedy, "The Presevation of Lindy," *Omni*, May.
Eileen Kernaghan, "The Weighmaster of Flood," *Ark of Ice*.
John Kessel, "Man," *IAsfm*, May.
Garry Kilworth, "The Cave Painting," *Omni Best Science Fiction Two*.
————, "Memories of the Flying Ball Bike Shop," *IAsfm*, June.
Kathe Koja, "Letting Go," *Pulphouse*, June.
————, "Persephone," *Asimov's SF*, Nov.
Stephen Kraus, "Bright River," *IAsfm*, Sept.
Nancy Kress, "Birthing Pool," *Murasaki*.
————, "Eoghan," *Alternate Kennedys*.
Marc Laidlaw, "The Vulture Maiden," *F&SF*, Aug.
Geoffrey A. Landis, "Embracing the Alien," *Analog*, Nov.
David Langford, "Blossoms That Coil and Decay," *Interzone*, Mar.
Roberta Lannes, "Dancing on a Blade of Dreams," *Pulphouse*, Mar.
Tanith Lee, "Exalted Hearts," *Grails*.
————, "The Lily Garden," *Weird Tales*, Spring.
Ursula K. Le Guin, "The Rock That Changed Things," *Amazing*, Sept.
Jonathan Lethem, "Program's Progress," *Universe 2*.
————, "Vanilla Dunk," *IAsfm*, Sept.
Richard K. Lyon, "The Secret Identity Diet," *Aboriginal SF*, Winter.
Ian R. MacLeod, "Returning," *Interzone*, Oct.
Paul J. McAuley, "Prison Dreams," *F&SF*, April.
Jack McDevitt, "Auld Lang Boom," *IAsfm*, Oct.
Ian McDonald, "Big Chair," *Interzone*, Dec.
————, "Fat Tuesday," *In Dreams*.

———, "Innocents," *New Worlds 2*.
———, "The Luncheonette of Lost Dreams," *Narrow Houses*.
Maureen McHugh, "The Beast," *IAsfm*, Mar.
———, "The Missionary's Child," *IAsfm*, Oct.
———, "Render unto Caesar," *Asimov's SF*, Mid-Dec.
Vonda N. McIntyre, "Steelcollar Worker," *Analog*, Nov.
Dean McLaughlin, "Mark on the World," *Analog*, July.
Sean McMullen, "An Empty Wheelhouse," *Analog*, Jan.
———, "Pacing the Nightmare," *Interzone*, May.
Barry N. Malzberg, "In the Stone House," *Alternate Kennedys*.
———, "Ship Full of Jews," *Omni*, April.
Diane Mapes, "Love Walked In," *IAsfm*, Mar.
———, "The Man in the Red Suit," *Asimov's SF*, Dec.
———, "She-Devil," *Interzone*, Sept.
Lisa Mason, "Destination," *F&SF*, Sept.
Paula May, "Memories of Muriel," *Universe 2*.
Beth Meacham, "The Tale of Ali the Camel Driver," *Aladdin*.
Bill Merrick, "Scoring," *Aurealis 7*.
Jamil Nasir, "The Heaven Tree," *IAsfm*, Feb.
———, "The Shining Place," *Universe 2*.
Kim Newman and Eugene Byrne, "Tom Joad," *Interzone*, Nov.
G. David Nordley, "Poles Apart," *Analog*, Mid-Dec.
Claudia O'Keefe, "Cameo," *Aboriginal SF*, Winter.
Lawrence Person, "Huddled Masses," *Alternate Presidents*.
Terry Pratchett, "Troll Bridge," *After the King*.
Paul Preuss, "Rhea's Time," *The Ultimate Dinosaur*.
Frederik Pohl, "The Martians," *IAsfm*, Mar.
———, "The Treasure of Chujo," *Murasaki*.
Tom Purdom, "Chamber Music," *IAsfm*, Aug.
———, "Sepoy," *Asimov's SF*, Dec.
David Redd, "The Blackness," *Interzone*, Feb.
Robert Reed, "Burger Love," *Asimov's SF*, Nov.
Garfield Reeves-Stevens, "Outport," *Ark of Ice*.
Laura Resnick, "We Are Not Amused," *Alternate Presidents*.
Mike Resnick, "Lady in Waiting," *Alternate Kennedys*.
———, "The Lotus and the Spear," *IAsfm*, Aug.
———, "Song of a Dry River," *IAsfm*, Mar.
Joel Richards, "Overlays," *IAsfm*, Feb.
Kim Stanley Robinson, "Red Mars," *Interzone*, Sept.
Madeleine E. Robins, "Willie," *F&SF*, Dec.
Mary Rosenblum, "Second Chance," *Asimov's SF*, Dec.
———, "The Stone Garden," *Asimov's SF*, Mid-Dec.
———, "Synthesis," *IAsfm*, Mar.
Kristine Kathryn Rusch, "Alien Influences," *F&SF*, July.
———, "Hitchiking Across an Ancient Sea," *Grails*.
Richard Paul Russo, "Just Drive, She Said," *Asimov's SF*, Mid-Dec.
James Sallis, "Ansley's Demons," *F&SF*, Sept.
Robert Sampson, "The Yellow Clay Bowl," *Grails*.
Pamela Sargent, "Danny Goes to Mars," *IAsfm*, Oct.
———, "The Sleeping Serpent," *Amazing*, Jan.
Karl Schroeder, "Hopscotch," *On Spec*, Spring.
Charles Sheffield, "Deep Safari," *IAsfm*, Mar.
Lucius Shepard, "'Beast of the Heartland," *Playboy*, Sept.
———, "Barnacle Bill the Spacer," *IAsfm*, July.

Lewis Shiner, "Sticks," *In Dreams.*
John Shirley, " 'I Want To Get Married!' Says the World's Smallest Man," *Midnight Graffiti.*
W.M. Shockley, "A Father's Gift," *IAsfm*, April.
Susan Shwartz, "Suppose They Gave a Peace . . . ," *Alternate Presidents.*
Robert Silverberg, "It Comes and Goes," *Playboy*, Jan.
————, "Looking for the Fountain," *IAsfm*, May.
————, "The Perfect Host," *Omni Best Science Fiction One.*
————, "The Way to Spook City," *Playboy*, Aug.
Dave Smeds, "Reef Apes," *IAsfm*, Aug.
S.P. Somtow, "Hunting the Lion," *Weird Tales*, Spring.
————, "Kingdoms in the Sky," *IAsfm*, Feb.
————, "The Steel American," *Grails.*
Martha Soukup, "The Arbitrary Placement of Walls," *IAsfm*, April.
————, "Plowshare," *Alternate Presidents.*
Brian Stableford, "Upon the Gallows-Tree," *Narrow Houses.*
————, "Virtuous Reality," *Interzone*, Jan.
Allen Steele, "Sugar's Blues," *IAsfm*, Feb.
Lorina J. Stephens, "Sister Sun," *On Spec*, Fall.
Bruce Sterling, "Are You for 86?," *Globalhead.*
James Stevens-Arce, "The Devil's Sentrybox," *Amazing*, Mar.
S.A. Stolnack, "Straw for the Fire," *IAsfm*, Mar.
Dirk Strasser, "Waiting for the Rain," *Universe* 2.
Tim Sullivan, "Anodyne," *Pulphouse*, Nov.
————, "Atlas at Eight A.M.," *Asimov's SF*, Mid-Dec.
Michael Swanwick, "In Concert," *IAsfm*, Sept.
Judith Tarr, "Death and the Lady," *After the King.*
————, "Persepolis," *Aladdin.*
Melanie Tem, "Trail of Crumbs," *Asimov's SF*, Nov.
Mark W. Tiedemann, "Shattered Template," *F&SF*, June.
————, "Thanatrope," *Asimov's SF*, Dec.
Larry Tritten, "The Lord of the Land Beyond (Book One)," *Asimov's SF*, Nov.
Harry Turtledove, "In the Presence of Mine Enemies," *IAsfm*, Jan.
————, "The Last Reunion," *Amazing*, June.
Lisa Tuttle, "Honey, I'm Home!" *In Dreams.*
Steven Utley, "Die Rache," *IAsfm*, June.
————, "Haiti," *IAsfm*, May.
————, "Look Away," *F&SF*, Feb.
————, "Now that We Have Each Other," *IAsfm*, July.
Jeff VanderMeer, "Mahout," *Asimov's SF*, Mid-Dec.
John Varley, "Her Girl Friday," *IAsfm*, Aug.
Susan Wade, "Living In Memory," *Amazing*, Oct.
Karl Edward Wagner, "One Paris Night," *Grails.*
Howard Waldrop, "The Effects of Alienation," *Omni*, June.
Ian Watson, "Swimming with the Salmon," *Interzone*, Sept.
Lawrence Watt-Evans, "Fragments," *Interzone*, July.
————, "Pickman's Modem," *IAsfm*, Feb.
Don Webb, "The Shiny Surface," *In Dreams.*
Andrew Weiner, "Seeing," *F&SF*, Sept.
————, "Streak," *IAsfm*, May.
Deborah Wessell, "The Cool Equations," *Universe* 2.
Leslie What, "King for a Day," *IAsfm*, Sept.
Wendy Wheeler, "June 14, 1959," *Aboriginal SF*, Fall.
Rick Wilber, "Ice Covers the Hole," *F&SF*, Dec.

Cherry Wilder, "Bird on a Time Branch," *Interzone*, Mar.
Jack Williamson, "The Birds' Turn," *F&SF*, Oct./Nov.
Gene Wolfe, "The Legend of Xi Cygnus," *F&S*, Oct.
————, "The Sailor Who Sailed After The Sun," *Grails*.
Dave Wolverton, "Siren Song at Midnight," *The Ultimate Dinosaur*.
Jane Yolen, "The Tale of the Seventeenth Eunuch," *Aladdin*.
Roger Zelazny, "Come Back to the Killing Ground, Alice, My Love," *Amazing*, Aug.